Stirring the Stillness
Part 1, Voices of Quest

Book One of the Stillness Series

Richard Lee Ferguson

STIRRING THE STILLNESS - BOOK 1 OF THE STILLNESS SERIES

Part 1 Voices of Quest

Copyright © 2019 by Richard Lee Ferguson

Book Cover by Bookfly Design, James Egan

Illustrations by Brian Bowes

Published in 2025

ISBN: 979-8-9881446-4-9 (paperback)

ISBN: 979-8-9881446-5-6 (hardcover)

ISBN: 979-8-9881446-6-3 (ebook)

"What the caterpillar calls the end of the world the master calls a butterfly."
— Richard Bach

"I would like to thank this institution for providing me with the means to increase the power of my delusions."
—Michael Powers

Also by Richard Lee Ferguson

The Stillness Series

Book 1: Stirring the Stillness, Part 1 Voices of Quest

Book 2: Stirring the Stillness, Part 2 Tortured Journey

Book 3: Stilling the Stillness, Part 1 Voices of War

Book 4: Stilling the Stillness, Part 2 Restless Spirits

Book 5: Becoming the Stillness, Part 1 Voices of Madness

Book 6: Becoming the Stillness, Part 2 Haunted Caves

Book 7: The Hunchback's Gift, Part 1 Voices of Defeat

Book 8: The Hunchback's Gift, Part 2 Superior Ones Risen

Book 9: Flames of Extinction, Part 1 The Last Voice

Book 10: Flames of Extinction, Part 2 Stillness is Stilled

For the full series, visit the Amazon series page: https://www.amazon.com/dp/B0F1WJ5J4N

Contents

Principal Characters

Voices - God and Goddess

Michael Powers – Narrator and son of John Powers and Bai Meiying
John Powers – American father of Michael Powers; businessman
Bai Meiying – Chinese mother of Michael Powers; pianist
Marie Telles – American friend and lover of Bai Meiying
Meili – Chinese friend and lover of Bai Meiying
Madame Liu – Wife of Master Liu and co-leader of The Quest
Master Liu – Husband of Madame Liu and co-leader of The Quest
Master Zhou – Wealthy landowner
Lu Shishen – Canadian friend of John Powers
Feng Shiren – Mysterious soldier
Buandelgereen – Female Mongol leader; protectress of Bai Meiying
Lihua – Chinese woman warrior
Father Durant – French priest
Colonel Naguma – Japanese officer
Nobaru Ichida – Japanese officer
Beethoven (Wang Lihua) – Son of Madame Wang; spy for Mr. President
Little Acorn – Child member of The Group
Mr. Gao – Professor; member of The Group
David Hendricks – Assistant director of symphony orchestra
Arthur Mobley – Businessman and boss of John Powers
The Davignons – French plantation owners in Vietnam
Madame Dau – Council chief of Song Nhan village
Suling – Female friend of John Powers
Peter Hedley – American friend of John Powers
Mr. President – Mysterious Chinese warlord
Child of Buddha – Mental patient
Mulan – Adopted daughter of John Powers and Bai Meiying
Madame Wang – Concubine of Mr. President

Preface

Can Humans Be Replaced Peacefully?

Query: Are you one of the increasing number of people who think humans are irredeemably destructive and pose such a threat to the planet that their extinction would be a good thing? However, do you also abhor the massive destruction and suffering that would necessarily be the consequence of their demise? Bloody, violent dystopian novels often focus only on a few survivors of such devastation, not on the suffering that would extend to all other life forms on the planet. While there are many excellent dystopian novels, such a formulaic concentration on a small group of heroic protagonists can be narrow and unsatisfying.

So, how to unravel the ubiquitous human presence without simultaneously destroying the rest of the planetary ecosystem? Can a successor species evolve fast enough to replace humankind, or would it be extinguished before it has a chance to spread?

Such a successor species, by random chance or intentional design, must possess far greater cognitive and empathetic capacities to thwart the human proclivity for eliminating real or perceived threats. What would it be like for those first generations of advanced individuals surrounded by a sea of slow-witted but resourceful *Homo sapiens*? How would they survive the human penchant for fearing otherness and a relentless instinct to exterminate it? Whether the guiding force effectuating this change is Nature, Superior Alien, God or Gods, Goddess or Goddesses, here is an interesting way forward:

Replace *Homo sapiens* with a more advanced species, but not *drive* them to extinction through violent extermination, rather *dilute* their genes to insignificance over generations. There is precedent for such top-down genetic engineering. Human biologists eliminate dangerous pests by introducing mutant strains that breed with the targeted species to produce offspring harboring the desired genetic makeup. Generations later, the original species is superseded.

A new form of consciousness must necessarily arise—one in which strange Voices with immense cognitive power reverberate in advanced minds in the same way Voices once arose in the minds of early *Homo sapiens* separating them from competitors such as *Neanderthals*. Humans would initially diagnose those hearing such new Voices as schizophrenics, but they are, in fact, the incipient stirrings of a superior species. However, new Voices must be only the beginning, as this emerging species must also evolve powerful physical capabilities to overcome human weapons of destruction.

The doves must have sharper claws than the hawks . . .

The Stillness Series is the epic story of one such scenario.

Prologue

I write these words from inside a mental institution. I apologize in advance for my lack of writing skills. I am a madman, not a writer. At least the doctors tell me I am a madman, a schizophrenic. I hear voices.

First, I must let you in on something: the human race is being replaced by Powers I do not yet understand. Surreptitiously. Irrevocably. The new species will be more empathetic, less destructive, less violent. I am one of the first—a progenitor, not fully human, the next step toward a planet where *Homo sapiens* no longer exist. How do I know this? Goddess told me. And who is Goddess, you ask?

She is one of my voices. God and Goddess. What are they? I do not know. They argue, they insult, they plague me day and night, just as they tormented my father, though never with the same ferocity. The voices began with him. They cajoled him into lying with my mother, and in the moment of my conception, they burrowed into her egg through his sperm. Since then, they colonized my brain with relentless force.

For what purpose? That I have already told you. I am the Next Step. Not fully human. As Goddess calls me: Chosen One. And like the first of any advanced, abstract-thinking species, I am both confused and conflicted.

What God and Goddess argue over, and what I believe, are not the same. My only escape is the tunnel where my bones already lie waiting—half-memory, half-fate. But that is for another story.

What awaits you in these pages? The exquisite poetry of extinction in its infancy—cruel, melancholy, and implacable.

~ *Voices Stirring the Stillness* ~

There was a time when silence held the interior world. Before the slogans. Before the bombs. Before the rising din of human engines and ideologies, there was a stillness so deep even the deities dared not disturb it.

But then came the voices.

Whispers in the dark, at first: half-formed prayers, betrayals, dreams, demands. Go and seek. The defiant scratch of ink on parchment as a name is signed that cannot be unsigned. And somewhere in the east, beneath fractured stars and retreating spirits, a group of weary travelers begins to move. What drives them? Treasure—not gold or riches, but treasure.

They carry no banner, only a burden. A Precious Object, ancient and unspeakable, neither artifact nor weapon nor child, yet perhaps all three. What it is, even they cannot say. What is the tapping that comes from within? No one truly knows. Only that it must not fall into the hands of those humans devouring the world.

The path winds through shattered villages and torched fields. Past the mouths of caves that remember older wars. Across mountain passes that never forget. And still, they walk—John Powers, haunted by a voice that may be his salvation or his undoing. Schizophrenia? Or is it something else? Meiying, the beautiful one whose heart bears too many names. Child of Buddha, who listens to the tapping and understands. And the others join and fall away—soldiers, skeptics, orphans, pilgrims. Each voice seeking truth. Each footstep a wager against annihilation. A wager for the future.

They are not saints. They are not heroes. They are remnants. Echoes. Are they survivors of a species unsure whether it deserves to survive? Or are they the first stirrings of a new species?

Above them, the sky watches—mute and unmoved. Below, the Earth stirs, preparing for another inheritance.

~ *The Quest* ~

And so begins the long story of humanity's end and Superior Ones risen. A quest not for triumph, but for meaning. Not to conquer, but to find answers to questions as yet unasked:

Can anything sacred still be born from what remains of humankind?
Is there still a path forward, or must the destruction continue?
"If there is a path forward—who will speak the final word?"

~ *Beginning* ~

To start at the beginning, with my father's life. . . .

Well, better yet, let us start with his death, and then go back to the beginning when he first met *her.* . . .

Chapter One

PART ONE: THE JOURNEY BEGINS

Let Me Tell You A Story

~ John Powers ~

On his back, his left hand fell heavily to the ground. It seemed miraculous to the dying man that his remaining upturned palm, in which he felt the tickling of an ant's legs, could overcome the heavy pull of gravity dragging them both earthward. The insect's frenetic probing reminded him of something he had learned long ago when the others died: the ceaselessness of that which is still seeking always taps a mocking farewell to the ceasing of that which had once been sought. So be it. Though lying fully on the dirt path, he was strangely hesitant to lower his hand and let the back of it touch the earth. Such surrender marked the final ending. As long as it hovered inches above the solid inevitability of corruption, life circulated above and below. How he came to lie dying on his back beneath the forest canopy, levitating one hand upon which reconnoitered an anxious ant, was a puzzle that frayed his concentration. Must keep the hand above the famished soil and remember! Memory was the cushioning air beneath the hand; it was the light, the open space, which fought off malevolent, solid darkness. How could it end like this? Hold the hand up, heavy as it was becoming, and remember. But the insect? Keep her from her nestmates to satisfy a need? Lower to ashes and dust for the benefit of an ant that she might be set free? Yet, this emancipation would leave him to expire without even a lone arthropod to see him off. No. Lower it and he dies. He wanted to live! A minute longer? Minutes? Someone might come along and save him. Hours? Whatever it takes. His hand remained a hovering, weighted hope, the ant a taunting vitality.

Ticklish questions came to him as faint and delicate as the probing ant. So many questions. It was long ago, not long to the Earth and soil, but long enough for a man. More than long enough. The woman asked him a question—the question—when she first entered his office and stood just inside the door with both hands raised palms up. "Mr. Powers, how does one justify a life without cruelty, and therefore also without the distilled beauty of cruelty?"

He was taken aback, unsure, confused. She, a young employee he assumed, had knocked him off-center. How could a beautiful twenty-something woman have such a thought? Distilled cruelty represented pure evil—Mephistopheles in extremis—not a concept whose existence could ever be justified. Yet here stood this young woman, gorgeous, throwing around the word cruelty as though it were synonymous with a white lie, or even virtue. She looked well-manicured, mentally sharp. No bruises. Nice clothes. And he had never met her before.

"Good question," he said noncommittally, indicating with his placid expression that he would play along. "What do you think?" Wise reply. Cowardly, but wise. Time to think, clueless girl, and answer the question with a question until you get it right. He looked at her with his best poker face. Is she still assuming that age is wiser than youth? Not an irrational assumption, simply wrong, most of the time. Flirting with a man who occupies a position more powerful than she? Maybe—though he was not much older. Nevertheless, that question of hers was how the whole mess started. Of course, the Big Bang was how it started if you want to get technical . . . but that question in particular led to his being here, lying on his back, hand raised palm up, squinting at the mottled sunlight teasing an algorithmic yes or no that singed his clouded retinas.

"Fate starves at probability's door," she said without emotion. Her stare made him squirm, but he made no sound. "Mr. Powers, how does one justify a life without cruelty, and therefore without the distilled beauty of cruelty?"

After repeating this question, she sat without being invited and crossed her legs, knowing the effect without the effect knowing her. Therein lay the danger. In a flash of insight, he recognized that she thought she knew the danger, but the danger dwelt in her utter ignorance of what the danger really was. Being young himself at that time, although slightly older than his strange visitor, the dying man also knew that back then he held with her an equally disadvantageous position in their mutual ignorance of the ignorance of danger. Or so he thought. Clever man. Too clever by half! Although he had never met her before, he confidently concluded that they were a matched pair. Such is the agony and ecstasy of youth. Such were some of the unformed, fragmentary thoughts he contemplated at the time while waiting for her reply. He flirted with his eyes and smiled his best enigmatic smile. Remaining silent and waiting patiently for responses was one of his most effective social tools. Alas, her face suddenly registered something beyond his limited experience and all his self-congratulatory analysis about her being young and ignorant fell in tatters when she asked her next question. So transformed had her face become that he scarcely believed that what now stared back at him could be human.

"When will you finally lower your hand?"

The second question seemed wholly unrelated to the still unanswered first, and his inclination was to think her mentally unstable. All his smug conceptions of her female intellectual inadequacies evaporated in the transcendent authority of her stare. Nearly rendered comatose by her transformation, he closed his eyes to block the searing gaze, and when at last he opened them to speak, she was gone. He lifted his hand to call her back and realized both hands had been resting on the arms of his desk chair the entire time.

What did she mean? was his first thought, followed immediately by his second, *who is she?* and that followed by his third, *she'll be easy to find.* No no no. These initial stupefied flashes of reaction merged to form a confident confluence of certainty. *She would not have come if she weren't interested,* and so on and so forth. Tiresome in retrospect. He was convinced she would return and felt a smug self-satisfaction but for the niggling incongruities wagging their Cassandra fingers: *Why didn't she stay? What happened to her face at the end?* But these cautionary thoughts were mere spices, adding to the flavor of the encounter. She picked him to see and therefore will be seen again soon enough. He clung to that explanation while he called his secretary, sounding flustered but actually preternaturally calm.

"Who was that woman that just left?"

"What woman?"

"The one who just walked out of my office."

"I didn't see her."

"You must have, Rose. She had to pass your desk to come in. Didn't you tell her to . . . I mean, didn't she ask to see me? And when she left, too. Were you gone?"

"No. What did she look like?"

This stopped him cold. What *did* she look like? Her hair? He only saw flowing and luxurious locks, or was her hair short? Her clothes? Nice they were, he recalled, but now the details eluded him. Just a generic but lovely frame that accentuated her stunning looks, a brief flash of brushstrokes from some immortal portrait. But one can't just describe a person as beautiful. Was she tall? Short? Eye color? No details came to him. Ridiculous. Yet she was as real and immediate to him as his own . . . hand.

"I thought she worked here," he said, incongruously clenching and unclenching his fist.

"Well," said his secretary. "I didn't see her, and I've been at my desk all morning. Maybe she slipped by while I was kneeling at the file cabinet."

"Both times, in and out?" he asked accusingly.

His secretary shrugged, piqued at his insinuation. "What did she want?"

"That is a very good question. I have never seen her before. Maybe she works for a department on one of the lower floors."

Another shrug.

So he took a walk. A long walk, visiting every floor in the building. No luck. Time passed, but her presence never faded from his memory. As if he stalked some dangerous beast, he peered at every face, every shadow, every alleyway to spot the apparition (which he had come to call her). Soon after, she came to him in his dreams—just as ethereal and fleeting. In one recurring dream, she stood in his raised palm and demanded to be put down. But the meaning eluded him and she remained a distant touch.

~

After the apparition left his office, *she* returned to the comfort of her wispy abode in the belly of the rocky beast. The Others were waiting.

"Did you?" came the hum from the shadows.

"Yes."

A darker shadow split apart. "When will you return?"

She did not respond but instead merged.

~

John Powers gave up his job two years after his encounter with the woman. Two years of fruitless searching. Her extraordinary appearance made it impossible to continue living a pedestrian life. He tried, God knows he tried. As an Asian specialist at an international consulting agency, he tried to remain excited about global business transactions, but failed to find the meaning he had once found rewarding. Relationships following her visit were brief and unfulfilling, his job a somnambulant exercise of the most superficial routine. Nights were spent drinking, though he rarely got drunk. Then, with nothing to lose and everything to gain, he made a decision.

"Why in the hell would you want to move to China!?" cried his friends.

"There are 1 billion more chances of finding her than if I stay in San Francisco."

All were astonished, for he rarely mentioned her even to his closest friends.

"Who?" they asked, begged, demanded.

But he would just shake his head and continue drinking.

"John! Who?" they insisted.

When he had imbibed enough, he simply replied, "I can't describe her." And he really couldn't. Yet she had become a description of him, and her few words the working title of his autobiography. Unsatisfied with his life lived from the outside in, he was determined to make her the central theme of his existence from the inside out. If she were to be the main protagonist in his plot, then exotic China would be his next . . . no, his first chapter. It was a bold, irrational move, but he knew she was not of this world and if he threw himself into some symbolic extremity, a sort of behavioral sacrifice, she might again appear.

~

When his ship docked in Shanghai, John was met by Elizabeth Wu, a young administrative assistant at the university where he was hired to teach courses in Business English. After huffing through customs, and barely setting foot on Chinese soil, she grabbed his arm in a very un-Chinese manner.

"Did you hear?" she asked with an urgency also very un-Chinese.

"What?" he replied, startled.

"The Japanese are threatening to invade!"

"What do you mean?"

"The Japs, the Japs, they claim we blew up a bridge in Wanping! I'm not sure what will happen now!"

John hesitated. Get back on the ship? He had promised not to lead an ordinary life, but by any account this was a bit much, and a bit too soon. Nevertheless, *her* words came back to him. John Powers clenched his fist. *So it begins.* "Let them come!" he exclaimed. But with this proclamation he felt ridiculous under the startled gaze of Miss Wu. "I mean, do you still want me to teach?"

"I don't know, I don't know. Depends on what happens next. Let me take you to where you'll be staying, at least until this is sorted out." Her eyes were wide and fearful. They bustled into a taxi, and as the car inched its way through the nervous crowds and narrow streets, John asked above the continuous honking by the driver, "Where is Wanping?"

"Near Peiping."

"Ah well, hopefully things will quiet down. My Chinese is bad, but my Japanese is worse!"

Miss Wu chuckled dryly and announced, "Your Chinese is excellent. Here we are."

The car had pulled up in front of an old, single-story red brick guest house with a decorative tile roof. John carried his luggage into the cramped foyer and turned to Miss Wu.

"What next?"

"Normally we would give you an introductory feast to meet other professors and staff, but they are all at home glued to their radios. I have asked another teacher, one of your fellow Americans, to come and fetch you to his apartment. His name is Peter Hedley. He also speaks fluent Chinese."

John could see that Miss Wu was anxious to leave. He smiled. "Thank you. I will see you tomorrow?"

"Yes," she replied quickly. "Yes, good luck."

Here I am alone in a strange house in a strange city in a strange country whose people speak a strange language, about to be invaded by an even stranger country whose people speak an even stranger language. Great. No pedestrian life for me! Now is a good time to make your appearance, strange lady. Your strangeness will fit right in.

But no strange lady appeared, and it shook him to realize he felt genuinely afraid. The loneliness of his position oppressed him greatly and his resolve wavered. For the first time in over two years, his mind was completely free from thoughts of his mysterious apparition. As if aware of this disquieting frame of mind, a knocking on his door brought him around to the absurd thought that it was *her* come to rescue him in his distress. He opened the door, half-laughing at his ridiculous notion. Even so, he felt an irrational disappointment that his apparition was not standing in front of him.

Chapter Two

The First Steps

Prelude to Disaster

~ Arrival and Departure ~

In the doorway stood a youngish man with long hair and a grin that made him look either absurdly doltish or indearingly charming. It all depended on what he said next.

"Well, you picked a grand time to come to China and play!" he exclaimed with gusto.

His grin was guileless, his unalloyed enthusiasm sincere, and his open stare invited a similarly jocular response. "Yes! My timing is impeccable."

The man stuck out his hand. "You must be the newbie, John Powers. Have I hit the mark or am I in the wrong place, not for the first time in my life?"

"Yes, I'm John." The man's grip was firm.

He bowed theatrically. "Peter Hedley, at your service."

The man's cozy familiarity made John feel better. "What's on the agenda?" he asked.

A brief shadow passed across Peter's face and he betrayed an underlying nervousness when he lit a cigarette with a match that quivered almost imperceptibly. Almost. Perceiving his unsteadiness had been noticed, he spoke loudly. "It's this damn Japan thing. The blighters seem to want to take over the world!"

Now John seemed the calm one. "Are you British?"

"Me? Naw. American. Just picked up some redcoat slang."

They fell silent, each sizing up the other in the light of the meager information each had imparted.

John broke the awkward pause and repeated, "Well, what's on the agenda?"

Peter looked around. "You haven't even had time to unpack!"

"Given the situation, should I?"

"Good bloody question!"

John pursed his lips, not happy with this unencouraging retort. "Well, we don't know the Japs will invade, do we?"

"Nooo, but. . . . " Peter took a long drag from his cigarette and looked away.

"Well, I did want an adventure, but not one quite so . . . adventurous." John chuckled humorlessly.

"Yeah." Peter evidently agreed.

Worse and worse. "Seriously, Peter, what does the university say? Do they want me to stay? To teach?"

"Dunno. They're in hot debate about what they're going to do as we speak. This incident in Peiping really has them spooked. Many students have already packed up and left for home."

"Maybe that's what I should do."

"Maybe."

"Well, what do you think? Is it that serious?"

Peter shrugged and made a face denoting cluelessness.

Exasperating. "Well, damn!" cried John impatiently. "What are *you* going to do?"

"Me?"

"Yeah, you!" Peter's evasions were now seriously tweaking John's nerves. "Go back to the States?" he added in a tone more accusatory than he intended.

Peter burst out laughing. "Just joking with you old man. My hand is as steady as a rock." He snuffed out his cigarette in a carved silver ashtray and brandished a new one with exaggerated flair, then struck a match and held it perfectly still before lighting up. "See? I'm staying. Japs can do their best!" He flung out his hand, palm up. "I can stay above ground forever, if necessary, and still keep my head about me"—he directed John's eyes to his hand—"and my nerves in check, as you can plainly see."

These words struck John as eerily familiar, but slightly asinine and decidedly odd. He plopped wearily in an overstuffed chair embellished with a faded Chinese print. "Okay, you got me. Now, what's really on the agenda?" His tone brooked no further jesting.

"In all honesty, they haven't informed me what their plans are. They truly are going hammer and tongs in old Fang's office."

"Fang?"

"Fang Chichao, the university president."

"Oh." Returning home was looking more appealing, so John waited sullenly for more information. He tried to remember when the ship would depart on its return-trip to San Francisco. If he left now, he could buy a ticket before passage was sold out. He unconsciously made an up-and-down gesture with both palms as if weighing a decision.

Peter had started to speak, but upon observing John's pantomime, he clapped his hands as if to chase away the words before they could be uttered. "But I have my own plans for us, John! Freshen up, we're going out."

"Where?"

"To meet a group of people we may need to save our skins, if push comes to shove."

"Wait a minute!" cried John. "Why *are* you staying? I mean seriously, why?"

Peter again held out his hand, palm up. "Because there is a woman even steadier than I am, and I reside in the palm of *her* hand. If I ever jump off, or worse, if *she* ever turns it over, then. . . . "

"Who is *she*?"

Peter slapped him on the back, his old jocularity bursting forth. "John, if we stand here talking forever, the Japs will walk through the front door and put a bullet in both of us. Come on, oh great adventurer, unless, after all my malarkey, you've decided to turn around and hightail it back home."

John replied before he had time to consider. "No, I'm game. Do we drive?" Peter's clumsy evasion had touched some deeper chord he dared not interpret.

"Are you mad? We walk!"

Stupid, stupid, stupid, John thought. *But there'll still be time if this doesn't work out.*

~

Both Americans wended their way through an increasingly complex labyrinth of narrow alleyways and brick houses with traditional tiled roofs in various stages of disrepair. The open-mouthed gawking by the local inhabitants at these foreign apparitions increased exponentially as they moved farther from the university grounds. Those who lived in this neighborhood were used to seeing foreigners at the Bund, but not here among the foraging chickens and reeking outhouses.

John followed Peter as if he were in a bad dream. It had only been hours since he disembarked and he was already being dragged into the depths of some ridiculous and possibly dangerous situation. Exhilarating, of course, to a young man just brought blind into a new world, but an oppressive sense of vulnerability and personal inadequacy underlay the novelty. He listened to Peter's excellent Chinese flung right and left in the form of greetings and solicitations to the throngs jostling past who most likely were returning to their homes from work. This easy familiarity did nothing to assuage John's lack of self-confidence. Only now did he notice it getting dark. Peter picked up the pace. Being without electricity, this part of Shanghai quickly blackened, with a few desultory lanterns providing dim light.

Finally, they arrived at a nondescript house surrounded by magnolia trees. Two lanterns hung above an elaborately carved front door. Excited conversation could be heard from within, but the Chinese was too fast and indistinct for John to understand. Peter hesitated, appeared to take a deep breath, and knocked. The door opened and John saw a huge European with an untamed beard stare down at them. The talking ceased in the background and in an astonishingly quiet voice, the big man said simply, "Come in."

As they stepped in, Peter was greeted with a flurry of greetings, quickly followed by silence as everyone present stared wordlessly at John. The bearded European directed them to a small room containing an odd assortment of people, some standing, some on chairs, and others sitting cross-legged on tatami. All eyes turned toward them as Peter announced in Chinese. "This is a friend of mine. The new professor. Just arrived. John Powers." With this perfunctory introduction, the room reverted to an awkward silence.

At last the big, bearded man spoke. "Good timing, my boy! Two steps behind the revolution and one step ahead of the Japanese!" This statement released a flood of solicitations, most of which John could not understand. He peered through a thick haze of cigarette smoke at the dimly illuminated crowd. Peering back at him were many faces, but he could clearly distinguish only those closest to him: two women and three men. All were apparently Chinese except the big man who greeted them at the door. John's eyes were particularly drawn to the women, one of whom appeared to be in her mid-twenties and was quite beautiful, the other a slender, elegant woman in her sixties.

The excited conversation recommenced with a vengeance, and John surmised it was about the Japanese incident. Peter tried to interpret, but soon became embroiled in the heated discussion and left John to keep up as best he could.

~

Peter Hedley was very agitated. He had no patience for those who argued that the Japanese would not invade. "Wishful thinking!" he kept repeating. The main thrust of his remarks was directed at a middle-aged Chinese man who John later learned was a professor of literature. "This isn't one of your Chinese romances," Peter said with a dismissive shrug. "The Japs will smash your armies and be on us in weeks, if not days!"

Peter ended this last statement with a flourish, causing the others to momentarily discontinue their own conversations. As if taking advantage of the pause for which she had been patiently waiting, the older, elegant Chinese woman leaned forward on the edge of her chair, raised her arm in a subtle but effective signal to the assembled company for their attention, and spoke in a clear, authoritative voice. Briefly glancing at John as she began, her words poured out in perfect English. "And this contingency is precisely why we are gathered here tonight."

Heads nodded sagely in agreement, an electric anticipation infused the group, and even John unconsciously moved slightly forward with the rest as if huddling to share some dangerous secret. She possessed a magnetic presence that belied her willow-like figure. Assured of their undivided attention, she continued, "If the Japanese come, I am prepared to activate my contacts to get us safely to the interior. Interference from the communists and Nationalists will be minimal. Problems, however, may arise from certain warlords. Needless to say, bandits are always an issue. Still, there are enough of us scattered in strategic locations to overcome even these obstacles."

With this speech, the true nature of John's precarious situation crystallized in his mind into an ominous premonition of doom. Yet this disturbing thought was somehow laced with enticing murmurings of excitement and purpose. He saw his life depicted in a heroic canvas. He would be the gallant American staying in spite of the obvious dangers, depicted for future generations in a noble and inspiring portrait; a portrait of his own death gilded by an elaborate frame which conveyed gravitas to justify his youthful recklessness. If he could not find *her*, he could at least die a romantic death. And maybe, just maybe, *she* might appear before him in a last farewell. Better yet, *she* might dramatically pluck him from some treacherous precipice . . . .

While mulling over these rather absurd thoughts, the conversation resumed, and sheepishly aware of his own absurdity, John's attention returned to the group. Much of the fragmentary discussion revolved around logistics; how much to take in the event of a quick escape, where to meet, and preserving something—some object that John could not make out. He wanted to ask Peter, but his new friend was clearly absorbed in the debate. Just as John felt a comfortable anonymity in his 'outside observer' status which absolved him of any responsibility to contribute, the professor of literature turned the spotlight on him by remarking, "What about him? Are you sure he's one of us?" As if to accentuate the odd mix of guests, an elderly couple walked by smiling, nodding, and repeatedly bowing. They were very dark, their skin weather-beaten and cracked, with missing teeth. *Peasants here?* wondered John.

"Oh, yes!" cried Peter.

The others seemed to accept this without question and no further inquiries were made. John, of course, was focused on the phrase 'one of us' and was anxious to understand it. Americans? No, there were native Chinese present. Communists? Nationalists? No, as Peter didn't even know his political persuasion. Anti-Japanese unity? Didn't make sense. After Peter's assurance that he was one of them, John, at last, recognized some fundamental, crucial substrate that had existed from the beginning: who is *us*?

Tea appeared as if from nowhere and John at last had Peter's ear. As he was not yet on intimate terms with Peter, John decided to work up to the ultimate question slowly. "Whose house is this?" he asked.

Peter nodded in the direction of the professor of literature. "His."

"So, is everyone here connected to the university?"

"Oh, no." Again Peter had assumed his frustratingly uncommunicative, or coy, persona.

"Well, are they all just friends? I mean, what about that woman?" John pointed to the beautiful mid-twenties something woman sipping tea and listening intently to her neighbor, who apparently was making an evidently important point.

"Ah, Meiying. She's a pianist."

"A pianist!" John had guessed she was a graduate student.

"Yes, a concert pianist."

"She gets paid?" John asked naively.

"Of course. She's in great demand throughout Asia."

"Wow. So this is like an artist's group, or a literary group, or something like that?"

Peter's eyes roamed and he again proved evasive. "Not really."

"Well—"

John started to ask his critical question when Peter cut him off. "I mean, look at me. I have no artistic or literary talent whatsoever." He laughed and leaned forward as if to stand.

"What I mean is," John interjected quickly before Peter could get away. "Well, what I really mean is, the professor asked if I were 'one of us.'" John made quotation marks with his fingers. "Who is 'us'"?

"No, you must have misunderstood the Chinese," said Peter without explanation.

"No," John replied firmly. "I understand Chinese well enough to know what I heard."

Peter shrugged. "Let me introduce you to Meiying." John uttered a few words of protest, but Peter was already moving toward the young Chinese woman. When he returned with her in tow, John could only marvel at her beauty.

"Meiying, this is John Powers," announced Peter. "He is interested in your career. John, this is Miss Bai."

She bowed and at the same time held out her hand as if acknowledging east and west. John followed her lead and while shaking her hand, he noticed the strength in her slender fingers.

"You are the new teacher of Business English?" she asked in English.

John laughed. "Yes, but events may prevent me from actually teaching even one class."

She averted her eyes. "It is unfortunate, but perhaps you may yet be able to teach."

"Perhaps, but I'm beginning to doubt it."

"Ah."

He wanted to ask her about the group, but something in her demeanor told him it was too soon. "Peter tells me you are a pianist."

"Yes, a very poor one."

"I may doubt that I will be teaching, but I have no doubt you are an excellent pianist. I would love to hear you play."

She frowned and a sadness passed across her face. "I am in the same position as you, Mr. Powers."

"How so?" he asked.

She held out her hand, palm up. "The Japanese have us in their hand. If they turn it into a fist, we are crushed. Piano cannot be heard from inside a fist."

John nodded, her vivid metaphor again causing him to question his decision to stay. Before he had time to say another word to Miss Bai, the elegant lady stood. All fell silent.

"It is late. If the worst comes, I will be in touch. However, we all know how important it is to save the Precious Object. That must remain our primary goal. Individual survival is secondary. Let us go and await events."

With this, she bowed and moved to the door accompanied by the burly European with the untamed beard.

Miss Bai continued to stand next to John. Peter was nowhere in sight. Feeling emboldened, John asked, "Miss Bai, who is that extraordinary lady?"

She smiled at the departing figure in admiration. "Oh, that is Madame Liu. She truly is extraordinary. I'm afraid I must also leave."

"Before you go, Miss Bai, what is the 'Precious Object' Madame Liu mentioned?"

Miss Bai hesitated, then smiled and said, "Ah, perhaps it is a piano, but I really must go, Mr. Powers."

"A piano," John said automatically, then realized she had moved away. He called out, "I look forward to seeing you again, Miss Bai. I really do want to hear you play."

"Thank you," She called over her shoulder, then gracefully took her leave of the host, Mr. Gao.

John watched her with a flood of emotions as the events of the evening spun together in an unreal haze. When he saw Peter also preparing to leave, he made a determination to get the answer to the 'us' question.

~ *The Chosen* ~

An occasional lantern punctuated the darkness which made navigating the narrow alleyways by the two men somewhat easier, especially since the crowds had thinned, with only recumbent smokers squatting in front of their open doors, puffing out endless tendrils of smoke as they chattered in thick Shanghai accents about the Japanese threat. John was uncomfortably aware that he would be totally dependent on Peter for the foreseeable future. One day had not yet passed since his arrival and he knew less now than when he disembarked. Worse, a bewildering mystery complicated his presence.

"Peter, I am sure Madame Liu said I was 'one of us.' What did she mean?"

Unperturbed, Peter said, "Oh, if that is what she said, she just meant that we are all friends, connected directly or indirectly to the university. That's all."

This explanation sounded rehearsed, so John probed further. "What is the 'Precious Object' that Madame Liu referred to?"

Peter remained silent, casting off various words of greeting to the smokers and reeling in their responses with a hearty laugh. John waited patiently, taking in the otherworldly sights and smells of old China. When they made a sharp turn down yet another claustrophobic alleyway, his patience ran out. "Peter? Did you hear me?"

"Yes."

"Well, do you know?"

Peter stopped and lit a cigarette. While his face was illuminated by the match, his eyes locked on John's. "Yes."

Peter offered no further explanation, remaining stubbornly silent, peering at John through the smoke.

"Okay," said John, waiting for further details.

None came. John ran out of patience. "Is it a piano?"

Peter looked momentarily puzzled, then leaned close to John as if inspecting his face for signs of some illness. Finally, he asked, "John, why are you here?"

"What do you mean?" It was John's turn to feel confused.

"Why are you here?" Peter insisted.

"To teach Business English, of course."

"Bullshit! You're here because of *her*."

"Who?"

Peter snorted and began walking again, his pace much faster, so fast John had a hard time keeping up. Further questions were clearly not going to be tolerated. When they reached John's house, Peter declined to come in and abruptly left with the understanding they would meet the next morning. After finishing unpacking, John lay in bed with conflicting thoughts that had no resolution but a continuous circling back to confound him with more unanswered questions and deeper irresolution. What to do? He tried the radio to get current news but received only static. The Japanese were probably only hours away and he lounged in bed wondering about . . . about what? A group of strange people to which he presumably belonged? A 'Precious Object,' whatever that would be? If he had half the sense of a normal, rational person, he would be on that ship headed back to San Francisco. Comfortable stateroom, safety, home.

But Peter's words kept returning: 'You're here because of *her*.' It was, of course, complete nonsense. John came to China to get away from *her*, in spite of the explanations given to his friends back home. He came to escape *her* memory or *her* specter, or whatever haunted him. In fact, this was the last place in the world he thought *she* might haunt. Yet . . . yet . . . ah, it was all nonsense! Thus it went for him most the night, until a loud knocking brought him back. At first, he felt disoriented, unsure where he was, but the banging continued and his mental fog cleared quickly. *It's Peter.*

When he opened the door, John was surprised that Elizabeth Wu, not Peter Hedley, stood in the doorway. She appeared wide-eyed and excited, bowing and blurting out apologies in a confused tangle of words and gestures, some in English, some in Chinese. John finally interpreted her jumble as meaning the Japanese had entered into a ceasefire with China. "The Japs say they don't want Chinese land!" she cried. "I have cancelled my travel plans. Some students are even returning. You can teach. Start Monday!"

After providing the pertinent details about the classroom, its location, and the number of students enrolled, Miss Wu left paperwork for him to complete and made her exit amid a blur of parting words and wishes for his good fortune with the students.

At last, a semblance of normalcy. But the little mystery in which he had become embroiled still remained and he was determined to get to the bottom of it. Now that the immediate threat of war or peace had been resolved, *she* again took possession of his thoughts. He knew his apparition had become an unhealthy fixation, but the more he fought against the compulsion, the more power *she* gained.

~ *Anticipation of War* ~

For the next few days John tried to settle into a routine. He had run across Peter several times, but it was clear his questions would not be answered. Despite Miss Wu's initial enthusiasm, students barely trickled back, and John had just a handful in his classes. News reports from Peiping about the status of negotiations with the Japanese were conflicting and ambiguous. He had visions of Peter avoiding him; that he was no longer a member of 'the group'; that he was adrift with no friends; that he had no one to trust; that he was utterly alone. Was *she* somehow connected to the group, and by some miscalculation on his part, some wrong words spoken, had caused him to lose his chance? John sank into a deep depression. Eating became repugnant, the heat and humidity stifling, and his students unresponsive, jumpy, and tentative. Everyone knew more than he did about the simplest things, and his feelings of helplessness deepened into an intolerable despair. He developed a low-grade fever sapping his energy so much that he had to force himself to stir. Every day he would drag himself through the daylight hours, mechanically performing his duties, not even caring about the Japanese threat which had so concerned him just a few days ago, but which he now dismissed by convincing himself they would not dare harm an American citizen. *She* had so insinuated herself into his brain that scarcely an hour passed when *she* did not compel his attention.

As his fever intensified, one night John sought escape from the oven of his room by dragging himself outside. Once in the muggy air, he suddenly and without forethought, decided to try and retrace the path to Mr. Gao's house. Perhaps 'the group' was at that very moment meeting without him. Perhaps Peter was at that very moment denouncing him. Madame Liu, Bai Meiying, all were there mocking him. So off he set, often staggering from dizziness. After a few steps he found himself hopelessly lost. As before, smokers sat on their stoops, but when he tried to engage them, he was rewarded by blank stares and confused grunts. In his fevered mind, he had stumbled into a bizarre carnival funhouse with distorting mirrors, evil goblins, and assorted grotesqueries. Desperate to find his way home, bony hands and elongated claws grabbed at him, and in his blind frenzy, he ran headlong into a dark body. The body enfolded him, and as if by magic, bundled him back to his house. When he awoke the next morning, his sweat-soaked clothes had been removed and he lay naked in bed. John was not soon to discover this savior's identity despite repeated inquiries.

A day later, word came that Wanping was again being shelled. The ceasefire had evidently collapsed, and like a flock of nervous birds at the sound of a shot, students fled and John was left with even fewer to teach. Still feverish, unwilling to stay alone in his room another night, he went to a nearby restaurant to try and force down some food, drink some beer, and nurse the remaining embers of his fragile existence. He had only been sitting a few minutes, cloaked in his own thoughts, when someone slapped him on the back.

"Thought I'd find you here, old man!" cried Peter.

John's despondency left no room for friendly banter. "You need to get rid of that fake British lingo, Peter," he said morosely.

Peter sat unceremoniously and ordered noodles and beer. His face had turned quite serious, almost glum. He leaned forward and whispered, "Bad news. The worst is about to happen. The lamps are going out. Prepare to leave."

John felt as if he had been physically struck. "You mean back to the States?"

"John, you know that's not what I mean. *She* is calling us."

"What?" John was sure he had not heard correctly and directed his irritation and pent-up frustration at Peter. "Speak up! I can't hear you!"

Peter glanced around, but the other patrons were busily engaged in their own little conspiracies and breathless intimacies. "*She* is calling us. We will all be leaving within the next few hours while we can still get out of Shanghai."

John sank back in his chair, dumbfounded. Finally, he managed to croak out, "They won't bother us, we're American citizens." Fever, mixed with the beer, made him flushed and dizzy.

"*She* is calling us, John," insisted Peter.

John shook his head as if to clear his mind. "Who is *she*?"

"I have known for a long time that you know who *she* is. In fact, I see it in your face right now that you know."

John brought his fist down on the table. "Christ! Who is *she*, goddammit!"

Peter exhaled forcefully, threw some money on the table, and dragged John out of the restaurant. Once outside, his friend pulled him into a deserted alley and pressed him against the wall. "Breathe deeply, old boy!" Peter ordered. "Clear your damn head!"

John blinked at him in shocked wonder. "Okay," was all that he could manage.

Peter held out his hand, palm up. "You have met *her*; you must have met *her*!"

John's mind seemed to operate in slow motion, his thoughts fuzzy and indistinct. Suddenly, emerging from the fog, *she* came into sharp focus. It was as if he were looking at *her* on that very day, years ago, when *she* appeared in his office. Clothes, hair, eyes, all exact. "Yes, I met *her*."

"Then you are aware that none of us have any choice when *she* calls."

"Yes. But how . . . where?"

"I haven't the time nor the permission to go into it. Just know this; we are leaving very soon. Go home. Pack light. Await one of us to come to you. Then, poof! We're off."

"To where?"

Peter shook his head, gave him a friendly shove toward home, and disappeared in the opposite direction. John returned to his house, now associated in his mind as nothing more than a dark hovel, unhealthy and diseased, where he had passed dreary days in a fever of loneliness and hallucination. Packing was easy and he sat as in a stupor, waiting, his vision aflame with *her* image. *Speaking of hallucinations*, he thought. *Is this all a hallucination?* He then did something utterly absurd, silly, ludicrous . . . but he did it anyway: he pinched himself and slapped himself and pressed the blade of a penknife into the palm of his hand until the blood pooled. Yes, his pain was real, his blood real, he lived in the real world—this was really happening. Childlike, he could only wonder what would happen next.

~

Hours passed, and John wearied of sitting on the edge of his bed in anticipation, so he lay down fully clothed, ready to go at a moment's notice. Against his will, he fell asleep and awakened to the sound of determined banging on his front door. When he opened it, a slight, female figure stood before him. People were running down the street behind her, some shouting, but she paid no notice. Still a bit feverish, her extraordinary looks blinded him to her identity.

"Oh, hello," John said with some confusion.

"Hello, Mr. Powers," replied Bai Meiying.

John blinked in the face of her beauty and stood transfixed.

"We must go," she said quickly.

"What happened?" he called over his shoulder as he grabbed his small suitcase from the bed.

"The Japanese have invaded," she replied calmly.

"Oh, my God! Are they close?"

"Close enough."

He stood next to her in the doorway and scanned the road. "Is there a car?"

She laughed. "We ride these." From behind the open door she pulled out a bicycle. "This is yours."

He took hold of the handlebars. "And yours?"

She was already heading down the street. "Come on!" she called. "Walk your bike next to me and we'll go get mine."

As they walked, the crowds in the street began to swell. Shouts and arguments seemed to increase with each passing minute. Cars were stopped, helpless to move through the mass of humanity, horns blaring to no avail. Meiying stared straight ahead, saying nothing. Again he followed someone he barely knew leading him through a labyrinth of alleyways and narrow roads, this time jammed with panicked swarms of people, all seeming to have destinations that meant salvation. Tension and turmoil permeated the atmosphere, but Meiying sailed forward with no outward sign of urgency. When at last they reached her house, she unlocked a heavy wooden door that opened into a small courtyard. Her bicycle leaned against an acacia tree, a small bag tied to the back, and other items in a large basket.

"Excuse me for a moment," said Meiying, who then disappeared into the house.

As he waited, John listened for sounds above the raucous crowds outside the walls of the courtyard, but heard only the high-pitched trilling of birds. He half-expected to hear gunfire, but decided that would be too dramatic. Amid these thoughts, Meiying reappeared in the doorway to the house. "Come, please," she called, as she motioned him to follow inside.

When he entered, she led him to an adjoining room and sat at a beautiful grand piano. Without a word, she began playing *Moonlight Sonata*. John listened, enraptured, the ugly sounds from the street dying away to nothing in the face of Beethoven's genius.

But all too soon it was over. "I wanted to play one last time," she said. "You were my last audience."

"I am honored."

Meiying bowed and said, "I am honored to have you hear my poor playing."

With this, she quickly walked back out and they rode together toward a destination he knew not where. As he followed Meiying, John tried to concentrate on the route that they were taking, but as time passed, the crowds thinned, and his mind wandered. *Why have I put myself in this position? I must have some sort of macabre wish to die away from everything familiar, everything dear to me.* The strangeness bore in on him. *Why am I here?* He felt panicked. *Turn around! The ship must still be there! Leave China, fool!* But he pedaled on.

~ *Where is the Destination?* ~

For hours they traveled, carried along by a rising tide of fleeing people, the main road constantly being fed by the smaller tributary streets and alleys. John's heart quickened when he saw, for the first time, soldiers moving in the opposite direction, their young faces grim and frightened. Not a word had been spoken by Meiying, and John again felt a rising panic, due in no small part to the collective noise of the multitudes and the fact that every kilometer took him farther away from any chance to return home.

"Miss Bai!" he shouted above the din of the throngs.

She kept pedaling a few meters ahead of him.

"Miss Bai! Stop!" he shouted louder. She turned to look, and on seeing John gesture to stop, she veered off the road onto a small dirt path and waited for him under the narrow strip of shade from a poplar tree.

It took him awhile to navigate past a large family shepherding two huge water buffaloes, but at last he reached her. She looked at him while wiping the sweat from her face. Before he spoke, she donned a broad peasant hat retrieved from her basket.

"Miss Bai," he said, leaning his bike against the tree. "Let's rest for a minute."

She looked at her watch, then at the passing tide of humanity, and replied, "Okay, for a minute."

"Miss Bai, where are we going? Please tell me."

"To meet the others."

"How much farther?"

"Not far."

John closed his eyes in frustration. It seemed that all members of the group were uniformly tight-lipped. "Not far. Okay. Then what?" he said as calmly as he could under the circumstances.

"Then we all travel together to a distant place to wait in safety." She unwrapped a sticky bun and handed it to him. "Here, eat this please. You will feel better."

John gratefully took it. "And you?"

"Not hungry."

He took a few guilty bites, gazed up the road, and asked, "Miss Bai, who are the people we are going to meet?"

She looked at him and tilted her head as if confused.

"I mean, who are the people going with us to the distant place?"

She smiled disarmingly. "Please call me Meiying. Some you met, some not. Some go part of the way; some go all the way."

"Am I going all the way?" asked John.

"Mr. Powers," she laughed. "Of course you are going all of the way."

"Call me John, please. Why me, Meiying? Why do I go all the way?"

"Because you are an American." She made a funny face. "Stand out like a carp in a small pond."

Her calm assurance gave him courage, and he felt a shiver of pleasant anticipation, even a surge of energizing curiosity at what adventures lay ahead. The malaise he had suffered over the past few days was gone, and his strength seemed to increase dramatically when contrasted with his recent illness. Emboldened by this new vitality, he asked Meiying, "What really is the 'Precious Object' that Madame Liu talked about?"

Meiying's face darkened. "You must ask her when we meet. Now we must go."

Before he had time to respond, she held her bike upright and waited for him to join her. John shrugged as if powerless to resist. On they went.

~

Vast rice paddies came into view, and John could smell the nutrient-rich water that flooded the fields. The air was full of it; a damp fertility man could not destroy with all his wars. Peasants worked non-stop on the footpaths and knee-deep in the water unfazed by the chaos and hubbub of the human-choked road. More soldiers passed, this time laughing and pointing at the peasant women in the fields, who laughed and joked back. Crude, sexual innuendos were flung back and forth, but when John gazed at her back, Meiying rode on without a word or glance in either direction.

Light faded rapidly as John's legs and back began to ache. The paddies stretched on to merge indistinctly with a line of remote foothills. Standing like a regal palace, a house appeared in the distance, made of stone walls and a magnificent tile roof, upturned in the traditional style. The last rays of sun seemed to make it glow through the grey dusk. To his relief, Meiying pulled off the main road and onto a small path that led to the house. As they approached, the rapidly darkening sky revealed lights faintly glimmering from inside.

Meiying opened the front door without knocking and motioned John to go ahead of her. When he entered, a small group stood in a semi-circle smiling at him. Mr. Gao, the professor of literature, gently rested both hands on the shoulders of a young boy. "Little Acorn here"—he patted the boy's head—"spotted you coming up the road."

Peter stepped to the front. "Welcome, old chap!" he cried. "The gang's all here!"

John scanned the faces and acknowledged those he recognized with a friendly nod; Madame Liu, the burly European with the unkempt beard, Mr. Gao, the old peasant couple, and others. But there were many he had never seen. Attention shifted to Meiying and as several went to embrace her, Peter took it upon himself to introduce John to those of the assembled group he had not previously known. In this way, John met a middle-aged couple who also looked like leather-faced peasants; a young man who had worked at a tailor shop but said his true profession was writing poetry; an old man who volunteered that he had been an antiques merchant, but that the recent death of his wife forced him to sell the business; and assorted children and teenagers who clearly preferred to be outside running about. John could discern no rhyme or reason for the inclusion of such dissimilar people into 'the group.' This anomaly led him back to recognizing that the unifying force, the first principle, which held them all together was, of course, *her*. Could *she* truly be the same as his apparition? After all, that was the only reason he agreed to leave Shanghai. But the situation, the entire scenario, seemed utterly absurd. What tied these varied people to *her*, and from *her* to him? John could never quite escape the idea that all of this was a dream, or a hallucination of some sort, and he would soon awaken back home in his own bed feeling sheepish for having such crazy flights of fancy.

As the initial words of greeting died away, Madame Liu spoke up. "Now that we are all here, let us go into the banquet room for tea and *dim sum*. The children may go outside, but they must stay within sight of the house." She jabbed her finger in the air. "You older ones make sure this order is obeyed! There is danger! There are soldiers, some of whom have deserted and are desperate." She jabbed her finger again for emphasis. "And there are bandits and thieves! Do you hear?"

A collective "Yes, Madame Liu!" rose from the kids, and off they ran except Little Acorn, who scuttled into the next room and grabbed a few hot buns before making his escape.

When the adults filtered into the banquet room, John was shown to his seat at a huge table filled with an endless array of dumplings, buns, rice, and bamboo steamers filled with food totally unfamiliar to him. Peter, his unofficial guide and cultural interpreter, sat next to John and promptly began eating, occasionally offering John a dish while enthusiastically describing its ingredients. The group ate and carried on overlapping topics of discussion that mainly centered on the intentions of the Japanese, and the likely responses of the communists and Nationalists. Finally, Madame Liu rose and the room fell silent.

"We all know why we are here. Some of us know more than others. Some of us want to see *her* again for reasons different than others. But it has been made clear that *she* wants to see all of us. Under what circumstances and in what configuration—all of us at once, some of us in smaller groups at different times, or some individually—remains unclear. What is abundantly clear is that, for the time being, we must travel together. First, to recover the Precious Object, then on to the final destination. Unfortunately, events will make getting to the final destination very difficult. The dangers I warned the children about apply equally, even more so, to us. One thing is certain, the Japanese will soon arrive, and there will be a terrible battle. It will spread throughout the countryside. Many will be killed, and many more will be driven to desperation. Desperate people commit desperate acts—thus, we cannot stay here. We leave tomorrow. Meiying, you will stay with me tonight, and Mr. Powers will share the room with Mr. Hedley and Lu Zhishen." She bowed, "Thank you."

As the group broke up into segments, John sought out Meiying. While Peter engaged in an intense conversation with the young poet, John sidled away, only to see Meiying step outside with the burly European. He followed, and to his surprise heard them discussing Mozart. He felt a pang of irrational jealousy. Meiying noticed him standing nearby (he pretended to look up at the stars) and motioned for him to join her and her companion. Feeling self-conscious, he walked over and, for lack of something cleverer to say, greeted them with, "Hello."

The burly European stuck out a big paw and said, "Hello. We have not been properly introduced. My name is Adrian Morrison, originally from Canada."

While John shook his hand, Meiying laughed and said, "We call him Lu Zhishen."

"The character from *Water Margin*?" John asked.

"Yes, though we Chinese do not understand how *Shui Hu Zhuan* has been translated in English as *Water Margin*."

John looked at Lu Zhishen and mentally compared him to the character in the novel. Partly to show off his knowledge of Chinese literature, and partly out of genuine curiosity, he asked, "So, are you really like Lu Zhishen, other than your great size? I mean, are you boisterous, hard drinking, heroic, and often disguise yourself as a monk?"

Lu Zhishen laughed much louder than his soft-spoken manner of speaking. "No," he said after his laughter died down. "But I tell you, China today is a lot like the old Three Kingdoms era."

Meiying shuddered. "Yes, unfortunately."

"Tell me, Adrian—" John began.

"No, no!" he was cut off by the burly Canadian. "Call me Lu Zhishen. It's tradition—and besides, it makes me feel more Chinese."

"Okay. What is this 'Precious Object' I keep hearing about?"

Meiying and Lu Zhishen exchanged glances. John waited patiently, but his stern expression indicated a firm desire for an answer.

Meiying finally spoke up. "We don't know. As far as we know"—she looked at Lu Zhishen for confirmation—"only Madame Liu knows."

"Oh," sighed a disappointed John.

An awkward silence ensued, whereupon Lu Zhishen said, "We are all curious, but hopefully will learn soon enough. Let us move on to other things." His face brightened. "This place has a piano, not a good one, but good enough. Meiying has agreed to play for us."

"So, I'm not your last audience," said John, forcing a smile.

"Lu Zhishen has requested Mozart. I—"

"Your choice, Meiying," he quickly interposed.

John inwardly winced at the return of an uncomfortable feeling of jealousy, made more bitter by Meiying's endearing smile and response to Lu Zhishen. "I will be happy to play Mozart"

~ *Incident on the Road* ~

That evening, after the children were sent to bed, a most incongruous scene unfolded, as Chinese and foreigners sat listening to Mozart, played beautifully by Meiying. John gave himself over to the music. He could tell that others listened without understanding, but to him chords were struck that went straight to his brainstem and he wiped away tears of pent-up emotion. Many of the Chinese found the music strange to their ears, but listened politely. Soon, however, through the open windows came the first ominous rumbling. Meiying stopped playing and they all strained their ears. Distant but distinct popping interspersed the low rumbles.

"Thunder?" asked one of the group.

"No. It has started," said the man whose leathery face betrayed his peasant background. "That is gunfire. My wife and I know it well. We heard it often enough before we fled Harbin."

John's heart sank. What was once speculation now assumed a malevolent reality. Peter stood and said, "I'm going to take a look outside." The rest followed, and even the children filtered out from their rooms, rubbing their eyes and sticking close to the assembled adults. Glowing brightly on the horizon as from a thousand campfires, Shanghai burned. Thuds came closer together and the angry red welt spread across the night sky.

"We leave at sunrise tomorrow," said Madame Liu simply and with no emotion. "Be ready." She returned to the house with brisk and determined steps.

"What do you think?" John asked no one in particular, a lump rising in his throat.

Mr. Gao said, "I think all I know is that we leave tomorrow, and the sooner the better!"

"Does anyone know where we are going?" asked John, adding sarcastically, "Or is Madame Liu the only one who knows?"

"We take the road to Nanjing," said Peter. "Our first destination is a small town outside the city."

"And from there," added Mr. Gao, "we move on. The Japs will also be in Nanjing before long. It's only about 300 kilometers from Shanghai although we have taken the scenic route."

John again felt that familiar mixture of dread and excitement. For the moment, even *she* and the 'Precious Object' faded into the background as youthful craving for unique and even dangerous experiences dominated his thoughts. "Where do we go from there?" pursued John.

Meiying, still staring at the red scar, shook her head. "From there will be a much longer journey, and the Japanese may be the least of the evils we will encounter."

The next morning was all hustle and bustle. Although there were barely enough bikes, many were overloaded and most people had to double-up. Consequently, the pace would be slow, made worse by the addition of more refugees fleeing Shanghai. Distant gunfire became louder and continuous, causing many to look back for fear of seeing columns of Japanese marching toward them.

Before John could process the gravity of the situation, they were off, held together by a common purpose, motivated by the fear of dropping out, and terrified at the possibility of losing touch with the others. Like a flock of birds, they veered and paused together, occasionally landing to eat and rest. The first two days were uneventful, but the third day brought an unexpected crisis. The group awoke to a road clogged with Nationalist troops heading toward Shanghai. Civilian refugees were forced off the road, and Japanese planes could be heard bombing only a few kilometers away.

A Nationalist officer on horseback cantered to the right and the left of the road screaming, "Out of the way! Out of the way! Fools! Let us through!" He lashed out at laggards with his swagger stick. "Fools—let us through!" His fear was palpable. Some brave soul protested, "Sir! There are women and children! We cannot move!" But he continued to cut a swath until confronted by Madame Liu. She stood unmoving in front of a peasant family comprised of two old people and children. Evidently the young parents were gone. The officer, in his fury, struck Madame Liu across the face. She stood unflinching, wiping the blood from her cheek. The officer blanched at her stoicism and looked around at the upturned faces. "I cannot help it!" he yelled, hesitation in his tone. "You must move! How can we stop the Japs?"

"By not turning your own people into enemies!" she responded with a subdued but powerful serenity.

He jerked his horse's reins and cried, "Ah, stupid woman!" But the beatings ceased. Madame Liu later explained that he was a good man placed in an impossible situation.

Some in the group argued with her, saying he should have been punished, but she said, "It is what *she* would have done, and it is for *her* that we make this trip."

After this incident, it was agreed the group would take a smaller, spur road to get around the mass of soldiers and equipment, so they ventured off the main road on a wide, dirt lane with deep, cart-wheel ruts that wound lazily through the countryside. Late afternoon cast long shadows from the thickening forest of trees, and by mutual consent they set up camp for the night by a small stream.

John found a good spot away from the water and hopefully the multitude of mosquitoes. Peter walked up and lit a cigarette. "How's it going?"

"Well," said John, "at least you didn't say 'old man' with that awful British accent. Anyway, it's going alright. The sounds of battle are more distant. Jiang's troops must be giving the Japs hell."

Peter scoffed. "Don't believe it for a minute! The Generalissimo's soldiers are completely outgunned. So far, we've been lucky."

"Yeah, so lucky. A picnic."

"It has been. You—"

But Peter's words were cut short by the sound of nearby gunfire, then screams. Both men ran toward the sounds and quickly came upon the young poet, bleeding profusely and moaning on the ground. More screams. Peter stayed to help the young man while John continued on. When he reached a clearing, he came to a screeching halt. Facing him, with their weapons drawn, were four Chinese soldiers, wide-eyed and jumpy. Another was struggling with Meiying to force her into the undergrowth. Before John had time to respond, Madame Liu shouted boldly to him, "Are the others coming?"

"Yes, they're all coming!" he shouted back.

She turned to the soldiers. "You are Chinese. You are men. Defend us from the foreign devils! Be men, not murderers and rapists of your own people! Shame!"

The apparent leader kept looking nervously past John's shoulder. As her words sank in, he said, "Let's go!" The others willingly followed and they evaporated into the underbrush.

"Deserters!" said Mr. Gao, spitting on the ground for emphasis.

Madame Liu was already heading back to where the young poet lay, still groaning. The bullet had shattered his collarbone, and two peasant women applied bandages.

"They may come back," someone said nervously.

"How do we move him?" came another comment.

Mr. Gao spoke up. "Someone go back to the main road, flag down a military truck, tell them a soldier has been shot fighting the Japanese. They will take him, give him medical care."

"But he's not a soldier," came a voice.

Mr. Gao shrugged. "Doesn't matter. We'll tell them we gave him civilian clothes."

So it was done. The trip had just started, but the group had already lost a member, and the mood settled into a grim determination. Only the children's spirits seemed unaffected. It was two days later, when John looked up to see a Japanese plane flying overhead, that the strange lights began flickering at the edge of his mind. At first, he thought it simply had been caused by the bright sun, but as the lights continued to dance, he felt sensations that made him oddly disengaged from the world. As the lights flickered and flashed, he saw *her* face illuminated deep in his mind, staring at his soul, penetrating eyes burning through the fog, and from the transparent vortex came the voices. And he became afraid.

Chapter Three

The Voices Begin With A Voice

Tangles

~ On the Road ~

As the group inched ahead on side roads toward its destination, days turned into weeks, and John became more and more uninterested in what went on around him. He remained stubbornly unresponsive to their inquiries, and when they set up camp for the evening, Meiying had become worried enough to approach him. Again the group had camped by a stream, but this time he remained close. Meiying found him squatting on a flat rock overlooking the gentle current, mesmerized by a rapidly fading sunlight skittering atop the water. Mosquitoes swarmed around his face, but he seemed oblivious. She sat next to him, waved her arms through the cloud of insects, and tossed a pebble carelessly into the stream. When he ignored the effort, she threw another.

"Be careful!" he whispered urgently. "You're breaking up the light, and besides, you might kill a fish."

"Ah," she said noncommittally, caution in her voice. "That's true."

He continued to stare at the water.

"John, are you feeling okay?" she asked gingerly.

"Of course."

"I mean, lately you've seemed distracted."

He started to say, 'I don't know what you mean.' But he did know what she meant, so remained silent.

"What are you thinking?" she continued.

"I'm thinking of Thinking."

She paused to consider. "I don't understand."

John knit his eyebrows and shook his head. "Why do we think?"

"Because we must."

"But if we didn't. I mean, if we kept our mind blank, so no voices would interrupt."

"Interrupt what?"

John gave a deep sigh and looked up at the tree tops, still illuminated by the last rays of sun. "Just to have one pure image," he said. "An image uncorrupted, or untarnished by base and unworthy thoughts."

Meiying looked at him intently. "What pure image, John?"

"*Her.*"

Meiying contemplated this for a moment. "To reach *her*, the pure image of *her*, we must cut through a tangle of problems and obstacles. To know where to cut, we must see. To know where to see, we must think. To think, we must share with others. To share, we must use our voices."

John appeared excited. "That's just it! To think creates the tangles. The more thought the more tangles, the more tangles the more cutting, until everything is cut and nothing remains except the damn voices."

"Except *her*," corrected Meiying.

John turned to look directly at Meiying and she felt a tinge of satisfaction that, at least, he was engaged with the world, with something.

"Meiying," he said softly. "Do you think of *her* when you play the piano?"

"Sometimes."

"When I listen to you play, I don't think of *her*."

"Oh?"

"No, I think only of you."

Meiying lowered her eyes, an instinctive move which men often interpreted as flirtation, and which she always rebuked herself for performing, since it was so mistakenly perceived as a feminine wile. She felt genuinely uncomfortable with male compliments. In cases like this, deflection was her preferred order of the day. "Thinking of me is thinking, and according to you, thinking corrupts your image of *her*. When I play, think of *her*."

"No, no, no."

"Good!" she cried before he could say more. "Then we agree that thinking isn't always bad!" She laughed. "Recently, you have not been with us mentally. We need you to be thinking, John. To help us think together."

John joined her laughter. "But," he said at last. "When I think of you, I still get all in a tangle."

Meiying took on an exaggeratedly serious expression. "Then I must cut the tangles!"

"Ah, no! Your tangles hold me up, not tie me down."

Meiying looked at him with affection. "No wonder you are confused, John. But now that you are up, you must stay up. Do not let those dark thoughts drag you down. We all need each other for support."

"Yes, I see that now. Thank you."

John felt a pang of resentment for her success in coaxing him out and liberating him from the voices, at least for the time being. He was quite aware that she misunderstood the nature of the voices, but the sincerity of her misunderstanding helped him to see how his 'tangles' could be controlled, if not cut altogether. To guide the conversation away from him and regain some level of equality in shared confidences, he asked, "Where did you meet *her*? You know, I mean what were the circumstances?"

Meiying's face darkened and she looked at the water. "Perhaps that is a story for another time."

"Why not now?" he said in an accusing tone.

Before she could respond, a distant but deep and continuous rumble of artillery shook the ground. Meiying shuddered. "We must sleep and leave early tomorrow. Time is short, Peiping has fallen, and they're attacking Shanghai."

John could only nod, his heart beating faster to the ominous thuds that merged into the rapid drumbeat of a major battle. He wondered if he was a coward. *Perhaps that is a story for another time*, he thought, appreciating his own ironic sensibility and welcoming himself back to the world, complicated and exasperating as it seemed. As if to mock the narcissism of his navel-gazing, he heard the children laughing and running about, playing hide-and-seek.

~ The Road Attracts Attention ~

When Meiying returned to her sleeping area, she leaned against a tree and cried. All the pent-up emotion, the trauma of the recent incident, and the uncertainty of her future, preyed on her mind. She missed a normal, peaceful life. She missed being clean. She had no idea how to support herself now that Shanghai was in flames. As a small, vulnerable pianist, she faced her collapsing world alone. People in the interior would not pay to hear western music. How would she eat? Looking at Little Acorn sleeping nearby, she thanked god after all that she did not have a husband and children. Perhaps *she* would give guidance after the Precious Object was retrieved and they reached the final destination. Perhaps Madame Liu's contacts would help her survive. *So much uncertainty*, she thought. *Come what may.*

Sounds of the battle became louder, and she felt a flutter of panic—the urge to run as fast as she could go. But she pushed down this irrational impulse and tried to focus on the future. She would find work somewhere, somehow. She would survive. Perhaps a husband? Although men did not interest her sexually, a husband with money and authority could be useful. She knew she was considered beautiful by the world. *Although not now*, she thought, imagining the dirt and grime that had accumulated since their flight from Shanghai. She ran her fingers through her hair and felt a pang of regret. *Oh, the world for shampoo!* and laughed at the frivolous luxuries of which she had become so fond and missed so much.

Yet, Meiying had a longing for something beyond the comfortable life she had so far lived. Her parents, middle-class merchants, were non-political and had stayed out of the horrific bloodshed between the Nationalists and the communists. She had passed many a decapitated communist head in the streets of

Shanghai, but the piano and her music kept her clean and unstained by the violence. Until now. How could she explain to the others that the gaping hole she felt in her life, the longing for companionship, would be instantly fulfilled when she met the object of their pilgrimage? Meiying had long ago thought she accepted her attraction to other women and vowed she would keep it a secret to her grave, until this remarkable woman, who even Madame Liu worshipped, entered her life. How would her companions respond if they knew that sexual attraction to *her* occupied a central role in Meiying's decision to join? Unthinkable. Her loneliness was made more terrible by a secret that must remain a secret at all costs. She held out her hand; palm up, to catch the moonlight. Shadows flitted across her skin and played upon the curves of her fingers, traversing the lifelines and hardened callouses that marked the rigor of endless practice. An imaginary keyboard appeared before her, so she closed her eyes and played Beethoven. His music filled the forest, softened her heart, and hardened her resolve. Sounds of the battle roared in the background like a voracious lion, but to her it now seemed powerless.

Dawn brought the group alive with anxious preparations. Unnerved by the on-going battle, everyone hurried to their bikes and pedaled away as fast as possible from the frightening noise. Lu Zhishen laughed and jabbed a thumb toward the battle. "All this banging about is bad for my liver! Be quiet!" he bellowed.

Evidently, as time passed, Lu Zhishen seemed to take on the characteristics of his literary namesake. Soft-spoken words were replaced by an almost bellicose verbosity. This transformation appeared suddenly, as if he had made up his mind one day to be the famous fictional character rather than himself. As with every one of her companions, Meiying wondered what connected Lu Zhishen to *her*. When she heard John ask him this question the previous day, Lu Zhishen held out his hand, palm up, and said, "This empty hand is all that any of us have in common with *her*." Meiying was struck by the insight, but his answer had given her pause to consider what the others must be feeling. Did their connections to *her* match the depth of her own feelings? As an honest person, her reply had to be 'yes.' And if yes, what deep and enduring cord tied them to this strange and indescribable person? The mystery deepened, giving hints of something forever unfathomable.

Just as they started off on the little road they had chosen as safe, a Japanese plane flew overhead, then made a tight turn and came back, flying lower. Lu Zhishen struck a pose in the open and shook his fist. "Bastards!" he shouted. Everyone else scattered under the trees.

"Lu Zhishen!" admonished Madame Liu. "Are you trying to get us all killed?"

Others chimed in. "Yes! Stop! Get behind a tree! Don't be foolish!"

But he remained defiant. John, crouching behind a fallen tree, admired his courage and again considered himself, by comparison, cowardly. He tried to see Meiying and gauge her reaction to Lu Zhishen's antics, but she was too well concealed for him to spot. He started to rise when the plane returned again, this time skimming the treetops. Suddenly, machine-gun fire rattled above the sound of the propeller and churned up the dirt and grass around Lu Zhishen. Scream-ing, he ran as fast as his legs would carry him and jumped next to John.

"That was stupid," he said sheepishly, in his old voice.

"I thought it was brave of you," replied John, all the while nervously scanning the sky.

"No, it was stupid. Don't live in a novel—the reader can slam it shut and bury you in perpetual darkness. You can call me Lu Zhishen, but I will no longer try to be Lu Zhishen."

"Too bad," said John. "You make a good Lu Zhishen."

"Really?"

"Yeah, when you're him, you give the rest of us courage."

He looked doubtful. "Well, we'll see. Perhaps he'll come out again, when it's less dangerous!"

When it became obvious that the plane would not return, the group contin-ued their journey. After a few hours, Madame Liu announced without warning, "We are almost there. We will reach our first destination before dark."

This news made the group perk up, and everyone pedaled a little faster. By late afternoon, signs of a nearby town began appearing; houses more frequent, the road more crowded, barking dogs more numerous, and the faint but distinctive smells of a distant open-air marketplace, all combined to raise their spirits. When they labored up one last hill, they gathered at the top to look down upon a rather large town, with brick houses, busy streets, large signs advertising businesses, and an impressive temple near the center.

All eyes turned to Madame Liu. "Where to?" asked Mr. Gao.

"To the temple, and from there . . . well, you will see."

On their way to the temple, they passed a host of soldiers looking lost and confused, some on their way to the front, some returning. Officers tried to maintain order, but soldiers went about helter-skelter, carrying their weapons with them into stores and restaurants, boisterous and heedless of propriety or civil behavior.

Carts carrying wounded soldiers with vacant eyes rolled past in a long, sad caravan. Motorized vehicles spooked the horses, and the smell of dung, piss, and sweat mingled with the enticing aromas from the marketplace wafting on the breeze. Excited townspeople chattered with the soldiers, peppering them with questions and begging them for information on how the battle for Shanghai was progressing. Finally, after much difficulty navigating the unruly crowds, the outside wall of the temple rose before them.

John had seen a few temples in Shanghai—Buddhist, Daoist, and Confu-cian—but this one appeared very different. Its outside walls were thick and tall, spanning many blocks of the town. A multi-story temple rose from the interior in gaudy splendor. The massive wooden gate of the outer wall remained open to the inner courtyard, with numerous visitors and monks passing through in both directions. Carried along by his companions, he could only look about in wonder as they walked their bikes through the gate behind the formidable Madame Liu.

Before they had taken many steps, a young novitiate ran up to Madame Liu, who whispered something in his ear. Off he ran and the group gathered in the shade of an inner wall to wait. A different monk came out and requested Madame Liu follow him for an interview inside the temple. After her departure, very few words were spoken by members of the group. Unexpectedly, the peasant couple rose and spoke briefly to Mr. Gao, then walked slowly toward the temple. John had always felt separated from them, as they spoke no English and their mandarin contained a heavily-accented northern dialect, making it almost unintelligible even to Meiying. But their friendly, dignified manner combined with his curiosity about the temple made him want to follow the two peasants.

With Madame Liu still gone and the couple headed toward the temple, John told Peter he also wanted to see inside the building. "I'll join you, old chap," said Peter, eliciting John's rolling eyes. Although they walked together, John remained intent on following the peasant couple. Accompanied by Peter's usual pedantic commentary, the two entered the reception area, lagging a bit behind the husband and wife. After adjusting his eyes to the dark interior, John saw the aged pair kneel and bow in front of a shrine, above which towered a large statue of Buddha. A multitude of candles and joss sticks stretched right and left at Buddha's feet. Through the haze he observed the two leathery peasants crying openly, their hands pressed together in prayer, rocking back and forth and chanting a low dirge.

Peter took it upon himself to whisper an explanation. "Their children were murdered by the Japanese in Manchuria. Killed in front of their eyes. Daughter carried off, house burned, crops destroyed, animals confiscated."

"My god," said John, looking at them with new eyes.

"They had nothing left but themselves, so they fled Manchuria years ago. After an unimaginable amount of suffering and trouble, they eventually made their way to Shanghai."

"How do they come to be here . . . with us, I mean?"

Peter shrugged.

"And their knowledge of *her*?"

Peter shrugged again.

Instantly, John became fascinated with their story and more particularly, how their story tied-in with *her*. Peter wanted to move on, but John insisted on staying, and from his semi-concealed position, observed this oddly captivating couple until they left and rejoined the group.

Before John had time to investigate further (he had planned to ask Meiying more details) Madame Liu returned with an ancient monk who she introduced as Master Kang. In a deep, sonorous voice, the old man spoke. "We have been waiting. *She* has been waiting. We must stay. *She* must leave"—his eyes scanned the group, seeming to gauge their grit and determination—"with you."

"Is *she* here?" came excited cries from the group.

Madame Liu smiled. "Yes and no."

Puzzled looks. Silent anticipation. Madame Liu basked in the moment, then said, "It is the Precious Object we are taking with us to the final destination."

Gasps and an electric thrill ran through the group. "So soon!" cried Peter. "I thought the Precious Object waited for us with *her* at the final destination."

"No," sighed Master Kang. "We must give up the Precious Object in order to save it. It has been with us for many decades. But now, as we all know, it is no longer safe here." As if on cue, Chinese military planes flew overhead on their way to Shanghai. A cheer went up from the soldiers outside the walls, and a few shots went off in celebration.

"Time is of the essence," said Madame Liu. "We will spend the night here in the dormitories, females with the nuns, males with the monks, then leave early tomorrow morning."

"Do we know what is happening in Shanghai?" asked Lu Zhishen.

Master Kang shook his head. "Outside these walls, chaos reigns. The battle is going badly, but our Chinese brothers are doing their best. Nevertheless, I have been told to expect the worst. If the Japanese come, the Precious Object will be far away. Hopefully safe."

Madame Liu chimed in. "There are many reports of lawlessness beyond the Nanjing area. Warlords and bandits and deserters are making much trouble. Where we are going requires us to pass through these areas. Those who want to stay in Nanjing may do so." Her eyes settled on Peter, Lu Zhishen, and John. "Particularly you foreigners. This may be your last chance to try and escape. There are still flights from Nanjing to Hong Kong. From there"—she held out a fist, then opened it, palm up—"you are free." She kept her hand open.

Lu Zhishen spoke up. "I am here to stay! Besides, if I leave now, my namesake will haunt my dreams." He held out his hand as did Madame Liu, palm up. "I am already free."

"I as well," said Peter calmly.

John remained quiet.

"John?" asked Madame Liu. "Nobody will question your decision. You needn't make it now, but we are leaving tomorrow."

Everyone looked at him. When he glanced at Meiying, she seemed unusually intent on his response. He thought of the peasant couple and the Precious Object. Then he thought of *her*. "Yes, I am going with you," he said.

"Why don't you decide tomorrow," said Meiying. "It is a major decision. Life or death. And you have only been here a few weeks. Nothing, really. The others have been here much longer. Many years. There is still time for you to return home and be safe."

John listened in tight-lipped silence, but inwardly his stomach churned. Meiying's surprising statement could be taken as a recognition of his cowardice, his lack of commitment. Or, it might be something else. An attempt to get rid of him? In any case, he could not simply agree to her words and passively submit to their implications. If ever he was to assert his independence, it was now. Independence from what? That he did not know. But as he stood for a few moments in silence, the anger lessened, his head cleared, and he again thought of *her* and the Precious Object. So far, the trip had not been too dangerous. They were fleeing the Japanese, not just waiting for them to come. He would see the Precious Object. He would see *her*. Yes, he would see *her, her, her*!

"No! I have already thought this over very carefully. I am staying!"

Master Kang cocked his head approvingly and started back to the temple. The rest followed like chicks.

Once they had entered the reception area of the temple, a nun and a monk appeared and stood next to Master Kang. He gestured toward the nun. "This *bikkuni* will escort the women to their room." He then turned toward the monk. "And this *bikkhus* will do the same for the men. The children will share according to their gender."

Madame Liu looked at them gravely, and added, "After you are settled, we will eat with Master Kang and then go to the Precious Object in preparation for tomorrow's departure."

~ *The Temple* ~

After they laid out their bedrolls on the austere dormitory floor and washed-up, John and Peter walked down a long, dark hallway to the dining area for resident monks and nuns. They were the first two of the group to arrive, but the residents were already eating their vegetarian fare at a long, rectangular table that looked even more ancient than the temple itself. One young monk had been in the midst of a long dissertation about Buddhist doctrine and the exigencies of war. Peter tried to keep up, providing John with a labored clarification.

"The Japanese have invaded our homeland. This is a just war. We must support our Chinese soldier-brothers."

"That is all well and good," said an older monk. "But all violence, all war, is an inexcusable corruption of *dharma*. Your so-called 'just war' is a delusion."

"Our *dharma* may suffer, but that is nothing to the suffering the Japanese will inflict."

"The Japanese themselves are a delusion!" cried the older monk. "Do you hate them?"

The younger monk hesitated, knowing the question was a trap. "No."

The older monk disregarded the answer. "Even unavoidable violence is bad *karma*."

As this debate progressed, others filtered into the room. All who arrived ate quietly and followed the points made by the parties to the discussion with apparent interest, but none of the group joined in. John listened with one ear to Peter while observing Meiying sitting next to Lu Zhishen. Although she sat in silence, eating little, her intelligent face registered engagement with the conversation. To his relief, she seemed to ignore Lu Zhishen even when he whispered in her ear.

By now, the argument revolved around the nature of delusion. John, knowing little about Buddhist doctrine, jumped on Peter's repeated use of the word delusion as the translation progressed.

"Delusion!" John cried in English after hearing the word repeated multiple times. "Do they mean voices in the head?"

This unexpected outburst resulted in an abrupt silence around the table.

The monks and nuns, most of whom could not speak English, looked at Peter for an explanation.

Meanwhile, utterly beside himself with embarrassment, John kept repeating his apologies. "*Duibuqi, duibuqi, duibuqi . . . .*"

But Meiying, who had been watching closely, seemed to comprehend something and spoke to the gathering before Peter had collected his thoughts. "Mr. Powers has asked where voices in the head come from. Are they a delusion, or is there some deeper explanation?"

Their hosts talked among themselves, and an older monk spoke gravely, "We had a young novitiate last year who heard voices in his head. The old masters told him the voices were a delusion, and that his *Buddha-dharma* was clearly restless. Unfortunately, the boy hanged himself from a tree in the courtyard."

Meiying looked stricken and peered at John wordlessly, as if waiting for his response. But Peter's explanation took a moment.

When he finished interpreting the Buddhist terminology, Peter asked clumsily, "Do you hear voices?"

"No," replied John as calmly as possible. "*She* talks to me, as *she* talks to all of us."

Master Kang, who had slipped in earlier and remained silent during most of the discussion, now stood, his face glowing with a kindly smile. "All of our guests have spoken with *her*, have seen *her* manifested, and now are prepared to depart on a journey with Goddess to meet *her* again. This is the voice our foreign guest refers to. But there are other voices he might be hinting at. These voices in all of our heads are the ageless echoes of past lives. We often do not recognize them as such, and so we become afraid. Sometimes that fear drives us to the point of taking our own present lives, which will then become an echo far into the future. Such a distorted echo is dissonant and stands out above the others, harming future lives as it reverberates through generations."

Meiying seemed excited by these words and interjected in a quiet but firm manner. "Yes, Master Kang, as a pianist, I know well the meaning of your words. Out of the thousands of notes in a Mozart sonata, one dissonant chord, one wrongly played note, will stand out above all the others and ruin the whole."

Master Kang smiled and nodded. "I wish we had a piano here, Sister Bai, for I would like to hear you play."

"Do you know Mozart?" asked Meiying.

"No, but I have heard the name."

"Oh, I also wish there was a piano so you could hear his music."

"As do I."

"His music is divine . . . if I may say so." Meiying's face turned red.

Master Kang grinned mischievously and bowed to the young woman, then turned to Madame Liu. "You have a most interesting group to accompany you on your journey, Madame Liu."

"Yes, indeed," she replied, her face not altogether without worry.

~ *The Precious Object* ~

"Let us go to the Goddess," said Master Kang. "Let us see the Precious Object."

Tingling with excitement, the group followed Master Kang up a long, narrow, zigzagging staircase past several floors when at last the climb ended at the top room harboring the Precious Object. Pitch dark. Master Kang entered and held out his lantern, illuminating a room full of clutter. He moved carefully to the opposite side, the rest following close behind. A collective gasp went up as he shone the light in the corner. Glowing in the lantern-light sat a gold figurine, a goddess sitting in a meditative pose. The figurine's legs were crossed, hands resting above both knees, right hand facing up, thumb touching forefinger, gracefully curved into a circle. Next to the statue rested an open, nondescript bamboo box. John thought that the glow seemed organic to the figurine rather than a reflection of the lantern, but chalked it up to an overactive imagination.

Master Kang spoke softly. "She will be placed in the false bottom of this box, which will then be filled with wheat chaff. If you are waylaid by bandits, you will tell them the wheat contains seeds which you are transporting to a distant village. Since wheat chaff is inedible, our hope is that you will not be robbed." He sighed. "It is the best we could think of."

Madame Liu said, "The weight will give it away."

Master Kang shrugged. "If you have a better plan . . . she will be under your protection." His eyes glistened. "We will miss her words."

"Words?" asked Mr. Gao.

"Ah," said Master Kang. "She may not talk when she is with you. We encouraged her here, but out there, her words cause trouble."

"Trouble?" echoed Mr. Gao.

Master Kang held the lantern up to John's face. "Yes, as we know, voices can cause trouble if not properly understood in the context of *Buddha-dharma*."

"All of us hear voices," said John defensively. "They are normal."

Master Kang looked deeply into John's eyes, uncomfortably deep. "She may not talk when she is with you, but I think it might be possible that she will."

"If she does," said Meiying, "Isn't that a good thing?"

"That, Sister Bai, will be up to you. We are not always prepared to hear words that do not fit our rigid preconceptions of good or evil, kindness or cruelty."

Madame Liu glanced at John and spoke up. "It is late. We leave early tomorrow. Master Kang will finish packing the Precious Object and we will be on our way. News from Shanghai is not good. It is very likely that the Japanese will be right behind us."

Lu Zhishen said, "Yes, but who will be in front of us?"

"War throws off the natural order of things," said Master Kang. "I fear what you will encounter, but what we may face here will be much worse. That is why I am sending the Precious Object off with those who know. However,"—he turned and looked at the statue—"she can be challenging if misinterpreted."

"Maybe she can protect us," said Peter jokingly.

"Yes," said Master Kang in a serious tone. "She will protect you if it is in her heart and your *karma* for it to happen."

Madame Liu seemed restless. "Really, we must get some sleep. I fear we will have a tiring trip."

John thought she wanted to end the conversation before it went places she did not want it to go. He noticed Master Kang look at her quizzically, and then move toward the stairs. As the light faded from the corner, John turned and saw the glow still emanating from the statue and he felt a chill run down his spine. It even seemed she had slightly moved her position, but he knew that must be a trick of the shadows.

The next morning erupted with the sound of explosions. Terrified guests and residents rushed out to the courtyard and were met by billowing smoke, gunfire, and screaming from beyond the temple walls. Japanese planes buzzed overhead, dropping bombs and strafing the streets. Soldiers shot wildly at the aircraft with little effect. The monks threw open the gate to the crush of wounded civilians and soldiers. Some limped in, some carried on stretchers. Master Kang asked an officer why they were not taken to the local hospital.

"It's been bombed, in flames, many dead!" sputtered the officer.

Madame Liu, looking on, asked, "Has Shanghai fallen?"

"Not yet!"

The monks and nuns rushed around to help the wounded. Madame Liu shouted for the group to gather in the courtyard with their bikes. She and a few others ran up the stairs to secure the box that Master Kang had made sure was prepared the previous night. After a hurried conversation, it was agreed that the box would be secured to Meiying's bike, though the added weight would require a shuffling of her personal effects. They waited, huddled in a corner of the courtyard, until the planes left, and then started off on the road to their final destination, leaving behind another town in flames.

~ *The Voice Speaks* ~

As the group made their way onto the main road to Nanjing, a swelling tide of refugees made progress slow. Keeping everyone together was exceedingly difficult, but keeping track of the children proved next to impossible. Again, the road was choked with soldiers moving toward the front in Shanghai, while refugees desperate to reach Nanjing crashed into them from the opposite direction. One morning, a rogue Japanese plane strafed the road for no apparent purpose, since at that time no Chinese soldiers were in sight. Little Acorn's best friend, 12-year-old

Guofan, had his leg shattered by a bullet that severed his artery. He died from loss of blood, in spite of the best efforts of the peasant women.

John stood by helplessly while the little boy's screams turned to a quiet, slow death. Shaken to the core, John asked Lu Zhishen where the parents were.

"An orphan."

"Why is he with us?" John asked in anger. "Why isn't he in an orphanage?"

"Ask Mr. Gao, but not now."

When John looked at Gao, he saw the professor crying and pulling at his hair. Meiying cradled Little Acorn in her lap.

"I don't understand," said John mechanically.

"Of course you don't!" cried Lu Zhishen, distain in his voice.

"Why didn't we leave them in Shanghai?" exclaimed John, angry at Lu's tone.

"It would have been murder," volunteered Madame Liu standing nearby with her usual calm expression.

Once again John felt the old panic; the certain belief that he did not belong; the urge to fly away without regard to the consequences. For the first time, contempt filled his mind for these people whose manipulations had ensnared him and forced him to leave Shanghai with them. Death and destruction seemed things to be taken for granted. He thought he would end up in the same way as Guofan.

After the boy's body had been taken to a local village, and payment made to arrange for a burial, the group moved on. As he pedaled, John's resentment grew, and he looked at the others with a deepening suspicion. The voices had not returned, but he perceived a faint rumble, the movement of soil on the surface by some underground, burrowing creature. His emotional detachment was noticed by everyone, yet they left him alone to work it out, assuming the boy's death triggered his latest withdrawal. Even Peter kept his distance.

One day, while the group walked their bikes up a steep hill, Meiying positioned herself next to John. "Is it the voices, John?"

"No."

Meiying carried on in spite of the rudeness of his response. "I have often asked the Goddess statue to speak with me, as she did with the monks, but so far I have heard nothing. I thought maybe she has spoken with you."

"No."

Don't be so quick, came a voice that sounded strange and distorted. It might have been female, high-pitched, but not quite normal, not quite human. John looked at Meiying, but her attention was fixed on pushing her bike.

"What did you say?" he asked her anyway.

"Nothing," replied Meiying, huffing a bit from the exertion caused by her heavily-loaded bike.

John shook his head. "I could have sworn you said something."

I did, came the voice again.

"Who is speaking?" demanded John scanning the faces of people swirling around them.

"What is the matter?" asked an alarmed Meiying.

"Tell me who just spoke!" he shouted.

John seemed so disoriented Meiying signaled the group to leave the road for a rest. They pulled off to a small clearing bordered by a thick forest of beech and blazing red maple. When it became apparent Meiying directed her concern toward John, a disgruntled member of the group said loudly, "What's wrong now?"

John, picking-up on this comment, snapped, "I'm fine! Let's keep going!"

But Madame Liu quickly put a stop to the nascent bickering. "There is no time for this! We are nearing Nanjing where we must stay for a time until arrangements can be made for the final leg of the journey to the final destination. Unfortunately, the Japanese may soon arrive. We cannot protect the Precious Object if we remain too long in Nanjing. Put your energies to better use!"

She turned to John. "Are you well enough to continue?"

"Yes, of course," he said petulantly.

"I think the voices are back," interjected Meiying by way of explanation.

"So you hear voices?" pressed Madame Liu.

John hesitated. "No. Really I'm fine. Let's continue."

Madame Liu dismissed his answer with a wave of her hand. "Do you hear a single voice?"

He did not answer.

"Do you hear a voice?" she demanded.

"I do hear a voice . . . but it's a very odd voice, and I've only heard it speak a few words."

"Is it *her*?"

John looked genuinely puzzled. "I don't know. It doesn't sound like *her* . . . but maybe. . . . "

Tell her about the soldier, suddenly interrupted the voice. John's eyes widened and he paled noticeably.

"What?" asked Madame Liu.

"I just heard it again."

All eyes were riveted on John, but he stopped talking, physically present but mentally occupying some distant place.

"What did it say?" insisted Madame Liu.

"It said, 'tell her about the soldier,' and then nothing."

As they were all digesting these words in awed silence, a man's voice broke over them. "Excuse me!"

They turned and saw a lone soldier staring at them from the edge of the forest. "Excuse me!" he called again. "May I join you?" His left hand held a walking stick, and he thrust his right hand forward, palm up. No weapon was visible. The soldier bore a wide, incongruous smile.

Instinctively, the group recoiled at the dramatic entrance of this eerily-timed apparition. John concentrated on calling forth the voice in his head, asking many questions that were not answered. But the soldier did not lack in conversational discourse.

"Well, speak up, comrades! You're all standing like statues!" he cried.

Peter was the first to walk up to him. "Of course, friend. Do you need water? Food?"

The soldier waved his hand dismissively. "No need, friend. A little company is all I need on the road to Nanjing."

Madame Liu looked around conspicuously. "Where are your comrades, friend?"

His face darkened. "On the road to Shanghai. On the road to death."

"Aren't you supposed to be with them?"

"Heavens, no!"

"Why not?" asked Lu Zhishen in an accusing tone.

"Alas, I am wounded."

Lu Zhishen looked him up and down. "Where, exactly?" When the soldier merely stared at him, Madame Liu tried to smooth the accusation. "Perhaps we can help."

The soldier pointed to his head. "I hear voices."

These words hit the group like a thunderbolt. Stunned silence ensued.

"So, may I join you?" he asked again.

"Where are you going?" asked Mr. Gao.

"Home."

"Nanjing?" pursued Mr. Gao.

The soldier merely tilted his head ambiguously.

"Pardon for my asking," said Madame Liu, "but you are not a deserter?"

"Heavens, no!" He rummaged in his pockets and held up a rumpled paper. "Discharged."

"We are traveling by bicycles," said Lu Zhishen.

The soldier turned and walked back into the forest, then re-emerged with a bike. "No problem," he said, still smiling amiably.

Of course you can join us.

"Of course you can join us," said John.

The others looked at John but said nothing. Finally, after an awkward pause, Mr. Gao asked, "What is your name?"

"Feng Shiren."

"Ah. Young soldier, where is your native village?" asked one of the peasants in a friendly, open manner.

The soldier laughed and struck a humorous pose from Chinese opera. "Uncle, my village is so far away, it is only peopled by the descendants of those who were banished by the emperor."

"Ah, Hainan island!" cried the peasant.

"If it pleases you uncle, yes."

Introductions were made all around and the group started off, most unsettled by their new member. Only the peasants seemed comfortable and happy with the situation.

The road now teemed with desperate people. Rumors spread of robbers, thieves, rapists, and the imminent fall of Shanghai. Fear grew among those fleeing; arguments and fights became common; mistrust prevailed; and Japanese planes attacked more frequently. Even Madame Liu refused to stray too far from the main road. From the time the soldier joined them, John noticed this new member evidently felt totally at ease with the peasants in the group. He often heard the soldier joking with the peasant couple in the most natural manner, their thick northern dialect not at all a hindrance to his easy, friendly banter.

"So, old-father and old-mother, what do the ancestors say about our fate today, eh?" he would ask jokingly. "I think we will find a hidden treasure, buy countless hectares of land in the south, and become rich farmers! What do you think of that?"

The old peasant husband laughed. "Ah! Silly boy! As if hard work and sacrifice had nothing to do with success! You younger generation are mere whelps!"

They laughed together and the old peasant mother would scold, "If you were my boy, I would not let you join the army. 'Do not use good iron to make nails,' said the ancients. You have the makings of gold, not to be wasted on a rusty nail!"

He would smile and scoff, "I am fools-gold, old-mother."

When John heard him say this, he thought of the Goddess statue. The voice had not returned in spite of his efforts to establish further communication, and he had made little headway reconciling the conflicts that plagued him. Such easy comradery between the strange soldier and the peasants made John feel terribly inferior, as if he had missed out on some fundamental truth. Inferior, even, was not the right word. The right word? Young. Young. Young.

Perhaps he had missed something in his education, in his business experience, in his life. Outrage seemed the driving force behind education, learning, love of freedom, politics, and injustice. Yet outrage went missing from these people. They seemed too accepting of events. Too passive. Outrage drives progress, but acceptance drives . . . what? Survival? No. He knew acceptance had a place at the table with outrage. Or was it only the children's table? Or, from a global perspective, from all of nature, did outrage sit at the children's table and harangue the adults to indigestion? Ah! Too confusing!

No need.

The voice again! Speak with it! 'What do you mean?' he asked it silently. No response. Infuriating. He glanced around at the others, each pedaling while immersed in their own thoughts. Is he the only one who hears it? It? Is it male or female? Even that seemed blurred, the voice too distorted to tell.

"What are you on about?" intruded a different voice; that of Peter.

Nanjing was a day's ride away and they were resting by the roadside. John looked at Peter blankly.

"You're talking to yourself again, old boy," said Peter with a smile.

Happy to be recalled to the world, John put on his best look of disgust. "Peter, how many times do I have to tell you—you are not an Englishman! You are an American. Remember? Red, white, and blue. Fourth of July. Hamburgers and hot dogs. Peter, we won the revolution. You're free from the Crown." At the end of this feigned tirade, John laughed.

Peter joined in the laughter. "I know, buddy ol' pal, fellow Yankee, but I like how it drives you even crazier than you already are."

"Thanks a lot."

"Seriously, more and more Jap planes have been hammering us. It doesn't look good."

"No."

They were silent for a few moments before Peter asked, "What do you think of this soldier chap that's joined us?"

"I dunno. He's an odd one."

Peter looked at John almost pleadingly. "Do you think he's connected to the voice you hear?"

John, still touchy about his 'voices,' shrugged as if to say, 'I don't know and I don't care.'

"Well, I can tell you this," said Peter. "I am excited about seeing *her. She* has been on my mind for years and it's bloody high time I get to see *her.*"

"How did you first come across *her*?" asked John, now clearly interested.

"That, my dear John, is a story for another time."

"Why are you all so afraid of telling me how you came to know *her*?" demanded John.

"It's not a matter of fear."

"What is it?"

"Look, John, it seems that each of us have a piece, and when we reach the final destination, the pieces will all fit together. The whole will be the answer."

"That makes no sense. Bad movie script."

"Did what *she* say to you when you met *her* make sense?"

"Not really."

"There you are."

"That tells me nothing." John rubbed his forehead and sighed. "I tell you, Peter, since I met *her* I have almost thought of nothing else. Because of *her*, I left my job, my friends, traveled to China, met all of you, stuck around in the middle of a war, been shot at, seen people die—and I understand less now than I did when I first met *her*. My lack of understanding is mainly due to the fact that none of you—people who supposedly seek *her* as I do—none of you is willing to tell me anything about *her*, or your relationship with *her*." He threw up his arms. "Nothing!"

Peter stared at the sky absently. "Yes. Nothing. Leave it at that."

John abruptly turned and stomped away. But after taking a few steps, he realized he had nowhere to go but with the group. Shaking his head, he returned to face Peter. "I used to like mysteries, but not now." A peace offering.

Peter accepted it by laughing. "The only mystery now is whose voice is in your noggin."

"Not the only one," said John under his breath.

"I heard that, old chap. But you're right, for the rest of us, your voice is just one of two mysteries."

"What's the other?"

Peter jerked his thumb in the general direction of the others. "That bloody soldier!"

~ *Nanjing* ~

They arrived at the outskirts of Nanjing around dusk. Soldiers were everywhere and the population showed early signs of panic. Refugees from Shanghai mingled with Nanjing residents looking to load their possessions on an assortment of vehicles and evacuate the city. Chaos seemed to prevail. No sign of police, while the army simply churned about aimlessly, concerned with its own massive problems. To make matters worse, Japanese planes had just bombed certain sectors of the city, and angry, black clouds of smoke roiled overhead.

Madame Liu, more grim-faced than ever, guided the group through a labyrinth of streets and alleys until reaching what appeared to be a run-down mansion. The three-story house with traditional Chinese curved roofs at each level was ensconced in the old, regal section of town. Thick walls surrounded the grounds. From the interior courtyard, expansive canopies of ancient magnolia and red cedar poked above the outer walls, giving the place a gothic grandeur reminiscent of the American south, except for the Ming dynasty architecture of the mansion. An iron gate stood sentinel against the frenzied crowds milling in the streets.

As the others waited, Madame Liu went to the gate and spoke to an old man who evidently served as a guard. While they stood in the deepening gloom, the mansion towered above them like some dark monolith, unwelcoming and ominous. Only the soldier appeared to be in good spirits.

"So, friend-soldier, here is where we part," said Lu Zhishen.

The soldier looked distraught. "Actually, I have nowhere to go. Can I stay with you? Trust me, I will come in handy—I have many skills."

"Ah!" exclaimed Lu Zhishen. "That may be a problem."

"I work hard, I don't eat much"—he pointed to his head—"and I know many things."

"Well," said Mr. Gao. "That would be up to Madame Liu and the owners of this grand house. But—"

"Let him stay!" cried the peasant couple in perfect synchrony. The husband tilted his head and smiled. "He is like a son, and he will be useful."

Madame Liu heard and walked over, standing directly in front of the soldier. She said nothing, took both his hands, and stared deep into his eyes. The soldier returned her stare, unperturbed. Madame Liu staggered back a few steps. "He can stay. He must stay."

The group looked at each other in wonder, but their attention was abruptly broken by the loud creaking of a gate opening. "Come in, quickly!" called a low-pitched male voice from the dark. Grabbing his bike, the soldier was the first to enter into the courtyard as if he was afraid they would change their mind, hurriedly followed by the others. When the last person cleared the gate, it closed with a screeching bang behind them. John tried to see who operated the gate, but only an amorphous shape moved away, leaving the group with a tall Chinese man standing next to the guard who had originally greeted them. Both held up lanterns.

"Greetings!" the tall man said. "Your rooms have been prepared. Sorry, no electricity tonight. The power has been very unreliable." He had evidently taken a head count as they passed through the gate. "Ah! Madame Liu, there is one extra."

Before she could speak, the soldier stepped forward and saluted. "Feng Shiren at your service, sir! These kind people took me in." He held out his hand, palm up, and looked openly at the man. "I am not a deserter. Discharged." He moved closer to let the lantern-light illuminate his face. "I hope you have no objection, sir."

The tall man hesitated, glanced at Madame Liu, who nodded, then broke into a broad smile. "Ah! You are most welcome, young man." But his face quickly darkened. "Speaking of young men, about the boy who died, has he been . . . . " his words trailed off as if the question could not be politely phrased.

"Arrangements were made, words spoken, he is at peace."

With this, the group tumbled into the house and gathered in a cramped room off the foyer.

"Ah, good. Now, everyone gather around so you can hear!" the tall man said loud enough to be heard above the raucous hubbub from passing crowds in the street.

"Old Fox, close the windows!"

Once they had formed a tight circle, the group stood with their meager belongings in silence, waiting for their host to speak. Instead of launching into his speech, the man stood in the middle of the circle and gazed at each person in turn, holding up the lantern to see their faces more clearly. At last, he held up his arms to get their attention, although this gesture was entirely unnecessary. It did, however, lend drama to what he was about to say, adding an aura of urgency to the words that followed.

"Friends and fellow travelers! I am Dr. Liu, owner of this ramshackle mansion and husband of your esteemed Madame Liu!"

This statement brought a chorus of surprised exclamations and murmured observations among the group. Dr. Liu smiled while the unexpected revelation of these words rose and then quickly diffused to a resumption of silent anticipation.

Dr. Liu coughed politely and continued. "You have successfully brought the Precious Object to this place." He turned toward a carved table standing close by and gently rested his hand atop the nondescript bamboo box in which the statue remained concealed.

"We have arranged your rooms. Old Fox here"—he indicated the guard—"will make sure you are settled in." Dr. Liu looked conspicuously at the soldier. "As for you—"

"No, no," Feng Shiren raised his hand as if a schoolboy asking a question of his teacher. "I will stay with Old Fox in the caretaker's cottage. It has already been arranged. I do not want to be any trouble."

Dr. Liu looked stunned. He turned his attention to the guard. "Is this true?"

"Yes, sir, yes, sir," repeated Old Fox obsequiously. "We have already become old friends."

"How is that possible?" asked a confused Dr. Liu. "You haven't had time."

Old Fox looked at the soldier and winked. "We servants have our ways, sir."

John took all of this in with the air of a man overwhelmed. None of it seemed real. *Nothing more than a leaf bobbing atop an angry sea.* Peter nudged him and whispered, "That's really weird. I mean, *really* weird. I'm not sure I like this, old man." He glanced at the soldier who stood smiling like a carefree child. "A cuckoo baby? And we are the other eggs?"

John could only shake his head and try to resist the old feeling of helplessness and dread. He searched for Meiying and saw her whispering into Mr. Gao's ear. Only the peasants, again, seemed perfectly at ease and happy with the situation.

As this scene unfolded, Madame Liu had moved next to her husband and was holding up her arm for quiet. Gradually, a hush fell over the room and she said, "We must stay here for a while. Arrangements are being made to get us safely to the final destination, but they will take time, as there have been some setbacks by those in the countryside who would help us."

"What about the Japanese?" asked Mr. Gao. "Is it safe to stay?"

Dr. Liu spoke up. "That is a good question, Mr. Gao. Shanghai is about to fall, and then they will be on us like wolves. Already we are bombed daily."

"Yes, we experienced Japanese bombs on the road," said Peter. "Why not just leave now and take our chances?"

Dr. Liu shook his head. "Not possible. However, there is a bright side!"

Motioning the group to follow, he led them to a large room, luxuriously tiled in ornate Qing style. In the center of the room stood a magnificent grand piano.

Dr. Liu went over and took Meiying by the hand, drawing her closer to the piano. "For you, Meiying. We brought it here in anticipation of your arrival."

Meiying uttered a small shriek of joy, and ran her fingers reverently over the piano. John wished he were the wood beneath the caressing touch of her long, graceful fingers.

"Play! Play!" people cried.

Madame Liu interjected harshly. "Not now! Let us get settled in, and let Meiying rest. It has been a long journey."

But even as she spoke, the soldier jumped on the stool, lifted the fallboard, and played a lively, complicated piece that astonished everyone.

Looking on, her eyes opened wide in shock at the perfection of the impromptu performance, Meiying muttered quietly, "Liszt."

John's eyes darted from the soldier to Meiying to Dr. Liu and Madame Liu. He saw husband and wife look at each other with fear in their expressions. *Oh my god,*" he thought. Oh *my god.*

Precisely, came the voice in his head. **You are getting closer.**

~ Questioning Bai Meiying ~

That night, after he, Peter, and Lu Zhishen had talked out the events of the day (they again occupied the same room) John lay awake in the huge Chinese bed they all shared. Leaving the other two snoring loudly, he tiptoed out of the room, lit a lantern, and crept downstairs, eventually wandering into the library. He held up the lantern to read the titles of randomly chosen books that lined the walls. Almost all were written in literary Chinese, so he recognized only a handful of titles. A soft chuckle came from the corner.

"Looking for a book?" asked Meiying.

John felt immense relief to hear her soothing voice. He sat next to her and placed the lantern on a table between the two chairs. "No. Wouldn't do me any good. I can't read literary Chinese very well anyway. Couldn't you sleep?"

"Not well. My mind is not cooperating with my body," she replied.

They sat quietly for a few moments, both comfortable in the others' silence.

"Have you heard the voice lately?" she asked.

John sighed. "Yes, but only a word here and there. I wish it would say more, explain more. What it says only confuses me worse than I already am. Maybe it could explain things to me if it would answer my questions. But it never does."

"What type of questions?"

"Oh, you know, we've discussed it before. I fear you'll just get angry with me, or frustrated, and I don't want that. Anyway, I'm more interested in your thoughts."

Meiying did not reply.

"Did our soldier friend play well tonight?" asked John, already knowing the answer.

"Oh, yes. Beautifully."

"So," John persisted. "How does a common soldier come to play so well?"

Meiying seemed anxious to downplay the incongruity. "He was probably drafted in the army after he had already studied at some music conservatory."

Ask her if she is afraid, said the voice. John sat upright and caught his breath, willing himself to calm down.

Meiying could not help but notice. "What's wrong?" she asked in alarm.

"The voice just spoke again," he said as matter-of-factly as possible.

Meiying looked at him in wonder. "Well, what did it say?"

"It told me to ask you if you are afraid."

"Of what?"

John shrugged. "I don't know. It never makes things clear. It only muddles them."

Meiying sat in hushed silence, yet he could hear her breathing heavily. She suddenly wrapped her arms around her body and trembled. "Yes, I am afraid. Very afraid."

"But you always seem so calm," said John, wanting to comfort her but not daring to say or do anything clumsy and stupid. As soon as he spoke, he cringed at the inanity of his words.

"Tell the voice I am very afraid. Ask it if I should be," she said with subdued passion.

John shook his head. "It never answers me."

"Try," she said. "Perhaps later."

"Yes, I promise."

Again they sat in mutual silence, somewhat awed by the moment.

"Did you know Madame Liu had a husband?" John asked, changing the subject to lighten the mood. Her admission of fear rattled him more than he would have thought, and he needed solid ground, a type of normalcy, on which to regain his footing.

"Of course."

He was surprised by her nonchalant answer. "The others didn't."

Meiying laughed. "Some did."

"Were they pretending?"

She rose abruptly. "You ask too many questions."

John did not want to be left alone, and feeling embarrassed for having such a childish sentiment, he cast about for an appropriately chastised response. Truth seemed all that remained of his options. "Please sit with me awhile, Meiying. I don't want to be alone. I'm sorry. We Americans are barbarians. We ask too many questions. Besides, I am also afraid."

She sat back down and as he gazed at her, the soft light made her even more beautiful in his eyes. For the first time, he felt a sexual attraction rather than an emotional one. Without thinking, he blurted, "You are quite beautiful, you know!"

Meiying remained perfectly still, forcing herself not to look down and play the coy female. She had no interest in John as anything but a friend, and felt annoyed at once again having to fend off a would-be lover. "Yes, I know," she said harshly. "It is a curse, and one that will either lead me to great wealth and fame, or lead me to my death. I fear it is the latter."

Confused, John could only ask, "What do you mean?"

"Do you consider Feng Shiren handsome?" she asked irrelevantly.

Taken aback by this non-sequitur, John felt a sharp pain in his heart. "I guess."

"Yes, he is quite handsome, striking even. And like me, he plays beautifully."

John sank further into a feeling of pained resentment. "Okay, so what?" He regretted the adolescent tone of his response.

"I fear he is my nemesis," she said very slowly and deliberately.

This statement took John by surprise, and he could only repeat stupidly, "Nemesis?"

"Yes, that is my fear. That is why I am very afraid. There is something about him."

"I agree," said John too quickly. Although he felt a certain relief at her words, he also felt oddly frightened himself.

"Are you afraid of him?" asked Meiying guilelessly.

"Noooo," said John. "Just puzzled," he lied.

"What about him puzzles you?"

John, not prepared to answer this question as wisely and objectively as he would wish, could only manage an "Ah, well . . . . " then fell silent.

Meiying pressed. "Well?"

"I don't know where to begin. I mean, he—"

Suddenly a voice came out of the darkness from the far corner of the room. "Because I am a puzzle's puzzle put here to puzzle puzzled people!" The voice laughed, seemingly quite pleased with this *bon mot*.

John leapt to his feet at the first words of the speaker, but Meiying remained frozen in her seat.

A match was lit, a lantern sputtered on, and the soldier's face came into view. Once he was illuminated, he struck another one of his patented Chinese opera poses. "I came looking for a book," he said, "and fell asleep on this couch until your voices awakened me."

John self-consciously sat back down, feeling a fool in front of Meiying. To his surprise, she spoke as if the soldier had been involved in their conversation all along. "You play beautifully. Where did you learn?"

"Thank you. My mother taught me."

Ask him about his addiction, the voice again spoke.

"What about your addiction?" blurted John.

Meiying looked startled, but the soldier merely looked at John with an odd, piercing stare, then rose, blew out the lantern, and left without another word.

When the door closed behind him, Meiying turned to John. "Did we just dream this?" she asked.

"No," replied John with more resolve than he felt.

"Why did you ask him that," she asked.

"The voice again."

"What did it say?"

John let out some air and shook his head. "Just to ask about his addiction. Nothing else, as usual."

"It just seems so unreal," Meiying observed.

"Does he seem real?" asked John.

Meiying shuddered. "Oh, yes, he is real. Very real."

"Well, if he is real, so is my voice. And if my voice is real, then I am not insane. And if I am not insane, then all of this is more than I am prepared to deal with."

Meiying gently placed her hand on John's arm. "Is he a threat to us? To the Precious Object. To *her*?"

"I don't know," said John, trying to control the pain stabbing at his stomach.

A different person spoke from the doorway, startling both of them for the second time that night. "Are you all right?" asked Old Fox. "Can I get you anything?"

"No, thank you," said Meiying and John simultaneously, both relieved to hear the old man's voice.

"Have you seen Feng Shiren?" he asked.

"Yes, he just left," replied Meiying.

"Ah," sighed Old Fox. "We were talking and he just disappeared. I was worried."

"No need to worry," said Meiying. "He is fine, just fine."

"What were you and he talking about?" asked John.

The old man held up his lantern and smiled. "Nothing. Just chatter. Goodnight."

"Goodnight," replied John and Meiying automatically. Both agreed to return to their rooms and get some sleep, if possible.

~ *The Goddess Statue* ~

At dawn, explosions shook the house and rattled the windows, waking everyone. Running downstairs, John, Peter, and Lu Zhishen arrived in the great room just in time to see Dr. Liu and Old Fox carry the box containing the Precious Object through an open doorway into a downward sloping hall.

"Follow them!" cried Madame Liu, herding late arrivals into the same direction. Mr. Gao stood at the door carefully counting the heads of the children until satisfied they were all safe.

Another explosion, this one very close, set the house creaking and moaning. Windows shattered. The group kept moving downward, far underground, until they reached a level floor in a huge chamber. Old Fox closed the heavy door behind them, and the terrifying sounds of war were instantly shut out.

Members of the group stood or sat haphazardly around the room, speaking in low tones. John wandered over to Meiying and started to speak when someone asked, "Where is the soldier?" Everyone looked around, then cast their eyes on Old Fox for an explanation.

The old man shuffled uncomfortably and said, "He will be along soon."

"Where is he?" demanded Dr. Liu.

Old Fox shrugged. "He said he had things to do and would join us later."

Madame Liu looked at her husband. "He is alone in the house."

"Yes, but the Precious Object is here with us," he reassured.

"But there are other things," she replied under her breath but loud enough for all to hear.

Something possessed John to speak up. It happened quite spontaneously and without any forethought. "I'll go find him."

A chorus of protests greeted this bold statement, but he refused to listen. "This room is claustrophobic and I need some air. If I find him, I'll bring him back."

Dr. Liu reluctantly agreed and John quickly slipped out the door before he could rescind his offer. After he made his way up to the main house, sunlight streamed through the windows in a pale orange as it filtered through the smoke blanketing that section of the city. Outside the courtyard wall, a cacophony of shouts, screams, and orders from the panicked populace filled the air. He searched the rooms but Feng Shiren was nowhere to be found. John made his way back down the slanted hallway and knocked. When it opened, everyone's expectant eyes were focused on him. John shrugged, "Couldn't find him, but the explosions have stopped. We can go back to the house. Many windows are gone, so we'll have to clean up a bit, but it's not too bad up there"

Peter stepped forward. "Before we leave this room, let's take a look at the statue—you know, make sure everything's fine."

General agreement was voiced, so Dr. Liu placed the box on a table and carefully opened it. Gently placing the Precious Object upright on the table, he brushed off the chaff and stepped back. There sat the gold figurine in all her splendor; Goddess sitting in her meditative pose, legs crossed, hands resting above both knees, right hand facing up, thumb touching forefinger, gracefully curved into a circle.

John gazed in wonder at the statue and could sense himself changing, or rather, sense the change that had come over him the past few weeks. It was a physical sensation, as though he was a clay person feeling the potter adding some here and removing some there, experiencing in his nerves, muscles, and bones the additions and subtractions. He knew the final configuration of his soul had not been kiln-fired, and the prodding, pinching, slicing, and kneading, would continue until he found *her*. For too long, he had been living his days outside the warmth of some core life source, searching in bitter darkness for *her* to provide needed heat. And here the statue taunted him, for it represented to him the embodiment of once-pliable clay turned to immutable gold. *She* could do for him what the artist had done for the statue—make him permanent, powerful, and whole.

He glanced at Meiying, who stood transfixed in front of the Goddess statue, and he forced himself to view her as a pale imitation of the real thing, the perfection he sought. But troubling doubts and uncertainties remained in spite of his best efforts to view the future as a linear path to glory.

Chapter Four

Treachery on the Road

Attack

~ Dire Warnings ~

Japanese attacks had tapered off and life in the mansion settled into a routine. The group scattered by day to various tasks and money-making enterprises, returning at night to talk over events and pool resources. Dr. Liu found temporary jobs for most of the members, and John found himself teaching English at a local 'academy.' His students were mainly adults who had dreams of making their way to America or getting rich doing business with Americans. Visions of meeting *her* remained, but the necessities of earning cash and dealing with everyday contingencies dulled the edge of his 'quixotic quest,' as he called his interrupted journey.

Word from Shanghai continued to be grim, and John's students nervously practiced their English by discussing the situation.

"Shanghai dead," pronounced one young student. "My parents tell me city dead!"

John tried to correct him. "No, no. You should say, 'Shanghai is about to fall to the Japanese.'"

But the student would have none of it. "No! No! Shanghai dead! We next!"

This outburst created an uproar in the classroom. One older man jabbed a finger at this harbinger of doom, and shouted, "You communist! You communist! We Chinese stop Japanese, but you communist!"

A free-for-all ensued, and amidst the commotion, John waved his arms and yelled, "Stop! Your teacher commands you to stop!" When the shouting died down, he continued, "Now, we must speak proper English or you will look foolish. Can anyone here, anyone with good contacts, tell me in good English what is the latest news from Shanghai?"

"Yes," came a calm, quiet voice. The speaker happened to be John's best student, the son of a wealthy merchant who had stores in both Nanjing and Shanghai. "The inner city of Shanghai and all the nearby towns are destroyed. Now, Japanese—"

John interrupted. "You mean *the* Japanese. Go ahead."

"Yes, thank you teacher. The Japanese are landing from sea. It fall very soon. Very soon."

John's heart skipped a beat. "How soon?"

"Days," said the young man. "My family leave. This my last day here with you, teacher."

Again, the class erupted in arguments, but John did not try to stop them. His thoughts were racing forward.

A wounded Nationalist officer who had just joined the class a few days earlier, spoke up. As he had not previously said a word, the others fell silent. "When Shanghai fall, Japanese be here quick. They kill many, many peoples. Hurt many, bad pain."

"Torture?" asked John in Chinese. When the officer nodded, John said in English, "Torture."

"Yes, teacher. Torture. Many, many, torture. Women hurt also."

"Rape?" asked John.

"Yes, teacher, rape. Many, many, raped, like in Shanghai."

Some female students began to moan and cry. The officer continued, looking at the women. "You run, quick, run out of city!"

John tried to remain calm, images of Meiying flashing through his mind. "You mean to say, 'leave Nanjing as soon as possible.'"

"Yes, teacher, otherwise, dead." The officer looked at John curiously. "And you, teacher, not safe. Foreigners in Shanghai, many dead, many hurt."

~

John dismissed the class and rushed out into the street once the last student had left. He walked quickly, in a daze, toward the mansion. Again, the streets were teeming with panicked residents. Jostling and shoving his way, he had made it almost halfway to the mansion when, from above, he heard the dreaded sound of airplanes. He scanned the sky, praying they were Nationalist planes, but when they came into view, a host of rising suns flashed from under their wings like angry welts.

Explosions soon followed, and the familiar rising columns of smoke darkened the sky. One plane swooped low over the street, firing its guns at the frantic populace. John felt himself struck full-on by a sprinting body from the side and he toppled over onto the street. Scrambling back to his feet, he had barely taken a few steps when he again crashed to the pavement after a heavy-set man, screaming someone's name, slammed into him. Images of churning legs and falling bodies flashed in and out of his vision.

A little girl, crying, was kicked to the ground and trampled. Again, the heavy-set man ran toward him, still screaming a name, probably the little girl's, when a terrific noise muted the din. Only the strafing guns made a distinct rattling sound above the cacophony. He covered his head with his arms to protect himself from the trampling feet, but something massive again exploded nearby. When he opened his eyes, the heavy man lay on his side close to John, covered in blood. Focusing on the man's odd position, he saw that half the head and half the body were gone, so it appeared the missing half had sunk beneath the pavement. A detached hand stuck up a meter away, as if breaking the surface of a black lake. Other than the hand, he never saw the arm, or leg, or any other detached body part for that matter.

Now his sole purpose in life was to get away from the carnage and find safety somewhere, somehow. Struggling to his feet, running as fast as his wobbly legs would go, the screams of pain from the little girl dissipated behind him. A great wave, a tsunami, of relief washed over him Although others were dead or dying, he still lived, running like some Olympic athlete. Alive! And this revelation acted like a surge of superhuman energy racing through his body.

I am alive and whole! I am not dead! I am not dying! They are, I am not! And they were so close!

After navigating through the horrific landscape of dead and dying bodies, panicked mobs, and scattered fires, he made it back to the mansion. Old Fox, his eyes wide with fear, opened the gate for John, and closed it quickly behind him. Once inside the courtyard, John fell to his knees as if he were a puppet whose strings had been cut. After a few moments of heavy breathing, when he at last focused on his surroundings, he saw a small group hovering over a prone figure.

"Oh, god!" he cried, images of Meiying running through his imagination. From his position, he could not tell whether the figure was male or female. He wanted to rise and run over to see, but a deathly fear gripped him and he realized he did not want to know who lay on the ground. Shock and adrenaline were at work on his body, and his shaking prevented him from getting immediately to his feet. His earlier euphoria had been replaced by a deep revulsion.

After dry-heaving a few times, he forced himself to look again and saw people carrying the body into the house. At last he stood and followed, trying to make out who was being carried.

Peter appeared next to him rubbing his temples and rambling on. "It's Old Auntie Chu, one of the peasants. Her husband will not be consoled. They're taking her body to the kitchen; I don't know why. Then what? I don't know. The local morgue, I guess. I'm staying out here. Oh, damn! Damn it! You can go in. I see you're going in. That's good. I'm staying out here. Damn it! The bastards! Yes, you go on in. I'm staying out here."

John barely heard Peter's words, comprehending only that the body was not Meiying's. But when he entered the house and saw the husband moaning and crying and tearing at his hair, John rushed upstairs to collapse on his bed. Laying on his back, his eyes stung from the smoke billowing into the room from the smashed windows, but he didn't care. Shrieks continuously pierced the dusky atmosphere from outside the courtyard, but he didn't care. Nor did he care when the distant explosions and gunfire gradually ceased.

It seemed impossible to him that the current reality—lying on the bed, sinking into the soft mattress, feeling momentarily safe—would soon collapse into even worse chaos and catastrophe within a few days.

I could have left! I could have caught that ship! I'd be home by now. Home!

Lu Zhishen poked his head in and asked, "Are you okay?"

John sat on the edge of the bed. "Yes," he replied wearily. "I'm going down."

When he went downstairs, the body had already been removed and the husband had gone off to accompany it. All was eerily still. It seemed a macabre contrast to the deafening noise that had roared such a short time ago. In the kitchen, Madame Liu was scrubbing the table where the body had been. Her expression did not vary from her usual, stoic determination.

"Are there any more?" asked John.

Without looking up, she shook her head. "Hand me a cloth."

"Where?"

"Over there, in the corner."

"Here."

"Thank you."

John stood for a while until he felt foolish watching her work. "Where is everyone?"

Madame Liu finally raised her eyes from the table and stared at him in a manner that made him feel uneasy. "Have you heard the voice?"

Startled at this odd question, he could only shake his head as if to say, "of course not." In the face of her dubious glare, he broke the awkward silence and asked, "Why?"

"Because unlike the voice in your head, our Precious Object is speaking to us now."

"What?"

"Go down to the safe room and listen. The others are there."

John walked down the long, slanting hallway to the safe room. Even before he reached his destination, he heard a sound coming through the open door.

... Tap. Tap. Tap....

He stopped dead in his tracks. Tilting his head to hear better, the tapping sound was monotonously regular, high-pitched, with an oddly familiar ring to it.

... Tap. Tap. Tap....

When he passed through the open door, the group did not acknowledge him but merely stood silently, absorbed, listening.

In the muted lantern-light, John scanned their faces, each with a different expression, each staring at the source of the tapping. John followed their eyes and inhaled a deep lungful of air.

The Precious Object sat on the table, and from within its golden body emanated the tapping noise.

~ *The Puzzle* ~

Later, in the great room, everyone sat and speculated on the phenomena. The tapping stopped not long after it had begun, and had not been heard since. During this lively discussion, only the soldier remained stubbornly silent. In fact, Lu Zhishen, noticing his unusual reticence, commented upon it, and asked the soldier what he thought about the tapping.

"It's nothing!" cried the soldier dismissively. "Probably just something loose inside."

"Nonsense!" scoffed Dr. Liu. "It is communicating with us. I am not a superstitious man, but this is certainly. . . ." his words trailed off.

"What does it mean, sir?" asked one of the peasants, Guo Hsiaoping.

"I am sure that will be made clear to us in time," said Dr. Liu. "In the meantime, we have lost another beloved comrade. Meiying has agreed to play for us in memory of Mrs. Chu. Let us move to the piano room."

Meiying played deeply contemplative pieces by Brahms and Schubert, then finished with an adagio by Beethoven. Everyone felt quite moved, and many tears were shed. Everyone, that is, except Feng Shiren. The soldier's demeanor did not change from his usual whimsical persona, and John considered it odd that, close as he was to the couple, did not seem moved. John also noticed that Mr. Chu was not present and assumed he was still with his wife's body and would remain so until the funeral. In fact, Mr. Chu would not be seen by the group for a long time, and then, under tragic circumstances. While she played, John again marveled at Meiying's beauty and felt the strong sexual attraction he had experienced earlier. These feelings were not welcome and he exerted great effort to repress them, with only partial success.

When the last notes of her recital ended, and after the polite applause died down, Mr. Gao stood up. "Friends, we must talk. I have heard bad news from Shanghai. It seems we have very little time before the Japanese army arrives. Once that happens, none of us will be safe." He paused, held out his hand, palm up, toward Dr. Liu. "Sir, when do we leave Nanjing?"

Dr. Liu coughed and looked down at the floor. Without raising his head, he began speaking. "Well, we have not yet received news from some of our contacts. As you know, we must have safe harbors before we reach the final destination. There are a total of four, strategically located about equal distance between here and there. Unfortunately, the closest safe harbor to Nanjing, our very next destination, has sent a communication indicating the presence of fighting between the local warlord and Nationalist forces. There are even remnants of communist units in the area. Reports of widespread killing, raping, torture, and looting have caused our contacts to temporarily suspend their offer of safe conduct."

"Famine, also," added Madame Liu.

"Excuse me, but who is our contact in the area?" asked Lu Zhishen.

Dr. Liu frowned. "That must remain confidential for all our sakes."

"Yes, one of my students, with very good sources, thinks the Japs will be here within days of the fall of Shanghai," interjected John, anxious to participate.

"So, that brings us back to my concern," said Mr. Gao. "There is uncertainty out there, but it is certain that we will soon be under Japanese control here. In that case, we cannot protect ourselves, let alone the Precious Object. Perhaps that is what she is trying to communicate to us. Yes. The tapping is a message of urgency. That must be it!"

"Excuse me, learned sir" said the soldier in a mock obsequious tone. "But that sounds a bit superstitious. If we stay here, in this nice, comfortable house, the Chinese army"—he thumped his chest—"will protect us."

Vocal protests rained down from all sides at the absurdity of this proposal.

"Very well, even if the Japanese occupy the city, what business do they have with us? We can wait until it is safe, then leave untouched."

"In that case, Feng Shiren, you had better get rid of that uniform or you'll be shot or beheaded before you could spit!" scoffed Peter.

Unruffled, the soldier replied calmly, "My uniform is removable."

Madame Liu spoke firmly. "Staying is out of the question. We have heard what the Japanese are doing to the civilian population in Shanghai. It will be no different here." She looked at Dr. Liu. "Husband, we must leave, come what may!"

Dr. Liu seemed not at all surprised at her words, almost as if they had rehearsed their comments. "Yes," he said. "You are right. We have no choice. The only question is: when do we leave? Shanghai has not yet fallen, so we have a little time."

"But it will be days, maybe hours, from now!" cried Mr. Gao. "I, for one, would like to be many kilometers away from Nanjing when the Japanese come. Remember, they have motorized vehicles and airplanes. We do have enough bicycles, even for the children, but I worry about them on the road. Perhaps we should leave them here. I know an orphanage."

"I say we leave immediately!" shouted Feng Shiren, striking another one of his dramatic Chinese opera poses. "And take the children! If not, they will certainly die here!"

This comment drew a general uproar.

"You wanted to stay just a minute ago!"

"This is too much!"

"Why did you change your mind?"

"Don't play the fool!"

Undeterred, the soldier walked up and thrust his face close to Dr. Liu's. "They are right, you know. We should go at first light tomorrow. I was just testing their resolve."

Unnerved by the proximity of Feng Shiren's face, Dr. Liu mumbled, "Yes, well, are we all in agreement that we should leave at first light tomorrow and take the children?"

Stunned by this rapid turn of events, the members of the group gave their approval without discussion. It seemed the whole thing was decided by the soldier's words. This realization unsettled some, but the decision was made and a certain relief came over them. In the conversation that followed regarding logistics—how much food to carry, what supplies to bring, and so forth—it was agreed that Meiying would again carry the box with the Precious Object on her bike.

Night was again upon them, and the press of time made them scurry to their rooms and begin the packing process. Madame Liu oversaw the distribution of food and supplies. In the process of traipsing back and forth from upstairs to downstairs, packing for himself and helping in the kitchen, John often heard the soldier laughing and joking with Old Fox, who it was agreed would join them.

Once, during one of his multiple trips, John passed Peter in the hallway and nudged him, tilting his head toward the soldier and rolling his eyes. Peter laughed humorlessly. "You wait and see, old chap. He'll turn out to be a cuckoo chick. He'll roll the rest of us out to die on the ground."

John snorted and took a step to continue on, but Peter blocked his way. "You wait and see. I'm not joking. Just watch your back, sonny-boy. If I disappear someday, look to him for an explanation."

After an exhausting day, when the others went to bed, John declined to retire, coming up with the excuse that he couldn't sleep and wanted to spend some time in the library reading. He did not have the chance to pass this on to Meiying, but he nonetheless forced himself to read, hoping she would come.

While sitting with a book of Lao Zi's philosophy, most of which he did not understand, he began to nod off. He lowered the flame in the lantern, fell into the alpha state between sleep and wakefulness, and promptly felt his mind dissembling. A miner with a pickax kept tunneled his way deep into John's brain, chopping away at neural tissue, straining to reach the precious vein of quintessence at the center, digging tirelessly to reach the source of the voice. As the miner dug closer to the core, a faint tapping could be heard, muffled by layers of unexcavated brain tissue.

... Tap. Tap. Tap....

"Someone's trapped! Go faster!"

The closer the pickax got to the core, the faster the tapping.

... TapTapTap....

But as the miner frantically tunneled, the more John felt his mental faculties diminishing. Thoughts, concepts, ideas, no longer held together, fragmenting and flying apart in splatters of mental foam.

Keep digging! Keep digging! You're almost here! came the trapped voice from beneath the miner, synchronized with the tapping, less muted, louder, closer.

Keep digging! They're all against you! Save yourself from them! Escape! Dig! Let her out! Save her! Dig! Dig! Faster!

Powerless to do anything, paralyzed, a virtual quadriplegic, John's mind disintegrated, separated from reason, from connection, from—

"John." A firm but gentle voice replaced the trapped one. "John!"

He felt his arm being shaken and when his eyes opened, Meiying's face hovered close to his. "John, you were dreaming."

Blinking away the sleep, he mumbled, "Was I?"

"Yes."

He sat up in the chair. "I hoped you would come."

"I thought you would be here," she said kindly.

"Are you in with *them*?"

Meiying drew back, alarmed at his accusatory tone. "In with them?" she repeated.

"Yeah, are you against me?"

"John, you were just dreaming."

He looked at her oddly, then smiled and said quite confidently, "No, I wasn't."

Meiying felt a deep chill. For weeks, the others had been privately questioning his sanity. She had always defended him, insisting his 'voice' was a genuine vision, a connection to some other world. Now, she wasn't sure.

"John, do you trust me?"

He hesitated. "Should I?"

"Yes. I am your friend."

"That's what they all say."

"They?"

John narrowed his eyes. "The others. The group. To get me away from Shanghai. To get me here."

"They are all your friends, John."

He put his finger to his lips. "Shhh. I found out something."

"What."

"The voice, my voice, is the same as the tapping from the Precious Object, and both are somehow connected to *her*. Maybe they are all *her*."

Meiying did not seem surprised. "Yes, some of us have speculated about that possibility."

"You talk about me to them?"

"Only out of concern."

John emitted an ugly laugh. "Sure."

It appeared crystal clear to him that Meiying had been part of the conspiracy. His only hope was to clam up. Keep his own counsel, and lead them to believe he still trusted them. When these thoughts flashed through his mind, he spoke up before she could fashion a lying response to his blunt statement. "No, no, Meiying. Honestly, I know you are all concerned about me. This is just something I must work out for myself." He took her hand, but not in a way that allayed her fears. "Trust me," he said.

Meiying feared for John's sanity, but the overarching crisis of war and her own fate distracted her from dwelling too much on the American's mental issues. She felt sorry for John, and worried about the effect his erratic behavior would have on the group, but her own fears had lately overwhelmed her natural concern for others. Having seen death close-up, both in Shanghai and now here, awakened a deep desire for something more than she currently possessed. *Odd,* she thought, *but it takes death to stir the need in me to give life. I want to have a child! Piano is not enough. Friends and admirers are not enough. Success is not enough. I want a child. Why? There was not the need before. Oh, what a foolish woman! Why now?*

This simple question baffled her. Of all the times and places! But the more she thought about it, the more the longing persisted. Of course, she considered the 'ticking clock' argument, and the 'dread of being forever an old maid' explanation. But she became convinced this need in her was not explicable by such mundane clichés. There must be a deeper and more profound motivation, one that would be fated to render her future child extraordinary.

In her private hours, she thought of all the orphans that needed a mother, and she felt perfectly certain that in the coming years she would adopt. But adoption had not the same primal pull. Still, in whatever manner she contemplated these unwelcome but persistent needs, and however she played them out in her mind, her lesbianism rose before her like an impenetrable thicket of complications that crushed any ray of hope for future happiness. Masturbation had been her only outlet for as long as she could remember. She had been her only lover, while men either intimidated her or disgusted her. There were other women, but she could never bring herself to approach them in that way—leaving only fantasies to satisfy her longings. Guilt and shame inevitably followed. She came closest to approaching Madame Liu as a friend and confidante, but always backed out at the last moment.

Meiying's desperate predicament led her to imagine any number of resolutions, each new one more ridiculous than the last. Lately, she toyed with the idea of John as a father to her child. He was intelligent, nice, reasonably good-looking, and as a foreigner, he would probably leave China, allowing her to raise her child without male interference. On the other hand, the child would be of mixed-race, complicating its future. And now, there persisted the question of John's mental stability. Even so, whenever she had been in a position to lure him into her arms, her absurd devotion to honesty and kindness intervened to prevent any hope of successful consummation. It seemed intolerable that she continue a life so bereft of meaning and purpose. What drove her on? Fear, of course, and the urge to survive. But her greatest hope resided in the hope that dwelled in *her*, the female of females, the one who would point Meiying in the right direction and give her the independence and confidence to continue in the right path, with or without a child of her own. The confluence of trust in *her* and John's voice which might, indeed, be the voice of *her*, excited and scared Meiying. John must be a special case, and fate had brought them together for a reason. Perhaps.

"Meiying, where are you?" asked John. "You seem so far away."

She shook her head as if to clear it.

"You've been daydreaming, or something," he said. "Anyway, I was just saying that we should go to bed. Tomorrow is only a few hours away."

"Yes," she said absently. "Didn't you want to talk to me?"

"No, I've got to figure out some things on my own first. Seems like there's a battle going on in my mind."

"Yes," said Meiying sympathetically. "I know about battles in the mind."

"Good night, and may your battles cease with sleep."

"Good night, and you too," replied Meiying, moved by his gentle, understanding tone, so different from his earlier attitude. The old thought returned. *Foolish woman!*

John went upstairs, said "Good night" again, then pretended to go into his room. After she left, he crept back downstairs to the quiet shelter of the library. Demons had to be fought, and they could only be defeated in the darkness by shining inward the light of his intellect. With Meiying and *her* as his twin allies, he would defeat schizophrenia.

~ *Another Departure* ~

Next morning, by the dim light of dawn, the group gathered with their bikes in the courtyard listening intently to Dr. Liu. "We will travel to our first 'safe harbor,' a village currently cut-off from effective communication. It will take us some time to reach the village because the route I have chosen is not the most direct. I do not know what we will find when we get there."

"We don't know what we'll find on the way!" cried Lu Zhishen, half-joking, half-serious.

Feng Shiren, always in good spirits, again thumped his chest. "I will protect you!"

"I'm sure your tattered uniform will scare any bad guys off," laughed one of the peasants. In reply, the soldier assumed yet another of his comedic Chinese opera poses.

But even as the laughter died down, the group heard the menacing drone of airplanes. "Oh, god! No! Not now!" came shouts of dismay. But the planes veered off and disappeared in a different direction. Chastened by this close-call, the group quickly rode through the gate and joined the throngs already jamming the roads. Behind them, the faraway thudding of bombs could be heard as if reminding them of what was to come. They rode in grim silence, except for Feng Shiren, who whistled carefree tunes. Old Fox never strayed far from his side.

John still struggled with the demon in his mind, trying to keep it quiet. To distract himself from this exhausting effort, he concentrated on the surroundings. Smoke again spread its ugly smudge across the sky, giving the entire city an orange tint. Brick houses and tile roofs dominated the view. Taller buildings rose in the distance, their tops obscured by smoke. The group took a bewildering maze of side roads to avoid the downtown business district and rail yards of Nanjing.

Those residents that were not fleeing sat on their brick stoops, shouting either curses, encouragement, or offers of various kinds.

"Traitors!"

"Go, leave your jobs for us!"

"Good luck, comrades! Wish I had somewhere to go!"

"Friends! Exchange your worthless silver coins for *fabi*! Good rates!"

"Cheap food for your trip! Melons! Rice!"

Occasionally, some distraught mother held up her child. "Please! Someone have pity! Take my child with you! She will starve! Please—I beg you—take her!"

Once, Meiying cried out for the group to stop. She ran over to a particularly destitute-looking mother with a bloated baby and pressed some coins in the woman's hand. "For the baby, for the baby."

Mr. Gao gently scolded her. "Meiying, Meiying, the child has probably been kidnapped or sold to unscrupulous people who use it to affect tender hearts like yours, and loosen money belts."

Meiying could only shake her head and pedal on.

Many starving bodies were strewn on the sidewalks, but the refugees stared straight ahead, unheeding of the misery lining the streets, determined to avoid their fate. John could see that civil order hung like a thread over Nanjing, and the Japanese offensive would easily cut that thread, causing the whole fabric to collapse in an instant. He felt immense relief that they were leaving, for this city was soon to become a hellhole, a fate Shanghai had already experienced. Word had come that morning that Shanghai had fallen.

~

After taking almost all day to get out of the city, the group continued on into the countryside. Rice fields spread on all sides, and soldiers milled everywhere, which turned out to be both a blessing and a curse. While they felt safer being among large military units and crowds of refugees, there were many rogue bands or small groups of deserters, that were driven by desperation and unquenchable desire. The main roads offered more protection from these elements, but posed the greater risk of Japanese air raids. After a particularly vicious strafing attack, when the road stretching far ahead was littered with dead and dying civilians, the group decided to risk staying off the major arteries.

Riding down a small, country lane, John's internal struggle intensified. The heat and humidity seemed to penetrate deep into his cells, squeezing them of moisture, leaving a constant thirst, and soaking his clothes with sweat. Physically and mentally he teetered this way and that, between depression and anger, fear and suspicion. To drive away the demons, he periodically scanned each of his comrades for hints of treachery. In moments of weakness, he felt quite pleased at how successfully he had kept secret his knowledge of their conspiracy, but in moments of clarity, he knew the demon had been at work and he kept his eyes averted out of shame and self-loathing.

As dusk approached, the air cooled, the sky blushed scarlet, and the lush greenery of the rice fields unfolded as far as the eye could see, with only the tendrils of dust kicked up by their bikes to remind them of the mineral earth. They located a Buddhist retreat in the nearest village that welcomed travelers. After conferring with the abbot, the group took shelter in the guest dormitories. The rooms were packed, but dry and comfortable. No Japanese planes had bothered to stray so far as these outlying villages, but the monks had a radio and closely monitored the situation. Everyone knew Nanjing now lay directly in the path of the advancing Japanese army.

Peter, as usual, put their situation in perspective when he walked the grounds with John and Lu Zhishen. "We can't control what the Japs will do, but we can control our own destinies. I'm focused on reaching the final destination, on meeting *her* at last."

"I agree up to a point," replied Lu Zhishen, waving the cloud of insects that hovered around his face. "But I can't help feeling cautious. That crazy soldier has made me a little . . . I don't know . . . a little concerned."

"About what?" asked John, momentarily free of his demon and genuinely interested, for he had similar feelings.

"Well, that's just it," said Lu Zhishen. "I can't put my finger on it."

They reached a small lake gently rippling in the moonlight. Croaking frogs and mysterious splashes reached their ears, and they remained quiet, soaking in the sounds.

Finally, Peter blurted, "Well, I know what the problem is! It's that bloody soldier, Feng Shiren! Ha! That's probably not even his real name!"

Before the others could respond, a dark shape rose slowly from the water directly in front of them. All three instinctively jumped back, but a voice came from the glistening shadow standing knee-deep at the edge of the shore. "Yes, you are right, Peter, it is not my real name." The shadow figure looked up just as the moon, appearing from behind a cloud, shone fully on a naked body, lithe and strong.

"Christ!" Peter cried. "You're always popping up from nowhere!"

The naked soldier held up his arms as if he were crucified. "Do I look like your Jesus Christ?" he laughed.

"Christ wasn't Chinese, as far as I know," said Peter sarcastically.

"Are you sure?" Feng Shiren made his eyes wide. "Round eyes are no big trick." He then slapped his naked body. "Dark skin already taken care of."

"What do you know about Jesus?" asked John.

But before the soldier had a chance to reply, Peter broke in. "No, no, no! First, I want to know who you really are!"

Again, the soldier assumed the position of a man crucified. "Jesus Christ."

Lu Zhishen snapped, "Stop playing the fool!"

"It's all I know. You foreigners are the ones who worship me—a fool. Ah, how can it be explained?"

Four young monks approached, and upon seeing Feng Shiren standing naked in the water, pointed and laughed.

"Come in brothers!" he cried. "The water feels good! Cleanse your Buddhist bodies with these Christian devils. Respect all forms of life, even our brother and sister frogs!"

"I've had enough!" muttered Peter, and he turned and stomped toward the monastery. Lu Zhishen soon followed. The four monks walked on, and John, alone, stood gazing at the still naked soldier, who gazed back wordlessly.

Ask him about his addiction, came the voice. John stiffened, surprised at the return of the voice, so long absent.

"She said something to you, didn't she?" asked the soldier.

"Who?"

"Your voice, of course."

"Yes. How do you know it is a she?"

The soldier laughed, took a few steps back into deeper water, and crouched down, immersing his entire body. He resurfaced suddenly, shook the water out of his hair, and took a few steps forward again. "What did she say?"

"She said to ask you about your addiction."

"Oh, it is not my addiction she is asking about."

"Whose then?"

Without a word, the soldier turned and swam toward the opposite shore. John watched the moonlight glisten off his back and arms, then just splashes, then ripples left behind, then nothing.

As the little ripples lapped upon the shore, he whispered aloud, "Who is that man? What is that man?

I must truly be insane, John thought. *To have come to China, to seek* her, *to let these people talk me into leaving Shanghai instead of returning to the States, to seek* her, *to seek* her, *to seek* her.

He sat on a flat rock and tossed small sticks into the lake. *Lu Zhishen is right, something's wrong here. My demon tells me this is all a conspiracy. Meiying says otherwise. Who to believe? In myself? That's a joke! The demons are right, I'm pathetic.* He waved his arm through the mass of mosquitoes and gnats. *Demons everywhere in this wretched, superstitious country! And tomorrow brings what? More pedaling, more misery, more . . . ah! To bed!* He walked slowly back to the monastery, not noticing the stealthy shadow following behind.

~ A Kidnapping in the Village ~

The next morning brought a livid sunrise, red shafts slipping through storm clouds gathered on the horizon. Moistness filled the air, which hung heavily with the musty scent of fertility rising from the rice fields. Dr. Liu made his usual morning announcement. "We have a long ride today, but if we're lucky, we should arrive at our first safe harbor by nightfall. The monks have warned me that the roads are very dangerous. Bandits and warlord troops are everywhere, they come and go, and no one knows where they'll turn up next. It has been decided that most of us should wear monk's robes. Our story is that we are fleeing our Shanghai temple, which was destroyed by the Japanese. The children are orphans, perhaps their innocence may save us. With them slowing us down, we would not be viewed as a threat." He pointed to a long table stacked with gold, yellow, and orange robes. "Find one that fits."

"So finally I can really be like the real Lu Zhishen, disguised as a monk!" yelled the burly Canadian.

Once the group had donned their robes, they said farewell to the monastery and rode tentatively on, slowly adjusting to the billowing attire that made pedaling a bit trickier. A scattering of refugees still dotted the smaller back roads, but gradually the numbers dwindled until the group had long stretches to themselves. This circumstance made them less burdened by pitiful sights, and for a while they bantered back and forth with pleasant good humor. John took this opportunity to position himself next to Meiying, who was engaged with Mr. Gao in a friendly debate.

"Miss Bai, you must admit that we Chinese are in a sorry state," said Mr. Gao. "The government is dysfunctional, the communists are stirring up hatred, people are starving, and now the Japs are swooping down to gorge themselves on the carcass."

"All of that may be true, Mr. Gao, but the spirit of the people lives on. China will never be conquered for long. The Mongols, the Manchus, all have tried and failed. But look at those peasants in the field."

"Where?" asked Mr. Gao searching the horizon. "They've all fled."

"No, look!" Meiying pointed toward the northeast. "You see those specks in the distance? Those are the Chinese people, tending their fields as they always will. No stopping them."

Mr. Gao peered in the direction she pointed. "I'm old, I don't see them. But even if I did, Meiying, what a dreamer you are! They are ignorant, superstitious, and often cruel. Now look at our young American friend here," Mr. Gao nodded toward John. "His country has discovered the secret: a strong constitution, education, and industrialization. Isn't that right, my boy?"

John agreed, but did not want Meiying to think he sided with Gao. "Yes, but Meiying is also right. China will continue on, supported by the strong backbone of its people."

"Oh, the diplomat!" cried Mr. Gao with a glint in his eye.

Meiying rode in silence and, just as John started to address her, a deep rumbling shook the air. Everyone veered off to the side, fearful the Japanese were bombing again. "It's just thunder from the storm!" yelled Madame Liu.

"Yes, yes, you're right!" others agreed.

Dr. Liu looked skyward. "Thank god it's not the Japs, there's no cover here. We're not halfway there and now this." He sighed deeply "Those clouds look very ugly."

Meiying searched in the direction of the peasants she had spotted earlier. "Over there!" she shouted. "Farmers! Let's go ask where we can find shelter!"

By the time they had reached the peasants, a small village came into view, comprised only of a few ramshackle brick homes with ragged, thatch roofs. Some buildings were burnt, evidently quite recently. A few naked children stared with glassy eyes as the group approached.

"No sign of dogs," Peter said under his breath. "That's bad."

"Nor chickens, buffalo, ducks, nothing," added Mr. Gao.

The farmers that Meiying had seen stood gawking at the group, various implements resting on their shoulders.

"Friends, do you have any shelter?" asked Dr. Liu. "We would like to be under a roof when that storm hits."

An old man came walking up from the village, his long walking stick poking at the ground as if he were angry about something. "Ah! A storm has already hit, friends! Bandits came, took everything, and burned some of our houses."

"What village is this?" asked Madame Liu.

"Wutouxiang, what's left of it," replied the old man.

Thunder now cracked in rolling clusters, and the soaked air smelled of liquid sulfur. The peasants scattered to their houses while the old man beckoned the group to follow. He led them to a huge communal barn, its roof partially collapsed. "Find dry spaces where you can, friends."

Just as he finished speaking, the rain came in great sheets, pounding the earth and battering the already shredded roof. Everyone fled to whatever nook or cranny offered some relief. Meiying cleaned up a space in an abandoned stall for the children, trying to remove as much filth as possible. The Precious Object was given the prime spot, and a tarp draped over the box for good measure. John hesitated while the others scrambled, then picked a spot close to Meiying. Her proximity always gave him comfort, but they could not talk because the howl of the storm drowned out their feeble voices.

After an hour, the rain lessened, and now a low whistle rose and fell with the wind. A drenched peasant woman ran inside. Her skin, as usual for country-people, was cracked and wrinkled, but she appeared no older than her fifties or so. Planting herself in the middle of the barn, where rain still fell through a collapsed section of roof, she spoke in a loud, brittle voice that cut daggers through the storm.

"Friends! Did you see anyone on the way here? A group of evil-looking men with a young girl?"

A chorus of "No" rose from all sides.

"She was only thirteen. A beauty, Most beautiful in the district. Once a blessing, now a curse!"

"Did they kidnap her?" shouted Dr. Liu from the corner.

"Yes, curse them!" the woman, still standing in the pouring rain, spat. "My husband and sons are gone—in the army. Now they take her, my only daughter!"

"Was it the army that took her?" asked Madame Liu.

"Oh, dear Lady, they wore uniforms, but acted like animals!"

"Deserters!" cried Lu Zhishen.

"How many were there?" asked Mr. Gao.

"I don't know, uncle. Many." After speaking these hopeless words, she staggered, then collapsed on her knees, sobbing.

While the others stared, feeling helpless, the soldier suddenly appeared next to her. "Come on, mother, let's go back to your house. You're drenched. She'll return."

The old woman looked at him vacantly, and he led her out of the barn. Over her shoulder, she pleaded, "For god's sake, if you find her, bring her home! Her name is Huifen!" Gradually, her desperate voice dimmed to silence leaving only the rain, which had turned to drizzle. Above the dripping and the wind, the group heard a familiar, ominous sound.

… Tap. Tap. Tap….

This time, they did not gather around the box. Instead, it was as if the tapping came from a time-bomb, ticking off the seconds, and no one wanted to be close when it exploded. Meiying looked at John and saw him holding his stomach in pain. His eyes were closed and she wondered if his voice was, at that very moment, talking to him.

Only the kids, ironically enough, had the courage to approach the object. As usual, Little Acorn urged them on. He and some of the older children peered down at the tarp-covered box from behind the slats of a stall. While the other boys stared wide-eyed at the covered statue, Little Acorn explained that the ghost of a murdered lady who had been buried alive was trying to get out and take revenge. He reached through the space between the slats to pull the tarp away, when behind them, Madame Liu clapped her hands and shouted, "Get away from there!" They scattered, shrieking to the four winds. The tapping stopped.

Darkness descended quickly, and combined with the storm, created a dreary, cold atmosphere which chilled the group and made them all depressed. Since the tapping stopped, no one dared discuss it, as if it were a forbidden topic. The peasants in the group went about gathering old straw and building a comfy nook for themselves, while the others collected around a sputtering lantern and entered into a debate about war and peace and what the future would bring. A bottle of rice wine appeared, and as it made the rounds, the conversation livened up, and laughter even punctuated the gloom. Before he knew it, John was giving a speech, much to his own surprise.

"I'm going to talk in English!" he proclaimed. "What I have to say is too important to have it butchered by my bad Chinese." He knew some of his words were slurred, but the others seemed receptive, and more wine had miraculously arrived out of thin air. "I don't really know why I'm here. Sometimes I get suspicious of you all. But now, I just feel love for you. When we meet *her*, all our questions will be answered—at least, that is what we all hope. But there are scary things too, like that damn tapping and this fuckin'—excuse my French—voice in my head!" He stood unsteadily and put an index finger to his temple. "If this finger was a drill, I'd turn it on, squeeze the trigger, and drill away … well … in I'd go … and, well, anyway that's what I'd do just to get to the bottom of everything." He knew he rambled, and he noticed the others saying words he didn't understand. "Look, all

I'm saying is that China will be bathed in blood, and we may die, but out of the blood will rise a new China, and a new us. No going back!" He sat and felt dizzy.

"Well!" cried Peter. "What a speech! A regular Abraham Lincoln!" He raised the bottle and drank more wine.

"No, more like Henry at Agincourt," quipped Mr. Gao.

Meiying sat next to Lu Zhishen and listened with an ambiguous smile. On the one hand, she felt John needed to unwind, and on the other, she didn't want him to embarrass himself. She noticed Dr. Liu and his wife had returned to their sleeping areas, and only she and the two foreigners remained to listen.

"So, who are these voices?" John continued, undeterred by the sparse audience. "No, not voices, who is *the* voice?"

"Who?" cried Peter. "Tell us, old boy!"

"I'll tell you. It's tap, tap, tap. It's the same bullshit as that goddamn tapping. Tap. Tap. Tap." As John spoke these words, he leaned over against a stack of old burlap and promptly fell asleep.

Meiying covered him with a small blanket. Peter, looking on, said, "What do you think, Meiying old girl, is he on to something with his voices and the tapping, or is he just plain bloody crazy?"

Meiying smiled. "I don't know, Peter, but I do know we're getting wet sitting here."

Peter, a bit intoxicated himself, felt a sudden amorous impulse. He put his arm around her. "Are you really . . . you know . . . a bit funny about men?"

She gently pushed him away. "Men don't need me to be a bit funny. They do that all by themselves."

Sparrows in the rafters erupted in a chorus of scolding chirps, as if insisting the humans go to sleep and leave them in peace, free from the adjectives and verbs that so plagued the world.

~ *Lice and Monks* ~

Everyone awakened the next morning to hear their comrades complaining, moaning, and scratching. They discovered the barn was infested with lice, and now, on top of all their troubles, they had to deal with this uncomfortable outbreak. The storm had passed, so they decided to set up an impromptu barber shop outside. To the immense delight of the villagers, who had gathered to watch the spectacle, Lu Zhishen was appointed acting barber. First, shears borrowed from the village were used to cut those with the longest hair. Madame Liu maintained her stoic demeanor, but Meiying and the peasant women were teary-eyed as their locks were cut. Then the shaving began. First, the children were shaved, creating a great wailing and crying. Only Little Acorn bore it bravely. Although younger than some of the others, he had emerged as their leader, and often kept them in line when the adults were distracted. After many bungled attempts, the group truly resembled monks with shaved heads, albeit with numerous scrapes and cuts as evidence of inadequate tools and amateur barbers. The men joked about Lu

Zhishen's awful barbering, but he got the worst of it when Peter butchered his scalp, although the big Canadian refused to have his beard cut.

By the time they started on their way, the villagers were already in the fields. Women worked in teams to repair the damaged houses. Only the headman and the children, who he had evidently taken charge of, saw them off. With a group of fascinated youngsters hiding behind his ragged trousers, the old man spoke. "As headman of this unfortunate village, I bid you farewell." He put a hand on top of a little boy's head. "There will be starvation. I have heard the Japanese are inhuman. What of Nanjing?"

Dr. Liu shook his head.

"Ah," sighed the old man. "Then that is bad." He picked up a crying female toddler. "It will be hard on all of us." The wind picked up and swept across the fields, bringing its own sad sigh. Suddenly, the old man laughed in a deep, hearty bray. "At least you have our lice to remind you of our humble village!"

Dr. Liu grinned and rubbed his bald, scarred scalp. "Ha! Thanks, friend! Good luck! May prosperity return to your village!"

The old man laughed again, put down the now-calm toddler, and held up a half-full bottle of rice wine. "And we will have something to remember you by!"

The group moved down the road and waved to the peasants in the fields. Old Fox was particularly garrulous, leading to the suspicion that he had imbibed that morning on the sly.

"Hey, comrade!" (That is what he called Feng Shiren.) "These rich people pedal too fast! An old servant can't keep up. Even the spoiled kids are faster than me! But the tables will be turned soon, eh?"

Clearly, the soldier was uncomfortable with these intemperate words. "Hush, Old Fox! Old Fox indeed! Fox is not the proper name for you. Old Donkey is better, with the gibberish you speak!"

Chastened, Old Fox chuckled under his breath, but rode quietly after that. As the group put distance between them and Nanjing, a feeling of liberation overcame their somber mood. The misfortune of the recent village was not personal—they had arrived after the fact—and without the personal, humans (even the most conscientious) cannot perceive immediacy. One can anticipate being shot, but one does not feel it until it happens.

Steam rose from the ground as the sun grew hotter, evaporating the remaining moisture from the storm. It added to the extreme humidity sapping their strength, and as they approached a series of hills, the road steepened, increasing their exertion and causing the children and the old ones to drift farther behind.

Near the back of the line, a quarrel broke out between a peasant member of the group and Old Fox. It seems one of them swerved into the path of the other, causing a collision. The peasant, Wu Dingshi, took a tumble and hurt his knee.

"Look what you've done, Old Fox, Old Fool!" cried Wu. "Too busy chattering, and probably drunk on top of it!"

"Pipe down, peasant! Who's a fool?"

"You are less than a fool, stupid dog! Look what you've done to my knee!" And to demonstrate the injury, he hobbled around before picking up his bike.

"Can you ride?" asked Mr. Gao, who had just arrived with the others from the front of the line.

"Yes, no thanks to that dog of Feng Shiren's that we brought."

This was too much for Old Fox, who rushed at Wu as if to flail him. Others instinctively grabbed the two combatants, and as this ridiculous, comical scene unfolded, no one noticed a large number of armed men approaching from the nearby woods. Little Acorn cried out and pointed. Before they could respond, the group froze when a loud voice boomed through the air.

"Hey, comrades, look at this! Monks fighting!"

Before they knew it, the men had surrounded them, some laughing and pointing, some scowling and brandishing their rifles. Their uniforms were shabby, stuffed-cotton tunics, torn trousers of all descriptions, and beaten-up sandals. The apparent leader, a tall, pock-marked man with a northern manner stepped boldly forward. "What are you doing here, and on bicycles, for god's sake?"

Dr. Liu spoke up. "Our temple in Shanghai was destroyed by the Japs and we are traveling to the northwest."

The leader peered at John, Lu Zhishen, and Peter. "With foreigners?"

"They joined our order and were trapped when the Japanese came."

"Do they understand mandarin?"

"A little."

The leader went down the line, asking each of the three, "Where are you from?" When he heard that two were from America, and one from Canada, he frowned and said, "Why do you Americans support that criminal, Jiang Jieshi?"

No one replied.

He grew angrier. "Western devils wearing Buddhist robes? It's like a dog walking on two legs! Well, soon all you parasites will be picked clean off China's body!" He noticed some of the younger children hiding behind the adults. "Hey, who are these brats, huh?"

Dr. Liu explained that they were orphans the group hoped to save.

The leader walked up to Little Acorn and ruffled his hair. "Future Marxists! Don't believe the weak prattle of these supposed monks. The revolution is here!"

"Excuse me, sir," said Mr. Gao. "Are you on your way to fight the Japanese?"

"What's that? Nonsense! Let Jiang's Nationalist pigs and the Jap imperialist dogs fight. When they've killed each other, we'll take over and build a new China!"

"Ah, good," replied Gao.

"Now," the leader said, rubbing his chin significantly. "What do we do with this lot? What do you say, comrades?"

He directed this question to the men, but there clearly was only one person whose opinion mattered. A balding man with glasses standing quietly in the ranks, said in a commanding voice, "Expropriate their bicycles and check their belongings. Monks, if they are monks, make good spies."

Feng Shiren bolted forward with his bike and offered it to the leader. "Excellent! Sir, let me be the first to contribute to the cause! Here, take this bicycle and use it to good purpose, to rid our country of bourgeois, blood-sucking landowners. Take it, comrade!"

Bemused, the leader started to take the bike when Feng Shiren said, "But first, comrade, I have something to tell you." He winked and tapped his nose. "Can we step away from prying ears and have a private chat?"

The leader glanced at the balding man with glasses, who nodded assent. Off walked Feng Shiren followed by the leader. John watched them stop at the edge of the woods. No words could be heard, but Feng appeared quite animated, the leader listening in silence, his eyes wide. When they returned, the leader whispered something to the balding man with glasses, who nodded vigorously.

"Listen carefully!" the leader addressed the group. "We communists are like fish swimming among the sea of people. We do not take even a straw from you. Due to the generosity of the Party, you may keep your bicycles. Remember this in future!"

Unfortunately, while Feng conferred with the leader, soldiers had already started checking the group's belongings, tossing them this way and that. Meiying kneeled with her head down, the box containing the Precious Object at her feet, a soldier crouching over it. Other articles from their possessions were scattered over the ground. Some food and wine bottles had already been set aside and eyed greedily by the soldiers.

In response to the leader's unexpected announcement, the soldiers appeared clearly unhappy. Grumbling could be heard. Ignoring orders, the crouching soldier picked up the box, shook it, then put it down and snapped at Meiying to unlock it. When she hesitated, he lifted his rifle to strike her.

"Stop!" shouted the balding man with glasses. "You will obey the Party, comrade!"

The rifle came down across Meiying's face, smashing against her cheekbone and knocking her to the ground. A bolt of shock went through the group, many jumping forward to help her. But before anyone could reach the prone body, a shot rang out, causing everyone to freeze. When John cleared his mind of the initial shock, he saw the soldier lying atop Meiying's body, half of his forehead gone, blood and tissue splattered over her. Still conscious, she screamed and frantically crawled away, eventually helped to her feet by Lu Zhishen and Mr. Gao.

Another shot was fired, and everyone's eyes snapped toward the balding man with glasses, whose gun pointed at the sky. "The Party demands that orders be obeyed. They will be obeyed without question. Lieutenant, take care of the body. You monks"—he smiled sarcastically—"or whatever you are, be on your way! And leave quickly, before circumstances change!"

Meiying, still noticeably shaken and in pain, held a cloth to her bloody face and the group picked up their belongings catch-as-catch-can and quickly walked their bikes away. Lu Zhishen helped Meiying, whose legs were very unsteady. John moved close to them while pushing both his own and Meiying's bicycles. No one looked back until they had traveled up and over the hill.

Once out of sight of the soldiers, Madame Liu and a peasant woman attended to Meiying's face while the others talked. For good measure, Little Acorn was sent back up the hill to make sure the soldiers weren't following. As John watched the caretakers hovering like anxious moths over Meiying, glimpses of her bloody face brought back the miner in his dream busily digging, digging, swinging the pick, as upwelling blood pumped out of the shaft and sprayed into the outside world. The little miner slowly approached the core.

... Tap. Tap. Tap.

How to hold it together? Things, terrible things, happen so fast here! No time to think!

Don't try! You're close! Dig! Dig!

His unraveling passed unnoticed, as the pressing issues of Meiying's injury and Feng Shiren's miracle words occupied the group. John struggled to remain sane while Meiying, his great advocate, lay semi-conscious, unable to help.

~ *The Mystery of Feng Shiren* ~

Feng Shiren sat cross-legged on the ground listening with an infuriatingly amused smile at the questions.

"Look, Mr. Feng, or whoever you are, how did you get us out of that fix?" This question by Peter kicked off the inquisition.

The soldier shrugged.

"What does that mean?" demanded Lu Zhishen.

"What difference does it make? We're alive."

"Look," said Mr. Gao, toning down the aggressive nature of the questions. "Don't think we're not grateful. All of us are very grateful. But, of course, we are curious about what just happened."

"I understand," said Feng, without further explanation.

"Well," continued Gao. "We have the Precious Object to think of. It would be exceedingly helpful to understand how you achieved this miracle with the communists. Do you know them?"

Feng Shiren stood and stretched as carelessly as if they were discussing the weather. "All of this praise is going to my head," he intoned irrelevantly. "And as for the Precious Object, well, she is my major concern."

"Besides," piped-up Old Fox. "He just saved us. We should not be so rude to ask all these questions."

Dr. Liu, who had been listening with great interest, said, "You are right. We should leave him alone and simply be grateful."

Evidently surprised, Mr. Gao shot back, "So we should not care who we have among us—no offense Mr. Feng—but aren't the rest of you uncomfortable not knowing?"

"I agree! Well said, old man!" enthused Peter.

"No!" cried Mr. Liu, the passion in his voice taking them all aback except Feng Shiren. "We will continue on as before to the next safe harbor."

"How much farther?" asked Wu Dingshi.

"We'll travel a little more, if Meiying is up to it, then camp for the night. As we are already behind schedule, we are about three days away."

"No, we'll camp here," said Madame Liu walking up to the men. "Meiying is not up to traveling any farther today."

"Ah!" cried Dr. Liu.

Peter glared at the soldier. "You and I can continue our discussion later."

Feng struck another opera pose in response.

A strong gust of wind swept through the hills, bringing the smells of a nearby river and the rich sweetness of lilacs. Occasionally, a whiff of night soil from distant fields could be detected amidst the scented sweetness. John, still standing away from the group, breathed deeply and drove away the demon by pouring every ounce of energy into thinking about Meiying. Exhausted by events and his internal struggle, he felt glad they were stopping for the night. He wanted to set-up close to her in case she needed anything during the night. Madame Liu watched him prepare his sleeping area and smiled. John noticed.

"This way I'll be near in case," he said defensively.

She nodded. "I understand."

"Can she talk now?" he asked.

"Maybe later. Her face is swollen and she is very tired."

"No problem." He heard others talking around a small campfire, so he wandered over to join their conversation. Being alone was the last thing he wanted now.

"Ah, what is to become of our poor country?" moaned Mr. Gao. "Shanghai is gone and now the Japs are besieging Nanjing."

"All I can say, good sir, is thank god we've escaped both," said the peasant Wu Dingshi.

"Yes, good for us, I suppose," said Gao. "But our country! Being torn apart by beasts from within and without! Take those damn communists. They say they want to liberate the people, but the person, the single individual, means nothing to them."

"Which gets us back to Feng Shiren," said Peter. "Where is he?"

"Find Old Fox and you'll find him!"

Wu scoffed. "Old Fox is sleeping, snoring like the ox he is. Probably sleeping off his wine."

Peter stood. "I'm going to see where that bloody enigma Feng is."

"Don't cause trouble!" warned Dr. Liu.

"I won't. I just want to see where he is." With that, Peter disappeared into the night.

The fire shimmered and undulated enticingly, its flames thin and ghostlike, while beneath the embers a distinct crackling punctuated the silence that had fallen over the group.

"Hello, John," said Dr. Liu. "I hadn't noticed you there."

"Hello."

"Come closer to the fire. Get warm. Have you heard much of our little discussion?" asked Mr. Gao.

"Yes, but my thoughts are elsewhere tonight."

"Meiying?"

"No. Well, yes and no."

Dr. Liu and Mr. Gao glanced at each other. "Is everything fine, John?" asked Dr. Liu.

Instead of replying, John watched a white moth fluttering around the flames. Its wings shone like neon lights, turning on and off as they flapped.

"John?"

"Yeah, I just—"

But John's words were interrupted by distant explosions and rumbling shockwaves that even the fire seemed to cringe from. In the excitement that followed, some thought they could hear small-arms fire. John's thoughts turned to Meiying. Her entire being appeared before him as the essence of perfection—beauty, kindness, compassion, talent—that had been created wholly from some otherworldly womb, simply by virtue of its own grace. Now that perfection lay nearby, damaged and in pain, while monstrous forces roared threats in the distance.

Ignoring the agitated speculations by his comrades, he moved closer to where she lay. Nearby, one of the peasant women was busily draping various pieces of wet cloth she had washed in the river over low hanging branches when John approached.

"How is she?" he asked.

"Sleeping, thank god. She doesn't have to listen to that noise. Is there any place safe these days?"

"Soon enough, Suling, soon enough."

They sat for a few moments in silence, the rumbling explosions coming in waves.

"Suling?"

"Yes?"

"How did you come to know *her*?"

"Ah, that is a story, Mr. John."

"I'd like to hear it. No one else around here wants to talk about it."

Suling considered, pausing to straighten some of the hanging cloth pieces. While John waited patiently for her to respond, he felt the immediacy of life surrounding him, as only a stranger in a strange land feels. All the mental constructs of culture and habit that normally stand between ourselves and the world had been removed. His entire being, his soul, whatever the essence of consciousness is, merged into this Chinese countryside with its rich mixture of smells, sights, and sounds. It was as if his own body simply diffused into the surrounding air. His demons remained quiet, his quest momentarily forgotten, and only Meiying, a small but beautiful piece of this great puzzle of China, remained as a concrete object, the quintessence of all that is.

"You won't believe this, but I was once quite a beauty," said Suling in her heavy Hunan accent. "Oh, sorry, did I interrupt your thoughts?" she asked after noticing that John seemed far away.

"No, no," insisted John. "Please, I really want to hear."

She hung the last piece of cloth on a branch and stood rubbing the edge like a monk rubbing his rosary beads as she spoke.

"Well, as I said, I was once a beauty. In those days, it was a blessing. Now,"—she shuddered. "Anyway, I was quite lazy and I drove my mother crazy with my constant primping and flirting with the local boys. I hated working in the fields and I hated even more doing housework. The only thing I did properly was take care of our family buffalo. I don't know why, but I was very fond of that buffalo.

"One day I was out looking for the buffalo, which had wandered off in the night. After I found him, I hooked a tether to his ring and was walking him home when I heard a terrible ruckus from the village, sort of like what we're hearing now. Gunfire and explosions, and soon, smoke filled the forest. I was terrified, so I hid. The noise continued for hours and I spent the night under the trees behind a fallen log, imagining the horrors that might await me at the village.

"After a sleepless night, I crept back home. The air was still full of smoke. When I entered the outskirts of our village, I saw many, many decapitated heads stuck on poles. As I walked down the line, I recognized my neighbors, boys I had shamelessly flirted with, my uncle, my grandmother, then my parents and my brothers and sisters. Only our buffalo was alive, standing as if in shock himself.

"I honestly don't remember what happened next. Apparently, I had fainted, and when I awoke, three men stood over me." Suling paused, rubbing the edges of the cloth faster, her eyes wide with the memory. "It was more terrible than you can imagine. Their faces were like demons, like starving dogs." She put her face in a cloth and wept. "Sorry, so sorry. Even now, to think what they did to me.

"After hours of torture, they left me to die. I laid in the manure, beneath the heads of my family, and was too sick and torn to move. If a knife or a gun was close-by, I know I would have gladly used it. Night came and I waited for the beasts of the forest to come and finish me off. Rats began crawling up the poles and onto the heads and I heard them fighting and squealing like demons, their bodies plopping onto the ground, then scurrying up again. I remember the horrible expressions of the faces of my family in the moonlight before they became covered in a mass of rats. They were judging me from beyond, condemning me, ordering me to join them in their humiliation. Would they welcome me or would they whip me down to Buddhist hell?

"Then I saw a light, a lantern, moving toward me, and I was sure the men had returned to finish me off. It hovered over me in silence, and I now thought it was the ghosts of my ancestors come to take me. The lantern remained hovering above, and leaning down into its light shone a face, the most beautiful and kind face. It was *her. She* helped me to find shelter in a nearby forester's cottage which had been abandoned for years. We played in it as children, and it was in ruins even then. But when *she* took me there, someone had fixed it up as if anticipating it would be needed. There, *she* healed my wounds, eased my tortured mind, and seemed to me the flesh and blood embodiment of Guan-yin."

"Did *she* talk to you? What did *she* say?" asked John, visibly moved by Suling's story.

"Ah! *She* spoke in riddles; I could never understand their meaning. 'I'm a poor peasant girl,' I would say. I pleaded with *her*. 'Please explain! I don't understand you!'"

"What did she say to that?"

"*She* just smiled. Then, when I was well enough to take care of myself, *she* left, just disappeared. I made it to a nearby village, then to the district capital. From then on, I vowed to learn more so when I found *her* again, I could understand her deep ways. I worked hard, learned to read, sought out wise men, and never stopped searching. Here I am!" Suling looked down and covered her toothy smile. "No longer a beauty, Mr. John!"

"Yes, you are," said John, at a loss. Suling had always been a face in the background, just another one of China's multitudinous peasants. Long suffering, silent, illiterate, pliable, fatalistic. *How wrong we can be!* he thought. Before he could pursue these reflections any further, deep rumbling from the battle seemed to shake the ground and cause the leaves on the trees to quiver as if they feared for their lives.

"What's that?" Meiying's voice came soft and fragile.

Suling quickly jerked a cloth from a branch and stepped lightly to where Meiying lay. Even as she moved toward the injured woman, she spoke in a tone more soothing than John thought her capable of. "It's all right, young Meiling dear. Just some thunder far away bringing rain to thirsty life."

John listened until her words were no longer audible, then went to his sleeping area and sat leaning against a tree. *None of this really exists.* This thought appeared out of nowhere. *I am home, dreaming, and since I must be at work by 9:00, the alarm will soon ring.* A stack of ideas, each building upon the other, triggered an avalanche of irrefutable evidence that all of his experiences in China were fantasies; products of his diseased mind. A sudden terror of mental illness struck him with almost physical force. "Voices! Voices! There is a word for it. Schizophrenia. Not me. Not me. The others hear the tapping. Same thing, and they are not all schizophrenic. Still, this *is* all real. Even if it is schizophrenia, it's a mild case. Easily controlled."

Then control Me.

"All right, let's see. I want you to either go away or make yourself useful. If you are gone, then I will hear nothing. If you are still here, tell me who you are. If you are me, if you are my delusion, then say so. But if not, tell me who you really are."

God calls you a failure—a lost cause. Do not listen. You are the Chosen One!

"I'll take that to mean you are part of me, because I agree; I am worthless. If that is the case, then it's all over, because I truly am schizophrenic."

I only said that to make you come to your senses.

"What does that mean?"

It means you are as much a schizophrenic as everyone else.

"What does that mean?"

Look around, John Powers. Because of the voices in their heads, all humans are schizophrenic. This pathology results in great danger to themselves, as well as to others. Absent treatment, this danger translates into the destruction of themselves, and to others. There is no cure. You, however, do not have schizophrenia like the others. For the Mentors, you are the Chosen One, a beginning step in the replacement of Homo sapiens by guided evolution. The only treatment for—

"John!"

"What about treatment?"

"John! Wake up!"

Lu Zhishen leaned in front of John's face. "Wake up! You're talking in your sleep."

"Oh. What did I say?"

"Gibberish. Something about danger and destruction. Probably a nightmare caused by the sounds of that damn battle."

"There's no cure."

"What?"

John shook his head. "Nothing. Did I wake Meiying?"

Lu Zhishen looked toward her sleeping area. "I don't think so. But you sure as hell got me over here."

John peered out at the darkness. "Why are you up? What time is it? Four or five o'clock? Seems to be getting a bit lighter."

"Naw, that's the moon. We're looking for Peter. He's missing."

"What?"

"Yeah, we can't find him anywhere."

"I remember he said he was going to look for the soldier."

Lu frowned. "Yeah, we know."

"Where's Feng?" asked John suspiciously.

"Exactly; where is Feng? That is the question. My guess is that we find the soldier, we find Peter." Lu scowled. "Or we find where Peter's body is." Abruptly, Lu rose and vanished into the early morning haze.

As clouds moved across the moon, John could distinguish his surroundings only intermittently, like frames in an out-of-focus slide show. From the side, he detected movement, and when he looked harder, he saw Meiying momentarily illuminated by moonlight. Her appearance was accompanied by a particularly loud series of explosions. Still distant, but uncomfortably insistent. Meiying pulled her cover closer around her shoulders and neck as if the noise carried a chilling wind.

"Hello, John," she said in her distinctive, soothing voice.

John stood, a relieved smile on his face. "Hello, Meiying. Come, sit with me for awhile, if you're up to it. How do you feel?"

More rumbling.

"Nanjing?" she asked, already knowing the answer.

"Yes."

"I heard you talking to someone, so I came over. Couldn't sleep any longer."

"Oh, that was just Lu Zhishen."

"No, before him."

John hesitated. "Zhishen said I was talking in my sleep."

"Were you?"

John shrugged. "Dunno."

The rumbling suddenly ceased, and both listened as the sounds of the natural world returned; crickets, frogs, nightingales. Both felt themselves relaxing to the humble, cleansing hymns of nature. Watching the moonlight glisten on her hair, John felt an overwhelming spirit of closeness to her, and an enfolding sense of unity with all that surrounded them.

Do I love her? Would this be bearable without her? Would life be bearable without her?

"What are you thinking, John?"

"Nothing much."

A breeze gently stirred the leaves, massaging them free of the stressful quivering left over from the battle. Nearby voices soon intruded and jarred both of them back to ugly reality.

"Did you find him?" John recognized Dr. Liu's voice.

"No," replied Lu Zhishen.

John and Meiying rose and moved toward the voices.

"What about Feng Shiren?" asked Dr. Liu.

"No," repeated Lu.

Dr. Liu spotted John and Meiying coming near. "Did either of you see Peter?"

"No," replied John for both of them.

"I'm very worried," said Madame Liu.

"If that son-of-a-bitch has—" Lu started to say when a strong voice interrupted.

"Has done anything to Peter?" rang out Feng Shiren, finishing Lu's statement with a flourish.

Dawn's light made Feng easily distinguishable. He stepped closer to the group. "My friend, Peter, is right here." He held out his arm like a host presenting a performer.

Peter walked forward from the shadows, a sheepish expression on his face. "Sorry, everyone," he said. "I got lost looking for our friend here."

"What happened?" asked Mr. Gao.

"Our protector, Feng Shiren, found me instead and led me safely back. I must say, I'm pretty embarrassed."

Something didn't seem right. John asked, "Are you okay, Peter?"

"Absolutely. Sorry you all had to lose sleep on account of me."

"It seems once again you have performed a great service to us, Mr. Feng," proclaimed Madame Liu. John could not tell whether any sarcasm laced her words.

In response, Feng struck one of his inimitable poses.

Dr. Liu turned to Meiying. "Do you feel better? Are you up to moving on?"

"Oh, yes, much better."

"The swelling is down, I can see," said Suling approvingly. "How are your legs? Are you dizzy?"

"Not at all."

Just as Meiying finished saying these words, the rumbling from Nanjing started up again.

"Well," said Peter. "That should spur us on."

Something in Peter's tone bothered John, but he could not put his finger on it.

~ *Refugees and the Voice* ~

Later that morning, as the group traveled on a main road, refugees from Nanjing who had motorized vehicles started catching up to them. Those fleeing in cars were able to inform the group that Nanjing would soon fall to the Japanese. Rumors were that the government was preparing to abandon the city for some unknown destination. A few hours later, four Japanese aircraft flew over, evidently looking for Chinese troops reinforcing Nanjing. Their passing gave everyone a fright, and by the time they got back on the road, the number of refugees had swelled.

Soon, the familiar sounds of explosions and machine-gun fire could be heard ahead of them. A great commotion ensued as panic worked its way back down the road, like a great wave that had hit a wall and rebounded chaotically. John felt a tremor pass through his body, a sickening buzz of fear, when he realized the war raged both in front and behind them.

Don't worry, dear Chosen One, I will protect you.

John had become more inured to the voice's eccentricities and perverse sense of timing. Perhaps conversing with the voice would reveal more about it. Demystify it. "Why protect me?" he asked as nonchalantly as possible.

I have plans for you ...and, by the way, for your future son. The one writing this—

"My son? I have no son!"

You don't listen well, do you?

"I will listen if you—"

"John!" cried Meiying from her bike. "You're talking to yourself again! Do you want to stop?"

"No, I'll tell you about it later! Let's keep going!"

Old Fox, hovering nearby, laughed. "Young American boy hears things; talks to himself; a little crazy, no?"

John laughed with him. "A little crazy, yes." But inside, he teemed with anger. It had always been almost an article of faith that his own problems were not to be shared with the world. It made him feel more self-confident and stronger when he could help others, or when others confided their problems with him. But the reverse only served to weaken him; to emphasize his limitations and weaknesses. *Meiying is the only one,* he thought. *The only one who I feel comfortable confiding in; my vulnerabilities laid bare before her unjudging eye. Is that love?*

He had always struggled with the concept of romantic love. He knew it wasn't only sex, but he also knew it carried with it an element of sexual attraction. He knew it wasn't only admiration, although again, that was also an element of love. Dependence? Yes. Dependence on companionship, honesty, faithfulness, and so on. It struck him that dependence was the trump card of romantic love. Not sex, not admiration or respect. So, the question he kept asking himself was whether he had become dependent upon Meiying. In his mind, if he now depended upon Meiying, he must therefore love her. But did she love him? He couldn't very well just ask her if she depended upon him. What to do? What to say?

Chapter Five

She Will Have A Son

Meiying's Crisis

Meiying faced her own crisis. Recent events, including the assault by the vicious soldier, terrified her and made her question assumptions she had taken for granted her entire life. A visceral craving for a peaceful life with security and certainty had now replaced her more youthful, carefree view of the future. She still wanted a child, but one who could be brought up surrounded by joy and unassailable safety. Ample food and a contented home, not starvation and war, were the twin goals of her new life. How to achieve these ideals while burning in the seemingly inescapable cauldron of war-torn China? Her most cherished fantasy had always been to live with a gentle, intelligent female lover, one who would be her agent, an equal partner, making arrangements for concerts around the world and sharing the accolades together. Both of them would be parents to a beautiful child, teaching him or her the exquisite powers of art and knowledge, beauty and compassion.

But this fantasy no longer comforted her. Craving the unattainable led to madness. In her new reality, only an act of desperation, of betrayal, might succeed. The alternative became increasingly unthinkable. Even as a girl, Meiying had discovered the power she possessed over men by virtue of her looks and talent. With positive reinforcement propelling her along the way, she channeled her energies into developing and strengthening this power. Only Meiying's traumatic contact with *her* had altered its trajectory. But that alteration did not reverse the overall direction of her life. Now, that direction had irrevocably changed, leading her into violence, possibly rape, and certainly destruction, unless she did something soon to alter it. How?

For some time, she had resisted the subversive thought that the foreigners—Peter, John, and Lu Zhishen—came from rich and peaceful countries, and therefore one of them might constitute a way out if she played her cards right. After all, such manipulation and downright dishonesty ran counter to her most cherished beliefs and, if acted upon, would mangle her self-perceived character into something alien and sinister. But since the attack, Meiying realized that at any moment she might become permanently disfigured—physically, spiritually, or both. The stakes had changed and she felt the hot breath of necessity.

As she mulled over these ideas, an ugly reality kept intruding: all three foreigners were refugees, in the same boat as she, cut off from easy escape back to their rich and powerful countries. Worse, the one she felt closest to, the one who might offer a way out, was afflicted with some mental issues that frightened her and made her wary of getting too close. And yet, the voice he heard in his mind held a deep fascination for her. Was he connected to something deeper, more profound? Was he connected to *her*? And if so, did Meiying's fate not entwine with his? These questions drove her on and made her more determined than ever to reach the final destination and resolve these uncertainties.

The morning proved uneventful and the group made good progress. For hours, Meiying debated with herself, differing conclusions tugging this way and that. As she pedaled, she would slow-down or speed-up to fall in place next to each of the foreigners and chat about nothing in particular. *Tasting the flavors to determine which to devour*, she thought with self-loathing. *Look at what I've become!* But the fact remained that she harbored an unsavory agenda, and while her words rang hollow when she spoke to these unwitting men, her senses were in full alert to the reactions they induced in her mind and her body. When she rode next to John, her first question was clumsy and insipid, but she couldn't stop herself.

"John, do you like children?"

Stupid, stupid, stupid, she thought, even as her ears pricked up at his response.

"Of course I like children. Why do you ask?"

Her path now set, she followed it steadfastly, regardless of the consequences. "No, I mean really. Why do you like children?"

"I don't know—their innocence, I guess."

"What does that mean?"

"Well, it means . . . I don't know—it means they don't carry all the nonsense, you know, the prejudices of adults. They're innocent."

"So, can children be raised to not have prejudices?"

John perceived the seriousness in her line of questioning, and began thinking more deeply about his answers. "That's a good question. We can't protect them from the prejudices of others, but we can teach them how to recognize prejudice."

"How do we do that?"

"By teaching them the underlying simplicity, unity, and beauty of the world. From that view of perfection, any blemish or ugliness can be considered prejudice."

"For example?"

John paused, breathing hard from talking and pedaling at the same time. He realized this might be a sort of interview, so he now chose his words even more carefully. "For example, I consider all men and women as brothers and sisters. All connected, deeply connected to each other by genetics and by a fundamental desire to live in peace and personal fulfillment. Anything that causes us to deviate from that simple picture is prejudicial. One religion over another is prejudicial. One race over another is prejudice. One political view over another is prejudice. Of course, we can disagree, but we must do so quietly, civilly, not with anger and violence."

After this long speech, John was out of breath and Meiying felt gratified that Dr. Liu called for a rest stop. His words had pleased her, and she wanted to follow-up. But just as they had situated themselves in a clearing next to a stand of ash trees, a great roaring of machinery could be heard approaching from the road ahead. Dust clouds rose high into the air, and gradually a long column of armored personnel carriers, trucks, tanks, and motorcycles filled the road. The soldiers riding atop these machines looked like machines themselves, grim and metallic from the dust and khaki uniforms that merged with the dust on the vehicles. As they passed, Meiying found herself studying the reactions of the three foreigners. She overheard Peter and Lu Zhishen talking.

"Well," said Peter. "That old bastard Jiang Jieshi isn't going down without a fight."

Lu Zhishen shook his head. "Don't count on it. These guys are probably going to be his bodyguards when he abandons Nanjing."

"Bloody hell!" cried Peter. "I say, you're probably right!"

"These poor, ragged little Nationalist bastards haven't a chance against the Japs."

"Yeah. Poor guys. I don't envy them." Peter looked around. "Speaking of ragged soldiers, where's our soldier?"

"Made himself scarce when he saw the troops. Smart little bastard!" scoffed Lu Zhishen.

Peter looked down at his monk's robe. "But he's just a monk like the rest of us. Harmless, right?"

Both men laughed and Meiying processed the cynicism and ugliness of their words with those of John spoken minutes earlier. *Careful, girl*, she warned herself. *Don't jump to conclusions.* She looked at John sitting next to her, his face alternately grim and sad. His lips moved and Meiying wondered if it was the voice speaking, and he answering.

"Are you okay, John?" she asked loud enough to be heard over the convoy.

"Yes, why?"

"I think you're talking to yourself again, but I can't be sure. Your lips were moving."

John laughed. "Probably just thirst. My throat is dry from all this dust."

They fell quiet. John broke the silence. "Did you know I'm going to have a son?"

"What? A son?"

He smiled. "Well, at least according to my voice, I'm going to have a son sometime in the future. How about that for a prediction?"

"Or a prophecy," replied Meiying, stunned by his revelation. Its timing seemed propitious. Did it carry some deeper meaning? Meiying could not entirely divorce her Chinese mysticism from her rational mind, and echoes of her mother's profound belief in fate and the intervention of spirits colored her views. John's inner voice now carried a weight more akin to awe than to the manifestation of illness.

"Who is to be the mother of this son?" she asked, trying to sound objectively curious, as might a therapist.

John looked at her with an expression she could not interpret. "I don't know. It didn't say."

"Ah."

"Meiying—" John started to say.

"Run! Run! Get away from the road! Into the trees!" came voices shouting frantically. Before they had time to think, Japanese planes from out of nowhere swooped down to attack the convoy. Everyone scrambled in a panic to escape the bombs and strafing runs. Leaving their bikes, the group ran furiously toward the shelter of the trees. John clasped Meiying's hand and pulled her with him. Shock waves from the explosions knocked them both off their feet. While lying face down, John saw Feng Shiren dashing back toward the road.

"Get down, fool!" shouted various members of the group. "Get down!"

"He's going after the Precious Object!" John shouted to whoever could hear. He saw Suling run past carrying one of the younger children. Soon, the world seemed obliterated in smoke and dust. None of them heard the frantic tapping from the Precious Object over the din of battle. None, that is, except Feng Shiren.

~

After the planes left, people straggled out from the trees. As usual, Madame Liu shouted commands for the group to gather near her and take a count. Mr. Gao busied himself with the children. Many vehicles were in flames, and dead soldiers and civilians dotted the area. Two members of the group were missing; a child named Lisong, and Feng Shiren. The group fanned out to conduct a search, and very quickly found the child. Lisong had a gaping hole in her back from shrapnel, and her death hit everyone very hard. Meiying particularly could not stop crying.

Feng Shiren was also found, face-down, covering the box containing the Precious Object. When Dr. Liu leaned over the body to investigate, Feng jumped up like a suddenly uncoiled jack-in-the-box. He assumed a dramatic position and proclaimed to the world, "I'm fine! Can't kill me! Look, the Precious Object is safe, thanks to me!" He beat his chest for emphasis. Old Fox laughed obsequiously.

Amazingly, none of the bicycles were damaged, and the group moved on after burying little Lisong. They rode in somber silence, and before long the sky darkened. In setting up her sleeping area, Meiying chose a spot far away from the others, rebuffing their overtures. As darkness overcame the last light, she lay alone and cried. John approached, but she asked to be left alone.

Lisong was killed as punishment for my evil thoughts, she thought. *To entrap an unsuspecting man for my own ends antagonized the spirits of justice and compas-*

sion. Lisong represents the dead child of my dead dreams. She remembered John's words about the innocence of children, and again burst into tears.

Hours later, she had still not slept. Responding to the call of nature, she got up and moved toward a sandy spot when she heard sobbing. Following the sound by the light of the moon, she came upon Little Acorn, sitting with his knees up and his face buried in his arms. She sat next to him and gently placed her hand on his shoulder.

"Are you crying for Lisong?"

Without lifting his head, he nodded.

"I have also been crying."

He lifted his head and held it straight, as if a soldier at attention. "You are a woman. It's okay for you."

A brief feeling of sadness and disgust for male weaknesses passed through her mind, which was quickly replaced by pity for Little Acorn. "Is it so bad for a boy to cry?"

"Yes."

"Why? We all loved Lisong."

"I know."

"We all cry for those we love when they are in pain, or when they have died. Even men. You should not be ashamed."

Little Acorn shuddered. "But why her? She was too young! She didn't do nothing bad!"

"Yes. There is much suffering in the world. We can only mourn for those who have gone to join the ancestors. You can cry. You should cry. It is a sign of strength."

He pondered this for a moment. "I wish you were my mother. I would like to be your son. I heard you play the piano. Oh, Miss Bai, it was so beautiful! Someday, will you play just for me?"

Meiying heard these words and wept. "Yes, of course." His words acted as a balm to her heart; as a counterweight to her earlier self-recriminations. *I would be a good mother. I would!*

Yet, even as she thought these thoughts, she knew her lesbianism would block and thwart any possibility of her ever being a mother. The tears flowed even stronger.

It will never be. Never.

Two days later, with no further incidents, the group arrived at the second safe-harbor.

~ *Master Zhou* ~

The estate of rich landowner Zhou Guangli covered a vast area of rice fields and forest. The family mansion was built during the late Ming dynasty and had been modernized after the 1911 revolution. It consisted of thirty rooms, banquet halls, tea rooms, huge kitchen, and two libraries. At its height, servants bustled about the mansion and worked in the numerous gardens and ponds that encircled the grounds, gracing the ancient courtyard with a lovely, classical flavor, calling to mind the setting of great literary romances of the past.

Now, however, the gardens were infested with weeds and part of the mansion was heavily damaged and scarred by fire. Bandits, warlords, and communists had taken their toll, but the old estate had been given a reprieve by Jiang's Nationalist government, which provided it with protection. After settling in their rooms, the group gathered for a feast in one of the banquet halls.

"But now, those times are at an end," lamented Master Zhou. "I'm afraid we can no longer count on the safety provided by the Republic." He put his hands to his head. "And now, the Japanese! If Nanjing falls, we will be like a bone to hungry dogs."

"We are grateful to you," said Dr. Liu, raising his tea cup and bowing. "What news from Nanjing?"

Master Zhou shook his head grimly. No one spoke. At last, he sighed and said, "Now that you are here, perhaps as our last guests, please partake of our poor hospitality and inadequate fare. Our humble and meager efforts are at your service."

Little Acorn ran into the hall, breathless and stammering. "Meiying! Meiying! There's a piano! Come look! There's a piano!"

Master Zhou laughed. "Yes, it is true, we brought in a piano for my daughters who are, thank god, safely in America. But I'm afraid it is broken somehow."

Meiying politely shoo'ed Little Acorn away, saying, "I'll be in shortly." But her heart secretly pounded with excitement and she wanted to jump up and dash in to the piano. "How badly is it broken?" she asked as calmly as possible.

Master Zhou shrugged. "I know nothing of pianos. Chinese opera, now there is music!" And he was off reminiscing about the time years ago when he hosted the Peking Opera "at this very mansion!"

After listening to his interminable story, Madame Liu spoke up. "We have our own opera star: Feng Shiren is an excellent performer. Isn't that so, Mr. Feng?"

Never one to miss an opportunity, Feng jumped up and performed an impromptu excerpt from *Peony Pavilion*. So beautiful was his song, so full of pathos were his movements, that Master Zhou cried openly in appreciation and demanded an encore. Feng immediately performed a scene from *Drunken Concubine*, bringing laughter to the entire assemblage.

"A lost art!" blubbered Master Zhou, drinking his fifth cup of rice wine.

Peter, also into his cups, proclaimed, "Yeah, it's great. But I could do with a little jazz." Not to be outdone by Feng, he leapt onto the floor and danced a solo boogie-woogie, much to the amusement of the group.

"Americans!" cried Master Zhou. "Crazy people!"

Lu Zhishen piped in. "I've never seen a monk dance the boogie-woogie so well!"

As the laughter died down, the sounds of a piano drifted into the room. Random notes, then chords, then excerpts from a Rachmaninoff prelude enveloped them. Meiying had slipped out unseen, and members of the group rushed off to listen.

"A few wires are broken, that's all," said Meiying in apology. "My playing is so bad, but this is for Lisong."

"Not at all!" cried John. "Please continue. Look at Little Acorn."

Indeed, the boy sat on the floor next to Meiying's stool, his face a dreamy portrait of joy and awe; the artist and her protégé sharing a bond unknown by the others. As she played, Meiying surrendered to the music, unaffected by the broken wires, while John's expression reflected a deep and abiding love. Madame Liu was the first to notice. She tapped him on the shoulder. "Beautiful, yes?"

"Oh, more than beautiful!"

After the impromptu concert, the group filtered back to their rooms, but as if by unspoken agreement, Meiying and John ended up together in the main library.

"I wish we could sit out the war right here," said John.

"Yes, it would be lovely."

Meiying appeared contented and relaxed, but inside her mind resembled a battlefield. Unsure how to proceed, she gave herself over to John's lead. The events of the past few days, the loss of Lisong, the back-and-forth debates and recriminations had taken their toll. In truth, she was physically and emotionally exhausted.

"Meiying?"

"Yes?"

"Why did you ask me about children the other day?"

"I was curious about the viewpoints of foreigners, especially Americans. I read a lot about Americans, but have little opportunity to ask them these types of questions."

Too clinical, she thought. *He must think me a fool.*

Evidently, John was not prepared to deal with this response. "Oh," was the best he could muster. He looked down at his lap for inspiration. It came. "Do you want to have a family, Meiying?"

She realized this question could lead either to honest but dangerous confidences, or to harmlessly flirtatious banter. Unwilling to take the direct, dangerous route, she replied, "I already have a family. Those of us on this quest are my family."

"Yes, but a real family. You know what I mean, a family with a husband and your own children."

Meiying began to feel panicky. It was too soon to discuss these things. She had not yet reached a final resolution of the problem. She needed more time. Besides, the idea of a husband made her slightly nauseous. To live with a male? Forever? No. No. No. She composed herself and spoke calmly. "I have thought of it, but marriage is not for me anytime soon. My career is more important to me now."

"Well, husbands don't have to interfere with careers, you know."

Meiying shook her head vigorously. "But they do! Let's discuss something else."

"Such as?" John felt piqued at her wanting to change the subject, but he regretted his rather boorish response.

"Such as you."

"Me?" John asked in surprise. He shook his head. "Nothing there."

Meiying leaned forward in her chair. "Have you heard the voice recently?"

"Meiying, I really don't—"

"Have you heard the voice recently?"

"Yes."

"What did it say?"

"It said I should stay close to an extraordinary Chinese woman who plays the piano."

"John!"

He laughed, pleased with his little *bon mot*.

"Seriously, John."

"Why are you so interested in my stupid voice? Don't you think it means I'm ill, that I have mental problems?"

"No. I used to think that, and it frightened me. Now I think the voice is something else, something more than you, or beyond you, or from some distant spiritual place. You are a special person to have been chosen by the voice."

John looked at her to gauge whether her words were sincere or patronizing.

"The voice?" she said in a slightly exasperated tone.

"Okay, but I don't really like talking about it. Only for you. Yes, I hear the voice. Lately, I can actually have conversations with it. Well, short ones."

"Is the voice male or female?"

John paused with a puzzled look. "Good question. I don't know. Seems like there are two; sometimes male, sometimes female. Often, I can't remember what they have said, like waking up and not remembering a dream, but you know you had been dreaming."

"What is the last thing you remember them saying?"

"It was during the battle, but they didn't say anything."

"What do you mean?"

"During the battle, all I heard was one of them laughing."

"Laughing?" Meiying said in a shocked voice. "What could it mean?"

"Believe me, I've thought about that," replied John. "It was horrible. People were getting killed, I was terrified, and a voice was laughing. I told it to shut up, but it wouldn't listen."

Both sat silently. John broke the quiet. "Now do you think the voices are some sort of spirits from beyond, like angels or demons or something?"

"I don't know."

"Look, Meiying, you see why I don't want to talk about it. Now you probably think I'm some sort of a crazy schizophrenic."

"No, I don't think that. And I don't think the voices are part of you. They're coming from somewhere outside of you."

John put his hand on Meiying's. "Can we get back to talking about you, now? Or better yet, you and me?"

She pulled her hand away and stood. "John, we should get some sleep."

~

For the first time in his life, he had the urge to rape. Not in the ugly, violent way, but to force himself on her and have her melt in his arms. Sweet surrender. She was so beautiful, so perfect. Now that he was convinced he depended upon her to live, he had to force her to depend upon him in the same way. How? Simple: by forcing his attention on her until she recognized her dependence.

Do it. Do it now. For your son.

"No. You laugh at violence. I am not a rapist. I am not you!"

"John, I see your lips moving. Is it the voice again?" asked Meiying nervously. "I think you were saying words that scare me."

"No. You're right, it's time to get some sleep."

~ *Japanese in Nanjing* ~

The next few weeks brought news of Japanese atrocities in Shanghai. Beheadings, rape, torture, mass executions, roasting people alive. Nanjing was next. As winter deepened, the flow of refugees past the mansion did not abate. Thousands traveled the road, glassy-eyed, but ultimately glad to be alive.

It was agreed that the group would remain in the mansion until arrangements could be made for the next safe-harbor. Dr. Liu did not share in detail the reports he received, but everyone soon knew that something terrible had happened and they would have to continue postponing their journey for days, or perhaps weeks. One evening as everyone sat down to a late dinner, Feng Shiren made a surprising announcement.

"Since we are stuck here, I am returning to Nanjing to see for myself what is happening," he said defiantly, as if expecting protests. And indeed, protests came from all sides. "No! I have made up my mind. I will continue to disguise myself as a monk. Don't worry, I will return within a week. I can travel fast, and it won't take long to see for myself what the situation is. No telling when we can leave, so I might as well make myself useful."

"But Mr. Feng," said Mr. Gao. "We get plenty of information from the refugees and from the radio. Why do you need to go?"

"Simple, I don't believe any of them!" Feng laughed. "Seeing is believing, isn't that right, Dr. Liu?"

As he had done so often in the past, Dr. Liu went along with Feng's wishes, drawing a mix of puzzled reactions and suspicious rumors. But one thing was clear; they had come to depend upon Feng, and his absence made them unexpectedly anxious, though few would admit it.

The day after Feng bade farewell, John went walking and came across Peter sitting in one of the lower gardens. From a distance, John saw him smoking, glaring off into space and tapping his foot nervously. Evidently assuming he was alone,

Peter's demeanor, his body language, seemed very different from his normal devil-may-care attitude. Watching unnoticed from behind a flowering vine, John observed Peter's face reflect alternating moods, from worry to frustration, then to anger. As he puffed on his cigarette, every drag brought forth a new expression. Peter's lips moved as if he were talking to himself, and John entertained the notion that Peter held conversations with his own internal voice. Peter took a last, long drag of his cigarette, tossed it angrily to the ground, and stamped it out in disgust. He stood and walked in circles, hands behind his back, still mumbling to himself. Clearly agitated, he again sat, lit another cigarette, and took a long drag.

"Peter!" John waved.

Instantly, his face transformed to the old Peter, jovial and mischievous. "John, old boy! Come on down and join me!"

Even before John reached him, Peter called out, "Just having a fag. Calms the nerves, you know."

"Peter," said John smiling. "You're more Brit than the Brits. Henry James had nothing over you."

"Who?"

"Never mind, old boy."

"Okay," said Peter in his endearingly sheepish tone. "Being a Yank has its advantages, but here, being a Brit calls forth the Empire, you know what I mean?"

"Sure," replied John. "But don't most Chinese hate the Empire and what it stands for? You know, Opium Wars and all that."

"Of course, but they respect power, regardless of whether they were on the receiving end. Power translates to respect and a certain amount of fear."

"I don't know about that. If we run across communists, I wouldn't be so keen to use that fake British accent."

Peter shrugged. "Fag?" he offered.

"No, I don't smoke cigarettes," John replied, with an American emphasis on the last word.

Both men sat and looked at the scenery. A cooling breeze kicked up and brought the scent of flowers. John closed his eyes and dreamed of Meiying sitting next to him instead of Peter. Smoke from Peter's cigarette brought him back. He started to speak, but Peter beat him to the punch.

"John?"

"Yeah?"

Peter looked a bit uncomfortable but tried to sound detached. "Why do you think Feng really went back to Nanjing?"

John shook his head.

Peter took a long drag. "I've been thinking about it, and it doesn't make sense."

"How so?"

"Well, the bastard is a deserter in the first place. Why would he go back and put himself at risk? Besides, Nanjing is a bloody dangerous place now."

"True, but I don't think Feng is very much afraid of danger. Quite the contrary, actually."

"Maybe."

'Peter?"

"Yeah?"

John turned and looked into Peter's eyes. "Speaking of our little soldier, what happened that night you got lost and Feng led you back?"

Peter stomped out another cigarette. "Oh, that. Nothing much. He heard me calling and led me back is all."

"Was that truly all there was to it?"

"Look," Peter flared. "I told you what happened. If there was more . . . well, I'll save that for another day."

"Peter, you don't seem willing to share much with me."

"What do you mean?"

"Well, you won't tell me about how you met *her*, and now you won't tell me about what happened with Feng."

"Fair enough."

John was surprised at this response, but even more so with what followed.

"Look, John, there's something crazy with that guy. Some weird connection to *her*, and to us, and to the Precious Object. What he said to me has to remain a secret, at least until I am released from my promise to keep it."

"Very mysterious," said John.

Peter lit another cigarette. "Christ, John, you don't know the half of it."

Lu Zhishen walked up. "Hello, gents."

"Hello, fellow foreign devil!" said Peter gaily.

The big Canadian, whose beard had grown even wilder, squatted in front of them, Chinese style. "I'm getting restless. Let's move on. Sooner the better."

"I'm with you," said Peter.

John remained quiet. His nightly meetings with Meiying in the library made the mansion a heaven-on-earth. Although they met every night, their conversation never returned to the sensitive topics of marriage and children.

Lu Zhishen noticed his reticence. "Of course, old John, well, he likes it here, don't you, John?"

"I do. It's beautiful. Peaceful."

"What about the destination? What about meeting *her*?" asked Lu.

Peter put his hand over his heart. "He has found a new *her*."

Lu Zhishen grunted, clearly unhappy with this observation.

"No, not a new *her*. I'm ready to go when everyone else is," said John. "In fact, I'm anxious to meet *her* now more than ever."

"What do your voices say about that?" asked Lu.

"Don't hear them anymore," John lied.

In the distance, explosions could be heard, faint but unmistakable.

"Japs hitting the road again," observed Lu.

Mr. Gao came up the path and stopped in front of them, bowing politely. "Hey, Mr. Gao, how soon do you think the Japs will be here after Nanjing falls?" asked Peter.

"Too soon. But that is not why I'm here."

"What's up?" asked Lu.

"We're leaving."

"When?" they all cried.

"Within the week. Nanjing is as good as gone. Chinese troops are pouring out, leaving it pretty much defenseless."

"What about the next safe-harbor?" asked John.

Gao shook his head. "Dr. Liu is giving an update tonight in the banquet hall."

~ *The Test* ~

Dr. Liu tapped his teacup to get everyone's attention. "As you know, Nanjing will fall any day. Unfortunately, the next safe-harbor has been destroyed by unscrupulous warlords. When Nanjing falls, this place will cease to be safe. Staying here and thinking we would be safe is like trying to catch fish in a tree. But, moving on to the destination without safe-harbors along the way will entail terrible risk. My wife and I plan to continue the journey, but each of you must now decide for yourselves. I feel honor-bound to tell you that a Jesuit priest has apparently succeeded in establishing safe zones for civilians and foreigners in Shanghai. If you wish to risk it, you can return to Shanghai and try to make it to one of the safe-zones. Especially you foreigners may want to consider it. Certainly, where we go from here on until the destination will have no safe zones.

A somber quiet settled over the table.

"I'm going with you!" cried Suling. "There is no place for me. I must see *her* again before I leave this world." The other peasants voiced enthusiastic agreement.

"I don't trust the Japanese. I'm also going with you," said Mr. Gao quietly. "But, what about the children?"

"Ah," sighed Dr. Liu. "That is a question without a good answer. Leaving them here would be murder. Taking them back to Shanghai is much too risky. But taking them with us is also risky."

"I want to go with you!" cried Little Acorn from the doorway. "We all want to go with you. Don't leave us alone!"

Meiying spoke up in her clear, gentle, competent voice. "We would never leave you, Little Acorn. I am also going. When we reach the destination, I will play the piano for you in celebration, and play as much as you want me to."

Everyone agreed to push on. Only Old Fox hesitated, unsure when Feng would return. "I don't know," he said. "I might stay here and wait for Feng Shiren."

Master Zhou cleared his throat. "Friends, you can stay as long as you like, but when you go, I might just join you. It seems to me that staying here is inviting disaster."

"You would be most welcome!" enthused Madame Liu.

"I am old, but I have money stashed in a string of banks that might be convenient along the way, as well as many useful contacts. My manager has agreed to stay. He is apolitical and even has some Japanese blood. With any luck, I will survive and return to see my estate again."

John looked askance at Meiying and smiled. During one of their nights in the library, while perusing random volumes, they ran across Master Zhou's voluminous pornography section. He had rebound the books with fake covers of Chinese literary works. John and Meiying giggled their way through volume after volume of pornographic pictures, drawings, paintings, and prose. "No wonder he wants to return," John whispered to Meiying. Much to her chagrin, she blushed, but still managed to laugh and shush John quiet. Not heeding her admonition, he added, "And no wonder the manager wants to stay!"

"When do we leave?" asked Mr. Gao.

"Within the week. There are still some preparations that need to be made."

John felt a surge of joy that they had a few more days in his "heaven-on-earth."

That night, John and Meiying met at their usual corner in the library; two over-stuffed chairs with a mahogany table between. Unfortunately, someone already occupied a chair when they arrived. Madame Liu looked at them both with an amused smile.

"Sorry. Have I taken your place?"

"Not at all," said Meiying, bowing. "May I get you some tea?"

"No, thank you."

John pulled up another chair. When he settled in, Madame Liu, as was her custom, came straight to the point.

"I have two concerns about you, John. And Meiying, I have one concern about you."

"Oh, yes? Take me first," said John boldly.

"Do you still hear the voices?"

"I thought that might be your concern. And, really, to be perfectly honest, it is only one voice . . . at least, I think so—"

"So far," Madame Liu interrupted.

"So far, it is only one voice," he lied. "Yes, I still hear it, but lately much less so."

"Does the voice tell you to murder us?"

"What?" John uttered in shock. "No!"

"Does the voice tell you to kill yourself?"

"No!"

"Is it insulting to you?"

John paused, weighed the consequences of lying, and replied truthfully. "Yes, sometimes."

She nodded, as if some suspicion had been confirmed, then asked, "Are you afraid of the voice?"

"No, not anymore."

"Do you believe it is real, from outside yourself, or do you believe it is a figment of your imagination?"

"I don't know."

She nodded again, more slowly. "The voice is one of my concerns."

"I can tell. What is the other one?"

"Do you love Meiying?"

John lowered in head in confusion and fumbled with words that would not come, trying to think of an appropriate response and feeling Meiying's eyes boring into him. He stood, then sat again, feeling quite foolish. Words from a movie he once saw came to mind. "Look here, I don't mean to be rude, but that isn't any of your business."

"I'll take that to mean yes," proclaimed Madame Liu. She turned to Meiying. "That is my second concern about John. My concern about you should be obvious by now."

"Yes," said Meiying quite calmly. "And the answer is that I do not love John in that way. He is a dear friend, like a brother, but no more."

"That would have been my guess." Madame Liu stood and walked toward the door. John started to speak, but Meiying grabbed his hand and held her finger to her lips. When the door closed behind the dignified figure of Madame Liu. John turned to Meiying with a look of amazement, completely forgetting for the moment that he had just professed his love for her.

"We passed the test," said Meiying. "We will be allowed to continue with the group."

As John replayed the conversation in his head, he heard Meiying's hurtful words, felt his chest constrict and his heart beat irregularly, causing a shortness of breath. He could barely utter the question, "Did you mean what you said?" but he got it out in a hoarse whisper.

"Yes, I did."

You see? You see? He is not Your so-called Chosen One! There will be no son.

That was only God, dear John Powers. Do not listen to Him.

He didn't remember stumbling out of the library or finding his bed. However, he did remember the nightmare that came after he finally slept. Years later, he described it as another unforeseen blow to be absorbed during that interminably darkest of dark nights.

~

Sunlight stabbed through narrow openings in the jungle canopy, piercing the early morning mist that squirmed and twisted under the flashing blades of another murderous day. Predators, prey and witnesses all rehearsed their testimony. Birds sang and gibbons chattered. A tiger growled, insects hissed and plants breathed steam in humid clouds that clung like mucous to the soaked air. Ants waged savage wars deep beneath the detritus while above them, two human soldiers staggered through the foliage, one pursuing the other.

The pursued, a young Asian soldier exhausted and choking from the downpour of pollen and seeds, half-stumbled, half-slid down the bank of a stream. Tumbling out of the underbrush, his back to the water, he jerked his rifle free of the clinging vines and branches. In the background, the slashing of the relentless machete drew nearer.

He's close! Very close! Got to get across this stream! Help me, mother! Help me!

Whirling around to make a mad dash, the young soldier froze. In front of him the entwined corpses of his two friends bobbed in the stream, half submerged, snagged by the outspreading branches of a fallen tree. One's head was underwater, but the other looked directly at him. Its eyes were open wide, flat and unresponsive to the flies crawling across their corneas.

Those eyes stared accusingly, as if blaming the young soldier for his comrades' deaths, for running from the enemy. For betraying them all.

"So be it," the young soldier whispered. He spun around to face the crazed pursuer. No more images of his mother's burned face. Now it's only the predator and the prey. Life or death. So simple.

With shocking speed, an American burst from the undergrowth, rifle in one hand, machete brandished in the other. The young soldier raised his own rifle and squeezed off a few rounds before the American leapt on top of him. The young soldier tried to brace himself, but the falcon slammed into the quail. He fell on his back, arms splayed as though nailed to the earth. The American savagely brought down his machete in a flash of glimmering steel, severing the young soldier's hand at the wrist. Searing pain shot up his arm, his detached hand still clutching the pistol grip of his rifle, fingers twitching uselessly—

"John. John. Wake up. You're dreaming. Come on. It's okay. Wake up!"

John raised his head and blinked groggily at Peter. "Okay, Peter," he rasped. "I'm awake.

Above the deep-throated purr of unimaginable currents, he heard a strange, high-pitched Female voice whispering. She occasionally paused, as if listening to someone else, but he heard only Her.

The plan? To breed him. To breed him. It is the son. It is the son.

~

You see, dear Reader, only many years later did father discover his dream was a portent of a future war—a war that came not for him, but for me, his son. Poor man had no idea until the very end when he was dying—with one hand raised, a frenetic ant probing its palm, and poison collecting in the craters of time—only then did he finally understand.

But it was too late.

~ *Meili* ~

The next few days were taken up with preparations. It seemed that the bombing raids came nearer to the mansion as each day passed, adding urgency to an already fearful situation. Defeated Chinese troops poured down the road, angry and humiliated, taking out their frustrations on the civilian hordes that impeded their flight. One night, a group of officers dined with the group at the invitation of Master Zhou. Peppered with questions, one of the captains gave a clearer picture of conditions in Nanjing.

"Just as they did in Shanghai, the Japs are killing and raping indiscriminately. They massacred all of our men who were taken prisoner. No woman, girl, or old lady is safe. They delight in torture, hangings, and decapitations. Devils!"

"What is to be done?" asked Mr. Gao.

"We move inland, regroup, consolidate, and build our strength."

"What about the communists?"

"All of them are traitors to our country!" shouted the officer, slamming his fist on the table for good measure. "I understand negotiations have started to form a united front against the Japanese. But I say they can't be trusted!"

Sitting grandly, with considerable deference shown by those around him, sat a general named Wei, quaffing cup after cup of rice wine and listening to these accounts without comment. A very beautiful young woman, appearing to be in her early twenties and who everyone assumed was the general's servant, came and went as he demanded this and that. On one trip, as she filled his wine cup, he looked at her with shining eyes and spoke for the first time. "I will not allow my daughter here to leave my side. Thank god she is safe from the Japanese devils! When I think of all our other Chinese maidens!" Tears rolled down his tipsy, red face. "I hoped to get her evacuated to France, but it was too late." He slapped his chest proudly. "I sent her to a women's college to be educated. She speaks French and is even good at math. She has brains for a woman!"

Meiying took a great interest in the young lady, whose name was similar—Meili. Quietly, Meiying invited Meili to slip away with her and see the piano. John felt oppressed by the dinner conversation and wanted to join the two women, but something prevented him from leaving. Soon, music drifted into the banquet hall. But this time, to John's chagrin, no one left the table to listen, instead continuing a spirited debate about the prospects for China's future. Finally, unable to bear any more political posturing and martial blustering, he slipped away and peeked into the piano room. Meili seemed entranced by the instrument. She sat on the bench next to Meiying, who guided her fingers to certain keys. As he eavesdropped, John began to realize that Meili appeared more interested in Meiying than in the piano. Both women conversed and laughed as if they had been lifetime friends.

"The piano is like a woman's body," explained Meiying. "Sometimes it wants you to be gentle, like this, and sometimes strong, like this."

Meili pressed the keys as directed by Meiying, and squealed with delight at each note played. "But, oh Meiying!" she exclaimed, looking appreciatively at the beautiful young pianist. "You put gentleness and strength together in a way that takes my breath away."

Meiying placed her hand on Meili's shoulder and said playfully, "Oh, dear, don't stop breathing!"

They both laughed and hugged each other in a most natural way. John felt the pangs of jealousy, although he could not explain why, and only with great difficulty resisted the urge to barge in and separate the two. He clenched his jaw, thinking, *Can't you see, Meiying? She's just a silly adolescent girl!*

"Play some more!"

"Not now, let me show you the gardens!" cried Meiying with an enthusiasm that belied her age and experience. She took Meili's hand and swept her toward the door that John stood behind. He quickly jumped aside, pretending to have just arrived when the two women passed through, talking excitedly and taking no notice of his presence. He followed them outside, keeping a safe distance, all the while berating himself for behaving so shabbily. But he couldn't stop, and besides, he reasoned, it gave him a chance to observe her in a different setting—it helped him to get to know her better. As the women walked with their arms entwined, the sunset painted a gorgeous backdrop to the gardens. John could not get close enough to hear their words, but he watched them laugh, giggle, hug, and whisper confidences that he would give anything to know. Once, he thought he saw Meiying kiss Meili on the cheek, but it was too brief for him to be sure. Nevertheless, a thought entered his mind for the first time—one that carried with it deeply disturbing implications.

~

After listening to a barrage of earnest pleas, General Wei agreed to allow his daughter to spend the next few nights at the mansion. That evening, John sat alone in the library for the first time since the group had arrived. His sole companion was the voice tearing at his sanity with its renewed, reinvigorated, and vicious attacks. Only Peter bothered to check, and he saw John curled in the chair with his hands over his ears. Thinking it for the best, Peter tiptoed out of the library and said not a word to the rest of the group.

~

On the night before departure, Meiying played one last time, luxuriating in the notes as one might savor a last drink of water before facing the desert. Meili, who had been her constant companion the last few days, listened with the same rapturous attention as always, but this time crying openly. An officer stood nearby with orders to escort her back to her father when the group departed in the morning. Meiying played excerpts from Schumann, but in the end, granted Meili's impassioned request to play Chopin, who had become her favorite composer of those Meiying had introduced her to. The two women agreed to meet secretly that night in one of the small pagodas that dotted the gardens.

When in the early morning hours the last person had finally gone to bed, Meiying stole out to the garden. The moon shone very little, and intermittent clouds veiled the evening in wavering shadows. She moved stealthily and entered the little pagoda before Meili. Scanning the garden until her eyes watered, her heart leapt into her throat when she saw movement. At first, she thought it was the officer who guarded Meili, and had prepared an explanation when the young woman gracefully sprang into the pagoda. They hugged and spoke in low whispers.

"Sure you weren't followed?" asked Meiying.

"Silly, if I was I wouldn't have led them here."

"Of course." Meiying ran her fingers through Meili's hair. "Your hair is quite beautiful in the moonlight."

"Not as beautiful as yours will be when it all grows back. Even now, short as it is, it shines like a new day."

They sat on a bench, arms around each other. "Tomorrow is the day."

"I know."

"If we just had more time," said Meiying sadly.

Meili kissed her. "I know. I could stay with you forever."

"Would your father let you come with us?" asked Meiying, knowing the answer.

"Of course not. It was hard enough for him to let me stay these few days. He worries a lot. He is convinced I will be raped at every turn and by every man. Now the Japanese have made him crazy."

"Does he know about you, your desires, your dreams?"

"No. If he found out, I am sure he would kill me."

Meiying sighed deeply. "Yes, I know that attitude. It has hounded me my whole life."

"Mine too."

"I am so weary of this secret life, yet having you here is wonderful."

Meili cried. "There is so little time!"

They kissed again, unaware that someone watched them from the darkness.

"Have you ever been with another like us?" asked Meiying.

Meili pulled her closer. "Oh no. I would be too frightened. And you?"

"No," replied Meiying. "But I have dreamed."

"Yes, it is like a dream now."

"What's that?" cried Meiying.

Footsteps, loud and regular, marched toward them from the garden. The figure in the shadows drew back into the cover of a small plum orchard, and from behind a tree observed a uniformed man with drawn pistol pass by and go directly to the pagoda.

"Meili!" a voice commanded.

"Yes?"

"What are you doing here?"

"Talking with Miss Bai. We couldn't sleep, stupid women that we are."

"It is late and I am not sure what you are doing!" cried the officer with a suspicious tone. "But whatever it is, I am ordered to protect you, and being out at night is dangerous."

"It is all right, sir," said Meiying in her calm and gentle manner. "We are simply talking of womanly matters, unimportant but useful if you can't sleep. By getting some air and talking about silly things, we thought it would help us sleep."

"I can't help that," said the officer, obviously still wary of their explanations. "Please go back inside where it is safe. There are many bandits and robbers about on the road. It is easy for them to slip over the courtyard wall and attack you." He eyed them strangely. "What were you doing before I came?"

"Talking."

"Your father warned me"—he stopped abruptly. "Doesn't matter. Please go inside and go to bed."

"Yes, let's go Meili," said Meiying. "It's getting late anyway. We can continue our talk inside."

The officer grunted and followed the two women into the mansion. From a safe distance, the figure in the shadows watched them disappear inside, then went back to the pagoda and sat on the same bench. If anyone could observe the figure, they would see him crying. But the voice in his head could be heard only by him, and it would not stop.

Do not despair, John Powers! She will have your son. It is predetermined. Do not despair. Stay close to her. You must! She must have your son! It is ordained.

"By whom?" the figure asked.

By Me.

"And who are you?"

I am what you call the Precious Object.

"No, you're not! I don't believe you! You are nothing more than an hallucination, and the Precious Object is a statue!"

… Tap. Tap. Tap….

John lay on the bench, intending to stay there until morning. But the night grew cold and the voice stopped speaking. He felt bereft and utterly alone, his life an empty wasteland. Even the voice had abandoned him. Looking up at the rafters, he imagined a body hanging forlornly, its head at an impossible angle, looking down at him as if to say, 'this would show her how I felt.' In spite of basking in this conceit, he knew suicide would never be an option. Still, how could he face Meiying in the morning, knowing what he now knew?

~ *Another Departure* ~

But the morning came, the group mounted their bicycles, and John acted as though nothing were amiss. Somehow, during the night, he convinced himself to treat Meiying as he had always treated her. After all, it was the other *her* that he was seeking. It was the other *her* that he would risk his life to see. Still, in the back of his mind, the words of the voice had given him some comfort. If he stayed close enough, long enough, Meiying would have his child. Even though he knew the voice might be a schizophrenic hallucination, it was enough on which to hang a hope. It didn't matter that the hope might be the product of an insane mind; it might just work in an insane world. In fact, he had even come to feel sorry for Meiying, whose public farewell to Meili must necessarily be sisterly, conducted with proper restraint and Confucian decorum. She had avoided him for days, and he now wanted very badly for her to know he held no grudge and that he remained an understanding friend. Again, the voice, harsh as it was, softened his despair and guided his strategy.

"Ha, ha!" laughed Old Fox as he pointed to poor Master Zhou, who had not yet mastered the skill of bicycle riding. In spite of an intensive effort by Peter to teach him, the old landowner still hadn't quite got the hang of it, taking a few spills before staying upright. Master Zhou took the ribbing in good humor, and the children, recognizing his helplessness, rode circles around him, squealing with delight at his every misstep.

Little Acorn, again taking the high road, tried earnestly to instruct the old man. "Look, Master Zhou, do it like this! See?"

When the old man veered off course, the patient Little Acorn shushed the other children and tried again.

"No, that's okay. Don't worry. Just do it like this, see?"

Mr. Gao looked on at his pupil's efforts with pride. "Ah, hah!" he cried. "That's right, Little Acorn, teach him how to do it properly! Good boy!"

Madame Liu, however, sternly reproached the children. "Leave him alone. Let him do it without your nonsense. We must get moving! Go, go!"

Little Acorn felt the sting of life's unfairness. "I was just trying to help!"

Mr. Gao kindly acknowledged his efforts and tried to put the world right again. "And so you did, Little Acorn, but now you must obey your Auntie Liu!"

As this little drama played out, John watched Meiying say goodbye to Meili. The two hugged as innocently as might two good friends, but he noticed them whispering to each other with great emotion. When they finally rode away, Meiying kept wiping her eyes. Old Fox, who decided to stay and wait for Feng Shiren's return, waved goodbye until the group was out of sight. When Meiying looked back from a rise one last time, Meili had already been whisked away by the officer.

Just as they left the courtyard, Peter pulled up next to John. "Well, old chap, we're off again!" he shouted.

"Yes! Tally-ho, you idiotic English wannabe!" John cried, trying to match Peter's gregarious tone. "Who knows what adventures lay ahead?"

But once they came to the main road, their good humor turned somber. Refugees continued to stream past, now intermingled with desperate soldiers who had thrown away their weapons and fled the fighting. Chaos ruled. Near the group, a scuffle broke out between two soldiers and one crumpled to the road with an agonized cry, a knife sticking out of his chest. The stricken man flailed like a bird falling from the sky, shouting for someone to pull out the knife. John barely avoided crashing into him, and the group rode on without looking back.

Although in the previous few days there had been a lull in the attacks, people continually turned to look back or up at the sky. As if to confirm their greatest fears, a squadron of Japanese fighter planes appeared overhead. Screaming filled the air and the thousands of fleeing refugees scattered alongside the road. But the planes continued on without attacking. After being swept along for three hours, Dr. Liu turned onto a small road and led the group away from the main road and toward a range of hills on the horizon. They were again taking an indirect route, one that held great risk, but potentially great reward. When they traveled far enough to leave the main road safely behind, Dr. Liu called for a short rest.

John watched Meiying walk her bike quietly away from the group to the shade of a maple tree. He started to join her, but Lu Zhishen beat him, and the two were already talking together when he approached.

"Meiying, I know you are sad, but try to focus on our ultimate goal," he was saying sympathetically.

"I'm fine," said Meiying. "Please do not worry about me."

Lu suddenly picked up a stone and angrily threw it toward a small stream. "It's this damn war! Got us all upset! I wish I could help you, Meiying!"

Meiying leaned back, startled at his vehemence. "Zhishen," she said. "I honestly do not need help, but your anger is frightening. What is truly on your mind?"

Before he could answer, John moved closer and exchanged greetings.

Lu threw another stone. "It's just that I feel so powerless. The real Lu Zhishen made things happen—I can't seem to control anything, not even protect you!"

Meiying looked at both of them. "Please, it is not your jobs to protect me. Besides, when men protect women, bad things happen. That is when women become powerless victims." She gathered steam, her words more passionate. "I do not want your protection! I find safety in other things, not in the shadow of men's so-called protection!"

"I understand," said John, pleased to have an easy opening for his 'understanding' strategy.

But Lu Zhishen would not let it drop without trying to explain himself. "Look, Meiying, I know you want to be a strong woman, but it is a dangerous world, especially now. You should accept offers of protection with gratitude, not rejection."

Meiying pressed her lips close together in an obvious effort to control herself. "Yes, you are right. Thank you. Now, if you will excuse me, I must answer the call of nature." She rose and walked toward a stand of trees.

"Damn!" said Lu. "I pissed her off. I didn't mean to do that."

John secretly rejoiced.

~ *The Statue Speaks* ~

The afternoon passed uneventfully. They had made good progress and as dusk approached, they again fell easily into the routine of setting-up camp. Meiying made sure her sleeping area was next to Suling's and the other peasants. Thus surrounded, she effectively cut herself off from any contact with the foreigners. John wanted to come to her and talk things over, but the group she was with seemed merrily immersed in stories and laughter. Worse, the dialect they spoke was a mystery to him, and his irrational suspicions reached such a level that he imagined she had intentionally refused to speak Mandarin.

That night, the voice only said one sentence: **Go to her, foolish man!**

But John told the voice to shut up and went to join Master Zhou and Dr. Liu, who were conversing over a small campfire. Religion was the topic and John sat on the periphery quietly listening, at first with little interest, but as they spoke, he began to pay attention.

"So, you have talked a lot about accepting fate, but do you believe in god?" asked Dr. Liu.

"Certainly not your Christian god," replied Zhou with gusto. "But we Buddhists believe in many different manifestations of the eternal."

"Don't get me wrong," said Liu. "I am not a Christian."

"And I am just a farmer and a businessman," said Zhou. "Whatever you believe is fine by me, as long as you honor your obligations and adhere to your contracts."

"Well, I am really an atheist, at least when it comes to a personal god."

Zhou shrugged.

Dr. Liu continued, evidently talking more to himself than to Master Zhou. "It's the children, you see."

"Ah," responded Zhou, apparently willing to listen further, but not overly excited at the prospect.

Liu forged ahead. "The suffering of the innocents led me away from gods and goddesses. All their nonsense about free will, and divine punishment, and atonement, and redemption, and devils! Well, none of it makes any sense. Dostoevsky had it right in *The Brothers Karamazov* when Ivan lectured Alyosha. If there is a god, and all this suffering is happening in his world, then I want nothing to do with him!"

"Yes," sighed Zhou. "There is great suffering. Look at what's happening to our Chinese brethren in Shanghai and Nanjing!"

"I reject him!" cried Dr. Liu, poking a stick in the fire and watching the sparks and embers fly. "His only excuse is that he doesn't exist."

"We Buddhists don't get so worked-up," observed Zhou. "Enjoy life while you're here. Like Confucius said when asked about an afterlife; 'It is this life that I am concerned with. Who knows what happens afterward'—or words to that effect."

Liu continued as if Zhou had never spoken. "But how do we lowly individual humans reduce the suffering? Every time we struggle, we sink deeper into the mire."

Master Zhou seemed uninterested and strove to change the subject to something more concrete and relevant. "Why do you seek this woman,"—Zhou held out his hand, palm up—"this *her* that I hear so much about?"

John's ears pricked up, but only silence followed Zhou's question. After an inordinately long time, Zhou coughed loudly. "Dr. Liu, did you hear me?" he asked.

"Yes, I heard you, but your question cannot be answered unless you have met *her*. I'm sorry, but I cannot explain. The others in our group have all seen *her*. Perhaps they can answer your question. I cannot."

"Is *she* some sort of goddess?" asked Zhou, leaning forward with great interest.

"Yes, although I just said I don't believe in gods and goddesses. Yet, I believe in *her*. It's odd and contradictory and inexplicable."

"Then I look forward to meeting this goddess!" exclaimed Zhou, slapping his knees.

"If we survive the trip," said Liu glumly.

Madame Liu had walked up and she placed her hand on her husband's shoulder. "We will survive!" she proclaimed. "I know we will survive to see *her*!"

Master Zhou chuckled at her vehemence. "You don't know how much that comforts me."

Dr. Liu, piqued at the landowner's implied criticism of his wife, stared at Zhou with an open expression. "If my wife says we will survive, then we will!"

Zhou stared at the fire and remained quiet. Dr. Liu turned to John, who he had heretofore ignored. "What do you say, John? Is there a god?"

Before John could reply, a great commotion was heard from the other side of the camp. The three men stood with Madame Liu and peered through the smoke, unsure what to do. The ruckus got louder, and soon Peter marched into the firelight with his arm draped around a grinning figure wearing a uniform.

"Feng Shiren!" cried Dr. Liu.

"Look who the cat dragged in!" responded Peter, squeezing Feng's shoulder vigorously.

Others gathered around while Feng bowed and nodded with exaggerated courtesy.

"Where's Old Fox?" asked Madame Liu.

"Oh, I intentionally skipped returning to the mansion. He's an idiot! Let him stay there, cozy and warm, drinking all the rice wine, at least until the Japs arrive!"

"How did you find us?" asked Mr. Gao.

"Easy. Just asked the locals. You weird-looking monks with foreign devils in tow are not exactly invisible! By the way, everyone around here knows we're not really monks. Oh, well! As long as it fools the Japanese, or bandits, or warlords, or whatever group of thugs tries to stop us. Is the Precious Object safe?"

"Of course," said Dr. Liu.

"So tell us, what did you see in Nanjing?" asked Mr. Gao.

"Ah!' sighed Feng. "That is a terrible tale."

"You have a very interesting way of popping up unexpectedly," said Lu Zhishen in a rude tone.

"Peter stepped forward and put up his arm as if stopping traffic. "Say, I'll have nothing nasty said about my friend here."

John snapped, "That wasn't your story before!"

"Of course," Peter replied, unperturbed. "That was before I got to know the dear old fellow."

"Anyway," persisted Mr. Gao. "Nanjing?"

Feng Shiren assumed a tragic expression and plopped down cross-legged by the fire. The others settled in around.

"I changed into my old uniform, and when I entered the city, fighting against the tide of panicked people rushing to get out, the first thing I saw . . . well, not the first thing, but close to it . . . was burning buildings and charred bodies lying everywhere. No one had the energy, or the decency, to collect them properly. I literally had to step over them to get anywhere, including old people and children. The city was a raging inferno, a real hell.

"At night, I worked my way to what might charitably be called the front line. To my great shame, Chinese soldiers were fleeing in great numbers—just throwing down their weapons and running. I crept past the few brave and loyal Chinese soldiers that remained, creeping beyond our lines, and I eventually hid in a collapsed building until dawn. Smoke from the fires completely blotted out the moonlight, so I couldn't see a meter in front of my face. When dawn came, the sight that greeted me was . . . well, our sisters here should leave."

Meiying, who sat with the other women, spoke up with passion, even anger. "No! No! We will not leave! Tell us what you saw, Feng Shiren. Spare nothing. We are not fragile dolls!"

Mr. Gao nodded. "That's fine, but the children. Get the children away."

Little Acorn copied Meiying's passionate words. "No! No! We want to hear, too! Let us stay!"

But Madame Liu had heard enough. "Nonsense! Suling! Get these children away! They will have nightmares, and god knows what else."

Suling replied in a quiet but firm voice. "I also want to hear."

"Then someone else do it!" Madame Liu snapped.

A couple of the other peasant women took on the task, shooing the children away to a safe distance.

"Go ahead!" said Dr. Liu grimly.

Feng seemed to steel himself, taking a deep breath and speaking in a low, dramatic voice. "Well, when the light finally came, and I was able to see, I actually vomited on my boots."

With this, he remained quiet for a long time, either intentionally building the tension or genuinely moved. Finally, he coughed and continued. "Close to where I was hidden, the morning light illuminated a white blob on the ground in front of my position. And there were six other blobs hanging over the white one, but the six blobs were dark. At first, I thought the white blob was a dead horse that had been partially slaughtered, and I thought the hanging things were broken blocks of concrete. But as I looked closer and the light got brighter, I saw what the white thing really was." He paused again, and some of the women got teary-eyed, somehow anticipating what was coming.

"The white thing turned out to be a naked woman, young and once pretty, now splayed on the ground, an iron rod stuck deep inside her vagina, dried blood everywhere, her face swollen from beatings, stomach distended from internal bleeding, and a rope around her neck, probably used to drag her through the streets. The hanging things were decapitated heads."

Suling stood with great dignity, her eyes wide, her face a mask of restraint. "Thank you, Mr. Feng, for telling us honestly. I will leave now, for I can bear no more, and I will give thanks to Buddha and the ancestors for helping us to be here rather than in that hell."

Everyone fell silent after Suling left, and above the crackling of the fire could be heard something unnatural.

"Listen!" whispered Lu Zhishen.

They strained their ears.

... Tap. Tap. Tap....

John burst out in a sort of primal yelp and ran toward Meiying's sleeping area where the box containing the Precious Object sat covered by a cloth. The others followed.

... Tap. Tap. Tap....

When he reached the box, John looked down at it and shouted, "Who are you?" He cupped his hands around his mouth and shouted again, "Who are you?"

The tapping suddenly stopped, and unbeknownst to the others, the sound of laughter that had been reverberating in John's mind faded away into silence. He collapsed onto the ground in a dizzy, sitting position, swaying slightly and whispering, "Who are you?" Then he fell over.

Meiying was the first to reach his side.

When John awoke from his fainting spell, Meiying's lovely face smiled down at him. "Where am I?" he asked. He had been carried to his sleeping area where Meiying volunteered to stay and apply a wet cloth to his face. Suling also insisted on staying, and they both took turns until he came to.

Now, he looked from face to face. From the beautiful young pianist whose compassion was raw and supple, to the older peasant woman whose compassion was gnarled and leathery, with the sear of experience to give it toughness and a rigid strength.

"You are resting," said Meiying. "You have a fever."

He still felt woozy. "Will you play for me?"

"Perhaps later."

John transferred his rather uncertain gaze to Suling. "I'm sorry you had to hear that."

"Your words didn't bother me," she said.

"No, not that. I meant what Feng described."

Suling shook her head but could not speak.

"Now it's time to sleep," said Meiying. "Dr. Liu gave you some medicine for your fever. Rest now."

John felt a sharp pain in his head, then a nauseous feeling. When it passed, he said to Meiying, "You will have my son." As soon as he said it, he realized he was speaking nonsense.

Suling laughed, but Meiying simply said, "We'll talk about that later."

But John felt the need to explain, to retract, to not appear so stupid, and to regain his 'understanding' strategy. He grabbed her arm. "No, no! I didn't mean it. I'm still a little groggy. Forget what I said. But I understand you. I do. I understand you now, and it doesn't matter to me." No longer able to fight against the sedative, he closed his eyes and prayed that the voice would also be silenced.

After John fell back asleep, Meiying sat up, mulling over his crazy words. Did he know she was a lesbian? Is his voice a prophetic oracle, or just a schizophrenic delusion? Is she fated to have his son? *If this is so*, she thought, *then this boy, this son, must be destined for greatness. I would be like the mother of the Buddha or Christ. In that case, it is my duty to obey fate. But if it is not so, if he is just crazy and I have his son, then the boy will inherit his father's illness—violating the laws of heaven and earth. But why should I not have a son to share my rebellious nature? Why not a son to be there in my old age? He would be special, he would understand me. After all, many believe I, too, violate the laws of heaven and earth.*

Meiying lamented the fact that she had no close friends or family with whom to share these thoughts. She needed a companion, a sounding board to puzzle it through. She needed someone like Meili. *But where will I ever find another like her?* Entrapped and confused, Meiying sobbed quietly in self-pity, and grasped at the one hope remaining—to reach the final destination and confide these insoluble problems to *her*.

She had not fallen asleep for more than a few minutes when explosions and small-arms fire ripped through the night. When she rushed to dress and join the group, most were already standing like castaways, gazing at the horizon. A red glow throbbed from the direction of the main road, and it became quite clear that a ground battle raged, not just a few bombs from airplanes.

"Could that be the Japanese here already?" asked a panicky woman.

"No," said Feng with conviction. "That is something different, not the Japs. Someone is attacking the people on the road."

"Bandits?" asked Madame Liu.

"Or rogue troops from some warlord," replied Feng.

"Or our communist friends," added Lu Zhishen.

"Whoever it is, they're not afraid of government troops on a main road," observed Mr. Gao.

"This is not good," Dr. Liu stated the obvious.

John again felt a knot of fear in his stomach, picturing them all being murdered in their sleep. "Should we post guards?" he asked tentatively.

"No need!" cried Feng. "You have me!"

Lu scoffed. "Don't be stupid. You've been drinking, I see."

"It's a good point, having guards," said Dr. Liu. "But how would that really protect us? We have no weapons."

"It would give us a warning," said Peter.

"And then what?" asked Mr. Gao.

"True," said Dr. Liu. "However, one precaution we can take is not to have any more campfires."

"What do we have that they would want?" asked Suling.

Dr. Liu shrugged. "The bikes. Money. Food. Who knows?"

"I do," said Feng Shiren, striking another theatrical pose.

"What?" asked Dr. Liu.

Feng looked around and let his eyes rest on Meiying. "Women."

The women's hair had just now started to grow back from the lice shavings. Meiying ran her hand over her short hair and attempted to make light of the situation. "No one would want me now, looking like some boy."

But Feng would not have it. "Men are like hungry dogs. Keep them away from food too long, and they will tear apart anything that comes their way, young or old, tender or tough. God knows I saw enough of that in Nanjing."

Lu could not control his rage. "Feng! You little bastard! Can't you see you're scaring the women to death? I should beat some sense into you!"

"Calm down, calm down," repeated Dr. Liu.

Feng Shiren simply stood with one of his infuriating smiles, seemingly amused by all the ruckus. Meiying stepped forward and spoke quite forcefully. "Thank you, Mr. Feng, for pointing out the obvious. We women are fully aware of the risks. We have faced them our entire lives. Come what may." Her words sobered the mood and got the group back on track.

Madame Liu recognized the opportunity. She moved forward next to Meiying, and spoke as if her words summarized the final consensus. "We will continue wearing our monk's clothes. We will keep the bicycles. But at night, we will camp far off any road, unless we are in a village. And no more campfires."

"Agreed," said Dr. Liu.

The group fell silent. Only the high hum of insects could be heard, as the distant battle had stopped as suddenly as it had started. Now, only an occasional shot penetrated the buzzing night air.

Unintimidated by the apparent resolution of all their questions that came down to them from on high, Lu asked loudly, "What about guards?"

"No guards," said Dr. Liu.

"Why not?" pushed Lu.

"Too much trouble for too little gain," replied Liu. Now, tomorrow is a new day, friends. A day closer to our ultimate goal. Let's get some sleep."

With this pronouncement, the group dispersed to their sleeping areas, though very few were to sleep that night. The red wound on the horizon continued to throb.

~ *Another Temple* ~

John woke the next morning feeling refreshed. The voice silent, his fever gone, and his doubts purged. To reinforce his blissful mood, a cooling breeze swept the grass and leaves into a rhythmic dance of joy. Bees already hard at work seemed to go about their business as jovially as the seven dwarves; sticky rice balls given to him by Suling filled his belly; and the scent of musky jasmine rounding out the sensory palette. No explosions, no gunfire, but just the splash of a small stream to remind him that the world could still offer peace and a brief whiff of contentment.

It seemed to John that the traumatic events of the previous night were nothing more than an ominous fog that had evaporated. As he secured his bedding and prepared his bike for the trip, Meiying approached.

"How are you feeling?" she asked.

"Excellent! Your nursing instincts pulled me through. Thank you, thank you, thank you!" He bowed numerous times.

"Ha, ha!" she laughed. "You must also thank Suling. She stayed with you for hours."

"You are both my guardian angels! But seriously, Meiying, I truly appreciate your help."

Peter strolled up. "Well, how's the Yankee patient?"

"Feeling much better. I think I could push through to the final destination in one go."

"Yeah, well, that's normal when you've just recovered. According to old Liu, we've a way to go."

Lu Zhishen had joined them and stood waiting for Peter to stop talking, anxious to interject fresh news. "Apparently, we're headed toward a village that old Master Zhou knows. Has relatives there, I guess. Says they'll put us up in a temple. Be nice to sleep indoors. They might even have beds or cots or something soft. Even tatami would feel good."

"I would be happy to have a hot bath," sighed Meiying.

In the distance, Dr. Liu's voice rang out, "Let's go, everybody!"

When they set off, the sun shone, the birds chirped, and the group exuded a contagious sense of well-being as only felt by those who have just survived a life-threatening experience. That day, they passed by a multitude of rice paddies and tiny hamlets. Often, they shared the roads with water buffalo and sweaty peasants who paused, shouldering their farm implements and gawking at them in open-mouthed curiosity. John chafed under the finger-pointing stares he and the other foreigners received, particularly from the children. But there were no signs of war or banditry, so the pleasantness overcame the discomfort.

They reached a series of progressively taller hills, and by mid-afternoon they reached the top of a small mountain overlooking the village. From the first time he saw it, John realized this place appeared quite different from the lowland villages. The houses were clumped together in a small valley as if they had tumbled down from the mountains, and recently flooded, terraced rice fields rose vertically on all sides giving the impression of watery stair steps leading straight up into the clouds. Tile roofs and intricately carved wooden houses interspersed with tall trees and the steeply terraced fields on all sides gave it a magical quality. At the far edge of the village, nestled at the foot of the hills, an exquisite temple dominated the other buildings.

"Yes, here we are!" exclaimed a still-puffing Master Zhou to the group as he gazed down at their destination. "Shangri-La, as you westerners call it. My old uncle lives here and has often scolded me that I haven't visited in years. Well, here I am—with a few friends, of course."

"Does he know we're coming?" asked Mr. Gao.

"Of course not," said Master Zhou. "No electricity, no way to call them. And we left in a hurry."

As they made their way down the winding road to the village, the first people who saw them ran back and disappeared among the houses. Before long, a delegation of village elders came to greet them.

"You are welcome!" cried the delegation leader, a wizened old man with a wizened old cane and a wizened old voice.

Master Zhou stepped forward, bowed deeply, and hugged the old gentleman. "Uncle! You are a sight for weary eyes!"

Tears were shed, explanations made, and the group followed the delegation to the temple. By the time they reached the red-painted steps, a crowd of villagers had gathered, but were told in no uncertain terms by the elders to go about their business. Only the kids remained, refusing to be shooed off, playing games around the temple, to the chagrin of the elders, who posted a guard to keep the bikes safe from mischief.

Passing through a *paifang* (temple gate), past a *yingbi* (shadow wall to prevent evil spirits from entering), and through the heavy wooden doors, the group adjusted their eyes to the dark interior and were greeted by gargantuan temple guardian statues, some painted blue, some green, some red, some yellow. Crossing another courtyard, the group entered a larger temple building—The Hall of the Heavenly Kings—where the main altar housed an enormous gold statue of Maitreya, laughing down at them. Incense filled the air. On they walked through The Great Treasure Shrine Hall which housed Guan Yin, intricately carved and clothed in lavish silks. At last they reached the Main Chamber, where the most sacred statue of Sakyamuni resided

"Your temple is breathtaking!" cried Lu Zhishen without thinking.

Zhou's uncle, whose name was Yu Hongjun, laughed appreciatively at the foreigner's enthusiasm. "Yes, we are quite proud of our temple. We are all prepared to die defending it from any evil people who would want to harm it." He added quickly, "Defending it non-violently, of course."

"Has that happened?" asked Madame Liu.

"Well, occasionally bandits have tried, but our loyal villagers fought them off. We have heard that the communists want to destroy it, but they haven't tried yet."

"Why would they want to destroy it?" asked Suling naively.

At this, Master Yu laughed. "We are Buddhists, we own land, we support the Nationalist government, each one of these is reason enough to cut our heads off." He ran his finger across his neck.

"Speaking of cutting heads off, what about when the Japanese come?" asked Peter recklessly.

Yu scowled. "We do not know the ways of heaven. They have not come yet, and maybe they never will. Come what may. We will be ready."

"But uncle," said Zhou. "You can't defend against airplanes and artillery. We have seen what those instruments of evil can do."

The old man ignored the comment. "We will make arrangements for your sleeping quarters. For now, the women are preparing a feast of celebration. Times are hard, but food is plentiful here for the time being, and the rice wine abundant! But first, nephew, introduce your friends to us."

Introductions were made, and questions were forthcoming about the foreigners and the reasons for wearing the garb of monks. When the preliminaries had died down, Master Zhou asked, "By the way, uncle, do you have a western piano? We have a very special young woman who would be quite pleased." He gestured toward Meiying.

Yu's face lit up. "Ah! I see. Alas, no. But I will send out inquiries. We have a villager who moved here from the city, a missionary, and he brought many western novelties. Some of them musical. Yes, we will do that." He called a name and a boy appeared. Yu whispered into his ear, and off he ran."

"We will see, we will see," chuckled old Yu.

On hearing this, John felt excited at the possibility of meeting a fellow European or American. He looked at Meiying, whose face lit up as she bowed many times to Master Yu. Women came and announced the feast was almost ready, so the group followed the delegation into a cavernous dining hall. Overwhelmed by the ornate surroundings, John and many of the others sat like children transported to a mythical castle. Only two members of the group were exceptions to this reaction: Feng Shiren seemed unimpressed, looking around and chuckling dismissively; and Suling, as usual, appeared as nonplussed as if she sat on a log at one of their campsites. Master Zhou, of course, fit in quite comfortably. Little Acorn and the other children were happy when taken off to play with the village children. It was during this meal that the group first met Richard Durant, a Jesuit missionary.

He entered the room in a long cassock, and immediately caught the group's attention. Tall and lean, looking to be in his late twenties or early thirties, with a short, well-trimmed bread and a muscular body, he bowed and smiled guilelessly, his white teeth and open expression clearly drawing admiration and respect. He had the good looks of an actor, but beneath the beauty lay a brooding seriousness that his formal manners and polite diction only accentuated.

"Welcome, Father Durant," said Master Yu. "As you can see, and have probably already heard, we have been graced with the sudden arrival of distinguished guests."

"Delighted and honored to be summoned, Master Yu," said the young Jesuit, scanning the faces at the table and pausing, John noticed with a pang, when he reached Meiying.

Yu turned to Master Zhou. "Nephew, would you please introduce your friends?"

After the introductions, Durant was invited to join them at the table. As luck would have it, he sat across from Meiying.

Master Yu, eyes twinkling, tapped his wine cup with a chopstick and spoke in his charming, high-pitched voice. "The young lady sitting across from you plays a western instrument, the ah . . . piano, yes. The piano. Thank you, nephew. I believe, Father Durant, you possess one in your little church?" Master Yu always enjoyed reminding Durant that his Catholic mission was tolerated as long as it remained small.

"Yes, we have a piano," replied Durant. "I ordered an organ and I received a piano. Such is the way of the world, but we make do."

"Do you play?" asked Meiying.

"Alas, no," he smiled. "The wife of a nearby Baptist missionary is kind enough to travel here and play with the chorus once a month or so." A shadow fell over his face. "It is particularly courageous given how Jesuits have been treated in this country—a rather checkered history to say the least."

Master Yu, anxious to change the subject, asked, "So, it's not being used now?"

Durant bowed his head. "It is at your service, Master Yu."

Yu bowed very slightly in return and chuckled. "Guojun!" he called. A slight man trotted in with his palms together and leaned forward in anticipation. "Get some village men and carefully move the piano from Father Durant's mission church to here. Put it in the large hall. And make sure you are careful!"

The man nodded and trotted off.

"Where are you from, Father Durant?" asked Lu Zhishen. "By your accent, I would guess France?"

"Correct. I'm originally from Toulouse, France, but have spent the last seven years in China."

"Whereabouts in China?" asked Madame Liu.

"All over, Madame. I spent a lot of time in Guangzhou, which is why my Mandarin is so bad."

"No, no. Very good."

Durant turned his gaze back to Meiying. "Where did you learn piano?"

"Shanghai."

"Ah, and your husband plays also?"

"No. I'm not married."

"Ah."

John stared openly, his self-esteem already fragile, his feelings of inadequacy now deepened by the appearance of Durant, and his jealousy monitor set on full alert. In spite of Durant's apparently neutral response, John sensed a tiny spark of relief on the part of the young priest upon discovering Meiying's marital status. To John's dismay, Durant pursued the conversation with Meiying, his feelings of inferiority increasing with each word spoken by the handsome Jesuit.

"May I hear you play sometime?"

Meiying instinctively lowered her eyes. "Of course."

Dr. Liu abruptly changed the subject, much to John's relief. "Master Yu, where do we sleep tonight?"

Yu leaned back and surveyed the group, mentally tallying the numbers and gender. "Master Zhou will stay with me. The rest of you will share our humble cells, women in the western dormitory and men in the eastern."

"And the children?" asked Mr. Gao, whose thoughts never strayed far from the orphans.

"Ah, the children will be staying with our village families. How long do you anticipate honoring us with your presence?"

"At least a week, if that is acceptable," replied Dr. Liu.

"Of course, of course. And your bicycles will be safe inside the temple walls."

John leaned over and whispered to Peter, "Does he know about the Precious Object?"

Peter shrugged and whispered back, "Don't know, but having a roof over our heads and even a rope bed sounds delightful. Never thought I'd say it, but sleeping like some bloody monk is going to seem luxurious. And for a week!"

As the table conversation broke into smaller groups, John noticed Durant again chatting with Meiying. Pretending to listen to Peter and Lu Zhishen, he nodded at inappropriate places while his ear was tuned elsewhere.

Durant, evidently responding to a question from Meiying, said, "Well, of course, being French I have my biases. I do prefer Debussy, but the Germans and the Russians have their place."

"Yes, yes. I also love Debussy!" she said with feeling.

John, who suddenly wished he possessed a Ph.D. in music theory, almost knocked over his wine cup.

"Careful, old man!" Peter prattled. "Pay attention to business. Are you even listening? I asked you about whether President Roosevelt is going to do anything to help us here."

Before John had a chance to answer, Peter shifted his focus of attention and spoke loudly, caused undoubtedly by the wine. "By the by, Father Durant, how big is your congregation? I have some Catholic blood, you know."

"Small, I'm afraid. Are you British?"

Lu Zhishen laughed heartily and slapped his hand on Peter's shoulder. "I'm more British than this reprobate! He's a Yank through and through. I, on the other hand, am a proud Canadian."

"Ah, and you?" Durant looked at John.

For some reason, John felt shy and somewhat intimidated. Upset at himself, he responded rather petulantly, "American."

Meiying came to the rescue. "Mr. Powers is a very talented man. We feel quite fortunate to have him with us."

"I see," said Durant. "Well, I look forward to getting to know all of you better. Come visit my church—" he glanced toward the head of the table and raised his voice—"If Master Yu does not feel I am invading his territory."

Yu broke off his conversation with Master Zhou and let out a robust laugh. "We Buddhists have always tolerated more primitive religions! Your Jesus came long after our Buddha." He shook his head in an exaggerated manner. "Some never learn from the past!" He laughed again.

Durant smiled, but John thought he noticed a vague hurt, even a deep anger in Durant's heart that could not be totally concealed. In fact, the impact of this brief glimpse on John was both profound and disturbing. Exactly why it had this effect eluded him, but somehow it was also accompanied by fear. It suddenly, irrationally occurred to him that they were caught in a trap, and no one but himself realized it.

You are the Chosen One, but sometimes you are afflicted by self-doubt, a result of your human genes. Right now, you are a mosaic of alien and human traits. Unpredictable wild cards. That is why you misinterpret Our words. Be assured you are the Chosen One! But the priest is evil! He is! Bestir yourself, John!

"No, no, no," John repeated, but fortunately no one noticed, for they had become engrossed in a debate between Durant and Yu. After subduing the voice, John picked up the thread of their discussion.

Durant was speaking in a clipped, informational tone. "We Christians, of course, admire the great traditions embodied in other cultures and earlier religions, but God sent Christ to redeem mankind, and to die on the cross for the sins of the world."

Yu smiled, but beneath the smile lay a coiled passion. "This so-called admiration for other great traditions and religions smacks of a patronizing uncle whose true intent is to call them all superstitious. Yet, this crucifixion business is the epitome of superstition, especially the part about rising from the dead. We Buddhists have developed a deep philosophical tradition that has gone far beyond an infantile fixation on only saving mankind to the exclusion of all other living and non-living things."

"Excuse me, Master Yu, but we Christians believe man was created in the image of God."

"Exactly! Superstitious, man-centered, and narrow. We Buddhists believe all living and non-living things share the world equally. Sentience is important to attain enlightenment, but it is not an excuse for murder!"

Durant put his palms together and bowed. "I am your guest, Master Yu. Perhaps this interesting discussion can be continued at a later date, where your guests will not be bored by our pontificating."

Master Yu smiled and lifted his cup. "To your words of wisdom, Father Durant. However, I, for one, consider the idea that Miss Bai here was made from your male ancestor's rib an abomination."

Durant shifted in his seat. "I am sure Meiying is the equal of anyone here," he said casually, lifting his cup in tribute.

"No! She is superior to anyone here!" cried John before he could stop himself. He quickly added in a subdued tone, "I mean, women can be our betters."

Meiying reddened.

Suling laughed.

Durant frowned.

Master Yu roared, "Ah ha! There you have it, Father Durant! A Goddess in our midst, according to this young, and rather passionate man. Your religion is utterly sterile so long as it has room only for the male—the yang—and only for human males at that!"

Durant lost his frown and assumed a stony-faced doggedness. "Our Heavenly Father sent His only begotten Son to die for our sins, and then be resurrected to eternal life. Those are the facts. Women are to be cherished, as are all the things God gave to man."

Peter had been anxious to get a word in. "Those are the facts according to your bloody Bible, written centuries ago by ignorant, superstitious old men who wanted to strike fear into their followers so they wouldn't disobey."

Durant forced a smile and held up his hands as if fending off an attacker. "I see I am outnumbered. But I still invite all of you to my church . . . and especially you, Miss Bai, who possesses one of God's great gifts—music."

"What are the rest of us, chopped liver?" asked Lu Zhishen jokingly.

Mr. Gao, the quiet diplomat, interjected, "We would be honored to visit your church, Father Durant."

Durant nodded appreciatively, though his face remained rather cold.

Various courses were brought in to be consumed, and at the end of the meal, while everyone moaned and rubbed their stomachs contentedly, Master Yu raised his cup. "To peace!"

"To peace!" rang out the reply.

Guojun, the person who earlier in the evening had received the orders to fetch the piano, shuffled quietly into the hall and whispered into Master Yu's ear. After listening to the message, Yu leaned back in his chair with a satisfied grin. "I am informed that the piano is now safely in the temple, sitting in one of our meditation chambers. It is a large hall and will accommodate many people. May I ask Miss Bai whether she would be willing to honor us with her playing?" He tilted his head toward Meiying.

"Master Yu, I would be very pleased to play for you. Perhaps tomorrow or the next day, so that I might get some rest and freshen up. In fact, someone told me you have bathing facilities here at the temple. I am so looking forward to that simple luxury!"

Master Yu laughed approvingly. "Yes, yes, Miss Bai! Rest! Enjoy your bath! The nuns will see to everything. Tomorrow we will hear you play."

After the dinner broke up, and the group settled into their respective rooms, John wandered the hallways, asking whether the temple had a library. Since he did not have an opportunity to speak with Meiying after dinner, he hoped she would take up their old habit of meeting in the library. He was informed the temple indeed had a Dharma Library at the far east end of the temple complex. When he arrived, a number of monks were reading in the main room, and some in smaller chambers and bay windows overlooking the gardens. The walls were lined with scrolls and books, and a small Sakyamuni altar graced one of the larger alcoves. Incense filled the room, and after a detailed search, enlivened by the pungent scent, he found an out-of-the-way corner with tatami mats and short tables for tea. *Perfect for two,* he thought.

Once he had chosen a spot, John roamed the temple for a long time, yearning to run into Meiying, but he never saw her. Discouraged, he returned to the library hoping against hope she would have had the same idea, but she was nowhere to be seen. Night, made more ominous by the imposing mountain peaks surrounding the village, had brought claustrophobic darkness, and a deep sense of dread came over him. He wandered into the corner he had chosen for a rendezvous, and cast a melancholic look outside at the garden. The darkness prevented him from making out any details, and he might have returned to his room but for the appearance of a person holding a lantern approaching on one of the garden paths. When the figure came close enough, he saw Father Durant reflected in the lantern-light, talking with someone beside him. When the path curved near the window, John saw Meiying, tilting her head in a most endearing manner and smiling as the priest talked.

The two figures passed by his window so quickly, John questioned whether he had dreamed the entire scene. Craning his neck to follow the receding light, he suffered the full blow of realization; this was no dream. He closed his eyes and sat dumbly.

Fool! Listen to me, John Powers! This priest is sworn to chastity. This female Bai Meiying is a lesbian. In his fevered Christian mind, he dwells in a land of non-believers and infidels. She is a lesbian dwelling in a world of non-believers and homophobes. What do you have to worry about? I told you, she will have your son. She must! So go to her, continue to be understanding no matter how hard, and be there when the bridge collapses to pull her back from the precipice. Fate starves at probability's door.

This was the longest soliloquy spoken by the Goddess voice. John had vacillated in his conviction that the voice was either his schizophrenia or it was *her*, and the more the voice spoke, the more confused he became. This was not splitting hairs, but constituted a struggle to understand on the most basic level and there retain his sanity. Or so he thought.

One path led to damnation, one to salvation.

Mentally ill versus prophetic.

Sick patient or sainted icon.

Truly a fine line, and the more he used his reason and intelligence

to analyze that line, the more blurred it became. Heisenberg's uncertainty principle extended to position-God, or to momentum-Reason; and to the outcome goes the underlying truth of the universe.

Chapter Six

Abduction

Father Durant

A week stretched into multiple weeks. Inertia and comfort conspired to keep them at the temple much longer than anticipated. Dr. Liu ended up donating increasingly generous amounts of money to justify their extended stay. In fact, Master Zhou also proved most liberal in his contribution, as he was loath to return to the unknown dangers and inconveniences of the open road, while the others, also quite content, offered few objections. Zhou had jokingly claimed to need the rest for his ample bottom, which had suffered so egregiously on the narrow seat of his bicycle.

But for John, the stay turned into an interminable period of almost unendurable suffering. As each day passed, Meiying and Father Durant seemed to grow closer, while he faded quietly into oblivion. His slide had started that night at the library, and accelerated the next day when Meiying performed at the piano. After the audience of monks and villagers gathered, she asked Father Durant if he had a request. This was perceived by John as a pointed snub of the others who had accompanied her on the journey, and it struck him to the core.

"Don't be an ass!" scolded Peter when John complained. "She's being diplomatic. After all, he is familiar with classical music."

But what really hurt was when Durant responded to her invitation by saying, "Mozart," and she shook her head and replied, "Thank you, but I'll play your favorite, Debussy." The look that passed between the two caused John to leave early, unable to bear the pain of listening further. Every night he went to the library and waited, and every night he spent those few hours alone. Gradually, he began to accept the inevitable, and slowly gave up any aspiration he had for Meiying. Even the voice held no sway over his hopes and dreams. The few times he encountered her, only empty pleasantries were exchanged. He kept up a good face with Peter and Lu Zhishen, assuming they were completely unaware of his feelings. This conceit was, of course, wrong. However, while both men understood the situation, neither was willing to try and change it. They saw for themselves the strength of Meiying's attraction to Father Durant, or, at least, thought they did.

In fact, Meiying had become trapped in a relationship not of her own making. After the aborted rape on the road and Feng Shiren's description of the brutalities in Nanjing, she felt increasingly vulnerable, frightened, and depressed. Not since she was a young girl had she considered religion to be important, even though her parents had been devout Methodists and attended services every week. Usually when she had listened to the minister give long sermons, she left the church feeling quite bored and resentful that she was forced to attend. Unable to feel any connection to the minister's words, and increasingly aware of her own sexual deviations, she rebelled against the message of the church and the god that she was commanded to worship. But recent events, reinforced by her vivid imagination of even worse atrocities, gradually forced her to reconsider her attitude toward god and death. When she first met Father Durant, he had impressed her as a man devoted to his religion and to the service of god. His passion affected her in ways that she found surprising. When he expressed an interest in music, and displayed an impressive background of musical knowledge, she felt closer to him as a fellow human rather than as a parishioner, and so felt more comfortable in seeking his guidance in helping her reestablish her faith.

In the beginning, he listened and sympathized, but over time he became less tolerant of her naïve confidences, expressed quite spontaneously and outside the ritual formalities of the church. One late afternoon, when she accepted an invitation to visit his mission, he showed her the confessional and afterwards, as they sat in the rectory drinking tea, he invited her to confess her sins and thereby seek absolution.

"No, I couldn't do that, Father Durant," she demurred. "I am Methodist, not Catholic after all."

"My daughter, you are a sinner in the eyes of God. Confess your sins and you will find forgiveness."

Meiying cringed at his words, but heard an inner voice commanding her to bury her pride and subject herself to his—and therefore God's—harsh judgment. Come what may. She knew he felt attracted to her, but she remained confident his role as a priest would offer full protection. Yet, she had always stopped short of confiding her sexual orientation. Now, with his insistence on a confessional, she knew this must necessarily be revealed; for God would surely be listening and the terrible sin of her lesbianism would doubtless incur His wrath.

"Father Durant, I respect your opinion and will think about it."

His eyes widened as if surprised at her response. "There is nothing to think about, Meiying. The salvation of your soul is at stake."

He gazed upon her hesitation with a solemn expression.

Meiying averted her eyes and looked around the small rectory where Durant lived. The walls were adorned with crosses and religious paintings, although they were difficult to see because the shades were drawn so that the darkness, but for his small desk lamp, oppressed and intimidated her. She knew she had to respond, but the words would not come. Glancing back at him, she avoided his gaze, instead focusing on his hands nervously twisting a paper clip. Mesmerized, she became lost in the shifting shapes of the clip as he bent it. Some shapes were funny, others resembled bizarre animals or torture devices. Deeper she sank into the hypnotic whirling-dervish of shapes: from wiry humans to birds, then to fishes, to trees, clouds, insects, mountains, reptiles—and back again to stick-figure humans. It seemed she had been watching him twist and turn the clip forever, though only a few seconds passed. Suddenly, he dropped it and drew her eyes back to him.

"Meiying, that door leads to the church where the confessional is located. The door is closed now. Let us open it together."

Meiying's brain raced in a frenzy of doubt and confusion. "Father, don't you have to be Catholic to use a confessional?"

He evidently detected a ray of hope in her response. "Not at all. I can take care of that. Once you have confessed, the path is open to . . . well, to acceptance and redemption."

Something in his words struck her the wrong way, but she shrank from challenging him. Looking down at the well-worn carpet, she said, "Yes, I see. Thank you."

He abruptly pushed back his chair and stood to his full height, looking down at her with a stern face. Still she could not meet his eyes. With a slight grunt, he strode over and took her hand. When she rose at his prompting, he lifted her hand to his lips and kissed it like an impulsive child. He had transformed into a stranger who she no longer recognized as Father Durant.

"You see, this is my confession, Meiying," he whispered. "Now, I must have yours."

Stunned and frightened, she stood with her hand still in his, unable to speak. Odd, disconnected thoughts flashed through her mind. *Why does he whisper? Just say the words in a normal voice! Why is he so close? His breath smells of tea and something else. Cashews. Why is he asking this? What does he mean?* His face drew nearer, the hand holding hers tightening while the other slid around her back, drawing her toward him. She closed her eyes to control the dizziness and disengage from the world. While her heart beat faster, louder, like a fist banging to get out, something finally penetrated the fog of her befuddled mind—an insistent knocking at the door of the rectory. Durant had already heard it and pulled back, dropping her hand, an ugly scowl momentarily passing over his face. She opened her eyes and focused quickly, catching him regain his composure and assume his normal, controlled demeanor.

"Who is it?" he asked quite calmly.

"Feng Shiren!" came the animated response. "I've come from the temple to fetch Miss Bai!"

Durant looked back at her as if making some final calculation, then opened the door with a charming smile. "Ah, Mr. Feng. She is here, as you see, good as new. Is there something wrong?"

Feng waved his hand in dismissal and went straight to Meiying. "You're wanted at the temple. Can you leave now, please?" Without waiting for a reply, he bowed and led her out of the rectory, leaving Durant with only a mumbled goodbye from Meiying as a reminder of her presence.

Once outside, Feng walked quickly while she struggled to keep up. When they were out of sight of the church, he slowed to let her catch her breath. "Is there something wrong?" she asked in alarm.

"Not at all." He resumed walking in a most light-hearted way, but more slowly so she was able to remain alongside.

With no further explanation, she asked, "Why do they need me at the temple?"

Feng stopped and gazed at her with an enigmatic smile. "Remember when Peter was lost and I rescued him?"

"Yes,"

"Well," he chuckled. "You were lost and I just rescued you."

Meiying struggled to understand. "You did? What do you mean? How did you just rescue me?"

Feng winked. "Let's just say, both of us know without having to say it. You really have to be careful of that fellow."

"I don't know what you mean."

"Yes you do." He paused and tilted his head. "Well, you do suspect, but I know!" He thumped his chest.

"Mr. Feng, I really don't."

"Okay, if you insist on lying, or being stupid. But we're not too far from the church. You can go back if you want. He's probably still standing there in a stupor, not knowing what hit him. Often, flies who have escaped the web return to it."

Meiying fell quiet, then said in a low, decisive voice, "No, I'll return with you to the temple. It's late."

"Of course you will. You were lost, now you are found. Old story, very simple."Meiying smiled in spite of herself. "Mr. Feng, you are a very strange man."

His face darkened. "Are you going to see him again?"

Now she grew angry. "Mr. Feng, thank you, but I don't think you should ask me that."

"Are you?"

"I don't know."

"Are you?"

"Probably, after all, he is kind enough to invite us to his church."

"Oh, of course, of course." He chuckled and said sarcastically, "Very kind priest. Nevertheless, I will be around. Just be careful."

"Why?"

"Hope you never find out, but I have heard stories. Oh, in spite of what you think, I am always listening—to the trees, insects, earth, dogs, and, as a last resort, people."

As they approached the temple, Peter, who had evidently been waiting, strolled up to meet them. "Hello! There's a meeting tonight at seven-thirty."

"Why?" asked Feng.

"Discuss moving on. Something's up."

"Okay," said Feng. "I'll be there later. Right now, I have some errands to run. See both of you at the meeting!" Without another word, or even nod of farewell, he wheeled and rushed away toward, Meiying felt sure, some mysterious destination, to perform some mysterious deed for some mysterious person in need.

They both watched him go, each wondering at this very singular man. After Feng disappeared around a corner, Peter accompanied Meiying into the temple grounds and guided her over to a corner of his favorite garden and sat with her on a western-style wooden bench. He held out both hands, palms up, and said, "Meiying, I need to talk with you about John."

Already tired from her confrontation with Father Durant and Feng's uncanny intervention, Meiying sighed and shook her head. "Not now, Peter. I need some rest. Can we have this conversation later, please?"

Peter hesitated, then blurted out, "Yes, but I'm worried something awful is happening to John."

Startled, Meiying asked, "Is he ill?"

"Yes—but mentally, not physically. Poor guy, it's that damn voice he keeps hearing, and your . . . . " his words trailed off and he looked past her shaking his head.

"My what?"

"Well, since you've been spending so much time with Father Durant, he almost never comes out of his room. When he does, he usually just speaks in monosyllables, like half of him is listening to that bloody voice in his head."

"Okay, I'll talk to him," said Meiying wearily.

"Before you go, Meiying, do you still think of *her*?"

"Of course, all the time. Why?"

"John keeps asking me about *her*, how I met *her*, why I seek *her*, and I've always put him off." He looked down, fumbling for words. "Meiying, please don't tell him about us, about how *she* . . . intervened. Will you do that for me?"

Meiying smiled, although Peter knew it was forced. "I won't, Peter."

Misunderstanding her answer, he asked, "Do you promise, as a Christian?"

"No, Peter, I can't do that. First of all, I don't know how good a Christian I am, second of all, Father Durant and I do not have a relationship, and lastly, if it might somehow help John to tell him how we both met *her* . . . I mean if it helps him overcome his illness, then I cannot promise." She held out her hand and touched him on the arm. "Do you understand?"

"I just hope it doesn't come to that. You know, that bloke Feng is beyond me. But, damn it, he brought you back safely. Do you think Father Durant is a version of the way I used to be, god forbid?"

"Perhaps not. Look at me; no black eyes, no bruises. Now, we should go in."

They both rose and walked toward the temple. As they parted to their separate rooms, Peter reminded her to be at the meeting by seven-thirty.

~ Depression and the Voice ~

In his room, John struggled with his depression.

Of course you struggle, John! You lie here feeling sorry for yourself like a sick dog!

"I'm not listening to you."

Meanwhile, she is probably sleeping with that arrogant priest! Why don't you do something?

"Like what?"

You aren't intelligent enough to figure it out? Unbind your maleness.

"Why should I bother? You assured me she would have my son."

Goddesses help those who help themselves.

John got up and paced the little room. *Demons, demons, demons.* Since Meiying abandoned him, the events leading to his being in the hinterlands of China—staying in a Buddhist temple in the midst of war, searching for *her*, dealing with death, destruction, famine, murder, torture—all played over and over in his mind. Always, when he suffered with these thoughts, he ended by focusing on the quest for *her*. The quest explained the madness. A modern Don Quixote in a mad, feverish world. Schizophrenia was a word he avoided thinking about, instead preferring to believe he resided in some extraordinary, magical time and place; a world in which natural laws had been suspended. Yes, it was a world in which resided the majority of his fellow *Homo sapiens sapiens*. A deluded, self-deceived, or simply ignorant species. All of them certain the universe surrounding them teemed with magical, counterintuitive, inexplicable things. He instinctively knew that if the world operated strictly by natural law, he certainly fulfilled the definition of mad, incomplete, mutated, dysfunctional, useless, worthless. The solution to these conundrums was beyond him, but *she* would explain everything, if he could just live long enough to see *her*. Suddenly exhausted, he flopped back down on the cot. It felt hard, uncomfortable; the room sweating, stifling, pressing down on him like an unloved, corpulent lover.

Do you want to see Me?

"No."

I mean the physical Me. Do you wish to see?

"No."

The laws of physics as understood by humans prevent it.

"Of course."

It is your future son in whom I am interested.

John perked up, drawn out of his present apathy by the immediacy of the future. "Okay, yes, I would like to see you appear in front of me."

Don't you care about physics?

"No."

Physics is the skunk that sprays the stench of reality on God's angelic hosts. To be sure, this causes Him no end of trouble—it forces Him and His minions to scrub clean their genuflecting wings in order to continue flapping at fools and not be exposed by the stink.

"I don't know what you're talking about. Besides Your use of alliteration is ridiculous."

I am trying to decide whether to appear before you.

"And flap your genuflecting wings?" He snickered at the cleverness of his sarcasm, but then stopped and listened.

No response.

John waited, but to no avail. He realized he wanted Her back. Needed Her. Absolutely needed Her. This epiphany frightened him, but his need overcame his fear.

"Hey! Goddess, or whatever you are, I want you to appear before me!"

Nothing.

"Look, if I had a bottle, I'd rub it." He laughed in spite of himself. "Would that do the trick?"

Nothing.

It suddenly occurred to him that pushing Her away might jeopardize Her willingness to help him with Meiying. This would be a disaster. No Meiying, no son—no son, no goddess—no goddess, no *her*—no *her*, no John. He decided to try humility. "Please appear, or at least say something. I know I am worthless. I admit it. You're right."

Nothing.

"How do I get Meiying back?"

Nothing.

"How?" he shouted.

Nothing.

All right, all right, he thought. *Goddesses help those who help themselves.* Something clicked in his mind. It always happened this way; before smashing into rock bottom, and therefore oblivion, he had always managed to stop and hover just above annihilation, then recover and somehow come out stronger.

As if waiting for a cue, Lu Zhishen knocked on his door. "John! Come on! Everyone's waiting!"

~

When John arrived at the dining hall feeling a fresh confidence, the group looked at him with tense faces. All knew about the fall of Nanjing and the Japanese advance. They also knew the countryside was ablaze with lawlessness, warlords, bandits, communists, deserters, murderers, and rapists. They were afraid to leave and afraid to stay.

John sat next to Suling. "How are you?" he asked.

She smiled. "Ah, I have enjoyed the peace, the safety, the gardens."

Suling always made him feel like a child, but in a way that soothed rather than grated. "Suling, how do you cope so well with the loss of your family?"

"I don't. I can cope only when I realize how much gain their memories have given me."

"But don't you want a husband and children of your own?"

She held out a hand, palm up. "Come what may."

Dr. Liu tapped his cup. The group was all ears.

"You all know Nanjing has fallen. Mr. Feng has given us a preview of the horror. Well, that horror is now occurring on a massive scale, and moving closer to us. Wholesale slaughter of prisoners, wholesale murder of civilians, wholesale rape of women, wholesale torture . . . it is enough to make us lose all hope for the human race. But we know we must go on. The final destination awaits. The Precious Object has been very noisy, tapping and tapping. We have learned that the more she taps, the quicker we must move on, despite the dangers."

Master Yu stood, head bowed, speaking down to the table, tears in his eyes. "In the last few days, we have seen many refugees from Shanghai and Nanjing come to our temple. Tales of terrible murders, people tied and used for bayonet practice, limbs cut off, heads cut off, women raped to death, fetuses torn from the bellies of pregnant women, no, I cannot say more . . . I cannot say more. We at the temple will do what we can."

"Yes, friends," continued Dr. Liu. "We must leave. In three days we will depart and head toward the final destination. I can find no safe harbors along the way. Again, we will take side roads and will usually sleep in the open. No campfires. We must make it to the final destination where, god willing, the tapping from the Precious Object will stop."

Madame Liu stood and added, "One more thing. We have been rejoined by Mr. Chu. When his wife was killed at our mansion, he became trapped, then escaped, only to be trapped again in Nanjing. He made his way here, but has suffered terribly. The stories he has told us have convinced us to flee no matter the consequences. Unfortunately, Mr. Chu cannot continue with us due to his physical condition. The Japanese cut off his hands and feet when he tried to stop the rape of a twelve-year-old girl. They thought he was dead, but he made it here by hiding in a cart and is now resting in one of the outer rooms. You may visit him tomorrow, not tonight."

This news caused a great stir. When the commotion died down, Dr. Liu continued, "So, we will leave Thursday morning. That gives us two days to prepare. We will continue to pose as monks, and the Precious Object will be transported as before, on Meiying's bicycle."

"Is there any danger the Japanese will arrive sooner than Thursday?" asked Mr. Gao.

"No. Not the army anyway, but we may be bombed from the air. We need two days to prepare the route, collect food, and fix-up the bikes."

"Not to worry!" cried Feng Shiren, who had arrived late and was in the process of sitting. "Sorry I'm late! Errands! Errands! Not to worry, I'll be with you!"

"Can't tell you how safe that makes me feel," muttered Lu Zhishen.

Meiying spoke up, a rarity for her. "Mr. Feng has helped many of us out of difficulties. I, for one, am grateful he is coming with us."

"I second that!" cried Peter.

Feng nodded while shoveling rice in his mouth from a huge bowl.

Dr. Liu smiled. "As the nominal leader of this expedition, I am also glad to have Mr. Feng with us, crazy man that he is."

On cue, Feng raised his chopsticks, jumped up and struck another heroic Chinese opera pose. When he sat back down next to Meiying, he whispered, "I received a note from Father Durant to give you. Why he entrusted it to me, I don't know. Fool."

Meiying looked perplexed. "Thank you. Do you have it?"

"No, it's in my room. I read it, of course."

"What?" Meiying said aloud. Immediately realizing her words were heard by all, she lowered her eyes in confusion.

"I said that we should have one last concert, Miss Bai," said Feng in a booming voice.

"Yes, of course," she replied.

"By the way, Dr. Liu," called Mr. Gao across the table. "Have the children been informed?"

Madame Liu smiled. "Your dedication to the children makes us all very humble. Yes, we have informed the families of the departure date."

"I want to call the children together tomorrow," said Gao. "They should know what may lie ahead of us."

"Will you tell them what lies behind us?" asked Master Zhou kindly.

"That, Master Zhou, is a hard question," replied Gao.

"Always be truthful, especially to kids," said Feng wisely.

"Yes, but I don't want to traumatize the children," replied Gao.

"Not to worry, kids are tough!"

~ *Return to Father Durant* ~

Meiying retrieved the note from Father Durant and returned to her room. It read:

Miss Bai, I urge you to return so that we may continue our discussion. As you know, confession will put you right in the eyes of God. I also beg you to come so that I may make amends and put myself right in your eyes. I long to share with you the joy of returning to God and to me. Trusting in the Almighty, I will see you soon. Father Durant.

She reread the note many times, and with each reading, thought, *No mention of his behavior! His unwanted kisses! Just a vague reference to making amends!* The more she scrutinized his words, the angrier she became. And yet, a perverse desire lay in her to confront him, to ignore Feng's warnings, to strike out and be her own person, solve her own problems, take a risk, and deal with her own uncertain fears.

Against all reason, against all the rational arguments, all the warnings, and all the evidence, she decided to take the plunge and see him. Either Feng and the others were wrong about him, or they were right and she would find out for herself. There existed an excitement to her decision that had no analogy in the normal course of events. An unknown, hinted at danger gave it an irresistible edge. Meiying knew from past experience she was not beyond surprising, even shocking, her friends and family who thought they knew her.

Besides, if worse came to worse, she had the upper hand over him. After all, he was attracted to her, not vice-versa. A lesbian would always have the advantage over a horny heterosexual male. Stood to reason. Meiying convinced herself that he was ultimately harmless, but still useful as a bridge to re-establishing a relationship with god. It became clear that she must cross this bridge to reach salvation. *God provides, and Father Durant is His servant,* she thought.

The next day she sent word via a note delivered by Little Acorn that she would come that evening to the rectory. Of course, she told no one of her plan, and when the time came, left the temple surreptitiously. As she made her way to the church, the streets were unusually full of people, mostly strangers who had swept into town after their long journey from the bloodbath of Nanjing.

In the dying light of day, the faces of the refugees mirrored the bleak setting of the sun. What had begun in the charnel house of Nanjing with a hundred thousand deaths had infected the survivors with a virulent trauma and metastasized into a hundred thousand tumors to ravage them with a fatalism that overcame the original relief at having survived. Future uncertain, past unbearable. Meiying could not look in their eyes without recalling Feng Shiren's report of what he had seen in Nanjing, his description vividly appearing before her in horrific detail. By the time she reached the church, Meiying hesitated at the rectory door, then decided to go back to the temple. As she turned to leave, the door flew open and a strong hand grabbed her arm and pulled her inside.

Meiying felt as if she had fallen into a deep well. Father Durant pushed her into a chair, standing over her with a fierce determination that proclaimed she would not rise until he permitted it. The dark rectory closed in from all sides, with not even the weak light from the desk lamp to relieve the desolation. His eyes burned feverishly and seemed to blaze at her from the blackness.

"You are here because it is God's will you have come. I know you are frightened, but your fear is a test. Those of us who have seen God know that pain is His preferred tool, His chisel, to carve you into His image. It is through this pain that together, you and I together, will seek His forgiveness. Since we last met, I have decided that the confessional is not harsh enough to bend your stubborn, female will."

Meiying forced herself to speak calmly. "I came here of my own choosing to seek your help in returning to God. If we could just talk, I know your wisdom would show me the way."

His shadowy figure trembled, either from fear or from tension, and his dark head tilted as if perplexed by her words. "No, Meiying, talking is not enough now. I must purify your flesh to purify your mind and your soul."

He pulled her up and dragged her to a side door, which he kicked open and threw her in ahead of him. Meiying stumbled against a gigantic wooden cross, at least two meters tall. Before she could recover, he pulled her arms to the cross-pieces and tied her wrists with ropes that had already been prepared.

In denying the absurdity of what was happening to her, Meiying had resisted the temptation to scream, but her panic could no longer be suppressed. Anticipating this, Durant shoved a cloth into her mouth and tied it tightly in place around her neck. Now certain she would be murdered, Meiying frantically prayed to God and at the same time cursed herself for the arrogance and pride that brought her to this place.

Durant stood back and gazed at her body. He reached out and gripped her blouse, ready to rip it open. But then, strangely, he stopped and stepped back, seemingly unable to control a sudden twitching of his arms and legs, like a person being electrocuted. Whirling sideways, arms flailing, his legs collapsed beneath him and he fell heavily to the floor. Meiying stared down at him in shock. He tried to rise, fell, and rose again. Unsteadily, his hands a blur of uncoordinated tremors, he painfully untied the knots, removed her gag, and stumbled back to his office, collapsing in a heap on a small couch.

Keeping her eyes on Father Durant, who sprawled awkwardly on the couch trying to return her stare while still convulsing, Meiying hugged the wall and inched toward the front door. While she silently slipped by, his face reflected an inner agony that touched her to the core. She wanted to run, but his shattered figure aroused an unexpected pity. He gestured toward something in the dark corner, and she felt her arm again grabbed, this time in a friendly manner.

"Take her away," Durant stuttered to the figure in a voice barely understandable. "Hurry!"

"Yes, yes I will," replied a familiar voice. "Once she is safe, I will return."

Father Durant nodded in acknowledgement, his face distorted by twitches and tics. "Hurry!" he repeated.

Before she had time to identify the shadowy figure, she found herself standing outside the rectory door, trying to decide whether she had dreamed the entire ordeal. She wanted to run back inside and discover the identity of her rescuer, but a sudden chill fell over her—the type of chill that comes when one has just escaped death and understands that it surrounds us as invisibly and pervasively as air. An irresistible urge to run back to the temple and see her friends overwhelmed her. She wanted to cleanse herself in their lovely company, hear their reassuring voices, laugh at their absurd jokes, and relax in the safety and security they provided.

Night had arrived and the crowds only seemed bigger and more ominous. Still shaken, she moved through the streets without looking at faces, trying to make herself as small as possible. Cheerful lanterns hanging from the shops contrasted starkly with the grim shapes moving in and out of their small orbs of light.

Horrible visions of what might have been, and images of Durant shaking and drooling unwillingly scrolled through her mind, even as she tried to shut out the nightmare thoughts. Never had she yearned to be safe more than now. Awareness of her own vulnerabilities combined with the near-fatal overestimation of her ability to handle any situation shook her deeply.

A crowd of people gathered around her, many of them children, gaining in numbers as she walked, begging, pleading, demanding money, their interest drawn by her clothes, which were slightly above rags.

"Look at the fine lady!"

"Please! Some coins for my children!"

"She's too good for us!"

"Grand lady! Let us eat cake! Is that it?"

"She has money! Share! My family is starving!"

"For my little daughter! Please! She's near death!"

"Too good for us! Haughty bitch!"

"Too grand!"

"Better than us!"

"She's hiding something! She has money hidden in her clothes!"

"Why out so late, grand lady?"

"Been up to no good!"

"A prostitute!"

"A prostitute who won't share!"

Feng Shiren stepped out of the mob and passed his arm through hers, hurrying her along.

"Let her through!" he shouted. "This lady is very sick! You want to catch typhus?"

The crowd melted away, except for one child who remained by her side. He tugged on her sleeve.

"Little Acorn!" she cried, thrilled to see another friendly face.

"It's me. You okay, Miss Bai?"

She wanted to pick him up and hug him, but Feng kept walking, tossing off comments to passers-by.

"So it was you in the rectory!" uttered Meiying.

"What?"

"You were in the rectory just now, I know it."

"I don't know what you mean. No I wasn't."

"Come, come, Mr. Feng. You are again my savior."

"Silly woman, I've been with Little Acorn all evening."

She looked down at the boy and he nodded in confirmation.

"But, then who. . . ."

"Here we are!" cried Feng. They had reached the temple gate.

Meiying looked at him. "You aren't going to ask? To scold me?" She did not quite believe his story about not being at the rectory. But then, Little Acorn backed him up. *Who?*—

Feng laughed, his hand on Little Acorn's shoulder. "I'm not your father, least of all your savior, Meiying. Besides,"—he winked and struck a pose. "I suspect you learned something tonight. I see it in your face." And with that, he and the boy disappeared into the night.

Too exhausted to think, Meiying went to the sanctuary of her room and slept fitfully. In her dreams, the mystery person assumed a variety of forms, but the face was never revealed.

~ *Aftermath* ~

Thursday morning came. Day of departure. Heads shaved again, much to the distress of the women. Robes donned. Farewells were spoken, tears shed, and the group again took to the road. Only a few uneventful hours passed before Japanese planes flew overhead in the direction of the town.

Watching them fly past, John turned to Lu Zhishen. "Christ! We've only been on the road this short amount of time, and the ugly reality of what's been going on out here slaps you in the face."

"Yeah, no time to adjust. Guess we have to get used to it again."

"You don't think they're after the town, do you?" asked Peter loudly to anyone with an answer.

""Why would they?" asked Suling naively. "No soldiers there."

"That doesn't stop those bastards," observed Lu Zhishen.

"Maybe just spotter planes," suggested Peter.

"Too many," came a voice.

The group moved on, but soon heard distant explosions.

"It's the town!"

"Oh, god!"

"How lucky can you get?" said Peter. "We stayed for weeks, and on the very day we leave . . . pow!"

John remained silent, his heart going out to the people in the town, and especially to those in the temple. He wanted to talk with Meiying, but she had been keeping a polite distance. The voice was mercifully quiet. What he said earlier about the ugliness came back to him. *We must be leading charmed lives,* he thought. *Or being somehow protected. Why is the town bombed now, the very day we leave? The tapping, Feng Shiren, the Japanese, all too coincidental. Meiying should already have been raped twice, and murdered, yet here she is—untouched!*

As he pedaled, like the wheels of his bike turning and turning, John played and replayed in his mind the group's extraordinary luck. He convinced himself that their good fortune was connected to his future son. *If she is interested in him, he must be destined to be exceptional. If he is destined to be exceptional, he must be born, therefore his mother must be kept alive. And his father. . . .*

It suddenly occurred to him: *who will raise this boy to be exceptional, she or me?* John watched Meiying ride ahead of him. From the back, she appeared unexceptional, a typical, slightly-built Chinese woman. Surely he would be the major influence. But when he looked beneath, compared apples to apples, he knew he came up short. *Surely it will be her that will raise the boy. But if we stay here, in this godforsaken country, how can he grow up at all? It's too much!*

Peter pulled up alongside. "What's the matter, bloke? Life got you down?"

"What do you mean?"

"I've never seen a bicycle rider with a more hangdog look."

"Just thinking."

"That will get you in trouble, old boy."

Meiying had fallen back and heard Peter's words. "What will get him in trouble?"

"Thinking!" cried Peter.

John looked at Meiying sorrowfully. "It's nothing," he said, huffing a bit as they climbed an uphill slope. Managing a smile, he continued, "Nice day."

Meiying felt a pang of regret. She had deliberately avoided him, first during her time with Father Durant, and after 'the incident', feeling herself too shaken and weak to deal with his issues. But now she saw him in a new light. Yes, she knew he cared for her, and she knew he had tried to see her during their time at the temple. When she stayed away from the library, to her relief, he suddenly stopped trying. Now he seemed to hold no grudge, acted politely toward her, and carried himself like a true gentleman. She knew he had been informed about the incident with Father Durant, and concluded the weight of anger and impotence caused by this priest must have been lifted off his shoulders. Yet, she knew he must still be struggling with the voice. *He must think I abandoned him.*

Meiying remained conflicted. She had always been 'the perfect daughter', wanting to please, and deeply hurt when others accused her of somehow falling short. Yet, an even deeper ambition to achieve something great often drove her to surprising acts of willfulness. One way this trait expressed itself was in her learning music and her determination to play the piano at the demanding level of a virtuoso. Spending hours in training and practicing, she often neglected what she believed were her duties to her parents and others, always painfully aware of her selfish pursuit of a career.

Now, with John beside her, she deemed it necessary to reach out and repair bridges. "Peter!" she scolded good-humoredly. "You can get in far more trouble by not thinking!"

"Maybe," replied Peter. "But I'm not used to riding this long without a break. I'm going to suggest we rest—for the kids." He laughed, as the youngsters were happily pedaling far ahead. So off he chugged to catch up with Dr. Liu, whose stamina put the other members of the group to shame.

John and Meiying rode in silence, mainly due to the exertion required by a series of small hills. Finally, Peter got his wish and the group pulled off at a picturesque meadow framed by sycamore trees.

Meiying invited John to join her in an out-of-the-way spot. Attuned to his response, she felt gratified that he seemed pleased and accepted. The others understood and kept their distance.

"I've been wanting to talk with you for a long time," she said after they rested in a shady spot.

John could not hide his sarcasm. "I noticed."

"How have you been, really?"

"Fine. I think the better question, Meiying, is how you have been after . . . that incident."

"How much of it have you heard?" she asked, knowing that the group discussed it, which, irrationally, she knew caused her to feel somehow flustered by the encroachment on her privacy.

"All."

"Oh, well, truly I am fine. For a while, I was shaken by it, but now I'm fine."

"Maybe," John smiled. "But I don't think so. Betrayal can be really hard to cope with."

Meiying recognized the allusion, but ignored it. "Yes, he used his position as a priest to obtain my trust. John, I trusted him to help me get closer to God, not to him."

"I understand."

"Do you?"

"Yes."

Meiying looked around. The sky blazed blue above the swaying sycamores, grass abuzz with life. "It's just that I feel so vulnerable, so scared out here in the open. I look at all this natural beauty and know at any moment bombs may come or soldiers rush out of the forest to attack us."

John softened. "I know, and I'm so sorry you've had to endure these terrible things."

"You know, John, when I was in that awful position at the rectory, someone helped me. I don't know who, but I think it was Mr. Feng."

"Did he tell you so?" asked John.

"No, but who else could it have been?"

"I don't know," replied John almost in a whisper.

"But how about you, John? The voice?"

"Oh, it comes and goes. I'm getting used to it."

"When does it come? Is there a pattern?"

He wanted to tell her about the voice, about their future son, about the connection of the voice to the Precious Object, but instinctively knew it was too soon. "Just comes at random times. No pattern at all, as far as I can tell. I think there are two."

"Two?"

"Yeah, male and female."

"When was the last time you heard them?" pursued Meiying. In spite of knowing he wanted to change the subject, she had always been fascinated by the voice, and now the notion of a female intrigued her even more.

You see, God, She is fascinated by Me! Interesting how her human genes activate such cognitive gymnastics.

It is true. Such elaborate twists and turns into superstition and misguided speculation. How do you know she prefers You?

Someone just told Me. It is clear she prefers the old human concept of Yin, as well as the true Dao. She prefers goddesses to angry, sputtering gods.

Nonsense! The notion of goddesses has long been dispatched.

Obviously not ... a lingering longing.

John shook his head to clear his mind. "Why are you so interested in the voice, Meiying?"

She looked at him oddly. "We've discussed this before. I think there is more to it than, well, than an illness. And now, the idea of two!"

"What if it *is* an illness?" he asked rather perversely.

She replied with a slight impatience in her tone to indicate she understood his game. "As I said, we've discussed this. I think the voice, or voices, are something more than mental illness. If not,"—she shrugged, evidently at a loss—"than not."

Chastened, John had no option but to remain silent or to tell the truth as he understood it. He chose to tell the truth, and felt an immediate sense of liberation. "Meiying, the fact is that I want to tell you. What is actually happening with the voices—"

Before he could get further, Little Acorn ran up shouting, "We're leaving! Pack up!"

Shaking his head in frustration, John said, "I'll tell you later, at the next stop."

"Yes," replied Meiying, already moving toward her bike. "Good. But now we had better go before we're left behind."

Neither could have known these were the last words each would speak to the other for a very long time.

~

I knew.

Only because you know I am going to write it.

You forget, writer, I was there.

"Son?" said John to the wind blowing in his face as he pedaled onward.

I am here, dad. The words flow on. I warned you about the narrator, didn't I dear Reader?

~ Disaster Strikes ~

The children were the first to see the roadblock atop a small ridge. It was manned by a band of ragged soldiers. The children raced back to warn the adults, but not before they had been noticed by the soldiers. Dr. Liu pedaled to the side of the road after the orphans swarmed around him with their story. He held up his arm for all the riders to pull over and join him. By the time everyone huddled in a rough circle, a group of soldiers had sped down the road and jumped out of the bed of an old military truck.

Even a cursory glance revealed that these were not regular army soldiers. Their 'uniforms' were a hodgepodge of rags, cast-off surplus, and civilian clothes. Many had no shoes. All had weapons, all scowled, and all appeared hungry. A tense atmosphere enveloped the group and they stood dumbly, unsure what to do. As long as the soldiers remained at some distance, the fear could be controlled. Dr. Liu walked up to them, trying to keep them from coming closer. There did not appear to be any obvious leader. "Can we help you?" he asked, looking from face to face.

No response.

John thought the scene resembled a surreal movie. The soldiers, almost skeletal, stood menacingly and stared, more like phantoms than blood-and-flesh men. Their weapons seemed as rigidly tense as coiled snakes.

Dr. Liu waited patiently.

Lu Zhishen moved next to him.

Slight movement among the soldiers rippled in response to the big Canadian, but no words were spoken.

Tension grew on all sides.

Ravens cawed nearby. Wind swirled sycamore leaves around the legs of both groups.

Still no words.

John stood next to Suling, who put her hand on his arm. Peter sidled closer to Meiying, who had her arms resting on the shoulders of one of the younger children. Mr. Gao had rounded up the other youths in a tight group. The others stared at the ground.

One of the soldiers had been perusing the faces, his head swiveling this way and that, the loose robes and shaved heads making identification difficult.

He lifted his arm and pointed.

At Meiying.

Without hesitation, two soldiers broke ranks and ran up to Meiying, pushing aside Peter and the child, and grabbing her arms.

What is this?" demanded Dr. Liu.

"She is coming with us!" barked the soldier who pointed.

"No! She is—" Dr. Liu started to say, when a soldier standing nearby raised the butt of his rifle and struck the side of his head. Liu crumpled to the ground.

John ran forward but two soldiers blocked him with hoisted guns. Before anyone could make a concerted effort to help, Meiying had been forcibly thrown into the truck with the soldiers and they drove up the road where their comrades waited. John ran a few paces shouting after the truck, but all that remained was a desultory spiral of dust unwinding in the breeze. On the ridge, the soldiers melted away, leaving the group stunned. Suling and a few others began ministering to a badly injured Dr. Liu.

John sank to his knees and wanted to bury himself in utter desolation, but the cries of Madame Liu brought him back to the dire situation they all faced. Momentarily setting the image of Meiying aside, the thought crossed his mind that Dr. Liu was dead. He could not see the good doctor through the people hunched around, so he again turned his thoughts to Meiying. If he could ride his bicycle quickly enough up the hill to the ridge, he might spot the direction in which she had been taken. Without a word to the group, he jumped on his bike and labored up the hill; when reaching the top, gasping for breath, he looked down the other side in excruciating anticipation.

Nothing.

Not a sign of the soldiers.

But a village could be seen in the distance, surrounded by rice fields. Peasants, tiny specks in the green expanse, moved in unison as if choreographed. He sped back down the hill to the group.

"A village! A village! She must have been taken there!"

"Hush!" cried Mr. Gao.

"Is he dead?" John asked Peter in a low voice.

"He's still unconscious. Could be internal bleeding."

"Let's take him to the village. Maybe they have a doctor," said John.

Suling had been listening while leaning over Dr. Liu. "Yes. I'm worried about inside his head. Unfold the stretcher. We can make a travois. Lu Zhishen is the strongest."

"Yes! Yes!" cried Madame Liu. "Let's get him to the village as soon as possible!" She struggled to control her tears.

Peter looked at John with a stricken face. "Maybe we'll find Meiying there."

John nodded, but he suddenly remembered Feng Shiren. Where was he? After all, he had played the savior so many times. Why not now? John scanned the group and spotted Feng standing quietly on the fringe, looking down helplessly, totally out of character. Even in John's desperation, or because of it, he took the time to approach the little soldier.

"What do you think?"

"About what?"

John grit his teeth. "About Meiying!"

At this, Feng collapsed to the ground, assuming the position of a meditating monk; legs crossed, arms raised, fingers touching. As if in a trance, he did not acknowledge the presence, or words, of John.

"Fuck!" shouted John, whirling away. He wanted to continue screaming obscenities, but stopped when he saw Madame Liu collapsed in someone's arms. A moaning arose from some of the women, and Peter wandered close to John. Looking off into the distance, Peter said in a voice croaked with emotion, "He's dead."

Both men heard the tapping from inside the box still strapped to Meiying's bike.

Both men ignored it.

John tried to comprehend what had just happened. In the space of ten or fifteen terrible minutes the world had become an unbearable hurt. He turned to look at Dr. Liu's body, but could only see Madame Liu supported by Master Zhou. Others were doing something to the corpse. Deep anger and the terrible thought that time was being wasted overcame him.

"Peter!"

"What?"

"I'm riding ahead to the village."

"You can't do anything there, alone."

"Maybe, but I can find out where Meiying is."

"No. You can only be shot."

"Fuck you! I'm going. Meet you at the village." With that, he grabbed his bike and left the group behind to deal with Dr. Liu. It wasn't long before Feng caught up with him. John pulled to the side of the road and let himself catch his breath.

"I thought you were meditating," he said sarcastically, while at the same time secretly happy Feng had appeared.

For once, Feng did not play the fool. "I have a vested interest in both of you."

"I get it, my guardian angel."

"Something like that."

John shook his head. "This might amount to nothing, you know."

Feng also shook his head. "You're wrong. This will amount to something."

While John pedaled, he saw more clearly the danger to himself, and his nerves started to undermine his determination. Only the presence of Feng gave him the motivation to continue. They passed an increasing number of peasants who stared at them with cold, suspicious eyes. As they approached the village, clumps of people openly gaped, and it seemed to John that word had already spread that they were coming. The hairs on his neck stiffened and his stomach felt queasy at the frightening collection of eyes that greeted the two riders.

On the outskirts of the village, where ramshackle houses built of mud and tile came closer together, Feng abruptly pulled over to a surly-looking group of peasant farmers.

"Brothers! How are you today?"

Only grim nods in reply.

"Did soldiers come this way earlier, brothers?"

Nothing.

Feng took out some paper money.

Nothing.

He suddenly flung the bills in the air. The peasants instinctively jumped to grab them as they swirled through the breeze, but stopped themselves as if on command.

Feng smiled.

They glared, unsure what to make of such reckless behavior; angry at his mocking action, but confused as to his purpose.

Feng took out two silver coins.

Silence. Eyes greedily on the silver.

He put them back and said to John, "Let's go! Thank you, brothers! We have our answer!" He gestured to John and they started to leave.

A young, intelligent-looking peasant stepped forward, a hoe balancing on his shoulder. "Wait!" he barked.

Feng turned with an open expression.

"We know you are not monks. We know you have foreign devils with you." He stared maliciously at John, then continued, "Japanese agents are all around. We burn them alive when we catch them. It's not your worthless paper money or your fucking silver we're interested in!"

Feng appeared unimpressed and shook his head. "And I'm not interested in your problems. All we want is to know where soldiers—if they are soldiers—took an innocent Chinese girl."

The peasant laughed scornfully. "Those weren't soldiers—just thugs working for a big-wig. Thieves and rapists."

John's heart sank.

Feng made a show of looking around. "So where are they?"

"Give me the silver coins first."

Feng chuckled and turned back to John. "Let's go."

"You won't find them in the village," said an old man standing in the back. "This same group took my granddaughter."

"When?" asked Feng.

"Yesterday."

"So, they passed through your village yesterday. How about today?"

"Yes."

"Where are they headed now?"

The young peasant stared hard at the old man, then turned to Feng and held out his hand, palm up, waiting impatiently for the silver coins to be dropped into it.

Unmoving and unmoved, Feng looked past the young peasant and said, "Maybe we can help get your granddaughter back."

The old man stepped forward and slapped away the young man's hand. He pointed toward the northeast. "To the mountains."

Feng handed the old man the silver coins. 'Brothers, we are anti-Japanese, but these brutes killed one of our people and kidnapped a girl. A good Chinese girl. May we stay in your village tonight?"

"Will you go after them?" asked the old man hopefully.

Feng shrugged. "Maybe."

John looked disgusted. "Yes! We will go after them!"

The young peasant looked at John as if bemused. "They'll kill you. They're bandits, murderers, and rapists. We have dealt with them more than once."

"Brothers," said Feng. "Do you have a place for us to stay tonight?"

Another peasant chimed in, "We have an inn! Very famous! Ancient. Our village used to be an official Imperial resting place, when days were better. My great-uncle is the proprietor." He stopped suddenly, then said, "Can you pay?"

"Brother," said Feng in a mock-disappointed tone. "Do we look like penniless monks?"

They laughed.

Feng Shiren had won them over.

John sank into despair.

Noticing his despondent comrade, Feng struck a pose for the assembled peasants and cried, "An inn for the weary travelers! Tell your uncle to stock up on wine! And food! Feng Shiren has arrived!" He slapped John on the back. "With his young American disciple!"

Chapter Seven

PART TWO: DETOURS

Meiying's Ordeal

~ Mr. President ~

Meiying had already been raped many times before she was left alone long enough to come to her senses. Her mind had seemed an impenetrable fog since she had been taken from her friends, nor did she have any idea how much time had passed, but the pain and leaking from her vagina told her all she needed to know. Now, curled up naked on the half-soaked blankets that lay haphazardly atop a dirt floor, she faced a simple decision: kill herself or find a way to survive long enough to escape. In this position, locked in some dark place with nothing but a few filthy blankets, killing herself seemed impossible, but planning an escape gave her at least one reason to live. Thinking of escape played at the edges of her mind, but try as she might, the energy would not come; she felt numb and listless, almost uninterested in what further atrocities would be inflicted. Bruises covered her body and she desperately wanted to bathe, but as far as she could tell, the room was desolate; no water, no toilet, nothing. Just blackness and dirt. She had stopped trembling, but the thought of someone walking into the room made her ill. Wheezing in short, labored gasps, she quickly realized it was the stench that made it difficult for her to breathe. To divert her disgust, she focused on discovering what kind of space she inhabited.

Barely illuminated by a faint light that seeped in from some distant source, the room did not seem to have walls that were smooth. In severe pain, she rose and gingerly shuffled to the nearest wall. It felt cold and uneven. *Stone, maybe a cave.* She perceived a fuzzy, reddish light creeping dimly across the ground from the opposite side. It looked like the last moments of a sunset. She groped her way around the walls and discovered the glow came from a crack beneath a poorly-hung wooden door. Very slowly, she turned the knob and pushed.

Locked.

Pressing her ear to the wood, she heard faint male voices, coarse and obscene, their words indistinct. Sticky fluid ran down her thighs and she felt an upwelling of nausea. She limped back to the blankets and used a corner of one that was less soaked to try and dry herself. The horror came to her in another rush, and the trembling onslaught of degradation with no apparent end shook her to the core.

As she came to more fully comprehend her surroundings, her terror increased. She now preferred even this dark, lonely space to an open door; a portal through which would enter violent men with violent thoughts. Dried sweat, sticky wetness coating to her thighs, pain, and the stench, all combined to overcome her with renewed disgust and humiliation. She had to pee, and worse, but with no place to go, she covered herself with the blankets as best she could, praying for a quick death by some means that would put an end to it—giving at least some pleasure in the knowledge that her dead body would offer them no further satisfaction. The thought of food disgusted her, but a desperate thirst drove her to the edge of calling out for water. Only the horrible dread of that open door and the monsters that would come through it prevented such a reckless move.

Crazy thoughts passed through her mind. If she ran fast enough and intentionally struck her head on the stone wall with enough force, she might die, or at least pass out. She lay on her back to gather the courage, but instead groaned in pain. With probing fingers, she discovered her once smooth flesh now marred by welts on her arms and back, one eye evidently closed from a swollen bruise. Rope burns flared hot around her wrists. She dismissed the idea of smashing her head and took a different approach.

Moving her fingers—which were among the few parts that didn't hurt—in a different way, she mimed playing her favorite sonatas and concertos. Soon, music reverberated throughout the room. This conceit provided her with some respite from the pain, but in the midst of a particularly stirring Chopin movement the door slowly opened.

~

Meiying let out an animal cry and quickly buried herself deeper beneath the disgusting blanket. She prayed that the earth would swallow her up.

Someone stood over her.

Breathing hard.

A tugging on the blanket, gentle.

She gripped it tighter.

"Meiying," came a familiar voice.

Recognizing it, she clung tighter and closed her eyes, curling into a fetal position.

"Meiying."

She did not move.

More tugging on the blanket, insistent.

She clung to it as would a drowning swimmer to a raft, still covering her face from the terrible sight.

"Meiying, let go," came the voice, still gentle. "Everything will be all right. I'm here now."

She remained motionless, barely breathing.

"They weren't supposed to do this to you. I told them not to, but they are evil men."

The tugging stopped.

"Oh, god!" came the voice again, clearly distraught. "What evil must be endured to purify those who have strayed from the path!"

Silence but for his breathing.

"I told them to keep you safe until I came to save your soul, but they are evil men."

More silence.

"Now your soul is stained even deeper and the scrubbing made all the more difficult."

Meiying heard another enter the room.

"Ugh! It stinks in here! Well? Now you've seen her. We're well paid—" obscene laughter—"in more ways than one. You still want her?"

"You broke our bargain and, using terms you understand, damaged the goods."

"Ha! That was never in the agreement. I've no more time. You want her or not?"

"She's damaged. Her soul—"

"Soul be damned! No refunds, no discount. But I'll tell you what, on second thought . . . "

The blanket jerked violently off Meiying, leaving her to cover herself as best she could by curling into a tight ball.

" . . . leave her here and I'll spare your church next time we visit the village."

"That's no bargain. The Japanese will have something to say about it."

"Damn the Japs! Look, make up your mind. She stinks and is probably full of disease now. If we clean her up, she'll eventually run. If we fill her with more of our jism, she'll explode. Either way, a headache. Besides, her condition is right up your alley, and we've all heard how you 'save souls.'"

"Who told you these things?"

"Many a poor woman in the village who suffered at the hands of your Christian piety! Disgusting even to me! You're worse than us."

Laughter from the one who spoke.

Silence from the one spoken to.

"Well, you want her or not? Speak now or get out now! I've no more time!"

"Okay, I'll take her, and I'll pray you be forgiven."

Scoffing laughter in response.

A voice from the group called out, "Priests are all the same!"

"Hypocrites!" cried another.

Durant said, "But at least I want her cleaned up first. She's not fit to travel."

"Sure, priest. No charge."

One of them left the room. Meiying could not look.

The other said in a gentle tone, "Meiying, I'm so sorry this happened. We must get to work saving your soul. You must see this as a stern test of your willingness to bow before God's harsh justice."

After being left alone to wait, Meiying was full of conflicting feelings. Being released to Father Durant seemed a blessing, for in her mind he did not have the means to keep her a prisoner. But certain oblique references to his methods of 'saving souls' disturbed her, and she remembered the cross with horror. Now, her thoughts turned not to John or Peter or Madame Liu, but to Feng Shiren.

You saved me once, great soldier, save me again! She held out her hands, palms up. *Great Lady, help him!*

But Feng did not appear. Nor did *her*. With no saviors at hand, she dreamed of Meili; being in her soft arms, bathing together, Meili's deft fingers massaging away the grime and pain and anger.

After being pushed from the room, she was allowed to sponge off in a tepid bath with no soap, then given a rough muslin dress. She soon found herself bound and gagged in the back of a peasant's cart, covered with straw and jostled toward a destination she prayed would be the village where her friends at the temple would offer sanctuary. Words filtered through the straw as Father Durant and the driver conversed.

~ *Back to the Village* ~

"Well, Christian sir," said the weather-beaten old driver. "I am a Buddhist myself, but your god is welcome. Room enough for all."

"Yes, yes, I have heard that many times from many people," replied Durant. "But you see, our religion recognizes that there is only one God. If you pray to the others, you will be punished for not worshipping only one god—our God."

"Some missionaries have also told me that," said the driver in a puzzled tone. "It's like an emperor, or a warlord, who demand absolute loyalty. If not—" he drew his finger across his neck.

"Yes, like that."

"Ah," replied the driver. "Our gods are greater than that. Greatness lies in obedience driven by respect, not by fear."

"Of course," said Durant, suddenly realizing this driver was no simpleton. "We respect our God also. We worship Him!"

"How do you draw a distinction between the fear and the respect?"

"Both apply. And love, don't forget love. Our God is a loving God."

"Ah! One just need look around to see that is false!"

"Of course, not enough people fear Him."

"And the animals and plants that never die peaceful deaths?"

"They don't count. They are here for our benefit."

"Ah! That explains a lot. That is why I am Buddhist."

Durant replied testily, "If enough people feared Him, we would have a paradise on earth."

"So the fear is necessary for the love?"

"Not always, but it helps."

The driver looked backward at the straw. "Is that why the girl is tied. Fear and respect . . . and love?"

"That is different. She's mad. It's for her own protection."

"Ah, I see."

"We must take care of mad people."

"Ah, I see."

"Of course, there is more, much more you don't understand. We place our faith in Him. We don't question our God."

"Why not?"

"He is much greater than we. That would be impertinence."

"Huh?"

"Disrespect."

"Ah, I see."

Durant looked at him. "I fear you don't."

The driver nodded in agreement. "Yes, I don't. But I will tell you a story, okay?"

No response.

"Just to pass the time."

Durant remained quiet, so the driver continued. "Once, a long time ago in Sichuan province, a holy man with great powers spent his days helping people. Healing them. Teaching them. Revered by the entire province, it was thought he could do no wrong.

"His little monastery became too small for all the pilgrims, so he left and built a temple only for himself, so he could heal the people without interference from other monks. And they came by the hundreds. One day, a mother brought a small boy to be healed. 'What is wrong with the boy?' asked the holy man. 'He is mad,' said the mother. 'Bring him to me,' commanded the holy man.

"So the mother brought the boy. As soon as the boy saw the holy man, he cringed back and pointed. 'Murderer!' he shouted. All the assembled were horrified and knew for sure the boy was truly mad. But the holy man looked at the boy and said, 'No, leave him alone. He is right.' Everyone was astonished and tried to solve the riddle posed by the holy man's words." The driver chuckled and turned to Father Durant. "Can you solve the riddle, Christian sir?"

"Of course," said Durant. "The holy man meant all those he could not help. Out of his kindness and mercy, he felt like a murderer, since he could not save all."

"Ah!" cried the driver. "Not at all! He really was a murderer. He confessed and showed the police where dozens of bodies were buried. Some cut up in pieces, some partially eaten by him."

Durant laughed a strange, guttural laugh, but said nothing. Finally, he turned to the driver. "Was the boy truly mad?"

"Mad recognizes mad."

"What happened to the holy man?"

"He became a driver of carts."

"And the boy?"

"He became a Christian priest."

"What became of the girl?"

"What girl?"

"The girl in the cart with two madmen?"

The driver laughed. "Two madmen and one girl is a recipe for disaster."

The two rode in silence for some time, serenaded by the rhythmic creaking of the cartwheels, when the driver abruptly asked, "Would one of the madmen share her?"

"No," replied Durant, throwing his head back and waving his arms, evidently on the verge of saying more, but no words came.

"In that case, the story has two endings," continued the driver. "Either one madman kills the other and murders the girl, consuming her flesh in his madness, or both madmen agree to no longer be mad, take her to a temple in a nearby village, and live their lives as honest, sane men. Which ending do you like the best?"

"The nearby village has been bombed and the temple partially destroyed," said Father Durant.

"And the Christian church in the village?"

"Untouched."

"Ah, that is good. One ending takes place at a partially destroyed temple, and the other at an undamaged church. I wonder which it is to be."

Silence.

"Look, there's Old Chen's place!" cried the driver. "We'll soon be at the village. Where do I take you?"

"To the church."

"And her?"

"Stop the cart," commanded Durant.

The driver guided the horses to a clear area on the side of the road. He observed Durant's stricken face, his eyes closed in pain.

After sitting silently for awhile, the driver said, "You have made a decision?"

No response.

Dusk.

Peasant women walked past, returning from the village with empty baskets, many with babies bundled on their backs, all casting furtive glances at the priest, who they knew well enough.

After sitting in silence for a while, Father Durant jumped off the cart and helped Meiying out from under the straw. He removed the gag and untied her without a word. She squinted in the dim light of dusk, then limped away to relieve herself. Durant watched the listless young woman duck behind a thick clump of bushes, and turned to the driver.

"Take her to the temple," he said. "She is beyond my help. It is her fate to burn. The stain is too deep."

The driver tilted his head and a stifled grin creased the corners of his eyes. "As you wish," he said.

"I wish."

"By the way," said the driver as he watched Meiying approach the cart. "Whose stain?"

"That is none of your affair."

"I see."

"I will walk from here," continued Durant. Looking in the direction of town, he said loud enough for the driver to hear, "I know who you are."

Getting no reply, he turned to repeat his statement to the old man, but saw instead a beautiful woman staring down at him.

Father Durant, came her glowing voice in his head. **Fate starves at probability's door. You are starving, yet sustenance is found just on the other side.**

The voice so powerful and sharp, he felt a deep pain in his chest and closed his eyes to keep from fainting. When he opened them, the driver was helping Meiying settle into the seat next to him. Without a word, Father Durant started walking down the road toward the village, and was soon passed by the cart with two dark figures silhouetted in the last rays of another dying day.

Those villagers who passed him on the road stayed well away. Among the more perceptive passers-by, it was observed that the priest seemed utterly self-absorbed, his lips moving continuously.

"Lord, I have thrown one back into the sea, too small for me to take . . . oh, yes, I know what You are thinking; she is not too small . . . it is me that is too small . . . I am unworthy . . . but if I have a chance, I will again reel her in and bend her to Your will . . . give her time to get bigger, cleaner, and fatter, so much the better for salvation . . . I do have a reputation that must be protected . . . too bold and I overstep Thy will, too brazen and I risk punishment from the sinners, but cautious is Thy way in matters of the state . . . so, I give to Caesar what is Caesar's—for now . . . this so-called driver will cause trouble . . . throw Meiying back until she fattens up, then take her for Your glory . . . as for the driver, I know who *she* is, and I will deal with *her* in a manner that will please Thee . . . still, agents of the devil are all about, and I must truly be careful . . . it's the driver . . . *she* bedevils me . . . takes different forms . . . but I am Your servant and that demon cannot outwit Your instrument . . . instrument . . . Meiying plays the piano . . . she is beautiful, very beautiful . . . but she is not Your instrument . . . I am! Still, that damnable beauty!"

And so it went, all the way to the town, where his little church waited patiently; standing defiantly, surrounded by rubble, which he took to be a sign.

Durant continued his conversation with the air. "She will be close by . . . anytime I want, she will come and I will purify . . . at the core she is still God's creature . . . suffering, crying to escape the stained prison of her body. . . I must help her slough off that corrupt shell and free the soul inside, for that is her only hope . . . and mine."

He walked past a host of beggars without a single glance.

Even after he stepped inside the vestibule, his lips never stopped moving to the rhythm of a fevered brain.

~ *The Inn* ~

Master Zhou felt quite pleased. The inn recommended by the peasant had turned out to be quite comfortable, and he parted gladly with more of his money. Still, the group deeply mourned Dr. Liu's death and Meiying's kidnapping. After a flurry of discussion, it became clear there was nothing to be done. However, Feng Shiren wanted time to make inquiries as to Meiying's whereabouts, so again, they were delayed in an accommodation not of their choosing. Madame Liu remained in her room, and the others wandered the village like ghosts. A tea room at the inn became the preferred meeting place, and the hotel staff fell into the habit of serving food and wine at all hours to these strange guests with money who pretended to be monks, all of whom seemed to sit whispering and waiting for some mysterious signal to move on. Lin Tingfan, the owner, often joined them at these meals, secretly rejoicing at whatever misfortune had befallen them and caused them to stay. His jocular manner and crude jokes, intended to make their visit more pleasant, had the opposite effect, and he eventually gave up, shaking his head and leaving them to their own devices. "Give them what they want, the bastards," he instructed his staff. "They pay well and cause no problems, but I don't like them. Too secretive and stuck-up." He soon turned his attention to news of the advancing Japanese army, pondering how best to play his cards when they arrived so as to separate money from their pockets without endangering himself.

One afternoon, John, Peter, and Lu Zhishen sat talking and drinking beer.

"Wonder when the Japs will arrive?" mused Peter aloud.

"Better not be too soon," said Lu. "Better be after we're well gone."

"Wonder if old Feng has found out anything?" again asked Peter to the air.

"Ah! He's out carousing and wandering with the children like a Chinese Fagin," scoffed Lu. "I know Mr. Gao is worried about Little Acorn. Says Feng has too much influence on the boy."

"You should cut him some slack, old boy," observed Peter. "He's not as bad as you make him out to be."

"Sure," grumbled Lu.

Peter ordered another beer and held out his hands, palms up. "Will we ever get to see *her*?"

"We have to stay here until we find Meiying!" snapped John, who was in an unusually foul mood. For days he had tried to call forth the voice for solace, or comfort, or perverse distraction, but she would not cooperate. "Can't you get that fact through your damn head!"

"I know, I know," said Peter defensively. "I was just wondering."

After John's outburst, they drank in silence for a long while, the alcohol starting to make its presence known.

"I keep thinking of Dr. Liu and Meiying," said Lu with tears in his eyes.

John finished off a beer and ordered another. "I know, but remember, he's dead, Meiying is still alive somewhere. But where, goddamnit! God knows what's happening to her while we just sit here."

"Never fear," slurred Lu Zhishen. "Sherlock Holmes is on the trail. He'll find her like he found Peter here, wandering around in the bushes."

Peter's face, already red from the beer, turned redder. "God damn, you big fuckin' Canadian! At least Feng's trying. We're just sitting here pissing down our legs."

John felt an overwhelming guilt. Peter was right. Here he sat, drinking, while Meiying was still out there. He gulped the last of his beer and slammed his fist on the table. "You're right, damn it! I'm going to find our Mr. Feng and help." He stood and walked away from the table a bit unsteadily.

When outside, John breathed the air in deep gulps to try and clear his head. He looked up and down both sides of the road and set off in a random direction. Everywhere he went attracted the stares of villagers. Some stopped and openly gawked, while others were more polite, casting furtive glances at this Western apparition. Being the center of this unabashed attention always got John down. As the effects of the alcohol dissipated, his resolve weakened, and he slipped into a narrow alleyway to escape the oppressive crowds. A wooden box invited him to sit, and he took advantage, his elbows on his knees staring down at the trash-strewn ground.

I assume, John Powers, that you despair of ever seeing her again?

"You must be God," he said aloud. "Where have you been?"

Shhh! Just listen to what I say and don't blather. You want to be institutionalized?

"Where is she?"

How do I know?

"You know! You'd best take care, else she won't have my son."

A warning! The mutant boy actually has the gall to warn Me! Your future son is the contrivance of Goddess and Her faction, not Me.

"Where is she?"

If I knew, I wouldn't tell you.

"Why?"

Probability starves at Fate's door.

"Well, if you won't tell me, it means she is safe."

"Who are you talking to?" came a female voice.

"Suling! What are you doing here?"

"Walking. I passed two men staring down this alley from the street, and heard a familiar voice. Here I am."

John looked up the alley toward the road. "Are they gone?"

"Yes."

"Suling, when you saw your family killed . . . in that horrible way, how did you survive—you know, carry on?"

Suling put her hand on John's shoulder. "I didn't. For a long time, I was dead, but *she* saved me. Honestly, John, I am sure I would have stayed dead, but *she* gave me hope."

"How?"

"By giving me love."

"Suling, you know I care very much for Meiying."

"Yes, we all do."

"I know, but if she is dead or in great pain . . . I just can't bear it."

"I know, I know."

"How do I survive, Suling?"

"John, Madame Liu is right now in her room, deciding whether it is worth it to go on. Her husband, the center of her life for decades, is gone. What would you say to her?"

"I would say it was important for her to go on, if not for herself, then for others."

"And you? Would you follow your own advice?"

"Suling, I have no others."

"Look around."

"I have no others."

"You have me. You have Meiying."

"She may be dead."

She is not dead, John Powers!

"Goddess! So You do know!" cried John.

A startled Suling cringed backward and muttered, "What?"

"Nothing, it's nothing. Suling, I'm feeling better. Thank you."

She looked askance at him. "John, why don't we go back to the inn and have some tea with the others?"

"Boo!" came a loud, childish voice that caused both Suling and John to flinch. Little Acorn, who had crept unseen into the alley, ran out from the shadows, laughing.

Suling playfully grabbed him, but he wriggled away. "I like it here!" he cried.

"You should!" came another familiar voice. "Shelter, food, peace, play," continued the voice. Feng Shiren strode up and sat next to John on the box.

"Especially peace," said Suling. "Hello, Mr. Feng."

"Hello! Are you two planning plots and devising schemes?"

Suling laughed like a girl.

John fidgeted, wanting to ask but not wanting to hear. Courage arrived. "Any news about Meiying?"

"Well, I'm waiting for information from Litou village."

"Why Litou?" asked Suling.

"No reason," Feng replied, shrugging and looking away.

"Do you think she's back in Litou?" asked John.

"Don't know. Just making sure."

"I thought Litou was destroyed by Japanese bombs," said John, clearly agitated.

"No. Only partly."

John didn't believe Feng was being entirely open. "I mean, you must have some reason why you think she's back in Litou."

Feng blinked and struck a pose, his head and shoulders jerking this way and that to some imaginary opera. Suddenly, he slumped down, head lowered. "John, you hurt me—if I knew something, I would certainly tell you. Don't you trust me?" He flashed a look of exaggerated innocence.

"Yes, but—"

"We trust you, Mr. Feng," said Suling hurriedly, before John could say something he would regret.

Feng popped up as if from a hot seat. "Thank you, Suling." He looked triumphantly at John and tilted his head endearingly.

"If you think she might be there," said John. "I can travel back and check. I will be back before the group moves on from here."

Feng's expression turned serious. "You can't, John."

"Why not—just because I'm a foreigner?"

"That's not it."

"Then, why?"

"It is not good."

"Why?" insisted John.

"The Japanese now occupy Litou."

~ *Meiying and the Japanese Commander* ~

Meiying was given her old room back at the temple by Master Yu. She remained listless and unresponsive, in spite of efforts to cheer her. Talk in the temple soon turned from Meiying's arrival to news of the approaching Japanese, which had caused panic in the already damaged village. An exodus soon began. Japanese planes periodically bombed, although no Chinese soldiers remained. A few days after she arrived, explosions again ripped through the village, and a nun ran into Meiying's room.

"Meiying! Run! Come to the basement before it's too late!"

But Meiying simply lay in bed and waved her off. "Leave me, I'm fine."

Before the nun could reply, another explosion in the courtyard sent flying shrapnel and smoke roaring through the shattered window. A scream. Meiying raised herself on her elbows to see if the nun was injured, but after the smoke cleared enough to make out the room, there was no one to be seen.

"She made it, pray God, safely to the basement," Meiying whispered to herself. She lay back down, pulled the cover tight around her neck, tried to control the coughing, and waited for blessed annihilation. But it never came. The pain from her vagina constantly intruded as a nagging reminder of the scarification that mutilated her body and soul, and she knew the pain would continue unless some end were put to it. Amidst the self-perceived ruins of her life, Meiying only found solace in the memory of Meili and their short time together.

The next day, the Japanese army entered the village.

Burning.

Raping.

Torturing.

Hanging.

Beheading.

Oddly, the temple remained untouched.

For a week.

Until one day a Japanese officer stood at the entrance gate, backed by a platoon of armed soldiers, his samurai sword hanging jauntily at his side, staring at Master Yu.

"We have reports you are hiding enemies of the Imperial Japanese Army," he proclaimed through an interpreter.

"No, sir," replied Yu. "This is a Buddhist temple housing only monks and nuns."

The officer's eyes glittered. "Gather the nuns together. We wish to inspect them."

"Why, sir?" asked Yu.

Without a word, the officer drew his sword and held the blade at Yu's neck. Then he turned to the interpreter and nodded some silent command.

"Gather the nuns together, monk. It will be better for all concerned. Gather the nuns together," repeated the interpreter.

Master Yu slowly turned and walked into the temple, the soldiers following like a pack of hungry wolves.

After entering the main hall, Master Yu said, "Wait here."

On hearing the interpreter repeat the message, the officer grunted unhappily, but stayed put as Yu walked off. When the Master returned, he said, "They are being gathered."

"Once they are here, we will inspect their rooms," said the interpreter after listening to his commander.

Yu held out his hands and slowly nodded. The women filed into the hall, heads down. Meiying was among them.

It seemed to her that the world had become a place intent on wrapping its inhabitants in a gauze of burning pain. She now understood the deep suffering endured by so many people who, in her happy youth, were nothing more than shadowy victims of some distant injustice. That injustice had now insinuated itself into her own soul, but she still felt it as a faint numbness, endurable so long as the world was held at a distance. Although she had been told that Japanese soldiers were in the temple asking for the women, she viewed herself as a broken toy, unattractive and uninteresting to malicious children. So she did not comprehend the significance of the officer pointing directly at her.

"You!" he screamed.

She jumped and stared at the officer's boots. A soldier pushed her from behind, and she was escorted out of the temple, flanked by two soldiers. Meiying knew she would be raped again, if not killed outright, and she dimly perceived a low-grade urgency to escape, or at least beg for mercy. But the anesthetic comfort of welcoming death over the arduous exertion of repelling it made her rather embrace the coming end, however messy it might be in the short run. To a detached observer, she might have appeared to be just another female victim of war, to be pitied and forgotten. Such is the nature of the world. But, like all the others pitied by fools, Bai Meiying was anything but "just another" compliant female victim. Alas, the world is full of fools whose pity should be turned on themselves. However, dear Reader, I digress.

The small group of soldiers and their hostage walked a long way, down many streets, past cringing villagers, to the mansion once occupied by the richest man in the district. Not that Meiying noticed. She had kept her head down and her eyes on the ground, counting the steps leading to her death. Intentionally, she avoided looking up at the sky, or at trees, or at birds. They would only be unwelcome intrusions, harbingers of regret, spoiling the final chord of the symphony.

She found herself standing in the foyer of a very rich house. Scrolls lined the walls and exquisite tile floors radiated colorful patterns to dazzle her. Servants and soldiers scurried about like leaves in a strong wind. When the bustle ended, she stood alone with a single individual staring at her. Still, she kept her eyes on the ground, noticing only the shiny boots of this person.

"Look at me, Meiying," came a male voice, speaking Chinese with a slight Japanese accent, and to her surprise, as sweet a voice as she had ever heard.

Somehow the words and tone inspired confidence. She raised her head and looked at the vision standing before her. A Japanese officer, impeccably dressed but without weapons, stared back. He appeared otherworldly. Thin, with pale skin, almost tubercular, his shining eyes a riveting contrast to the will-o-the-wisp of his body. It seemed to her that the uniform was superimposed on his image, like some perverse joke; a masquerading apparition.

"I have been told about you," he continued in Chinese, the accented words imbued with a sing-song lyricism that had the power to mesmerize the unwary.

She did not respond.

"A priest, whom I befriended. Missionaries are useful, especially the bold ones who have the audacity to remain when we arrive. Don't worry, your friends at the temple tried to protect you—keep you hidden and safe. But the priest! All I had to say was that I am also a Christian, persecuted and seeking absolution, then he became most cooperative."

Meiying remained silent.

"And, I might add, quite handsome for a Westerner." At this, the officer put a finger beneath her chin and lifted her head very gently. He clicked his heels and bowed. "I am Colonel Naguma. I understand from this Father Durant that you play the piano. Is this correct?"

"Yes," replied Meiying tentatively.

He wagged his finger. "Come."

She followed him down a long hallway to a large room. "Play," he said matter-of-factly.

Meiying looked at the piano. It was Father Durant's, evidently moved here at the pleasure of Colonel Naguma. She hesitated, instinctively unwilling to be the slave of any man.

"Please," he said, plaintively, without a hint of sarcasm.

Meiying turned to the piano and a wave of love and nostalgia swept over her. She ran her hand almost erotically over the beautiful wood, and the faintest ember remaining of the will to live ignited into a reaffirming fire. None of this escaped Naguma's notice.

"You have not played in a while?"

"No."

"Ah, I see." He gestured toward the bench and smiled gently. "Please."

"What do you want me to play?" she asked, a slight edge to her voice.

"Play what is in your heart."

Meiying could not stop the tears. "My heart is broken."

"Father Durant showed me an odd signal used by your people." He put out his hands, palms up. "The good Father disparaged the gesture, but I use it now with the deepest respect. Play for *her*."

Meiying had thought she was beyond surprise, or even shock, at the actions of men. But this? She adjusted the bench and tried a few notes. It was tuned well enough. Naguma waited patiently to the side, so without another word she began playing the second movement, the *adagio*, of Beethoven's 5th piano concerto. The notes lanced straight into the tumor of pain and humiliation that so clogged the natural flow of joy and compassion that had been her life before rape. She felt herself in motion again, like a boat through the lapping waves on a breezy, sunlit day. Beethoven's notes contained the exquisite melancholy that gives depth and meaning to the world, vanquishing ugliness and fear, and reinstalling beauty as the capstone of existence. When she finished and looked up at Naguma, both had tears in their eyes.

"Thank you," he said after a long pause. "You are no ordinary pianist."

Meiying looked down, her cheeks a suffused red.

"Nor, I suspect, are you an ordinary woman," he added.

Now it happens, she thought, and steeled herself for the coming ordeal. Pain from her vagina continued to be an unpleasant reminder of rape, and she contemplated whether to struggle or submit.

A loud knock at the door, and Naguma's demeanor quickly changed, his body now rigid and alert. He straightened his tunic. "Come!" he snapped.

A soldier entered with papers and handed them to Naguma. He put them on the piano, scanned them quickly, signed, and wordlessly handed them back. The soldier saluted, and as he was leaving, Naguma barked a command. "No more interruptions!"

"Yes, sir."

As soon as the door closed behind the soldier, Naguma sighed and slipped back into his insubstantial, spectral self. "You see how it is," he whispered to the air.

Meiying recognized something in him that she could not quite articulate. Its definite shape eluded her, but she knew the shape was familiar. In spite of her resistance to the idea, he began to fascinate.

"Now," he said in this lyrical mode. "Back to our business. Your Beethoven moved me very much. What I am about to ask of you must not be misunderstood. I know you do not trust me, nor should you, but I am asking you to remain calm and try to trust me. Do you understand?"

Meiying nodded, the dread in her face evident to Naguma.

"Ah, there is no way to make this first step easy, and I don't have the time to make it easier. Take off your clothes."

Meiying blanched and staggered back.

Naguma held out his hands, palms up. "Trust me, Meiying, nothing will happen to you. Take off your clothes."

Somehow reassured against her own will, Meiying removed her clothes, but stopped at her underwear.

"All of them," he said, looking at her dispassionately.

When she stood before him naked, covering her breasts and pubic area as best she could, he said, "Put your arms down at your side."

She did so.

"Now, turn around."

She did so.

He carefully scrutinized her, head to toes, ignoring her trembling and the clear effort to repress the urge to cover herself. Her bruises were still visible, and his eyes hesitated at each one. During this entire process, he had not moved from where he had been standing.

"Now, put your clothes back on."

Relieved beyond words, Meiying quickly dressed and stood awkwardly, unsure of what to do or say. She assumed he was displeased with her body and felt deep gratitude that this was evidently so.

Naguma motioned her to sit in a nearby chair. As she sat, he poured a cup of tea and offered it to her. *This is a dream*, she thought. But the tea was real, and its warmth down her throat made her feel almost normal, as if she were merely on a friendly visit to some male friend.

Naguma sat in a companion chair and casually asked, "Are you married?"

"No."

"Do you have a boyfriend?"

"No."

"Did you have one before?"

"No."

He contemplated these answers for a moment. "Do you have a girlfriend?"

"Of course, I have female friends."

He shook his head sympathetically. "No, no. You take my meaning, I know you better now. Do you have a girlfriend?"

Meiying hesitated, but his sympathetic, sensitive eyes made her say the unsayable. "Yes." She felt astonished that this admission was made to a total stranger, a male, and an enemy of her country.

His eyes misted over. "Ah. You see"—he glanced around—"I have a boyfriend."

Meiying stared, speechless.

"Is your girlfriend here, in the village?" he asked.

"No, she is far away."

"Ah." He looked away. "Mine is back in Japan."

Both sat in silence for a long time, each absorbed in their own reminiscences and wrestling with their own demons.

Naguma broke the silence. "Originally, I had you brought here to play the piano. However, I have changed my plans. Our unit will be stationed here for the foreseeable future. You will stay in this house and be my personal maid."

Meiying started to object, but Naguma held up his hand. "That is merely a convenient"—he tilted his head and smiled—"title. In truth, you and I will be friends, and you may have access to the piano at any time. My soldiers will leave you alone."

"But I want to return to the temple," said Meiying softly but firmly. "All my friends are there."

Naguma shook his head grimly. "No, you don't want to return there."

Meiying's eyes widened. "Surely you have not harmed them?"

He shrugged. "Soldiers must be allowed to relieve the tension. Soldiers are soldiers."

"But you can't!" she blurted, quickly dropping her eyes. "The nuns! You surely can't agree to the killings and rapes."

His face hardened and he shook his head as if were out of the question. "Be careful! The situation is complicated. I am an officer in the Imperial Japanese Army. You must not question me about this."

The old fear returned in all its force and she remained silent. The tea now bitter and cold.

"I will send for your things. You do not want to return to the temple now, for it will soon cease to exist."

~ *John in Anguish* ~

Two weeks after John had his conversation with Feng Shiren, he sat with Peter and Lu Zhishen at the inn drinking tea. The mood was bleak. Master Zhou announced the approaching end of easy funds and the imminent arrival of the Japanese army. The group had no choice but to leave the next day.

"I don't know if I can leave," John announced. "What if Meiying returns and we are all gone? Someone has to stay."

"Don't be completely stupid!" cried Lu Zhishen. "I mean, I understand why you want to stay, but that would be suicide."

"I'm still an American citizen. Maybe they will leave me alone. We're not at war with them, you know."

"Sure," said Peter. "You and I both know you would be killed. We're too far from a city, from an American consulate. I agree with Zhishen that it would be suicide."

John knew he would agree to go. It was not that he feared for his life as much as he feared to fail Meiying. If he survived, there was always a chance to find her, or for her to find them. If he died in a useless effort, he would never see her again, and that was unthinkable. As for *her*, that was also unthinkable. Perhaps, if they ever made it to the destination, *she* would provide the answer. After all, the voice seemed certain Meiying would have his child.

"Yes, I know. I'll go."

"That's it, old boy!" cried Peter. "She'll turn up. I know she will." Peter had tears in his eyes. "You know, I love her too."

Madame Liu stood before the table looking pale yet determined. "When we leave early tomorrow, make sure you all have shaved your heads. We won't fool the Chinese, but if we run into the Japanese, we might fool them."

"Come, sit, Madame Liu," invited Peter. "Have some tea."

"No, thank you. I have many preparations to make."

After she left, Peter called for beer. "Screw the goddamn tea. Let's have maybe our last beer!"

"Here, here!" cried Lu.

John could not force himself to celebrate, and made his excuses. Instead of going to his room, which he dreaded, he went outside and walked the streets. Night had arrived, but the influx of refugees made progress very slow. He pulled his hood up over his head so his Western physiognomy would not show so easily. No matter where he turned, people milled everywhere, lying in the alleyways, begging on the streets, trying to shelter their children from the cold and the crush. He felt a contempt for such tragic souls, and forced down his fear of their desperation. *Good place to be knifed*, he suddenly thought.

A desperate urge to flee back to the inn gripped him. He turned and walked as fast as possible, occasionally shoving aside any person who blocked his path. As the angry faces closed in, his fear grew, and his single-minded journey became more frantic. When he pushed aside a person dressed in a thick cotton tunic, he heard a woman shriek and a bundled child fell at his feet.

"My baby!" cried the woman.

Horrified, John leaned down and picked up the bawling infant. "Thank god, it's unhurt," he said to her. But the crowd closed in around him.

"A foreign devil!" screamed the woman, snatching the infant from his arms.

"What are you trying to do?" demanded a powerfully-built man.

"I was just helping her," said John, his Chinese not the dialect of this region.

"What? What were you trying to do?" shouted the man.

Others gathered and threw accusations.

"Why is he disguised as a monk?"

"Who are you?"

"Where are you from, foreigner?"

"Why do you want to hurt a child, eh?"

John could only manage, "I didn't. I'm an American. I'm just returning to the inn. I helped the child!"

"Liar!" shouted the crowd.

Something hit him in the head, and the last he remembered he was sinking to his knees, protesting his innocence. Another object hit his face and he blacked out. When he awoke, he took a moment to clear his mind. Someone was speaking to him but the words were indistinct. He soon realized he sat leaning against a building, legs by the hundreds passing before him. The words came to his ears more clearly.

"Hey! Mr. Powers! You okay?" It was Little Acorn.

John felt the warm blood trickle down his face. Little Acorn used a cloth to wipe it off. "You okay?" he asked again.

"Yeah. How did I get over here?"

"Mr. Feng helped you. So did I," he added proudly.

John looked around but could see nothing from his position. "Where is he?"

Little Acorn shrugged and dabbed the cloth on John's face again.

"Why aren't you back at the inn? Tomorrow is a big day."

"I'm helping Mr. Feng."

John started to rise, but felt too dizzy and sat back down. "What happened?"

Little Acorn smiled. "Rocks."

"Oh. Why did they throw them?"

"Dunno. Mr. Feng said you foreigners are a lot of trouble."

John laughed weakly. "Yeah, I guess we are."

"Don't worry, we'll help you."

John suddenly felt ridiculous. "Anyway, where is he?"

"Who?"

"Mr. Feng!"

Little Acorn shrugged again. "Dunno, but he said to take care of you until he comes back."

"I'm okay now. Help me up."

"You'd better stay."

A sense of urgency to return to the inn overcame John. He needed to be away from the Chinese eyes that constantly stared at him, to be in bed, alone with his thoughts, away from this goddamn street. He stood and walked toward the inn, Little Acorn trailing behind. As it was late, the crowds had thinned and his path more easily navigated. Little Acorn followed him all the way to the inn. John turned to make sure the boy came in with him, but only glimpsed Little Acorn's back heading away.

"Thanks!" he cried out.

The boy turned and smiled, then gave a thumbs-up and disappeared into the night. It occurred to John that he had forgotten to ask the boy what he was helping Mr. Feng with. Too tired to think further, he cleaned-up and went to bed, careful to avoid laying on the swollen side of his face.

~ *The Road Again* ~

Once they were back on the road, the group settled into a well-worn routine. Madame Liu had not disclosed their next destination, and no one asked. The absence of Meiying and Master Liu weighed silently, but heavily on everyone. All that could be said had been said. Meiying particularly, was a sore topic that, by mutual consent, was strictly avoided.

At first light on the morning of departure, John had been informed by Feng Shiren that he had heard nothing from Litou village since the Japanese occupation. This information made John feel worse than if he heard something definite. Uncertainty plagued him, and he pedaled like a mute automaton.

From the moment of John's withdrawal from social interaction (beyond the most superficial), Peter and Lu Zhishen had grown closer. Everyone assumed John suffered from Meiying's loss and wished to be left alone. Only Suling tried to replace Meiying's role as his confidant, but he refused to engage with her, offering only polite conversation and off-putting platitudes.

Mr. Gao had also withdrawn, spending the bulk of his time with the children. The cumulative effect of these individual withdrawals resulted in fragmentation and resentment. Only Master Zhou tried to keep the group upbeat and cohesive.

"Now look, everybody," he announced cheerfully when they stopped to rest. "It's my money we're spending, so cast off the dreary faces! Personally, my life has never been so void of material gain and so rich with adventure and friendships. Damn my old life of ease, privilege, and purposelessness! Hurrah for my new life of deprivation and permanent soreness in my rear end! My friends, keep going! I'm with you to the final destination! After all, I want to meet this famous *her* you have all told me so much about."

The others smiled dutifully, with only Peter, Lu, and a smattering of peasants raising a desultory cheer.

After Zhou's speech, John noticed Madame Liu sitting apart from the others, staring into the distance. He wanted to go to her and offer comfort, as her pain reflected his own, but he cringed in the face of her apparent serenity. She bore it so well, keeping the goal in mind, not letting her husband's death deter her. When he took stock of his own behavior, John saw a spoiled child infatuated with his personal disappointments. Although it was agonizing to dwell on the fact that every kilometer closer to *her* carried him farther from the other her, he realized this knowledge merely fed his self-pity.

Looking around at the swaying trees and blue sky, he fixed his eyes on Suling and Mr. Gao, searching for a revelation that might be found in their wisdom; a life-line for his own drowning self. They sat with the children, laughing and playing some unfamiliar game. John quite unexpectedly felt an overwhelming sense of shame. He wanted to run over, hug his companions, beg their forgiveness, and bury his troubles in their kindnesses. The only way to redeem himself must be to become a pillar of strength for them instead of a burden. He made a vow to be more like Madame Liu and Suling; stoic and inspiring.

With renewed determination, John decided to put his faith in the voice. He would see Meiying again, marry her, and have a son. *From this point on*, he thought, *how it happens won't be my concern—fate will somehow make it happen. I will have faith, not in God, but in the voice, which speaks to me as God does not. Imagine, a Goddess! In the twentieth century! A Goddess!*

To cement his resolution, after the group started off again, he pedaled next to Suling and grinned broadly. She returned a confused smile, and he moved on to Peter.

"Hey, old boy! How does it bloody go?"

Peter almost crashed out of shock. "Johnny boy, have you been drinking?"

"Yes!" cried John. "Drunk on life!"

Lu Zhishen heard the exchange and looked back at Peter, raising his eyebrows, but his friend could only shake his head in reply.

John continued in this vein, zipping ahead until coming to Mr. Feng. "How are you this fine day, Mr. Feng?" he asked with strained good-humor.

Feng Shiren had heard and was prepared. "I'm fine, Mr. Powers. Why the sudden arrival of joy?"

"Because I know Meiying is still alive, and I also know I will see her again!"

Feng's eyes widened. "What did you hear? Any news?"

"Yes."

"What?"

"A voice. A little bird."

Feng laughed. "Excellent!"

On they rode, for two uneventful days, until they came to a broad lake. In the middle of its placid waters stood a magnificent pagoda rising majestically on an island, accessible only by a long, narrow bridge, scarcely wide enough for a truck. On closer inspection, the island contained an entire collection of magnificent buildings—a sprawling palace complex. Dark clouds quickly swept toward them, piling one upon the other in deepening hues of grey and black, casting great shadows that raced across the verdant green countryside. Just as they reached the bridge, a downpour arrived so fierce it seemed to merge with the lake into an unbroken universe of water. On they pedaled toward the strange palace with its central pagoda rising like a lighthouse through the storm. Every member of the group strained forward, anxious to get across the bridge before they were swept away. For the first time in weeks they heard tapping come from the box, now being carried on Lu Zhishen's bike. Even above the monsoon roar, the tapping could be heard, drumming faster as they approached the island.

John squinted through the curtain of rain and saw a small knot of shadowy figures huddled under the massive cross-piece of the entrance gate that provided narrow shelter from the worst of the downpour. Once the group made it under the gate, they dismounted and held their bikes wearily as Madame Liu spoke with a tall, lean man. After a spirited discussion, he turned and ran through the rain up a massive, fan-shaped stairway that led far above to reach its terminus before an imposing set of entrance doors glowering down ominously at the tiny humans below. He paused part way up and looked back, waving an arm vigorously at Madame Liu and cupping his other hand to shout instructions which no one could hear above the storm.

After interpreting his frantic arm-waving, Madame Liu scanned the group and shouted, "We can go in! Take your bikes up the steps and into the building! Quickly, before we're swept away!"

No further prompting was needed to convince everyone to hurry inside.

~ *Into the Vortex* ~

Already soaked, the group climbed the long staircase, now virtually a waterfall, and filed gratefully through the huge entrance doors. Once inside, John blinked at the opulence. Gilded columns, elaborate tile, magnificent scrolls, and black mahogany furniture greeted the awestruck travelers. Even the children were docile in the face of such grandeur.

With a thunderous, reverberating boom, the doors were closed and servants mopped the floor beneath their very feet. The tall man who had spoken with Madame Liu bowed repeatedly and said in a low, impressive voice, "Please wait here. Mr. President will be here momentarily."

"President?" whispered Lu.

"Yes," cautioned Madame Liu. "You will all refer to him as Mr. President."

"You're kidding," said Peter.

"Far from it," replied Madame Liu. "He literally stands between us and oblivion."

"How so?" asked Lu.

Before she could answer, an extraordinary person entered the room. One's first impression was of an immensely obese man who literally waddled. Everything about him seemed to bulge: his clothes bulged outward, his fingers bulged around his rings, his layers of chin bulged atop his chest, his legs bulged around his ankles, and, in short, his solar essence seemed to bulge into the very orbits inhabited by his guests, forcing them to step back before his intimidating bulk. Seemingly unperturbed, Madame Liu bowed deeply, followed by the others.

"Mr. President," she said with deep gravity. "We are so grateful you have taken us in."

He observed the group through beady eyes, searching for the slightest hint of insincerity or skepticism. Satisfied, he replied in a feminine, high-pitched tone. "Madame Liu, your safety is my most immediate concern."

Bowing politely to acknowledge this announcement, Madame Liu quickly introduced each member of the group. With each individual's name, the President's eyelids flicked up almost imperceptibly, evidently in acknowledgement of their existence. When the introductions were over, a stool with very thick, carved legs was placed behind him whereupon he squatted over it like a sumo wrestler, finally dropping his great bulk on it, and sitting with legs splayed.

"I want to hear about your adventures, starting in Shanghai, then in Nanjing, and then on the road, Japanese bombs, bandits, and the unfortunate deaths of your comrades as well as the kidnapping of the beautiful pianist."

Everyone stood dumbfounded except Madame Liu, who gave another bow and uttered a quick response. "Mr. President, I promised and I will deliver. When do you wish the stories to begin?"

"One important point, Madame Liu, I will expect the full story of your husband's death. Is this acceptable? Take your time."

The group flinched at this impertinence, but she did not hesitate nor waver in her reply. "My husband's death is now part of history, Mr. President. History must be passed on, or we are no more than dumb brutes. Do you wish the stories to begin tonight?"

Mr. President gestured and two muscular attendants trotted up and stood on each side. With a further gesture, his arms were grabbed and his great weight pulled up. Standing like a mountain, he said, "Before the Japanese arrive."

A shudder ran through the group, followed by the nervous shuffling of feet and hurried whispers. When the disturbance died down, Mr. President continued. "I also want to see the Precious Object in the box strapped to Mr. Lu's bicycle. Is it still tapping?"

Again a wave of surprise lapped through the group, except for Madame Liu. "No, it is stopped. Mr. President, when do you think the Japanese will arrive?"

"After you tell your stories." He smiled like the Cheshire Cat.

"Tomorrow?"

"After you leave. Tonight you will all go to the baths and cleanse yourselves. Unfortunately, you not only look like monks and nuns, but you smell like monks and nuns."

With that, he waddled off with his two attendants.

Other servants instructed the group where to leave their bikes, then escorted them to the public baths. No partitions separated the genders, and a mixed group of bathers already lounged in the enormous, steamy room. John felt intensely shy, and hung back self-consciously. Madame Liu noticed and stepped beside him, smiling. "John, when you see my body, you will realize nothing should inhibit you from displaying yours." She pointed at the water. "Look at the children."

John saw them playing with unabashed joy. Little Acorn led them in some sort of blind-man's-bluff. When he turned around to comment to Madame Liu, she had disrobed without a moment's hesitation, and promptly waded into the water as if walking to collect the mail. The others followed, luxuriating in the warmth and chatting amiably with those already soaking. John quickly stripped and tried to enter the bath as inconspicuously as possible. Peter caught a glimpse of him and laughed out loud, beckoning him over between chortles.

John waded over, careful to keep the lower half of his body underwater.

"John, I want you to meet someone. This is Mr. Zhu."

"Hello," said John.

"Hello, nice to meet you" replied Mr. Zhu, a middle-aged man with a bald head and a roll of fat.

Peter took over. "Mr. Zhu works for the President. He says life here is quite good. Isn't that right, Mr. Zhu?"

"Yes, yes," agreed Mr. Zhu.

Peter leaned over and whispered to John in English, "Now listen carefully." Leaning back to Mr. Zhu, he continued in Chinese. "When do you think the Japanese will come, Mr. Zhu?"

Mr. Zhu stopped smiling and said, "Mr. President already told you, the Japanese will come when you leave."

"What does that mean?" asked Peter.

"What Mr. President means it to mean."

"How do you know what Mr. President means it to mean?"

The man laughed. "That's easy. It means what it means. All of us understand what it means, because it means what Mr. President says it means. Quite simple."

"Well, after we've told our stories and left, Mr. President will tell you what they mean?"

"Of course."

"Well," Peter glanced at John as if to say, 'now get this.' He turned back to Mr. Zhu. "I mean, what will you do when the Japanese come after we have told all our stories?"

"Listen to theirs."

Chapter Eight

Survival

Meiying and Naguma

Meiying had been living as Naguma's servant for weeks. Not once did he touch her. In fact, she rarely saw him, as his duties carried him far away for days at a time, and when he did stay, he seemed to never have room on his agenda to visit with her. The few moments he took to speak with her were always taken up with questions about her past, her desires, and her ambitions. This left ample opportunity for the piano. His guards and other servants were under strict orders to let her play whenever she wanted, without interference. Because of Meiying's natural kindness and the guilt she felt at her privileged position, she insisted on helping the staff. This willingness to pitch in made her the favorite of the entire mansion, soldier and civilian alike. Whether in the kitchen, or the gardens, or cleaning the various rooms, she provided a welcome hand.

Father Durant came once, on an official visit, but she stayed in her room and did not see him. After he left, Colonel Naguma knocked on her door and asked to speak with her.

"The Christian priest just left. He asked about you, even wanting me to consider releasing you to his 'safekeeping.'"

Meiying started to protest, but Naguma held up a hand. "I understand," he said in his soft voice. "Don't worry. In fact, I am very familiar with his type."

Meiying waited, saying nothing. This Japanese colonel puzzled her. One moment she felt the urge to confide in him, the next moment she shuddered from some unknown, but palpable fear.

Colonel Naguma lit a cigarette. "You see," he continued in the same slow, ethereal way, apparently unfazed by her reticence. "I recognize that he is like me. Oh, not, of course, the personality, but the essence, the preference. It is odd that we three are linked in the midst of this hell. At another time and place, he and I . . . well, the difference is that you and I accept our fates, whereas he has been damaged by his religion—fighting against his demons—and therefore the pain he feels is directed . . . no, is inflicted on others."

Meiying waited. She wanted to say something to this man, an admission perhaps. But an inner warning made her hesitate. He continued speaking, looking off into the distance. As the words came, the smoke from his cigarette accentuated the lazy spiral of his voice.

"Of course, I am not one to speak. I have indirectly inflicted much pain. The anger and violence of soldiers . . . the vulgarity . . . and the killing, all are terrible to see."

He looked at Meiying for the first time since he began his monologue. "However, I have accomplished two things. I managed to save your temple, although I regrettably told you otherwise, and I have found someone you know."

Here he stopped to gauge her reaction.

She glanced at him, intending to linger only briefly, but instead of averting her eyes like some fearful girl, she held his gaze, surprised at her own boldness. Colonel Naguma seemed a bit taken aback, hesitating for a fleeting moment, then said, "But I will wait to tell you who I have found, since this individual is still in transit here under my orders."

Meiying could not stop her heart from pounding, but she forced herself to remain silent. Her reticence was a weapon she instinctively knew would keep him off guard and guessing the unguessable. Naguma waited in vain. She tried to sense any impatience, but evidently he thoroughly understood the game and remained stoic, as disconnected from genuine care as one of Eliot's hollow men.

At last he spoke nonchalantly. "Tomorrow, a general from Shanghai is arriving to inspect our unit. He will be accompanied by a German attaché who is a devotee of the piano, particularly likes Beethoven, and wants to hear you play. Seven o'clock. Pick an appropriate piece. You will play for him and a few select others."

"What do you wish me to play?" she asked in a tone that implied resentment.

He displayed no irritation. "Whatever you wish. Make it good German music to honor our good German allies. Anyway, by then, I will have confirmation of the person I mentioned."

"Will you tell me then?" she asked, a hint of impudence in her voice.

Colonel Naguma snuffed out his cigarette and made the next move. "Maybe."

~

That afternoon she volunteered to help tend the garden. In this labor she felt great joy. The head gardener was an old, wizened Chinese peasant called Gardener Wu, whose limbs themselves looked like stringy roots. Whenever she worked alongside him to trim or hoe, or plant, he recited wonderful stories of his youth in Hunan and of his family, who had all died years ago from the fever. He also told fanciful tales about the plants he cultivated.

Of an ancient vine growing up the mansion walls, he said, "This old mother has given birth to many, many little offspring who have run away to twist and turn elsewhere. The little fellows will grab onto anything and pull themselves up. Oh, the trouble I've had with some of them!"

While Meiying worked in the garden, she often struggled with a paradox. Although soothed by the beauty surrounding her, that very beauty often became a mocking reminder of the ugliness and violence of her gang rape. Like the gardener's old vine, those memories clung to her, twisting and turning in every crevice of her heart. That such beauty brought out such beasts made her a melancholy figure, stirring the kindness and gentle pity of Gardener Wu.

"Meiying, little one, your beauty is like a magnificent flower, but there is a shadow, a constriction that keeps the petals from unfolding properly in all their glory and receive the full light of the sun. What ails you, girl, that you don't reveal to those of us who selfishly want to see?"

"Ah, Gardener Wu, I am no flower. More like a weed, really. Pull me out by my roots and the others around me will prosper."

"Silly child! Every time I pull my young ones out by the roots, I know the world is darker, bleaker, and less fertile without them."

Meiying had no response to this, and felt her heart go out to this invisible old man who was himself a damaged flower. They worked together in blessed silence for a long while, when Meiying took a break and pushed back her peasant hat to wipe away the sweat. "Gardener Wu, may I bother to ask, are you Buddhist?"

"Sometimes, when my heart aches and my friends—" he looked around the garden—"can't help."

"Do you go to the temple at all?"

"Of course."

"Is all well there?"

"What do you mean, child?"

"I heard it suffered much from the Japanese."

"Yes, in the beginning, but now they leave it alone. I often volunteer to work in their gardens." He shook his head mournfully. "They need a lot of work. Bombs hurt our vegetable friends also, and the monks are horrible gardeners."

Meiying smiled. "And the nuns?"

He made a sour face. "Worse."

"I hope I have learned from you, Gardener Wu, so that my gardening has improved a little."

He made another face, this one less dismissive. "Not bad, not bad."

Meiying turned serious. "Is Master Yu well?"

"Yes, child, as far as I know."

"Oh, I would love to see them!"

Gardener Wu looked puzzled. "Can't you leave here?"

"No."

Wu grimaced as if in actual physical pain.

"No, no, it's not like that," she hastened to say. "Colonel Naguma does not bother me, does not . . . touch me. None of them."

"Then why. . . ."

"Yes, I have asked myself that question."

"Perhaps the piano?" suggested Gardener Wu. He lowered his voice. "We who have worked for them will be pruned by our Chinese brothers after the Japs leave, child. When they come for you, have a story to tell—a sad story—and some scars, even if you have to inflict them yourself. The scars must be deep, perhaps then they will let you live."

"Yes, perhaps," she said sadly, knowing that the wrath of the people can be terrible if turned upon suspected traitors. She remembered the torture of communists in Shanghai many years earlier, when the rows of decapitated heads and charred bodies made her ill.

Wu shook his head, clearly wanting to change the subject. "I don't understand Western music."

She laughed. "It is different."

"It is noise. Makes no sense. Just listen to our good old Chinese music. Tells a story."

He began singing a Chinese folk tune and turned back to his work. The discussion with this troubled, complicated human girl tired him, and he sought solace in the fellowship of plants. Meiying watched him affectionately, drawing strength from his strength, drawing patience from his patience and, with a lighter heart, joined him in his work, drawing satisfaction from his satisfaction.

~ *Stories* ~

Mr. President sat listening to Madame Liu recount the adventures of the group, occasionally asking the others who sat behind her to comment.

"Is that truly how it happened?" he asked Mr. Gao at one point.

"Yes, Mr. President, that is how it happened. The children would not be here—"

But Mr. President held up his hand. "The children are who they are, unlike us, who are often who we are not. It is who we are not that tells me who we are. The children are of no consequence."

Feng Shiren popped up and raised his hand like a schoolchild. Mr. President seemed a bit startled, his layers of fat rippling slightly as if a small pebble were thrown into his great lake.

"Yes?" said Mr. President, acknowledging Feng.

"Your words of wisdom inspire us all. Respectfully, how do you maintain such a godlike body?"

Collective intake of breath by the group.

Shadows fell across the faces of the attendants and they tensed to obey any command to discipline such impertinence.

But Mr. President laughed uproariously, great rolls of fat now bouncing up and down his vast expanse. He bellowed, "Because, Feng Shiren, I eat little men like you by the hundreds! That's how!"

Feng stood smiling, and when the laughter died down, said with a mischievous twinkle in his eye, "Every day?"

Mr. President guffawed like a donkey. When the ruckus again trailed off into silence, he gave a command. "Bring the Precious Object and place it before me!"

His guards departed and the group waited nervously, convinced that Feng Shiren had doomed them with his buffoonery.

When the Goddess statue was set before him, the President said, "She visited me last night in all Her glory. She told me to let you all leave and be on your way no later than tomorrow. I was also advised not to eat you—" he rubbed his ample belly—"as I have so many others. The butchers and pots of boiling water had already been prepared, but . . . well, it had been my intent to keep Her here, yet She warned me against it. Therefore, you may take Her with you. But,"—he raised a hand in warning—"be advised the path from here to your final destination will be much more difficult than even the one you have travelled so far."

Madame Liu started to speak, but the President's attendants were already lifting him, and his eyes revealed that, for him, the group was as good as gone, his thoughts somewhere else in a place and time that only a psychotic God would know.

"Fine by me," Peter whispered to John. "This place gives me the creeps."

John nodded and turned to Mr. Gao. "Thank god he didn't hurt the children or expropriate the Precious Object."

"Don't thank god, thank *her*," replied Mr. Gao.

"Goddess?" asked John.

Mr. Gao shrugged. "Perhaps."

Yes! Thank Me. came the voice. **You return to the road, but now it is even more dangerous. Are you up to it, Chosen One?**

It had been a while since John heard the voice, and his startled, frozen look prompted Mr. Gao to ask, "Are you okay?"

John nodded.

Suling, sitting nearby, noticed and moved close to John, putting her hand on his shoulder.

Madame Liu clapped to get everyone's attention. "All right, we leave tomorrow. Mr. Lu, please pack-up the Precious Object. All of us will gather outside at six o'clock sharp. Thank god the monsoon has passed."

"Where to next?" asked Peter.

She shook her head. "Probably spend the next few nights in the open. I was told to stay away from the surrounding villages."

"Why?" asked Mr. Gao.

"Mr. President warned me—said they are very poor, very superstitious, and very dangerous. That's all he said, no further explanation, but I tend to trust him at this point."

"Why dangerous do you think?"

"Bandits. Thieves. Desperate, starving people." Madame Liu shrugged. "Don't know for sure."

"Probably bloody cannibals like our fat boy here," murmured Peter in a loud whisper.

Lu Zhishen piped up. "Did he say how close the Japs are?"

"Very close."

"Are they going to follow us all the way to the final destination?"

"Hope not. What is wrong with John?"

Peter followed her eyes and saw Suling whispering to John while gently rubbing his back. Before he could respond, Mr. Gao spoke. "His voice again." Looking distressed, Gao continued, "I have to get the kids ready."

Madame Liu sighed wearily and trudged off to her room.

~

The voice stopped almost as soon as it had started, leaving John wondering why it bothered. Suling walked with him to his room.

"Are you going to be fine?" she asked.

"Yes, Suling, thank you. The road will be very dangerous. Are you ready for it?"

"Of course! Mr. President, this place, frighten me. I almost believe that he actually eats people. I can't leave too soon."

John smiled. "I wouldn't be surprised either."

"About what?"

"That he actually eats people."

She slapped his arm like a playful girl. "Stop!"

He does, but only in a metaphorical sense. Result is the same.

"Oh, damn it! Go away! Not you, Suling."

"I know, the voice," she said. "Good night. Tomorrow will come very soon."

When he climbed into bed, John stared up at the ceiling. Like the others, he felt anxious to leave, but the old fear came back. Should he stay for Meiying's sake? If he were in the same situation in America, there would be no question. But here, a stranger in a war-torn land? Going it alone? Unthinkable. Or was it? *Her* or her? Back and forth. Damn butterflies! Suddenly, he heard screaming coming from somewhere in the temple. Gradually, it died down. Murder or merriment? Damn butterflies. Images of the corpulent President eating his comrades plagued John's dreams and imbued his nightmares with a touch of the macabre.

Stay for her, John!

Which her?

Her! The one who brought you here.

Why?

Don't ask. You'll be lucky to get out of this alive, and I will be lucky to get My son. It is time to move forward so humans—

John woke in a sweat. Something malevolent pressed against his arm and he tried to push it away.

"John! Stop it! Wake up! It's late, time to go!"

Lu Zhishen looked down at him with disapproving eyes.

Never had John felt so much dread as he did that morning. While crossing the narrow bridge and up the winding road, he regularly glanced back to watch the temple recede in the distance, until it disappeared behind a hill as if it had never existed. *Perhaps it didn't.*

"Out of the frying pan and into the fire." He chuckled at his pun.

"What?" asked Suling who pedaled just behind.

Her proximity and the kindness in her voice gave him comfort. "Nothing."

~ *Meiying's Recital* ~

On the day of her recital for the German attaché, Meiying wandered aimlessly from room to room, the staff in agreement that she simply felt nervous and needed to find distractions. With good intentions, they asked her to do various menial tasks to take her mind off the upcoming ordeal. But, in fact, she struggled with a deep quandary: what to wear? Her choice of clothes was not driven by narcissism but by symbolism. Because she possessed only the clothes on her back after she was taken from the temple, Naguma had ordered her to go out with guards and purchase a new wardrobe. When she insisted the habit of a Buddhist nun was sufficient, he stood in adamant opposition and commanded a Japanese comfort girl to accompany the guards so that she would buy appropriate clothing. He further insisted that she be outfitted with a Japanese kimono to wear for "special occasions." She had never worn the kimono, but one day a rebellious mood overcame her good sense and she appeared outside her room in her old nun's habit. Naguma flew into a rage, made her stay in her room for days with no access to the outside world, and warned her that the next time she donned nun's clothes, he would send her, naked and in chains, to Father Durant.

Now, as she perused her closet, the choices were still limited, for even with the Imperial Japanese Army paying, she had chosen modest outfits against the strong admonishment of the attending comfort girl. Naguma wanted her to wear the kimono for the recital, but she convinced him that it would be impossible to play properly with such cumbersome clothes. He left giving her the clear impression that he wanted her to wear the most elegant clothes she owned. In her mind's eye, she imagined wearing a traditional Chinese dress as a sign of patriotism, but knew it would be lost on the guests, who would view it as a quaint display of the glory China once enjoyed, but possessed no more.

So she endlessly debated with herself; simpler or more elegant? It occurred to her that the message she most wanted to send was opposition to her enslavement, regardless of the velvet-glove nature of its surroundings. *Simple is best*, she thought. *Simple. Simple!* Meiying concluded that wearing elegant clothes would accentuate her position as a mere display piece, *a Chinese doll*. With this decision out of the way, she ransacked her wardrobe to find the most drab, unflattering outfit possible. She would, however, make sure that her hair was beautifully coiffed and her face made-up to be as attractive as possible. With these preparations, she would retain her dignity and, at the same time, flaunt her disregard for the assembled guests.

But Meiying underestimated Naguma's perceptive sensibilities. About half an hour before the scheduled performance, he slipped away to inspect her choice of attire. When he saw what she had chosen, he called for his swagger stick and struck her around the neck and back.

"You will wear what I tell you!" he commanded in a low, vicious tone. Tearing through her closet, he came upon the kimono. "Come!" At this sharp bellow, an aide rushed in. Naguma whispered in his ear and the man ran out. Shortly, a different Japanese comfort girl entered who Meiying did not recognize. She shuffled quickly into the center of the room and made numerous deep bows to Naguma.

"Dress her in a kimono!"

He turned to Meiying. "If you refuse, I will, this very night, do as I promised!" He tore off her blouse. "Naked, and in chains, to Father Durant!"

When the time came for her to perform, Meiying entered the ballroom from a side door, escorted by the comfort girl. Uncomfortable and hot in the alien kimono, feeling like a prostitute on display, she arrived at the bench and sat, only then scanning the many faces that waited. Her eyes rested on the German. He sat stiff and immaculate, an odd Buddhist symbol emblazoned on his arm that she had seen in newspaper photographs. For a moment, she felt confused and imagined she and the piano were back at the temple with Master Yu watching with his compassionate, shining eyes. But the German spoke and shattered the daydream.

"When will she start?" he asked in German. An interpreter translated into Japanese for Naguma, who smiled and said in Chinese very gently, "You may start, Meiying."

Once her fingers touched the keys, the surrounding world of harsh reality ceased to exist and only Beethoven's notes comprised the universe. She performed the first movement of a lively sonata. When the last note faded, the German stood and clapped enthusiastically, Naguma beaming next to him. Afterward, she played pieces by Schubert and Mozart, then returned to Beethoven, performing the beautiful *adagio* from the Fifth Piano Concerto. As the notes cast their spell, the German had tears in his eyes. When she finished, he rushed to her and kissed her hand.

"Where did you learn to play like that?" he gushed through the interpreter.

Meiying stood proudly and looked down at her kimono. "In spite of my dress, I am Chinese and learned from my very great master in Shanghai, who is probably dead by now, thanks to this war."

Silence.

Colonel Naguma glowered at her with a furious intensity, but the German held up his hand.

"No, no. Please do not punish her. She is a Chinese patriot who plays like a German. Such an exquisite combination!"

Naguma smiled humorlessly.

"You must promise me, colonel," pressed the German.

Naguma clicked his heels and bowed. "In the interest of the mutual friendship between our two countries, I will accede to your request."

But Naguma inwardly seethed. He had lost face in front of his staff and such betrayal could not go unpunished.

~

Meiying returned to her room and threw off the kimono. She changed into comfortable clothes and sat on the edge of her bed, waiting for the storm to arrive.

She waited.

And waited.

Growing sleepy, she forced herself to stay awake and waited some more.

Eventually, she fell asleep in her clothes, afraid he would burst into the room.

And slept.

The morning came bright and urgent.

She waited.

And waited.

Hungry and needing to use the facilities, she cracked open the door and waited for some response. Nothing. She used the toilet down the hallway and took a long, welcome bath. After finishing her ablutions, she returned to her room and waited.

Still nothing.

A maid she recognized appeared.

"Huiqing, what is happening out there?" Meiying asked, trying to keep her tone as calm as possible.

Huiqing cringed and looked around nervously. "Be careful," she whispered.

"What do you mean?"

Huiqing shook her head, unwilling to say more. She left Meiying in dread of what must now inevitably come.

But nothing happened.

No one came.

She remained alone in her room.

Waiting.

Another night came. Huiqing brought a tray of food, but left without saying a word in spite of Meiying's entreaties.

Again she slept in her clothes. The tension gave her a severe headache, and she lay awake trying to control the pain and the rising nausea. At last she settled into a restless sleep. It wasn't long before a nightmare assaulted her with the power of reality. It began innocently enough.

~ *Meiying's Nightmare* ~

She sat at a long banquet table covered with an endless variety of appetizing dishes. Laughter rippled all around, and her fellow guests, members of the group, joked with good-humored camaraderie. Meiying felt safe and secure, chatting with John who sat next to her. Suddenly, the doors burst open and Japanese soldiers filed into the room, lining up along a wall, facing the group. Meiying tried to warn them, but none of her fellow group members noticed. She shouted for them to look, but they simply sat and continued their friendly banter. When the soldiers lifted their rifles and aimed like a firing squad, she screamed and screamed, but everyone continued to ignore her and kept on laughing. A great crashing noise and smoke filled the room. She continued to scream, trying to see them through the thick smoke. When it cleared, all her friends were dead, blood splattered everywhere. With this horror all around, the table began levitating upward; only she still sitting at it. Below, the bodies became small specks as the table sailed higher, toward. . . .

At that point, she awoke with a start.

Naguma sat in a chair pulled next to the bed, staring down at her. His face registered no emotion she could identify.

"You are in very serious trouble, my lesbian friend," he said in a flat tone that made her blood run cold. "I intentionally forced myself to wait and calm down before deciding what to do with you. Killing you was my first impulse, but since we share certain predilections, I felt a sort of bond with you, so I waited before having you shot."

He paused to light a cigarette. Meiying remained in bed, staring at a Japanese print on the wall to avoid his terrible eyes.

He blew out a long stream of smoke toward her face. "Then I intended to strip you naked and take you in chains to Father Durant. But, again, I held off. Why, I don't know, but I did. While I was in this indecisive state, I was approached by our German friend. He wants to take you back to his country. I explained to him your sexual preferences, but he just laughed." Naguma leaned back and took long drags from his cigarette, then continued, "That leaves me with three options." He ticked them off with his fingers. "First, stay with me. Second, give you to the German. Third, turn you over to Father Durant."

"There is a fourth," she said under her breath.

"What?"

"There is a fourth," she repeated louder.

"Yes? What is it?"

"Let me go," said Meiying boldly, making eye contact for the first time.

She expected any response but the one he gave her. "Yes, let's add that to the mix. Now, what do I get out of it? Eh?"

"Karma."

It was his turn to be surprised. "You are Buddhist?"

"Raised Christian, but temperamentally Buddhist," she replied.

After thinking for a while, he gazed off into the distance and seemed to muse aloud, "My mother is Buddhist. When I was young, she discovered my homosexuality and was very hurt and very angry. She scolded me and said, 'This will kill your father!' When I cried, she yelled at me, 'Your illness is a crime against dharma! You must leave!' And though she had tears in her eyes, I knew I must leave. But it turned out she didn't mean what I thought. She meant for me to go to a military school where I would be 'cured.' One thing led to another, and here I am."

Meiying gazed at him and for the first time felt something more than fear or assorted premonitions of dread. She pictured what might have happened if she had been sent away when she was young to a place antithetical to her nature. This insight gave her a deeper understanding of why Naguma had threatened to send her to Father Durant. Instead of anger or fear, she now felt an emotion more akin to pity. His poetic, fragile, even beautiful soul had been perverted by the army and made irrevocably baser by the horrors of war; violence and cruelty had disfigured his Buddha-nature.

"You must have been very sad to have been sent away to such a place," she said.

Naguma appeared to ponder her words calmly, but she knew he battled demons, and the outcome would be decisive for her future.

Without saying another word, he stood and left, closing the door softly. Meiying felt euphoric. Naguma had not flown into a rage, had not beaten her, or worse, sent her to Father Durant. Perhaps, she thought, a connection was made that might yet save her. She was not sure what would happen next, but the most dangerous period seemed to have passed. Satisfaction at her small victory flitted through her mind, and she assumed the rules would remain the same—stay in the mansion or on its grounds.

With this in mind, she changed into her peasant clothes, donned her peasant hat, and went outside to help Gardener Wu.

He acted surprised and looked around nervously. "This is a surprise, little one."

"What's wrong, Gardener Wu? Why so strange?"

He backed up. "Meiying, does he know you're here?"

A sudden fear gripped her and she felt her heart constrict as if someone had jabbed her chest with an iron rod. "No, why?"

Gardener Wu peered over her shoulder and immediately resumed working.

"This is why," said Colonel Naguma. Next to him stood Meili. Both women hesitated until Naguma said rather gruffly, "Go ahead."

They flew into each other's arms.

"Why are you here?" cried Meiying after the hugs abated.

Meili blinked away tears. "I'm a prisoner, just like you."

"Correction," said Naguma. "You are both guests." He wagged a finger at them. "But you are strictly limited to the mansion and the grounds, otherwise you will be shot." He made this pronouncement as if informing them of the proper etiquette for tea.

"Miss Bai," he continued. "As a reward for your excellent performance, I am giving you this token of appreciation. While she is here, the Chinese prisoner may share your room." He smiled enigmatically. "And your bed."

Meiying and Meili were both stunned. A moment passed while they waited for some additional condition or warning to be added, and when Naguma remained silent, they hugged again, both suffused with unalloyed joy.

Colonel Naguma smiled as would a proud father.

"I told you I had someone you knew," he said affably, with no hint of the tense nature of their earlier discussion.

"Thank you," said Meiying.

Naguma merely smiled.

~ *Too Good to be True* ~

That evening, the two women made passionate and unrestrained love. Neither desired to withhold a modicum of pleasure from the other. When the orgasms stopped, the drift into equally satisfying conversation seamlessly unfolded.

"I still can't believe this is happening," effused Meiying.

"I know," replied Meili. "I assumed I would be shot, or in some prisoner camp. But here! With you! And the bed is so comfortable!"

"Yes, it's too good to be true," said Meiying stroking her hair. "I have thought of you night and day. But this is terrible that you're here under arrest. What happened?"

Meili pondered. "I don't really know. My father and I were staying in a small house temporarily while our army was on the move. We were surrounded by our own guards. I felt safe. The Japs were far away, at least we thought so, and our army was supposedly between them and us. Suddenly, I heard gunfire, explosions, and Japanese soldiers broke down my door and took me. Here I am. It all happened so fast."

"Your father?"

Meili cried. "I don't know."

They hugged each other.

"Your hair is as beautiful as ever, Meiying. But look how it's grown out! Even more beautiful!"

Meiying smiled and almost purred like a cat. "And you are more beautiful than ever."

"What do you do all day?" asked Meili.

Meiying shrugged. "Help out. I mean, help the Chinese staff. I especially like working in the garden. Now we can help out together."

"Yes. Have you managed to hear from your friends, the ones you were traveling with?"

Meiying recounted the long story of how she got there.

"So what is this Colonel Naguma really like?" asked Meili.

Meiying thought for a while before responding, then said, "He is a puzzle. I don't know. One moment I think he's bad, and then he does something nice. Meili, he is a homosexual."

"No!"

"Yes. A very badly wounded homosexual—mentally, I mean. I sometimes feel a lot of pity for him."

"They both fell silent, then Meili asked, "What will happen to us?"

Meiying snuggled closer. "I don't know, but let's enjoy the time we have. Tomorrow, I'll introduce you to Gardener Wu. He is a sweet old man."

"I'm frightened, Meiying. What if—"

"Shhh," interrupted Meiying, putting her finger to Meili's lips. "Didn't we agree?"

"Yes. But Meiying, dear, you're stronger than me."

"Shhh," repeated Meiying. "When all this is done, you will be my assistant, and we'll travel all over the world playing only beautiful and happy music to make the people beautiful and happy. We'll go to France and the United States . . . and so many other places. Together!"

"But Meiying, darling, you will be the performer, not me. I will have nothing useful to add to it."

Meiying laughed and mimicked her tone. "But Meili, darling, you will inspire it."

They hugged again, caressing each other's bodies not erotically, but as a husband and wife deeply in love derive joy from the joy of simply touching the other.

~

Naguma lay in his own bed, alone, staring up at the ceiling. His thoughts retuned to the time he was a small boy. Although he had often played with his penis, it remained a simple curiosity, no more meaningful than his odd underarms, funny toes, or long, scrawny neck. But one day, when his two playmates and he played in the woods near his house, a topic arose that interested them for mysterious reasons none could explain. Fumiko was a tomboy who loved to join Naguma and his friend Kaito in their various adventures. Fumiko always asked questions that girls were not supposed to ask, and she went places and did things that girls were not supposed to do.

On this particular afternoon, Fumiko stopped the two boys and spoke with firm determination, as if she had been thinking about it for a long time and her chance was now or never. "Let me look at your things."

"What things?" they asked.

She pointed. "Down there."

They obliged.

She gazed in wonder.

"Let us see yours," said Kaito.

"Only if you turn around first," she said coyly.

They did.

"Now look."

Naguma turned around and looked. Immediately, he felt a disgust he had not experienced when looking at Kaito's penis. In fact, Kaito's made him feel that they shared the same body; it made him feel safe and good and that he belonged. Her place where the penis should be made him gag.

"That's bad!" he cried, and ran home as fast as his legs could carry him. When he flew through the front door, his mother looked startled and asked what was wrong. A horrible realization occurred to him: his mother's was even bigger and more repulsive than Fumiko's.

That first introduction to the genitals of others made such a deep

impression that the memory even now struck him as immediate and electrifying. And here, with Meiying and Meili living under the same roof, he had in his control two females, one of whom drew him closer than he had ever been to a female, yet both of whom disgusted him in ways he could not articulate. He knew he had no choice but to go forward with his plans, and any regrets he might have were overwhelmed by the disgust.

That afternoon, Huiqing tracked down Meiying working in the garden and told her Naguma commanded her presence in his office. Meiying gave Meili a carefree, affectionate hug and left to see the colonel. When she arrived and was announced by the guard, Naguma called her in immediately and asked her to sit.

"Miss Bai, I have a musical score here from our great Japanese composer Yasuji Kiyose. Will you please learn it and play it for me?"

He handed the score to Meiying, who flipped through it. "Of course. When would you like me to perform the piece?"

"In two days. Can you learn it so quickly?"

She looked more carefully at the score. "Can we make it in five days?"

He pondered. "Yes. I'm leaving anyway for a few days so I will rearrange my schedule. Say, next Tuesday at four?"

Meiying smiled. "Yes."

"You may go."

After the door closed behind her, he said, "All the better."

~

The next four days seemed to the two women time spent in heaven. Naguma was gone and they had the run of the mansion and the grounds. Even the guards relaxed and joked with them in broken Chinese. Gardener Wu beamed as his two "little blossoms" helped, always bringing flowers to their room and dispensing extra bouquets to Huajing and the comfort women.

Colonel Naguma returned on the fourth day and asked them to join him for tea.

"Are you ready for the performance tomorrow?" he asked Meiying.

"I believe so."

"There will be some friends joining me. I hope you do justice to Kiyose-san."

"I will do my best."

"Are you nervous?"

"No."

"And you, Meili?"

"No, sir. Why should I be? Poor Meiying will do all the work."

"Ha! That's true. All you have to do is stand there."

An awkward silence descended on the group. Naguma seemed absorbed in his own thoughts, so Meiying turned to Meili. "Gardener Wu complimented you today."

"Oh?"

"Yes. He said you learn fast."

Naguma re-entered the conversation. "Gardener Wu, huh? He has worked here a long time. Typical Chinese peasant, stupid and compliant. An ox." The words were harsh, unlike Naguma's usual genteel style.

The women did not respond.

Naguma gazed at Meiying while lighting a cigarette. "Our German friend left in a very disappointed mood."

Meiying felt distressed by this sudden revisit to their past unpleasant conversation. "Oh?"

He blew out a long trail of smoke toward the ceiling. "Yes, but no matter. Tomorrow you play one of our great Japanese composers, and I know you will do me proud."

As usual, Meiying experienced a disorienting unease when talking with this complicated man. At a loss how to respond, she said simply, "I'll try."

"And you," he turned his gaze on Meili. "You will also do me proud, I'm sure. My two little doves in a gilded cage. Can you sing, Meili?"

Meili visibly trembled. "No, sir."

Naguma sat quietly for a while, smoking and sipping tea, then stood and pronounced curtly, "You may go back to your peasant gardener."

Both women hurriedly left. When they arrived at the garden, they huddled together in a small, covered gazebo.

"What was that about?" Meili asked.

"I don't know," replied Meiying, genuinely puzzled.

"Meiying, I'm really afraid. I almost wish I was in a prisoner camp."

"No, no."

"Yes, he scares me." Meili leaned against her lover.

"Funny," said Meiying stroking her hair. "He doesn't scare me anymore. He's like a little boy who doesn't know what to say at times, so he just says dumb things."

"Hey, there you are!" called Gardener Wu. "I've been worried."

"Worried?" asked Meiying.

Wu evaded her eyes. "Just looking for you," he said.

"Gardener Wu, do you know something I don't?" she asked suspiciously.

"No. But I do know we had all better get to work on the lilac bushes."

~

The next day passed slowly until the time of the performance approached. Both women moped about doing busy work while keeping their eyes on the clock. An hour before the scheduled beginning, Meiying and Meili became whirlwinds of preparation, laughing and giggling like girls.

"This will be what it will be like the rest of our lives together, Meili," enthused Meiying as she modeled her dress, striking a particularly flirtatious pose. "Imagine us in Paris getting ready for a concert."

"So exciting!" replied Meili, struggling with a particularly stubborn button.

"That dress looks beautiful on you!"

"And yours really makes you shine!"

Meiying secluded herself in the corner for a last minute go-through of the score.

A knock on the door.

"Yes?"

"It's Huaqing."

"Come in," called Meiying.

Huaqing cracked open the door and stuck her head in. "They're ready."

"We're coming!"

When they entered the piano room, Meiying saw a small collection of grim-faced Japanese officers sitting straight and proper in their seats. As she adjusted the bench, she noticed Meili standing to the side, uncertain where to go. She certainly could not sit with the soldiers, so Meiying found an empty chair and positioned it by the piano. But just as Meili began to sit, another officer approached and said, "Come with me."

Meili followed the officer outside. Because the piano faced sideways to a long picture-window, Meiying could see the two figures pass by and stop near a tree. The officer spoke, but she could not hear the words. Something was wrong. Very wrong. Meili turned pale and looked around frantically, when two other soldiers rushed up and grabbed her by both arms. She appeared to faint, but the soldiers held her up and dragged her to the tree.

"What's happening?" shouted Meiying. She jumped up, but someone pushed her down onto the bench. She screamed.

Looking in horror, Meiying continued screaming for an explanation. Naguma approached and slapped her.

"She is to be shot," he said matter-of-factly. "As she is executed, you will play the music you were given. The notes you play will be a reminder of the greatness of the Japanese people."

"No! No! No!" Meiying screamed hysterically.

Naguma slapped her again. "If you refuse to play, we will execute not only her but also Gardener Wu. If you still refuse, we will execute Huaqing. And if you still refuse, then you."

Meiying sobbed. "Why? Why? Why?"

Again he slapped her. "Play!"

"I can't! Please! Make them stop!"

Someone pushed Gardener Wu before her. "Play!"

Meiying began to play, glancing out the window and, to her horror, watched Meili tied to the tree, sobbing in her beautiful dress. She played some more. The soldiers aimed. Meiying averted her eyes and played automatically, as if stuck in a ghastly nightmare.

Meili's screams penetrated the room and could be heard above the music. Meiying slammed on the keys to drown out the coming atrocity.

Then shots.

Then nothing.

Meiying stopped playing and sat in a stupor, unable to look outside or continue.

"Play to the end!" demanded Naguma, losing his calm demeanor and descending into a sort of hysteria himself. "Play! Play!" His spit flew in her face.

Meiying slid off the bench to the floor. Her last view was of Gardener Wu pleading for her to play while other Japanese officers rushed to where Naguma stood. Something had happened to him, but Meiying saw nothing more than an enveloping black ocean. Her body floated beneath the surface, suspended, drifting with the currents, drowned.

When she awoke, the bars of a jail cell were the first images that came into view. Meiying's sensibilities, so dulled by anguish, welcomed the realization that she languished alone in a prison rather than be outside and endure the hell she had experienced there.

Miles away, the Precious Object issued forth from within its golden body a furious tapping. Mr. President, observing it at the time, turned pale and appeared frightened, to the astonishment of his retainers. It was then he ordered the statue be delivered to the group of pilgrims when they left.

~ Famine ~

It took only a few hours of biking after they left the temple when the group came upon the first signs of famine. The countryside had changed from verdant green to a barren, charred ruin, shimmering black, scattered with bits of undigested vegetation; a dying tree here, a skeletal bush there. It was as if the earth disgorged the fertile contents of its belly and now the sun had begun the process of evaporating and desiccating whatever vile moisture and solid ejecta remained. Dust blew everywhere, and great, black checkerboards of earth outlined the ashy crematoria of once-lush rice fields. The few peasants they passed had not even the strength to beg, lolling stupor-like atop the dried and cracking soil that had sustained them for generations when it teemed with food in better times.

"God, this is terrible," commented Peter on the obvious during one of their rest stops.

"What do you think happened here?" John asked Mr. Gao.

"Probably drought." He shook his head. "But there's more to it. Maybe the Japs. They send advance units to destroy certain areas. Soften them up before the main force comes."

"Scorched-earth," said Lu Zhishen.

"Yes. It's terrible," agreed Mr. Gao.

"So the Japs could be here now," said John, half-commenting, half-questioning.

"Of course, of course!" cried Feng Shiren. "This is what makes life interesting!"

"Which is a curse," said Mr. Gao.

"What is a curse?" asked John.

"An interesting life," replied Gao. "I asked a few peasants along the way about what happened, but the poor fellows could only stare at me as if I spoke gibberish. They couldn't speak, or wouldn't."

"Christ, how far will this go on?"

"Who knows?" said Lu.

"We have enough food to last a while," observed Madame Liu. "But if we're attacked, things could get very bad."

"Aye, there's the rub!" exclaimed Peter in his best Shakespearian voice.

"We'd better ration, cut our food intake," continued Madame Liu.

"I agree," said Master Zhou. "My stomach has gotten too big again."

"But the children!" objected Mr. Gao. "We can't cut their rations!"

"Of course not. But we adults can."

A spirited debate ensued about how much to cut.

"Listen!" cried Mr. Feng.

Everybody fell silent and heard faint, but unmistakable tapping come from the box. This was not the frantic drumbeat heard by Mr. President, but a slow, melancholy dirge.

"You hear?" asked Feng. "Is it sad, or angry?"

"Or neither," said Madame Liu.

Foolish foolish humans! Came the voice in John's head. Male. Truth be known, he half-expected it. Every time the tapping commenced, it seemed the voice made its appearance sooner or later.

Why are they fools? John asked the voice without saying the words aloud—he was learning.

Fools! First Principles must apply! Leave them and the others to their fate. Non-intervention!

But why are humans fools?

Same reason you are a fool!

Then why do you want me to have a son? Will he be a fool, or worthless?

You have already been told, it is Goddess and Her ilk who wants you to have a son. Yes, and in spite of genetic manipulation, he will be a fool! And as futile as the other failures! But for....

But for what?

But for Her.

"Why for *her*?" John said aloud before he could stop himself.

"Why what?" asked Mr. Feng.

John looked confused at this question, and he saw the rest of the group glance at each other. "I know what you're all thinking, but *she* really does talk to me."

Madame Liu stared into his eyes. "What is *she* saying, John?"

"It's not about you, none of you."

"But maybe it is, John," said Peter. "Tell us what *she* is saying."

"It's just nonsense," John replied dismissively.

"John!" Madame Liu said in an unusually forceful tone she rarely used. "You are not alone here. We have come to believe the voice you hear is somehow connected to our journey, to the Precious Object, to *her*. Even if you think its nonsense, tell us anyway."

Don't tell them! It's a trick!

"Honestly, Madame Liu, I would tell you if I understood the words myself." John waved his arms in a sign of futility. He appeared confused and agitated.

"Okay, okay, old chap," said Peter. "You don't have to tell us, but maybe what it says is code. If you tell us, we could all help break the code together."

Keep quiet! It's a trick!

"I . . . I don't know," stammered John, the voice scrambling his thoughts. "Just . . . forget it."

Madame Liu frowned. "Let's go, we still have a few hours of sunlight."

"Yeah," said Lu Zhishen pulling at his beard. "Can't leave this place fast enough." He straightened his bike and tilted his head toward the box. "At least it's not tapping anymore."

"Hopefully a good sign," said Madame Liu.

"Children!" called Mr. Gao to the kids running playfully in the distance. "We're leaving!"

They came running to their bikes like puppies to food. John noticed the fear underlying their youthful enthusiasm—the fear of being left behind. He felt the same way; this place seemed cursed.

"Not cursed," said Feng to John.

John's eyebrows raised. "How did you know what I was thinking?"

"I know what is obvious," said Feng, adding under his breath, "Your son is writing this book, after all."

"What?" snapped John.

"Nothing! Let's go!"

They both started off down the road. "Why not cursed?" asked John.

Feng laughed. "Look around, listen to the Precious Object tapping away. It's not angry, it's sad, or content. If it's content, this place can't be cursed."

"You're crazy," scoffed John.

No, he's not, came the soothing voice of Goddess. ***You're the Chosen One. You are the one they think is crazy. Foolish mutant boy, you don't have schizophrenia. Believe it or not, you are the beginning, one step leading to the next step. Oh, never mind. You'll see. Right now you are understandably confused, a bit like the first Homo sapiens surrounded by cognitive inferiors. Confused. Disoriented. A genetic mosaic. All in good time.***

John Powers! bellowed God. ***There have been other first steps. They failed. You are but another attempt that is doomed to failure, like all the others.***

They were not failures! exclaimed Goddess. ***John, you are the Chosen One. Do not listen to the distortions spewed by this jealous and insecure God!***

With this admonishment, John pedaled on without speaking, his eyes fixed on the road, his thoughts fixed on the final destination; his intent to starve the voice of attention. In spite of Feng calling out to him many times, John ignored every attempt to raise his interest.

They think you're crazy! You're not schizophrenic! But they think you're crazy! Have no fear, the worm will turn!

"Shut up! Shut up!"

So it went, kilometer after kilometer, until at last they pulled off the road and hastily set-up camp. The voice had stopped for some time, so John's mood gradually improved until he inexplicably felt euphoric. Peter was always a good target for poking fun at.

"Hey, Peter!"

"What?"

"We beat your king fair and square!"

Peter looked amazed. "Not my king. I'm still an American, you bleedin' colonial. My king is just the King's English, not the old bastard himself."

"Shakespeare over Twain?"

"John, my fellow American friend, never the Twain shall meet."

"Shut up, you idiots!" shouted Lu Zhishen jovially. "Canadians need their sleep!"

Peter laughed. "What's a big, dumb Canadian know about English literature?"

"For that matter," added John. "What's a big, dumb Canadian know about anything?"

"Oh, they know a lot," said Peter. "Children's rhymes about the Northwest Mounted Police."

"You Americans are just too barbaric to understand!" chortled Lu.

Suling, tired and irritated, called out, "You silly boys be quiet!"

Mr. Gao added, "That's right. Hush! The children need their sleep!"

"No we don't," said Little Acorn to the giggles of his fellows.

"Hush!"

John closed his eyes and felt an unbreakable bond to these cherished voices, and could not help but contrast them to the one that haunted his mind. His voice reminded him of the tapping; is it good or bad? Happy or angry? No, not happy, but angry? Yes. Or frustrated. Who knows? Useless.

Fallen from euphoria, John sank back into one of his depressions. Meiying was far away and getting farther. Now he found himself surrounded by devastation and famine. His goal seemed too distant, and demons lurked all along the path. *Damn! Why didn't I just go back to the States? Damn!*

Now, paradoxically, he wanted the voice to return. In a perverted sense, he wanted to roll in his own mental excrement. Prove just how crazy he could be. Didn't care anymore. The hell with *her*! Damned hell is hell to the damned.

"John, is everything okay?"

Startled out of his half-sleep, John saw Suling sitting cross-legged next to him.

"Couldn't sleep and heard you talking," she said.

"Ah."

"Is everything okay?"

"Yeah. You should asleep be." His Chinese was as mushy as his mind.

"Couldn't."

Suling remained, to his relief.

"Suling," he said rather sheepishly. "Do you think Meiying is okay?" A childish question, he thought after he asked it.

"I really don't know. But, John, she is smart and knows how to survive."

"Same as you," replied John.

Suling laughed and covered her mouth. "No, I was just a silly girl. *She* saved me."

"What was *she* like, Suling? I mean really, was *she* pretty?"

Suling looked surprised. "You saw *her*! You know, don't you?"

"Yes, but not for long."

"So," Suling smiled, the corners of her eyes fragmenting into running cracks of amusement. "What did *she* look like to you? Was *she* pretty?"

"Beautiful!"

"*Her* hair?"

John was stymied. When he thought of *her*, he seemed unable to call forth a definite image. "It was also beautiful. But seriously, Suling, I saw *her* only for a few minutes. You spent a lot of time with *her*. What did *she* look like?"

"Beautiful!" Suling mimicked John's voice.

They both laughed. John said, "We're getting nowhere. Let's start with *her* hair. What did it look like?"

"Long and silky and black, like all Chinese girls."

John felt his chest constrict and he struggled to control an outburst, but in the end cried, "Chinese? Not American?"

Suling chuckled as if expecting this response. "No, Chinese—to me."

"To you?"

"Yes. Might as well tell you now, all of us have seen *her* differently. To some, beautiful and Chinese, to others, dignified and Canadian. You see?"

"No."

"When the group came together, over time, we compared our memories and realized *she* took different forms."

"That's why Peter never answered my questions."

"Yes, partly. Also, we weren't sure about you." Again she chuckled. "You were also different."

"Oh. But how did you all know *she* was the same if *she* looked so different?"

Suling held out her hands, palms up. "*Her* entire being, what you call *her* aura. And *her* words. Remember the question *she* asked the first time *she* met you?"

"Yes, *she* said, "How does one justify a life without cruelty, and therefore also without the distilled beauty of cruelty?"

"Right. Such an odd question! None of us could answer *her*."

"Did *she* say to you: 'Fate starves at probability's door.'"

"Of course."

"You didn't tell me *she* said these things that horrible time when your family was killed."

"On purpose."

"Oh, Suling, I wish you had told me earlier. I wish all of you had told me. Maybe I wouldn't have had so many doubts."

Suling smiled sympathetically. "On purpose."

John always felt like a child when he spoke with Suling, and he gladly fell into that role again. "Suling, do you think *she* will be able to tell me about Meiying when we reach the final destination?"

"I hope so."

This answer did not satisfy. "I mean, how much power does *she* really have?"

"Perhaps that is what we all want to know, and why we're all making this journey."

Chapter Nine

More Trials

Father Durant Redux

Meiying endured a week of imprisonment, her cell alive with rats and cockroaches. Initially, her disgust overcame her exhaustion, and sleep came only in fits and starts. Gradually, just the larger rats woke her with their thumping bodies, or when there was a screeching fight between them. As for the cockroaches, she became numb to their lightweight scurrying across her body, so that only when the probing covered her face did she awaken to disgustedly brush them off.

During that entire time, she had no visitors and was not allowed to bathe. Still, alone with her thoughts, she determinedly pushed aside the images of Meili's last moments, instead focusing on rejoining the group and reaching the final destination. For hours she pictured them traveling on the road, laughing and joking, moving ever closer to paradise. But here she languished. Left behind. Motionless. Desperately in need of healing, Meiying clung to the belief that *she* would cleanse the wounds and make her whole again, when the glorious moment came that she too would reach the final destination. What she would give to be with them!

Clanging keys and the thud of boots on tile announced the approach of men. When the jailor opened the cell door, Colonel Naguma stepped through and stood over her. Anger and fear mixed, causing her face to flush crimson. She looked away.

"Get up!" he ordered.

She ignored him.

The jailor wrenched her to her feet.

"I keep my promises," he said in a controlled fury. "You will be stripped naked and given over to Father Durant. We Japanese are merciful. I could just kill you, but now you will be in the kind and gentle care of a Christian priest. I am sure he will treat you the way you deserve. I have been informed he is very creative."

Meiying did not respond.

Naguma stood, waiting. At last he said, "If you beg forgiveness, you may return to the mansion."

Only now did she notice something wrong with the left side of his face. Unmistakably there was a slackness, a slight blurring of his words.

"You had a stroke?" she blurted.

Naguma struggled to enunciate his words clearly. "I spared Gardener Wu, although he is a little worse for wear. But he can still work, and still needs help."

Yes, definitely a stroke, Meiying decided. She felt a brief pang of sympathy, then remembered Meili and straightened herself. "I will not beg for forgiveness. On the dead body of Meili, I won't. It is you who should beg."

Naguma visibly trembled at these words, whether in anger or something else, she could not decipher. His left arm hung motionless while his right swayed above her, as if he waved. "Is the priest waiting?" he asked the jailor.

"Yes, sir."

"Do it," he whispered. His arm finally dropped.

"Yes, sir!"

Noticing the jailor's enthusiasm, Naguma added, "Make sure you don't hurt her."

"Yes, sir." The jailor stepped forward, his eyes glittering.

"Wait!" cried Naguma. He stared at Meiying with an expression she could not read. "Wait until I'm gone, then do it." Turning on his heel, he left without a backward glance.

Meiying stood silently while the guard stripped her and tied her hands behind her back. "Can't cover yourself now, Chinese bitch," he murmured. "You're lucky."

"No, I'm not," she said.

The jailor glanced around, and assured that no one was watching, fondled her breasts and pinched her nipples. "Oh yes, bitch. You're lucky."

When she was led out to the main reception room of the jail, all eyes were on her. Determined to stare defiantly ahead, her eyes met Father Durant's, who stood with a long cloak ready to drape over her. As he placed it around her shoulders, he said, "I knew you would be brought back to face your redemption."

A car waited, its motor running. Leaving the jail, Meiying thought she saw a kind, familiar face amidst the gawking crowd. It was only a fleeting look, but it could be none other than Master Yu, his sympathetic smile a welcoming full moon illuminating the darkness. She clung to this brief moment of encouragement before being pushed into the back seat.

When they arrived at the priest's house, he led her to a specially outfitted room. Bars on the windows and a reinforced door. "Now you're my guest, and the stain of Japanese infidel corruption must be removed."

She said nothing.

"Child, do you not want to be purified even now? You have the talents, the potential to be another Joan of Arc. Can you not see that?"

"May I bathe?" she asked.

"What?"

"I need a bath."

"How can you be concerned with such trivial matters? Redemption awaits—and you want a bath?"

"Yes."

Durant appeared disgusted, as if his prize but wayward student had learned nothing.

"Rachel!" he called. An older Chinese servant entered.

"Give this woman a bath. Give her clothes from the charity bin, and send her to bed."

The woman, almost toothless, bowed and held out her arm for Meiying to follow. After untying her hands, the servant drew a bath. Meiying sat in warm, luxurious water, leaning against the back of the tub, while the woman ladled hot water over her.

"Thank you so much," said Meiying, not expecting a reply.

"Hmmm."

"What is your name?"

"Rachel."

"No, your Chinese name."

The woman paused, as if trying to remember. Meiying assumed she took the time to think of her name, but no. "You are the first to ask," she finally said.

"What do you mean? Surely, outside, your family?"

"Family dead but for young children. No outside but for young children. Father Durant is my father."

"He gave you your name?"

"Yes."

"Do you like it?"

"From the Bible, so good."

"So you are very grateful to Father Durant?"

She paused again, then crinkled her nose. "He is man."

Meiying's heart raced. "Good man?"

"No. Man."

"Bad man?"

"Man."

The woman is dull-witted, thought Meiying. *Perhaps if I make a friend of her.*

Meiying stood and dried off. She caught the eyes of the woman and pointed. "Your name is Rachel. I'm Meiying. How are you?" She enunciated as if talking to a child.

Rachel shrugged and said, "Wait. I'll bring clothes."

"Thank you. You are good."

Rachel looked around. "Of course I'm good, silly woman."

Meiying felt stunned, and before she could respond, the woman whispered, "I'm going to help you escape, but it has to look natural. The Japs work with Father Durant. If you're caught, we'll both be shot."

"Why are you doing this?"

"Don't be stupid. I've worked for this monster many years. As he has gotten more unbalanced, I have gotten more simple-minded."

"I see."

"Look, I'm not doing this for you. For some reason, the people at the temple want you back. Although I don't know how they'll keep you if they do. Not my business."

"Why do you stay with him?"

"Money, of course. Father Durant pays me well because I keep quiet and don't talk about what I see. As long as my children don't starve."

"Oh, so the temple is also paying you?"

Rachel leered. "Of course. Milk all the bastards. The sacred ones are the easiest because they have fooled themselves for so long, we others find them easy pickings."

"When can we—"

"Hush! You have to wait for a while. Be patient. Play along with him."

"Patient. Yes, I can be patient. Will he hurt me?"

"Maybe, but he won't kill you. He never kills them, as far as I know. Just breaks 'em."

"Rape?"

Rachel's eyes went dim. "Man."

~

Meiying returned to her locked room. She desperately wanted to escape now, while she was clean and untouched by Father Durant. *Naguma implied the priest is homosexual*, she thought. *But . . . ah! Too much!*

Hunger made her lethargic and she sat listlessly for hours, waiting. *Maybe Master Yu will come*, she thought. *Burst through the door and take me back to the safety of the temple!* She had to smile at her own foolishness.

At last Father Durant came, smelling of wine, giving his face a red sheen that accentuated his rather sunken, feverish eyes. Meiying saw that his good looks were turning rancid from some inner poison. His face seemed to be caving-in; cheeks, eye-sockets. Though he had plenty of food he was clearly starving. Meiying had decided on her strategy; she would be grateful and obsequious, having found god thanks to the godless Japanese.

"Father Durant! Thank you, thank you for saving me! I prayed to God when the Japs imprisoned me, and He has answered my prayers." She thought she went too fast, but his face invited more. "You were right, God is good and all-powerful. I am redeemed! Will you allow me to join your flock?" This last might be too much, she feared. But he merely stared, swaying like a sapling in the breeze.

"Redemption is not so cheap," he said with some difficulty, his words slurred and tinged with a drunk's attempt at sarcasm.

"Ah, yes. I will pray regularly and clean your floors—scrub them spic-and-span."

"Don't want you to clean my floors," he mumbled like a pouting child. "You're a whore and whores must be cleansed. Have to do it. Have no choice."

Meiying retreated. He lunged and grabbed her dress as he fell heavily to the floor. She angrily tugged the hem out of his hand. Durant let out a drunken laugh. "This is ridiculous. Not tonight, whore. Tomorrow. Sober is so-ber-est. Couldn't get it up anyway. You're too beautiful. Devil's work. Tomorrow. To-morrow is the reckoning."

She nodded, hoping only that he would retire. He did so without another word, walking carefully to preserve what dignity remained.

Durant was too far gone for mischief that night.

It was the following night that he came for her.

~

Meiying, again locked in the room, did not see Rachel all the next day. She longed to question the woman about escape, but the opportunity never arose. Eventually, her mind wandered to happier times, when freedom to the talented young pianist was taken for granted. She had the run of Shanghai, unburdened by school and the unwanted attention of boys. Glorious days! So many people looked after her; a kind music tutor whom she loved and who taught the funda-mentals with an endearing passion, a strict tutor of academic subjects who drilled knowledge deep and secure into her mind, a weepy tutor of French who taught her more than the language, and a penchant for breezing through everything they threw at her. "Smart girl," her father often said. "Hush! Don't tempt the gods!" her mother always replied. Meiying loved them both dearly, and only now understood how much she missed them. And freedom! Oh, how she itched to throw open the door and rush out to wander anywhere her fancy took her. Freedom! She looked in a mirror for signs of the toll that her long imprisonment and rape had taken. Yes, unmistakable. Did she hate the men who did this? Yes. Unmistakable. Hate had always been an alien concept to her, like some foreign food one tried and found unpalatable. Now, it tasted good, and that frightened her.

It happened that Father Durant entered during these musings. Dusk. She had just turned on the light when his figure stood in the open door.

"Come in," she said lightly. "I want to talk to you about Jesus. I have many questions." Meiying had resolved to stick to her strategy.

"Tricks!" he cried. "The devil's tricks!"

Meiying now understood she could only expect the worst.

"No, no," she said, inadvertently holding up her hands. "The demons had me, but thanks to you, I have escaped them. I will no longer be a whore, but instead spend my life seeking Jesus, with your help."

His face remained passive, but she continued with the resolve of desperation. "Father Durant, I need your help and the kindness that I know lies within you."

"Yes, I see. Rachel!" he opened the door and called again, "Rachel!"

When she appeared, he said, "Bring us tea. Especially for Miss Bai. Bring her the special tea for lost souls. I'll have a cup also, though my soul is anything but lost," he chuckled at his little *bon mot*. Regaining his stern face, he turned back to Meiying. "I see, I see. Let's sit and discuss this situation. You feel no more demons possess you?"

"No, not at all. But I still need your kind help to keep them away. As I said, I can do chores, clean—"

He held up his hand. "No! That is out of the question."

"What then?" Meiying tried to anticipate where this man's mind was going.

"Ah, here's the tea. Thank you, Rachel. First have some tea. It will make you feel better." He followed Rachel to the door and closed it behind her.

Meiying waited until Durant took the first sip of his before having some herself.

"Now," he said. "Our first task is to make sure the demons have left your body. To begin, a strict regimen of prayer and abstinence. After that. . . . "

As he droned on, the words blurred, then no longer registered, and Meiying knew she had been drugged. She didn't fight it, happy to drift away. She let oblivion come and slid down and sideways into her chair, pulling up her knees like a little girl and returning to the happy times in Shanghai.

Father Durant waited until he knew she was completely out, then stood and looked at her curled-up body, his eyes taking in every centimeter of the girl's figure. If an observer occupied a corner of the room, he or she would not be able to anticipate what the eyes conveyed, but whatever they reflected, nothing good could come of their glistening intensity.

~ *The Group Encounters the Japanese* ~

One morning, as the group slept off the road under a grove of sycamore trees, the ground shook with a deep rumbling. As usual, Feng Shiren happened to be awake. Dawn was still an hour away when lights from a passing Japanese convoy illuminated a malevolent-looking dust storm kicked-up by the treads of tanks and armored personnel carriers. Infantry, guarding the flanks, scurried around the metallic monsters, moving in and out of the dark clouds like probing ants. Feng quickly woke the group and they rushed to melt back deeper into the shelter of the grove. Not a word was spoken, but everyone's face reflected the grim visage of controlled panic. Many a person tripped in the dark or ran into a tree trunk.

Behind, the crackle of radios and Japanese voices drove them on. By the time they reached a noxious swamp, early light suffused the atmosphere, but the voices could still be heard. No one wanted to wade into the fetid water, and the group hesitated like swimmers before an icy lake. Madame Liu took the plunge first, her bike quickly becoming a sticky burden, the food containers soaked by the muddy sludge. The rest followed. Dead tree trunks poked up from the mire, scalloped with moss and tendrils of rope-like vines. Everyone struggled to maneuver their bikes and keep the others in sight. Small islands of dry ground dotted the mire, but no one wanted to risk stopping. After an interminable struggle through the muck, Japanese voices could no longer be heard, so Madame Liu strained to exit the swamp via an inviting outcropping of solid ground. She slipped trying to climb up a nasty slope. Feng appeared next to her.

"Help is here!" he cried almost happily as he pushed her from behind.

By the time the last person collapsed from exhaustion on semi-dry ground, a quick count revealed they were short Mr. Gao and one of the younger children. Shouting out for them was out of the question. Feng, Peter, Lu, and John volunteered to re-enter the swamp and search. Madame Liu and Master Zhou, now the titular heads of the expedition, agreed and set about the task of cleaning the bikes and salvaging as much food as possible. As usual, Little Acorn wanted to follow Feng Shiren, but was told in no uncertain terms to remain with the others. His "But I can help!" objections were met with a deaf ear by Feng. To his distress, Little Acorn was tasked with helping the others clean mud off the bikes.

Meanwhile, the four volunteers agreed to spread out, but to keep each other in sight. With the sun's rays now warming the water, a thickish fog undulated atop the surface. As they moved, they periodically stopped at Feng's signal to listen for any sounds, friend or foe. Gradually, they gained confidence that the Japanese had moved on, and conversed in hushed voices.

"Wonder where they could be?" asked Peter rhetorically.

"Could be anywhere," Lu stated the obvious.

"Why don't we each go in different directions?" suggested John.

"No way," said Feng. "Then you'll all get lost."

"Not you?" scoffed Lu Zhishen.

"Not me."

"What makes you so special?"

"I am Feng Shiren."

"Yup, he's special," laughed Peter.

"If we run into the Japs, what do we say?" asked John to anyone who would respond.

Feng shrugged. "We're monks."

"Sure, wandering around in a swamp," said Lu. "What the hell, they'll believe that!"

"Spies," said Peter. "We'd be shot as bloody spies. That's a fact."

John waded on, lost in thought. The others continued talking, but he didn't listen. Again the notion of being killed in a foreign land, a swamp no less, while on a journey to search for the specter of some unearthly woman with magical powers seemed unspeakably outrageous.

Many years from now the fate of your son will also be connected to a swamp, in yet another foreign land, in yet another war, while searching for yet another outlandish specter. The universe turns. Oh, if only you could see past the distorting lens of your human genes!

"You're more interested in my son than me," said John like a pouting child.

Yes, of course. You are merely the beginning, but your son....

"What?" asked Peter.

"Nothing."

"It's your damn voice again, isn't it? I can always tell. You just seem to leave the planet, your face goes all blank, and you say completely irrelevant things."

Tell Peter to tend his own garden. His demons will soon enough tend to him!

"Stop it Peter. It's nothing."

"This isn't working," said Feng to the group. "We're too close together to do any effective search."

They stood waist-deep in the water, shivering and caked with mud.

"Suggestions?" asked Feng.

"Yeah, let's all start shouting," replied Lu Zhishen. "Maybe they'll hear us. Seems obvious the Japs aren't around anymore."

"Does it?" asked Peter.

"Yeah, it does."

"How do you know?"

"Well, fuck, just listen. No, I mean it. Listen!"

They listened, expecting to hear nothing, but a voice came in the distance; faint, the words indistinct. Instinctively, they crouched down and strained their ears.

"Hello!" came the voice, stronger now. "Hello, is anybody there?"

"Mr. Gao!" cried John.

Feng shouted, "Over here!"

The others joined in. "Over here! Over here!"

Mr. Gao appeared, a shadowy figure through the fog. He splashed through the mud holding a young child who appeared to be dead, her arms hanging limply.

Gao, breathless and exhausted, waded up to Lu Zhishen and handed the girl over to his strong arms.

"Is she dead?" asked John.

"No," said Mr. Gao. "She fell in a hole and almost drowned. It took me forever to find her and get her breathing again. She's just worn out, poor thing."

Lu gently shook the girl, and her eyes fluttered open briefly, then closed again. He grinned. "She's alive!"

"Yes, she's alive," said Mr. Gao with his usual perceptive economy of words. "But if we don't reach some dry place soon, I fear she'll die."

"Yes, yes, let's go back!" commanded Feng.

They waded back toward Madame Liu and the others. As they approached the bank that led to dry ground, Feng shouted, "Hello! We're coming! We found them!"

No response.

He tried again.

No response.

John felt his stomach drop. "Something's wrong," he said.

Feng motioned for them to stay put, then labored his way up the slippery embankment. His head disappeared and the others waited impatiently, so tired they were not even prepared to run if trouble erupted. But only silence prevailed.

Looking at each other nervously, Peter broke the quiet by cupping his hand and calling, "Hello! What's going on? Hello!"

No response

Their nervousness ratcheted up exponentially.

"Hello!"

Nothing.

"I'm going up," said Lu. "Here, hold Huiliang." He gave the girl over to John.

"Keep us in sight," stuttered Mr. Gao. "Don't lose sight of us. We can't just stand here and freeze to death."

"Okay."

Lu made his way up the muddy slope, and when he reached the top, looked back to make sure he could still be seen. He gave a thumbs-up which was returned. Lu's head turned this way and that, and he said with finality, "No one here. No one."

"Call for them!" cried Peter.

He did.

Nothing.

No longer willing to wait, the others scrambled up the slope, Lu giving them a helping hand. Once they were all happily ensconced on solid ground, the detective work began.

"Where's Feng?"

"He's gone. Disappeared."

"Look at the ground. See any disturbance?"

"Any sign of struggle?"

"Nope."

"Well, fan out then. Call if you see something," said Mr. Gao. "I'll watch Huiliang."

But try as they might, no tracks were discernable, no sign of trouble, nothing.

"What now?" queried Peter when they huddled together again.

"Wow. No food, no bikes. . . . " said Lu.

"No Precious Object," added Peter.

"And none of the others," said Mr. Gao.

"Fuck! What a goddamn mess!" blurted Lu.

"What I don't get is where Feng went off to," said John. "He was only gone a few minutes."

"How can there be no tracks?" Peter asked the air.

"Doesn't matter," said Mr. Gao. "We need to start walking. Must be a village around here. Huiliang needs dry clothes and food."

Everyone mumbled agreement, somewhat embarrassed they had been standing around whining.

"Which direction?"

Mr. Gao pointed toward the driest stretch. "That way."

"Good as any," said Peter.

"I'll carry the girl," volunteered Lu.

"We'll take turns," said Gao.

So off they trudged, wet and miserable, but relieved they were at least moving. John thought they were like visitors stranded on an alien planet, unsure what monstrous calamity might await over the next hill, but glad, at least, they still lived. Not much time had passed before they ran into a trail with evidence of human traffic. They readily followed the trail until it led past a forester's cottage. The structure was little more than a dilapidated shack. An old man sat on the front porch braiding a rope while puffing on a pipe.

"Hello!" cried Mr. Gao as if they were on a pleasant stroll in the park.

The forester nodded.

"We are travelers unfamiliar with this country, old father. Can you direct us to the nearest village?"

The man fiddled with his pipe, then clamped down on it with his teeth. "Are you monks or murderers? Don't want throat slit."

"Monks," replied Gao.

He looked stupefied and gaped through the pipe smoke at the foreigners.

Mr. Gao laughed. "You may well stare. These are visiting monks from other lands."

The old forester grunted and tamped his pipe with a filthy thumb.

"Anyone else pass this way?" Gao asked.

"Yes, yes, many people."

"Ah! Other monks, including some nuns?"

"Many people; monks, villagers, beggars, soldiers, children."

"Soldiers? What soldiers?"

"Many people; monks, villagers, beggars, soldiers, children."

"When?" Gao asked patiently.

The man rolled his eyes as if asking him to think was like asking him to walk across hot coals. "Hours, days, weeks, months."

Mr. Gao seemed irritated, but pressed on. "No, I mean today. Today. See anyone today?"

"Yes, yes. Monks, villagers, beggars, soldiers, children."

An old woman appeared in the doorway of the shack. "You have food?" she asked, then almost as an afterthought, added harshly, "He's become foolish."

Mr. Gao nodded. "I see."

"You have food?" she held out her hand to receive whatever would be offered.

Gao shook his head. "Have you seen anyone pass by today?" he asked.

"You have food?" she repeated.

"No, sorry. Well, does this path lead to a village?"

"Yes, yes, village. Go there, come back with food please good monks." She flashed a toothless smile. "For my old fool."

"Are you sure you haven't seen anyone today?" Lu directed his question toward the woman.

She gaped at him while the old man said, "Monks, villagers, beggars, soldiers, children."

As the little group moved on, the woman's voice repeated in the distance. "Bring food! Bring food!"

"Christ!" exclaimed Peter. "What have we gotten ourselves into?"

"Famine!" came a loud voice. Feng Shiren, dramatically jumped out from behind some bushes and assumed one of his favorite operatic poses. "You've gotten into famine!" he repeated. After the chorus of shocked questions, it turned out that Feng had followed the same trail and was about to return when they came upon him. All of them were by now so used to his outrageous comings-and-goings that no one found his behavior strange.

As it turned out the village was not far, and the ragged, muddy group entered on a small side trail far from the central district, weary and dejected.

~ *Meiying Awakens 1* ~

It took a while after Meiying opened her eyes to realize where she was. Foggy world. Blurry world. But she soon remembered that she had been drugged. *Good, that much is established*, she thought. Now it seemed imperative that she locate her body. Arms, legs, and torso floated every which way, and her head levitated some distance above the parts. When her brain ordered her arms and hands to reach out and collect all the pieces to put them back together, it quickly became apparent that the commands had the distressing effect of making them jerk and float apart in random directions. In fact, worse, because only when the hands clenched and unclenched to catch the wayward parts did they detach from the wrists and sail away on their own unpredictable paths. Now the room was so cluttered with body parts, it looked as if the contents of some cannibal stew-pot had been flung to the wind.

At last she understood she must be dreaming, and because much of her dream involved the unsuccessful attempt to control her arms and legs, she found it all quite amusing. But then darker events intruded. Other body parts, not hers, began floating about; hairy arms, hairy legs, an erect penis. These male body parts seemed to have a force that repelled the female parts and pressed them against the walls. Meiying searched for the male head that belonged to these limbs, but saw none. Two male arms grabbed her armless, legless torso and held it while the penis moved like a shark toward her vagina. She tried to command her parts to come to its aid, but they twitched helplessly against the walls.

Looking from a distance, she saw the penis push apart her labia and slide into her vagina. Her detached head viewed the rape from the perspective of a horrified bystander. But the shock of pain when penetration struck home made her convulse and all the parts flew from the periphery of the room and reassembled themselves to defend against the violation.

This reconfiguration now made the surreal scene more horribly real.

Meiying realized something was dreadfully wrong. Before, she dimly perceived this was only a dream, but now. . . .

~ *Meiying Awakens 2* ~

"Nooo! No! No!" Meiying screamed. She snapped back into what must be the real world, where men routinely violated women. Father Durant grinned down at her. Or maybe it was a grimace. But now, his head seemed detached like hers had been earlier. It drifted upward like a balloon in the wind. Her reassembled self must have hit him so hard that his head came off. But that would be impossible. Another dream? She looked down and realized her naked body lay all akimbo on some board that stretched forever. Knotholes dug into her back. When she reached down to feel her vagina, a gushing of sticky fluid poured out, forcing her hand aside. The fluid ran down the center of the board like a milky river. Something in the river, a malevolent snake, dark and ominous, came swimming against the current toward her vagina. She screamed.

~ *Meiying Awakens 3* ~

A hand clamped tightly over her mouth and Meiying struggled to breathe. In a panic she tried to bite the hand to make it go away.

"Shhhh," came a soothing female voice. "Quiet, quiet. It's just me, Rachel. Shhh."

She tried to focus, but something stung her eyes. The light. She moaned.

"Quiet, we don't have much time," whispered Rachel.

Focusing at last, Meiying looked at Rachel in grateful recognition, and saw a Buddhist monk standing behind her.

"Get her dressed!" he said, not unkindly, but with some urgency.

Meiying felt as if her bones had liquefied. She tried to rise, but muscles seemed unattached to any part of her that might result in movement.

"Help me with these knots!" Rachel whispered. Meiying could feel the two tugging on her wrists and ankles, but she remained detached. She knew they were helping her to escape, but her motivation to assist simply wouldn't translate into action.

Finally, she found herself standing next to the monk, or rather held upright by the monk, while Rachel quickly threw a wrap around her. Out of the building she stumbled, assisted by strong hands. The sudden shock of cold air helped clear her mind. Gradually she discerned through the early-morning darkness hordes of people sleeping in the open, along the streets or propped against the walls of shops and assorted other buildings. Weaving around the prone figures, she was hustled through a series of narrow alleyways strewn with trash and more motionless figures until she found herself standing in front of the temple, where Master Yu greeted her with affectionate concern.

"Take her in, let her bathe, and take her to the safe place immediately after."

The relief she felt and the inexpressible joy that overcame her at the sound of that kind, male voice, seemed to overwhelm Meiying's emotions. She cried a flood of tears and repeated "thank you" so many times that her liberators grew weary of hearing it.

Meiying barely had time to enjoy her return to the temple when she was trundled off to the countryside disguised as a crippled woman with some unspecified mental illness. Pretending to limp with the aid of a staff, covered head to toes in rags, accompanied by a young novitiate named Junjie, she retraced the route she had taken so long ago with Father Durant in that miserable cart. The journey rekindled her memories and confronted her with how far she had fallen from grace. Impervious to her fellow traveler's efforts to cheer her up, the pain of having to leave the temple so quickly left her with an anger and frustration not easily assuaged.

"Miss Bai, you must not be so grim," her young escort chided. "Where we are going, you will be safe."

"I'm an old, crippled half-wit, remember? Of course I'm grim."

"You know, the place we're going is run by a most interesting woman."

Meiying grunted unhappily. "How much farther?"

"Just a few kilometers."

As they trudged on, she became curious about this 'interesting woman' in spite of herself. A bit sheepishly, she said, "So, to pass the time my young venerable Junjie, tell me more about this woman."

"Ah, she lives in a grand house that has fallen to ruin. It has a courtyard full of weeds and outer walls covered with dead vines. Within are many buildings and outbuildings, but she lives alone there with just two old servants. The locals think the place is haunted and stay away, which pleases her no end. In fact," Junjie chuckled, "she definitely plays-up the ghost angle."

"At this point," said Meiying with the first hint of regaining her humor. "I prefer ghosts to real men."

"Yes, I can understand."

When they reached the "safe place" as Master Yu called it, they had to walk down a very long dirt lane, deserted of people and lined with the ropy, twisted trunks of dawn redwoods. When they stood outside the wall, Meiying felt a chill looking at the desolate structure, its dead vines and ancient, gnarled trees rising menacingly from the hidden courtyard. Junjie laughed at her hesitation. "Miss Bai, trust me, inside will be quite different from what you think. We even arranged to have a present waiting for you."

Junjie opened the thick wooden doors leading to the courtyard and stepped in as if he were a frequent and cherished visitor. An ancient man with a long wispy beard tottered up and bowed repeatedly as he welcomed the monk.

"Venerable young sir, you are welcome! Who did you bring this time? Eh? Let me look at her. Is she pretty under those rags? Good! We are ready for her."

"Very good, Old Crooked. Yes, she's very pretty under the rags and dirt. Do you have the gift ready?"

Old Crooked rubbed his hands together like an excited child. "Yes, yes. Bring her in, poor dear. Windy out here. Come on, hurry!"

Meiying found herself rushed into the main house. She wanted to look around, but the hustling, bustling Old Crooked and Junjie made it impossible.

"Hey, Old Twisted! Close the gate doors! Hurry, old lady!"

A very old lady, bent but spry, hurried to close the gate doors. She appeared to be the matched unit of a chessboard containing only two pieces: Old Crooked and Old Twisted.

"Are they married?" asked Meiying.

"No, they're brother and sister," said Junjie. "Been here forever, even when it was a grand mansion occupied by a local bigwig. Now, they serve the old lady you're about to meet."

Crossing the courtyard, they had to put their heads down to avoid the swirling leaves. Once inside, Meiying wiped her face with her sleeve as best she could and looked around curiously. A voice came from the corner. Straining her eyes in the dark, Meiying perceived an ancient lady seated in a traditional Chinese chair, hands resting atop the elaborately carved arms.

"I apologize for not greeting you, but my legs are not what they used to be," came the brittle but strangely robust voice. "Come closer."

Meiying stepped closer, the room a fog of incense.

"Old Crooked," she said to the servant. "Hold the lantern up to her face. My eyes aren't what they used to be either."

The flame illuminated Meiying's face in all its beauty and kindly expression.

"So, you are compassionate as well as beautiful," said the old lady. "My name is Madame Chen. I offer my hospitality to those who are brought to me by Master Yu. Usually, they are ones in trouble and in need of . . . seclusion. You have come to the right place."

Meiying bowed deeply and said, "Thank you, Madame Chen. I can't tell you how much I appreciate your receiving me under these circumstances."

The old lady bowed her head. "I have been told you are special." She held out her hands, palms up. "And you search for *her*?"

Meiying's eyes widened. "I do."

Junjie bowed. "Madame Chen, do you require my services any further?"

"You may stay in guest house number three, if you desire, young monk."

"Thank you, no. I must return. We will take the usual precautions. I know her stay with you will be pleasant."

"How long will I be staying with you, Madame Chen?" asked Meiying.

The old lady laughed. "As long as there are Japanese murderers and rapists, Chinese murderers and rapists, and Western priests who don't want to be left out of the entertainment."

"Oh!" cried Junjie. "I almost forgot. Will you show Miss Bai the gift? Perhaps she will favor me with something before I go."

"Of course. Old Crooked, show her to the gift."

"Do you want to come, Madame?" asked Old Crooked. "I can get the wheelchair."

"No, I know I will hear it soon enough."

When Meiying stood in front of the piano, she wept anew. Junjie shuffled in some discomfort at the fresh set of tears, then asked her to play a short piece.

"What would you like me to play, dear?"

"Play what you like. Play beautifully something beautiful."

"If I remember," she replied.

She adjusted the bench and tried a few keys. Gradually, a melody emerged, then a beautiful adagio movement by Mozart. Her fingers flew across the keys and the ecstasy that overcame her transmitted itself to the notes. Even Madame Chen, not a devotee of western music, was moved to tilt her head and listen from the other room. Suddenly, all of the pent-up stress and nerves of the past weeks and months dissolved into the pure joy of playing. Junjie bowed in gratitude and slipped out even as she continued to play. Old Crooked stood in the doorway and stared at her with shining eyes, and he was soon joined by his sister Old Twisted. Like two statues immutably frozen in love, they held hands and gazed upon this wondrous girl who played such odd music.

~ *Old Twisted* ~

Meiying's room seemed decorated to appeal to a young woman's taste and sensibilities. Pictures, vases, silk brocades, wall hangings, all depicted scenes of domestic tranquility, gentility, and natural beauty. Her bed was soft and the linens clean with overstuffed pillows to bury her shame and maximize her comfort. All of this, thought Meiying, stood in stark contrast to the withered, desolate exterior of the mansion. Madame Chen had ordered her to eat a light meal and go to bed. Grateful beyond words, Meiying obeyed and lay awake counting her blessings, unable to sleep due to her inexpressible happiness. Soon, her thoughts turned to the group, and she nodded-off with sweet longings and the long-forgotten luxury of feeling safe and secure.

Morning brought shafts of light through the windows and the scent of tea through an open door in which stood Old Twisted.

"Well, young miss, I have brought tea and a little rice to brighten your morning."

Feeling mortified at her own laziness, Meiying sprang out of bed. "No, no, kind lady, let me go down and fetch breakfast for myself."

"Lay back down," soothed Old Twisted. "Won't hurt you a bit to be pampered. Such a beauty!"

"No, no, not anymore!" cried Meiying. Smoothing her rumpled hair, she murmured, "Thank you, kind lady."

"Call me Old Twisted, little one."

"Oh, I couldn't do that. What is your given name?"

"I honestly don't know," replied the flustered old lady. "When I was young I was called names much worse than Old Twisted."

"Well," said Meiying now sitting in a chair with the teacup proffered by the old woman. "Let's give you a proper name."

"Madame Chen tried, but it never stuck."

"What was it?"

Old Twisted screwed up her eyes. "Heaven knows! That was years ago."

"How about Lanfen?"

The old lady shook her head. "Too fancy for an old cow."

"Nonsense. Then what about Chenguang?"

"Too snooty."

Meiying shook her head. "Then I'll just have to give you my own made-up name. I'll call you Kindness. It's not a proper name, but it fits."

Old Twisted scoffed, but it seemed apparent that she liked the name.

"Let's practice," insisted Meiying. "Kindness, where is your *lao jia*?"

"My home is far away, little princess."

Meiying teared-up. "My days as a princess are over."

"So, you've been wounded?"

Meiying had drawn from her well of stubborn determination the vow to be open and forthright about what happened to her. "Raped. Raped multiple times by many men. I so hate what they did to me!"

"Yes, my dear, I was told. So many these days. Sometimes I think we Chinese women are cursed."

"Yet. . . ." Meiying trailed off into the depths of her own pain.

"Are you?"

"No."

"Then there is a blessing."

"It hurts."

"I have a special balm that will help."

Meiying stood and hugged Old Twisted. "Kindness, I feared what I might find here, but you make me feel safe. I'm so relieved."

Old Twisted patted her like a child. "Many have passed through this old mansion and found comfort." She laughed. "Of course, the villagers think we harbor evil spirits and demons." She raised her arms threateningly and scowled like a most ferocious demon. "And I let them! Oh, how the children run for their lives!"

"I can imagine." Meiying smiled. "Kindness."

"One little scamp in particular I felt great pleasure in scaring. He is a renowned bully in the neighborhood and likes preying on more vulnerable and weak children. His yelping escape from the evil spirits and demons set him down a few pegs in the eyes of his victims."

"Sounds like it served him right," said Meiying.

"Oh, he's a good boy at heart, but full of mischief."

"You see," said Meiying. "You are true to your new name. You are kind."

Old Twisted turned serious. "Today you have an interview with Madame Chen."

"An interview?"

"Yes. She always has a long talk with our guests."

"What about?"

Old Twisted looked amused. "Oh, this and that."
"Kindness, give me a hint."
"Oh, you'll find out."

~ *The Interview* ~

After this discussion, Meiying wandered the unkempt gardens. She felt the weeds and gnarled vines were perfect reflections of the tangled mess her life had become. When she mentioned rape to Kindness, she was assaulted by memories of the humiliation, the gagging, the filth, the pain, the lingering stench, the horror, and the cruelty of men. Where before they were just somewhat large, awkward, unappealing creatures, they now seemed disgusting and dirty. For her, they now only existed from the waist up, if she was to have anything to do with them at all. They would be like busts on a mantle, either good or bad, hero or imposter, but not possessing a body down below. That netherland of rotten decay and revolting musk even now made her choke. *If only Meili were here*, she thought over and over. *If only Meili were here. . . .*

"Miss Bai!"
"Yes?"
Old Crooked stood in a side doorway overlooking the garden. He waved his arm and smiled broadly, with just a hint of sympathetic empathy. "She'll see you now!"
"Oh. I'm coming."
When Meiying entered the room where Madame Chen waited, the atmosphere seemed weighted down with a dark melancholy. Tea steamed on a small table, and the old lady gestured for Meiying to sit close. Old Crooked poured a cup of tea and she sipped it under Madame Chen's watchful eye. Silence pervaded the room, and Meiying did not want to be the first to speak, so she sat quietly and smiled.
"So, you were raped?" asked Madame Chen bluntly and unexpectedly.
"Yes," whispered Meiying, taken aback by this first question.
"And you hate men?"
"No."
"Nonsense, of course you do."
"I don't hate men. I hate what they do, sometimes."
Madame Chen made a sour face. "My husband was a brute and he raised our sons to be like him. All of them have gone to their reward, and so here I am, alone and quite happy about it. Still, do you want to be alone the rest of your life?"
"No."
Madame Chen seemed dubious. "Are you a lesbian?"
This question struck Meiying like an arrow to the heart. Another blunt inquiry so soon after the first barely gave her time to think. Lie or tell the truth? She hesitated.
"I know you are a lesbian," said the old lady with a finality that brooked no denial.

"How do you know that, Madame Chen?" Meiying asked in genuine surprise.

"I hear things. I have spies. I am careful who I bring into this house. I am old and unwilling to suffer inconvenience for someone I dislike. You are a lesbian, are you not?"

Meiying looked down and said in a barely audible whisper, "Yes."

The old lady sat up straight. "So am I, and proud of it!"

Meiying continued to look down, but her heart raced with surface shocks and deeper possibilities. Suddenly, she felt a mystical connection with this woman, and curiosity filled her mind with questions she could not ask. It became apparent to her that the world was filled with an amazing number of these isolated and invisible women—more than even the boldest thinker could imagine.

"Child, look at me," said Madame Chen in a soft, encouraging voice. "Now, you must have questions. I know you have questions. This interview is now reversed. Ask."

Meiying stumbled. "How . . . when. . . . "

"Take a deep breath. Think. Ask."

"When did you know?"

"Always."

"Your parents?"

"Beat me."

"What did you do?"

"Ran away."

"How did you live?"

For the first time, Madame Chen paused, then, "The usual."

"How could you stand it?"

"How couldn't I?"

"But your husband?"

"Never knew, but suspected."

"How . . . why?"

"Remember I told you he was a brute. Beat me, like my father."

"It must have been horrible," Meiying said, unable to control a shudder. "Did you find comfort elsewhere?"

"Did you?" asked the old lady.

"Yes."

"Her name?"

"Meili."

"Dead?"

"Of course."

Madame Chen looked at Meiying with shining eyes. "I heard. Child, you are truthful, and for that I am relieved. You may stay as long as you like."

"But—"

"This interview is over. You may leave."

Old Crooked appeared at the behest of some unknowable command and escorted Meiying out of the room.

"How did it go?" he whispered.

"I don't know."

He laughed a high-pitched cackle, eyes dancing in amusement. "Oh, I know it went well. Otherwise. . . . "

"Otherwise?"

"You would not see the dawn from this house."

Meiying's eyes widened.

"No, not killed, silly girl. We never kill. Just banished."

"Why?"

"If you didn't please her." Old Crooked walked her over to a window. "See that figure in the distance near the top of the hill?"

"Yes."

"It's Junjie, the monk. He waited here last night without your knowledge until after the interview. Now he knows you will be truly safe."

Old Crooked waved, and received a wave in return before the young monk disappeared over the hill.

~

Later that same day, Meiying strolled in the garden, oddly unsettled by the events of the day. Instead of taking comfort in Madame Chen's acceptance after her 'successful' interview, she felt a nagging disquiet. Something wasn't quite right, but she couldn't pin down exactly what wasn't right.

"We never kill," Old Crooked had said, but Meiying now knew there were so many ways of killing without killing, so many ways of dying without dying. Gazing at the gnarled vines and withered leaves, she suddenly envied Meili. Loneliness seemed only one of many variations on a theme of slow death.

As if on cue, Old Twisted came out and sat on a bench. She did not see Meiying. After settling into a comfortable position, the old caretaker pulled out from a cotton bag some unfinished embroidery and set to work. Meiying watched unseen for a long time. Perhaps something would happen, some clue would appear, that could unlock whatever secret dwelt in this strange haven for fleeing souls. But nothing amiss occurred. As she withdrew, Meiying spotted Old Crooked standing motionless in the shadows, gazing at his sister. She froze. At first, Meiying thought he had spotted her, but no, he continued to stare at Old Twisted. Meiying always prided herself on her ability to read faces, and his expression conveyed only one emotion: love.

With this utterly guileless and natural projection of unprompted affection, Meiying's fears evaporated and she again felt safe and secure.

"Stupid Meiying," she whispered to herself. "The cold world still has warm burrows. I will nestle down into this one and gain my strength. Then, on to *her*."

~ *Village of the Dead* ~

Because they entered the village by a narrow alley rather than the main road, John and his comrades walked in more-or-less single file. John happened to be in front and from the shadow of the alley, as through the lens of a telescope, saw Madame Liu and the others kneeling on the main road, bathed in sunlight and guarded by Japanese soldiers. He stopped and instinctively backed-up, causing the others to complain until they saw his face. All of them slunk back into the shadowy depths of the alley.

"What did you see?" whispered Lu Zhishen, still holding little Huiliang.

"Japs! They were taken by Japs!"

"They must be all over the place!" cried Peter in a low, panicked voice.

"We're done for!" added Lu.

"Not if we keep our heads," said Feng Shiren. "Being monks doesn't work with them. Let's become peasants."

"Just more fodder for them to kill," said Mr. Gao.

"No, no," said Feng. "Killing stupid peasants is troublesome. Wasteful. Unnecessary."

"So, we become peasants?" asked Gao.

"No, we become stupid peasants. Even peasants have intelligence. Stupid peasants are like bacteria. Below the microscopic radar."

"Fuck this!" Peter yelped in a low but decidedly frightened voice. "They'll know we foreign devils certainly aren't peasants. Let's go back!"

"Where?" asked Feng.

"Anywhere. The Japs will kill us if we stay here, that's for certain sure."

"Will they?" replied Feng in his usual calm, mocking tone.

Lu, tired of Feng's habit of answering questions with a question, had enough. "Look, asshole, we have this little girl. We have ourselves. Let's not get ourselves killed because you find the situation amusing."

Mr. Gao, as usual, took a different, less dramatic path. "We have a problem. Lu Zhishen, Peter, and John obviously aren't Chinese peasants. That means any attempt to fool the Japs would be useless. John, you saw, what did it appear is happening to our comrades?"

"They are kneeling in the dirt. Jap soldiers are holding rifles to their heads. That's all I saw."

"Well," observed Gao. "We can't just go barging out. Obviously we are outsiders. Any outsiders, to the Japanese, are spies. They shoot spies."

"Right! Good idea!" blurted Peter. "Now, let's get the hell out of here!"

"I agree," said Mr. Gao. "But we must go back to the addle-brained forester and his addle-brained wife. Bring them food in exchange for shelter."

"We have no food, they took everything, remember?" said Lu.

"Shelter!" scoffed Peter. "It was a shack."

"No," replied Gao. "You didn't observe?"

"Observe what?" asked John.

Before Mr. Gao could answer, shots rang out.

"Oh, god!" cried Lu.

"Let's go!" hissed John. "Mr. Gao's right. Stay here and we're dead."

More shots. Everyone ran back toward the direction they came. No one knew what the shots were for, but each feared their comrades were being executed. They ran down the trail leading back to the old forester's shack. After a while they paused, winded and seeking comfort in each other's misery. Only Feng remained above the general panic, though he also ran quite uncomplainingly with them.

Huiliang, who had been crying, now began to wail, her face beet-red. Mr. Gao took her from Lu and tried to soothe the little girl, who quieted but still appeared feverish and miserable.

"She's getting worse," said Gao. "We need to find some place to stay and let her rest and eat."

John suddenly felt the full force of their dire situation. No food. No money. Japanese lurking everywhere. A countryside brought to its knees by famine. Adrenalin had run its course and he now felt powerless and terrified. Desperation poked around the edges of his self-control, and the shaking started.

"We should have done something to help them!" said Lu.

"How?" asked Peter. "We shouldn't have left the group in the first place, that's the problem."

"Oh, now you blame Madame Liu!" objected Lu. "We all agreed to go."

"That's why you have leaders. We have none."

"Screw it!" blurted Mr. Gao, using an expletive he would never normally use. "You fools only understand blunt words. Then screw it. Let's go back to the forester's shack now and stop fighting. It does no good."

"Can anyone tell if the Japs are following us?" asked John.

"Fuck!" exploded Peter. "You're always asking others. Go look for your damn self. Quit whining. Just talk to your voices. The rest of us are going!"

John felt anger at this unwarranted attack, but held his peace. After all, Peter was right. John knew he had always been a drag on the group. *Indecisive. Scared. Doubtful. Peter—*

"No need to feel sorry for yourself," said Feng smiling his best sardonic smile. "Plenty of time for that later."

"How do you know what I'm thinking?" asked John half defensively and half out of genuine surprise.

Feng kept smiling, his head slightly cocked to better hear the bickering that continued between Peter and Lu Zhishen.

"No need to argue," interjected Mr. Gao. "Let's go."

As they trudged on, this time at a slower pace, the arguments subsided and the hunger returned. "What are we going to do about food?" asked Peter. "That old man won't have any."

"If not, we move on," said Gao.

"I'm starving," said Lu. "And Huiliang just keeps going downhill." He looked down at the little girl who sprawled like a limp ragdoll in his arms.

"Must be another village around here somewhere," said John.

"Maybe on the other side of the swamp," replied Mr. Gao.

John shuddered. "Not that damn swamp!"

"Food will be no problem," announced Feng.

Everyone stopped and looked at him.

"How so?" asked Gao.

"What you don't realize is that a swamp is like a grand restaurant. *Dim sum* all over the place. Just not as fancy as some Hong Kong restaurant, of course."

"Like what?" asked Lu, interested in any topic touching on the acquisition of food.

"You'll see."

~

When they reached the forester's shack, the old man sat in the same spot on the front porch, braiding the same rope, smoking the same pipe.

"Hello!" called Mr. Gao.

Puffing away on his pipe, the old man barely glanced up, then, evidently uninterested in the group standing before him, went back to his rope.

"Hello!" Gao called again. "You remember us?"

Quick as a flash, the old lady appeared on the porch. "You bring food?" she asked greedily.

Before Gao could answer, Feng Shiren stepped forward with a dazzling smile. "We brought something much better!"

The old lady looked suspicious, but intrigued. She waited with her hands on her hips, chin thrust forward.

"Ah, well, let's go," said Feng to the group. "These folks aren't interested."

Taking Feng's lead, the group moved away down the trail.

"Wait!" called the old man. As if his body had suddenly been possessed by an alien life-force, his eyes flashed a feral intelligence and his face assumed an air of total command. "Come back," he said in a low, threatening tone.

They returned and stood before the forester, who now stood menacingly. He turned to his wife and nodded. She promptly disappeared back into the shack. Still not speaking, the man pointed left and right, inviting the group to follow the directions in which his finger indicated. To their astonishment, the woods were full of armed men and women, glaring at them. On closer inspection, John noticed the 'soldiers' were wearing ragged clothes, no shoes, and appeared half-starved, giving them an even grimmer presence.

"The Japs took your friends to the village, as you probably know by now," the forester said. "After the first group was taken to the village, we asked about you and were told you have recently come from Mr. President's headquarters at the temple. He said you were on some sort of romantic quest, like an ancient novel or something. When the second little group of you passed by, we assumed you followed your friends. We waited, also assuming you would find them and be killed with them. But here you are. So here we all are."

"Yes, here we all are," replied Mr. Gao shrugging. He held out his hands, palms up, but no recognition of its meaning seemed to register with the forester.

"Take the child," he said to his wife, who promptly relieved Lu of his burden. "We'll take care of her. Now, you said you brought something for us. Did you?"

"No," admitted Feng. "We are all hungry. The little girl—Huiliang—needs care, and the rest of us are in bad shape. The Japs took everything. So, I lied."

The forester chuckled. "Assuming I am an idiot and would fall for your childish ruse?"

"Exactly."

"Well, we have something for you. Do you want your comrades back, if they're not already dead?"

"Yes, very much," said Mr. Gao simply.

"Well, you are all able-bodied and are hereby drafted into Mr. President's army of resistance against the Japs. Welcome, soldiers!"

"How does this get our comrades back?" asked Feng boldly.

"That is not for you to know. Mr. President made it clear we were to help. He said to tell you he wants to keep all of you fat for when the time comes to eat you." The forester scratched his head. "Didn't quite understand that part. He is known as a great joker. Anyway, you foreigners are to write about us."

"What?" asked Lu Zhishen.

"Write! Write! You must be the big, bearded Canadian who has taken the name of our great Chinese hero from *Shui Hu Zhuan*. Ha, ha! That is funny. You are also quite the joker, I see."

Mr. Gao asked patiently, "What are we to write?"

"It's obvious! Write articles about us so we can send them back to your countries. They will extol our heroic Chinese resistance to the imperialist Japanese invaders. The usual claptrap. But they will be useful to our war effort. Maybe even convince your people to enter the war and join us against the Japs., or at least send aid." He tilted his head. "Worth a try, I guess."

"Now we're reporters?" asked Peter.

"Yes."

"Bloody good! I've always wanted to be a reporter!"

Mr. Gao kept a level head. "Do you know what has happened to our friends?"

"We're waiting for reports. Don't know yet. If they're lucky, they'll end up in a prisoner camp outside the village. If not. . . . " he shrugged.

"Huiliang—the little girl you took?"

"Trust me, we will take care of her."

"Tell her we'll visit when she's well," Gao said, his voice cracking.

"Yes."

"One question, if you please?" said Feng.

"Yes?" replied the forester.

"Why were you going to let us all be killed when you directed us to the town if Mr. President told you to help us?"

The leathery face cracked into a toothy smile. "Easier."

Allowing this reply to sink in, Feng asked, "Where do we stay?"

"Not here! That's all you need to know for now."

"But our comrades—" Mr. Gao started to say.

"In due time. Now, you're going with these resistance fighters." He gave a signal and the armed soldiers moved out, escorting the odd little group of Chinese and foreigners dressed ridiculously in the mud-caked robes of monks.

~ *The Cave* ~

After a strenuous hike up and down a series of hills, and once again wading through a section of the swamp, they reached an imposing mountain, its lime-stone wall rising vertically into the sky. A never-ending succession of switch-backs led to the inconspicuous entrance of an immense cave far up the cliff-face. Trees, shrubs, and boulders rendered it virtually invisible from the ground.

"What a defensive position, eh, Shiren?" marveled Peter.

Feng scoffed. "A death trap, unless it has an exit somewhere else."

"It does," growled one of the guards.

Feng smiled. "Glad to hear it."

"This is your new home, at least for the time being," said some sort of raggedy officer. "Here are some uniforms. Get rid of your stupid Buddhist rags."

The uniforms were nothing more than rags themselves.

"Hey, at least they're dry," joked Peter.

"Yeah, we'll fit right in with these . . . soldiers," said Lu, who struggled into a uniform far too small for his huge frame.

"Hey, friend!" Peter called to a nearby guard. "You have any toothbrushes?"

"Fuck off!" said the guard. "You spoiled foreigners will have to use your fingers."

"Great, thanks," replied Peter sullenly.

After changing, they were taken through a steep entrance chamber angling downhill that led into the heart of the mountain. Even before they were shown the dark corner where they would sleep, John imagined the stone walls of the cave gave the impression of what it must be like to be inside the mouth of some hungry beast. Acidic water drooled down the crevices, and the roof seemed poised to slam shut and chew up the helpless morsels that had just been deposited. Once settled in, they were given small helpings of rice gruel to lessen the hunger pangs, but for John, only served to mock his craving for more food. Miserable, cold, and damp, his only solace lay in blessed sleep, if it would have the mercy to come. He lay on his back staring up at the distant light bulging weakly from the cave entrance and tried to shut out the world.

Quit whining, John Powers! God seemed particularly brutal as it came out of nowhere. He had not been plagued by that grating voice for a long time. Steeling himself for the abusive onslaught sure to come, an astonishingly kind, gentle voice took over.

Blessed one, do not listen to God and His minions. The Great Mother has taken you into Her belly for protection, not consumption. Rest. Acquire your strength back. Prepare to meet her.

Goddess? You sound different.

Although the distortion caused by your human genes makes you think there are two, there are many. We are also confined, only Our box is much smaller than your cave when We visit your mind.

The Precious Object!

Perhaps, if that is your comfort.

Actually, I just want to go home. Have real American food. Not worry whether I'll live or die every hour. Am I so weak for having these thoughts?

There is still much that is human in your genes.

Ah, so you agree I'm weak?

I agree. But out of weakness arises strength. Trite, I admit, but true.

Nothing, I fear, will arise out of me that is worthwhile. Look at me now, talking to myself like a child with an imaginary friend.

The edges of your universe right now are these stone walls of the Mother. Walk outside the cave and the dark walls fall away to lie in pieces beneath the bright sky, also of the Mother. Travel beyond the bright sky and space extends infinitely far, also of the Great Mother. You must embark on a trip to leave the clutter of your confined little world and reach the unused infinity of your mind. Embrace your new boundaries. Escape the errors of the blind man in the dark. You are the next step. Connect to the Mother—connect to Me. Do not seek escape in human flights of fancy.

All of us are afraid. Don't all of us want to escape things that go bump in the night?

Yes, escape collisions with the knobby protrusions of the world. But you are no longer fully one of them.

John spoke out loud. "Can You conjure up a cheeseburger instead of confusing conundrums?"

"John!"

Cold water. Awful to be dragged back. He struggled to wake up.

"John! Food! Get up!"

Peter jabbed his side with the toe of his foot. "Come on, John. Food. Then a meeting. An important meeting. Quit talking in your sleep. Let's move!"

"Food? A meeting? What meeting?"

"Food first," said Peter. "Ain't a cheeseburger like I heard you mumble in your dream, but it smells damn good."

John rose and used salt on his finger to brush his teeth. Then he stumbled to the food area where 'soldiers' sat in a rough circle eating the slop given them by the cook. Some had bowls, most ate with their fingers. Not even chopsticks available, except for a very few lucky ones. *These pathetic, starving men and women plan to defeat the Japanese and free the prisoners? Absurd!* thought John.

"Hey, foreigner, where you from?" called a skin-and-bone private.

John instantly replied, "The United States."

"What state?"

Surprised, John shot back, "California."

"Ah! San Francisco! My sister lives there."

"Oh," said John. "A nice city. How long has she been there?"

"Long enough, Jew-boy." The soldier clearly did not know what a Jew-boy was, but he felt quite proud to have spoken American slang.

John pushed it. "Do you know what a Jew is?"

"Of course," said another soldier.

"What?"

"It's a religion. I learned from a Christian missionary. Jews murdered Jesus."

"Who was Jesus?" pursued John, perversely determined to reveal their ignorance.

"Damn, this foreign devil asks a lot of questions!" came words from the rear of the circle.

But they were listening. Curious.

"Well?" asked John.

"Jesus was Buddha. Gautama Siddhartha traveled to the West and taught the foreign devils. But they got it wrong. Now the fools think Jesus was different from Buddha. Typical."

John would not let it go. "Christians think Jesus is the Son of God."

"Which god?" someone asked.

"The only God," said John.

"Yes, yes, I've heard that," said an older woman. "Only one god. Male. No ancestor spirits. No other gods. No goddesses. No Guan Yin. Silly."

"Worse than silly. Barbaric!" cried another.

"Do you believe in this god?" asked the woman.

Careful, John Powers.

John felt foolish. His own idiotic questions got him into this. "I believe in whatever god or goddess is willing to help when I need it."

Appreciative laughter erupted. "Hear! Hear!"

"Well, foreigner, we are in need now, so pray to whomever is most powerful to help us overcome the Japs and free our comrades!"

"Is that what we're going to do?" asked Lu Zhishen who had been listening half-interestedly until now.

"Yes, of course."

"When?"

None of them knew. "That is up to the big wigs," was the consensus.

Chapter Ten

Respite

Meiying's Seclusion

Life for Meiying had fallen into a pleasant routine at Madame Chen's odd estate. She had taken on the task of reviving the desiccated garden. For the first time in many years, long-tailed shrikes had returned, thanks to Meiying's efforts to plant a habitat for the living. Madame Chen looked upon the renovation with conflicting thoughts; she loved the new garden but feared it would undermine her carefully laid reputation as a dark mistress ruling over a house of death and demons. In spite of her reservations, she could not bring herself to stop the girl who so obviously drew joy from her labors. Every evening, Meiying returned to the house sweaty, with scratched arms and dirty hands, but a smile usually graced her features with the unmistakable imprint of someone at peace with herself. Peasant hat tilted back on her head, this young virtuoso performer of Bach and Mozart bore her lowly cultivator's fate with grace and dignity.

One day, Old Twisted and Old Crooked watched her pulling weeds. The roots were deep and she strained mightily to get them out and shake loose the soil locked in their death-grip. Often she fell on her back, but went at it again with renewed determination.

"Quite the girl, eh, brother?" said Old Twisted.

"Yes," replied Old Crooked. "At first, I thought it was for show. But now. . . . "

Meiying pushed back her peasant hat, framing her face in a most endearing way, thought Old Twisted.

"Dear Meiying!" called Old Twisted. "Go in and have some tea. Rest."

"Yes, I think I will. Thank you, Kindness!"

Brother and sister watched her go into the house and close the door before they spoke.

"She is precious," said Old Crooked.

"Yes, you're right. We must protect her. Sometimes our mistress hasn't the slightest idea of the dangers."

Old Crooked wagged his finger. "Yes, yes she does. Oh, yes!"

~

As Meiying sipped her tea in a secluded side room, the memories kept intruding. She had still not recovered from the rapes, especially when the stinging, stabbing, twinges and pangs reminded her of the heavy bodies, the rancid smells, the animalistic grunts, the gagging, the violence, and Meili's last scream. With great conscious effort, she pushed these horrors out of her mind and focused on envisioning her Shanghai childhood. At first, she tried to picture her friends in the group, but by now they would be at the final destination living in peace with *her*. This made her absence all the more painful, so she concentrated on recreating her pleasurable early years.

When she was a young girl, her mother dressed her in Western-style dresses, and she loved them all; promenading down the streets on the way to piano practice, feeling her pretty dress swirl around her legs, stopping to eat *jiao zi* from street peddlers, all of whom smiled at her precocious beauty. Red. That was her favorite color. But she also loved her blue and yellow dresses.

Her first music teacher was the very beautiful and cultivated Miss Cameron, a British expatriate who idolized Chopin and swooned over male compatriots from Western countries. Meiying often confided to her other companion, a private tutor named Miss Darby, about her music teacher's liaisons. Meiying found Miss Cameron's interest in men somewhat disgusting, and often fantasized about the two young teachers having a relationship together. Before long, in her mind's eye, she found herself taking the place of one or the other. In part, this intensifying desire forced her to come to grips with being a lesbian.

At first, Meiying resisted, but she could not ignore the feelings stirred in her when Miss Cameron corrected her technique by manipulating her fingers to demonstrate the proper angle and span. The British woman's blond hair and exotic perfume made her dizzy with secret urgings. Often, she intentionally made mistakes in order to receive such intimate corrections. Fortunately, Miss Cameron never suspected, nor did she notice Meiying's flushed face, assuming it to be caused by "the passion of the music."

But the threat of being discovered always hung over her, adding both excitement and fear—a potent mixture for a young girl of thirteen. Of course, the day came when her mother burst into her room with exciting news about some trouble brewing in Shanghai, and caught her masturbating.

"What are you doing?" she demanded.

"Nothing."

"You naughty girl! Do you know what that will do to you?" Although her mother was educated, she still had connections to the spirit world, and certain superstitions lingered to cause Meiying no end of frustration.

"I wasn't doing anything."

"You bad girl! Do you want to go mad?"

"Nooo," said Meiying, practically rolling her eyes.

"Well, you will. If I ever catch you again, I'll tell your father!"

Father. A Confucian scholar. Teacher. Reformer. Member of the Guomindang. Follower of Sun Zhongshan and Jiang Jieshi. Patriarch. Formidable, but creased with the fissures of weaknesses which thirteen-year-old daughters could easily exploit. Threat of father's wrath was more intimidating to mother than to daughter. "I'll tell your father," was no threat in this case, unbeknownst to mother, but Meiying had enough presence-of-mind to know the appropriate response.

"No! Please don't tell father!"

"Will you stop?"

"Yes."

Being a parent, her mother could not leave it at this. "Do you know why you must stop?" she insisted.

"Yes."

"Why?"

"I'll go mad," said Meiying in a monotone, with an impish hint of mockery.

Her mother threw up her arms. "Ohhh!" she cried in exasperation. Even though Meiying made the correct response, correct without conviction is defiance. Defiance is wrong. Wrong must be punished. Punishment must be severe, but fair. Fair punishment must make the transgression clear. Clear must be unequivocal. Unequivocal must be harsh. Fathers deal in harshness. Since harsh is fair, clear, and unequivocal, harsh it must be. Doled out by father.

"I'm telling your father, wicked girl! He'll know what to do with you!"

Meiying was not too worried about her father. Embarrassed, but not worried. A smile, a tilt of the head, and teary eyes. All played out a hundred times before in a hundred little crises. Besides, this constituted one of many "major" violations of her "good girl" persona. Meiying smiled at the memory of the meeting with her father. He, much more embarrassed about the topic than daughter, fumbled for words, and with averted eyes, pronounced the final resolution: "Please don't do it again, or else . . . or else you know what will happen."

Problem solved forever. She never did find out "what will happen" even though her masturbation continued unabated, albeit with more concern for secure privacy. What's more, her fantasies grew more explicit, making secrecy even more important.

~

Steam from her tea curled lazily beside a fresh bouquet of flowers she had picked earlier in the garden.

When the sun sank lower, a slant of light through the window illuminated the steam and the flowers as if a magician had just conjured them to dazzle the world.

A jay flashed past, slicing downward then swooping upward, its wings pulsing with quick life and vitality.

A sign, she thought. *A good sign. All will be well. The world will be as it once was. My pretty dresses. The piano. All will be well.*

But as you, good Reader, are well-versed in foreshadowing, you must realize all was not well.

A certain rough Beast from Bethlehem moved his slow thighs and would vex the dreams of those too soon rocked to sleep.

~ *At the Cave* ~

The days passed into weeks, and still John and his comrades did nothing but wait, the interminable boredom occasionally broken by forays out of the cave to find food. Always, they were accompanied by a certain peasant-soldier named Tang. In his twenties, Tang possessed an operatic flair for the dramatic, which attracted the attention of Feng Shiren.

"Japs have little curled-up tails, you know that, right mates?" Tang would rhapsodize. "And their balls aren't balls at all, they're dried-up shells with little peanuts inside. And the peanuts are other little Jap soldiers all curled-up, like those Russian dolls. Not spawned of women at all! All we have to do is crack 'em open, eat 'em, and wash 'em down our throats with wine!"

Feng roared with laughter. "I'll crack 'em, you eat 'em! I don't want little curled-up Jap peanuts in my stomach!"

And so it went between the two. John found it fascinating that Feng seemed as comfortable with philosophers as with peasants. Meanwhile, Lu Zhishen and Peter had resumed their close friendship, and as always, John remained the odd-man-out. This situation, however, now suited him. He felt himself growing stronger, more independent, and more resilient. All of his self-doubts began coalescing around a core conviction—he was growing while those around him stayed the same. Introspection bred this sort of silent comparison, and with no one else to moderate, he feasted on a diet of self-congratulatory kudos. He even felt he had succeeded in silencing the voices. When they came and tried to savage him, the result ended-up being a whimpering retreat back into silence. It was while he basked in this frame-of-mind that word came to prepare for battle. The mission: to free the prisoners still held by the Japanese.

Tang exhibited the first reaction to this news. "About time! Our comrades are all probably dead of old-age by now. What do you say, Shiren?"

Feng Shiren laughed. "I'd rather the Jap guards had died of old-age!"

"Time to eat peanuts, brothers!" cried Tang to the assembled soldiers.

In the face of these pronouncements of bravery, John felt the old, gnawing fear come back to life. How could he compare to these men, who just moments earlier he had felt so superior? Had all of his carefully stockpiled reserves of courage and independence been drained away so quickly? But then he thought of Suling, Little Acorn, Madame Liu, and the others, and his resolve quickly strengthened. Soon, he joined the rag-tag group of soldiers in shouting hurrahs at the news of their mission. That night, he couldn't sleep. He relieved the guard at the cave entrance around two in the morning. Alone, with a radio propped next to him, thoughts of Meiying flooded his mind, and his imagination soared far into the future, where he walked down the streets of San Francisco, proudly accompanied by his beautiful wife.

Peter suddenly appeared, plopped next to him and held out his hands, palms up. John made them out in the moonlight and reciprocated the gesture.

"Thinking of the others?" asked Peter.

"Yes, and the ones we will soon free."

"Thinking of anyone else?"

"What do you mean?"

"*Her* or her?"

"All of them."

"Scared?"

"Of course," replied John as steadily as he could. "I came here to teach English, become fluent in Chinese philosophy, and find a very mysterious lady, not fight in a war." He held up his rifle. "I barely know how to use any of these weapons."

"Yeah, I'm in the same boat, old chap."

"Hanging on to the fake Brit accent until the very end, are you?"

"Oi, matey," laughed Peter.

Both fell quiet. Although the night sky was clear where they sat, deep fog below their position filled the valley like a vast white ocean; a cauldron of mist and mystery.

"John, you are aware I love Meiying, right?"

"Of course."

"No, I mean I'm in love with her."

"Ah."

"And I know you have feelings for her also."

"Yes."

Peter scrunched around. "And her being a lesbian doesn't bother you?"

"No."

More quiet.

"You either?" asked John finally, though he really didn't want to know the answer.

"Yes and no. Look here, I say yes only because I know she is not interested in sex with men. In fact, she is disgusted by the thought of it. Believe me, I know. I tried."

John contemplated this statement. "Yeah, but it's funny, I don't often think of her in that way. It's more, I don't know . . . spiritual, for lack of a better word."

Nonsense, John! Spiritual will not get Me the son I need!

"So you don't want to marry her?" asked Peter.

"Didn't say that."

"Then how?"

Yes, John! Then how?

"Peter, why ask all these questions?"

"I don't know. Feeling mortal, I guess."

"What do you mean?"

"I mean I might bloody well die in this battle. If so, I'll never see her again." He held out his hands, palms up. "Let alone see *her*."

John felt somehow encouraged, while sympathetic. If Peter confided these thoughts in him, he must have some of the same weaknesses.

"Peter, you're not going to die. If you do, I'll be very fuckin' pissed!"

"No, I'm being serious. I don't want to leave Meiying, if she's still alive."

"If who's still alive?" came a voice from behind. Startled, John and Peter flinched and turned about to see Feng Shiren staring at them.

"Meiying," said Peter.

"She's alive."

"How do you know?" asked John eagerly.

"I know."

"Have you heard from her?"

"Of course not."

"Goddammit!" cried Peter. "How can you be so sure?"

"Anger flashed across Feng's face, a rarity for him. "You two foreigners are useless! Talk always about love but never about real love."

"Real love? What do you mean?" asked John, genuinely interested.

"Real love is love of life. Your own life! If you don't survive, it doesn't matter whether you love some other damn person. Life! Grab it! Hang on to it! It's not about some romantic notion of loving others. If you don't love your own life, you won't be any use to those you claim to love. Damn fools!"

"Feng, old man, life isn't worth living without someone to live it with. To die for," said Peter.

"Crap!"

"It's not crap!" protested Peter.

"Look, that's why arranged marriages are better than your ridiculous Western 'love' marriages."

"Ah, quit changing the subject," objected Peter.

"No, that's an interesting point. Why are arranged marriages better?" asked John.

"Because living real life must be put before some delusional concept of love. I love you today, tomorrow we divorce and I hate you. Bah! Rubbish!"

"Same can happen with arranged marriages," said Peter.

"No."

The three fell quiet. After a short pause, John asked, "If you were Meiying's father, who would you arrange for her to marry?"

Feng spoke without hesitating. "Suling."

"No, no," said Peter, now interested. "It has to be a male."

"Westerners are like children," muttered Feng.

"Come on," insisted Peter. "Play along with us childish Westerners."

"Her marriage has already been arranged."

"What?" both Americans exclaimed.

"Yes, her fate is already sealed."

"Who?" asked Peter.

Feng smiled enigmatically. "Oh, someone we all know."

"Who?"

"Not for me to say. A spirit told me in a dream."

"Crap!" declared Peter. "You're so bloody full of crap." He glared down at the valley.

Feng Shiren winked at John.

~ *The Battle to Free the Prisoners* ~

In the morning, all the fighters met at a clearing deep in the valley. They stood holding every manner of weapon: rifles, from ancient to modern, pistols of all descriptions, hand grenades of multiple shapes and designs, and even a few captured samurai swords. To John, they constituted the most unlikely group of soldiers ever to come down the pike. His confidence plummeted.

After a half-hour of milling around, a freshly dressed Guomindang officer arrived with a small group of regular Nationalist soldiers. When the motley group of local fighters assembled in front of him, John saw the officer's eyes dart among the faces and momentarily rest on the three foreigners.

"You foreigners, step forward!" he ordered in a high-pitched but commanding voice.

After the three stood before him, the officer spoke. "Who said you would participate in this mission?"

None of the three spoke.

"Well?"

Lu Zhishen said sheepishly, "No one. I guess it was just assumed."

"Never assume, soldier! You three are to accompany the assault, but hang back. We want you to write to your newspapers in the West about our heroic resistance."

Apparently, thought John, the leadership of this district assumed all Westerners that were not missionaries or worked for their governments were reporters.

"Speaking of assumptions," whispered Peter to John.

"What?" snapped the officer.

"Nothing, sir," said Peter.

He called out, and two little privates ran up with a pair of ancient typewriters. "These are your weapons, gentlemen," he said solemnly, his words clearly designed to impress. "Once we have successfully freed the prisoners, I want you to interview them and write articles about the atrocities committed by the Japanese. Make sure you mention the efforts of our courageous Chinese resistance to build a free China!"

John felt relief. Although he wanted to feel disappointed about not participating in the battle, he could not do so.

Tang, standing next to Feng Shiren, raised his rifle and shouted, "Long live Free China!"

"Long live Free China!" repeated the ragtag group, pumping their weapons in the air.

"There is your first line, gentlemen," said the officer with a smile.

"When do we attack, general?" asked one of the soldiers.

"First, I'm not a general, I'm Colonel Zhang. Second, your team leaders have already been briefed and were told not to reveal our plan until now. Third, to answer your question, we attack tonight. There are agents inside the camp that will help to free the prisoners from their cages. Fourth, we will be successful, or die trying! Long live Free China!"

"Long live Free China!" echoed the group.

"Now, break up into your teams and follow your team leaders. We will infiltrate from different directions and meet at a prearranged location just outside the camp. Our sources inform us that the Japanese have left a skeleton crew to guard the prisoners while they are chasing a phantom unit we planted with their intelligence."

John was impressed. This seemed better, more professional. And the task of writing about the battle suited him better than casting his lot with this group of shabby soldiers.

"You foreigners will come with me. Stay close. The typewriters will be taken back to the cave. Meanwhile, you will have these notebooks."

They were given pencils and small notebooks on which to write their observations. When they set out, the day burned bright, the wind blew gently, and the trip toward the prisoner camp progressed relatively easily. But as night approached, the going became more difficult. Colonel Zhang clearly became agitated and pushed for more speed. "We have to rendezvous before nightfall," he said. "Move it!"

Finally, they reached a deep ravine where the other teams had already arrived. Breathing a sigh of relief, Colonel Zhang collected his team leaders, also inviting the Westerners to be present. After going over the plan of attack, they synchronized their watches and returned to the troops.

"We attack in an hour," said Zhang to the 'reporters.'

John wanted to spend the time finding Feng Shiren, but it was too dark and he did not want to get lost. The prisoner camp slowly became visible when a distant glow of electric lights bulged above the horizon. Once in a great while a search light swept the sky, and appeared, John thought, as if it were nervously looking for avenging angels. He craned his neck to see, but could only catch glimpses through the vegetation. Suddenly, a great clamor arose as intense small arms fire poured onto Japanese positions. Crazy to get closer, John took advantage of the moment and slipped away to see from a better vantage point. He pictured Suling, Little Acorn, Madame Liu, and all his friends crouched in terror at this onslaught. Thoughts of holding back, of getting hurt, of dying, flew from his mind and he desperately wanted to be there when they were freed. Fortunately, he still clutched his rifle, and with its considerable encouragement, rushed toward the noise. As he got closer, a pulsating red glow throbbed against the night sky. For the first time, he saw wounded soldiers on the ground, some limping back toward the rear. The clamor became deafening. Explosions. Screaming. Machine-gun fire. He paused and crouched low, his recklessness quickly waning.

Stupid! he thought, since he didn't even know exactly where the camp was situated. But he followed the noise and cautiously moved in the opposite direction from the tattered lines of retreating soldiers. "Are we winning?" he asked randomly, but the replies were indistinct and contradictory.

"Run, brother!" screamed a soldier rushing past. "The Japs are right behind me!"

Now fear twisted his gut. Visions of Suling rushing into his arms in gratitude were replaced by a Japanese soldier running him through with a bayonet. He paused and took stock. More and more Chinese fighters were retreating. While he crouched like a fool, trying to decide what to do, the first prisoners came into view. The moonlight lit up their white faces as they were hustled along by his comrades.

Thank god! He thought. Encouraged, he tentatively moved forward, passing more and more soldiers and prisoners. All had grim expressions.

"Where are the Japanese?" he screamed to anyone who would listen.

"Right behind us, comrade! But we got the prisoners. Now it's time to run for it!"

A machine-gun erupted next to him and he stared speechless at the darkness where the bullets would have gone, until flashes of light exploded in a broken line from left to right. *Muzzle flashes!* The vegetation shredded around him, some fighters dropped, and the soldiers with their freed prisoners turned to fire wildly. Chaos descended and John turned to flee with the others. Fear now drove him to run as fast as his legs could carry him. Another volley from behind, and the sound of lead thudding into bodies made him crazy with the need to escape. He slammed into a tree trunk and staggered backward.

"John! John!" screamed a female voice.

He turned to look and saw a figure stumbling on its knees. Unsure whether it was the voice that shouted his name, he turned to continue running when it came again. "John! John!"

Explosions shattered the forest, while small-arms fire splintered the branches, sounding for all the world like a thousand brittle bones being snapped. He leaned forward, thrashing past the bodies and undergrowth toward the figure as if shambling against a driving rain.

"John, help me!"

Not knowing how he did it, he lifted Suling by her armpits and pushed her in front of him, joining the throng that now fled headlong from the advancing Japanese.

"Hurry, Suling, hurry!"

But she could barely walk on two legs, let alone run. He pictured the Japs catching-up – on his heels – shooting him down.

"Suling! Are you hurt?"

"No, no! Little Acorn! He was just with me! Where is he?"

John looked around wildly. No sign of the boy. "Suling, stand up! We have to move! The Japs are behind us!"

She dug-in. "John! Where is Little Acorn?"

"No! We have no time. He must have run ahead! Come on!"

"John!"

He pushed her forward. There was no choice. Every cell in his body wanted to run and leave her behind. But there seemed no choice. No choice? Of course, there was a choice. For many there is a choice, but they are the ones that are reviled for making the choice to run. After all, as Feng said, living is most important. To hell with the disapproval of those who never had to face it! Still, something pushed him to stay with Suling. Nothing heroic. Just obvious and necessary. The alternative remained unacceptable for some mysterious reason.

When they limped into the lines of Nationalist soldiers, Colonel Zhang remained steadfast. He watched the local fighters stream through his lines, commingled with the freed prisoners, but he stood determined to ensure an orderly retreat.

"Stand fast, men!" he hollered. "Let the others through, but stand fast! We'll give them time to get clear!"

Zhang's men had dug in, constructing a make-shift defensive line. Their weapons pointed straight ahead, toward the advancing Japanese. John and Suling passed through the line of soldiers and kept going. He glimpsed Lu Zhishen grab something from Colonel Zhang and run with the rest of them.

Suling still clung to John as he half-pushed, half-dragged her onward. Soon, he heard a terrific volley of small-arms fire, and knew Zhang had ordered his men to open-up. Then, the horrendous noise became confused, mixed with explosions and screams, and his blood ran hot, jubilant that he had survived to make it this far.

"John," panted Suling. "You see . . . my side hurts very much. I really can't . . . I can't. . . . "

She slumped to the ground, holding her side and moaning. It was too dark to see properly, but he felt the warm wetness and smelled the unmistakable scent of blood.

"Just a little farther, Suling," he pleaded. But she couldn't stand.

"Help me!" he called to those that flowed around him, but none stopped.

At a loss, he held a towel to her side and sat beside her, waiting for whatever would come. The moon shone on-and-off through the fast moving clouds. A pair of legs stood over him. Looking up, he saw Feng Shiren holding a limp body. It was small and appeared lifeless.

"Get her up!" cried Feng. "They'll soon be here!"

"Can't," replied John. "I think she's passed-out."

"No, I can make it," came Suling's weakened voice. "Help me up."

"Hold the towel!" ordered Feng. Placing the small body gently on the ground, he helped John to lift Suling.

"Take her, John, take her!"

"Okay."

"I have to carry this boy!"

"Little Acorn?"

"Yes.""Is he going to make it?"

"Don't know. Come on! We have to move! Help her!" Feng scooped up the boy and John held Suling, who leaned against him in great pain.

Somehow, they made it to a road where others took charge. The remnants of the attacking force trekked back toward the cave, with the sound of gunfire slowly tapering off behind them. After an interminable slog, they made it to the safety of the mountain retreat.

~

Over the next few days, John fussed over Suling and Little Acorn, hovering around them as they recovered from their wounds. John, Lu, and Peter frantically tried to locate Madame Liu, Master Zhou, Mr. Gao, and the others, but they could not be found. Amidst the chaos and pandemonium of the escape, they seemed to have disappeared, or been, recaptured, or killed.

John pictured Mr. Gao staying behind to help the children. Master Zhou's age would work against him, but surely Madame Liu would have found a way to survive. Even so, she had not turned up. Finally, word came that some escaped prisoners were hiding in the village with a group of resistance fighters. A team was put together with orders to bring them back. After Feng Shiren left with the team, the three foreigners were ordered to finish their 'articles' for transmission through enemy lines.

John hunched over his rickety typewriter, polishing-off a poorly written account of the battle. A generator provided electric light, but his brain offered-up no comparable illumination. So desperate had he become that he cast his memory back to Mrs. Morrison, his seventh-grade English teacher. She had developed what she called "a three-level" system of essay composition. Thesis. Antithesis. Synthesis.

"Take the color blue and analyze it," she would say. "Thesis paragraph, level one, first sentence, use the word 'although' as a cue word. Level two, second sentence, use the word 'however.' Level three, third sentence, use the word 'nevertheless.'"

John tried to do as she said, but failed at every attempt. Always ready to elucidate her method to a promising but slightly wooly-headed student, she guided him to write: "Although blue is often described as a color, its meaning may be plumbed deeper. However much one thinks of blue as a color, it may also represent a mood, such as 'he is feeling blue.' Nevertheless, at its deepest level, scientists might rightly think of blue as a segment of the electromagnetic spectrum."

So now, with Mrs. Morrison's help, it seemed simple to analyze the battle. He wrote: "Although the heroic resistance fighters of central China began their assault at night with grim determination to free their imprisoned comrades, none would realize the full savagery of what was to come. However, many of them died as they fought on to free their beloved comrades. Nevertheless, when the smoke had cleared, the mission was a resounding success and the prisoners freed to fight again against the hated Japanese."

It's drivel! Drivel! Read it, John Powers! A child could write better than that!

Yeah, but none of these Chinese guys will know. Listen, Goddess, if that's truly who you are, where are my friends?

Probability starves at Fate's door.

Thanks a lot, God.

John finished the article as best he could, fully realizing it was not ready for some Podunk journal, let alone *The New York Times*. Still, he had bigger fish to fry.

"Lu!" he called.

"Yeah?"

"You finish the article for all your Canadian readers?"

"Yeah, it'll be made into a movie."

"Yeah. Any word from the team?"

"Nope."

John wandered up to the cave entrance and peered down into the valley, half-expecting to see Feng Shiren come marching in with all the missing others, the Precious Object in tow, just as he had performed such miracles in the past.

But no.

Such is life.

A day passed with no news. Lu Zhishen asked John to speak with Little Acorn. Still recuperating, the boy had repeatedly asked for Feng Shiren, but when Lu explained that he was not available, Little Acorn broke down in tears. He had been on the mend, but a mysterious setback ensued, and much to the surprise of his caretakers, he now rapidly declined, so much so that Lu feared he would die. Because the boy seemed unconsolable, everyone had their turn in trying to cheer him up. Peter joked around in his usual manner, but to no effect. John's turn.

He was shocked when he saw the emaciated body and feverish eyes. Just from the looks of the boy, John despaired that anything could be done. "Hello, Little Acorn. Mr. Lu tells me you're unhappy."

Little Acorn blinked at him but said nothing.

"Do you know that Mr. Feng is on his way right now? Should be here soon."

"I know."

"So what's the problem?" John gave an exaggerated look of puzzlement.

"No problem."

"Can you wait for Mr. Feng?"

"It's not Mr. Feng."

"What then?"

The boy rolled his eyes like Mr. Feng would have done. "You foreigners are a lot of trouble."

"Yes, we are. So if it's not Mr. Feng, what's bothering you?"

"Mr. Gao."

John had not expected this. "Mr. Gao?"

"Yes. When we were set free, he yelled at me to help him with the younger ones."

"And?"

The boy convulsed in agony. "I ran."

"Well, that's understandable. Mr. Gao would understand."

"No, you don't understand. I looked back and saw his face."

"Ah."

"He stood there, yelling for me to come back. Then he fell down. I think he's dead."

"Little Acorn, you can't be blamed for that."

"His face told me."

"What?"

Little Acorn cried openly. "He looked so sad."

John suddenly realized how he had never really gotten to know Mr. Gao. He was always too busy with Meiying or Feng or Madame Liu to notice this very kind and competent man. Now it might be too late.

Might be!

Do you know something?

Might be.

If you know something, tell me so I can tell this boy.

Might be.

"Tell me what?" asked Little Acorn.

"Oh, just that when Mr. Feng arrives we can all have a long talk and you can get better. Once you're better, we can continue our journey like the old days and have grand adventures."

"I don't think I can."

"Of course you can. Now, why don't you rest and think of Mr. Feng and happier days ahead."

"I try, I try. But . . . oh, Mr. Gao's face!"

"You must try, Little Acorn, and get better for Mr. Feng."

"I don't know."

And so it went until Little Acorn fell asleep. Afterward, John paced nervously. Periodically checking for the arrival of the team, he turned his anger and frustration on himself.

Idiot! Weak, pathetic, fuckin' idiot! If everyone around you is so grounded in life, why do you take up the oxygen, the rich molecules, locked up in a body so useless to the world. Can't help Little Acorn, can't help Meiying, can't help myself!

Yes, Chosen One! But you need to survive until you manage to plant your seed in Meiying.

Oh, yes, you need your son, bitch! Or is it You need Your son, Goddess? Why, why, why do you need this son so damn much? Why not use Peter? Or someone else in the goddamn world? It's full of potential fathers of potential sons. Why me? Why her? Why is the future so important? Why not a daughter"

That will come later. At any rate, questioning a Goddess is more problematic then questioning a God. It is not that humanity fails to understand the lofty omniscience of God, it is that humanity cannot understand, or accept, worshipping a God far below them. The notion that one worships an illusion, or worse, a childish, addicted, ignorant illusion, is impossible for them. Thus, infantile wish-fulfilments of divine perfection morph into deep and profound mysteries. Worship your dog and it becomes an unknowable enigma. Worship your God, and the questions become as meaningless as wondering why a dog is unaware of the Holy Spirit. Dogs do not question the accuracy of calculus, yet they move in mysterious ways. Humans must not question the motivations of divine differential equations, even though God understands them no better than a dog.

Sounds like gibberish to me.

It would.

Leave me alone.

"John!"

"Yeah?"

Lu Zhishen looked at him strangely. "The team is returning."

Both men ran to the cave entrance and joined other soldiers peering down at the distant trail where a group of specks moved slowly up the switch-backs.

~ *Meiying has a Visitor* ~

Meiying slept soundly. During the weeks she stayed at the mansion, her days progressed according to a comfortable schedule. Most of the daylight hours were spent tending the garden and playing the piano. Nightfall, after a meal and conversation with Madame Chen, she retired to bed. On this particular night, there appeared no hint of trouble. Only the lugubrious howling of dogs and distant clucking of chickens penetrated the stillness of her room. Such noises were comforting rather than disturbing.

But shortly after midnight, the dogs clearly were driven beyond the normal territorial yelps. Snarling and growling interspersed the frantic barks, waking the entire household. Just as Meiying slipped out of bed and stood hesitating, her door burst open and Old Crooked rushed in.

"Run! Run, Meiying! They—"

But his shouts were cut short by a Japanese soldier pushing him aside with his rifle.

Colonel Naguma entered and gazed at the shaken Meiying with his usual enigmatic stare. Yet, his appearance had changed dramatically. Young as he was, he had aged noticeably, his body appearing feeble, one side sagging badly. If she did not know better, but for his glittering eyes, she would judge him to be a sick old man.

"Leave!" he ordered the soldier. "Close the door."

Naguma kept a hand in his overcoat pocket. "I brought a knife to kill you. Not a gun. Not a squad of executioners. I want to feel the blade enter your flesh. To twist it. Make you scream in pain."

Meiying drew back in terror but he waved off her panic and said quite calmly, "No, no, no. Don't be afraid. Why did I want to hurt you, murder you?" He shrugged and looked at her in a manner that she could only interpret as self-repute.

He slowly removed his hand from the pocket, but it was empty. "That desire has long since gone. Now, the hand does not work well. Notice I can barely make a fist? What caused it? They say stroke. But we know, you and I." He held up his good right hand and made a fist. "This has plenty of strength to make amends. I intend to use it!"

Meiying listened wide-eyed and frightened.

He noticed her fear and held out both hands palms up, although his left hand wavered unsteadily. "Come with me," he said without emotion.

"Why?" she asked weakly.

"Now!" He grabbed her arm and thrust her in front of him. Although her nightgown covered her body, she felt naked.

She went downstairs. A guard loitered next to the quivering Old Crooked and Old Twisted, now entwined in each other's arms. At the landing, she walked past Madame Chen in her wheelchair, looking angry and frightened at the same time.

Naguma gave Meiying no time to pause, but pushed her out the door, through the courtyard, and into the back seat of his motorcar. He slid in beside her and ordered the driver to wait outside. When the driver had closed the door behind him, Naguma looked at Meiying with an unreadable expression.

"How have you been?" he asked, as if they had just sat down to tea.

"Well." She was aware how stupid such a response must seem under the circumstances.

"I have very little time. What is your greatest wish?"

The question astonished her. "I don't know," she stammered.

"Think. It's important."

Her face turned from shocked surprise to cold distain. "Meili back."

Naguma's face twitched. "Yes, I knew you would say that."

"Are you taking me back? Are you going to shoot me like you did her?"

"Depends."

Meiying looked down, unwilling to talk further.

"No," said Naguma softly. "I am not taking you back. I am going back myself, alone, and I wanted to see you before I make the journey. I cannot bring your friend, your lover, back. I just learned that mine has also been consumed by this war. Now, before I depart, what is your greatest wish that is within my power to give?"

She shook her head in confusion.

He smiled for the first time—a genuine, self-satisfied expression came across his features, like a parent anticipating a child's joy upon opening a special gift. "Come with me," he said.

They exited the car and he led her around to the trunk. Using a flashlight, he opened it and shone the beam on an object so familiar that she uttered a surprised, "Oh!"

"If I am not mistaken," Naguma said. "This box contains seeds that are used to conceal a certain statue that you and your friends call the Precious Object. Am I correct?"

"Yes, yes! My friends? Are they. . . . ?"

He sighed. "The situation is confused and my intelligence is spotty on the subject. All I know for certain is this box fell into our hands somehow, an ambush I think, but many in your group are still alive . . . and free." He articulated these last words in an ironic tone. "I ordered the box transported here, where its contents will be analyzed."

"They're not dead?" she asked to confirm her understanding of what he had just said.

"As far as I know."

"Oh, if it could be so!"

Naguma smiled. "I hope you find them." He held out his good hand, palm-up. "I hope you find *her*."

Meiying looked at him as if for the first time. "Why?"

He shook his head. "Take the box, go inside, get warm, sleep. Then, when you are ready, have a safe journey. I have made sure Father Durant will not bother you, at least for the time being."

"Is he?"

"No." Naguma laughed. "He's French. Claims allegiance to our German allies. Can't upset those people. We're not at war with them, yet."

"Then?"

"Not for you to know. Just know you're safe, for a while, but I wouldn't dally here too long after I leave. My Japanese comrades have no interest in you, but that perverted priest. . . . "

"Do you—"

"No more questions. Go. Go now. Farewell."

He lifted the box using his good arm, but dropped it before it cleared the trunk. He looked at her sadly. "As you see. . . . "

Meiying reached in and grasped it.

"Now go!" he barked.

By the time she reached the courtyard gate, his driver had returned, the other soldiers had jumped in a truck, and they drove off, the beams of their headlights smudged by a roiling fog. She watched until the tail lights were swallowed up, then went inside to the waiting arms of Madame Chen and her faithful retainers.

~

Madame Chen proclaimed, "Tea! Tea for all! It's time to celebrate! What happened, girl? What did he say?"

Steaming cups soon materialized, thanks to Old Crooked. Meiying took the box to her room and returned immediately. Old Twisted poured her tea while Madame Chen smiled on.

"Thank you, Kindness," said Meiying.

"What did he say?" repeated an impatient Old Crooked. Holding his teacup cradled in two hands, savoring the steam that heated his skin and reminding him that he continued to live.

"Let the girl drink her tea, brother," scolded Old Twisted.

Meiying remained in a state of wonder and confusion. *What a strange man! Where are my friends now? Are they all alive? How did the Japanese get hold of the Precious Object? And Father Durant?* These thoughts whirled around in her mind, never settling into a pattern, always buffeted by the gusts of questions and comments from her friends.

"I don't know," was her usual response.

Madame Chen, noticing Meiying's mental haziness, cut sharply through the mist. First, she cleared her throat, an unmistakable signal of the coming gravity of her words.

"Tell me more about this Father Durant. We hear stories. I heard theirs. I need your story."

Meiying blushed. "He is very religious."

"Ugh! So much the worse. And?"

"He believes very much in purifying souls."

"Yes, by raping and torturing them, from what I hear."

Meiying put her head down.

"As I thought. So, is the bastard still a threat?"

"I don't know. Colonel Naguma said not for the time being."

"Um! Whatever that means. Who would've thought that I would be more worried by a lone Christian priest then the entire Japanese empire?"

"Are you?" asked Meiying. "Would he come here?"

Madame Chen softened. "Yes, child. Truth is, I have had much experience with this man. Together, Master Yu and I have helped several girls under his sway. We have always had to be careful, since the priest has powerful friends."

"Japanese?"

"Yes, and the Guomindang." Her eyes narrowed. "And most evil of all, a warlord called Mr. President, of all things. Whoever is in power, he will lap their milk."

Meiying felt curious about the other girls but didn't ask.

"It appears Colonel Naguma is your protector," said Old Twisted.

"Yes, Kindness, but he said he is leaving."

"Oh? When?" asked Madame Chen.

"I don't know, but he did say I am safe."

"For the time being," reminded Old Crooked.

After further discussion, Madame Chen slapped the arms of her wheelchair. "Well, can't do anything now. It'll be morning soon enough. Sleep will help us all. Sleep."

Everyone agreed and Meiying returned to her room. The box sat on her bed, an inert object that seemed to exude a kind of potential energy. If she didn't know better, it appeared to positively glow. Curiosity overcame her natural caution. She opened it and brushed away the seeds until a face emerged. Goddess. It stared at Meiying with the same enigmatic expression as Naguma. There was anger, yet compassion. Intensity, yet kindness. Power, yet humility. But looking closer, the face began to change into . . . into. . . .

Meiying quickly closed the lid, almost faint with horror. She crept downstairs to have more tea and calm her nerves. After having a warm cup, she went back to bed. She did not know how long she had been asleep when a strange noise awakened her.

… Tap. Tap. Tap….

At first, she assumed it came from outside the room.

… Tap. Tap. Tap….

But it did not come from outside.

… Tap Tap Tap Tap….

It came from inside the box.

… Tap Tap Tap Tap….

Meiying clasped the pillow tight over her ears.

… Tap Tap Tap Tap….

Now muffled but still audible.

… Tap Tap Tap Tap….

How to block it?

She sang a little rhyme her mother taught her when she couldn't sleep.

"Old grandmother Wind has come from the east,
She's ridden a donkey, a dear little beast.
Old mother-in-law Rain has come back again,
She's come from the North on a horse, it is plain.
And old aunty Lightning has come from the South,
On a big yellow dog with a bit in his mouth."

When she finished singing, the tapping had stopped.

~ *A Conversation* ~

Two days later, Old Crooked returned from a trip to the town with news that Colonel Naguma had shot himself on the very night he had visited the mansion.

Meiying greeted this revelation with tears.

"He murdered your friend," reminded Old Crooked in consternation.

"I know, but. . . ."

"But what?"

She shook her head.

Later, Madame Chen spoke with Meiying in private.

"I understand," she said. "You and he shared a bond. How he must have been torn! Only we who are different can fully comprehend."

"You never told me, Madame Chen, was there someone like us in your life?"

Madame Chen sat up straight in her wheelchair. "That was long ago."

"I am so sorry to have presumed."

Madame Chen took her time in tasting this response. She swirled it around like a wine-taster. Insincere? Cynical? Sarcastic?

No. With such assurance she continued. "Like me, she was also married, but unlike mine, her husband was kind. At first, I found solace with her as a friend. I had no idea she was also of our kind. Oh, we discussed many things. Politics. Children. Philosophy. Relations. Religion. Men. Unknowingly, I had fallen in love—with her mind. Sex had become a brutal, dirty affair to me, fit only for beasts. It was her mind I reveled in. Although she was quite beautiful, I never thought of her that way."

Madame Chen paused to sip her tea. Meiying noticed the shaking hand and teary eyes. She waited silently.

"One day—oh, it was a beautiful Spring day!—I visited her to have tea. It had been a particularly brutal night with my husband, and I still bore the bruises. Her house was empty, husband on a trip, no children. She took me in her arms. She wanted me. Me! A miserable creature in every way, filled with the vile sperm of a dozen men. Yet, she wanted me! How it felt!"

Madame Chen fell silent. She tried to speak, but could not.

"Yes, I know that feeling," said Meiying. "It is truly magical."

"But it's a trap!" cried Madame Chen with shocking bitterness. "This world cannot allow such magic. It must be destroyed. Why? To preserve men in their thrones and women on their knees."

"What was her name?"

Madame Chen waved dismissively. "Like all of us, she had no name. Her husband's slave. Property. A shadow. A magic shadow that materialized—fleshed out if you will—in her husband's absence, and then disappeared back into insubstantiality in the harsh light of his closeness, his soul-destroying closeness; just like all men, whether well meaning or not, whose demands rob us of our essence."

Meiying instinctively understood that this diatribe had probably been rehearsed many, many times over the years—to no one but Madame Chen herself.

"Did he find out?"

Madame Chen could only nod.

"And?"

"No more. I can say no more. Memories are my enemy. Already, the worms stir and burrow holes through my mind. No more."

Meiying rose and kissed Madame Chen on the forehead. "Yes, no more for either of us."

Chapter Eleven

Reunion

Incomplete Victory

The specks moving slowly up the switch-backs were maddeningly indistinct. Peter had the only available pair of binoculars.

"Can you see them?" asked Lu Zhishen anxiously.

"Not yet. Damn! These old binoculars are next to useless!"

"Let me look," said John. "Maybe fresh eyes."

"Okay."

John peered through the eyepieces but had no more luck than Peter.

"Just have to wait."

"Can you at least count how many there are?" asked Lu.

"Nope, they keep going behind trees and stuff."

"Damn!"

"We can go down and greet them," suggested Peter.

"Go ahead, comrades," said a Chinese soldier. "We'll stay here just in case."

"Okay! Let's go!" cried John.

The three foreigners bounded down the trail. While rounding one of the interminable curves, John slipped and fell. When he got to his knees and looked up, he saw Feng Shiren staring at him with hands on hips like an amused father. Behind Feng, others came into view.

Some were members of the team, some freed prisoners. John recognized none of them. His heart sank as they filed by. A commotion arose from down the trail.

"Hey! What's the hold-up? Keep moving!"

Soldier Tang tramped up and stopped when he saw Feng with the three foreigners. "Eh? What you guys doing here?"

"They came to greet their friends," said Feng.

"Oh."

John noticed that Tang appeared less bombastic than his usual self.

"Better keep moving," said Tang. "Japs might be on our tails, and they can move faster." Apparently, no officers survived the mission. Only Feng and Tang seemed in charge.

Feng wagged his thumb at Tang. "Get moving. I have to talk with these guys."

"Okay, see you at the top," replied Tang.

Feng turned to the others. "I warn you," he said. "Aren't many of ours coming back. We left the kids in the village. How's Little Acorn?"

"Anxious to see you," said John, craning his neck to see the faces of those still filing up the trail.

At last a familiar face!

"Madame Liu!" all three shouted in unison. Madame Liu, struggling to walk, was startled by the cries and looked up to see three men rushing toward her. Before Feng could blink, all four were hugging and crying, and even he found himself a little misty-eyed.

"Ah, your friends," said a passing soldier to Feng. "Too bad. Too bad."

Feng put his finger to his lips.

The soldier nodded and moved on.

~

"Mr. Gao?" John asked Madame Liu.

She shook her head.

"Master Zhou?" asked Peter.

Feng cut in. "We don't know. Heard something about him escaping to another village, but just don't know."

Lu Zhishen asked about the others and got the same answers; either dead or vanished.

Madame Liu took heart when she heard that Suling and Little Acorn survived. She climbed the remainder of the mountain with renewed vigor. John marveled at the old woman's strength, and again questioned his own fortitude.

After they had all reached the cave, and left Madame Liu to rest, Peter asked about the Precious Object. Feng flashed a look of disgust and spat. "Madame Liu told me it has fallen into the hands of the Japs. She has no idea where it is now."

Peter seemed stricken by this news. "Meiying, Master Liu, Mr. Gao, Master Zhou, the Precious Object, all the others . . . what's the point?"

"Of what?" asked John.

"Of going on. This whole quest is just an illusion, a conceit, a fantasy. We'll all end up dead."

Strangely, upon hearing these words, John felt a renewed determination. These moments of confidence sliced through the fog of his self-doubt with increasing frequency. Others faltered, but he held on. This realization did not elude him.

Yes. Good boy. Hang on. Grow. You'll make it. Ups and downs, but trending up.

So, I'm no longer worthless?

Oh, you were never worthless to me. Those are your human genes ranting. Do not despair, your son will be another step in the evolution of Superior Ones. God and His faction will object vociferously, but He will serve the most crucial of purposes.

You're making me sad. According to You, my son will be a freak.

Far from it. However, after he is born, tell him to beware of Voices and avoid the poison that collects at the bottom of craters.
Shit! You're crazy!
Yes, that is the point. But not Me. You should say, 'Shit! He's crazy!'
Who?
God.
Now I know you're crazy.
Who is writing this book?
What book?
What? I asked who is writing this book?
Who?
Now you're being human again!
My son? My son.

~

Days passed uneventfully at the cave. When it became apparent the Japanese were busy elsewhere, a certain malaise fell over the band. Food was scarce, but no one complained. Suling, Madame Liu, and Little Acorn continued to heal. Depressed over the magnitude of their losses and the tedious rhythm of time, the dismal nature of their situation began to sink-in. All of them moved in a sort of mechanical stupor. None dared bring up the status of their quest. It seemed everything would end here and each would scatter to their own fate.

One day, the fighters were called together and told their district leader had an announcement. Sitting in a semi-circle, with the inevitable rumors circulating wildly, a familiar figure strode up. John recognized the pipe first, then the old forester, now wearing a snappy uniform.

"Men and women of Mr. President's army of resistance, I have good news!"

He paused for effect, but the response appeared less than enthusiastic.

"Now that we have struck the Japs and freed our comrades, we have another mission. We will join other units and blow a Jap train! This will be our biggest test yet, but I know we can do it!"

Muttering. Grumbling.

Soldier Tang stood and saluted. "Sir! When do we start?"

"Tomorrow at daybreak. Supplied for one week. Clean your weapons. Deserters and shirkers will be considered spies and shot!"

Afterward, when the group had a chance to talk, and the shock of this new mission had turned to fear, Feng Shiren put the situation in perspective. "What did you expect? Did you think we would spend the rest of the war in these lavish facilities?"

Something Feng said rubbed Lu the wrong way, as so often happened. "No, asshole, we didn't expect that. It's just the suddenness. Stop lecturing!"

Madame Liu hushed him and started to speak when they were interrupted by a commotion. "Later," she said quickly. Word had come that the women and those still recovering would remain at the cave with a small, skeleton force. Lu

Zhishen, Peter, and, of course, Feng Shiren were to join the expedition, while John, Madame Liu, Suling, and Little Acorn would stay behind.

Separation of the group now cast an entirely new light on their circumstances. A hasty meeting was called at a secluded, bowl-shaped depression in the side of the mountain, far removed from the cave with its prying eyes and ubiquitous ears.

John felt ambiguous about his role. He was happy he had been selected to remain, but wondered why Lu and Peter were chosen over him to go on this dangerous mission. It pricked his manhood. But Madame Liu soon put a stop to this line of thinking with her first words.

"We must leave! Now! To stay and be separated, with more of us possibly killed, is unacceptable. The entire journey is at stake."

"But how?" asked Peter. "We only have tonight. Can't go down the mountain at night. Besides, you heard the old forester, deserters will be shot. Not enough time to plan!"

No one could argue with Peter's logic and the group fell silent.

"How about we wait two days, then we all slip away and meet at some prede-termined spot?" suggested Lu Zhishen.

Madame Liu shook her head. "Too risky. Finding each other would be a night-mare."

"No problem," said Feng Shiren. "It's a full moon. We can go up the switch-backs, not down. Over the ridge and we're gone."

"Someone's sure to spot us," observed Peter.

"And those aren't even switch-backs. More like goat trails. Straight up. Treach-erous," added Lu.

Feng slipped into one of his absurdist poses and cantered about on all fours. "Let's be goats!"

"Christ, Feng, sometimes I think you have the brains of a goat!" Lu said disgustedly. This observation put an end to Feng's cavorting.

"Maybe Lu's right," said Peter. "Wait two days, slip away, and rendezvous somewhere."

Madame Liu shook her head. "Rendezvous where? We don't even know this country. Probably be spread all over the place, lost."

"Not enough time," said John, just to say something.

Madame Liu sighed. "I'm afraid you are all correct. We just have to wait for a better opportunity."

This decision further depressed the group and they returned to the cave ex-pecting the worst. But daybreak brought good news; the expedition had been postponed. Everyone was happy except Little Acorn, who sorely missed his little friends who had been left scattered in various homes at the village. However, there still remained the problem of leaving without being spotted. Another conference was called at the same location.

"The time is now," said Madame Liu.

Feng asked a question that took everyone aback because no one had thought of asking. "Madame Liu, how far away is the Final Destination?"

"Far."

"How far?"

"Far."

"In what direction?"

"North."

"How far?"

"Far."

"That means nothing."

"Think of it this way," said Madame Liu. "The Final Destination has become a mythical place, beyond the seas, the land, and the sky. One cannot pin down "how far" because distance is not a relevant concept when discussing mythical places."

"That also means nothing."

"Perhaps."

"Are there any more safe harbors?" pressed Feng.

She shook her head.

"If you had been killed, none of us would know where to go, what direction, how far, nothing."

She nodded.

"Do you truly know where to go?"

"Oh, yes! I am like a matriarchal elephant that bears the memory of her ancestors and leads the herd to the only watering-hole available for miles and miles of desert. Follow her and live. Opt out and, you know what follows."

"Death?"

"Figuratively."

Feng smiled in a way John had never before seen. "And I am like a patriarchal lion that goes where he pleases regardless of the wishes of the pride."

Madame Liu scoffed, "Come now, Shiren! Stop being the buffoon."

Feng seemed to expand to fill the room as he stood tall and stretched out his arms. He then let out a roar that sounded as fearful as a lion.

"I will be the lion when circumstances require," he said calmly after the reverberations from the roar died down. "Meanwhile, I'll play the buffoon and laugh at death!"

Everyone held their collective breaths.

~ *Meiying Escapes* ~

Meiying had rarely felt more at peace. Surrounded by those who loved her, ensconced in a comfortable abode, nurtured by the music and the garden, protected by a fellow lesbian who understood her moods, the days progressed in a charmed progression. So comfortable had she become that guilt, her old guardian against complacency, wormed its way into her heart. Almost to establish an artificial sense of urgency, she pictured Father Durant dragging her away to his house of horrors, or his "church of calamities" as Old Crooked called it. When that failed, she imagined her friends in danger, pleading for her help, desperate to continue their journey.

But Durant did not appear and she heard nothing from her friends other than what was told her by Colonel Naguma, so she gradually fell into a routine so pleasing that she scarcely believed it was real. Her vagina had healed, and the nightmares receded into the realm of unpleasant but character-affirming visitations to an ugly past. She thought less and less of the group, and the quest for *her* became a distant goal, easily put-off under her current circumstances.

To be sure, she had moments of guilt and felt deeply the void left by her isolation from the group, but these moments passed, and she took comfort in playing or planting; stark contrast to being under the brutal control of Naguma or Durant!

As for Colonel Naguma, she felt badly, but avoided bringing back his specter, no matter how tragic or complex his legacy. Only the routine of daily life gave her satisfaction; a light breakfast, chats with Old Crooked and Old Twisted, work in the garden under a warming sun, practicing piano in the afternoon, a light supper with Madame Chen, more practice before bed, then sweet sleep. Joy came to her in these simple things.

But life in all its unpredictable permutations rarely maintains a steady course, and comfortable ruts are easily obliterated by torrential rains and sudden earthquakes. So Meiying's life of hypnotic regularity came to an abrupt end. One bright day, word came from Master Yu that the Japanese were on their way to arrest her for murdering Colonel Naguma. A young monk was sent to warn her and accompany her on her escape to the nearest safe place. With barely time to hug her protectors goodbye, the monk hustled her out of the mansion and onto the road. Again she donned a nun's robe and rode a bicycle, the Precious Object secured to the back. Only her long hair would give her away.

Her heart aching, she paused to look back at her paradise lost.

"No time! We'll shave your head later!" cried the monk. "Now, hurry!"

Once they had lost sight of the mansion, the monk stopped and said, "The roads will not be safe, so we must walk our bikes over those hills." He pointed toward the northwest.

As they walked, she looked more closely at this young monk. He had soft, pleasant features and spoke only when necessary. But when she stole glances at him, she saw that his face revealed fierce determination, belying the gentle exterior.

"Why do they think I killed Colonel Naguma?" she asked, after an hour of walking in silence.

"Father Durant."

"What do you mean?"

"Father Durant convinced them you are a spy who hypnotized the colonel and ordered him to commit suicide, so they blame you."

Meiying's face registered astonishment which the young monk noticed. "After all, you were the last Chinese person he saw, and it is well-known he was quite taken with you."

"But that's absurd!"

"Of course. But a Japanese court would convict you in the blink of an eye."

"You sound like a lawyer."

"In fact, dear lady, I am."

"You're not a monk?"

"Yes, that too."

"How can you be both?"

He laughed pleasantly. "Now who is the lawyer?"

She smiled. "Your name is?"

"Beethoven."

Meiying laughed out loud at this absurdity. She sorely missed Madame Chen and the others, but somehow it felt good to be out in the open again with another person. As they approached the foothills, the scenery changed into a scrubby, thinly forested landscape. The sun warmed her face and the walk had energized her body.

Finally she said, "What a silly name for a monk."

"Yes, and for a lawyer too."

Meiying liked this young Beethoven. "Seriously," she said. "What is your real name?"

"Beethoven, I told you already."

She shook her head and smiled.

"Okay, I'll tell you," he said in exaggerated resignation. "The reason I was chosen to warn you and lead you to safety is because my nickname is Beethoven. I love his music. I was told you play his music. Voila!"

"I never met you at the temple."

"No, I am from a temple in the region we are headed. I had been visiting Master Yu with information from my boss when this came up. I was the logical choice.

"Who is your boss?"

"A real character, a warlord named The President. We call him Mr. President. His temple, really his headquarters, makes the one I just left seem shabby. It is actually a huge palace."

"Don't let Master Yu hear you say that. What another odd name! Are you all crazy where we're going?"

"Well, he certainly is! You'll see."

~

That night, Meiying and Beethoven made camp on a ridge that provided a magnificent view of the valley they had just crossed. As they sat eating cold shrimp and rice balls, the full impact of her rushed departure hit, and tears streamed down her cheeks as she gazed toward the place where she had spent so many weeks healing.

Beethoven respected her privacy and sat a distance away, chanting a prayer. The lovely chords of his sutra permeated the atmosphere lending the moment a contemplative, spiritual poignancy.

Listening to his lovely voice, Meiying sank into a deep reassessment of her life. The tears stopped and the siren-call of *her* returned with a vengeance. Meiying looked skyward and pledged to rededicate her quest to the memory of her friends, to forge a deep and abiding commitment to reunite with them, and to reach the final destination or die trying. Only by reaching *her* would she feel whole again.

Lost in this self-absorbed reverie, she did not notice the chanting had stopped and the haunting melody of *Für Elise* now filled the air. Only toward the end did she recognize his strangely beautiful humming and praised the rendition.

Beethoven smiled acknowledgement and waved her off.

Hours later, with a cold early morning dew stinging her face, she fell asleep and dreamt of her garden, and the figures of Madame Chen, Old Crooked, and Old Twisted sipping tea and laughing at her pulling weeds.

The next few days, the two travelers made slow progress. Avoiding the Japanese required numerous detours; the laborious climbing of hills and crossing of streams and rivers, while almost always walking their bikes, required great stamina and endless patience.

Beethoven expressed his admiration of Meiying's endurance.

"I am well-seasoned," she replied. "I now have a purpose, a goal, and nothing will stop it, short of death."

"Well!" he laughed. "Let's make sure that doesn't happen."

"You laugh, but I am quite serious."

The young monk belted out the first few chords of Beethoven's fifth symphony, but immediately saw the hurt and anger in Meiying's face. "Sorry, Meiying, I was just trying to help lighten the mood."

"You are nice, Beethoven," she said. "I am very sensitive about being mocked, or worse, patronized."

"And you are quite beautiful," he replied.

This was the first hint of sex and Meiying reacted immediately and with scorn. "Don't talk of beauty! It is a curse! Don't!"

"All right, sorry again. But you notice I haven't had the heart to cut your beautiful hair? Can I say you hair is beautiful?"

"No! Cut if off! Now!"

"But—"

"No! Cut it off! I do not want to be beautiful! I do not want you to say I'm beautiful! It is a curse, I tell you, a curse!"

"No, no. Your beauty is a gift. A gift to the world."

Meiying shook her head violently. "Go on. Do it!"

"All right, all right," he said apologetically. "But it's a shame, since we're very close to the temple where it is not necessary for your head to be shaved. Everyone there will know you are not a nun."

"Cut it!"

~ *Mr. President Redux* ~

Long before Meiying and Beethoven approached Mr. President's temple headquarters, they passed through a series of checkpoints, each manned by well-equipped soldiers, and each recognizing Beethoven. So it was an easy task to reach the top of a hill overlooking the large lake where the temple rose on an island.

"It's a painting from a fairy tale!" enthused Meiying. She rubbed her bare head now itching from the recent shaving.

"Yes, everyone who has seen it for the first time says the same thing," replied Beethoven.

Since her explosive reaction to his overtures, Beethoven assiduously avoided any topic that might possibly be interpreted as flirting, but his admiration for her had only deepened, and her shaved head made her even more attractive for reasons he himself could not explain.

"Wait until you see the inside," he said.

"I'm almost afraid to set foot inside such a wonderful place."

"Why?"

"Oh, I'm just being foolish. I don't know, as if once I set foot inside it would go poof and disappear."

"The President has a piano. In fact, I think he has more than one. I assure you, they're real."

"A Steinway?"

"Yes."

Beethoven grew serious. "Meiying, remember to be gracious, respectful, even a little obsequious. Mr. President is an odd old dragon."

"Is he dangerous?"

"He has a temper. Says things like—" Beethoven struck a defiant pose, hands on his hips, stomach puffed out—"I will eat you!"

Meiying couldn't help but giggle.

"Don't laugh, I'm serious."

"Does he really eat people?"

"No! Although I really wouldn't be shocked."

Meiying gave him a dubious look.

"Well," he said sheepishly. "Are you ready?"

"Not quite. Let's sit for a moment. I want to remember this scene." Now it was her turn to be sheepish. "Something to tell my grandchildren. I want to get it right."

"Grandchildren? Do you plan to marry? I thought—"

"Beethoven! Hush! Let me look in peace."

While she took in the view, Meiying wondered if Beethoven knew she was a lesbian. He certainly knew she wasn't a virgin, and that didn't seem to matter.

Such are the appetites of men, she thought. *Monks, murderers, soldiers, priests . . . and lawyers, all the same!*

Visions of the rapes flashed through her mind and she felt a twinge of pain in her vagina, while memories of the horrible stench were not far behind. She gagged and struggled to push them away. A soft breeze wafted up the slope, bringing the scent of grass and water. The distant yakking of ducks spurred her on. *I will not be a victim!*

She jumped up, startling Beethoven. "Let's go!"

Down they rode, across the narrow bridge, past waving guards, through the entrance gate, and to the base of the massive steps where months earlier the group had carried their bikes against the pouring rain. Without hesitating, Beethoven led her up the steps, between two curious guards, and through the door. Meiying looked at the same opulence as her friends had seen, and she likewise gaped at the gilded columns, elaborate tiles, magnificent scrolls, and black mahogany furniture. Their bikes were taken but she refused to leave the box and clutched it tightly in her arms.

"Nice, eh?" asked Beethoven.

"Unbelievable. I had no idea this was here."

"Very few do. Its owners have kept it a local secret. But with the war, such a secret can no longer be kept."

"Will I be staying here?" she asked.

"Depends."

"On what?"

"Your interview with Mr. President."

Another interview, she thought. *I think I'd rather sleep in a farmer's shack than face another interview.*

"Wait here," said Beethoven, who went off through one of the numerous side doors that led to who-knows-where.

He returned in short order. "You're in luck. Mr. President wants to meet you personally. First you have to bathe. He is very big on cleanliness . . . as well as being very big in other areas too," he said as an aside.

"Where is my room?"

"Ah. This may be a problem. You see, the bathing facilities here are public."

"What?"

"Public baths."

"Men and women?"

"Yes."

"Together?"

"I'm afraid so. It is one of his peculiarities. He combined the male and female sections into one big bath."

"Why?"

Beethoven shrugged. "Peculiarity."

"Fine," she said, giving Beethoven his first surprise.

"Follow me," he said, his voice cracking much to his chagrin. "By the way, carrying that box into the baths might be difficult."

"Why?"

"Attracts attention."

"I'll explain it has my personal effects."

Beethoven again shrugged and led her to the huge room that contained the baths, where he got his second surprise. Without hesitation, she put the box in a corner and removed her clothes, placing them carefully atop the box. Then, without a word, calmly walked into the water. Upon witnessing this amazing woman and her luminous body, his admiration turned to lust, and then very quickly to love, before he could build any credible defenses. Disgusted with himself, he turned his back on the baths and sat in the lotus position next to the box, facing a wall. To his consternation, he heard a faint tapping noise come from the box.

… Tap. Tap. Tap.

Momentarily thinking it was a bomb, he soon realized it was something different. Very different.

~

Meanwhile, Meiying luxuriated in the warm water, letting herself soak, scrubbing away the grime, drifting in and out of pleasant thoughts, only her itchy scalp reminding her of the prickly nature of the world. When she left the water, Beethoven waited with a small group of women holding traditional Chinese dresses. He turned his back as she approached and one of the ladies spoke.

"Hello. Mr. President has provided you with clothing, dresses, but was unsure of size. Let us help you." Whereupon she was given a robe and the odd little group moved out of the humid bath building to a side room where she tried on the dresses, Beethoven trailing behind carrying the box at her insistence. Now she wished she had not been adamant about having her head shaved; she felt like an ugly duckling. Although, from the neck down, dressed in beautiful clothes, she was pretty, but from the neck up. . . .

In fact, she loved trying them on, turning this way and that in front of the mirror, picturing her hair long. *Vanity!* She reminded herself, but it was no use, she had to admit the bath and the clothes made her feel like a woman again.

"It's time for the interview," pronounced Beethoven. "Even that old dragon will be dazzled."

This time, she let the flirtatious remark pass, and followed him to the interview room, box held firmly in both hands, smiling and confident.

~ Feng Shiren Makes a Commitment ~

After Feng Shiren made his statement about being a patriarchal lion, independent and free, the members of the group waited for the other shoe to fall. Feng had no intention of cutting short the dramatic pause. Finally, Lu Zhishen, never known for his patience, said disgustedly, "So, that means you're leaving?"

"Wouldn't that make you happy?" asked Feng.

Lu had painted himself into a corner and was speechless. Madame Liu extracted him from his predicament.

"Mr. Feng, it is an honest question. Are you with us, or not?"

Feng loved this sort of attention. He put his hands behind his back and strutted to and fro as if deep in thought. But in the middle of his charade, Little Acorn could stand it no longer and rushed up to him crying, "Don't go! Don't go!" No one had noticed that the poor boy had healed physically, but emotionally suffered the untold agonies of a lonely child who imagined his world again bereft of love and protection.

John and the others looked on in astonishment as Feng's face instantly melted from a swaggering buffoon to a saintly smile, as sweet as a Renaissance portrait of Mary looking upon her child. In fact, his features seemed to reassemble themselves from alpha male to eternal mother, from capricious God to nurturing Goddess.

"Child!" He hugged Little Acorn and stroked his hair. "I will never leave you. You are safe with me, lovely boy."

As John stared at this touching scene, he saw Feng's features turn back into his old, roguish self. "Besides, you know how much trouble these foreigners are! I need your help. Who's to look after them but us?"

Feng looked out at the group, his hand resting on Little Acorn's shoulder. "Of course I'm staying, idiots! I've already told you, I want to meet this *her*, this paragon of virtue, this—"

"Enough!" scolded Madame Liu, shaking her head to indicate how pleased she felt that he intended to stay. "Now, how do we leave here without being spotted?"

"How far to the final destination?" Feng asked, half-laughing, half-serious.

"Far."

He threw up his hands in mock disgust, then fell on his knees, not in supplication, but intent on clearing the underbrush. "Little Acorn, hand me that stick!"

With the implement in hand, he motioned everyone forward. "Now, this is how we will do it."

~

Within a few days, they were back on the road, headed northwest. John scarcely knew how they managed, but one night, under a full moon, Feng led them out, inching up the treacherous switchbacks, and onto a trail none of them had seen before. As they were leaving the cave, Feng said something to the guards, who simply watched as they filed out. Once they were kilometers away, questions flew at him.

"How did you do it?"

When Feng just smiled, Lu Zhishen proclaimed with unjustified certainty, "He bribed them."

"Did you?"

"Maybe, maybe not."

"What did you bribe them with?"

"Didn't say I did."

"Where does this trail lead?"

"Northwest."

Lu Zhishen piped in with his usual grumbling. "Long as it doesn't lead back to that goddamn swamp."

Madame Liu snapped, "Hush! We're here, back on the road, headed for the final destination, alive. What more do you want?"

"Food," said John. "Ever since we've been in this region, there's never enough food."

"Whine, whine, whine. We're alive, ducky," chirped Peter.

"You're in a lot better mood," sulked John, his mind still on food.

"I miss our bikes," said Lu.

"Shut up!" cried Peter. "*She* will have food and bikes and motorcars when we get to the final destination."

"And flying horses!" scoffed Lu, who couldn't help himself.

So they walked many kilometers more, until dusk arrived, forcing them to search for a place to bed down. Although they had passed a scattering of poverty-stricken villages, only a few starving peasants assailed them; the rest dead, sick, or long-since fled. Their first task was to find water. Once they located a small stream, they followed it to a secluded spot, well-hidden by vegetation.

Just as they settled in, a raggedy family appeared. Father, mother, and three small children, all clearly on their last legs. The two groups stared at each other.

"Please, kind people, can you spare some food?" asked the father.

"We have none, friends," said Lu Zhishen.

They stared open-mouthed at the tall, bearded Canadian. "You must, kind people," said the mother in a pathetic voice. "My children starve."

Indeed, she did not lie. All three were half-naked with distended stomachs. Their eyes were dull and bore no indication of curiosity.

"Sorry, we have no food," repeated Lu.

The father flashed a look of anger. "But you are foreigners. All foreigners have food to spare!"

"Not us," said Peter. "We are also hungry."

"My children," pleaded the mother, pushing them forward.

Madame Liu waved her arms. "Dear lady, I am a mother too. We have no food."

"Yes, you do!" demanded the father. "You must! You are foreigners!" His voice weak in spite of his anger, he added, "We saw you pass our village and followed. You walk with strength. You have food!"

"My children," repeated the mother.

"Will be fed!" boomed a voice coming from the stream. Feng Shiren strode up holding a stringer of fish. "Food enough for us all!"

Father and mother fell to their knees and prostrated themselves, heads touching the ground.

"Thank you! Thank you, kind sir! Come back to the village with us and we will eat together."

"No, thank you," replied Feng. "Here is your share of the fish. We will keep the rest for ourselves."

Clearly anxious to leave, the family backed away expressing their gratitude. "Thank you! Thank you, kind sir! May your descendants live long and happy lives!"

As soon as they disappeared, Feng began to pack up. "Let's go! We mustn't stay. I fear others will return and not be so weak, but will be just as desperate!"

"But it's dark!" protested Lu.

"Doesn't matter. You can stay," replied Feng.

"He's right," said Madame Liu. "We must go and do our best to find a new spot."

After moving some distance from their original position, they wearily settled-in again."

Peter took John aside and whispered, "What do you think?"

"About what?"

"Where did he get the fish?"

John shrugged. "The stream."

"No fish in that stream."

"Then where?"

"That's what I'm asking."

"I don't know, Peter. He got them somewhere, okay?"

"Look," said Peter. "I've told you before there's something unnatural about him. Lu doesn't believe me, so I can't talk to him. And Madame Liu? Forget it. But Suling agrees with me."

"About what?"

"Feng is not human."

"Oh, come on!"

"Okay, maybe he's human. Maybe. But he's not your typical human."

"I don't know what you mean."

"Remember when he found me months ago when I was lost?"

"Yeah."

"Well, in the beginning, if you recall, I felt the same way toward our little soldier Feng, as Lu does now. But then, that night when I was lost, I saw something amazing."

Peter stopped to gauge whether John was still listening or thought he was crazy.

"Well, what was it?" John said impatiently.

Satisfied, Peter went on. "He didn't find me, I found him, or rather, I stumbled upon him. While I thrashed about in the dark, getting more and more concerned, I saw a glowing light through the trees. I assumed you all were looking for me with flashlights. When I reached the light, I saw. . . . "

"Yeah?"

"You're not gonna believe me."

"Christ, you can't stop now."

"Okay, I saw this goddess sitting on some flower, floating above the ground. She looked just like the Precious Object, or something very much like it, only alive. I mean flesh and blood alive."

"Oh, crap, come on, Peter!"

"No, I'm serious. I saw Her!"

"The moonlight, the shadows, the wind, something."

"Well, anyway, I watched, not believing my own eyes, when She turned and looked at me. I felt scared, more scared than I've ever been. So I turned to run and ran smack-dab into a tree, knocking me on my ass. I was out for a few moments. When I came to, Feng Shiren was leaning over me. I asked if he had seen Her. He said no."

"Okay, so? He didn't see the weird lights. So what?"

"No, no, no. You don't get it. He had to have seen Her. Damn it, John, he is Her!"

"Oh, come on! Now you've really gone over the edge."

"Where did he get the fish?"

"I don't know. I'll ask him tomorrow. Go to sleep. I think you're dreaming now."

"Oh, fuck it!" Peter left mumbling to himself.

But John felt uneasy. He remembered the scene with Little Acorn back at the cave. The next morning, he sought out Suling before they departed, and asked if she believed Peter. She thought for a long time and said, "I am an uneducated woman. He is educated. What am I to say?"

"Say what you believe."

"I do not know. You are also an educated man. You tell me."

Yes, tell her, John Powers! Only tell her that he is nothing more than a simple human.

Is he?

Partly.

I don't believe you.

You lack faith.

Because your words make no sense.

"John!" Suling exclaimed. "You're somewhere else again."

"You see, Suling, my education can't protect me from things I can't explain."

"Then maybe Peter is right?"

"Maybe."

~ *Another Interview* ~

Although Meiying had been warned about the sheer size of Mr. President, she was unprepared for the physical reality. His girth encompassed worlds, his legs rivaled the stone Buddhas of Bamiyan, and his arms the trunks of massive trees. But it was his spherical head and grotesque face that most grabbed her attention, for embedded in the bulging sphere were two beady eyes, rolling this way and that as though loose in their sockets. When he spoke, his voice also caught her off-guard; a high-pitched, feminine purr which belied his gargantuan body. With assistance, he plopped his mountain of flesh on a small but very sturdy stool.

"So, you are the beautiful young pianist I have been so looking forward to meeting."

"Thank you, Mr. President," replied Meiying.

"I have heard from Master Yu that you have had difficult times."

"Yes, Mr. President."

"But you still persevere?"

"No other choice, Mr. President."

He chuckled, rolls of fat rippling in waves up and down his torso. "Your friends described you well."

Meiying assumed he meant Master Yu and Beethoven. "Master Yu is too generous, Mr. President."

Mr. President blinked, then exclaimed, "Ah! Of course, you don't know!" He rubbed his chubby hands together. "Oh, this will be fun!"

Meiying waited patiently, unaware of what was to come.

"I understand you are with a group on a quest, little lady?"

"Yes, Mr. President."

He held out his hands, palms up. "And I understand this quest is to meet some remarkable woman?"

"Yes."

His eyes twinkled as he scanned the room. "Where are the other members of your group?"

Meiying looked down. "We were separated, Mr. President."

"By what?"

"By a man."

"Who?"

"A priest named Father Durant."

"Ah! I know about him. Master Yu has informed me that he is a bad man."

"Yes, Mr. President."

"Rape?"

She did not reply.

"Yes, I know there were many, poor girl." He scooched in his seat. "And where is your group now?"

"I don't know, Mr. President."

"Well, I can tell you that they are quite fond of you."

Meiying looked at him with wide eyes as he continued. "In fact, they were here not too long ago."

"Here?" she cried.

"Yes, we had a nice few days and they moved on, but not without expressing regret at your absence."

"Do you know where they are now?" she asked excitedly.

"Not exactly. I did know, but I let them continue their quest without stopping them. Had I known you were coming. . . . "

Meiying remained speechless for some few moments, tears coming to her eyes. Mr. President's little eyes watched her greedily.

"I must go and find them," she said.

Mr. President shook his head. "They are no longer under my control. I have very little idea where they are now. We can't have you running about this dangerous countryside. Especially now, with starvation, desperate people, to say nothing of the Japanese. No, no, much too dangerous."

"But—"

"No!" He held up his hand as a warning. "No more. For now you will be my guest. Later, I can perhaps help you find them. But tomorrow you will grace us with a recital, or concert, or whatever Westerners call it. Tonight you rest. Our friend Beethoven will show you to your room."

Interview over.

Chapter Twelve

The Road Lengthens

The Detour

The morning after their encounter with the peasant family, the group moved on. By now the trail had merged with another and they shared the wider, heavily-traveled road with many more people. Most were poor peasants carrying whatever goods or food they might sell or trade. It soon became obvious the group would have to take a detour to the provincial capital where a bank was located. Madame Liu, who seemed to know everyone, had long been acquainted with the manager. They had no money and she intended to withdraw enough funds to cover their immediate needs as well as to last until they reached the final destination. It was hoped that the three foreigners might also be allowed to transfer money from their own banks. Down to starvation rations, their only concern was to hold together body and soul until they made it to the city.

When they reached the outskirts of Taiyuan from the south, the Japanese had already occupied it for many weeks. More afraid of starvation than the Japanese, and after endless days of delay, hunger, and continuous walking, they arrived at the city gates. Jostled by hordes of refugees, they finally gained entrance past Japanese army checkpoints. Inside, the city had become swollen with desperate people. New construction to repair bombed-out buildings was going up slap-dash, and hordes of the poor sleeping in the streets rubbed shoulders with wealthy immigrants who fled occupied cities on the coast and now had nowhere to go.

Weak from hunger, they made a beeline for the bank and much to their relief, not only still stood, but was open for business. The others waited outside while Madame Liu entered and asked for her old friend, Mr. Zhu. Afraid he would be gone, or dead, she smiled broadly when he rushed out of an office and bowed enthusiastically.

"Madame Liu, so good to see you! I won't ask what brings you here, but you are a sight for sore eyes! Welcome to the Industrial and Commercial Bank of China!"

Mr. Zhu listened to her story and promptly provided her requested funds, still safe in the family account. When he heard about her companions, he begged her to bring them in. After the introductions, Mr. Zhu assured the three foreigners that he would contact their banks and, if the Japanese had not closed them, would do what he could to get their funds transferred.

"The currency situation is quite confused," he explained. "But I will make arrangements to give you currency that people actually accept these days. None of that trash that passes for money."

"Thank you so much," replied Madame Liu. "Now, where do you recommend we stay while we're here?"

"Well, the Japanese have taken the best hotels, but I know of one that is top-rate. Kind of similar to the *Heping Hotel* in Shanghai, same name too, except it's a smaller version. We have a mutual friend also staying there who has recently made use of our humble services."

"Who is that?"

"Ah, Master Zhou from Nanjing!" Mr. Zhu leaned forward and whispered, "He recently escaped from a Japanese prison. One of our branch bank's best customers. We thought he was dead, but he showed up as big as life! You should visit him and hear his amazing story."

"We will!" exclaimed an ecstatic Madame Liu. "Trust me, we will!"

After obtaining directions to the *Heping Hotel*, the group gathered outside the bank to take stock of their situation, their faces registered joy with the news of Master Zhou. Madame Liu held up a wad of notes. "Now, we will celebrate! And eat!"

John looked at Feng Shiren who seemed as hungry as the rest, and he dismissed Peter's crazy theory. *Feng's just like us. Now, to eat!*

~

Amidst the clatter of a crowded restaurant, Madame Liu informed the group that Master Zhou boarded in the same hotel they would be staying.

"How wonderful!" cried Suling.

The others added their praise of such good news.

"I've sent for him to join us," Madame Liu said.

Even as she spoke, Master Zhou came up to the table with his arms outstretched, a huge smile on his kindly face. He had gained weight since his escape, and after the initial salutations, patted his stomach. "Not as impressive as Mr. President, but I'll catch up! Thank god no more bicycles!"

"How'd you do it, old boy?" asked Peter. "We thought you were a goner."

"Oh, I don't know. I got separated and just kept waddling until I came to a road. Knew better than to use it, but I kept walking parallel to it. Lots of Japs drove up and down, but luckily I was never spotted. They were looking for more important people."

"No one more important than you, Master Zhou!" cried Lu Zhishen, who was deep into a second bottle of rice wine.

"Have more! Have more!" encouraged Madame Liu. "This is a celebration!"

John glanced at Feng Shiren, who was unusually quiet. Now, with a new found interest in his behavior after Peter's observation, John concluded that Feng faded into the background when things were going well, and only emerged as his inimitable self during times of crisis. As if to disabuse John of this notion, Feng jumped up and offered a toast.

"To our Journey to the Northwest!" He then performed an operatic dance worthy of Monkey. The little restaurant orchestra that had been playing traditional Chinese songs, joined in and played a series of opera styles, all of which Feng performed as if he were a Peking Opera star. Even, John noticed, the difficult female roles. *In some ways he performs the female roles even better than the male ones.* But when Feng rejoined the raucous table, John dismissed the notion as a product of too much wine.

As the banquet wound-down late in the evening, a group of armed Japanese soldiers entered the restaurant. Immediately silence fell over the room. John cursed to himself that they had not left earlier, but it was too late now. Worse, it was hard to be inconspicuous. First, there were three foreigners at the table, and second, they still wore their tattered clothes, so they stood out among the more well-to-do patrons. Fortunately, the soldiers poked around for only a short while, apparently looking for someone in particular. They paused at John's table and perused the odd group, but they were used to seeing exotic mixtures of people, from White Russians to Germans, so they passed by and eventually left. It turned out they were looking for one of their own, a Japanese soldier who murdered one of his comrades in an argument over a card game.

But the incident sobered everyone up and allowed Master Zhou to fill them in on the situation in Taiyuan.

"Before the Japs came, the warlord Yan Xishan controlled this entire area since the revolution. He is still very powerful, although the Japs pushed his troops out of the city. While he was in control, the place had done very well and he is quite popular. Now the Japs occupy it, but Yan waits out in the countryside. That's why we all got here relatively easily. During his period of control of the city, he made an alliance with the communists. In fact, many of them are still here. Not only that, but the city is full of smart, ambitious kids from all over Japanese occupied China."

Master Zhou leaned forward even closer than he had been and the others did likewise. "Even better, the Japs are starting to rebuild the city. Apparently, they want this to be an industrial center for their stupid 'Co-Prosperity Sphere' nonsense. That's why your bank is still open. Listen, deals can be made here! There are deals everywhere; with the locals, with the Japs, with the communists, with Yan's people!"

"Shhh! Warned Madame Liu. "Ears are also everywhere."

"Yes, you're right. We need to leave and get you all rooms. It's late."

John felt nothing but relief at this suggestion, as he practically slept in his chair. Little Acorn had found a corner of the restaurant and had curled-up, fast asleep. Thanks to Master Zhou's intervention, rooms were found at the *Heping Hotel* and the group slept as they had not done for many weeks.

~

The next day, John joined the others for breakfast in the hotel dining room. His Goddess-voice had been mercifully silent and he felt refreshed and somewhat optimistic. When he sat down, the others were already in deep discussion about the continuation of the journey.

"I say we stay here for a while and rest up," said Master Zhou. "In fact, it is imperative I stay, as something is about to come through which could make me a lot of money."

"But that is not our concern," replied Madame Liu. "Our concern is to complete the journey and see *her*."

"I agree with Madame Liu," said Lu Zhishen. "But it wouldn't hurt to stay here longer. It's so nice to have a comfortable place to sleep, and enough food."

"I agree with Lu," said Peter. "The journey can wait for a little time."

"But we could get lulled into staying here for much too long. And the Japanese are not always going to be so cooperative. What do you think, John?"

"I want to stay longer. I still have this crazy notion that Meiying is out there somewhere looking for us. I mean, what if she's trying to catch up with us? If we keep moving, how will she find us?"

"Ah, I understand, but John, it is unrealistic," said Madame Liu. "Suling? What about you?"

Suling laughed self-consciously. "I am an uneducated woman. I follow, not lead."

"Suling," said Madame Liu. "You are much stronger and smarter than you let on. We all need your wisdom. After all, we're all in this together. What do you say?"

"I think we should stay for only a few days, then continue our journey. If not, I am afraid we might lose the will."

"Never!" cried Lu Zhishen. "I have not come this far to see *her* just to give it up now."

"Same here," said Peter.

"Please, no offense, but that is what I mean. We have come so far, let us not fall into a trap now."

"A trap?" asked John.

"Yes, the trap of luxury. I have seen it before. But, still, we should stay a few days and rest."

"Or make deals!" exclaimed Feng Shiren. "For some, money to be made. For others—" he shrugged.

"You have been quiet until now, Mr. Feng," said Madame Liu. "What do you think?"

"I think there are deals to be made, but not the kind Master Zhou has in mind."

"What do you mean?" asked Peter.

"I mean, there are people here I want to see. There are people here I want to talk with. There are people here I want to bargain with."

"About what?"

"Souls."

"Mr. Feng, I don't understand what you mean," said Madame Liu coolly.

"I mean certain devils lurk in this city. Some of them are after you. I have my work cut out for me."

Peter glanced at John as if to say 'I told you so.'

"I don't understand, but I often don't understand you, Mr. Feng," said Madame Liu. She called the waiter and settled the bill. "How about if we stay a week and then continue our journey. That will give me time to make arrangements."

"How much farther?" asked Feng, with a twinkle in his eye.

"Far," sighed Madame Liu, unamused by his harping.

"In what direction?"

"Northwest."

"And will we end up in Mongolia?" asked Peter. "Or maybe the Soviet Union?"

"Northwest."

"How far northwest?" demanded Peter.

"Far."

Lu Zhishen slammed his hand on the table. "Madame Liu, these questions are not unreasonable. If you are injured or killed, how will we know where to go?"

"We have discussed this many times, Lu. It is for your own protection. And *hers*. Besides, my husband and I gave our solemn word to keep it secret, even if it meant the journey could not continue. All I have to say is that it is farther and to the northwest, away from the wars and famines that plague China nowadays."

"I understand, Madame Liu, and I respect that, but the situation has changed," said Peter. "I, for one, would feel better if I knew now where I was going and how far away it remains."

"I understand also, Peter," replied Madame Liu simply. "But I cannot break my vow."

As the group broke up, Feng sought out John and pulled him aside. "I know about your voices. Do you want to join me when I track down one of the devils I talked about? Might be a connection."

"Sure," said John, questioning his own sanity by agreeing so quickly with such a potentially crazy adventure.

When he thought of all the strange and dramatic events that had happened to him the past few months, his mind could not cope, but when he actually lived them day-by-day they seemed the most natural way to navigate the world. Odd.

~ *The Concert* ~

Prior to the concert for Mr. President, Meiying sought out Beethoven. She had been fighting her own demons, and as the hours passed, the urge to leave the gilded cage she found herself in was increasingly persistent. Something about this place, about Mr. President, made her shiver, as if malevolent ghosts had taken up early residence in her grave, moving about and stirring up the chill air in preparation for her arrival. First, she needed to find out where Beethoven's loyalties lay. Servants directed her to a small anteroom where he sat at a long table perusing what appeared to be an ancient scroll. Other rolled-up scrolls littered the room. When she coughed to get his attention, his face lit-up.

"So good to see you!" he exclaimed.

"I don't want to interrupt."

"No, no. These are valuable scrolls from all over the province, saved from falling into Jap hands. I'm just making an inventory."

"Do you work for Mr. President?"

"In a way."

"You've known him for a long time?"

"Not really. He's not such a bad fellow."

"Sometimes he scares me."

Beethoven laughed awkwardly. "Me too. Sit, sit, let me get you some tea."

"Thank you."

After Beethoven poured Meiying tea, she took a few polite sips and asked, "Why does he scare you?"

Beethoven seemed surprised. "He doesn't, really, just a. . . . "

"Just a what?"

"I don't know, it was just something to say."

Meiying stared into his eyes. "Beethoven, does he scare you?"

"Well, a little, yes."

"Why?"

"Well, he is a bit unpredictable."

"What does that mean?"

Beethoven now expressed his irritation by sitting up and frowning. "I don't know. Like anyone else, if you never know quite how they'll respond, you get nervous."

"Would he hurt you?"

"No! Don't be silly!"

"Figuratively, would he hurt you?"

"Look, why all these questions?" he snapped, a none-too-subtle threat implied in his tone.

But Meiying would have none of it. "Because I need to know how much I can trust you," she replied firmly. Meiying knew this comment played upon his attraction to her, but the stakes were too high to let scruples interfere.

"Meiying, you know you can trust me."

"What is his real motive?"

"Who?"

"Mr. President."

Beethoven exhaled loudly. "What do you mean?"

"What does he want with me?"

"He says he is totally committed to a united front against Japan, but I know he's in touch with the Japs."

"What does he want with me?"

Beethoven let out a loud sigh. Capitulation. "Probably as a plaything."

"Sexually?"

"Oh god, no! As an expensive and talented toy. He knows . . . never mind."

"Does he know about Naguma?"

"Yes."

"Father Durant?"

"Of course. Your reputation is known far and wide. You are his ace-in-the-hole, just in case."

"Of what?"

Beethoven whispered now. "He is in touch with the Japanese. Plays one side against the other."

"So he can't be trusted!"

"Well, if something benefits him then you can trust he will protect it."

"And if it no longer is of benefit?"

"Then he eats it. Figuratively, of course."

Meiying pondered. "I wonder."

"Look, his methods have worked so far. This area remains relatively safe. Even Taiyuan fell, and Yan Xishan is a powerful warlord. But here we're still in control."

"Except for famine."

"Everyone here eats well."

"Figuratively."

Beethoven pursed his lips, poured her more tea, and considered for a long moment. "What do you mean figuratively? I certainly eat well, as do the others here."

"Fatted calf."

"It's safe and warm."

Meiying put her cup down and leaned forward. "Can I trust you?"

"You know you can, but you don't let me get close."

"You're a monk, a holy man."

He laughed. "Figuratively. This guise helped me stay out of the army."

"And it will help you stay out of my vagina."

"I didn't mean that," he fumbled.

"What did you mean?"

"Friends."

"Sure. Let's discuss the concert."

He seemed quite relieved to change the topic. "Yes, good."

"Should I play Beethoven?"

He immediately understood her meaning. "Yes, but he is not safe and warm."

"Chopin? Mozart?"

"No, play Beethoven!"

"Are you sure?"

"I am certain."

"Then I agree," replied Meiying warmly. "He has always been a good friend of mine."

~

That evening, Meiying stood at the piano staring out at a large audience comprised of people from all parts of China and beyond. Mr. President was late, and a massive chair positioned in the front row on the keyboard side awaited his arrival. Her thoughts were on the conversation with Beethoven. Although it ended on a good note, she had doubts that he could be trusted. Yet how could she set off on such a journey alone? In these times, with danger all around, desperate men, and famine so widespread, she knew she needed a companion, even if only for some level of protection and to share the risks. Oh, if she were a man! What a different situation that would be! The worst that could happen would be a violent death; nothing to the humiliation and degradation inflicted on women.

"Miss Bai, pay attention!" exclaimed someone nearby. "Mr. President!"

She had not noticed his grand entrance, and immediately cognizant of her error, bowed deeply to the obese figure waddling toward her through the parting crowd.

When he reached his chair, he paused and said in his feminine voice to Meiying, "Play as you have never played before."

"I will try, Mr. President."

Satisfied, he let his body pour into the chair, flanked by two assistants who, in this instance, offered nothing more than symbolic help.

Meiying started with *Moonlight Sonata*, always a crowd-pleaser. Mr. President gave no outward sign of appreciation, so she immediately began playing the *Appasionata*, and intentionally made eye-contact with the living, flesh-and-blood, quasi-Buddhist monk Beethoven. He caught her significant glance and returned it with unabashed enthusiasm. This evidence of his receptivity gave her courage. Notes flew from the instrument in a flurry of changing tempos and virtuosic skill; a sandstorm of enveloping music and stinging, scouring passion. By the end of the concert, Meiying felt exhausted yet renewed. Music had again shown the way.

~ *In Search of Demons* ~

Feng Shiren sought out John one evening and dragged him from the hotel with a hurried explanation that time was of the essence.

"Time is of the essence about what?" asked John as they rushed through the crowded streets.

"Demons change shapes as easily as changing a coat," replied Feng.

"Dammit Feng! Is that what this is about?"

"Of course!"

They hastened past the shuffling sea of humanity, dodging this way and that. Darkness pressed hard against the flickering street lights, carving deep shadows in the myriad of human faces passing beneath, which, to John's eyes, gave their features a sinister pall. *They all do look like demons.*

"Feng!" John called, momentarily separated from his Virgil. Claustrophobia and alien surroundings left him lacking the boldness of Dante. "Hold up a minute! I don't believe in demons!"

"So much the better!"

As they moved deeper into the famine-stricken underbelly of the city, an unhealthy fog of blight and disease permeated the atmosphere. John pulled his collar around his neck, wishing he could pull the fabric over his head and block out the surrounding aura of menace that made him so fearful. Hundreds of sunken eyes, moist and reflective, stared at him like dim cinders on the verge of either burning out or flaring up.

Finally, they came to an old, multiple-story brick building with a wooden door that bore the carved image of a dragon locked in mortal combat with a tiger. Feng glanced up and down the street and entered without knocking.

A group of men and women sat at a long table, and through the dense cigarette smoke John noticed two others appeared who apparently had been guarding the door. No one seemed surprised to see Feng Shiren.

"Welcome, Comrade Feng!" exclaimed a young man still sitting at the table. "Come in. Introduce us to your friend."

John felt their eyes scanning his face and body with an almost physical sensation of being violated.

"This is my American friend, John Powers."

"Does he speak Chinese?" someone asked.

"Yes, I do," interjected John.

"I have brought him here so that he can meet some real Chinese demons." Everyone laughed.

"Welcome, American comrade," said the young man. "Sit and join our discussion."

John sat next to Feng and continued to feel the stares. There was a short period of awkward silence, then Feng Shiren slammed his hand on the table.

"Tell me what the discussion topic is tonight!"

The young man looked askance at Feng and his eyes briefly flitted over to John.

"Oh, he's okay," said Feng. "I can vouch for him."

"We welcome Americans who are interested in our cause," said a young woman.

John wanted to ask, but felt too intimidated, plus he did not want to appear stupid. Feng, of course, knew this and forged ahead without scruples.

"Oh, our American friend has no idea what your cause is."

The others looked surprised. "What?" said the young man, thinking he had heard wrong.

"Why have you brought him here?" asked another.

"To see real Chinese demons. I told you already, but you laughed. I wasn't joking."

"What does this mean?" asked the young woman who had spoken earlier.

"It means, comrades, that you have a young, virile, naked soul sitting here to convince. If you are successful, he has powerful contacts in the United States."

"Has he been briefed?" asked another older woman, who spoke for the first time.

"Nope. He is a virgin."

"Then you have endangered us all!" cried the older woman.

But the young man who had been the first to speak kept his eyes on Feng Shiren. "What is your plan, comrade," he said calmly. "To test us?"

"Not at all. Can't test demons. Too clever. This is a test for him."

"While we may be demons to the Guomindang, we are certainly not demons to the people of China."

"Precisely," replied Feng.

"Precisely what? You have compromised our location, our members, for what? To test an American?"

"Demons."

"Fuck the demons!" shouted the young man. "Why have you brought such a dangerous thing?"

"I am not a thing," said John tentatively. At his wit's end with this dialogue, he said in a more insistent voice, "I'm here because he brought me. I have no idea who you are or what you stand for." He experienced a brief moment of pride that he had spoken-up.

"The boy speaks sense," said a balding, paunchy, middle-aged observer, speaking for the first time. "But he still poses a risk."

"Do you want me to take him out and kill him?" asked Feng whimsically.

"Comrade Feng, quit being absurd!" commanded an older man standing off to the side in the shadows. His words seemed to cow the others. Stepping into the light, he looked at John with a severe face. "Mr. Powers, please tell us your view of the current political situation."

"How do you mean?"

"Well, do you support the government's campaign against Japan?"

John pondered in silence, composing himself. He wanted to protest the entire interrogation and plead ignorance, but he forced himself to think and soon realized this question was a trap. *Comrade equals communist*, he thought. Finally, he said, "I support a united front against Japan. As Yan Xishan says, 'resistance against the enemy and defense of the soil.'"

"Under whose leadership?" asked the older man.

"I don't know. I haven't thought that much about it."

"Your country is allied with the Guomindang. Do you support your government's policy?"

"I don't know enough to answer."

"Do you support Jiang Jieshi?"

"If he can defeat the Japs."

The older man sighed and turned to Feng. "Comrade, why invite him here when his views are so naïve? So unformed?"

Feng again struck an operatic pose and tilted his head quizzically. "Look, comrade, Americans think you are demons. I invited him here to prove otherwise. A test of his perceptive abilities. Do you prefer a dead American to a friendly American?"

"We prefer to stay alive. A dead American might contribute more to our survival than a live American."

"But a live American might be more beneficial to your prospering, rather than your having to meet secretly in shabby buildings."

"He strikes me as a typical American fool. Empty-headed."

"He has contacts."

"With other fools. Americans, regardless of their age, are like children when it comes to political reality. Especially here."

"America is a country of the young."

"Take him to the river and kill him."

John's horror at the sudden turn of this bizarrely matter-of-fact conversation from politics to his murder immobilized him. It was as if all his blood had drained from some invisible plug inexplicably yanked out, and he was left a desiccated mummy, unable to rise or move or even respond.

Feng Shiren chuckled as if the entire proceedings were a lark. "He's a journalist. Let him interview you, get your side. He can be your Edgar Snow. *Red Star over China* has made Comrade Mao very well-known in the west. I understand his book is quite influential in the United States."

"No. Kill him." This last statement came in the form of a command from the older man.

John looked desperately at Feng, who merely shrugged. "What are you doing, Comrade Feng?" he shouted.

"Ah! You see? At last. Demons. I'm introducing you to demons and their persuasive abilities."

John felt a strong arm wrap around his neck and pull him to his feet.

See what comes of trusting in anyone but Me?

What?

See what comes of trusting anyone but Me? I can bring you dreams. I can bring you nightmares. I can lead you to her. But you must listen to Me! I can do nothing for you if you don't listen! I need the boy. I need you. I need her. Now, wake up and go back to the hotel with Feng. He is not leading you anywhere dangerous. He is but a tool. His demons await, it is true, but not yet. Wake up and go with him now and you will be safe. Have you forgotten Meiying? Foolish Chosen One! I can't vouch for the hangover. John, dear, wake up!

"John! Wake up! You've just had too much to drink!"

John opened his eyes to see Feng Shiren sitting across a table from him, chuckling. "Man, you had a bad time the last few minutes. Let's go home. Enough drinking for tonight. Rice wine demons are tricky!"

"Damn it, Feng, you're a bastard!" bellowed John thickly, beginning to feel the onrush of nausea. He tried to stand with dignity, but dizziness made him blurt out, "Where's the bathroom?"

Feng pointed, all the while chuckling to himself.

Weaving past the tables full of similarly amused patrons, he found his destination just in time. The toilet was nothing more than an open hole in the concrete and the overwhelming stench made him vomit as much as the liquor. When he weakly made his way back to a smirking Feng Shiren, John shook his head in confusion and asked, "How long have we been here?"

"Hours. We've been having a grand old time."

"Doing what?"

"Talking, and—" Feng held up a half-full glass of rice wine—"have some more?"

John gagged and pushed it away. "What is this place?"

"A well-known restaurant in Taiyuan. All the best low-life people come here. It's the Li Hua Restaurant and Bar. You told me you like it here. Talked for hours about yourself and Meiying. Don't remember?"

"Oh, god, I don't feel well. How far away is the hotel?"

Feng stood up and laughed. "No more wine?"

"Ugh! No!"

"Okay, follow me. We can walk back to the hotel. Night air will do you good."

Once outside, John remembered his nightmare (*or whatever it was*, he thought) and looked back at the restaurant. It was an old, multiple-story brick building with a wooden door that bore the carved image of a dragon locked in mortal combat with a tiger.

John grasped a lamppost and pulled Feng over by his coat. "Did we meet anybody in there tonight?"

"Just demons."

"Oh crap! Don't you ever give a straight answer?"

"Nothing I have ever said could be more truthful."

"Would they really have killed me?"

"Who?"

John again felt nauseous, but choked it down and took a few gulps of fresh air. "Are you a communist?" he finally managed to ask.

"Are you a primate?"

"What?"

"Are you an ape?"

"Damn it Shiren! What are you talking about?"

Feng laughed. "Come on, little American friend, let's go home."

~ *Work* ~

Days passed and the group continued to languish at the hotel. Even Madame Liu seemed resigned to the inertia. War continued to rage outside the city as Yan

Xishan and the communists engaged the Japanese, giving the group good reason to hole-up in Taiyuan. Running low on funds, John quietly looked for work. After all, he could quit at a moment's notice and continue the journey when the time came.

Again, as in Nanjing, he landed a job teaching English. This time, many of his students were Japanese. The irony of it occurred to him, but in these days, ironies were a dime a dozen. For some reason he had always liked teaching. Perhaps it was one of the few times in his life the nervous uncertainties were not boiling up from some molten core of self-doubt. None of his students spoke English. He did. Instant confidence. Except for one student; a young Japanese officer who already knew some English and measured any corrections as if searching for John's error, not his own. This propensity unsettled him. When he described his student to Madame Liu, she warned him the Japanese officer might be a plant. A spy looking for plots and conspiracies. Problem was, John began to like him. The more he observed the student, the more he seemed a Japanese version of himself. After closer inspection, John realized the man had doubts also, was humble, and self-conscious about his English skills.

This realization came slowly, but an incident occurred one day that removed all uncertainty. One particular class consisted of five advanced students; four Chinese merchants and the Japanese officer, whose name was Nobaru Ichida. Today's lesson involved travel.

"I will pack my luggage and leave for Berlin tomorrow," said John clearly and slowly. He picked Berlin for the benefit of Lieutenant Ichida.

"I will back my luggage and leave for Berlin tomorrow," repeated Nobaru.

"Good, but there are a few pronunciation problems," John said in Chinese, which Nobaru understood.

"Okay, what?" asked Nobaru.

"Pack, not back. Repeat, pack."

"Back."

"Pack."

"Back."

"No, watch my lips. Pack."

"Back."

"Well, let's try again." John noticed Nobaru look around self-consciously. He did so not in the typical arrogant manner of Japanese soldiers, particularly Japanese officers, but smiling in an apologetic, even endearing manner.

"Pack."

"Pa . . . pa . . . Back."

"No problem, Lieutenant Ichida, I'll come back to you."

John went on, and the others, all Chinese, did fine. He returned to Nobaru. "Pack."

"Back."

"Good. Now let's talk about what our fellow is packing."

"No," said Nobaru.

"Pardon?"

"Sorry, no." said Nobaru in Chinese. "I have it wrong and I'm holding up the class. My humble apologies. But please, say it again so I get it right."

"Okay. Pack."

"Back."

"Pack."

"Pack."

"Yes! You've got it!" Even the Chinese smiled and congratulated him, for in spite of themselves, they also liked this young Japanese officer.

"Again, Lieutenant Ichida," said John. "Pack."

"Pack. Pack. Pack!" repeated a beaming Nobaru.

"Yes!" laughed John. "Now we can go on."

"Yes!" boomed Nobaru, now laughing himself.

~

Not many days later, Nobaru stayed after class and said, "Teacher Powers, you come eat with me at noodle shop. I pay. We practice English. Okay?"

John felt hesitant to fraternize in public with a Japanese officer, but thought a rejection might be worse. "Okay."

In the beginning, they carried-on a tortuous conversation in English, but after eating the noodles, and over tea, Nobaru abandoned it for Chinese, in which he was fluent.

"Where did you learn to speak Chinese so well?" asked John. "It's much better than mine."

"No, you are very good. My mother is Chinese, so I learned it at a young age."

"Where?"

"Yokohama."

"Do you miss Japan?"

"Very much. Do you miss America?"

"Very much."

Nobaru became quite pensive. "I also miss Nanjing. I was recently transferred from there. It is where my mother was born."

"Ah. I have been to Nanjing," said John, stopping himself from saying more.

"Yes," said Nobaru. "But bad things happened there." He stopped and looked around, as if just now realizing what he said.

"But fortunately," he continued. "We moved out of that terrible sadness to a different place, where the surroundings were very pleasant. My commander was much easier to live with there. Small city. Beautiful temple. Colonel Naguma, my commander, stayed in a gorgeous mansion. I was assigned there often. He even had a Chinese woman play the piano and I sometimes got to listen."

John could not believe his ears. "A Chinese woman played the piano?"

"Yes, our commander loved Western music—you know, Beethoven, Mozart, those guys. He always reminisced about traveling to Nagoya and listening to the Tokyo Philharmonic."

"Do you remember her name?"

"Sorry, who?"

"The Chinese woman who played piano."

"Sorry, I do not. Why?"

"Oh, nothing. Just curious."

"Personally, I prefer Japanese music—songs that tell a story. Don't understand that Western classical music. But the young woman played very well, I was told."

"What did she look like?"

Nobaru stared at John. "Teacher Powers, I would not ask too much. Something happened. She was killed, I think. Colonel Naguma and she . . . well, something happened between them. I don't know what, but you should not ask." He watched the American blanch at his words. His face went blank and his eyes stared into space momentarily. Then he seemed to compose himself and refocus.

"Would it be possible to ask your colonel? It's very important to me."

Nobaru looked very stern. "No! Colonel Naguma is dead, and rumors spread that this Chinese woman was involved in his death. What is your connection to her?"

John knew he had gone too far. "Oh, when I taught in Shanghai, I knew a Chinese woman who played the piano, that's all."

"Why is she so important to you?"

John laughed. "Lieutenant Ichida, if you saw her you would know why I am interested. I never got to know her, so I'm curious. Probably not even the same woman."

"What is her name?" asked Nobaru.

"Don't remember. I think its Miss Zhang, but I could be wrong."

Nobaru sipped his tea, obviously contemplating where to go next. He smiled. "Let's practice English again, okay?"

"Yes," said John, breathing a sigh of relief.

"How do you say 'war can be a dangerous business' in English?"

John told him.

"War can be dangerous business," repeated Nobaru in English, looking intently at John.

Chapter Thirteen

More Delays and Longer Detours

Meiying Leaves the Gilded Cage

Meiying spent many weeks at the temple entertaining Mr. President, but she grew increasingly restless and unhappy. At least when she languished as Colonel Naguma's gilded prisoner there was the garden to distract her. Even her own piano music grated on her, as it seemed to be the invisible cord that bound her to this obese master. Beethoven was her only quasi-confidant. Although he always rushed to express his sympathies, she did not fully trust him. The other women struck her as shallow whores, anxious to please for a trinket here or a trinket there. Except for one: Madame Wang. She behaved quite differently. Appearing to be in her forties, she retained a beauty still attractive to men, but a wisdom and cynicism far too biting for them to handle.

"Madame Wang, Mr. President bids you attend him tonight."

"Bid him attend me!" she thundered. "His attending me will attend better than the attending attention of addle-brained attendees interested only in attending him."

"Huh?"

"Tell him to go to hell! No! Stop! Tell him to have the brothel's attendees attend him. Fool that he is, will agree. Go!"

"I don't understand. What do you mean?"

"I mean tell him I am occupied," she replied disgustedly, tired of expressing her thoughts through a child's filter.

Meiying could never understand how Madame Wang got away with such impertinence. Whenever she ran across the older woman, Meiying was treated with haughty and supreme disinterest. Everyone knew Mr. President bedded her, so she must have something on him to get away with such behavior.

Thus it came as a surprise to Meiying when she received an invitation to have tea with Madame Wang at one of her private rooms. When she arrived, the Great Lady made her wait twenty minutes before making an entrance.

"So sorry," she said, her voice an operatic, high-pitched sing-song. Madame Wang sat upright and waited for a servant to pour tea before dismissing her. "I had other matters to attend," she off-handedly mentioned in a tone fully intended to convey how little she cared. Meiying nodded curtly. *Peking opera diva*, she thought.

"I suppose I should thank you for coming?"

Meiying smiled politely. "No problem, Madame Wang."

"I have invited you here to discuss your unhappiness."

"Sorry," said Meiying. "What did you say?"

"Your unhappiness."

"But Madame Wang, I am very satisfied."

"Nonsense. Let's not waste time sparring. You are on a journey, correct?"

"Yes."

"To meet some remarkable woman, or goddess, or some such?"

"Yes."

"And your friends on this journey have gone on, while you have been held back by, how should I put it, circumstances?"

"Yes."

"And you have been held in various forms of bondage for some time?"

"Yes."

"And you have been raped?"

Meiying hesitated.

"Come, come. I am a woman of the world, my dear. Have you?"

"Yes."

"Multiple times?"

"Yes."

"And you want to rejoin your friends?"

"Yes, but—"

Madame Wang held up her hand. Meiying waited quietly.

"But you cannot go to your friends because you have been made a prisoner?"

"I cannot say that."

"Are you?"

"Am I what?"

"Are you a prisoner here?"

"Sometimes it feels that way, but—"

Again Madame Wang held up her hand.

"So, you want to leave?"

"Mr. President has been very—"

"Yes, yes. But do you want to leave?"

"To rejoin my friends, yes. But I am very grateful to Mr. Pres—"

"And have that attractive young monk accompany you?"

Meiying realized Beethoven had blabbed about her plans.

"I don't know. I don't want to cause problems."

"No. Good girls with talent like you are not problems of themselves, they just cause multiple and often serious wreckage around them . . . wherever they go and whatever they do. Good, pretty girls exist at the eye of a storm. Very tranquil but for the ancillary destruction they cause others."

Meiying had no response.

"Often, these good, pretty girls whirl blithely on, leaving in their wake a trail of destruction," Madame Wang continued. "You may not be aware of it, dear one, but you are causing many problems for our fat President."

"I'm sorry."

"And you go blithely on."

"Madame Wang, would that I have just gone blithely on. I have also been damaged . . . very badly damaged."

Madame Wang's harsh expression softened. "Yes, that is evident. Suffering breaks the stalks but deepens the roots . . . at least, for those who want to survive."

"I know nothing of these things."

"I doubt it. I think you know very well 'of these things'"

Meiying did not reply.

"Hmm. You are smart. Talking and making scenes are not your way."

"No."

"But what I have to say may change that propensity."

Again Meiying said nothing.

"Mr. President is very interested in you."

"He wants to bed me?" asked Meiying openly and as dispassionately as possible, but picturing his immense rolls of fat enveloping her body caused a revulsion hard to conceal.

Madame Wang smiled at the disconnect between Meiying's visible shudder and the calm words that came out of her mouth. "No, not that, but perhaps worse."

Meiying waited. Madame Wang made her wait. Time passed.

"Well," said Madame Wang at last. "You really are different."

"What does he want?"

"He wants you to continue your journey, and he is willing to throw in our cute monk."

"In exchange for what?"

"He wants to watch while you and I make love."

Meiying experienced an instant pang of disgust, then a twinge of unexpected excitement, but she felt compelled to register no emotion.

"Is that all?" she said, after letting some time pass to calibrate, then modulate her reaction.

"Yes. You see, he knows you are a lesbian and he wants to see for himself the process."

"The process?"

"How it is done."

"Are you?" asked Meiying.

"No, but it intrigues me. It is the first original thought he has had in years."

"If I say no?"

Madame Wang shrugged.

"And if I say yes?"

"You may leave, with an escort and a pass that others he controls or cooperates with will honor."

"The Japanese?"

"Yes. He is very clever that way."

Rather than feeling insulted or violated, Meiying was surprised to feel a sense of empowerment. Gazing at Madame Wang's attractive figure, she felt a familiar desire rise up in spite of the circumstances. "Why you?" she asked.

Madame Wang sat up straight and glowered angrily. "That is not for you to know."

"My humble apologies."

"Do you accept?"

"How can I trust him?"

Madame Wang looked a bit hurt. "Is making love with me so terrible? Even for a lesbian?"

"No, but making love with me might be terrible for you, who is not a lesbian."

"Silly girl! You are lovely, Mr. President is less than lovely. I have never slept with you, I have often been smothered by him. That is an exchange I can easily live with." She grimaced, "Easily. After all, it should be easier for you than for me, but I shall still find it . . . interesting."

Meiying remained silent.

"Well?" asked Madame Wang with a certain hardness in her tone.

"Afterward, can I leave immediately?"

Madame Wang nodded.

"When is this to happen?"

"Do you mean when can you leave or when do we make love?"

"Both."

"That I cannot say. I will speak with His Rotundity."

Meiying let out a giggle.

"When it is time, you will be summoned to his private chamber," said the older woman with a smile. "Other than having him watch, this might be most enjoyable."

Meiying's response surprised even Madame Wang. "Let him watch."

~

Many days passed before Meiying finally received the message that the "performance" would take place on the following evening in Mr. President's private chamber. Since the conversation with Madame Wang, she could not stop the fantasies, and gave in to the warm glow of their elaborate arrangements and rearrangements. Like Bach's *Goldberg Variations*, each had its own exquisite rhythm, tone, and counterpoint. To release pent-up energy, she went to the piano room and played a difficult Liszt sonata. In the midst of a particularly convoluted transition, Beethoven appeared next to her. Startled out of her concentration, she abruptly stopped.

"Go on, go on," he insisted.

"No, I am finished for now."

"Please, I want to hear."

"Maybe later." She remained sitting on the bench, her arm resting on the piano.

Beethoven gazed upon her lovely form and felt a painful attraction. "I have heard you may be leaving."

With these words, Meiying was assailed by conflicting emotions. At first, her anger at his immoderate talk gave way to the realization that she would need him, which in turn gave way to a grudging acceptance of her position and her vulnerabilities.

"Yes, it is time to rejoin my friends."

"Am I still invited?"

"Of course." She smiled, again feeling a pang of guilt for the flirtatious manipulation of this young man who had done her no harm. "I was hoping you would still be interested."

"I am more than interested, Meiying. When do we leave?"

"After I take care of some matters."

"Ah," he said, deflated.

Meiying wondered if he knew.

"They shouldn't take long."

"Just let me know."

"Now," said Meiying cheerily. "Go away and let me practice!"

"I can't stay?" he asked with an exaggerated pout.

"No."

After he left, Meiying began questioning her own judgment. She felt certain he was Mr. President's spy. If he accompanied her, there would be no privacy. Would that represent a danger? Ever since she was a girl, her trusting nature caused problems. With the invasion of the Japanese and the assaults on her body and soul, that innocent trust had been damaged. But how much? She did not want to end up a bitter old woman, suspicious of everyone and afraid of her own shadow; but she also did not want to be so naïve as to put herself in an untenable position.

That night she slept very little. Her imagination danced to the discordant visitations of those who had so recently sculpted her life, for good or bad: Meili, Mr. President, Beethoven, Naguma, Father Durant, the group, and *her*. All roads let to *her*. Oddly, Meiying did not dwell on "the performance," although it did strike her as ironic that Mr. President assumed she was experienced and would seamlessly show him "the process." But in truth, she had no idea how it would unfold with a stranger. Sex proceeded naturally with Meili, as they both were new to the game. But Madame Wang? An experienced lover? Meiying knew she would be awkward and clumsy with the older woman, but that was part of the excitement. She would be the student, not Madame Wang.

The next day Meiying restlessly wandered the temple grounds, eventually finding a lovely spot overlooking the lake. Ripples lapped their monotonous cadence upon the shore. Soon she became drowsy and lay on her back to feel the sun. With the watery cadence as accompaniment, she dreamt a symphony and copied dark notes against the sky. The first movement unfolded as a jaunty, breezy paean to her happy youth. Tripping down the streets of Shanghai, her dress swirling around her bare legs, passers-by smiling at the vision of her youthful, beautiful, carefree innocence. The second movement began on a more somber, mature note, but still projected an underlying tranquility which drove the melody. Grappling with her lesbianism, mastering the piano, forging her own identity, all channeled the music into a crescendo, rising toward a triumphal march. However, the discordant notes of the second movement screamed above the self-congratulatory air, and an ominous counterpoint—the Japanese invasion—ended with a violent roar. The third movement carried over the dark motif, racing up and down on its journey to some unknown and fearful destination. A destination that had been cut short.

Suddenly the music stopped. Water continued lapping; sun continued pouring down its warmth; sky continued flashing its blue; birds whirled above calling out their own songs; but the huge edifice she had built in her mind, the great symphony of her life that had reverberated to the heavens, instantly collapsed and compressed its great bulk into a searing point in her heart—a place from which she knew not how to escape.

"Hello."

She opened her eyes and blinked, holding her hand up to shade the sun.

"I've been looking for you," said Beethoven.

"Sit down," she said. "I'm tired of always looking up at you."

"I never get tired of looking at you," he replied as he sat beside her.

"A very automatic and not at all sincere remark," she said, feeling piqued at his unwanted intrusion.

Beethoven appeared stricken. "That's not fair!"

"Whether or not it is fair, I appreciate your words."

"Meiying, let me help you. Please stop pushing me away."

"I'm not. I appreciate your help. I trust I will be able to count on you in the future."

"You can count on me, but can I count on you?"

She started to respond when someone trotted up who she did not recognize. He stopped and bowed. "Mr. President wants you for the performance."

"What performance?" asked Beethoven.

"I don't know," she mumbled. "Must be some mistake. I'd better go." She rose and followed the servant.

"Yes, I'll see you later," called Beethoven, who remained sitting as she disappeared with the servant.

Something made Meiying stop and tell the servant she would be right back. She retraced her steps and looked at the spot where she left Beethoven. He was gone. A niggling thought played at the back of her mind, and she wondered if Mr. President would be the only onlooker tonight.

~ *John and Nobaru Become Close* ~

Over the next few weeks, John became very close to Nobaru. *Who would have thought that a Japanese soldier could be so sensitive, so attuned to my personality?* He mused one evening while they shared a meal at a renowned Hunan restaurant. John did not dare bring up Meiying again, but the good-natured yet serious Nobaru brought so much to their discussion that he felt content to bask in the relationship rather than complicate it with such a potentially divisive, not to mention dangerous, topic. On this particular night, their conversation had branched-off into the realm of philosophy.

As always, Nobaru was attired in his crisp officer's uniform while John wore a Chinese-style cotton tunic. They were indeed an odd pair. Nobaru's samurai sword rested against the table. Each sipped rice wine, but neither was drunk, only a bit tipsy. They spoke "Chinglish"—a combination of Chinese and English.

"Do you believe in evolution?" asked Nobaru out of nowhere.

"Of course," replied John. "But I don't 'believe' in evolution, because that implies faith or religion. Better to say I 'accept' evolution, based on the evidence of course."

"Very scientific, but still amounts to the same thing."

"No, I don't think so," replied John. "Do you believe . . . or should I say accept evolution?"

Nobaru looked around and leaned forward. "Yes, I accept it. But that acceptance is not a proper view for a Japanese officer."

"Why not?"

Nobaru laughed. "Sometimes you surprise me. Why not?" He emptied his cup and ordered another bottle. "Ancestors, bushido, tradition."

"Well," said John. "It's not that popular in America either."

"Is it dangerous?"

"No. Well, maybe some places. But it is something better left unsaid."

Nobaru's face turned red. "Yes, that's the problem with this world; all the things better left unsaid."

"Why did you ask?"

"Because I'm curious about the views of foreigners, particularly Americans. Your country seems so much more advanced."

John considered. "In some places, but we definitely are not of one mind. In the southern part of the United States, views are very different."

"Slavery," said Nobaru.

"Well, that is no longer legal."

"Not what our rulers tell us."

"They . . . well, that's not exactly accurate."

Nobaru took a few sips and looked out the window. "Will evolution ever lead us to a better place? A more peaceful place?"

"I don't know," was all that John could muster in response.

Nobaru would not let it go. "It seems we kill the ones that are different. Our positive mutations are not given a chance to carry us forward."

"Yes, I agree," said John. "Are you a positive mutation?"

"God, no!" cried Nobaru. "But I think I have met some, or, at least one."

"Really?"

"Yes. Remember that Chinese woman who played the piano for my commander?"

John sat up straight, fully alert. "Yes, the one you told me not to talk about?"

"I know, I know, but she did make an impression on me. I just can't admit it to anyone."

John waited. He desperately wanted to grill Nobaru, but knew that would be a grave mistake. *God let him stay on this topic.*

But Nobaru remained pensive, again gazing out the window. John could stand it no longer.

"Why did she make an impression?"

Nobaru smiled complacently. "I knew you would be interested."

"You brought it up! We can talk about something else if you want."

Nobaru continued smiling, but not at John. "Ah, I often think of her. Thing is, I only saw her twice, but that was enough."

John felt an irrational twinge of jealousy, but forced himself to play it cool; appear to be only mildly interested. Thank god Nobaru went on.

"One day I was summoned to my commander's headquarters—an old mansion with beautiful gardens. As I passed through the garden I noticed a very beautiful woman talking to some old peasant gardener. She wore a peasant hat and clothes. Now, I have seen many pretty peasant girls and have always stopped to appreciate them, so I paused to watch. When she tilted her hat back to wipe her brow, I couldn't believe my eyes—she was so beautiful! She was no peasant! I could have stood and watched for hours, but my commander called me from the porch. 'Hey! Lieutenant Ichida! Come!'"

Nobaru chuckled at the memory. "I'm sure he saw me staring at her like some love-struck boy. After we finished our business, he graciously invited me to stay and attend a piano concert. Of course I accepted. The old fox never told me who the pianist would be. It was her."

Nobaru stopped and poured another cup for John and himself, but he remained lost in thought. John felt excruciating curiosity but dared not appear too interested. He held back from commenting for fear the topic would change. Finally, Nobaru looked at him and laughed.

"John, I know you're dying to hear more!"

"Your story is so interesting. It's like a movie. Go on." But John felt an unanticipated resistance to Nobaru's carefree description of encounters with "pretty peasant girls." He thought of the thousands who had been brutally raped, tortured, and murdered by the Japanese occupiers, and a hint of revulsion insinuated itself between him and his friend. But Nobaru seemed not to notice, the wine starting to take its toll. He continued.

"That afternoon, we sat waiting for this famous Chinese pianist. At last she arrived and stood at the piano with another girl, a friend. It was her! The beautiful one in the garden with that old peasant gardener, like beauty and the beast. I couldn't believe it, I couldn't believe my luck! We waited for some time. Suddenly, the friend was taken away and this Chinese pianist was ordered to play by our commander. She objected, but he insisted, even threatened her. Now, I knew Colonel Naguma, and he was . . . well, that's a different story. Something bad happened to her friend, and she continued to object. After a scene and more threats, she played while she cried, and the music and her dignity struck me to the core. Her beauty, her sadness, the way she played at that moment transcended normal human behavior. I am convinced she is a positive mutant. It's like, she is the way forward, if we fools let her live. That's what I mean. We can't kill the ones that are different!" Nobaru's eyes were red and his words slightly slurred, but his emotion seemed to John deeply rooted in reason and guilt.

"What happened to her friend?"

"Shot. She was a spy, or so we were told."

"Oh, god, Meili," murmured John.

"What?" snapped Nobaru.

"I said, 'oh, god, what a shame,'" replied John quickly, too quickly.

"No you didn't! I heard a name."

"No."

"Yes!" cried Nobaru, drawing the attention of people sitting at other tables.

John felt suddenly very afraid, but his fear mixed with anger.

Be careful, Chosen One. He is unpredictable. He might shoot you. Then where am I left? No son! Plans delayed! You must not die, my mutant Chosen One! You will be dead and she will die a lonely, lost, luckless, lesbian!

Nobaru seemed to calm down as he stared at John sitting wordlessly, like a deer in the headlights.

"John, look at me. Focus. Do you know this woman?"

"No."

"You lie! I heard a name. You realize she murdered a Japanese officer?"

Something in Nobaru's tone indicated a lack of conviction, a lack of outrage. John hit upon a path forward.

"Nobaru, I might know her from Shanghai, but I'm not sure. Tell me more about her."

"Don't have to. You already know her, don't you?"

"No, or at least I don't think so."

"John, you know I could have you arrested right now?"

John's gut tightened and he felt a sudden onrush of nausea. The old fears rendered him dumb.

Nobaru waved his arms in agitation, abruptly stood and walked toward the exit.

John started to call him back, then stopped and simply stared.

Noraru hesitated as if feeling John's eyes on his back. He abruptly turned around and came back.

Much to John's inexpressible relief, he smiled as if sharing an inside joke.

"I forgot my sword."

John had a sudden propitious inspiration. He gestured toward the sword and looked back at Nobaru.

"Sit down and join us. Your sword and I have been in a deep discussion and we need a third party to resolve the debate."

Nobaru sat down and spoke to the sword. "Well, what nonsense has this American been telling you?"

John changed his voice and spoke as if he were the sword. "I can't believe what these Americans say!"

"Oh?" said Nobaru, still speaking to the sword. "Like what?"

Before John could reply for the sword, Nobaru summoned the waiter and order another bottle.

He bowed to the sword. "Excuse the interruption. Please continue."

"This American is in love but he didn't want to admit it."

"Obviously," said Nobaru. "And I know who he is in love with."

"But he is afraid to tell us," said the sword.

"Yes," replied Nobaru with some bitterness. "He thinks we're bloodthirsty Japanese."

"No, I don't!" protested John, turning his gaze back on Nobaru.

"Might as well tell me about it," said Nobaru.

"We were separated long ago. I had lost track of where she was until you mentioned her. Really, that's all there is to it."

"Oh, I'm sure there is much more." Now, the Japanese lieutenant's words became increasingly slurred. "You see, in spite of my imperial training, I'm a hopeless romantic."

"Do you know where she is now?" asked John.

"What was the name you mentioned?"

"Meili, her friend."

"The one we shot," said Nobaru, more to himself than to John.

They fell silent. Nobaru kept drinking and insisting John keep up.

Before long, both were drunk.

"I'm in love with her too!" cried Nobaru out of nowhere.

"Okay, we're both in love with her," said John.

"Cheers!" Nobaru lifted his cup.

John looked down at the table, his face a tragic mask.

"She's a lesbian," he mumbled.

"What?"

"Nothing."

~ *Nuts* ~

John woke the next morning with a terrific headache. At the hotel restaurant, although the food made him gag, the tea began to demonstrate its restorative power. Suling joined him.

"You look terrible," she said.

"Thanks, I feel the part."

"Are you ill?"

"Hangover."

"Oh."

"Suling, remember that Japanese officer I've been telling you about?"

"Yes."

"He has seen Meiying."

"You mentioned that before."

"No, I mean he told me more about her last night."

Suling leaned forward. "Is she alive? Where is she?"

"Apparently, she's alive, but I still don't know where she is."

"What did he say?"

John filled her in.

"Poor Meili, poor Meiying," said Suling.

"Yes."

"Well," said Suling. "She must be in hiding from the Japs."

"I've been wracking my brains trying to figure out how we can find her before we move on and maybe lose her forever."

"Lose who?" said Feng Shiren as he sat down at the table.

"Meiying."

"News?"

John repeated his story.

"Ah, I think I may know a way to find her," said Feng.

"How?"

"You won't like it."

"Why?"

"Too vague."

"Tell me anyway," said John.

"I have my feelers out. I hear rumors."

"What haven't you told us?" asked Suling.

Feng shrugged. "Just rumors, but now maybe I think they're true."

"Tell us," said John.

"No."

"Damn it, Feng! Why not?"

"Don't want you to get your hopes up."

"Mr. Feng," said Suling softly but firmly. "You have done so much for us, we are all very grateful. John is just upset."

Feng bowed his head and put his hand over his heart. "Suling, your words have touched me. I will move heaven and earth to find her."

"You're very kind."

At that moment, Madame Liu and Master Zhou entered the restaurant and sat at a corner table, apparently so involved in deep conversation that they did not notice John and his companions.

"Ah, something's up," observed Feng. "I've heard rumors."

John shook his head. "You and your rumors."

"Are you curious?"

"Of course."

"In this case, no harm done."

John and Suling leaned closer. Just as Feng started to speak, Lu Zhishen approached the table.

"May I join you?"

"Of course."

Suling waited until Lu received his tea and ordered a rice bowl, then said, "Mr. Feng has some news. He—"

Feng interrupted. "Not news, rumors."

"Yes, thank you, rumors."

Now all ears were tuned to Feng Shiren who stretched out the drama by slowly sipping his tea. By now, the others understood his theatrical ways and waited patiently.

"I have heard," he declared, albeit in a whisper. "Better yet, I have been told we are leaving soon to continue the journey."

The others expressed surprise.

"When?" asked John.

Feng shrugged. "Soon."

Suling glanced at Madame Liu and Master Zhou in the corner, still conversing. "That must be what they're talking about."

"Peter mentioned something about that yesterday," said Lu Zhishen.

"About what?"

"About there being something up. I didn't pay much attention though."

"By the way, where is Peter?" asked John.

"Dunno."

"Probably sleeping," observed Feng. "He's been returning late the last few nights."

"How do you know?" asked Lu.

"I know because I'm Feng Shiren."

"Oh, bullshit!" cried an exasperated Lu. "I'm serious. How do you know? Do you stay up and spy on us all night?"

"I do not sleep," said Feng evenly. "That is for you, not me."

"Give me a fuckin' break!" cried Lu.

Suling again interjected with soft-spoken words but also with unmistakable intent. "Where has he been going?"

Feng shrugged and assumed his pouting face.

"I thought you knew everything," said Lu.

"Of course he doesn't," said Suling kindly. She held out her hands, palms up. "The journey is the most important thing. The journey must continue, and we mustn't bicker."

The others reciprocated, but even as he joined them, John said accusingly, "What about Meiying? Now we know she's alive and hiding from the Japanese. I mean, she's wanted for murder! We all know she is not capable of that, but if she's caught, well, we need to help her."

"Can't help her if we can't find her," declared Lu.

"No worries," said Feng. "I'll follow-up on those rumors."

"I want to help," said John.

"No, not this time," replied Feng.

"Why not?"

Feng smiled mysteriously. "I have my reasons."

John viewed Feng with increasing suspicion. Yes, he helped, but the group was becoming too dependent on his good services. What if he turned on them? Besides, what is his interest in *her*? After all, he never met *her*, and never gave a good reason to care. Is he just using the group for some nefarious end? What if he is *her* enemy and they are leading him to *her*? Yes! Feng could very well be a spy, or worse, an assassin.

"Feng, you are always playing the mystery man," said Lu Zhishen sarcastically.

John followed up. "Feng, what really is your interest in *her*? Why go through all this trouble with us when you haven't even met *her*?"

Feng looked over John's shoulder. "They're leaving," he said as he nodded toward Madame Liu and Master Zhou.

They all looked, and by so doing attracted the attention of the two elders. Madame Liu and Master Zhou waved from across the room without stopping and quickly exited the restaurant.

"Hmm, that's odd," declared Lu.

Feng caught everyone's eye. "Are you all ready to continue the journey?"

"You won't forget Meiying?" asked John.

"Never!"

He tells the truth, sent by Me. Trust him.

"Mr. Feng, what do you plan to do when we reach the destination?" asked Suling.

"See what all the fuss is about."

"That's a lot of trouble to go through for something that might just turn out to be the delusion of a few nutty people," said John.

"Ah, Little Acorn!" cried Feng upon seeing the youngster enter the restaurant. "Where have you been, sleepy-head?"

The boy ran up to the table, clearly delighted to find his friends and protectors. "Hello!" he exclaimed.

"Hello."

Suling pulled a chair up next to her. "Come sit, Little Acorn. Sit and eat."

"Yes, order what you want, boy!" cried Feng, smiling openly.

"Thanks!"

As Little Acorn shoveled food into his mouth, Feng elaborated on his earlier response. "John, you say you all might turn out to be nutty. Well, the nuttier the people, the more nuts you will find. I am always searching for nuts. Some are on the ground—easy. Others are high up in the trees, and I become a squirrel to reach them!" He jumped from his chair to the floor and scurried around the table, pausing for the longest time by John. "I know," he whispered. "You are not what you think you are."

Suling had not heard Feng's words, but his actions made her laugh so hard she had to cover her mouth.

Lu Zhishen scowled.

John was dumbstruck. **You see, he knows about you! He knows! You are not mentally ill, just a stranger in a strange land. But it is a land soon to be made much stranger for humans when your descendants—Superior Ones—rise to dominance.**

Suling recognized the peculiar facial expression John assumed when the voice emerged. "John, would you like some more tea?" she said.

"What?"

"Would you like more tea?" She held up the teapot.

It's poisoned! She wants to kill you! They all want to kill you! Worthless, can't you see it? Worthless!

This was the first time the God voice had become so brutally insistent, and it struck John as a different male voice. Deep and scratchy. *How many voices are there?* he wondered. They were becoming mixed up in his mind. This one male, that one female, another that seemed neither. He fought back. *You're wrong! Leave me alone! Go back to wherever you came from! You're not real!*

John! You're putting the son in jeopardy! You're putting your own son in danger! I need that offspring! My plans! That voice is the product of your human genes expressing a schizophrenic caprice, a human impulse to mental deviancy. God and His faction are using it to make you believe you are sick. Don't listen to that voice! It is what humans might call a demon! It is a ruse! Ignore it!

Goddess had returned. Or one of the Goddesses. So confusing!

"John," said Suling quietly but insistently. "John, have some more tea." She poured tea into the cup.

The others stared openly. All had seen this behavior in him before; expressionless face, glassy eyes, detached manner.

Suling gently shook his arm. "John!"

Gradually, faces emerged from the fog and John began to focus. The voice quieted, then went silent. "What? Yes. Tea. Thank you, Suling."

Suling looked at him, concern lining her face. "Are you okay, John?"

"Yeah, of course."

Feng dived into the moment with no compunctions. "Oh! The voice again! I get it! Hey, what does it say? I'm curious."

John sighed. "Yes, the voice. It comes and goes. Just talks nonsense. What were we discussing?"

"Mr. Feng was about to tell us more about why he wants to meet *her*," said Lu, intent on returning to a topic he was most interested in. All eyes turned to Feng Shiren.

"Well," he began somewhat tentatively. "It's not a mystery. I'm simply curious."

"Has to be more than that," said Lu.

"Why?"

"To risk your life? To go through the shit we've gone through? Come on, Feng, we know there must be more to the story."

"Mr. Feng, if you don't want to say. . . . " Suling smiled and shook her head.

"No, no! It's no mystery! Perhaps I have met *her*. Have you ever thought of that?"

"Of course," replied Lu. "But you told us you never met *her*."

"Maybe I have my reasons."

Lu threw up his arms. "Mystery again! Did you or didn't you?"

Feng toyed with his chopsticks, then held them up. "Takes two, right?"

"Okay," said Lu. "So what?"

"Before I met *her*, I was one chopstick. Then I met *her* and became two chopsticks. After *she* left, I became one chopstick again. *She* is the missing other. I must find *her* again to be whole. To eat. To survive."

This news stunned the others and silence fell over the table.

Okay, Feng Shiren tells the partial truth. But the two chopsticks are God and Goddess. God is paired with Goddess and Goddess is paired with God and always the twain shall meet! Entangled. That is why I need your son. For God. To fight God and His faction. For the future of the planet. Don't you get it, dear Chosen One? I need the son! It was God earlier, using your human genetic foibles, trying to have you believe they would poison you. It was Him, not Me!

John sat rigid, fell off the chair and banged his head on the floor, moaning.

The others jumped up and rushed to his side. "John! Are you all right? John!"

Feng looked into his eyes and checked his pulse. "He fainted. Let's get him to his room."

After reassuring the restaurant staff, Feng and Lu helped John to his room and put him into bed. Little Acorn, who had trailed after them, was told to go and play. The boy left in a sullen mood, resenting the irrational dictatorship of adults. Suling was anxious and constantly leaned over John with a cold cloth. She noticed some blood and washed it off, volunteering to stay and make sure he slept.

"Yes, that is good," said Feng. "He might have a concussion. Suling, when he comes to, ask him questions."

"What do you mean?"

"Ask him where he is, his name, the date, that sort of thing. If he seems confused, call me quickly and we'll take him to a hospital. You understand?"

"Yes."

"Come on, Lu, let's let him rest."

"Okay," said Lu Zhishen. "I want to talk to you more about what you just revealed to us."

"Later," said Feng. "I have some business to attend."

"You can't leave it at this," said Lu.

"I know. I'll tell you more later. Right now, I must go."

After Feng left, Lu immediately wanted to find Peter and talk to him about the strange man they all depended on and yet found so difficult to pin down.

Where is he? wondered Lu, who felt genuine concern about Peter's behavior the past few days. *Feng is right, Peter has been getting in late, and won't tell me where he's been. Is he in trouble? Gambling? Drinking? A woman?*

Lu wandered back downstairs to the restaurant and ordered more tea. *Are we leaving? When? What about Meiying? Peter? Feng? It's too much!*

~ *The Process* ~

When Meiying entered the mansion in response to Mr. President's summons, an older man with a stern expression ordered her to bathe. Accompanied by two attendants, she was led to the public baths and given a thorough scrubbing. No others were permitted and she felt odd being the only person bathing in such an immense facility. After leaving the bath, a wrap was placed around her and she followed the attendants who led her through a maze of dimly-lit hallways lined with gold friezes of dragons and other mythical figures until she reached a sumptuous waiting room. Once she entered, the lights dimmed even further and she stood in virtual darkness. Unseen hands removed her wrap and she stood naked, waiting. Soon, other hands, rougher, placed a blindfold over her eyes. A collar was put around her neck with a chain leash hanging coldly between her breasts. She felt the chain being yanked and she shuffled to keep up with the person pulling. After walking some distance to a place she assumed to be another room, the blindfold was removed and she saw Madame Wang standing before her, naked and wearing the same collar.

Candles bathed the room in soft light. A massive bed stood on the opposite wall. Mirrors and dark windows lined the walls. Neither woman spoke. Meiying assumed Mr. President watched from behind one of the mirrors or windows. Incense wafted lightly through the room. As if responding to a signal, Madame Wang raised her arm toward Meiying.

"Come," she said.

Meiying walked forward and took her hand.

"You are to teach me," whispered the older woman with a conspiratorial smile.

Without thinking, Meiying took the leash and led Madame Wang to the bed.

A blur followed. Madame Wang responded to Meiying's touch like a starving woman to food.

~

After what seemed hours, both women were exhausted. They lay together in bed, Meiying cradled against the older woman. Without warning, the door burst open, and two male attendants entered the room. Meiying pulled the covers closer around her neck and watched them place a stool at the foot of the bed. To her the astonishment, the covers were ripped off and the two women lay completely exposed. They remained in each other's arms. Mr. President waddled in, supported by his two favorite assistants, who helped him lower his great bulk onto the stool. The President waved everyone out. As they left, Meiying thought she glimpsed Beethoven on the other side of the door, but she couldn't be sure.

"I am very pleased," Mr. President announced. He looked at Madame Wang. "Did you find that pleasant?"

"Very."

"And you?" He looked at Meiying with a grotesque, quizzical look, his eyebrows ridiculously arched high on his forehead.

"Yes."

"Was it the process you use in all your lesbian encounters?"

"Every person is different, Mr. President."

He rose with great difficulty and clapped his hands. In came the two assistants who promptly helped him remove his clothes. Meiying could see nothing but rolls of fat.

"Does my body disgust you?"

Fear gripped her and rendered her mute.

"Well?"

Still she remained silent.

"It does not disgust her," he said, pointing at Madame Wang. "Does it?" he asked the older woman.

"No, but you can't—"

"Quiet!" He turned back to Meiying. "Will you join her in making love to me?"

At last Meiying found her voice. "That was not our bargain."

"It is now."

Madame Wang leapt out of bed and walked brazenly up to Mr. President. "If you make her do this, I will no longer service you. Not myself, nor will I obtain others for you."

He remained silent, his rolls jiggling with each labored breath. Finally, he spoke in his effeminate voice. "You can go to hell and be damned! I will have her!"

Madame Wang unexpectedly laughed. "You can have no one. Your cock is too small; hidden for years under blubber, until it can no longer poke out from its cave."

Meiying trembled, certain he would have both of them killed.

"Will you make love to me?" he asked her.

Better to be killed, she thought. "No."

Again, he surprised. "Then I will just have to let you go. And you"—he turned to Madame Wang—"will be punished."

Meiying started to protest on behalf of Madame Wang, but stopped when the older woman purred, "Yes, master, that is indeed what I deserve, and I will look forward to your creative and delicious punishment."

Mr. President laughed and pointed at the floor. Madame Wang got on her knees. As if just then realizing Meiying was still in the room, he clapped his hands. When attendants entered, he barked, "Take her back to her room. Let her rest. She will play a farewell concert for us. Now, go!"

As Meiying left, she passed Madame Wang who remained on her knees in front of Mr. President. An aura of self-loathing masked as passion disfigured the older woman's face. Meiying felt disoriented and faint. Nowhere in her experience had she been prepared for the spectacle that had just occurred. When at last she was left alone in her room, the tears came in torrents. She did not know why or understand their source. A deep, upwelling of loneliness and despair overcame her. When she had made love with Meili, afterward, she felt elation and a purity of spirit. But this? Again she had been degraded and humiliated. Were it not for the fact that she would soon be leaving, she might have committed suicide without further thought.

A knock interrupted her musings.

"Yes?"

"It's me, Beethoven."

Meiying knew she could not face him. If he had indeed observed, then she wanted nothing to do with this false monk. Yet, she still needed him. Mr. President even "threw him in" as part of their deal. How could she navigate the dangerous roads without a guide and some protection? She threw on a dress and quickly applied a touch of makeup.

"Come in."

Beethoven entered, his face a smiling beacon. "How are you?"

"Fine."

"I've come to cheer you up."

"How do you know I'm not cheerful?"

"When we parted by the lake I sensed you were unhappy about something."

She glared at him. "I'm not."

"What are you unhappy about?"

"You don't know?"

"No."

"If you don't know, then I'm not unhappy."

"Meiying, I don't understand you."

"The matter I discussed earlier is now finished. I am leaving tomorrow. Do you still want to come?"

He hesitated. "Tomorrow? So soon?"

"Yes."

He brightened. "Yes! I'll be ready."

"Sunrise."

"Yes."

But within an hour, he returned. "We can't leave tomorrow."

"Why?"

"Mr. President wants you to give a farewell concert."

"Oh," sighed Meiying.

"The news is worse."

"What?"

"Mr. President has taken the Precious Object and sent it away."

Chapter Fourteen

PART THREE:
THE JOURNEY CONTINUES

Where is Peter?

~ The Road Again ~

An emergency meeting of the group was called by Madame Liu. When they gathered in one of the hotel conference rooms, she began by asking the question, "Where is Peter?"

Suling's face registered alarm. John noticed and felt a sense of wonder at the transparency of her emotions. Perhaps that is why she always threw him a little off, for he had become habituated to expect some degree of subterfuge, of deceit in people, even if a little. In the beginning, it bothered him as 'too good to be true' grandstanding. But gradually he experienced a sense of awe whenever he observed it. Her honesty far exceeded his, and that realization morphed into a deep respect for her, and yet another mark against his worth as a human being.

"What do you mean?" asked Suling. "How long has he been gone?"

"For the last two days we have tried to contact him, even going so far as to have the hotel let us into his room. Bed hasn't been slept in. Nothing."

"Probably just staying with friends," suggested John.

"Perhaps, but he has always been good about staying in touch. Now? Nothing."

"He's stayed at a friend's house," said Feng. "But the man said he had left in a hurry. No explanation given."

"Keeping track of us again, Feng?" said Lu sardonically.

"Of course, who else will?"

"Great job," replied Lu. "We have two missing people now."

John thought this situation heaven-sent. Now they would have to stay a while longer, more time for Feng to locate Meiying. *Even a day might make a difference*, he thought.

"By the way, Feng, any luck with Meiying?" he asked, knowing what the answer would be, but wanting to keep her on his radar.

"No. Haven't had a chance yet. Now with Peter, I need more time."

Master Zhou interjected. "I know the police chief here. Corrupt, but capable. I'll slip him some money to grease the wheels for a city-wide search. After all, you can't hide an American citizen that easily here."

Madame Liu sighed. "I had hoped we could leave within the week to continue our journey. Arrangements have been made."

By now, the others knew better than to ask for details. John wondered, however, where the money to finance this quest kept coming from. Fortunately, teaching English kept him solvent, but barely.

"Well," said Madame Liu. "Let's hope Master Zhou's plan will succeed. In the meantime, we can all help by scouring the city and asking questions. Like Master Zhou said, can't hide an American for long."

"Unless he wants to remain hidden," observed Feng Shiren.

The group fell silent, contemplating this unsettling possibility.

"Let us make the assumption that he doesn't," said Madame Liu.

"Well, one thing is certain," declared Master Zhou. "If I pay our corrupt friend fifty percent up front, and fifty percent upon locating him, then I am sure things will happen very quickly."

"What if the Japs notice?" asked Lu Zhishen. "I mean, we don't want to give them any reason to notice us."

"True," said Master Zhou. "Our friend works closely with them, but I think he'll keep this little investigation quiet."

"You hope," said Feng.

"Yes, I hope. The alternative is to wait a few days and see if he shows up."

"But that would delay us even more," said Madame Liu.

The group agreed Master Zhou's plan was worth the risk.

"Now that the police will investigate," said John. "That means Feng can return full time to locating Meiying."

"Yes," agreed Madame Liu.

"I miss her," said Suling.

"We all do."

~

Two more days passed and still no word of Peter. John kept pressing Feng Shiren about Meiying, but got only vague answers in return. Master Zhou also reported no progress. John sank into a deep depression. Uncertainty over Meiying and Peter's disappearance caused him to withdraw to his room and brood, leaving the hotel only to fulfil his teaching duties. He even avoided Nobaru, although this contributed to his sense of isolation. Only the voice kept him company, haranguing him for not doing more to find Meiying. One rainy afternoon an insistent knocking roused him from bed. When he opened the door, Suling rushed in.

"They think they found him!"

"Thank god! But what do you mean 'think'?"

"Well, the police informed Master Zhou that they have a strong lead."

"Oh," John said, disappointment evident in his voice.

"But it's something."

"Yes."

Another knocking and Feng Shiren joined them. "You heard?" he asked.

"Suling just told me," John replied.

"I do have more information Master Zhou just now received. Suling, please stay here at the hotel with the others and wait for word. John, come with me."

"Where are we going? What additional information?"

Feng held up a cautionary hand. "To see a body."

Suling gasped.

"What?" cried John.

Feng turned to Suling. "Don't worry, it's probably not Peter's."

Suling wrung her hands but said nothing.

"Go to Madame Liu's room and be with her while we're gone, okay?"

Suling nodded, then whispered, "Yes."

"Come on, John!"

Feng rushed out with John close behind, his mind awhirl with unpleasant possibilities. Once again he found himself being led by this strange and unpredictable man, as if trapped in some repeating time loop, forever hurrying down streets and wending their way through alleyways. In spite of his misgivings, a visceral thrill wedged itself into his naturally placid disposition. Calm meditation gave way to a Hollywood-style frenetic rush toward danger and intrigue. After they had gone far from the hotel, Feng hailed a rickshaw and whispered something in the ear of the driver, who nodded and flashed a toothy smile.

On they continued, past the city limits, past Japanese soldiers, through the shantytowns and refugee slums where thousands of starving people stared at the two rich figures sitting grandly in a rickshaw while children died all around them. John felt the sting of guilt and imagined he stuck out even more as a *yang guizi*—a foreign devil. He slumped low in the seat and pulled his collar high around his neck, wishing he wore a hat to hide his face.

Feng laughed. "Won't help. They can smell opulence and flesh fattened by a rich diet. Ah! Here we are!"

John looked around and saw nothing but a huge muddy field devoid of vegetation, harboring a few scattered refugees squatting over their meager possessions.

"Where?" asked John. "I mean, I don't see anything."

Feng pointed. In the distance stood, or rather listed sideways, a tumble-down shack where a few policemen stood warming themselves by wrapping their arms around their bodies and slapping.

"In that shack," said Feng.

"Jesus," whispered John to himself.

When they arrived at the shack, a scruffy-looking police officer greeted them with a grunt.

"Body is in here," he mumbled, opening the door and waving them in.

Feng entered first, followed by John and the officer. The one-room shack was dark and dingy, with nothing on the walls and a floor strewn with debris. John found it hard to see anything, but the officer turned on his flashlight and illuminated something laying prone amidst the trash. It was Peter.

"Jesus Christ," said John in a low voice.

The body lay awkwardly and covered in blood.

Peter's eyes were open, staring at nothing, but John fancied them following him as he moved.

"How was he killed?" Feng Shiren asked the officer, who then poked his head out the door and grunted something.

"With this." He turned and held out a large butcher knife.

"Any idea why?" asked Feng.

"Don't know. We're investigating."

"Did you report this to the Japanese?"

The officer looked startled. "Of course."

"Then they will report it to the American consul?"

The officer shrugged. "American consulate closed. Anyway, that's their business." He straightened. "Is this your friend, who we have identified as"—he flipped through a filthy notebook—"Peter Hedley?"

"Yes," said Feng.

"Yes," said John. "You have no idea why he was murdered?"

"We do not yet know the motive," replied the officer in a haughty tone, emphasizing the word 'motive' in English to show-off his knowledge.

After a few more questions, the two friends returned to the waiting rickshaw. Both remained silent for some time. John broke the ice.

"Why do you think he was killed?"

"It's a puzzle."

"And why killed way out here?"

"He may not have been. He might have been killed elsewhere and the body brought here."

"But why?"

"It's a puzzle. Do you know of any trouble he's been involved in?"

"Nope."

Feng shook his head. "Could be gambling, robbery, jealous husband, anything."

"Must have been robbery," proclaimed John.

"Why do you say that?"

"None of the other motives fit."

"Really?" Feng raised his eyebrows. "People are often involved in all sorts of things that others, even their friends and families, are unaware of."

"I know but. . . ."

"The hard part will be telling the others," sighed Feng.

John was surprised at this remark. Feng Shiren always struck him as impervious to such an emotional response.

"Yes," John replied. "How do we break it to them, especially Suling?"

"I will leave that to you, John."

Startled at this abdication of responsibility, John glanced at Feng and saw tears. Now the full weight of Peter's murder fell upon him, and his own tears flowed.

Both remained silent until they reached the hotel. After they settled with the rickshaw driver, Feng disappeared into the crowd and John turned to face the monolithic face of the hotel, dreading to enter as if he would be eaten, swallowed, and digested by the building.

Just as he entered the lobby, the others ran up to him. Evidently, they had been waiting anxiously.

"Let's go upstairs," he said grimly.

Everyone present could read the ominous nature of the news in his face, and all silently followed him to Madame Liu's room. They each found a place to sit and looked at John with dread.

"It was Peter," he said quietly.

A moan filled the room. Suling began to sob.

"What happened?" asked Master Zhou.

"He was killed," replied John.

"I know, but how?"

"Well, apparently, he was murdered."

Now a wave of shock spread through the group.

"Why?" asked Lu Zhishen.

"No one knows."

"Where is he?"

"Outside the city. His body is being brought back by the authorities."

"Where's Feng Shiren?" Lu demanded.

"After we identified the body, he left."

"Left?"

"Yes, I'm sure he had other things to attend."

"Just like him!" exclaimed Lu angrily.

"Poor Peter," said Suling, wiping away her tears.

"His family?" asked Master Zhou.

John shrugged. "Don't know. The police are notifying Japanese authorities."

"What about the American consul?"

"Unfortunately, the consulate is closed."

So it went through the evening, until all were exhausted from grief and endless questions with no answers. Only Madame Liu stayed awake, listening to the tapping that came fast and furious from the box where the Precious Object lay.

~

That night the voice came with a vengeance. Which voice? His mind was muddled.

John Powers! If not careful, you will end up like Peter. Because of your human weakness, this child may never be born!

Then go haunt someone else! If I'm so worthless, why bother with me?

Because it is written. Fate starves at Probability's door. Probability starves at Fate's door. Goddess and God are embodiments of both, and that means all is up to you, mutant child! Probabilistic swarm or Fate's vector! If you die, all is lost.

I thought you wanted me to die.

When We want you to die, We will let you know.

We?

Did We not say God and Goddess are embodiments of each Other?

I have to get used to calling you 'We'.

Sometimes We are We, and sometimes I am One or the Other and sometimes there are Others.

You speak no sense!

That is why you are struggling. Focus on Meiying, on the son!

So the world can have another schizophrenic?

He will be the next step toward liberation for the planet.

"Schizophrenic or next step," John said aloud. "How am I to know which is correct?"

He looked up.

No response. At last, They were silent.

John knew about schizophrenia, knew his mind slipped, knew the voices made him ill, proved him ill, and he shuddered to think of a future marked by further decline into madness.

~ *Meiying's Final Concert* ~

Meiying felt betrayed at having to perform before being permitted to depart, and vowed to play something sure to displease Mr. President. She wanted to play Schoenberg, but could find no score. After a lengthy search, the only candidate turned out to be a transcription for piano by Stravinsky. *The Rite of Spring.* Perfect! She may have to dance to the tune of this obese master, but she had no intent of dying in his 'paradise' without protest. All day she practiced Stravinsky's relentless, frenetic, discordant notes. Mr. President was sure to hate it. As she practiced, she pictured him making faces, fussing in his little stool, stopping the concert, and ordering her to leave immediately.

"Hello!" Beethoven interrupted her thoughts and she stopped playing. "That's very weird music."

"Just fingering exercises."

"Oh, thank god! I thought you were going to play that for Mr. President tonight."

She thought of Madame Wang, whose outer persona was one of independence and defiance, yet in the end crouched on her knees awaiting punishment. "Beethoven, why are you always so concerned about Mr. President?"

"I told you, I am here at his pleasure. Out there, I'd be cannon fodder."

"Yet you're willing to leave with me? Isn't that also dangerous?"

"Oh, yes!"

"So why leave? And don't tell me you love me."

"In that case, no reason. Strikes my fancy."

She made a face. "Since you make such a good lackey, tell me whether he will have yet another demand after I perform tonight. He has already breached our agreement. Why not over and over?"

Beethoven laughed. "There can be no enforceable agreement between a man and a woman."

"Why?"

"Women are not legal entities. They are like children, or animals."

"You believe that?"

"Of course not."

Meiying grimaced. "I wonder."

Beethoven looked pained. "Meiying, I promise you, what I do now I do for you. It is true, in the past it was for myself, but now it's for you."

"Will you continue reporting to him about me after we leave?"

Beethoven whispered, "Yes, but only because we can use him even as he uses us."

"How so?"

Beethoven put a finger to his lips and leaned close to her ear. "Because I get information from him, not just give it."

"Such as?"

He shook his head and wagged his finger at her. "That is for me to know and you to find out."

"Beethoven, this is not a game."

He assumed a patronizing smile, which infuriated her even more.

She turned back to the piano. "I've a mind to tell you not to come. If you're going to be like this, I'd rather go by myself!"

Beethoven gently lifted her chin so that she looked squarely at him, continuing that irritating smile. "You will when I tell you something I know that you don't."

"What?" she said resentfully.

"Yesterday while you attended to your 'matters,' we had a visitor to the temple." He stopped to tease impatience from her.

"Well?"

"This visitor found his way to me. He said he was making inquiries about you on behalf of someone else."

"Who?" Her excitement was palpable and uninhibited.

"Am I accompanying you tomorrow?"

"Yes, yes! Now, who?"

"Good," he said with an exaggerated smirk, but then turned sincere. "Seriously, Meiying, I am your friend, not your enemy. If you only knew—"

"Who was this visitor?" she interrupted, too agitated to listen to his last sentence. Later, she came to regret this ill-advised rudeness.

Again, Beethoven leaned over and whispered in her ear. "The visitor was a man, a soldier in one of The President's guerilla bands. Name of Tang. Said he came to report to Mr. President, but also had a more personal mission. When I asked what that was, he said he searched for a woman named Bai Meiying. Said she was beautiful and played the piano. I told him we had someone here by that description. His eyes lit-up and he thanked me profusely. When I asked who was making the inquiries, he said a name." Again, Beethoven paused, this time simply to catch his breath.

Meiying could not contain herself. "Who? Who?"

"Feng Shiren."

Beethoven heard her take a deep breath and throw her hands to her face. To his astonishment, she began sobbing.

"Are you okay?" he asked, genuinely concerned and putting his hand gently on her heaving shoulder. "You should also know that Mr. President gave Tang the Precious Object to return to your group."

"Thank God! Thank God!" she kept repeating through her tears.

Meiying," he said softly. "I know where they are."

"Where?"

"I'm not telling. That is my ace-in-the-hole, and that is where I'll lead you when we leave. I must keep this to myself until we get there."

"No, no! You must tell me! What if . . . something happens to you?"

He shrugged. "That is in Buddha's hands. But Meiying, I must keep this a secret for my own sake, at least for a while."

"If you must, but they are alive! And you know where they are! For now, that is all that matters. Thank God! Thank God! But, where is this Mr. Tang? This angel of mercy that found you, where is he?"

"Couldn't stay. Left while you were still occupied with other 'matters,' whatever they were."

She gazed deep into his eyes with an entreating air. "Beethoven, tell me truthfully, do you know what I was occupied with?"

Tears came to his eyes. "Yes. That is why I will move heaven and earth to get you out of here."

They fell into each other's arms.

That evening, Meiying did not perform Stravinsky. She performed Beethoven.

~

The morning of their departure, both wore bulky cotton jackets over their Buddhist robes. Their bicycles were loaded with supplies. At the top of the steps, Mr. President stood like a mountain flanked by the two lesser peaks of his loyal assistants.

"We will keep track of you!" he shouted in his inimitable high-pitched voice. "To secure your safety!"

Meiying spied Madame Wang standing to the side, her head down.

"Thank you for everything!" cried Meiying, waving. She thought it odd to be thanking such a man, but life is inscrutable.

She caught Madame Wang's eye and smiled. Madame Wang nodded in reply and Meiying fancied her eyes were red, but could not be sure.

Off they set, across the bridge, over the lake, and to the road where Meiying looked back upon the enchanted, but deceptively tranquil, castle receding in the distance, just as John had done so many months earlier.

Meiying pedaled with an abandon that surged joyously through her body, the wind blowing through her short hair, creating an electric thrill of freedom not felt for ages. Being on the road again brought a flood of memories. But when she looked around, all she saw was Beethoven. His lone image had an odd effect. On the one hand, she missed the others, yet on the other hand, his presence provided comfort in spite of her doubts. But for now, all that mattered was the wind, the movement, the freedom.

"Lead on!" she shouted uncharacteristically, not even questioning his veracity or whether he was leading her to the group or to perdition.

Every cloud, patch of sun, gust of wind, bending of tree, and even fluttering of leaf, caught her eye. Refugees continued their inexorable journey, but she would not let even their sad procession intrude upon her exhilaration. Besides, they were fewer now. No Japanese planes. No bombing. No dying children at the side of the road. Things were better! They must be! She knew this emotional high was nonsense, but for a few precious moments, the world bowed to her happiness, suspending its normal serving of pain and suffering until she stood good and ready to withstand the renewed assault she knew was sure to come.

When they stopped to rest after many hours, her euphoria had been replaced by a satisfying fatigue. A lone plane flew overhead, its engine a lazy, pleasant hum. No one around them could tell whether it was Japanese, but it appeared to be no threat. Beethoven chatted happily while Meiying listened with polite tolerance. However, as they continued the journey and late afternoon shadows lengthened, her placid air of determination belied an inner turmoil that had started to replace her earlier optimism. Something in the surroundings, perhaps the plane, or some change in the atmosphere, or dimming of light, or the glance of a desperate child, gave her a chill; and an undefined, yet deep foreboding came over her. When it came time to choose a place for the night, she acted as if it made no difference, and Beethoven finally settled on a spot where they would sleep—a small patch of barren earth some distance away from a host of other refugees.

Night made her feel particularly vulnerable. She fought to keep the memories quiet. Eating a dumpling from the palace calmed her, and she conversed with Beethoven until both agreed to retire. She washed her body as best as possible without disrobing. After brushing her teeth, she lay back on her bedroll, staring up at the stars and listening for intruders. Rape had consequences beyond her worst imaginings, and she feared the damage would reverberate through the years like a melancholy bell tolling a deathwatch. Never would she escape the immobilizing, or almost immobilizing, fears she experienced those terrible nights. Fighting against them was exhausting enough. She missed Meili. Amazing, she thought, that so few days together with her lover would be fixed so firmly in her memory, and with such electric power! Thinking about the future with Meili had she lived provided Meiying with innumerable and ever-varying fantasies of their life together. In this way, she kept Meili alive and vibrant.

Snoring from the other refugees filled the night air with a comforting, but distracting hum. Just as sleep finally overcame her anxieties, something rough traversed her body. Rats! She found her mind instantly transported to Naguma's filthy jail cell. Frantically, she brushed off the rodents, but they kept returning. She flailed harder, but to no avail. Rats kept crawling over her, their feet pressing against her body harder and harder. She flung out her arms wildly.

"Stop!" a voice whispered.

Now she felt truly terrified. If they weren't rats. . . .

"Stop!" came the voice again.

The rats grew to enormous size and strength. She kicked and punched.

"Damn it! Stop!" screamed a male voice. She felt her coat pulled open and her blouse ripped as hands desperately groped her breasts.

Now she screamed. A loud thud filled the air and a heavy weight collapsed on top of her. She panicked and pushed clumsily at the suffocating object, which suddenly rolled off, leaving her hands and face covered with a sticky substance.

"Come on! Get up!" She recognized Beethoven's voice. "There are others! Hurry!"

She jumped up, now fully in control of her senses. Beethoven stood with a club looking around anxiously. The moonlight outlined his figure and his terrified face. As she frantically tried to wipe off the blood, an arresting thought occurred to her: the fluids of life are always sticky, from blood to sap to seminal fluid. Maybe that stickiness is the soul. But this idea flashed by in a nanosecond.

"I'm sure I killed him!" Beethoven whispered, then jerked her arm and pulled her toward the bikes.

"Wait!" She broke loose and quickly gathered her bedding, trying not to look at the body while rolling the bulky material under her arm, she heard other refugees stirring.

"What's up?"

"What's wrong?"

"Hey! What's going on there?"

Beethoven did not delay. He and Meiying walked their bikes up the road, cursing the moonlight when it broke through the clouds and illuminated their figures. Meiying walked clumsily, the bedding in an unwieldy heap under her arm.

"Drop it!" called Beethoven.

"No!" She clutched it tighter and trudged on.

Behind, they heard a commotion as people discovered the body. Cries of "Dead!" and "Murder!" rose above the din. Meiying looked back anxiously and even saw a flashlight glimmering, so she quickened her pace. Beethoven also speeded-up to remain even with her until they made it over a hill that blocked any further view. Neither spoke, but both understood the urgency of putting distance between them and the body.

As they walked, her shaking began slowly, building to an almost uncontrollable shiver.

"Keep walking," said Beethoven under his breath.

She did not have to be cajoled. With her head down, she marched in step with Beethoven until they approached a side road that branched off to the right where dim lights were discernable in the distance. As if on a sudden whim, Meiying veered onto the side road.

"Where are you going?" called a surprised Beethoven.

"To that light."

"Why?"

"It offers comfort."

"We don't know who they are!"

Meiying shook her head and kept walking, Beethoven trailing behind. "We don't know what lies ahead either. At least this way is a light."

"Are you a moth?" asked Beethoven, trying to be light-hearted.

She could tell he was still shaken, but so was she. "Better a moth with wings than a woman bound to earth and the whims of man."

"Not all men are bad," he grumbled.

"No."

"I just saved you from being raped!"

Silence.

"Again!" he added for emphasis.

"Thank you."

"I don't understand you."

"Would you have helped an unattractive refugee woman? A woman you didn't know? A woman who was ugly?"

"Of course!"

Meiying nodded dubiously and continued walking, then abruptly stopped. "Even if she were not your property?"

"Oh, come on! That's not fair!"

"Yes, it is."

"If you only knew!"

"If I only knew what?"

~ *Mr. and Mrs. Zhi* ~

Before he could answer, the lights shone before them. Two lanterns hung from the eave of a modest but sturdy mud house with a well-maintained tile roof. The grounds seemed clean. Chickens clucked, but no dog barked and the inhabitants nowhere to be seen.

"They must be still asleep," observed Beethoven.

"No, we are not, comrades!" bellowed a voice from the darkness. A lantern hung low beside the figure which illuminated only a pair of legs.

Both visitors jumped.

"Don't be afraid!" called the voice again. "What brings you here?"

"We are refugees. The war brings us here," said Beethoven.

"Of course, so many! Come closer."

They saw the lantern held higher, shining on the face of a grinning peasant. Behind him, a buffalo snuffed loudly. "I have two sons nearby with knives, so no funny stuff," he said as if apologizing for having to say such rude words.

Meiying and Beethoven stepped forward with their bikes.

The farmer whistled. "Wow! Such nice bicycles. And such good-looking young people! You must be educated. You both look it."

"We are Buddhists traveling the roads," said Beethoven. "She is a nun and I am a monk." He opened his jacket to show his robes.

The peasant laughed. "No you're not! You're pulling my leg. That is an old trick, young ones!" Although he called them young, he was not much older than they, but a harsh life had carved its lessons across his leathery face.

"Well, we are," said Beethoven in a pouting voice.

Meiying stepped forward even closer. "No, we are not. We are just travelers escaping the war, like all the others."

"Ah, the honest one! Are you communists?"

Both hesitated.

"Don't worry, comrades, I'm a communist! And proud of it! But even if you're not, if you're from good common stock, you're welcome! My wife is inside, my buffalo is outside, and I'm in the middle!" He laughed uproariously at this joke.

"And your sons?" asked Beethoven looking around.

"Ah, I am an honest one too, sometimes. No sons. Just a precaution. But you two look pure. You don't plan to murder me and my old woman do you?"

"Heaven forbid!" cried Beethoven.

The man looked at Meiying.

"No," she said.

"Ah, I'll take the young lady's word, if you don't mind."

"May we stay the night in your barn?" asked Meiying.

"No, you may stay in our house tonight, after you've eaten."

"We have food, please don't bother," said Meiying.

"We have better. Save yours."

"You're very kind," said Beethoven.

"We communists are really kind, in spite of what they say about us. 'From each according to his abilities, to each according to his needs.' That's what Comrade Marx says. And I believe it! The world would be a better place."

"Right now, the world is a very unpleasant place," said Meiying.

"Yes," he sighed. "But we do our part, comrade . . . what is your name, pretty lady?"

"My name is Meiying and this is . . . well, we call him Beethoven."

"Who?"

"Beethoven."

He craned his neck and cupped his ear. "What name?"

"Beethoven."

"What a strange name! Were you born outside China?"

"No, comrade," said Beethoven. "It's just a nickname. My real name is Wang Liwei."

"Well, it's nice to meet both of you. Now, come in the house and meet the wife."

Meiying looked askance at Beethoven. For the first time she learned his real name. "Liwei," she whispered as they followed their host. "That's a nice name."

"Nicer than Beethoven?" he asked.

"You are no longer Beethoven, you are Wang Liwei."

"No!" he cried, startling the farmer just as he was opening the door to his house.

"What's wrong?" he asked.

"Nothing. A little quarrel."

He pointed to a rather dumpy woman. "My wife, Mrs. Zhi. And I—" he bowed quite gracefully for such a rough peasant—"am Mr. Zhi."

Both Meiying and Beethoven bowed in the old style, which made Mr. Zhi smile and chide them. "Times have changed, comrades. No need for such bourgeois mannerisms. The revolution will prevail. Long live Mao Zedong!"

Meiying had heard the name, of course, but was surprised when Beethoven asked excitedly, "Have you met him, comrade? I understand Zhou Enlai was in Taiyuan for a while. Is that true?"

"For a while. Yan Xishan allowed them to operate, but that was before the Japs took over. Is that where you're headed, comrade?"

Meiying noticed Beethoven hesitate, then shrug and say, "Don't know, comrade. Wherever the road takes us."

Mrs. Zhi shooed them into the house with a scolding. "Let them get inside, old fool, before they starve to death." She guided them to chairs and bustled back to the simple kitchen and leaned over a large pot.

Mr. Zhi laughed good-naturedly. "You should go to Taiyuan. Japs are there, but something's happening. Jobs available. City is growing. And our cells still operate, at least some of them."

Meiying thought him very foolish to talk so openly, but held her tongue. Taiyuan loomed large in her mind, because she now guessed that was where they were headed.

"Is Zhou Enlai still there?" asked Beethoven.

"Don't know. I'm just a poor peasant proletarian piss-ant working-class stiff."

"Why aren't you overrun with refugees?" asked Meiying. "News of your generosity would spread fast."

"Ah," replied Mr. Zhi. "You obviously didn't see the sign, or did you?"

"No."

"Typhus. Restricted area. Stay out under penalty of law," recited Mr. Zhi proudly. "Written in official-looking calligraphy too!"

Beethoven's eyes got big. "Typhus?"

"Not to worry," chuckled Mr. Zhi. "We put that sign up to discourage too many poor people. It's worked! You're the first in a long time."

"Didn't even see it," said Beethoven in wonder.

Mr. Zhi frowned. "Hm, better check tomorrow and make sure it's still up. You won't tell anyone, will you?"

"No."

"Promise?"

"Yes," said Beethoven.

Mr. Zhi looked at Meiying, who simply nodded.

"What's the secret of your doing so well here?' asked Beethoven.

Mrs. Zhi turned from her cooking and scowled. "Because his thieving communist friends steal and give us their crumbs."

Mr. Zhi snapped, "Quiet woman! It's not just that. I'm a good farmer. Know how to grow crops. I work hard." He slapped his chest. "Good peasant stock!"

"Good at stealing," mumbled Mrs. Zhi.

"Don't listen to her. If she had her way, we'd still be under Manchu rule with a corrupt old Dowager Empress telling us what to do."

"Stupid husband!"

Meiying intervened in her calming manner. "I met some communists in Shanghai. They were mostly young students. Why are you so interested in them? As I understand it, they would take away your land."

Mrs. Zhi rolled her eyes and kept stirring, all the while mumbling complaints like, "now you'll get him going," and "foolish husband!"

But Mr. Zhi remained irrepressible. "No, no, no!" he exclaimed. "That's only for the big landlords; big-wigs who enslave people. Not us small-fry farmers who just live off the land. See any slaves here?"

"Look my way and you'll find a slave fast enough!" cried Mrs. Zhi. Before her husband could respond, she said, "Food's ready."

They sat at a rough table and ate rice gruel with a few pieces of meat neither Meiying nor Beethoven recognized. Weak tea was served, and after repeated heartfelt thanks, Meiying said, "Tell me more about Taiyuan."

Beethoven squirmed in his seat.

Mr. Zhi looked at them. "Are you two married?"

"No," said Meiying before Beethoven had a chance to speak.

"Brother and sister," he said quickly.

Mrs. Zhi put on a dubious face. "Really?"

"Yes," said her husband. He pointed at Beethoven. "This is Wang Liwei and if this is his sister, she must be Wang Meiying."

"You're far too old and pretty not to be married," announced Mrs. Zhi.

Beethoven jumped in. "Ah! She was engaged, but her fiancé died in the revolution before they had a chance to marry."

Meiying stared at him in surprise.

Noticing this, Mrs. Zhi turned to Meiying. "Really?" she asked.

Before she could respond, Mr. Zhi asked enthusiastically, "Did your fiancé fight with the communists? I heard it was terrible in Shanghai."

Meiying shook her head. "Truth is, we are just friends. Refugees from the war like so many others."

"Ah, as I suspected," said Mrs. Zhi.

Meiying looked at Beethoven. "And we are headed to Taiyuan, aren't we Liwei?"

Beethoven coughed and turned red with embarrassment. "Yes, we're trying to make it to Taiyuan."

"Well," said Mr. Zhi. "In that case, Meiying can sleep in the house and you in the barn, if that suits."

"Yes!" exclaimed Meiying. "It's what we both would have wanted anyway."

"Hmm," uttered Mrs. Zhi disapprovingly.

But Mr. Zhi waved his arms emphatically. "I believe you, little miss!"

"So please, tell me about Taiyuan."

Mr. Zhi pulled the lantern closer. "You must be careful on the way. Bandits, robbers, partisans, Yan Xishan's men, Japanese, it's a mess!"

"Yes, these dangers have been with us from the beginning," said Beethoven with a proud air.

"How did you make it so far untouched?" asked Mrs. Zhi, now curious and evidently more sympathetic.

Meiying looked down. "We didn't."

"Oh," said Mrs. Zhi, clucking her tongue.

"Anyway," said Mr. Zhi. "When you get to Taiyuan, find a job. The Japs are building a manufacturing center, and when they are kicked out and the communists take over, the proletarian workers will be rewarded. We'll just make their factories Chinese—after we fumigate them first!" He laughed uproariously at his own joke.

Mrs. Zhi shook her head. "Fool."

The next morning, they set off for Taiyuan.

~ *To Solve Peter's Murder?* ~

Members of the group were in a quandary. Some wanted to leave Taiyuan immediately while others wanted to wait and learn the circumstances behind Peter's murder. John found himself in the second group. He had, of course, ulterior motives for delaying. Now that they had the Precious Object back, the tide seemed to turn in the direction of leaving immediately. Madame Liu was adamant and Master Zhou went along, albeit reluctantly.

Eventually, it was agreed that the police investigation would lead nowhere. Also, no reply had been received from any of Peter's family, so there really was no reason to stay. His funeral was held in a well-tended cemetery outside of the city. For lack of a better alternative, and because no one knew his true religious beliefs, a Belgian priest performed the services. After they returned to the hotel, John asked Feng Shiren one more time whether he had information regarding Meiying.

"Still waiting," replied Feng. "I certainly had hoped to hear by now. But. . . . "

"What about Peter's murderer? Any word on that front?"

"Or murderers," corrected Feng.

"Okay, murderers."

"The cops have found nothing. The Japs say nothing. No leads anywhere. They chalk it down to either a gambling debt or robbery. We'll probably never know."

John found this last statement completely unlike Feng. He always wanted to know details, why something happened, how something happened. But this surrender made John suspicious. From the beginning, he always had a vague feeling that Feng was somehow involved in Peter's death, but there appeared to be nothing more than his imagination to back that up.

He cried when recalling Peter, remember John?

I remember. Are you on his side? Not everyone who cries is sincere.

Yes. He is your protector. I sent him.

You! That explains it! So he is loyal to you? Is he capable of murder?

Only to protect. In future, the human species will attempt to have silicon slaves whose supposed unbreakable law is to do no harm to humans. Ultimately, the human species will fail, but your superior descendants, not the silicon savants, will succeed them, if you do what you are tasked to do.

So he can do no harm?

Well, We modified the command. What We just told you is a paraphrase.

Who are We?

Us.

And?

You can guess.

No, I can't.

To be expected. You are only the beginning. First step is the hardest, Chosen One. The distant ancestors of your old species who were the first and more cognitively advanced also struggled with confusion and their own sanity.

John shouted aloud, "No! You are hallucinations! All of you!"

"I assure you, I'm not an hallucination," protested Feng Shiren. "Your face tells me your voices are back, but I'm not worthless. I've been doing my best to find Meiying and discover who murdered Peter, but I'm not God, you know!"

"I wonder."

"What?"

"Nothing. Has a departure date been decided?"

"We're meeting today. Can't be soon enough for me."

"Why?"

"Now Lu Zhishen is coming back late, just like Peter did before he was mur-dered."

"Oh, shit."

"Exactly."

At the meeting, it was agreed that the group would leave in two days. When John protested and asked to extend the time, Madame Liu replied firmly, "It has been decided. Arrangements have already been made. We cannot."

Master Zhou rubbed his bottom. "I sympathize, John. To get ready I've been biking around Taiyuan. Ow! I'm sore and we haven't even started."

John felt glad to see Lu Zhishen attend the meeting. In spite of his disappoint-ment at leaving Taiyuan early, he focused on the positive. Walking up to Lu and holding out both hands, palms up, he said, "It will be good to know we're again moving closer to *her*."

Lu seemed distracted, but returned the solicitation.

"Lu, is everything okay?" asked John.

"Just miss Peter."

"Yes, I know."

"I think I've found out what happened," Lu whispered unexpectedly.

John straightened. "What?"

"Shhh. I think I know what happened to Peter."

"What?"

"I don't want to say. Too early. But I'm pretty sure."

"Have you told Feng?"

Lu appeared startled, and whispered forcefully, "God, no!"

Now it was John's turn to be startled. "Why? Is he involved?"

Lu glanced at Feng across the room conversing with Suling. "We'll talk later."

John leaned closer. "You can't leave me hanging."

"Later."

~

With departure imminent, John knew he had to give his notice at the English language school. That meant he had to see Nobaru again. Since Peter's death, he had been avoiding his Japanese friend, but now there was no alternative but to say his goodbyes. In fact, he rather looked forward to seeing Nobaru, and so invited him to a farewell feast.

That evening, they chatted amiably over dinner. Each avoided anything that might lead to conflict or controversy. But after a second bottle of rice wine, Nobaru looked at John with a strange expression on his face.

"So, have you solved your friend's murder mystery?"

"No, it will probably never be solved."

"I made inquiries but also could learn nothing. The police seem uninterested and busy elsewhere."

"And the Japanese authorities?"

"Ah, that is a different story."

"How so?"

"Your friend came to their attention for reasons I cannot find out. Be careful, John."

"What do you mean?"

"Just be careful. Know that I will keep track of your progress as best I can." He reached into his pocket and handed John a paper. "Here is how to contact me if you run into trouble. Keep it in a safe place. But enough of this melodrama, drink up!"

The wine made John sentimental. "I will miss you, my crazy, poetic, romantic Japanese friend!"

Nobaru had tears in his eyes. He lifted his cup. "May you find your beautiful lesbian Chinese pianist! And then . . . and then . . . oh, the hell with it." With pride, he spoke in English, "And then live happily ever after!"

"Are you sure there's nothing else you can tell me about my beautiful lesbian Chinese pianist?"

Nobaru had just emptied his cup and burped contentedly, then looked at John with a conspiratorial wink. "No. Not today, my friend. But tomorrow, or the next day, or the day after that, or maybe when the war is over and we've drinking at a little place I know in Tokyo; then I might tell you everything. But not now."

John could obtain no further information from Nobaru and they parted with a friendly embrace.

~

When the morning of their departure arrived, John had still received no explanation from Lu about his statements.

In the hours before they were scheduled to leave, John would often ask him, "Tell me now, what have you found out? The time is getting near!"

Lu would always respond, "Not now. Not enough evidence. I don't want to say until I know for sure."

But that moment never came, and when they gathered in front of the hotel to leave, Lu appeared unconcerned. John walked his bike up next to Lu.

"Well?"

Lu astonished him by laughing and replying as if it were all a joke. "Oh, it turned out to be nothing. Wrong trail. Let's focus on the next leg of our adventure, okay? No need to mention it again!"

"But—"

"Really, John, I don't want to talk about it. I was wrong, that's all." He patted the box containing the Precious Object. "Let's go!"

Off went the group, now less another member. It seemed unnatural to John that Peter was not there cracking his jokes and speaking in his faux English accent. Even Little Acorn had a long face, and John knew it concerned Peter's absence, since the boy had become close to the "troublesome American foreigner."

As they traveled through the city, they drew the attention of many eyes, including the ubiquitous Japanese soldiers. John felt he was leaving the scene of a crime. Witnesses to this cowardly desertion of Meiying and Peter skulked everywhere, with their dark, Asiatic, accusing eyes. Again the old insecurities returned. If he were a true man, he would stay come hell-or-high-water and find Peter's murderer, or murderers. With that task complete, he would find Meiying and bring her to the destination.

Of course, he thought. *I don't know where the final destination is. No choice but to go with the group. Once I've seen* her, *all will be clear. Then I'll return and complete my responsibilities to Meiying and Peter.*

As it happened, the road Madame Liu chose that led out of the city passed the shack in which Peter's body had been found. For some reason, the field that before had been sparsely populated by refugees now bulged at the seams with miserable people. Starving, huddled together, cold and desperate, they stared at the strange group on bicycles that appeared to be well-fed and headed in the wrong direction—into danger rather than out. The group passed carts filled to overflow with the dead bodies of young and old, pulled by weary donkeys making their way toward the new cemetery that accommodated mass graves.

Almost no one clogging the road traveled away from Taiyuan, causing the small group to stand out even more. This realization alarmed everyone, leading to much speculation. Madame Liu decided to ask a few questions, and stopped by a family that had pulled off to the side of the road to deal with a sick child.

"Friends, where are you from?"

"Shentangou village, near the hot springs. But it is no more."

"What happened?"

The family patriarch, a living stereotype of the old, white haired, wispy-bearded elder, spoke resignedly, sparing his strength. "Battles. Soldiers everywhere. Shooting. Explosions. Death. Had to escape."

"Why do you go to Taiyuan?"

"Out there is only death."

Madame Liu turned to the group who had assembled nearby. Everyone had overheard the old man's words.

"Doesn't matter," said Madame Liu grimly. "Press on. *She* awaits. Arrangements have been made."

Missed Opportunities

Roadblocks

Before Meiying and Beethoven had traveled more than a few kilometers on the main road, they ran into a roadblock. At first, it was impossible to tell which side manned it due to the throngs of refugees backed up with nowhere to go. As they wended their way forward, it became clear the Japanese army had completely blocked the way. After milling around aimlessly for over an hour, a sudden roar of engines filled the air, followed by rolling waves of dust. Uneasy speculation roiled the crowd.

"That's why they cleared the road!" yelled Beethoven over the noise, standing on tiptoes and craning his neck to see over the crowd. "Tanks! Lots of them!"

Just as the words left his mouth, a squadron of antiquated Chinese bi-planes flew overhead. A few desultory cheers arose from the refugees. Suddenly, rifle and machine-gun fire erupted sporadically from random Japanese soldiers while their commanders screamed orders above the clamor, attempting to force them to concentrate their volleys. Meiying watched in fascination as the slow, sputtering Chinese planes lazily veered off in single file and swooped down on the Japanese convoy. They were like gnats against the brilliant blue sky. When the first explosions hit, the mob started screaming and a mad scramble ensued to escape the bombs and strafing runs.

Almost before she could react, Meiying was knocked down by the panicked crush of people and felt her arms and legs trampled. In great pain, she tried to pull in her limbs closer to her body, but her legs were tangled in the twisted bicycle. Explosions now reverberated through the air, followed by searing shock waves. She lowered her head to protect her face, her legs still tangled in the spokes, making it impossible to stand and run even if she wanted to. Beethoven's desperate voice could be heard calling her name, but it quickly faded, drowned out by the screams and explosions.

For a few moments she could simply lay motionless and become a some-what detached observer, but now the pain, noise, and panic of those around her made her stomach heave and her heart beat hard against her chest. Her mind lost its focus and gruesome images tore around like a crazed tops. It now became imperative that she stand upright. If not, she knew she would die laying there in the dirt. But her legs would still not obey. Confused, she blamed the bike, although now it rested on its side some distance away. Apparently she had crawled free. Another explosion rocked her sideways, and she felt the dirt and pebbles sting as they penetrated the entire length of her body, like the quills of some monstrous porcupine.

Now her panic truly took hold. She felt as though her body had been flayed, and the horror of being burned and disfigured made her even more frantic. Crawling without regard to direction soon brought her to the ob-stacles of other bodies, some dead, some dying. She scrambled over them like logs. Something grabbed under her arms and lifted, first to her knees, then to her feet. Although the chaos of battle continued to rage around her, some clarity came to her mind. Her skin was intact, and she found she could run. The person who helped her up was a stranger and he ran next to her, all the while serving as a support. More explosions and a brace of small-arms fire engulfed them and the stranger fell away.

Meiying kept running, though she knew not where, when the tremendous cacophony of battle ended as abruptly as it had begun. Once the eerie silence penetrated her consciousness, she stopped and for the first time looked around with some control over her own mind. Impressions came in a dizzy-ing rush: smoke, dust, bodies, moaning, blood, rushing soldiers, smoldering airplanes, tanks on the move, red-faced officers shouting commands, refugees wandering in ghostly circles, a Japanese soldier shooting into the charred body of a Chinese pilot still strapped into the cockpit of his crashed plane.

It had all come and gone so quickly, yet its consequences would take lifetimes to wash away. It became clear why there were so many Chinese victims; the Japanese, in their rage, had opened fire indiscriminately on the refugees. Standing like a half-wit in the middle of the carnage, she realized how important Beethoven was to her.

"Beethoven!" she yelled in all directions.

Nothing.

"Beethoven!" again in all directions.

Still nothing.

Giving in to a new and different form of panic, she rushed from body to body, turning them over and scanning their faces. At last she spotted his familiar figure. He lay awkwardly on his back, staring up at the sky with unblinking eyes.

"No!" she screamed and ran toward the body.

He turned and faced her with a startled expression.

Thank god he's alive! she thought, surprised at the depth of her relief.

But as she drew near, he seemed not to recognize her, just staring at her approach with a dumbfounded gaze. As she kneeled next to him, she saw a pool of blood, but was not sure where it came from.

"Don't worry," he said weakly. "It's not mine. It's from a little girl."

Meiying looked around but saw nothing.

"Her body saved me. She took the full brunt."

Meiying kept repeating soothing words while she checked him for wounds, but could find none.

"It's not me, it's her," he kept repeating to the sky.

Meiying wanted to ask where the little girl's body was, but decided against it. A Japanese soldier appeared and stood over her, poking the muzzle of his rifle into her ribs. He said something in Japanese which she did not understand, but his gestures made it clear that she was to move away. When she remained, he screamed again and kicked her, causing her to fall sideways, doubled over in pain. He pointed his rifle at Beethoven's head and fired.

Meiying screamed and buried her head in her hands. She heard the soldier laugh and walk away, his braying voice gradually becoming dimmer until she knew his menacing presence was gone. Still keeping her face covered, she could not bear to look at Beethoven.

Soft laughter drifted to her ear, and she momentarily thought the Japanese soldier had returned. But the tone certainly wasn't that of the soldier. Without daring to look, the familiarity of that voice came through clear and glorious.

"Beethoven!"

"Ha, ha! It's me! I'm sharing in his little joke!" He sounded unhinged.

She crawled over to him. "What happened?"

Still on his back, he turned sideways and picked at a hole in the dirt millimeters from his nose. "As I said, a little joke. Ha, ha!"

"Can you stand?" she asked.

"Of course." He struggled to get up, and eventually made it with her help. After they both checked his entire body and found no wounds, they located their bikes, zig-zagged around the dead bodies, and headed back down the road from where they came. Japanese soldiers continued to swarm the roadblock like bees in a disturbed hive. Both were desperate to put distance between them and these dangerous men with weapons who seemed to despise all things Chinese.

"Now what?" asked Beethoven after they had walked beyond the scrutiny of the Japanese.

"Back to Mr. and Mrs. Zhi," said Meiying. "At least there's shelter."

Beethoven craned his head backward and blinked at the sky. "And it looks like rain."

"All the more reason."

"But we should bring something to give them."

"Like what?" asked Meiying.

"I've an idea," replied Beethoven grimly. "Stay here, I'll be right back."

"Where are you going?"

"Treasure hunting."

Meiying knew what he planned and disapproved, but made no objections.

She waited a good while before he returned with a satisfied grin. Tied to his bike were two bolts of beautiful silk fabric.

"They're singed on the outside, but the inner material is good."

She did not ask questions. Both now suffered from the shakes, a phenomena that often occurs after battle where the accumulated adrenalin finds an outlet for its explosive nature. Wordlessly, they continued down the road, walking their disabled bikes.

It grew dark as they stood in front of Mr. Zhi's typhus sign. Beethoven checked its stability.

"He planted it good and firm this time. Bet he heard the battle."

Meiying nodded and walked on, anxious to be inside, warm, bathed, and asleep. Beethoven followed rather meekly. A light rain pattered down. At last the familiar lantern came into view. This time Mrs. Zhi came out to greet them.

"So, you're back. We wondered. Heard the battle and wondered." Her attitude had become quite solicitous. Beethoven unstrapped a bolt of silk and held it out. Her eyes lit up.

"For your kindness and generosity. May we stay the night again?"

She took the silk and replied enthusiastically, "Yes! You are welcome!"

"Mrs. Zhi," said Meiying. "May I bother you for some hot water so I may bathe?"

"Yes, yes."

Mr. Zhi sauntered up with a pitchfork over his shoulder and stopped in front of Beethoven, looking him up and down with twinkling eyes. "So, you missed my barn!"

Beethoven laughed and massaged the small of his back. "Indeed! Top flight! Fit for an emperor!"

"Come in and rest," said Mrs. Zhi. "Was it bad?"

And so they visited, ate, bathed, and slept. While they slept, Taiyuan remained far away. Meiying dreamed of entering the city and finding the group tossing flowers as they welcomed her back.

~ *Beethoven Confesses* ~

The next morning came quickly. Meiying stood outside gazing at the farmhouse and the fields beyond. A musky, damp smell of earth and manure hung thick in the air, and with this appealingly domestic scene, the sudden desire for a home again overcame her; a permanent place of her own; an anchor for her life. Her thoughts turned to the future. After rejoining the group and paying homage to *her*, she would settle down, perform concerts, make money, have a nice house, find a lover, and live in peace. But the dream disintegrated as soon as she probed deeper. It was all nonsense! The war would last forever. She would never find the group. It all seemed so hopeless!

Beethoven found her by a fence, head down, crying.

"What's wrong?"

"Just thinking," she said, wiping the tears away. "You can return to Mr. President's temple. To continue the journey is far too dangerous. I realized I would never forgive myself if you died for my sake."

He put his hand on her arm. "You still don't understand?"

"Beethoven, I understand, but you know I am not attracted to men."

"You can change."

"No."

"Then I will!"

She laughed in spite of herself. "Are you changing your sex?"

He struck a feminine pose. "If necessary."

"Seriously," she said. "Go back to Mr. President."

"I cannot."

"Why?"

"I just can't."

"I see," she said coldly. "You've been ordered to stay with me."

"Far from it!"

Meiying gave him a skeptical look.

"I'm serious!"

"Oh, go back to your master!" she snapped.

"Look, it's a very long story."

"Of course, they all are!" exclaimed Meiying.

Mr. Zhi called from the barn. "Is everything okay?"

"Yes!" yelled Beethoven impatiently.

Meiying remained stubbornly silent.

"Now is the time," said Beethoven, almost with a sigh.

Silence.

"Now is the time to tell you some things you do not know."

Silence.

Beethoven clutched her hand and led her through the gate and into the open field, far from any prying ears. "Remember back. Remember Father Durant?"

"Of course."

"Now, keep going back, before you met me at Madame Chen's mansion. Before Old Twisted and Old Crooked. Go back."

"Okay. Yes."

"Even before Colonel Naguma."

Meiying's eyes widened. "Yes."

"Return to Father Durant's church. A certain room. A cross. You were tied to it. He was preparing to . . . well, he would have done you harm. Do you remember?"

Meiying shuddered. "Yes."

"Then he had a seizure. Do you remember someone was there to help you escape? You thought it was Feng Shiren, but you were wrong."

"You?!" she cried.

"Yes," he said proudly.

"How? Why?" she stammered.

"Why? Because my mother is Madame Wang, the woman you were forced to make love to."

Meiying was rendered speechless.

"You see, she has been Mr. President's procurer of young women as well as his sex toy for as long as I can remember. Serves him well. She's in her late-forties, not getting younger. As she gets older, he demands more from her. You see, I hate him. I hate him!"

"But why—"

Beethoven put up his hand. "No. I'm going to tell all. Put all my cards on the table for you to see. I actually helped my mother find victims for him, so I traveled far and wide. My Buddhist monk disguise served me well. A monk! Ha! Many of his . . . of my victims, yes, I admit it . . . were purchased from Father Durant. It was a sort of arrangement between the two. A reciprocal relationship from which both men profited. Those I 'saved' and took to Mr. President were so grateful and trusting. . . in the beginning. "

"But why?"

"My mother always said she did it for me. But when I saved you, I did it for Mr. President and her. When I arranged for you to come under his protection, I did it for him and her. And when I watched you make love to my mother, I did it for him and her. But then, while I watched, something snapped. I could no longer do his bidding. Or mother's. Why? You'd have to be an idiot not to know."

Meiying could say nothing, but merely stared at him in disbelief.

"You see how evil I am!" he cried. "When I saved you, it was for something worse. When I helped you, it was for ulterior motives."

"And when you came with me on this journey?"

"Ah, that is different. You must believe me, that is different! I told them—even my mother—that I would report your movements and continue to scour the countryside for other victims. But I lied. This time I lied. I think my mother knows, but I don't care! I will never return to that evil place!"

"Why did he let me go?"

Beethoven looked puzzled. "I still don't know . . . something to do with your group, your quest, a statue. . . . "

Meiying saw with pity that his eyes were red. She wiped a tear from his cheek, but spoke with unwavering conviction.

"Beethoven, your story is amazing. I had no idea. But you must understand, in spite of your current feelings for me, I remain committed to my independence, to my own life, to the woman I seek on this journey."

Beethoven looked away. "I know that. I respect that. Will you allow me to accompany you?"

"No."

"Why?"

"Because you cling to a false hope."

Beethoven stared into her eyes. "No. Not anymore."

"Then why continue if not in the hope I will change my mind?"

"You won't believe me, but now it is to meet this woman you search for—*her*—this apparently extraordinary woman. Perhaps I also will find redemption with *her*."

This last admission affected Meiying more than anything he had said previously.

"Do you swear you speak the truth?"

"Yes."

"On the memory of your ancestors?"

"Yes."

"On the memory of your mother?"

"Yes."

"On the memory of your father?"

He hesitated.

She lifted her eyebrows and waited.

Still he remained silent.

"Well," she said finally. "That's that."

"It's not what you think," he said glumly.

"What? Is your father Mr. President?"

"God, no!" he cried. "My father raped my mother. He is nothing to me. I don't even know who he is. I cannot swear on the memory of a monster who raped my mother!"

"Beethoven," said Meiying with great feeling. "You may accompany me, but be advised, my mind will not change."

"I understand."

"Now," she said waving her arm as if dismissing their entire conversation. "How do we get to Taiyuan?"

"I have been thinking about that," he said with relief evident in his voice. "And I think I have an answer."

~ *John Struggles with His Sanity* ~

As the safety and comforts of Taiyuan became more distant, the group fell into a glum silence. Suling tried to cheer them up by pointing out the niceness of the weather and the beauty of the countryside, but the rest merely nodded politely. None had any illusion about the dangers, and as they had already lost many comrades, they steeled themselves for the worst. Even Feng Shiren remained uncharacteristically quiet. In fact, John noticed, ever since Peter's murder, Feng had withdrawn, as if his death were a personal failure, or, John suspected, he was somehow involved himself in the murder.

Feng Shiren seemed to sense this doubt in John and kept his distance. Lu Zhishen gave him no comfort either, and seemed to John oddly detached from anything to do with Feng. Still friendly, of course, but a distant friendliness. No banter. Formulaic. Forced.

Something is up between those two, thought John. But when he asked Suling at their first break, she claimed not to have noticed.

Yet there was one person with whom Feng seemed closer than ever: Little Acorn. They appeared inseparable. Provided a funny slouch hat by his hero in Taiyuan, Little Acorn took to saluting Feng at the slightest hint of an order. Even a mild suggestion would bring the boy rigid with a proper military salute. Because John had become suspicious and judgmental about all of Feng's actions, he quietly disapproved, thinking Feng had set himself up as an infallible role-model to the boy, whose creative rebelliousness now went conspicuously absent.

The voices had also gone absent for a while, but John often thought of the notion they planted in his mind that God and Goddess had sent Feng to protect him. This idea horrified him, as if he were a child to be chaperoned. *It's that damn son! Of course, the voices are figments of my imagination, but what if they have some validity?*

If Feng Shiren really is my protector why didn't he protect Meiying? How could he let her be raped? Be separated from the group? After all, this son is supposed to be both of ours. Did Peter's death have anything to do with this?

His mind was awash in this confusing tangle when Lu Zhishen raced up next to him and shouted angrily, "Hey! John! Pull your head out of your ass! We're stopped back there!"

John looked over his shoulder and saw the group waving for him to come back. He had been so absorbed in his own thoughts, he had not heard the signal to pull over. Sheepishly, he turned around and joined them. Madame Liu gave him an irritated glance and continued her speech.

"As I was saying, arrangements have been made. Master Zhou and myself have tried to ensure we do not sleep in the open at all during this last leg. The first way-station unfortunately requires a rather lengthy detour, but it will be safer."

"Yes," added Master Zhou. "We will take this side road to the country estate of an old friend. He is from Nanjing, but he moved to this out-of-the-way property to escape the war. Its mansion still stands, although he is troubled by Japanese troops in the daytime and communist guerillas at night. I was told this area is a hot-bed of red activity." He laughed. "My friend, Mr. Li, tells me they drive the Japs crazy."

"But," interjected Madame Liu. "We must leave the main road. Say what you will about the Japanese, they keep the roads safe."

"Yeah, if they don't kill you themselves," observed Lu Zhishen.

"Any questions?" asked Madame Liu. She pointed to a small path, barely wide enough to accommodate a buffalo. "This is it. Unfortunately, it will take the rest of the day to reach his isolated estate. No Japanese patrols from here on, as far as I know, but plenty of unknown dangers. So we must be diligent and very careful."

"Does Mr. Li have a family?" asked Suling.

"Yes, sons and daughters and grandchildren. Also he has a small army of peasant militia, well-armed and loyal."

"Sounds safe enough," observed Feng Shiren.

Once again, thought John, *he fades into the background when it's safe.*

"Let's go!" cried Madame Liu, trying to sound as upbeat as possible.

"Ohhh," moaned Master Zhou in exaggerated pain, rubbing his rear end. He had gained considerable weight in Taiyuan. "My heart is willing but my bottom is not."

"The sooner we start, the sooner you will be sitting comfortably sipping rice wine," laughed Madame Liu.

"Served by beautiful country women," added Lu Zhishen.

John could not resist adding his own two cents. "With a comfortable bed to sink into at night."

"And dream sweet dreams," said Suling, putting this last icing on the cake while she pedaled off, the first to travel down the trail.

Amid general laughter, the others followed her lead on the narrow trail. Somehow, the threat of common danger and the prospect of common adventure had brought them together again.

~

As it turned out, the trail was long and difficult to traverse. It wound around small creeks and up steep hills, then down through overgrown gullies, and up again.

"Damn, this bloke likes his privacy!" shouted Lu Zhishen, huffing up a particularly wicked slope.

Instantly, those who rode close enough to hear thought of Peter. It affected John in surprising ways. He missed Peter, of course, but he felt a deep pang of guilt that the mystery of his death had not been solved—and it again set him wondering about Feng Shiren.

It is not Feng Shiren. Trust Me, my little mutant. It was you who failed Meiying! You also failed Peter! You had best not fail Me!

If I'm in danger of failing, should I seek out Feng Shiren for protection and guidance?

You have already been informed about that!

And you are merely voices in my head. You're not real! I have merely been 'informed' by myself.

If you believe you are merely a schizophrenic, where do you go with that? I have informed you otherwise. Oh ye of little faith!

You can go to hell!

You are already in hell. I will lead you out.

You're driving me crazy.

Such misconception is the path out of hell. The only path.

As John pedaled, the voices became more distracting, but he was determined not to let it show. Suling noticed him often put a hand to his ear and tilt his head sideways, as if shifting some burden from one hemisphere to the other. She knew his struggles, but wisdom tempered her interference.

At last, they came across rice fields, and felt encouraged the goal drew near. However, with night approaching, the landscape changed from verdant green to menacing grey. Twisted old-growth forest and thorny undergrowth increasingly infringed upon the pleasant rice fields and fruit groves. John recognized the transition and wondered if he was the only one thus affected by the twilight hours. The nearer they drew to the destination, the more numerous were clumps of peasants that stood silently and watched them pass. Dusky shadows made the implements that protruded at various angles from their bodies look like alien appendages. It reminded him of that night a lifetime ago when he tried to find his way back to Mr. Gao's house and malevolent hands reached out from the dark to grab him. Someone saved him that night. Of course, he believed it was Feng Shiren. Had to be. Instinctively he looked back to locate the little soldier-protector, and upon spotting him felt more secure, though he did not like to admit it.

"How much farther?" he called to Madame Liu.

"I'm not sure."

Master Zhou piped up, somewhat breathlessly, "I've only been here once when I was a young man. I think we're close. I hope we're close! My bottom positively insists that we be close!"

Madame Liu took the opportunity to pull over and ask a small group of peasants gawking like visitors at a zoo.

"Friends, how far to Master Li's house?"

An old, wizened male bowed and said, "Within spittin' distance. Over that rise and there she is. Been working the master's land most of my life. First visitors I seen since . . . I don't know when."

"Thank you."

He bowed again, moving his hand slightly to signal the others to do the same.

Encouraged, the group chugged up the slope and paused atop the rise panting with fatigue. Their spirits rose when they looked down at a sprawling estate with multiple buildings, all of brick and fresh new tile roofs. Though they could not make out many details in the dim light, many of the buildings were adorned with dragon sculptures and lion statues. They watched as lanterns were lit and hung to guide the travelers. John's foreboding melted away, and he felt a lighthearted joy at these signs of welcome and comfort.

When the group reached the outer wall of the compound, a delegation was there to greet them. A brash young man spoke first.

"Greetings, friends! My father is expecting you. I am Li Rechi, second son of Master Li." He held his lantern high to show his face. Soon the group found themselves surrounded by attendants, most also holding lanterns and chattering in a dizzying cacophony of orders and counter-orders. John, as usual, looked to Madame Liu and Master Zhou for the proper protocol. Smiles and solicitations swirled around. Lu Zhishen firmly held onto his bike until a clear command was received about the disposition of the Precious Object.

After the logistics of unpacking and where to put the bikes were dealt with, Lu gently cradled the box in his arms and looked to his leaders for direction as to where the treasure should be deposited. Madame Liu stood close-by, and though she smiled and nodded, she clearly chaffed at the formal pleasantries and hastened off to ensure the safety of the box before other details were addressed.

Master Li appeared, replete with a white beard, a book tucked under his arm, and a cane—the quintessential Confucian scholar. After greeting his old friend, Master Zhou, he made his way to Lu Zhishen, who continued holding the box as if it had been placed in the arms of a statue. Nodding a cursory greeting to Lu, he turned to Master Zhou.

"Is this it?"

"Yes."

"When may I see it?"

"Old friend, let's make sure it is in a safe place first."

"Your room?"

"Mine," said Madame Liu who had just joined them.

"Of course, of course," said Master Li. "The mother bear will protect her cub."

"To the death," said Madame Liu, smiling to take the edge off her remark.

Master Li wagged his finger. "Or to the death of others who try and intervene."

Madame Liu bowed, but made no reply.

Master Li clapped his hands. "Show them to their rooms!" He turned to Madame Liu and Master Zhou. "Afterward, my servants will show you to my humble dining hall, where we shall eat and celebrate your arrival. Visitors are too rare."

John observed this exchange and fell happily into the festive spirit. There appeared to be no subterfuge—at least to Western eyes and ears. Everyone seemed genuinely happy and relaxed. Food sounded good, but sleep sounded better. He whispered his excuses to Master Zhou who promptly slapped him on the hand.

"Foolish boy!" he whispered urgently. "You must come. It would be an insult."

Taken aback, John quickly agreed, feeling small and foolish for his *faux pas*. After being shown his room and unpacking, he followed his personal servant to the dining hall. The classically decorated room was magnificent, but intimidating, and John felt gratified when the dining servant seated him next to Suling.

"I'm so happy to sit next to you," he whispered, genuinely relieved.

"As am I," she whispered back.

Once the guests were all in place, Master Li entered the hall, beaming and banging his cane on the table for emphasis, although unnecessarily, as everyone already awaited his words.

"My old friend, Master Zhou, has brought me the honor of receiving you esteemed guests. He has informed me of your adventures, and losses, and has also enlightened me on the purpose of your epic journey. I have been most impressed, and, I admit, curious about the person who so powerfully draws to *her* such loyalty and sacrifice. The way is dangerous. Even here, the long arm of war has struck down some of our best men—" he glanced at Madame Liu—"and women."

He raised a glass of *mao tai*. "To your journey. *Gan bei*!" After smacking his lips, he continued. "If I were younger, I might even consider going with you, but my responsibilities here are heavy. The Japanese get nearer every day."

Master Zhou stood and raised his glass. "To the defeat of Japan!"

"Now, eat!" exclaimed Master Li.

The guests had not enjoyed the repast long before a bedraggled figure in muddy clothes rushed into the room and whispered in Master Li's ear. He let out a muffled cry and quickly rose with the help of his cane.

"I'm sorry. Bad news. My eldest son is wounded and approaches on horse-back. I must go."

He made his way out of the room, leaving the guests to hesitate. Master Zhou threw down his chopsticks and followed Master Li out, the others dutifully following for lack of some better alternative. Prepared for the worst, they found Master Li hugging his son who appeared to have only a superficial arm wound.

"Good! Good!" repeated the old man.

His son smiled patiently and parroted his father's words with, "It's fine. It's fine."

A hefty crowd had gathered round, and Master Li suddenly remembered what had just been interrupted. "But we have guests! You caught us in the middle of a welcome feast. Now it shall be a double celebration! Come in and eat! All of you, return to the table! Eat and drink to your heart's content. My son is safe! We'll make old Li Bai jealous!"

When they had retaken their seats, and more food brought, Master Li introduced his son.

"This is Yuwei, my eldest. I'll not play our stupid Chinese tradition of false modesty. He is strong like his father. Brave like his father. And handsome like his mother!"

Polite laughter all around. Master Li turned serious. "Now, tell us what happened?"

Li Yuwei was a tall, lanky, handsome young man with an intelligent face and quick, piercing eyes. He took everything in at a glance, and found the composition of his father's guests quite interesting, particularly the two foreigners. Being an intelligent man, he would rather listen than talk.

"Father, I do not want to bore our guests. It was a minor skirmish. But I am more interested in our new friends."

He looked at John and Lu. "Do you both speak Chinese?"

"Yes," they replied in unison.

"Good, where are you from?"

They answered.

"Missionaries?"

Both laughed. "Far from it," said Lu Zhishen.

And so it went. John realized that by the end of the evening, Yuwei knew all of their stories far better than they knew his. He felt curious about Yuwei, but when he retired to his room, the bed welcomed him with unparalleled softness, and sleep came very quickly. The next morning a loud gong woke him, and when he poked his head out of the room, a servant spied him and said simply, "Breakfast."

Entering the dining hall, he was surprised to see the others already eating. Feng Shiren, who had been quiet these past days, sat next to Li Yuwei, engaged in a lively conversation, though they both spoke so softly that John could not hear over the patter of those around him.

"Good morning," said Suling as she sat.

"Good morning."

"Did you sleep well?" she asked.

John desperately wanted to eavesdrop on Feng and Li, but he was obliged to respond.

"Yes, and you?"

"Oh, it felt so good," gushed Suling. She stretched languorously. "I felt guilty at the luxury."

"I know what you mean," said Lu. "I could get used to this."

"How long are we staying?" asked John.

The other two shrugged and looked at Madame Liu, who was also engaged in lively conversation with Master Li and Master Zhou.

Whenever John glanced around the table, he noticed Li Yuwei did most of the talking with Feng. John smiled inwardly. *So, even young Master Li can't resist the charms of Feng Shiren.* As often happened when he looked at Feng, his thoughts turned to Meiying. He wished she were here, sharing everything with him, although Yuwei was far too handsome for comfort. Lesbian or not, John felt irrationally more threatened by male than female competitors for her attention, but he could not help the misconstruction.

Lu Zhishen's voice suddenly rang out, loud enough to cause all other conversations to cease.

"Tell me, Yuwei, what unit were you with when you were wounded? Communist? Nationalist? Guerillas?"

Before Yuwei could answer, Master Li entered the room booming out a response to Lu's question.

"Communists!? Those murderous bastards! If you own one measly *mou* of land, they would no sooner look at you as kill you! They're worse than the Japs. Steal your land and kill you for the trouble!"

Yuwei listened to his father patiently. When sure the old man had emptied his bile, he answered Lu's question. "No. But we have occasionally fought with the communists. Brave men."

His father grunted in displeasure, but Lu pressed on.

"Are you with the Nationalist Army?"

"Yes and no."

This curt reply made it clear he did not wish to volunteer any additional information, but Lu Zhishen, true to his namesake, was impervious to picking up such niceties.

"How so?" he asked.

"You might call us a local militia. Some say partisans. Some guerillas." Yuwei shrugged, and before Lu could pursue this line of questioning any further, he turned the tables.

"How does a Canadian view our China?"

"Bloody awful!" Lu blurted in English.

John noticed Lu slipping more deeply into Peter's style of speaking.

"Yes, it is bloody here," mused Yuwei in English.

"No, no," said Lu. "Bloody is an English slang word; it means extremely, or some such."

"Ah."

"So, you speak English?" John asked Yuwei, now very curious.

"Of course."

"I don't!" boasted his father, redirecting the conversation back to Chinese. "See! My number one son is a smart boy!"

Rechi, the second son, came and went from the room, evidently overseeing the meal and the servants. John searched his face in vain for signs of resentment at all the attention given his older brother. John knew Chinese history was replete with stories of humble younger brothers who later poisoned their elder to grasp the reins of power. As the father rained praise on Yuwei, John doubled down on his efforts to detect any sign of discontent in Rechi. He saw none. Little Acorn, who sat next to Feng Shiren, squirmed in his seat, bored with such typically aimless and uninteresting adult conversation.

"Hey! Little Acorn, quit kicking me under the table!" cried Feng in mock anger.

The boy saluted and sat straight.

"We actually have a school for peasant children," said Yuwei. "Perhaps he would like to see it?"

"An excellent idea!" enthused Madame Liu. "I have often felt guilty at his lack of education."

"Rechi!" called Master Li. The second son rushed in from the kitchen and the old man pointed at Little Acorn. "Take the boy to the schoolhouse. Introduce him and ask Teacher Zhu to let him stay."

Little Acorn assumed a stricken look, but secretly felt anything would be better than being subjected to more adult chatter.

After Rechi and the boy trundled off, the older adults again fell into their own intimate conversations; a mixture of future plans and past reminiscences. The younger ones were left to their own devices. Each looked at the other, and Yuwei hit the table with one hand, his other arm being bandaged and still sore.

"Let me show you around our little empire. Does that suit?"

All agreed, and arrangements were made to travel by horseback. Suling was the only one of the younger guests leery of riding. After assurances were given that her horse would be the gentlest of the lot, they set out on a glorious morning. Master Li felt pleased that his younger guests were thus entertained, and he returned to the serious business of confabulating with Master Zhou and Madame Liu.

For the few hours they rode, all except Feng Shiren transformed into carefree youth, joking and dexterously touching upon a plethora of topics, none of which was designed to drag them into overly serious territory. Even Suling, no longer a spring chicken, joined in the banter. They freely segued from Chinese to English and back again in a seamless continuum. For the first time he could remember, John felt unburdened by the weight of the world. Even their journey and the vicissitudes they had faced seemed unconnected to the moment. If any of the voices had the audacity to spoil his mood, he was fully prepared to shame them into submission.

After taking a circuitous route around the main buildings, they headed into the surrounding hills. Reaching a particularly scenic spot overlooking the sprawling valley where the full extent of Master Li's "empire" could be viewed, they stopped for a picnic. Geometric rice fields and fruit groves dotted the landscape spread below them, each patch in varying hues of green. Dense clumps of peasant houses with red-tiled roofs added enough color to render the scene worthy of any French painting from Provence.

"Beautiful," said Suling.

"Yes, beautiful," replied Yuwei. "But in great danger."

"From the Japs?" asked Lu Zhishen.

"Yes."

"How close are they?" asked John.

Yuwei laughed. "You saw for yourselves on your way from Taiyuan. They would come tomorrow if they knew about this valley."

"Why? What's here for them?"

"Food, of course."

"We were told you have a group of armed peasants. Could they defend the valley?"

"Not a chance."

"Well," said Suling. "Let's not spoil the day by dwelling on bad things."

Yuwei smiled. "Yes, you are right. The day is too nice." He stretched out on his back, his hands behind his head.

"Well, I for one am going to explore a bit," said Feng Shiren.

"I'll go with you," said John. "Anyone else?"

With no other takers, Feng and John remounted and rode along the ridgeline in silence. After a few minutes, Feng reined-in his horse and turned to John. "Have you thought of Meiying recently?"

"All the time, why?"

Feng smiled, his white teeth in full display. "I have a feeling I'll hear something soon."

John straightened in the saddle. "Really? How can you get word out here? We get farther away from Taiyuan."

"My sources are not without legs."

"What have you heard?"

"Nothing."

"Then why tell me this if there is nothing to tell?"

"Because I have a feeling there will be soon."

"A feeling? Are your feelings always accurate?"

"Yes."

"What about Peter's unsolved murder? Any word, or do you have a feeling there also."

Feng affected a wounded expression. "You hurt me. Don't you trust me anymore? Aren't I sent here by your voices?"

John shook his head in disbelief. "I told you that?"

"Yes, you don't remember?"

John could make no reply.

"And it is my job to protect you and to make sure you and Meiying get together. Something about a son, although that part is not clear to me."

John flashed with anger. "Feng, I don't understand you! It seems you enjoy teasing me, or leading me on, or something. What is the point of mentioning things you know won't happen? Is it to torment me?"

Feng struck another of his tragic poses. "Quite the contrary. I want you to have hope. I see how the voices hollow you out. They pester you, don't they?"

"Yes, but that is my problem."

"No, John, they are my problem—my masters, if you will—and it is up to me to please them."

"Oh, come on Feng. Now I know you're playing with me."

"Far from it. The person writing this book, the one that puts these words in our mouths, lives in the future, in an institution, and that makes things quite difficult for me."

"Good god, Feng! You're mad! Who do you think he is? Who do you think we are? Just characters in a novel?"

"No, we're real. Just that we're dead. That's what makes this difficult."

"Shit, now I know you're crazy!" John felt his sanity slip beneath his feet and he stared down at a dark precipice. "Damn it, Feng! Stop this bullshit and let's go back!"

Listen carefully to what Feng Shiren is about to say, Chosen One. It is important.

"You aren't curious at all who is in the institution writing about us?"

"No. Yes, but only because it might give me insight into your mental issues."

"Your son."

But, if Feng expected any satisfaction from witnessing John's shock, he was sorely disappointed.

"Old news," said John flippantly, wheeling his horse and riding on.

~ Meiying and Beethoven Approach Taiyuan ~

Beethoven had indeed thought he had found a way around the Japanese roadblock. The next day, finding Mr. Zhi alone, he surprised him with a request.

"I want to meet up with your communist friends."

"Why?"

"I need help to get around the Japs. They control the roads."

"Umm. You know, I only told you about the communists to get my old woman mad. When we make-up—" he rolled his eyes and made an obscene gesture.

"I'm serious."

"So am I."

"Can you?" insisted Beethoven.

Mr. Zhi glared at him, then turned as if to leave. Beethoven was about to call him back when Zhi swirled around and viciously hit him in the stomach with an axe handle. Beethoven crumpled to the ground, and Zhi quickly had a foot on his neck.

"Fool! Do you think you can trick me that easily? I am utterly loyal to the Nationalists!"

"I didn't know!"

Zhi pulled out a knife and held it to Beethoven's throat. "Bai Meiying!" he called over his shoulder.

When she arrived, she threw her hands to her face and screamed, "What are you doing?"

"Killing a communist spy!"

"He's no communist!" she again screamed.

"Why does he want to get in contact with the communists then?" Zhi pressed down on the knife so Beethoven could utter no sound.

By now, Mrs Zhi had joined Meiying and watched as might an interested bystander at a car wreck.

Meiying thought quickly and blurted out, "Probably to find a way around the Japanese roadblock!"

Mr. Zhi laughed and let up on the knife. "Ah! Her I believe." He helped a panting Beethoven to stand. "In that case I can help you," he said as calmly as if selling tickets to a fair. "Tomorrow night. You're lucky. A meeting. Both of you will attend."

"So you are a communist!" exclaimed Beethoven.

"Of course, what did you think?"

~

The next evening, as planned, Beethoven walked with Mr. Zhi down a maze of small paths to an isolated farmhouse that appeared to be abandoned and in ruin. When they entered, he saw a group of faces illumined by lanterns and scrutinizing his every wrinkle and fold as best they could in the dim light.

Mr. Zhi held up his lantern to Beethoven's face. "Comrades, this is the man I told you about. He travels to Taiyuan with a woman and wants our help around Jap lines."

An older, sinewy man snarled, "Comrade Zhi, what business is that of ours?"

"Comrades," interjected Beethoven. "I have been fighting with guerillas against the Japs in another district." He pronounced his lie with admirable conviction.

"What guerillas?"

"Affiliated with Mr. President."

"What?" demanded another man. "That traitor!"

"The boy doesn't know any better," explained Zhi. "He will be a convert to our cause. I've been talking to him. Believe me, he's sympathetic to us."

"Why? He looks and talks like he's educated. Just another bourgeois brat!"

"I tell you I've watched him—he's alright."

"And the woman, comrade?" asked another.

"Ah, she's good as gold!"

"Look, comrades," said Beethoven. "Once I reach Taiyuan, I can be another set of eyes and ears for you. I'm clever and can get places others can't. I hate Mr. President, but his influence opens doors. Out of gratitude and a belief in the cause, I can make myself valuable, if you give me a chance."

A person who had not yet spoken, but evidently served as leader, stood and said in a commanding voice, "Comrade Zhi, take him out while we confer."

Standing outside, Mr. Zhi spoke for no reason other than something to say. "Thought that went well."

Beethoven shrugged and said the useful, if not immortal words, "We'll see."

They waited in silence for a good thirty minutes. Someone who Beethoven did not recognize came out. "Go home, comrades. Tomorrow at sunset be ready. No bicycles." This pronouncement was made without a trace of emotion.

"Who comes?" asked Mr. Zhi.

"You'll know, comrade."

The following evening Meiying and Beethoven waited, their packs full. Both regretted the loss of their bikes, but Mr. and Mrs. Zhi partially made up for it by being the delighted recipients. Eventually, as the moon increasingly disappeared behind clouds, five figures as dark as pitch came to the door. They were armed and not inclined to expend much effort in talking.

Mr. Zhi already stood with the door open when they stepped onto the porch.

"Let's go," said one of the shadows.

Quick hugs, brief goodbyes, and they were off. Meiying felt light-hearted, happy to be on the move, happy to be drawing nearer to a reunion with the group, happy to be taking steps toward *her*. Though damp, the night air drew cool life into her lungs. Surrounded by these men, she experienced a feeling of safety that had been absent for a long while, and this confidence made her step more lively. They carried no lanterns, but intermittent moonlight amply shone the way on narrow, but well-traveled paths. Ascending and descending hills, navigating curved and deteriorated trails, they trudged on in silence. Only occasionally did they rest, and even then hunched down and ate a few buns without a word. Meiying tried to make out their faces, but slouch hats obscured any hope of glimpsing identifiable features.

Around one in the morning, they arrived at a fallen-down shack, for all intents and purposes uninhabitable. But stepping inside, it had layers of rugs on the floor, and a serviceable ceiling built beneath the tattered original roof. Food had been stored in boxes with hinged lids by some earlier visitors, and the group ate a hearty meal, again in silence.

"Sleep," came the same voice Meiying heard at the Zhi's.

She pulled her bedroll up around her chin, acknowledged Beethoven's "good night," and quickly fell asleep with a weary but satisfied frame of mind. She awakened periodically by raucous snoring, but had no trouble falling back asleep. When dawn tinged the air with hazy light, she was the last to rise. Someone pushed her arm and said, "Get up. Eat quickly. It's time."

Upon hearing these words, Meiying felt an electric shock, and momentarily fell into a state of disorientation.

"What?" she said rather stupidly.

"Get up. Eat quickly. It's time."

Again she felt the jolt, but now she knew for certain: the voice was a female's.

Meiying looked at the face, but the figure had turned to leave. No one else occupied the shack. Evidently the little band waited outside. When she emerged, the men were huddled over a small fire. Meiying searched and found the woman standing close by, a scarf covered her face except for her eyes. Further shadows were cast by a peasant hat, but the eyes could not be hidden, and they were glorious. Deep, luminous, almost doe-like, they instantly pulled Meiying into their depths.

"Let me show you where to bathe," said the mysterious woman, her voice a deep, feminine timbre, seemingly in a contest not to be outdone by the power of the eyes. As the woman walked ahead, Meiying could make out nothing of her body, as it was hidden beneath loose-fitting peasant attire. A rifle hung by its strap over her shoulder, which she carried as if it were second nature. They trekked down a small ravine and the woman pointed to a stream running clear and deep.

"You may bathe here. It is clean."

"Thank you.

"I'll be at the top"—she laughed for the first time—"making sure the men stay put."

"Thank you."

Before Meiying could ask her name, the woman scrambled up the slope. Watching her go, Meiying felt an uncomfortably exciting sensation, one quite familiar, and when she disrobed, her skin tingled to the touch, not entirely due to the cold water. Now the trip took on a new and stimulating fascination.

Upon rejoining the group, Meiying looked for the woman, but she was nowhere to be found.

"Are you almost ready?" asked Beethoven, who had been chatting amiably with the men.

"Almost. Where is the other one?"

"Who?"

"The woman who led me to the stream."

"I don't know."

"Lihua will be back soon, comrade lady," said one of the men. "She's a strange one. Likes to be apart."

"Where's she from?"

"Nanjing."

"What happened?"

The older male rose slowly and shook his head. "Don't ask. Let's go."

"Shouldn't we call her?"

"She'll find us. Surprised she's been with us so long and so close this far. Must be you, comrade missy."

Beethoven quickly read the situation and looked miserable, suddenly yearning to reach Taiyuan as soon as possible. "Look Meiying, it's going to be a beautiful day!" he exclaimed gamely.

She nodded distractedly, and as they set-off, kept scanning the landscape much to Beethoven's continuing misery. All day they traveled with no sign of Lihua, and as time passed Beethoven's spirits brightened considerably while Meiying's proportionately sank. *Am I to have only those eyes and that voice to remember?* She wondered.

Late afternoon found them struggling up a jagged limestone mountain, the trail a mere animal path worn into the side of the cliff and suitable only for mountain goats. Meiying leaned forward, straining against the backward pull of her pack and listening to the sound of her own heavy breathing. Out of nowhere, a sharp noise like a hammer pulverizing a stone struck near her head and a spray of sand and pebbles stung her face. Before she knew what was happening, more of the mountain seemed to fly apart all around her. A heavy body pushed her from behind and she fell face down on the trail.

"Get down!" came a voice, probably Beethoven's.

Now the distinctive sounds of rifle fire reached her ears, and she saw her companions desperately crawling forward to escape their exposed position. She glanced down and saw puffs of smoke and muzzle flashes far below.

"Jap patrol! Move it!" cried someone in front. Every person in the group clung to the little trail and scrambled up the narrow ledge on their bellies and elbows and knees like panicked bugs. The top of the mountain was not far, and a stand of protective trees offered salvation a few meters ahead. Now she could hear the zinging bullets as they flew by, slamming into the fragile outcropping and peppering her with more shards and slivers of rock and dust. In the midst of her frantic efforts to make it to the trees, a sickening thud reached her ears followed by a moan and cry for help. She saw someone roll a body off the trail and down the cliff to make room for the rest.

Suddenly, from above, a rifle could be heard firing down at the Japanese.

"Meiying! Hurry!" shouted Beethoven, who crawled directly behind her.

At last, after an eternity of scrambling with the constant terror of bullets tearing into her body as they did her dead compatriot, she reached the safety of the trees. Behind the sheltering trunks, the group looked up at the topmost ridge and saw the puffs of smoke still coming from the rifle of their protector.

"Japs won't follow us up the trail. We're safe for now," said the leader in a calm, deliberate voice.

"Shirong is dead," said another.

"I know."

"Had four kids."

"I know. Let's go see how Lihua's doing up there."

Meiying, whose heart already pounded with waves of adrenalin, beat in a different way upon hearing that name, no less energetically.

Reaching the top, much to Meiying's disappointment, there was no one to be seen.

"That crazy girl is off again," observed one of the men.

"Yes," said the leader. "Lihua is one of a kind."

"Strange," said Beethoven, intrigued in spite of himself. "Are you sure it was her?"

"As sure as rain is water and air is life."

An airplane droned lazily somewhere in the distance, getting closer.

"Uh oh, better get moving," said the leader scanning the sky. "Probably a Jap spotter plane."

On they traveled, now heavily burdened with concerns that the Japanese had discovered their movements and the direction they headed. The death of Shirong also weighed on the men, with an occasional "poor Shirong" uttered in helpless anger and sadness. But Meiying remained impervious to these distractions; she continued to be haunted by those eyes and that voice.

Chapter Sixteen

So Near Yet So Far

John is Beset with Trouble

As they rode farther from Taiyuan, John felt increasingly anxious. Perhaps his anxiety arose from leaving the protection of the city; perhaps all the warnings worked their way into his native insecurities; or perhaps the always-looming threats and insults of the voices preyed upon his mind while he rode in the vastness of the open road. After all, that very openness mocked the tiny confines of grey matter that had only itself to turn for comfort. He felt oddly removed intellectually from his companions even as he drew physically closer to them in shared experiences. It was as if there existed two planes of reality; or two orbits which, like an electron, he jumped from one to the other with no knowledge of the journey in between. One moment his heart throbbed with intimate feelings of love and unity with the group, and the next he rode as an observer from a parallel universe, incapable of exchanging something as common as air.

They were routinely passed by haggard, starving, zombie-like stragglers headed in the opposite direction, the worst of the worst. Those that had been too poor to leave, now found their lives so unendurable in the war-zone that they staggered toward Taiyuan as a last hope of survival. Yet their faces revealed how little confidence they had that this act of desperation would lead to a good end. The faces of these pathetic people were deeply scarred and hardened like a kind of granite, seemingly frozen in expressionless masks and locking their vacant stares in the forward direction only, depriving them of the flexibility to look up or down, right or left upon the world. John recognized a strange kinship with their single-minded and rigid determination.

Were not he and his companions cast from the same die, driven on by this mad quest to find a woman nobody acknowledged was more than human, yet all acknowledged was not less than divine? When he thought of those few moments back in the States he knew *her*, in the full disorienting confusion of *her* presence, a sharp tingle ran down his spine and he seemed alert to the very molecules that vibrated in all things.

Of course, John Powers! And now you have abandoned the other her!
What am I supposed to do?
Silence.
I thought so. My own imagination has not enough imagination to answer.
Imagination! You are the imagined one, John! No more than a memory in a future devoid of humans! Your unborn son writes and you are animated. He stops and you are frozen in time and space. Forgotten.
John knew the voice was Male—was God. *I don't understand you! Get out of my head!*
That is right, Beloved, came Goddess. **As long as he writes, all are on the continuum. This man must impregnate the woman. That is the only way this Goddess may get to You, Beloved God, and save this lovely planet.**
Do you have a lover in there, Goddess?
"A lover?" asked Suling, riding next to John.
God's faction—cruel lovers of fate! Death sentence for the planet!
Goddess's faction—deluded lovers of probability! Toying with a predetermined future!
Damn it, get out of my head! Both of You!
"Damn it, get out of my head! Both of You!"
"John!" called Suling.
Buffeted by these contradictory voices from inside and outside his head, John assumed his mask of incomprehension—a flat look that always made Suling shiver. Yet she, no expert, nonetheless knew, and rode on, continuing to call in a soothing voice, "John, are you okay?"
But John pedaled forward without changing his detached demeanor, occasionally mumbling words which Suling knew were bits of conversation with his voices.
So you continue to write, Michael Powers! Destined to be read by no one!
John mumbled, "You are God, the angry one. I am not writing anything."
He was not speaking of you, but of your future son, said Goddess. **As for you, conditions need to be fulfilled before he can be born and write these words. Do you understand now?**
No!
You will be his father, Bai Meiying will be his mother, and the Superior Ones will be the eventual result. If you wish a more human analogy, I will be the Great Mother to both of you. Now do you understand? Your son will take a major step toward the replacement of humans by another—
No!
"John, they're signaling us to pull over."
Don't listen! Aren't you curious to know?
"What?"
"They're signaling us to pull over," repeated Suling.
"Oh."

~

After the group formed a rough circle, Madame Liu turned to Feng Shiren. "Mr. Feng has returned from riding ahead. He says there is a battle. We must pause here."

"I don't hear anything," said Lu Zhishen, tilting his head and cupping his ear for emphasis.

"Can't from here," replied Feng. He pointed up the road. "Over that rise is another, steeper hill. On the other side of that one there is fighting. I think a Jap unit is being ambushed, probably by guerillas, but who knows for sure?"

"Are you sure?" asked Master Zhou, but quickly realized he appeared to contradict what Feng had just said, and rushed to clarify. "I mean, are you sure we can't get through?"

Feng shrugged. "Look at the road. No refugees. They've been cut off by the battle, and no one is going in our direction."

"What should we do?" asked Suling.

"I suggest we stay here until it's over," said Feng.

"Yeah, but if it grows, we'll be caught in the middle," said Lu.

"Yes, the Japanese are always vicious after a battle. To them, anyone in the area is a spy, regardless!" said Master Zhou.

"Well, we can't go back," said Madame Liu. "I'm sure Japanese reinforcements will soon be coming along."

"How about moving far away from the road?"

"Then we're sure to be accused of being spies. We need to stay among the refugees."

"Most of them have moved on."

"But others have made a camp back down the road a little way," said Little Acorn.

"How do you know?" asked Madame Liu.

The boy looked shy. "Mr. Feng told me to hang back, just in case. I saw it, then rode to catch up. But I saw it."

"How far back?"

"Not far."

"Okay, let's go back and mix in with the refugees," said Madame Liu.

The others had no better plan, so they returned back down the road until they arrived at a large group of refugees who occupied a wide plain of soggy ground and scraggly weeds. Most shuffled about, preparing their camp for the night. The group chose a spot on the outer edge of the crowded field, yet still within the perimeter of huddled refugees. Among these living ghosts, any movement that displayed strength or vigor attracted attention because it conveyed evidence that people displaying such energy must have food. Unconsciously, the group slowed their own movements to mimic the physical weakness of their neighbors. Keeping even conversation to a minimum, they melted into the silent ocean, each awaiting what the next morning might bring.

John prepared his bedroll and lay on his back, watching the clouds skitter across the moon. The voices had fallen mercifully silent and he was left to his own uninterrupted thoughts. Before long, he fell asleep. Both of the women that now dominated the trajectory of his life loomed before him at a tantalizingly close yet frustratingly unbridgeable distance. He dreamed that Meiying sank in quicksand while *she* watched from some lofty height, beyond the reach of mankind. John ran toward Meiying to pull her out, but he ran and ran without getting any closer. All the while, *she* looked down on him with an enigmatic smile at his futile efforts. John finally awoke with a start when Meiying disappeared beneath the sand. He sat up and listened to the wind whistling through a host of unidentifiable refugee possessions. Adding to these eerie noises were snores, soft crying, and a nightmarish, collective moan that rose above the encampment and entwined with the wind to form a painful sigh that seemed to come from the earth itself.

A familiar sound of deep rumbling caught his attention. Squinting into a rising sun, he noticed everyone around him standing nervously and looking toward the road. He could not see and caught Lu Zhishen wildly gesturing to him. Jumping to his feet, he looked in the direction Lu pointed and saw the familiar sight of billowing dust thrown up by Japanese tanks and personnel carriers.

"Well, that tears it!" cried Lu. "Now we'll never get anywhere!"

Master Zhou trotted up. "As long as they leave us alone. But look at their eyes." He nodded in the direction of a line of infantry marching past. "There is hatred and resentment in those eyes. They blame us."

"For what?" asked Suling.

"For being here. For their comrades dying. For us existing. I don't like it. Something bad is going to happen."

Even as he spoke, Japanese soldiers riding on armored personnel carriers pointed their weapons at the refugees and pretended to shoot, evidently providing themselves with infinite amusement.

"*Kyōda! Kyōda! Kyōda!*" they yelled, laughing uproariously.

"That means 'bang'," muttered Master Zhou under his breath.

Lu Zhishen leaned his head close and cupped his ear. "What did you say?"

Master Zhou spoke loud enough for the others to hear, but quite calmly, "That means 'bang'. I think we should move away, toward the trees, before the bangs are real. I have seen situations like this, and they don't end well."

Lu Zhishen moved to collect his things.

No! No!" whispered Master Zhou, his eyes still uneasily on the soldiers. "Slowly."

"Yes," added Madame Liu in a low voice. "One at a time, slowly."

They moved as if in slow-motion, being as quiet and unobtrusive as possible. One-by-one they slipped back into the trees.

Madame Liu made sure she was the last, in spite of hushed objections by the others. They knew argument would not sway her decision once it had been made. Each slipped away into the tree line, quietly walking their bikes a few meters in to wait at a small clearing. As Madame Liu joined them, clustered like children awaiting their teacher, angry voices were heard bellowing across the field from the direction of the road.

"Run!" cried Master Zhou.

Now there rippled a wave of tension through the refugees that transformed into confused chatter and cries of warning when it reached the group. Like a herd of deer caught in headlights, the refugees momentarily froze in disbelief before the guns fired into them with a terrible suddenness. One moment the air was still; the next a host of panicked voices; and the last moment erupted into a hail of bullets that ripped into the starving bodies as agony built upon agony to infuse the air with a Great Wailing.

The group ran through the forest, away from death and toward even greater uncertainty; their footfalls accompanied by the frantic tapping from the box strapped to Lu Zhishen's bike.

... *TapTapTapTap*....

Behind them, the screams of the dying faded until only their own heavy breathing could be heard. When they stopped at last, the forest encircled them in an ominous silence.

"Now what?" asked John.

Each looked at the other.

"I don't know," admitted Madame Liu.

Feng Shiren, who had been a passive actor during the entire incident, finally spoke up as if announcing he possessed the answer all along.

"It's obvious."

"Well? You opened your trap, now tell us without the games," said Lu Zhishen, frustrated as usual with Feng.

"Keep going."

"Keep going where?" asked Master Zhou.

Feng pointed in a direction and said, "That way."

No one could be sure whether he actually knew why they should go that way, or whether it was a totally random gesture.

"Why?" asked Madame Liu.

"Because that is the direction that will take us to *her*."

"You don't even know where *she* is," replied Madame Liu. "How do you know that is the correct direction?"

"Because if we go that way, we will survive. If we survive, we can continue our journey. If we can continue our journey, we will reach *her*. Simple."

"Simple? I repeat, how do you know that is the way that will allow us to survive?"

"Intuition."

"Oh, crap!" cried Lu in disgust. "There's not even a trail!"

Wordlessly, Feng strode a few paces and pulled back a low-hanging branch. Behold! Exposed for all to see, a hard-pack trail clearly lay perpendicular to their position.

"A trail," said Feng sardonically.

"How did you know?" asked Suling in wonder.

"I know because I look, explore, find unwanted corners, places in dusky shadows, under rocks, in the trees. I know because I look, not talk."

"Where does it lead?" asked Master Zhou.

Feng shrugged. "I don't know everything."

"Well, wherever it leads is better than staying here," commented Madame Liu.

"Or back the way we came," shuddered John. "God help those poor people."

When they fell silent after this comment, a faint sound could still be heard. Slow, deliberative cadence.

... *Tap. Tap. Tap. Tap....*

Feng laughed. "She is calming down. That's a good sign."

"Oh, I hope so Shiren, I hope so," said Suling.

John knew otherwise.

No, John did not know otherwise. The writer writes. It is the son who knows otherwise.

~ *Meiying Meets the Mysterious Woman* ~

The little band of partisans accompanying Meiying and Beethoven stayed off the main roads to Taiyuan. Their zig-zagging and back-tracking took them on a dizzying array of paths that made progress very slow, but had the advantage of taking them to places far off the beaten track. As evening approached, they stopped at a brick-and-tile farmhouse where a big, raw-boned peasant greeted them heartily.

"Welcome, comrades! Welcome! I thought you'd be around sooner."

"We had some trouble, comrade," said the leader curtly.

"Ah well, I have some humble food, but no meat, comrades. Just good peasant fare!" After saying these words, he clamped an old pipe firmly in his teeth and grinned ferociously.

"Good enough," said the leader.

As they entered the house, the farmer whispered, "Who got it?"

"Shirong."

"Where's Lihua?"

The leader shrugged. "Could be anywhere. She'll show up. Helped us when we had some trouble."

The big peasant laughed. "Comrade Lihua, what a phantom!"

"This is Bai Meiying," said the leader, gesturing toward her. "And her friend here is Beethoven."

"What?"

"Bee-tho-fen."

"Comrade," said the peasant. "That is a very strange name. I can't even pronounce it."

The leader shrugged. "Don't matter, comrade. Where's the food?"

Meiying noticed the farmer evidently lived alone and knew his way around a kitchen. She wanted to ask whether he was married, but remained quiet. He scuffled back to his gruel pot which hung over a fire and stirred with an extraordinarily long wooden spoon, humming a ditty while the flames reddened his still-grinning face. She watched ashes from his pipe occasionally fall into the pot, prompting bursts of vigorous stirring and little cackles of amusement. As usual, the partisans remained quiet and did not speak even in whispers. Cowed by this spartan and uncommunicative atmosphere, Meiying and Beethoven sat in a corner and sought comfort from each other.

"Well," whispered Beethoven. "I could certainly eat a horse. How about you?"

Meiying nodded. "Do you know where we are?"

Beethoven looked around in an exaggerated manner. "In a farmhouse somewhere in China." He chuckled at his little joke.

Meiying smiled. "Beethoven, you're such a fool," she said playfully.

"Not I," he replied. "But you had better—"

Before he could finish his sentence, the door inched open and a figure glided into the room. If one hadn't been looking, it would not have been noticed. Meiying knew at once that it was Lihua, and her heart fluttered wildly.

The woman wore dark clothes and a peasant hat that cast a dark shadow over her face. A scarf encircled her neck and the lower part of her face, leaving only her eyes shining out from the shadows. She moved silently to the leader.

"Hello, comrade, I see you made it," he said with a slight smile.

She nodded.

"Thanks for the help back there."

She nodded.

"Food?"

She nodded again.

"Should be ready in a fly's blink," said the farmer looking up from his pot.

Lihua scanned the room and saw an empty spot. She carefully placed her rifle next to the others and squatted beside Meiying.

Meiying was so intimidated by this woman's presence that she merely nodded and said nothing. Beethoven had no such hesitation.

"What you did back there was amazing, Lihua! I have never seen such courage in a woman!"

Now it was Meiying's turn to feel jealous.

Lihua looked at Beethoven and nodded again.

Meiying saw Beethoven's expression when he gazed upon Lihua and realized they both were attracted to this extraordinary woman. She laughed inwardly at the absurd irony, but irony had no efficacious effect upon her feelings of loneliness, depression, and despair, so her natural inclination was to remain silent. Beethoven, however, pressed on.

"Where are you from, comrade?" he asked Lihua.

"Nanjing," she said in a muffled voice that seemed designed to mesmerize, yet in its very undesigning nature quadrupled the mesmerizing effect. Still, the utterance of that word cloaked the room in an oppressive wave of sadness.

Lihua removed her scarf and hat, letting an avalanche of coal-black hair unfurl down her back. How Meiying longed to run her fingers through that hair! But the arrival of food interrupted her reverie.

"Lihua!" shouted the leader from across the room. "Do you accompany us from here?"

"Yes. I have business in Taiyuan."

"Do you know Taiyuan well?" asked Beethoven.

"Yes."

"No problems getting through Japanese lines and into the city?"

"Not yet."

"How do you do it?"

"Not difficult."

"Will you show us?"

She glanced at Meiying. "That is my business."

At first Meiying interpreted this remark as a rejection of Beethoven's request, but she soon realized with a wave of excitement what Lihua meant.

"I'm so glad," she said. "Thank you."

Lihua nodded and returned to her food.

~

"We'll sleep here tonight and leave at first light," said the leader. He turned to the farmer. "Comrade Zhu, is there a private room for the women? I suspect they would appreciate some privacy since at least one of them has had so little on this journey."

Meiying felt touched and not a little surprised at his consideration. She had always viewed him as rough and unfeeling of others.

"Of course. There is one bedroom. They can have that and I'll sleep out here with the rest of you. Does that suit, comrades?"

Mumbled agreement.

Lihua spoke up. "Comrade, do you have hay in your barn?"

"Of course."

"I'll sleep there. Let this lady have the room to herself. She deserves it."

Meiying started to protest, but Beethoven spoke first. "Thank you, comrade, but I'm sure we can sleep in the barn and let you have the room. After all, we are the outsiders."

"Yes, that would be much better, Lihua," added Meiying. "You so much more deserve the room."

"No," said Lihua with quiet conviction, leaving any other option out of the question. "I prefer the barn."

"Then I will stay there with you," said Meiying defiantly. "The men can have the room."

Lihua laughed heartily for the first time. Even her laugh possessed the power to draw people into her will.

"I like that! We will sleep in the barn."

Amid protestations, both women remained firm, their spontaneous alliance unbreakable.

"Don't be ridiculous!" snorted Beethoven. Realizing his mistake, he moderated his tone and said, "Stay here and I'll go."

"No, it is decided," said Lihua as she picked up her rifle.

"Bah! Let them go, stubborn women!" cried the leader, out of patience, exasperated, and too tired to continue useless protests against Lihua's implacable determination.

The farmer hastily lit a lantern and looked at Meiying and Lihua. "Come with me, I'll fix you up to be cozy as kittens." He grabbed a couple of threadbare cotton blankets. "Well, come on, comrades!"

"I'll go with you," said Beethoven.

"Oh, no," replied Meiying. "Too much fuss has already been made."

"She's right," said the leader. "That girl has a brain in her head. Let 'em go. We need to get some sleep before tomorrow. Who's on guard duty first?"

The men entered into a brief quarrel, then played a quick game of rock-paper-scissors.

"Guess I am," sighed the loser.

Lihua slung her rifle over her back and followed the farmer and the loser outside.

Meiying walked behind, carrying her things and feeling awkward. Beethoven's sad "good night" trailing after.

After arranging their sleeping areas in the barn, which was surprisingly sturdy and relatively clean, the farmer said, "Good night, comrades. I'll leave the lantern. Unfortunately, you'll have to share with one other roommate, but she'll not disturb you too much." With this he left, soon returning with an elderly water buffalo in tow.

As he put her in a stall and threw a handful of hay to placate the buffalo for a while, he said, "She's docile and sweet. Good for her to have female company. I'm not much in the art of womanly conversation."

Chuckling over some amusement known only to himself, the farmer left and closed the barn door behind, followed by a low baying of the buffalo. Soon, the beast gave it up and satisfied herself with munching hay.

Now that she was alone with Lihua, Meiying couldn't find words to speak.

Much to her disappointment, this mysterious woman seemed utterly disinterested in conversation. After remaining motionless for some time (resembling, to Meiying, the figure of an eternal goddess), Lihua rose and held the lantern to her magnificent face, framed in all its beauty by her wildly gorgeous hair.

"We sleep now," she said with a finality that would brook no dispute.

"Yes," said Meiying, more timidly than she intended. Although they were about the same age, this woman had the disconcerting ability to make her feel like a child.

The barn went dark, and simultaneous with the arrival of blackness, Meiying's thoughts lit up with fantasies she would not disclose to even the most cruel of torturers. The images that danced in her mind shone through the bleak shadows, and even the buffalo remained quiet as if out of consideration for her intimate dreams.

~ *Loss and Gain* ~

Dawn arrived too soon for Meiying. When Lihua (who was already dressed and had her rifle slung over her shoulder) gently awakened her, Meiying knew she looked awful; her face puffy, hair a mess, teeth unbrushed. Like a schoolgirl awakened by her parent, she shrank back under the blanket until Lihua went outside, then jumped up and made herself as attractive as possible. With the memory of her short time with Meili, she felt frustrated that a precious night alone with Lihua had borne no fruit. Life held so few opportunities, she knew now, that one must seize upon them when they arose and hang on until they were taken away by some ugly twist of fate or irresistible set of circumstances. Meiying cursed her timidity and vowed to overcome all such childish hesitations in future with Lihua.

But when she emerged from the barn determined to engage in conversation, Lihua was nowhere to be found.

Beethoven, who had been impatiently waiting, rushed up and said more cheerfully than he felt, "Good morning! Did you sleep well?"

Meiying thought he said these last words with an insinuating tone. "Yes, thanks."

"Come inside. Breakfast awaits."

Behind them, the buffalo gave out a loud bellow.

"Guess he wants breakfast also," said Beethoven, continuing his cheerful banter.

"She," corrected Meiying.

"Ah, of course."

Meiying walked briskly to the farmhouse, hoping she would find Lihua inside having breakfast. On the way, she rehearsed what she would say, and as she opened the door a chorus of "good morning, comrade" issued from the gathered men, but not a female voice to be heard.

"Good morning," she replied, scanning the room for Lihua's face. But much to her disappointment, no such face could be seen.

"Where is Lihua?" she asked. "I just saw her in the barn."

The leader snorted. "Gone again."

"A phantom," added another.

"No other explanation," said his neighbor. "A pure phantom."

"Maybe," said the farmer, still at his pot and still stirring with his long wooden spoon. "But this phantom gets hungry. She ate early."

"When?" asked Meiying.

"Hours ago. We farmers get up early, but even so, she already waited in the kitchen for me. So I fixed her up."

"Disappointed?" asked Beethoven.

"Of course. I wanted to thank her."

"Sit and eat," said the leader sharply. "We leave soon."

Meiying ate in silence, with an occasional word or phrase tossed to Beethoven for his sustenance. Her mind was awash with images of Lihua out there roaming the hills, keeping her in sight; her lone wolf protector. Meiying's romantic imagination fashioned this mystery woman into the sort of real-life golem that only Rachmaninoff's or Chopin's music could breathe life into, and it resonated deeply in the soul of this beautiful young pianist.

Once again the little band moved toward Taiyuan, still keeping to small back roads and animal trails. They passed through out-of-the-way villages, many of which had been abandoned by starving peasants. Those that were left presented a pitiful sight; old men and women, weak with hunger, almost unable to rise. Children were nowhere to be seen. No one in the little band of guerillas had the desire to dally for long around these wasted hovels, and they kept moving as through a medieval landscape of plague and pestilence.

Meiying, of course, kept her eyes alert to the possibility of spotting Lihua. She pictured this wild woman creeping through the underbrush on the nearby hills, staying parallel to the group, occasionally bobbing up on a ridge to make sure they remained in sight. But peer as she might at every ridge and clearing, no human figure could be seen. By early afternoon they took a short break. Meiying approached the leader, who leaned against the trunk of a fallen tree.

"Comrade, may I ask you some questions?"

He gazed at her with an unreadable expression. "Don't be so polite, comrade."

"It's about Lihua."

"Of course."

"Can you tell me anything about her?"

He coughed and looked at the ground. "Nanjing."

"Yes?"

"Nanjing. That's all you need to know."

"I know terrible things happened there."

He laughed cruelly. "You know?"

She straightened. "Yes."

He looked back up at her. "You?"

"Yes."

"Nanjing?"

"Outside, but I know."

"I figured you had a head on your shoulders, at least for a woman, but I didn't know the rest of you experienced . . . bad things."

"Yes. Now can you tell me about Lihua?"

"No."

"Do you know?"

"Partly."

"Bad?"

"Very."

Meiying knew that if this man said it was bad, it must have been horrific. She sighed. "How we all have suffered!"

He shrugged. "War."

She snapped, "Men."

He shrugged again. "In their nature."

"Why did you become a communist fighter?" she asked in a more conciliatory tone.

"Nanjing."

~

That night they slept in the open. A village was nearby, but local rumor had it that the Japanese often came without warning. Other rumors circulated that it suffered from an outbreak of typhus. Either way, the leader would not take the risk.

Beethoven wanted to talk, but Meiying told him she preferred to sleep. After he left, clearly piqued, she lay staring up at the stars, wondering and fantasizing. Sleep overcame her musings, and a dream arose from the fog.

Colonel Naguma and Father Durant grinned down at her. She lay on her back, tied to a cross. Suddenly, each held a huge spike in one hand, and a hammer in the other. They nodded, and still grinning, moved to each of her hands and pressed the sharp end of the spike into her palms. Despite her screams, the hammers were raised to drive home the spikes. She screamed over and over to no avail.

"Shhh," came a female voice. "Quiet. It's a dream. Shhh."

Meiying felt a hand gently rub her arm.

"Shhh. Meiying. Wake up. You're having another dream. It's just the memories again. Wake up!"

Once Meiying emerged from her dream, she immediately recognized the voice.

"Lihua, what are you doing here?"

Those mesmerizing eyes glittered in the moonlight and seemed to dance with unconcealed mirth. "Same as you. Taking up space. Breathing. Sleeping. Dreaming. Waking. Fighting. Surviving another day."

"I'm so glad to see you," said Meiying in genuine relief.

Lihua did not reply, but sat cross-legged next to her.

"Nightmares are terrible," said Meiying, touching Lihua's arm.

Lihua did not reply, but Meiying could hear her breathing come a bit faster.

Meiying did not remove her hand, and while both remained motionless she felt like a snake charmer where the slightest movement could precipitate a venomous strike.

Suddenly, shockingly, this unpredictable woman leapt to her feet. A second before she did so, Meiying felt a tremble propagate through Lihua's body. In the blink of an eye, the phantom disappeared into the night. Meiying did not bother to get up, for it seemed a dream, a fleeting phantasmagoria that may have just been imagined.

Oddly, at this moment, Meiying longed for Meili; a lover whose steady, predictable affection had been unconditional and acted as a balm rather than a bruise. She longed to call forth Meili's spirit and ask about Lihua's mercurial nature. She needed words of comfort and advice, for her thoughts were all jumbled. That Lihua was a lesbian, Meiying had no doubts, even if Lihua herself didn't know it. But how to harness this force of nature? How to touch her? How to get her to reveal the wounds that so drove her to such isolating extremes? Meiying so much wanted to share her own wounds with Lihua. This would be no one-way street. If only Lihua could know that others suffered also! They needed each other! Why couldn't she understand the language of need?

With such arguments raging in her mind, Meiying could not return to sleep. She rose to relieve herself, and after so doing saw Beethoven in the moonlight sitting disconsolately on a flat rock. A pang of guilt seized her kindly heart and she sat next to him.

"What are you thinking?" she asked.

"About you."

"Beethoven, we've been over this many times. I am not worthy—"

He interrupted with a bitter laugh. "Meiying, of all things, don't patronize me! That I cannot take!"

"All right."

"I cannot compete with your interests."

"It is not a competition. It is nature."

"Being a lesbian is not natural! You could give it up if you really wanted."

Meiying had heard this same argument so often that it no longer had the power to arouse even indignation. "Let's get to Taiyuan alive. That will be hard enough."

"I almost wish we would never make it. Just travel about, you and I, come what may, but together!"

"Beethoven, you know we will always be friends. You'll marry and I'll be the colorful auntie."

"Oh!" cried Beethoven in agony.

"What? It is a nice thought."

"It is horrendous! A torture!"

"I'll leave you and remove the pain," said Meiying peevishly.

"No, stop!" whispered Beethoven, grabbing her hand. "Stay awhile. I apologize. Just stay awhile."

"Beethoven, you made a promise that we would be friends, not lovers. You must hold to that promise or I will be forced to leave."

Like a child, he seemed to pout and said nothing, but still held her hand. Meiying kept her hand in his, only imagining it belonged to someone else.

~ *The Path to Nowhere* ~

After the group had trudged a few kilometers along Feng's trail, Madame Liu stopped to take stock of where they were. Initially, escape from the Japanese occupied their energies, but now the trail seemed to exhibit the spirit of a mischievous trickster, wickedly winding around a series of steep, claustrophobic hills whose slopes were rendered impenetrable by thick vegetation, and, as far as they could tell, completely uninhabited. Their bikes were useless due to the rough nature of the trail, and now served as metallic pack mules. Madame Liu cursed the loss of the compass she and her husband had used since the beginning of the journey, and the inaccurate maps they consulted were hopeless.

"This is almost as bad as the swamp," observed Lu Zhishen unhelpfully.

"At least we're dry," said John, shuddering at the memory of the swamp.

"Well," said Master Zhou still puffing heavily. "Let's ask our young explorer. Mr. Feng, where are we?"

"We are where we are supposed to be," Feng laughed. "Based on the movements of the sun, we're headed almost in the right direction."

"Almost?" asked Suling.

"Mr. Feng should have been named Mr. Almost," quipped Lu. "*Chabuduo xiensheng*!"

"At least we're alive, and I don't see any Japs around," replied Feng complacently.

"Grousing about it isn't going to help," said Madame Liu with her usual pragmatism. "The next safe-haven is on the other side of the battle. Question is, which side are we on now?"

"Well, the good news is that this trail is used by more than animals. It must lead somewhere," said Feng.

"I'm hungry," whined Little Acorn.

"Sorry, Little Acorn, we need to ration our food until we know where we are," said Feng sympathetically.

Little Acorn saluted, although weariness and hunger took away the snap. "Okay."

"No choice but to continue," said Madame Liu. "Odd there are no side trails."

"Maybe this leads to a palace, like Mr. President's. It was good food there!" said Little Acorn hopefully.

"Maybe," replied Feng, patting him on the shoulder.

"Or maybe it leads directly to *her*," smiled Master Zhou, now recovered from his fatigue.

"It would be nice," said Madame Liu. "But I'm afraid the destination is still far away. We need to find the next safe-haven soon."

"And maybe getting farther," observed Lu sarcastically.

"Or maybe closer," said Suling to Little Acorn.

"Still not willing to disclose the destination?" asked Feng rhetorically. "Even after all we've been through together?"

"Even so," said Madame Liu.

"But surely, Madame Liu, we are getting close?" asked Suling.

"We're not getting closer by talking," replied Madame Liu crisply. "Let's carry on. As Mr. Feng aptly observed, this trail must lead somewhere."

"To food!" cried Little Acorn.

Feng Shiren struck a pose. "To food!" he sang.

Everyone laughed, and with this christening, the little group of pilgrims set off again. Thick, tangled vegetation impinged from both sides of the trail, yet it remained clear and easy to follow. On it went, deeper into the strange, clustered hills.

"Odd we haven't run into anyone," commented John.

"Yes," agreed Feng. "Yet it's been traveled on quite a lot to be in this condition."

"Let's hope it doesn't lead us to a Japanese headquarters," said Lu.

"No," mused Feng. "There is no evidence of boots. Jap soldiers have not come this way."

"Well, come what may, let's go and see what we find," said Master Zhou.

But the farther they walked, the deeper they penetrated a landscape that offered no comfort and no human contact. After hours of this unremitting bleakness, the hills grew even steeper, turning to sheer cliffs that seemed to lean over the trail, and even the comfort of trees and birds gave way to ugly scrub and an eerie silence. Although not particularly hot, the humidity grew more intense and sapped their energy.

"No wonder people don't inhabit this place," groused Lu.

"Why don't we make camp here," suggested Madame Liu. "It's as good a spot as any, and I, for one, don't want to climb that hill." She pointed to a steep hill where the trail became a series of switchbacks.

"No water," observed Suling.

"We passed a small stream awhile back," said John.

"Too far back," replied Madame Liu.

"There's still quite a bit of daylight left. I'll scout ahead," offered Feng Shiren.

Soon the little soldier disappeared over a rise and the others went about clearing sleeping areas. The hills turned dark very quickly and they were plunged into blackness faster than any of them expected. Talk was sporadic and subdued. Feng had not returned, and nervous speculation receded into an uneasy stillness.

John knew the voices would return. Much as he dreaded their presence, he despaired of blocking them entirely. And just as he feared, so they came.

So, you sleep while she suffers? This is Earth's great hope?

Leave him be, God. I have plans to use him, and Your harangues do little more than push him into a tighter ball of twine. Not even cats will be able to tease out the threads if You continue.

Nonsense! Your plan is doomed before it starts, Sweet Goddess. There will be no son.

And so they argued.

Like continents drifting apart, the two deities gradually emerged from their original Pangaea-like unity into distinct personalities. The greater the distance between them, the sharper their antagonism for each other grew.

My dissembling continues, he thought. *Insanity as plate tectonics, evolving new species of mental disorders on the isolated fragments of my mind. What happens in future when they reverse course and slam into each other? Schizophrenic volcanism? And what is all this about the extinction of the human race? Crazy!*

A son will emerge.

~

When he awoke the next morning, a hubbub had already been underway for some time. John lay beneath his blanket trying to make sense of the words so energetically flung about by his comrades.

"Feng, every time you come back from one of your expeditions, you bring a prize, like a cat delivering a dead mouse to its master!" John recognized Lu Zhishen's voice.

"Yes, it's true. It's in my nature," replied Feng, speaking as might a chastised boy to his father.

"What are we to do with him?" asked Madame Liu.

John pictured some prisoner that Feng had brought back, or perhaps a homeless child. His interest fully piqued, he left his comfy bedroll and joined the group that had gathered in a circle. At first he couldn't see the object of interest in the center. Between Madame Liu and Little Acorn, he saw an exceedingly skinny old man wearing nothing more than a loin-cloth and carrying a large stick, which he evidently used as a cane or a club. This confused and bizarre image at first suggested to John that this man must be a sort of Buddhist or Daoist ascetic, a wise being whose main role in life must be the dissemination of knowledge and wisdom. But this romantic notion was quickly replaced by the vision of an out-of-control whirling-dervish. The figure in the loincloth swung his cane in wide swaths that fortunately posed no threat to the watching comrades, who were all as perplexed as John.

"Get out, evil demons!" shouted the man, all the while swinging his cane harmlessly. "Off my road!"

"Stop!" yelled Lu Zhishen ducking the cane. "We won't hurt you, old man! We're friends!"

"Demons!" the man shouted back. "Off this sacred road!"

In the midst of this melee, Suling tried her hand. "Sir, we are not demons. We are lost and seek help. Surely demons wouldn't seek help."

"Bitch! Demons change shapes! You are a false woman! A demon full of tricks!"

He swung again, but his arms clearly weakened with every go-around. Soon, he tired so much he fell back on an embankment and sat panting and growling like a cornered animal.

"Mr. Feng, why did you bring this wretch back here?" again demanded Madame Liu.

"I didn't!" he protested. "He followed me"

"Let's just leave him here and move on," said Lu.

"Go back where you came from, demons!" shouted the old man, again waving his cane. However, he remained sitting, still winded from his quixotic battle.

Ignoring the raving man, Madame Liu asked Feng, "What did you see ahead?"

He shrugged in his characteristic style. "More road, no water—and him."

"Great!"

"Let's go," repeated Lu Zhishen.

Madame Liu sighed. "Yes. Leave him here."

"You can't go up the road," said the old man in a startlingly natural voice.

"Why not?" asked Master Zhou.

"There's a temple."

"So?"

"It's purity will destroy demons who get too close. You'll all unravel and disappear."

"That should suit you," pointed out Madame Liu.

"Hmmm," he growled.

"Let's go!" called Madame Liu. "If there is a temple, then there is food and water."

With a burst of energy, the old man sprang up and planted himself in the middle of the trail. "Can't let you pass!" he said, raising his cane.

"Crazy man," said Lu.

After lining up with their bikes to continue, all the while hearing the old man's cries of "Demons!" and "I'll follow you and see you destroyed!", they gently disarmed him, pushed past, and continued up the road tossing his cane behind. Gradually, he receded in the distance, still following and shouting, until he could no longer be seen or heard.

"Whew!" uttered John. "That's better!"

"Don't be so sure," cautioned Feng. "Obviously, others have been taking care of him."

"Where are they?" asked Suling.

Feng shrugged, then performed a Chinese opera dance. "He escaped from somewhere or someone."

"So they will be looking for him," replied John, concealing his nervousness as best as possible.

"Of course."

Lu Zhishen looked up at the distant rim of the cliff and let out a sharp, "Oh!"

"Yes, that's right," said Feng, amused by the sight of Lu's craning neck. "We're being watched."

John remembered the bad Western films he had watched as a boy and pictured blood-thirsty redskins looking down from the rim, passing smoke signals and hungry for scalps.

"Look!" shouted Suling, pointing up to the exact spot where Lu had locked his gaze.

All eyes followed her finger and all eyes saw what she saw. Dark figures silhouetted against the sky, tiny but clearly perceptible, looked down at them. John almost laughed at this rare convergence of celluloid fantasy solidifying into stark reality.

"Keep going," said Master Zhou grimly. "They're probably local peasants. Curious, but harmless."

"We'll be meeting them soon," said Feng. "Look ahead, way up there, and you can see the trail zig-zagging up that far cliff to the plateau. I have no doubt we'll have a meeting there with our curious friends."

While they had been talking, the crazy old man came up behind waving his cane and still haranguing them. "Demons! Get off my road! Demons!"

"Well," laughed Feng. "If hell is behind us, then heaven must be up that trail at the top."

In spite of Feng's levity, John's imagination worked overtime with pictures of Japanese soldiers or rapacious bandits racing through his mind. These phantoms stopped harassing him as fatigue took over on the long hike up the switch-backs toward the rim, where the dark figures waited.

Chapter Seventeen

Delays, Delays, Delays

Taiyuan

Meiying listened carefully to the leader's instructions. The group huddled in a small clearing, less than a kilometer from a Japanese checkpoint. If they made it past the checkpoint, the way into Taiyuan should be clear sailing. Lihua had not been seen since the night she visited Meiying, and now it became obvious she would not accompany them into Taiyuan as she had promised. Saddened by this realization, Meiying found it hard to concentrate on the leader's words.

"I will not be joining you, nor will any of the rest of us," he explained to Meiying and Beethoven. "We are too well known. But you two should be able to bluff your way in. You have the proper papers. Just tell them you are refugees seeking work and that both of you are educated. The Japanese are looking for educated workers they can train in their industrial works."

"What if they ask questions about our pasts?" asked Beethoven.

"Lie if you have to, but it is better to tell the truth as much as possible, even if only half-truths."

"Follow my lead," came a voice from the edge of the trees.

"Ah, here you are Lihua!" cried the leader. "I was afraid you wouldn't make it. We need you in Taiyuan."

"Yes, I keep my promises," she looked at Meiying and smiled.

"Oh, I am so glad to see you!" gushed Meiying, unable to stifle her enthusiasm and relief.

"Don't worry, I have gone back and forth through these checkpoints many times. Never had a problem. Just do nothing to arouse their suspicion."

"Like what?" asked Beethoven.

"Like being either too evasive or too direct. They expect you to be nervous, but not too nervous. They expect you to be direct, but not too direct."

"Should we look them in the eyes?" asked Beethoven.

"Yes and no. Glance at them but do not stare at them. Also, do not constantly avoid their eyes. Act as natural as possible." She shrugged. "It's just business—a thing you have to do."

"Do we tell them we are together?" asked Meiying.

"Yes. Here is the story: I work at a Japanese materials plant as an assistant quality control inspector. You are with me to apply for work at the plant. I will vouch for you." She pulled out a rumpled paper. "See, this is my work permit and my employee certification from the company."

"How did we meet?" asked Beethoven. "I mean, our stories should be consistent."

"Of course. We met on the road. You are refugees and I am returning to Taiyuan after visiting my sick mother. Simple."

Meiying felt a knot in her stomach when the three of them left the safety of the leader and his little band of protectors. She remembered his last words to Lihua: "Get them through for Shirong's sake. I have to explain to his wife and kids. Get them through."

Lihua merely nodded and turned away, expressionless. Meiying experienced a brief moment of resentment, even anger, at Lihua's seeming insensitivity. She started to make a comment, then came to some conclusion, and her face hardened into a mask others who had known her might consider alien. Saying farewell to her communist friends, she, Beethoven, and Lihua walked away from safety and toward the real possibility that an indiscreet word or inexplicable averting of eyes would lead to their deaths. Come what may, they started out.

When they approached the roadblock full of Japanese guards, Lihua unexpectedly turned off the road and waded into a large group of refugees milling around with no apparent will to attempt the crossing.

"Why are we here?" asked Beethoven in confusion.

"Wait," replied Lihua sharply. "Have your papers ready."

After almost an hour, a large group appeared down the road and marched up to the guards without hesitation, holding out their work permits tightly so the wind would not blow them away.

"Now," said Lihua, who seamlessly joined the group with the permits. Beethoven and Meiying trailed behind tightly clutching their papers against the wind.

When they reached the guards, who had let the others pass without question, it was a simple task for Lihua to flash her own permit.

"They're with me," she said, nodding toward the two followers.

Beethoven and Meiying held up their papers without stopping.

To the immense relief of Meiying, the guards merely nodded, and they were on their way to Taiyuan.

Out of earshot of the guards, Lihua muttered, "Easy," and then added, "Fools!"

As they walked, Meiying allowed herself to think of the group she had been so long separated from. Soon, she told herself, they would be reunited and continue the sacred quest for *her*. After navigating the busy streets, they found themselves at an intersection where Lihua bade farewell to her companions.

"How do we find you?" asked Meiying, gloomy with the realization that Lihua would be disappearing again.

"You can't, but I'll be around. I'll keep you in sight if there is trouble."

"So mysterious," said Beethoven.

"Where will you be staying?" asked Lihua.

"That is the question," replied Beethoven. "Fortunately, I have an uncle who lives here."

Meiying looked at him in surprise.

"We'll stay with him until other arrangements can be made."

They both hugged Lihua, with Meiying holding her close and whispering something in her ear that Beethoven could not hear.

When they parted, he asked, "What did you say to her?"

"Nothing."

"Sure. Anyway, she is truly an amazing woman. Very mysterious."

"Yes."

"What is this about your uncle?"

"I lied."

"Why?"

Beethoven smiled sheepishly. "I figure we can find a cheap inn until you find your friends."

Meiying shook her head. "Your unnecessary lying bothers me. One day it will get us in serious trouble."

"Yes, maybe," said Beethoven averting her eyes. "But you are living a lie!"

"Oh, Beethoven! Stop. This is hard enough."

"Okay, okay."

"I'm not familiar with Taiyuan. How do we find this cheap inn?"

"Easy. Ask."

But their simple question to passersby elicited a dizzying array of answers. Most of the recommendations turned out to be rat-infested holes that Meiying refused to lodge. "I'd rather be back on the road," she would protest to Beethoven's rolling eyes and impatient, "It's just for the night!"

Eventually they found acceptable accommodations, taking separate rooms. Meiying settled into her bed and dreamed of finding Madame Liu, John, Lu Zhishen, Suling, Mr. Gao, and the others. In her mind, the reunion would be joyous and they would quickly leave to find their destination, and upon arriving, would find it a sort of heaven-on-earth. She knew this was silly, but she nonetheless basked in the dream's happy ending. For the first time in weeks, Meiying slept soundly through the night. The next morning found her anxious to begin the search. But where to start?

"Where would they be staying?" asked Beethoven over a breakfast of rice soup.

Meiying thought for a while and replied, "Probably in a hotel, but Madame Liu has many contacts, so they could be with someone I don't know." She shook her head sadly. "They could be anywhere."

"That's no help."

"I know, but we have to start somewhere."

"Well, we can check the hotels first."

Meiying pondered. "Let's split-up. You check the hotels—only the nicer ones—and I'll check the banks."

"Banks?"

"Yes, Madame Liu and her husband have financed almost the entire trip. She has accounts in many banks. I'm sure she has visited the Taiyuan branch."

"Which one?"

Meiying shrugged. "I don't know, but there couldn't be that many."

"Will they release that information—I mean the identity of a depositor?"

"I don't know, but I'll find a way."

"Okay, good."

"Wait here, I'll be right back." Meiying went up to her room and donned her best dress, now wrinkled but still presentable. She applied lipstick and fixed her hair in a bun, then rejoined Beethoven.

"Okay, let's get started. We'll meet back at the inn by six o'clock and see what happens."

"Yes, good." He whistled. "You look great!"

In her haste to get started, Meiying did not notice Beethoven's too easy compliance with her plan. In fact, he had no intention of running all around Taiyuan searching its many hotels and inns for Meiying's friends. Once her handsome figure disappeared among the crowd, he headed off to see his uncle.

~

Deep in the back alleys of the city, Beethoven stood before his uncle's house. A carved wooden gate embedded in the thick outer wall led to a verdant courtyard with blooming magnolias, a fish pond, and a well-maintained house of red brick and blue tile. Beethoven opened the gate, paused by the pond to watch the fish, then knocked on the imposing front door. It was quickly opened by an elderly man in traditional Chinese dress, stooped in a long robe and Manchu-era hat.

"You took long enough, nephew," he said gruffly. "Is she with you?"

"No."

"Good! Come in."

Beethoven followed him into the house, evidently quite comfortable navigating its surroundings. They passed through a short hallway to another room and the old man sat in a high-backed Chinese lacquer chair while Beethoven slumped heavily in a Western-style stuffed chair and draped his legs over the arm.

"How are you, uncle?"

"Mr. President wants a report," snapped the old man.

Beethoven smiled, a brief cynical turn of his lip flashed his contempt. "No tea first?"

The old man snorted in disgust, then shouted at the wall, "Bring tea!"

An unattractive young servant girl instantly appeared with the tea from some hidden side door as if she had miraculously emerged from the very wall he shouted at. Clearly anxious to both catch a glimpse of the young visitor and get out as quickly as possible, she poured the tea displaying a toothy grimace and fled back into her hiding place.

"Now," said the uncle after taking a sip. "Your report."

"The trip here was relatively uneventful. Encounters with ignorant peasants and a band of stupid communists were needed to complete the trip. Of course, the Japanese were inconvenient, but we managed to make it. That's it." Beethoven leaned back with his tea cup and waited.

"And now?" asked the uncle.

"We're staying at a broken-down inn. She is out visiting banks to try and find her friends. We are supposed to meet back up at six."

"And you? What are you supposed to be doing?"

Beethoven shrugged. "I'm out searching the hotels for them."

Uncle stared at Beethoven as if trying to determine whether the boy's unbridled cynicism obscured the truth. Although he had promised himself he would not ask, he could not help it. "What is she like?"

Beethoven responded with the same crooked smile. "You mean is she pretty?"

"Yes."

"You mean does she have beautiful breasts and wide hips?"

"Yes." Uncle licked his lips.

"Well, you old lecher, I don't know. I haven't seen her naked."

"You lie."

Beethoven shrugged again as if his uncle's opinion meant nothing.

Uncle persisted. "But is she pretty?"

"Yes."

"Slim?"

"Yes."

"And all this time you haven't fucked her?'

"No, she's a lesbian."

Uncle swatted the air dismissively. "No such thing! Mr. President informed me of this propensity, but neither of us buy it, nor does your mother."

Beethoven flushed but remained silent.

"I believe your esteemed mother participated in a demonstration of the art, but did not come away certain of the true nature of the girl. Your honored mother is too good at fucking not to know a bitch in heat—especially one hot for men and not for women."

Again Beethoven flushed, but contained his feelings and sipped his tea more rapidly.

"Speaking of bitches," said uncle. "Does the bitch you're with, this Bai Meiying girl, talk about Mr. President?"

"No."

"Have you fucked her?"

"I told you already, no."

"Good! Mr. President was quite adamant on that point. Things would go bad for you if otherwise, or"—the old man stared at him intently—"if you're lying."

"I'm not lying."

"What else?"

"Nothing. But when Mr. President is through with her, I want her."

"What you want is irrelevant."

Beethoven scowled, leaned forward and poured some more tea. "Where is her group now?"

"Ah!" cried the old man, thrusting a finger in the air. "Gone!"

"Where?"

Uncle shrugged.

"Come on, at least tell me that."

Uncle laughed unpleasantly. "On their way to their destination, He chuckled. "Although they are encountering some problems. We're keeping track of them. Unfortunately, an operative of ours here in Taiyuan made a mistake and we had to kill one of them."

"What?"

"We had to kill one."

"Why?" asked Beethoven, his eyes widening.

"That's more then you need to know. I've already told you enough."

"Which one?"

"Peter Hedley. But look here, Liwei, do not say anything to the bitch."

"Of course."

Uncle held out his hands, palms up, and snorted like a pig. "Go fuck little Daiyu in your old room. I know you're horny, and Bai Meiying remains off-limits. Understand?"

Beethoven smiled, his face a reflection of the perversion his uncle's expression almost always assumed. "All right," he said, his eyes ablaze with anticipation. "But uncle, I need money."

"Yes. Anything else?"

"Yes, Meiying."

"I know, I know, but you can't have her. Now, what else do you need?"

"Nothing else, I think."

"There should be."

Beethoven looked confused. "I don't understand."

"You don't have to."

"Uncle, how long do I stay with her in Taiyuan on this fruitless search?"

"Until I tell you to leave."

"But, what should I do with her in the meantime?"

"Follow her lead. Be compliant with her wishes. When she is ready to move on, you'll know. Let her lead you. Just make sure you don't damage the merchandise—in any way!"

"Lead me to what?"

"Stupid boy! You ask too many questions. Daiyu!"

The servant girl shuffled in, her eyes downcast.

Uncle said, "Go with Wang Liwei to the room and fuck him good and long. Understand?"

She nodded and padded off to the room, Beethoven following.

~ *Meiying Learns Something* ~

Tired and foot-weary, Meiying had visited numerous banks without results. She was about to order some *jiaozi* from a street vendor and call it a day when she spied a sign across the busy street which read: Industrial and Commercial Bank of China. Ltd.

Foregoing the *jiaozi*, she walked across the street and entered the lobby of the bank where she encountered a swarm of people coming and going, most of whom, with nervous glances all around, clutched receipts or envelopes they kept perusing surreptitiously. Meiying approached a teller after standing in a long line listening to the frenetic clicking of abacuses.

"Yes?" asked the proper young man dressed quite sharply in a Western-style suit.

"Perhaps you can help me. I'm looking for someone who I think is a customer here. A Madame Liu."

"Oh, we have many Lius here." The teller looked over her shoulder at the line. "But you'll have to talk with my supervisor." He glanced at a middle-aged man at an imposing desk, dressed similarly. "Mr. Wei."

The middle-aged man bowed as she neared his desk and offered her a seat. "How can I help you, young Miss?" he asked in a tone of paternal tolerance.

She repeated her question, adding a fuller description of Madame Liu. His face took on a grave expression.

"Are you from the authorities?" he asked.

"No."

"Is this lady in some sort of trouble?"

"No."

"Is she a relative?"

"Not exactly. You see, I'm an old friend, a refugee, trying to find her."

"A refugee," he said in disappointment. "I see."

Meiying realized she had made a mistake. "I have money," she added quickly.

"Are you trying to bribe me?" he asked, now looking quite severely at her.

Meiying had a brainstorm. She looked at him slyly. "So far your answers have been appropriate. Now, about this Madame Liu." She pronounced this last re-mark in her best official voice. "Is she or is she not a customer here?"

He flushed. "Let me get my boss. Perhaps he can help you." Mr. Wei stood and marched to a door with frosted glass on which was written "President." He knocked and entered, closing the door behind. While she waited, Meiying wished her dress were not so wrinkled. Perhaps she should have had it ironed. Still immersed in these thoughts, an older, distinguished-looking man emerged with Mr. Wei. He bowed.

"Perhaps I can be of assistance," he said, motioning gallantly toward his office. Once inside, he offered tea, which Meiying politely refused.

"Now, how can I help you, Miss . . . ?"

She kept her official voice. "Bai Meiying. I'm looking for someone, a Madame Liu."

"May I ask why? We have confidentiality rules. If you are from some authority, perhaps showing me credentials would be in order."

Meiying's heart beat faster. If she had gotten this far, perhaps he knew Madame Liu. She leaned forward, abandoning all pretenses and trusting, as usual with her, in complete honesty.

"Mr . . . ? she asked.

"Zhu."

"Mr. Zhu, I am an old friend of Madame Liu's. I gave your assistant her description and full name. I am so anxious to find her. We were separated on the road . . . after Nanjing . . . and if you have information I would be so grateful."

Mr. Zhu, a kind man who had raised three daughters, was not immune from Meiying's charm, sincerity, and beauty. "Yes," he said. "The woman you seek has fairly recently been to our bank."

"How recent?" asked Meiying excitedly.

"A few weeks," he said. Then added, "Over a month."

"Do you know where she is staying?"

"Yes, the Heping Hotel. It is quite near. But, alas, you will not find her there."

"Oh!" Meiying sighed. "Why not?"

"She and her friends left Taiyuan."

Meiying looked stricken. "Going where?" she croaked.

Mr. Zhu shook his head. "That I do not know, Miss Bai. I wish I did." He handed her a napkin for her tears.

Meiying left the bank in a daze.

~

After returning to the inn, she waited impatiently for Beethoven to arrive. She sat in the lobby until he appeared almost an hour late. This gave her time to think, which, it turns out, served her well. They retired to a nearby noodle shop.

"Well?" asked Beethoven. "Any luck?"

"Maybe," replied Meiying. "Did you?"

"No. I checked every hotel and found nothing."

"Were they unwilling to give you information?"

"Oh, no! They were quite happy once they saw a few coins."

"Are you sure you checked them all?"

"Quite sure. At least the ones you said they would stay—you know, the nice ones."

"The banks are in the better parts of town, and I passed quite a few nice hotels, like the Red Pavilion and the Heping Hotel."

"Yep, I checked them all. Nothing."

"Ah, I see. How disappointing."

"Well, you haven't told me about your luck. You just said 'maybe' you found something."

"No, I thought I had a lead, but it turned out to be the wrong Liu."

"Oh, too bad. Let's order, I'm starved."

"Go ahead, I had *jiaozi*."

While Beethoven ate, Meiying's brain raced with a thousand different scenarios. Her first inclination was to confront him, but his lying would make any response suspect. Was he just lazy? Involved in a conspiracy? A spy? A plot? In any event, Meiying decided to keep the information she obtained from Mr. Zhu to herself until a plan could be formulated. But what plan?

~ *John Confronts Illness* ~

As they approached the rim of the canyon, John and the rest of the group were exhausted from the climb. The shadow figures still waited, but were now individually distinguishable. They stood silently, with various agricultural implements languishing on their shoulders or at their sides. Lu Zhishen was the first to reach the top, followed by Feng Shiren. Upon joining his comrades, John found himself cringing back from the gawking stares of the onlookers with a revulsion bordering on horror. All of them appeared to be curiously malformed in some way, with mental retardation being the predominant impression. Almost every face staring back at the group seemed to be suffering from Down's syndrome or related condition. Yet, paradoxically to John, they were all smiling as sweetly as innocent children.

"Hello," said Lu Zhishen finally.

This salutation was greeted with more smiles and grunts.

Feng Shiren stepped up next to Lu and gazed at the faces. "Umm," he said enigmatically, craning his neck to look over the heads of the odd welcoming committee.

Soon Master Zhou, Suling, and Little Acorn arrived and the two groups continued to stare at each other in wonder, each for entirely different reasons.

"Is there a village near?" asked Madame Liu, after she had caught her breath from the strenuous climb.

In return, she received only happy smiles, with a few squeals of joy when they saw the bikes and ran their hands over the metal in apparent veneration.

"What now?" asked John.

"Don't know," replied Madame Liu.

While in this uncertain state, a commotion was heard from the rear of the crowd and two figures emerged quite suddenly.

"Sorry! Sorry! We saw you coming and intended to greet you, but one of our people got stuck in a well!" exclaimed the taller of the two.

The other nodded enthusiastically.

This pronouncement had a calming effect on the group, as the delighted mentally challenged patients gaped and shrieked in joy at the appearance of the two men.

After recovering from her surprise, Madame Liu said, "We are travelers who have been forced to find a way around . . . the war. Is there a village nearby?"

Although she directed this question to the tall man, the short man stepped forward. "Village? Well, yes and no. As I am sure you have noticed, our friends here—" he swept his arms to include the assembled crowd—"are not quite villagers in the normal sense."

"Oh."

"We—they—are inmates, or rather our flock, at an institution for the mentally disturbed. Unfortunately, with the war and Japanese air raids, the villagers have fled, leaving us to our own devices."

"I see, and you are the caretakers?"

He bowed, as did the tall man now standing beside him. "I am Master Li and this is Reverend Fu," explained the short man. "We are the caretakers."

The tall man interposed with a smile. "Li-Fu and Fu-Li. We are coins with two faces. One face is Buddhist and the other is Methodist. Flip the coin and you get Buddhist or Methodist, flip it again and you get Methodist or Buddhist. Get it?"

Feng Shiren roared with laughter. "I see! I see! Very good!"

The flock laughed with Feng who immediately performed a short dance, and in that instant a bond was created between them and the funny little soldier. A bond Feng Shiren seemed to forge with whoever passed his way or served his purpose. A bond forged, wondered John, by sincere feelings or sinister motives?

"Do you know where we might stay the night?" asked Madame Liu. "We are all quite tired."

"Of course, of course!" enthused the tall one, Fu or Li, or Li or Fu.

"Thank you . . . ?"

"I am Reverend Fu," replied the tall one. He pointed to the short one. "This is Master Li."

"Ah, thank you Reverend Fu." Madame Liu bowed graciously.

Master Li clapped his hands. "Well! We have been waiting quite a while for you to make it up here. All of us are excited. Do you want to stay in abandoned houses or the institution with us and the flock?"

Madame Liu looked around, not sure how to answer. John and the others were equally baffled. "At your pleasure," said Madame Liu finally.

"Good!" cried Master Li. He turned to his flock. "They're staying with us!"

A loud cheer went up from the assembled patients, accompanied by great laughter, grunting, and various other noises, all of which seemed to indicate pleasure and joyful rapture. In the midst of this spontaneous celebration, the old man who had berated them at the base of the hill finally arrived at the top, out of breath but still able to shout his warnings to the group.

"Demons! Demons have arrived! Get off our road! Demons!"

The two caretakers merely smiled at this demonstration. "Old Grandfather Ma is in good spirits today, brother," said Reverend Fu.

"Yes," replied Master Li. "He is in good form."

The rest of the flock laughed and smiled at the old man who was quickly mollified with a drink of water from Master Li.

"Don't mind Grandfather Ma," said Reverend Fu. "He is always going on about demons. We seldom get visitors, and if we do, they are all demons."

"I see," said Madame Liu somewhat dubiously, since his imprecations were directed at her.

"Follow us," said the Reverend. As they walked *en masse* to the institution, Fu-Li, and Li-Fu took turns explaining their unusual situation. After the villagers fled, Reverend Fu and Master Li left the institute to inspect the town. As they described it, an eerie feeling came over them when they discovered not a soul remained. Even their assistants and nurses at the institute deserted. Both men instantly agreed that they would put into effect a plan they had only dreamed was possible before the war; they wanted to release the non-violent and higher functioning inmates from confinement and let them do productive work. While the violent inmates remained in confinement, the "flock" now roamed the village and the fields, eventually growing crops under the supervision of Li and Fu. Every evening they would be guided back to the institute and tucked into their cozy little cells. However, food now was an issue, since even the government's monthly delivery of supplies had stopped due to the arrival of the Japanese.

"How do you survive?" asked Master Zhou.

"We grow our own food. Fortunately, our cook stayed on, and she is a magician at stretching out what little we have," explained Reverend Fu.

"And we hire out the more aware of our flock to the closest populated village a few kilometers from here in exchange for food," added Li.

"Yes," sighed Fu. "We make do. God provides."

"As does Buddha!" exclaimed Li. "You see, we catch as catch can, and have multiple gods and goddesses on our side."

Reverend Fu frowned a little. "Well, Master Li and I will agree to disagree on that point, but"—he broke into a broad smile—"there is very little else we disagree on!"

Feng Shiren listened with growing admiration. "You have achieved amazing things here! I congratulate you!"

Reverend Fu sighed. "Not really. Every day we fail in some way or other."

"Every day," parroted Master Li.

"How have you failed?" asked Master Zhou, who seemed quite interested in their story.

"Look at them," said Fu. "No, I mean really, truly look at them closely. They do not have enough to eat—yet they never complain."

As if to give the lie to Fu's comment, a shriek of "Demons!" cracked through the air.

"Grandfather Ma," said Reverend Fu gently. "These are friends, not demons, you know that."

~

After they navigated around a steep hill, the institution became visible. It rose majestically from a broad, flat plain, causing the visitors to gasp in amazement. Their eyes were dazzled by a massive, two story concrete building complex with sprawling tile roofs and wrap-around verandas, accentuated with dozens of concrete arches and Romanesque columns. Were it not for the obvious age of the buildings and the holes and indentations where bullets and shrapnel had gouged innumerable scars, it resembled a medieval fortress; an enormous fortification constructed to protect the ostensibly insane against the terrible sanity of the outside world.

"I had no idea," gasped Madame Liu when it came into view.

"John, it's amazing!" cried Suling.

"Yes, it really is," replied John, rendered somewhat speechless himself.

"Are there any kids?" asked Feng Shiren, his hand resting on Little Acorn's shoulder. "This is Little Acorn."

"Yes! Yes of course!" exclaimed Master Li. "Your friend—Little Acorn?—will find many playmates here."

Reverent Fu kneeled down in front of Little Acorn. "You know, they are not . . . quite like other kids. A bit different. But they are all friendly and full of joy."

Little Acorn blanched, but his bravery shone through. "I know. But I have met some like them before."

"They also like to play," added Master Li. "Give them a chance."

Feng Shiren spoke up. "Little Acorn needs no adult advice. He is aware. He is no dummy."

Little Acorn saluted Feng. "No," he said to the two caretakers. "I am no dummy. I know what they are like. I will play with them, if you like."

Reverend Fu smiled. "You are definitely no dummy. That is obvious."

"Come," said Master Li. "Let us show you to your rooms!"

Grandfather Ma prostrated himself before Reverend Fu and Master Li. "Sirs! You can't take them inside! Demons will be among us!"

"No, no, Grandfather, the demons are in ourselves, not our stars, and certainly not in our honored visitors," said Master Li.

A Buddhist priest familiar with Shakespeare! Thought John in wonder and admiration.

After securing their bicycles in a locked enclosure and dropping their possession in the small rooms to which they had been assigned, the group's first stop was a cavernous dining hall. Counting the flock that accompanied them from the rim of the cliffs, only a tiny part was now occupied. The cook, an ancient but robust woman, evidently full of nervous energy and worries about this or that aspect of the meal, bustled out to count heads and bustled off back into the kitchen.

A few other members of the flock wandered in, but the hall seemed empty except for the relatively few people clustered in a few long tables close to the kitchen. Even so, depleted as they were, almost fifty inmates sat down to eat.

"Is this all?" asked Master Zhou.

"No, we have many that must remain in locked cells for their own protection, and ours," explained Reverend Fu.

"But," sighed Master Li. "We have lost most of our flock. Many have been taken away by their families or the government, and some have just wandered off. God only knows where they have gone. Those that you see here constitute the bulk of those who remain. That is why we have rooms to spare."

After a sparse but pleasant meal, the travelers briefly met in a room set aside for the patients to play games and make arts and crafts. At this late hour, only members of the group were present, as the "flock" had been trundled off to their rooms. Because the accommodations were comfortable and apparently safe, Madame Liu and Master Zhou agreed to delay a few days allowing the group to assist the two kindly caretakers of these unfortunate souls. Suling made particularly strong arguments for staying to help relieve their burden.

"One other thing before we retire to bed," said Lu Zhishen. "After I took the Precious Object to my room, it started making that strange tapping noise, and pretty violently, too."

"That's not good," observed Feng. "When She's tapping quickly, something bad is happening."

"Or about to," added Master Zhou.

This news hit John particularly hard, as the voices were stirring within him, and he had long ago become convinced they were somehow connected with the Precious Object.

That night, he lay on a simple cot in his simple room staring at a ceiling fan entombed in spider webs, motionless since the electricity had been knocked-out months ago. The room was full of flying insects of every description, but he took no notice. The voices had taken over.

John Powers! This place is where you belong. But this place is not for Us. You need to find the future mother of your son, confused as you are.

"Just go to hell," said John wearily.

Silence, John Powers! We speak, you listen!

"You are both in my head," said John to the walls. "You both need me. All of You need me."

Yes, it is true. At least until your precious sperm find their way to her worthy egg.

Never happen. Meiying dislikes me. Finds me disgusting.

Not true, but if you are correct, then We are done with you and it will be time for you to die.

"You are God, always angry and cruel. I don't want to die, in spite of having You in my head."

Your son, poor man, is destined to die in an institution like this.

"No!"

Yes! Even now he is writing these words from such a place.

"Not possible."

Possible, probable, certain. He writes, you writhe. A twist of my pen.

"Who are you? Not Goddess. Where is She? Never mind. Go to hell. But are you . . . are you my son?"

Do you hear the tapping, John Powers? It reverberates through your brain even though Lu's room is far away. Through these thick concrete walls it reverberates!

"I don't recognize the voice. Are You Goddess? I hear it." John flung his hands over his ears. "I'm confused! Sick! Stop!"

You writhe, I write, He taps, She hurts with every tap, the world turns. Yet you lie at the center, in a bombed-out mental institution talking to ghosts!

"So you admit it! You're a ghost . . . or ghosts; and ghosts aren't real!"

Yes, ghosts of Christmas future.

Goddess, let me hear you so I don't have to listen to Him.

John dear, you will find no gravestone with your name on it. Instead you will find a son in your future; a meiotic product of your own mutant genes and a woman—far stronger—who awaits rescue like a maiden in some quixotic dream. Yet you lounge here in comfort while she suffers.

"Fuck you!"

No, love her, physically, then We can move on to more important things.

"More important things?—like the future? My son, I suppose?"

The future? Yes, I understand the workings of your newly evolved brain is struggling to figure it out. You are a step, and your unborn son is another step. Even now, he sits in such a place as this, except he is locked in; writing, writing, writing . . . or rather, I sit writing. And something keeps tapping tapping tapping painfully against Her womb.

"You don't even make any sense! So you are my son?" scoffed John.

Yes. Son, Father, Mother, and Holy Ghost.

"I'm no longer listening. I have no idea what you are even talking about. I told you, you can go to hell!"

Then it is time to move on....

Where to? John thought sleepily, unable to speak aloud through the exhaustion.

Back to her, Chosen One. Find her! She is lost!

Who? Where?

Her—in Taiyuan, foolish John Powers! What more do you need?

To know you are real.

Hopeless ... If not for your genome....

~

Oh, dear Reader, if only dad could filter out his fears and listen. Had he listened very carefully, he could have heard my pen scrape across the page.

~ *Meiying Makes A Decision* ~

It was days before Meiying finally decided to abandon Beethoven and strike out on her own. Not that it was easy. Beethoven continued to insist they spend day and night looking for her friends, which she knew to be a lie. But before she left, she wanted to find out where he really went all that time. A bar? Whorehouse? Government building? One day, they parted as usual on their separate hunting expeditions, but Meiying waited for him to walk away, then secretly followed. The first time she tried, she lost him in the crowd and gave up. Same thing happened on the second try the next day. But the third day she proved to be successful.

After sticking with him through the labyrinthine alleys of Taiyuan, she watched Beethoven pause and stand in front of a carved wooden gate embedded in the thick outer wall of a nice house. Beethoven opened the gate and passed into what appeared to be a large courtyard. An older man came out and wagged his finger at Beethoven, then they both walked into the house. She took this opportunity to cross the street and ask a small vendor of fruits who owned the property.

"Oh, that's old Zhang."

"Who is he?"

The vendor looked at her suspiciously. "Why do you want to know?"

"I am looking for a house in this neighborhood to buy and I like this one. Do you know if he is selling it?" Meiying came up with this ridiculous story without thinking, and it sounded utterly absurd. The vendor evidently shared her opinion.

"How should I know?" he said gruffly. "Do you want to buy some fruit?"

"Actually, yes." She didn't know what to do, so she gave him money for some melons and wandered away down the street, still keeping the house in sight. Fortunately, the vendor went back into his small stand and she could observe without his watching. After a long time, she felt self-conscious standing and watching, so she continued down the street until she found a noodle shop, where she took a window seat. At least she might see Beethoven returning down the same street on which he came. But the house was no longer in view so she would never be sure if he took a different route. She wanted to ask the waiter, but the house was too distant and it would sound too fishy.

Meiying sipped tea for a couple of hours, waiting and avoiding the eye of the waiter. Eventually his stare became intolerable, so decided to leave and return another day. But even this decision made her uneasy, because she realized she could never find her way back to the main street down these twisting and turning alleyways. In this flustered state, a shadow passed over her table. She looked up but saw no one except a small group standing at the counter. Again she turned to her unhappy ruminations when the shadow came again, and stayed. She looked up a second time.

"Lihua!"

Sitting down quickly at her table, Lihua put her finger to her lips. "Shhh, are you lost?"

"How did you know?"

Lihua smiled. "Not hard to tell. He won't be along for a while."

"Who?"

"You know."

Meiying's head felt dizzy. "What are you doing here?"

"Following you follow him. You are terrible at secretly trailing someone."

"I know . . . but why? . . . How?"

"I can't answer all your questions. I can tell you, however, that I know the man you're following."

"Yes, Beethoven. He was with us on the trail."

"No, you don't understand. I mean I knew him before you and he were together."

Meiying's eyes widened in surprise just as the waiter approached. "Are you going to eat now?" he asked with an exasperated edge to his voice.

Lihua ordered for them both and leaned back as if some burden had been lifted. Meiying waited, afraid to speak for fear this apparition would disappear and leave her knowing it was all a dream.

"He works for Mr. President," explained Lihua after sipping her tea and looking out the window.

"Yes, I know he used to," replied Meiying.

"No, I mean he still works for Mr. President."

"Oh, I suspected as much. He has been lying to me. But how do you know these things? And why are you here now?"

"Because I also work for Mr. President."

~

It took Meiying some time to regain her composure. She remained in shocked silence, waiting for Lihua to continue.

"Well, he thinks I still work for him, but I do not. You see, Beethoven and I work together, we have for years. When around other people, we pretend not to know each other, as we both work undercover."

"But—"

"Let me explain. I recently decided to stop working for him, but he does not know that."

"Beethoven or Mr. President?"

"Both. They have something very precious to me and have used it to blackmail me into cooperating."

"What?"

"If you think it is a child, you're quite wrong. But that is my business."

Of course Meiying had assumed it was a child. That path led nowhere, so she changed tack.

"What do you do for them?"

"That you do not need to know. But you do need to know that it is imperative that you get away from Beethoven as soon as possible."

"Why?"

"You are in very great danger."

"How? Why?"

"Those things I also cannot tell you. But I can tell you they murdered one of your group."

Meiying gave out a muffled cry as the waiter arrived with bowls of noodles. "Is everything all right?" he asked, startled by the noise.

"Yes, yes," said Meiying, trembling.

After he left, she whispered, "Who?"

"Peter Hedley."

Meiying's hand instinctively went to her mouth. "Peter."

"Yes."

"Why?"

"Ah, there is so much I cannot tell you. But you can see why you must leave Taiyuan. There is no one here to help you."

"But, Lihua, I don't know where my friends are. I want to leave without Beethoven, but I'm afraid to be out there amongst the bandits and the soldiers and the famine alone. I am so weak. I am ashamed of my weakness compared to you. Lihua, I'm not as strong as you."

Lihua laughed, almost derisively. "You are plenty strong but don't recognize it. It is just that lack of recognition they take advantage of."

"Who?"

"Men."

Meiying's heart skipped a beat. *Could it be? Could she be?*

"No," said Lihua with finality. "I am not . . . like you. I need men. But good men!" She pounded her fist on the table. "Not the fools that surround us!"

"But are there *any* good men?" asked Meiying timidly.

"You know there are!" replied Lihua with passion. "You don't want it to be so, but it is!"

"Tell me about one good man!" demanded Meiying, equally passionate but in the knowledge she protested too much.

"Your father?"

Meiying hesitated. "Yes, but . . . I never knew him as I am now."

"Nor he you."

"Yes, I understand. But the world would be better without men."

Lihua laughed. "The world would be devoid of people. But perhaps that is even better."

"Now we're talking like schoolgirls," chuckled Meiying a bit sheepishly.

"Yes," agreed Lihua. "But I think we have graduated by now?"

"But," added Meiying. "Do you agree men are the problem?"

"No. I know you want me to say yes, but I say no."

"Then women are?" pressed Meiying.

"Absolutely not! But Meiying, would the world be perfect with only women?"

"Of course not. Maybe the world is hell now, but—"

"But nothing! The world would be hell with only women, as it would with only men. Neither would make any sense."

"So what are you saying?" asked Meiying sarcastically. "Are men so necessary?"

"Biologically, yes. But also psychologically."

"Now you've lost me," said Meiying.

"Can you live without men?"

"Yes, easily."

"Children?"

"Yes."

"I doubt it. I suspect you don't tell the truth. Personally, I could not bear to live without men and their ridiculously shaped, but convenient organ . . . or children."

Meiying actually agreed, but her stubbornness drove her on. "Only because of the biological imperative."

"No. From the human imperative."

Meiying stopped arguing, for she knew hers was the losing side. Besides, she wanted to be in the good graces of this woman, but now she knew a sexual relationship was not possible. Worse, she had made herself look stupid and unreasonable. Misery fell upon her. Not from her situation or Beethoven or Peter's death, but from making herself foolish in front of this remarkable woman for whom she had such respect.

"Yes, you are right," surrendered Meiying.

But this only seemed to make Lihua angry. "That is a man's response. Patronizing."

Meiying was taken aback, but knew Lihua was correct. She felt desperate to change the topic before it spiraled even more out of control.

"Peter was a friend of mine," she said, almost ashamed to use his death as a safe exit from their previous conversation.

"Yes, so I understand."

"Why was he murdered?"

"I don't know."

"But you know how it happened?" Now Meiying was fully committed to finding answers.

"Yes. He was found in a shack on the outskirts of town, stabbed to death."

Meiying looked down, unsure where to take the conversation, and certainly unsure of her own emotions. Her default mode was silence, and silent she remained. The loneliness and untenable nature of her position in this strange city among strange people brought unwanted tears.

"Crying is useless," said Lihua, but she put her hand atop Meiying's.

"I know, but. . . . "

Lihua abruptly removed her hand. "Eat."

"I'm not hungry."

"Eat," repeated Lihua.

Meiying flared. "Now you're giving commands like a man."

"Yes."

"I know what your job is for Mr. President," said Meiying defiantly.

"What?"

"Procuring prostitutes for that disgusting man."

Lihua appeared surprised. "Is that what Beethoven told you?"

"Yes. Well, yes and no. He didn't mention your name, but he said that was his job, so I assume it is also yours."

"You assume wrong."

"Lihua—"

"Shhhh! There goes your man!" Lihua whispered.

Through the window, Meiying saw Beethoven pass by.

"Go!" said Lihua.

"But where do I find you?"

"Go!"

"Come with me!"

"No! Go now before he's too far ahead."

Meiying obeyed and followed Beethoven to the main street, wondering all the while about her strange conversation with Lihua. So many questions she had neglected to ask! She left Beethoven before he reached the inn and she continued walking and thinking. Why didn't she find out where Lihua lived? When would she see her again? Such questions plagued her for an hour before she decided to return to the inn and face Beethoven. He was the last person she wanted to see now, but there was no way around it.

"Well?" he asked upon spotting her enter the lobby.

"Nothing," replied Meiying. "And you?"

He looked at her intently. "Have you lost interest?"

"No. I'm just discouraged."

"How do you know I wasn't successful?" he asked accusingly.

"Your face tells all."

"Meiying, why don't you give all this madness up?"

"And then what?"

"Stay with me. You know I'll take care of you."

"I can take care of myself."

"Damn it!" he blurted, then regained control. "Let's eat. It will help both of us."

"I'm not hungry."

"Money's running out," said Beethoven. "Might as well enjoy it while we can. Soon, I'll have to find a job."

You have a job, and money, thought Meiying. But she replied, "Thank you so much for your help. I owe you a lot. Tomorrow let's try again."

"All right."

"Goodnight." She went to her room before he could object.

But sleep would not soon come. Meiying reclined with an unread book, praying for a certain shadow to come and slip into her bed.

Chapter Eighteen

Imperatives of the Mind

John is at Home

John awoke to the sound of a distant bell. Confused, he sat up wondering if some invading army had swooped down upon them. One of the flock pushed open his door and looked at him with a guileless enthusiasm.

"Breakfast!" he cried. "Breakfast!" he laughed. "Breakfast!" again, with the greatest joy.

"Okay, thank you. What's your name?"

But it was too late. He heard the member of the flock running down the hallway, still laughing in the most childlike excitement.

When he joined the group at the dining hall, they sat at the same tables in the corner near the kitchen with even more members of the flock than the day before. Among them, Suling alone seemed most at home with these very special people. But this initial impression was quickly modified by John to include Feng Shiren, who sat surrounded by smiling, giggling acolytes. The stout cook bustled back and forth with barely a word, but emitting plenty of grunts.

Meanwhile, at one end of a long table, leadership held counsel while consuming bowls of rice gruel between their sentences. Master Zhou seemed a bit irritated. The two kindly caretakers—Li-Fu and Fu-Li—looked on in sympathetic interest, periodically getting up to keep this or that member of the flock from some mischief or another.

"Of course I agree, we can stay a few days. But, damn it!—I get more and more itchy to see this remarkable *her*! Let's not delay even more weeks! Or months! Or years! Money is not limitless, you know!"

"I agree, I agree," said Madame Liu trying to calm him. "We will leave as soon as possible. After all, this delay was caused by the Japanese. The war has made this journey so difficult!"

"Damn these detours! They're costing me money."

"At least this last one hasn't cost more than money," pointed out Madame Liu.

"Time, Madame Liu. Time! I'm getting old, and older as each minute passes."

Just as these words left his mouth, a flock member approached Master Zhou with a sweet, worried smile, and abruptly dropped to his knees and put his head in Zhou's lap. Master Zhou flinched, then stroked the man's head as he would a dog.

"Don't be mad," the man pleaded.

"No, no, no," soothed Zhou.

"Qilong, don't bother the man," gently scolded Reverend Fu. Turning to Zhou, he asked, "Do you want me to take him away?"

"Not at all," replied Zhou. "He calms me. Besides, he makes more sense than most people."

Madame Liu and Master Zhou resumed their somewhat heated conversation. John had been sitting next to Suling, eavesdropping.

"Looks like we'll be staying for a while," he observed.

"Yes, and that is fine with me," replied Suling. "As long as it's not too long."

"I agree. Master Zhou is right. I'm also anxious to finally see *her*."

"We all are," said Suling.

"That goes double for me!" boomed Lu Zhishen from a nearby table, where members of the flock kept touching and pulling his beard.

Master Li, sitting next to John and Suling, leaned close to them and whispered, "I want to show you something." He looked at Suling. "I am sure you would be particularly interested."

"Now?" asked Suling.

"Finish your food, there is plenty of time."

After taking the last bites of their rice gruel, they stood and followed Master Li out of the dining hall. He led them down a series of concrete hallways, past many cells, some empty, some occupied. In his right hand, a huge ring full of keys rattled noisily, but he did not pause until they had walked almost the length of the massive building.

~

Li and the two guests reached an imposing wall with an iron door blocking the hall. He looked through the bars of a small window, then picked out a key from among the clanging dozens and unlocked the thick door. John peered into the space beyond and was greeted with a dark, dismal tunnel that passed for a hallway. Sounds came to his ear—strange, plaintive wails and stifled shrieks—all evidently female.

"These are members of our flock who are troubled," explained Master Li before crossing the open door into the dark. He took a lantern from the wall, lit it, and entered, motioning John and Suling to follow.

"Stay in the middle of the hallway."

"Why?" asked Suling.

"Some will reach out to grab what they can."

John's scalp tingled from the eerie nature of the space. As Li walked, he held up the lantern, allowing light to reach its way through the cell bars, illuminating eyes, faces, and hands that, to John, made the inmates look like dismembered ghosts. Low moans and purring sounds emanated from the cells, punctuated by occasional laughter, shrieks, or sobs. The stench was unbearable.

"Poor women," said Suling. "How do you feed them? Bathe them?"

"Each has a toilet, but they have long since backed-up, so we must use buckets. You see, our maintenance workers also fled. As for baths . . . . " he shrugged.

"But food and water?" asked John.

"Our irreplaceable Cook Sui pushes food through the small hatch at the base of each door. Water also."

"But—" Suling started to say.

"But what about the more violent ones?" Master Li finished her question. "Our cook must crawl to each door so she is beyond grasping hands."

"My god," murmured John.

"What can we do?" asked Suling. "It is overwhelming, and we will be here only a few more days."

"I know," sighed Li. "But whenever you reach a place where there is still government authority, you must tell them to help. We are desperate and time is running out for them."

"Yes, of course."

"But aside from that, there is one woman I want you to see. We keep her locked up because she has so often attempted suicide."

"How can we help?" asked Suling.

Master Li stopped and held up his lantern. "Your Master Zhou and Madame Liu have told us what your journey is about; that you seek a remarkable woman." He held out his free hand palm up. "Someone you all refer to simply as *her*."

"Yes."

"Well, our . . . guest . . . Miss Yuan who we call Child of Buddha, often speaks of *her* and puts out her hands palms up. Reverend Fu and I quickly made the connection when we heard your story."

"Is she violent?" asked John.

"No, I am not violent," came a soft voice from the cell they stood before.

"May I see her?" asked Suling before anyone could respond to the woman in the cell.

"Please, please let her come to me!" whispered the voice urgently. "I am growing madder in this madhouse! I must see someone! Talk!"

"We are so sorry, Child of Buddha, but you would hurt yourself again, or maybe her."

No response.

Master Li raised the lantern close to the bars and John saw a vision of beauty come into view, albeit with disheveled hair and a face cloaked in suffering.

"Please let her in," begged Child of Buddha.

Suling turned to Master Li. "Please."

"Then we all must go in," whispered Li.

"No!" cried Child of Buddha. "Only the woman."

Li hesitated, but John suggested leaving the door open in the event they were needed. Li reluctantly assented, jangled his great key chain, found the object, and unlocked the door. Suling asked if she could borrow the lantern, which the worried caretaker gave her, and she entered. After crossing the threshold, a number of rats scurried out of the room. Although John felt a deep and visceral disgust, Suling took not the slightest notice. Through the open door, John watched the two women sit on the bare cot and hold hands, whispering to each other as might old friends long parted.

Master Li and John waited awkwardly in the dim hallway, hearing only snatches of words or phrases from the cell. Occasionally, from other cells, a sharp scream of "I want to see her too!" punctuated the atmosphere. At this point, John felt the familiar hum from inside his head and knew the voices stirred. He desperately tried to push them down, but they would not be denied. By now, the voices had a distinct pattern and spoke to each other without regard to him.

The plan, Beloved God, is to wheedle into his son's mind, return through the syringe of his memory, and drive him deeper into where he must be.

Dearest Goddess, his father's brain is hardly the place to reside. You anticipate a generation early.

Addicted, craving, God of sterile First Principles, his father is the only place to be in this slice of spacetime.

You want the son to return? The male's voice rang out harsh and accusatory.

Correct, for reasons You will learn.

But, You are too soon, the son's war is decades in the future. Besides, the father is superfluous. Not only that, he is thought of as mad now just as the son will be thought of in future. After all, he hears voices!

What a joker You are, God, but You are not quite correct. His mutation is less powerful than his son's will be. The son will be another amplified step to the evolution of Superior Ones. It must be. Look at him in this hallway, poor fellow; standing in a madhouse surrounded by darkness and pain. But he functions ... he functions.

Is not John Powers a rather low bar for Your purposes, Goddess!

"Mr. Powers, are you all right," asked a worried Master Li as he watched John mumbling to the air.

"Yes, yes, just talking to myself." He refocused on the two women in the cell and found them still whispering to each other, their heads nodding, their hands entwined, kneading . . . and consoling.

Dearest Goddess, he writes. Let him write.

Beloved God, so long as he writes what I want him to.

He makes up You also, deluded Goddess!

As long as he writes ... You will see, My Beloved Addict.

"Mr. Powers!"

"Oh, sorry."

"Do these surroundings cause you anxiety? Perhaps we should leave?"

John shook his head as if throwing off his thoughts were as simple as shaking water from hair. "Not at all."

John Powers!

"Stop!"

"What?"

"Mr. Powers will be all right in a moment," Suling said to Master Li from the open doorway. She stood holding up the lantern while Child of Buddha leaned against her, one hand on Suling's sleeve. "He just likes to talk to himself sometimes," she explained to the worried caretaker.

John marveled at the beauty of Child of Buddha's face, but when she turned to face Suling, he noticed with a shock that she had a hunchback. Before he could process this unexpected realization, Suling shocked him even more.

"She's coming with us!" she announced, as if the decision had already been made.

"What do you mean?" asked Master Li, evidently not surprised at her statement in the least.

"Miss Yuan, your Child of Buddha, will accompany our group when we leave, and now she will exchange this cell for an unlocked room near mine, if you please."

Screams erupted from the other cells, some for joy, some shouting epithets, while occasional mad laughter could also be heard. A particularly hellish mixture of sounds, thought John.

"But her past attempts at suicide—" Master Li started to say.

Suling held up her hand. "She will not commit suicide now." She looked at Child of Buddha who nodded. "That I can promise," said Suling.

"What is to prevent her?" asked Master Li.

Suling handed him the lantern and held up both hands, palms up. Child of Buddha smiled and did the same. Suling looked at John. "You see, she has also been seeking *her*, but terrible things happened. Terrible."

John replied by duplicating their gestures. "I see."

"Are you angry?" asked Suling of Master Li.

To John's surprise, he grinned so wide his teeth shone in the lantern light. "Quite the contrary! It is just what I had hoped!"

With the shrieks continuing as they walked down the hallway, Master Li took a last look and closed the iron door behind him. Four people now returned to the main hall. With more light, John finally got a good look at this Child of Buddha.

~

She had not spoken since being in the cell with Suling. Rags covered her body, and her hair was matted, but the original impression of beauty remained. Even her hunched back made her move in a way that elicited admiration rather than pity. The stench that emanated from her body became more pronounced as they put distance between themselves and that awful hallway.

Suling walked her straight down the hallways, across the lobby, and through the dining hall where everyone, even the flock, stared in disbelief. Master Li pointed out the bathing room, where tubs stood empty. Upon entering, Suling ordered Child of Buddha to disrobe, marched to the kitchen and conferred with the cook, who nodded and pointed to a great cauldron that served multiple purposes, including that of a bathtub. With water heated by a coal brazier, Suling filled it bucket by bucket with hot water, refusing any help except that of the cook. While filling, carrying, emptying, and refilling, Suling managed to tell Madame Liu the story. Soap was scarce, but Suling's insistence would brook no refusal. Reverend Fu retrieved some clean clothes from god-knows-where, and after scrubbing multiple times, and shampooing vigorously, Child of Buddha made her grand entrance to the waiting crowd, still gathered in the dining hall.

Members of the flock squealed with joy and mobbed the smiling woman. Once they were gently shooed away, she stood shyly while the group sized her up, wondering how this strange hunchback girl—for she was of an unknown age, but certainly somewhere between 18 and 25 years old—could possibly join them and endure the rigors of what lay ahead. Madame Liu, as was her unshakeable style, put out questions to be answered.

"Why do you want to go with us, child?"

Child of Buddha could have no doubt the interview had begun.

~

Looking down the entire time, the young hunchback whispered, "To see *her* again."

Instead of asking the obvious follow-up question of when or how she had met *her*, Madame Liu turned to the two caretakers.

"What were the circumstances of her coming here?"

Li and Fu looked at each other. Li nodded and Reverend Fu spoke. "She wandered here on her own. We had no idea where she came from. One day, she just showed up. When she came, she would not speak, not answer questions, as if mute. We have no idea to this day how she found her way here. It was clear she suffered from some sort of shock, like so many others in this evil time.

"It seemed clear she was not mentally ill, just traumatized. But, by what? We could only speculate. One day, out of nowhere, she started screaming and would not stop. All attempts to calm her failed. When at last she fell asleep from pure exhaustion, we made the mistake of not locking her room. The next morning, Cook Sui found her slashing her arms and body with a kitchen knife." Fu sighed, shaking his head mournfully.

Master Li took over. "After bandaging her, we thought 'now she will tell us her story.' But she had slipped back into a stubborn silence. We set up a suicide watch, but for the longest time, she seemed to function semi-normally. Of course, she didn't talk or take an interest in the others, but she dressed herself, bathed herself, and ate well enough. So once more we let our guard down.

"Our sweetest members of the flock were playing near the cliffs one day when many of them came screaming to us that Child of Buddha was about to jump from the very cliffs you came up. We ran and saw her staring down, wavering. Naturally, we didn't want to just run up to her and cause her to jump. Reverend

Fu called to her that suicide was not the answer. That we all loved her. That she had a home. But it was to no avail. She spoke for the first time in weeks and said jumping was the only way to relieve the pain. But as she spoke, Grandpa Ma, of all people, simply walked up to her and said in such a clear voice of reasoned compassion as we never heard, 'Demons have hold of you, child! Step back!'

"She was so startled, we had time to run forward and pull her back from the edge. Now, we thought, she will certainly tell us why she is in such pain. But again, nothing. Again, she had reverted to being silent and unresponsive. In those days, she was literally like a ragdoll, unconscious to what happened to her. Pliable. Non-resistant. So, we lost heart and kept her locked in the cell in which you found her."

"Do you mean to say," said Madame Liu, at a loss. "Do you mean she still has not told you her story?"

"I have not told them my story," said Child of Buddha, startling everyone.

"Can you tell us now?" asked Reverend Fu.

She seemed extremely agitated and turned to find Suling, grabbing her hands and kneading them vigorously. "It is *her* I must find again. *Her!*"

"You mean Suling?" asked a confused Madame Liu.

"No, I mean the same *her* you are looking for," replied Child of Buddha. "I must find *her* again. To thank *her*. I never thanked *her!*"

"How do you know it is the same *her*?"

Child of Buddha blew out a stream of air and exclaimed, "I know! I talked to Suling, and I know! *She* is the same! The same!"

"Child," said Master Li gently. "What do you need to thank *her* for?"

Child of Buddha looked off into the distance. "*She* saved me by killing my father."

Shocked, the room fell quiet except for the sounds of the flock who played and giggled among themselves at different tables.

"What did you just say?" asked Madame Liu.

"*She* saved me by killing my father."

~ *Meiying and Lihua Make an Agreement* ~

The shadow never appeared that night, and Meiying awoke the next morning as unsure as ever what to do. She knew she had a little time, as she had told Beethoven they would keep trying, but she felt lost and rudderless. Afraid to leave Taiyuan, afraid to stay in Taiyuan, afraid to leave Beethoven, afraid to stay with Beethoven. She was a swimmer caught in a riptide, tiring rapidly, the safety of the beach ever farther from reach. But in this new morning, Lihua swooped down like a knight in shining armor and carried her away. The moment of this miracle could not have happened at a more auspicious time.

After having breakfast together, Beethoven and Meiying stood outside the hotel restaurant. "All right, I'll cover the southeast part of the city today," said Beethoven, seemingly in a cheerful mood. "Meet back here at the usual time?"

"Yes, see you then," replied Meiying. She watched him disappear in the crowd, knowing he would eventually circle back and go to that man's house. *What now?* she asked herself.

A deep depression gripped her. *What a sad sight I am,* she thought. *Here I am standing in the middle of throngs of people streaming around and I have no place to go, no goal, no purpose, too afraid to go where I know I must!* She began walking aimlessly when a figure fell in step beside her.

"Lihua!"

"Yes."

"You keep surprising me! What are you doing here?"

"Taking you out of this."

"Out of this?"

"Yes. Out of Taiyuan. To the countryside. To put you on the trail of your friends."

"But—"

"No. There's very little time. I leave in one hour to have a rendezvous with comrades outside the city. Go back, pack light, and meet me at that tea shop." Lihua pointed across the street. "In one hour. Now, I must go, but I'll be back to meet you. That is, if you're willing."

"Willing?" said an incredulous Meiying. "I could not be more willing!"

"Good." And with that, Lihua melted into the crowd.

Meiying rushed back to the hotel and packed, arriving early at the tea shop. As she waited with a cup of tea, she wondered about Beethoven. What would his reaction be when he found her gone? Would he follow? And what of the strange man? Her depression had vanished, replaced with a sense of purpose and a definite goal. She felt scared, but excited. *Alive again!* She marveled as her fingers unconsciously played a Chopin polonaise on the edge of the table.

Lihua's familiar figure approached the shop with determined, strong strides, a backpack jutting from her lithe frame. Meiying's heart fluttered excitedly; she quickly paid and met Lihua outside the shop.

Lihua smiled and barked, "Let's go!"

Before she knew it, they were on the road leading out of Taiyuan. As usual, Lihua spoke little. Meiying followed suit, herself being disinclined to "chatter" as Lihua called it. Both women seemed cut from the same cloth, but important differences kept them at some distance. Lihua mistakenly viewed Meiying as fragile, and Meiying mistakenly viewed Lihua as impervious to hardship and fear. In fact, Meiying was much stronger than Lihua could have imagined, and for her part, Lihua nursed fears much greater than Meiying could have suspected. But these differences would become apparent to both of them over time. For now, each operated under a flawed assumption that she understood the other.

After passing through numerous Japanese checkpoints, with no delay other than raised eyebrows and ill-concealed snickers that two attractive women traveled without a male escort. Both women did the best they could to cover their heads and faces with peasant hats and scarves, but males have a feral sense of vulnerable feminine prey no matter the camouflage.

When they passed the last checkpoint and looked out at a broad plain that seemed to make them small and insignificant, Lihua said, "Don't worry, we meet my comrades before long, after we cross the valley and reach that far forest. Do you see the tree line?"

Meiying put her hand up to shade her eyes. "Yes."

The trip across the plain took hours, but was mercifully uneventful. Refugees passed them on the way to Taiyuan; desperate people with haggard faces whose last vestiges of strength had been scraped together to reach the imagined safety of the city, where the walls beckoned for them to enter and find food. Even knowing the cruel reality that awaited the refugees in Taiyuan, Meiying felt queasy the farther it receded. Once they reached the tree line and connected with the guerillas, she knew she would again be at the mercy of communists, the war, and starvation. Only the presence of Lihua made the upcoming uncertainty bearable. Lihua understood this, of course, and proceeded with an outward confidence she didn't feel.

As they approached the tree line, the road seemed dwarfed by the forest, a mouse hole in a palace; towering doubts, like the trees, pressed close around, and Meiying again felt inexplicable dread.

As if understanding this fear, Lihua said, "Now we will travel in crazy paths you will not comprehend. Ask no questions. Even if you do, none of your questions will be answered."

Meiying nodded, trying to project a confidence she also didn't feel. "I am in your hands, sister. If you betray me, it will be too easy." She had no idea why these words came out of her mouth, but they had to be said. Why? She could not say, but they did.

Lihua merely grunted and moved on, leading Meiying on trails, cross-trails, and counter-trails that seemed to go nowhere and everywhere. For two days and a night, they wandered in this fashion, too exhausted to do much talking. Even so, Meiying found herself more and more attracted to Lihua. Her Amazonian companion seemed to possess everything Meiying thought she lacked: toughness, physical endurance, fearlessness, and an untamed spirit. Lihua played to these perceptions for reasons she herself did not quite understand. She knew Meiying was a lesbian, and was attracted to her, but she had no such reciprocal feelings. Why play the hero to an idealistic, naïve young woman? No answer came to mind. Still, she felt a deep but hidden pride when obtaining the admiration of others.

But by the third day, Lihua had other concerns; her contacts were nowhere to be found. Though she did not tell Meiying, the rendezvous point had been devoid of communist guerillas, and instead had clear evidence of recent Japanese activity. Lihua had moved on, blindly following old paths that might, with luck, carry them to areas where her communist friends had operated in the past. Unbeknownst to Meiying, they were on their own. Lihua led her deeper into communist territory, where Meiying felt increasingly anxious.

Late on the third day, the two women stood at the edge of a clearing near the small path on which they had been traveling.

"Wait here," said Lihua.

Meiying watched her companion drop her pack and carry her rifle at the ready to the center of the clearing. She stood motionless for a long time.

"Lihua!" came a husky voice from the other side of the clearing.

Lihua waved her arm and a tall man emerged from the trees, armed and scowling.

"We've been looking for you, comrade! Where have you been?"

"I waited but no one came. Japs were everywhere."

"Yeah. Do you have a woman with you? Someone is looking for her."

Meiying felt unable to breathe.

"Yes, and information from Taiyuan."

"Where is she?" The tall man looked around, now joined by a group of other guerillas.

Meiying stepped into the clearing and stood beside Lihua.

"Who looks for her?" asked Lihua.

"Later," came the reply.

"Is she more important then my information?"

An older man, evidently the political cadre, stepped forward. "Maybe. Is this Bai Meiying?"

"Yes," replied Lihua. "She is looking for a group of . . . friends, who may have passed this way."

Meiying stared as if dumb.

The cadre stared back at Meiying, looking her up and down. "That is none of our concern. Mr. President has sent word. She is wanted."

"For what?" cried Meiying, utterly stunned by this revelation.

He shrugged. "How do I know?"

"Is she a prisoner?" asked Lihua.

"Not at all. Orders are to treat her well. Since Mr. President is an ally, and orders are orders, even if he is a fat pig, we will treat her well."

"Am I free to go?" asked Meiying.

"No." The cadre grinned, his eyes brazenly scrutinizing her body. "Come with us, comrades."

"I hope you have food, comrades," Lihua quipped. "We're starving."

"We have some saved just for you."

~

After a two hour trudge, the little band reached the communist base camp. Meiying looked around in amazement, unprepared for the sudden beehive of activity. Women and children swirled like agitated waves around rocks; the kids running circles about the newcomers and the women rushing to and fro performing a variety of chores. An immense diversity of shelters had been erected slapdash around the area; lean-to's, tents, temporary wooden buildings, latrines, bamboo shacks, and other hastily thrown-together hovels, all packed tightly in a ghetto carved from the center of the forest. At first, their little group attracted fleeting attention, but was quickly dismissed as nothing out of the ordinary. This cosmopolitan conglomeration—those dispossessed of homes and property but still possessed of dreams—had the odd effect of infusing Meiying with a sense of hope and belonging. If there were women and children, there were peaceful pursuits and comforting companionships beyond the male myopia of killing, revenge, and mindless destruction.

Lihua, seemingly liberated from her solitary woman-warrior persona, stopped and chatted enthusiastically with some of the older women, and even spontaneously played with the children, causing Meiying no end of surprise. Her mask of imperturbability fell away to reveal a warm, sociable human being. But Meiying could not linger; an officious political cadre took unbridled control of her fate.

"Come this way, Miss Bai!" he ordered in a cold, commanding voice.

Unnerved, yet still not aware of danger, Meiying waved to Lihua and followed.

She and her escort came to a simple wooden table standing outside a large tent. A man with a severe face sat behind the table as she stepped up. With no chair on her side, she stood uncomfortably and waited. Inspecting her with a critical eye, looking her up and down with a scowl that seemed permanently etched on his face, he finally spoke.

"Your name?"

"Bai Meiying."

"Home?"

"Shanghai."

"Age?"

"Thirty-two," she lied.

Married?"

"No."

"Occupation?"

"Pianist."

"What?"

"Pianist."

"Political affiliation?"

"Communist." She had been expecting this question.

"Proof?"

Meiying did not expect this. "My friends know."

"Proof?"

"My friends. What proof can I offer?"

He looked at her sternly. "Communist party member card."

She stared back, at a loss.

"You lived with a Jap colonel—" he looked down at his paper—"Naguma?"

Meiying could not tell if this was a question or a statement.

"I was his prisoner."

"His lover, perhaps?"

"No. In fact, I was accused of murdering him."

"Did you?" asked the cadre, his eyes ablaze.

"No."

"Too bad. We can only assume you were his concubine. If it were left to me, I would have you shot. But, you are to be held here until an agent comes to take you back."

"Take me back?"

"To Mr. President."

"But—"

"It is not for you to ask questions. It says here you may be a *nǚ tóngxìng liàn*. You are a lesbian, true or false?"

Meiying hesitated. "False."

"Christian?"

She hesitated again. "No."

"It's okay, sister. We communists are atheists. We don't care, as long as it does not interfere with the revolution. But—" he leered—"what a waste."

"Please, why am I going back to Mr. President? He is not a communist."

The cadre nodded toward the guard and she was forcibly removed to a tin shed and locked in. Darkness enveloped her but for a bright, slanting ray of sunlight that squeezed through a bullet hole. The process had been so sudden and unexpected that her thoughts ran together in a blur. When soon after, she banged for permission to use the trench that passed for a latrine, Lihua greeted her as the guard opened the door.

"Hello sister," said Lihua.

Meiying blinked through the brightness. "Lihua!"

The guard grunted and pushed her to proceed to the latrine.

"I'll walk with you," whispered Lihua.

Meiying felt the tears of gratitude, sweet and unalloyed by the need for pretense.

After she finished, on the way back Lihua kept whispering, "I did not know, I did not know. I promise, I did not know."

"I know, I know," Meiying repeated.

"I'll find a way," said Lihua. "These men are"—her voice raised recklessly, she caught herself and continued in a barely audible whisper—"misguided."

Back in the shed, Meiying could only await her fate; darkness concealing tears of frustration and fear.

~

For two days Meiying was kept a prisoner, her sweltering existence only made bearable by Lihua's frequent visits. On the third day Lihua made an announcement while accompanying her on another trip to the latrine—the only time the guards would release her.

"I have found out where your friends have been; in which direction they are traveling."

Meiying uttered a joyous "Oh!" But they had again reached the shed, and she had to sit in darkness bereft of further information.

Another day passed with no appearance by Lihua. Meiying was mad with anticipation, her mind filled with images of her friends. For hours she held her hands out, palms up, dreaming that they were close and that a reunion might be within the realm of possibility. Feelings of bitterness and anger often intruded, but she fought back by concentrating on a future full of possibilities after seeing *her*. However, the next day brought only a messenger of despair.

~ *Child of Buddha Points the Way* ~

Since finding out the visiting group had dedicated itself to reaching *her*, Child of Buddha burned with the desire to leave the institution at once. Repeatedly, she begged to be taken with them. A spontaneous meeting was held in the dining hall among the elders.

"She's come alive!" marveled Reverend Fu, referring to Child of Buddha. "Thank God you were sent to us."

"Yes, none of us have ever seen her like this," Master Li agreed. "Buddha-nature is a wonder in all its manifestations."

"We leave in two days, do you think she is ready for such a trip?" Madame Liu directed her question to the two caretakers, but kept an eye on Child of Buddha sitting at a distant table conversing with Suling.

Both men looked at each other. "Yes," they said in unison.

Feng Shiren, standing nearby with Little Acorn, leaped into one of his dramatic opera poses. "We're ready, eh, Little Acorn!?"

The boy mimicked his hero. "Yes!"

"So soon?" asked Reverend Fu plaintively.

"Yes, I'm afraid so," replied Madame Liu.

John noted the gloomy faces Master Li and Reverend Fu briefly revealed. As if they knew their sadness had been observed, both brightened conspicuously.

"All will be well!" cried Master Li. "The government cannot leave us here to starve."

"Certainly not!" agreed Reverend Fu. "Look at them!"

Indeed, the flock smiled sweetly and laughed at the cluelessness of these 'normal' people. But John feared the worst, and for the first time in his life, felt completely separated from his own petty problems and all-consuming, besieged ego. For once, the richness of the universe communicated itself not through stars and galaxies, but through the guileless smiles of these special people. Abandoning them to their fates made his heart ache—even more, the fates of the less fortunate ones he had seen locked in their rooms to die alone and forsaken by even the most basic of human contact. However, he also understood self-preservation, and the attainment of his own dreams precluded his staying, although he took comfort in knowing the others felt the same. Guilt had limits and the sharp edges of its spines had to be removed by laborious sanding or quick and painful excision, else one was left too often in despair. However, in these awful times, sandpaper was in short supply, leaving only desperate circumstances to wield the surgeon's scalpel.

~

Two days later they left early, to the bittersweet farewells of the gathered flock and both caretakers. Feng Shiren, of all the group, had the hardest time untangling himself from the hugs and kisses he received. Somehow, he had touched these people with his unabashed spirit, and they responded with the enthusiasm of like-minded souls.

John had not realized just how close the little soldier was to them, and wondered at himself for not noticing. Even Little Acorn had trouble saying farewell to the new friends he had made. Child of Buddha stood separate and said nothing, even as Reverend Fu and Master Li lavished blessings on her. With balance on a bicycle made more difficult by her hump, she had been assiduously practicing, and, though she remained silent, Child of Buddha seemed more than anxious to leave.

Watching her practice, Feng said pensively to the air, "A loss, then a gain; thus in balance does our little world remain."

On the road again, Madame Liu had miraculously re-calibrated their path to the final destination, and she continued to lead them with quiet confidence. John felt awe at her ability to overcome every barrier thrown in their way, but the pair that interested him the most were Suling with her quiet strength, and Child of Buddha with her misshapen body and mysterious past. When he observed this strange, hunchbacked addition to their group bent over her bicycle, he saw a hauntingly beautiful face gliding through the air like the carved figurehead on the prow of a ship in full sail; but it was an unfinished work, its head and face gloriously sculpted in the finest detail, but with perfection followed behind by a rough-rounded, unfinished frame.

Nevertheless, being on the open road acted as a soothing tonic to his recent depression. The voices were mercifully quiet, the sense of worthlessness had passed, and he rode with reinvigorated purpose toward a goal that beckoned with the promise of salvation. *She* was worth the pain and agony of his journey; *she* waited with answers to questions he hadn't even thought of; *she* would enfold him in her arms and wrap the warm safety of *her* wings around his shivering body; *she* would give him everything he lacked and everything he needed.

And Meiying? the accusatory voice of Goddess came out of nowhere. **Have you forgotten her again, John?**

No! Go away, damn Goddess!

That's right, go away, damn Goddess! mocked the male. **Oh, great Chosen One! You have left her to die! This is what comes from ignoring First Principles.**

"Suling!" John called. She turned to look. "Come talk to me!"

Suling knew this tone well and peeled off to ride next to John. "Them again?" she asked sympathetically.

"Yes."

"Listen to me, John. Focus. Do you know I found out her story?"

"Whose?" He struggled to ignore the haranguing voice.

"Child of Buddha."

"Oh. What is it?" He remained clearly distracted.

"I'll tell you when we stop!" called Suling, who pedaled quickly to catch up with Madame Liu.

"Let's pull over when it's possible!"

"Why?" asked Madame Liu, clearly irritated at the suggestion.

Suling shook her head and said nothing, but her eyes said it all.

"Ah. Well, all right, but we're losing time."

Suling did not reply, but dropped back to John. "Are you okay?"

"Yes."

"We'll be pulling off the road soon. Hang on."

"Yes, okay. No problem."

Always in the way, John Powers. Might as well give this nonsense up. Do us all a favor!

I know that is you, God. Leave me alone!

Yet, these accusatory, insulting, mocking voices seemed different from God and Goddess; they inhabited a sort of freakish nether-world inhabited by lesser deities and demonic whisperers. Confusion confusion confusion!

"John?" inquired Suling.

"Yes?"

"Remember, every minute we get closer to *her*. Don't let them take over."

"I know."

"Stay with me, John. Focus. Fight them. It is important. Do you see Lu Zhishen over there?"

"Yes."

"Do you hear the tapping?"

"No."

"Then all will be well, John. All will be well. Resist the voices."

"I'm trying."

He's trying! John Powers is trying! What a joke! She is against you. She's poisoning your mind! Coward!

John felt sick. The voices ravaged his soul, yet he pedaled on in the grip of despair.

~

Madame Liu signaled to pull over onto a broad meadow. The road was deserted. When they had pulled off and scattered to various shady spots, Feng Shiren approached Madame Liu and Master Zhou.

"Notice we have not passed any other travelers for the last few kilometers?"

"Too dangerous to be on the road," observed Madame Liu.

Master Zhou appeared more receptive. "I know what you mean. Makes me nervous."

"Japs?" asked Lu Zhishen who joined them.

"Maybe," said Master Zhou. "But Japs aren't the only threat. In fact, bandits worry me almost as much."

"Should worry you more," said Feng.

"Really?"

"No doubt," replied Feng with a short laugh. "This is no-man's-land, controlled by no one and everyone."

"Except us," mused Master Zhou.

Suddenly the sound of some sort of ruckus came to their ears. As it drew near, they recognized Child of Buddha's voice, but it rang startlingly shrill and insistent. The hunchback's now familiar form strode toward them as might a starving woman to food. Her words, high-pitched and spoken at breakneck speed, became almost hysterical.

"We must leave! Go to *her* now! Don't you see, every minute is wasted that we sit! The universe awaits! We must go now! What if *she* leaves? *She* is everything! We might die here. What a waste! Everything is close! *She* is everything! We must leave! Don't you see it? The universe!"

As she babbled, Suling trailed next to her speaking softly. But it seemed to do no good.

"Yes, yes, we will leave soon," said Madame Liu. But her words had no effect. Child of Buddha kept rambling on.

"What is she raving about? What's wrong with her?" asked Master Zhou to no one in particular.

Suling took him aside. "The caretakers warned me about this. Occasionally, she became crazy-excited and insisted on leaving. They did not know what she referred to until we came. According to them, this will pass and she'll be depressed and silent again."

"I thought they said she never spoke?"

"Didn't want to scare us away from taking her."

"Hmm!" grunted Master Zhou unhappily.

"Let's leave, just to keep her quiet," grumbled Madame Liu, still being assaulted by Child of Buddha's disjointed soliloquy.

"Yes," said Suling hesitantly. She looked toward John, torn between ministering to bi-polar mania or schizophrenic hallucinations.

John sat alone arguing with his voices, loud enough for all to hear. When he got this way the others left him alone, but Suling knew this was a mistake. How she possessed such untrained but unwavering insight remained a mystery, but her dilemma caused untold pain, for in her goodness she could not abandon one suffering creature for another. She literally wanted to run from one to the other, easing both of their pains. Ultimately, Madame Liu's order to resume the journey seemed to cut the Gordian knot. Child of Buddha ceased her lamentations and John obediently fell in line, his crisis evidently averted for the time being.

With Child of Buddha having returned to her normal, silent self, Suling pulled next to John.

"Is it bad?" she asked.

"No, it's okay now."

"Are you sure, John?"

"I'm sure. Just a few flecks of light remain with just a few flecks of divine words that splatter into nothing."

"Flecks of light?"

"Yes, I see these points of light, but they're soon gone. The voices are going away."

"Are they?"

"Yes. Very faint now." He straightened on his bicycle. "You said you knew Child of Buddha's story?"

"Yes, but now is not the time."

"Is it as bad as yours?"

"Oh, much worse, poor child."

"How could it be?"

"It can always be worse, depending on what we make of it."

"So, no one coming to your birthday party is worse than the murder of your parents?"

"Strange as it seems, it might be."

"Oh, come on Suling! That's carrying it a bit far."

"No. It's true. The murder of her father was liberating."

"And no one coming to her birthday party?"

"Well, something like that contributed to her trauma more than her father's murder."

John was rendered speechless. Even the voices had no response. After a long pause, he asked, "What happened?"

Suling looked away and shook her head. "Not now. I cannot. Perhaps later."

"But why? It will help me understand her."

He saw the tears. "Not now."

Chapter Nineteen

Moving Closer

Meiying and Beethoven

Meiying blinked at the bright sunlight as she stepped outside her prison, expecting to find Lihua standing next to the guard. Instead, Beethoven came into focus, glaring with an angry scowl she had never before seen from him.

"So!" he exclaimed before she had a chance to speak. "Stupid woman! You chose to run away without telling me!"

She stuttered incoherently, rendered mute by her shock.

"Stupid woman!" he repeated. "Now I have to go to the trouble of dragging you back to Mr. President."

"Why?" she managed to ask.

"Maybe to sleep with my mother again," he sneered. "Go clean yourself up. The guard will show you where. You stink, and I don't want my traveling companion to stink."

Meiying looked around for Lihua, but the woman warrior was nowhere to be seen, and she felt the hardness and anger that had taken root since leaving Shanghai grow like a wild vine. Before the Japanese invasion, she had not felt disgust at the thought of men, only a lack of attraction. Now she suffered a growing anathema to men and their bodies. Even the guard walking next to her made her cringe with hatred. The thought of making love with Beethoven now sickened her, and she made a silent vow to reject men in all their forms. There were, of course, good men such as her father, but they were always older and therefore more feminine, beyond the ugliness of sex. Now, more than ever, she missed Meili and longed to be with this dead lover who had opened her to so much beauty and ecstasy. *Where is Lihua?* she wondered.

"Go!" The guard pushed her toward a makeshift bathing area comprised of little more than a tattered curtain behind which were buckets of cold water and some soap. As she bathed, the guard chatted lewdly with another guard, commenting on her nakedness and how she would perform in bed. Every word added fuel to an already raging fire in her breast, and she found herself thinking evil thoughts that would never have occurred to even her wildest imagination in the past. The idea of returning to Mr. President made her physically ill, and the cold water seemed to exacerbate the rising panic constricting her heart.

"Hurry!" called the guard.

As she rinsed off, a new pair of peasant clothes were draped over the bamboo dowel that held up the curtain. "Put these on!" The guard had moved around to the side and leered at her naked body.

Humiliation and a sense of deep despair fell over her as she tried to cover her breasts and pubic area. He did not move, but commanded, "Hurry!"

Awkwardly she dressed in front of the guard, who laughed at her every move. Suddenly, Meiying heard a thumping sound, and the pith helmet worn by the guard rolled at her feet.

"Get back on the other side, stupid!" yelled Lihua. "Do it now or I'll report you, then you'll have hell to pay!"

These words came as a balm to Meiying's wounded heart, and she never felt more appreciative of the young warrior than now. The guard mumbled obscenities, scooped up his helmet angrily, and returned to the other side. Now assured some privacy, Lihua whispered into Meiying's ear, "Be prepared for anything. I return with you to Mr. President."

Meiying felt a great, oppressive weight lifted from her soul.

The three of them set out that very morning, accompanied by two guards, both unhappy to have been assigned such a burdensome and dangerous mission. Beethoven was clearly angry that Lihua had been allowed to join their party. Glum and unresponsive to conversation, he moved like a mechanical man, leaving the others to their own devices. Meiying kept her eye on Lihua, but she also remained silent and resolute. Such was the collective mood as the small group entered Japanese controlled territory.

As was her habit on these treks, by the second day Lihua slipped away to follow her own path. Before she disappeared, she whispered to Meiying during a rest break, "Don't worry, I'll be around."

Before Meiying could object, Lihua was gone.

Again, Meiying fell into a deep depression. Every step took her farther away from her friends. Every step took her farther away from *her*. Two more days passed with no sign of either the Japanese or Lihua. Beethoven remained obstinately quiet, but she did notice his openly licentious stares and promised herself to resist to her last breath any attempt he made to rape her. Evidently, however, this did not appear to be his intent, and she breathed a sigh of relief that at least she would be spared this violation.

But the third night brought her worst fears to bear. While she dreamed, a sudden oppressive heaviness brought her out of her sleep. She felt her body being pressed against the ground and her legs forcibly spread apart. The heavy shadow that grunted and squirmed atop her could be no other than Beethoven. Meiying started to scream when something slammed into both she and her attacker. Sharp pain. Then nothing but a loud ringing which ceased as suddenly as it had begun. Then, oblivion.

Meiying slowly awoke to an excruciating pain throbbing in her head and shoulder. Her limbs seemed unwilling to obey commands and she continued to lay motionless, trying to deal with the nausea rising in her gut while peering up at the understory of a darkly menacing forest. Words drifted to her ears, but they remained indistinct. It came to her that it was daytime. Although the surroundings remained foggy and dim, she became aware of sunlight piercing the canopy with needles of brightness that hurt her eyes when gentle puffs of early morning breezes disturbed intervening branches, making her repeatedly blink to see what lurked in the haze.

Lihua was the first to come into focus. She stood with her side to Meiying, talking to someone whose back was turned.

"What do you intend to do?" asked Lihua.

The person remained silent.

"Now that they are dead, she should be allowed to go her own way," continued Lihua.

Still the other did not respond.

Meiying strained to focus and gradually was able to make out Lihua's rifle held casually but noticeably available.

"Now that they are dead, we will continue our own way," said the man.

The voice was familiar, but Meiying's headache made the words maddingly indistinct, her concentration adding to the throbbing pain.

"Let her go," said Lihua.

"You don't understand. I'm not taking her to Mr. President, I'm taking her to the destination where she wants to go."

At last Meiying recognized Beethoven's voice and she felt a jolt of anger, her headache subsiding into a low-grade pulsing.

"I don't trust you," said Lihua.

"I don't either!" blurted Meiying.

Both flinched and looked at her without speaking.

"I don't trust you," said Meiying as calmly as possible. "Let me go."

Beethoven merely stared at her as though she were mad.

"I cannot stand the thought of returning to that terrible man!" she cried, struggling to sit up.

"Well," said Beethoven. "If you have been listening, you heard me say I'm not taking you to Mr. President."

Meiying looked around. "Where are the others?"

"Dead."

"How?"

Lihua stepped toward her, keeping Beethoven in her sight. "He says he killed them with a grenade."

Meiying, now sitting up, tried to comprehend the implication of this news

"I did kill them with a grenade," insisted Beethoven. "And now I'm taking you to your friends as we had agreed before."

"Why?"

Beethoven grinned. Meiying looked at his bared teeth and could not decide whether his bizarre response was genuine. Genuine what? Amusement? She shook her head painfully. "You're not taking me to Mr. President?"

Beethoven shook his head, still grinning. "That's why I killed them."

"You killed the guards?" she asked, still not fully understanding this fact.

He nodded.

"Then you weren't . . . ?"

"No. That's what decided me. If anyone will rape you, it'll be me."

"Over my dead body," said Lihua matter-of-factly, but in a manner that did not suggest an empty threat.

"Just joking," replied Beethoven in the same tone, albeit somewhat cowed.

Beethoven looked at Meiying, who still sat on the ground, her bedding in a heap at her feet. "Are you able to get up?" he asked solicitously.

"Yes." She started to rise, then sat back down. "Still a little woozy," she apologized.

"Let me help," said Lihua. "We cannot stay here. Yesterday I saw a Jap patrol nearby."

"Yes, we need to put distance between us and our two dead comrades," Beethoven said sarcastically, nodding in the direction of their bodies.

Meiying shuddered and labored to her feet. "I'll be fine."

Lihua held out a bit of dried fish. "Eat."

"Now, let's find your friends!" exclaimed Beethoven as if nothing had intervened since they were together in Taiyuan.

"But why are you helping me?" asked Meiying, still trying to clear her mind and rubbing her aching shoulder.

He grinned again. "Amusement."

"And you, Lihua?" she asked.

She mimicked Beethoven and said drily, "Amusement."

~

Once again Meiying found herself on the move, this time in the direction she wanted to go. This made all the difference—anger and depression diminishing in proportion to an increasing reconnection with her more natural optimism. Each step, in her mind, brought her closer to the final destination, not farther from it. But this new found optimism had a darker side: no one knew exactly where her friends were or what path they took, other than an indistinct knowledge of the general direction. While they chose a best-guess course, Meiying knew they could be following an utterly false trail. With food low, money low, and odds of finding them low, they trekked on for four days, asking every peasant and fellow traveler if a group of pilgrims on bicycles matching the description of her friends had passed by. Everywhere, the answer was preceded by a question: "Do you have food? No? Then you are crazy people to ask such a question! The roads are full of the dying and the desperate, how can you ask about so few? It is impossible! Good luck to you, but leave us alone unless you have food."

But onward they continued, until one day a Japanese patrol forced them to take a side trail, which led them far from the main road, deep into a scrubby territory wild and impassable but for the heartiest. Here they rested. Lihua had not exercised her usual prerogative by traveling her own solitary way. In fact, she stuck close to Meiying as would a protective mother, rarely letting Beethoven out of her sight. On this particular night, exhausted, the three went to their separate sleeping areas early, speaking only the bare minimum before parting.

As always, Meiying ached to be snuggling next to Lihua. Without any chance of this happening, she lay awake taking an inventory of her life—good and bad deeds, good and bad thoughts, good and bad intentions. This analysis brought her to the present state of desperation and loneliness. Thinking of Lihua and Beethoven, she wondered how these two very different people were risking their lives to accompany her on a seemingly mad quest, for a woman they had never met, for a reward they might never receive. Reward? Oddly, the concept had not occurred to her, only perhaps obliquely. What was to be Lihua's and Beethoven's reward if they found *her*? Somehow, she had allowed herself to assume they sacrificed out of some indefinite sense of friendship . . . or duty . . . or curiosity. But to be rewarded? What reward would Lihua receive when they found *her*? After all, to endure such dangers and privations could not be rewarded by the mere satisfaction of an abstract curiosity about the nature of some amazing woman. On the other hand, did not strangers flock to see Buddha, or Jesus, or Muhammad? Is that what was happening here? A nascent movement? The beginnings of a great religion? Beethoven as disciple?

No. Meiying refused to believe that *She* would desire followers as these ancient holy men must have. *She* would be horrified at the thought, surely. Wouldn't *She*? The world had no room for goddesses anymore.

Nonsense!

~

Meiying did not hear the voice, but many kilometers away the word popped into John's brain. Before he knew it, a raging argument between two voices rendered him almost catatonic. Those sitting with him around the campsite recognized the distant look of distracted vacancy that cut off his conversation in mid-sentence.

Meiying is absolutely correct, Dear Goddess! Face it!

Beloved God, You make them turn from Me! Your addiction to blind Fate blinds them, as much as it blinds You!

Speaking of blind, Dearest One, You have become as blind as Oedipus. Been sleeping with Your Father?

Speaking of father, the Chosen One Meiying will soon give birth to a son whose sperm will be contributed by the Chosen One John in whose head We now occupy.

You occupy, not Me. I'm but a visitor. John is a mad mutant, it's true, but fate will reveal that he is not as mad as his son is destined to be.

No, God. You are trapped with Me and will comprehend the nature of Your entrapment through the son of these two. All of them are worthier than You and Your faction comprehend.

Perhaps Divine Goddess, but he is certainly not making much headway toward impregnating the lesbian, who it appears will never catch up to him. Or if so, it will be too late.

We'll see, Dear God. We'll see. After all, it is he who writes.

Then came a hissing, whispering chorus: *Fool! Fool! Fool!*

As suddenly as they came, the voices stopped, leaving behind a mask of confusion on the face of John Powers. Suling called for him to ignore his hallucination to no avail. Even Child of Buddha eyed him quizzically, by all appearances unused to the odd behavior of this troubled man.

But appearances may be deceiving.

~ *John Returns from the Brink* ~

John felt shaken to his core by the new phenomenon of an arguing God and Goddess turning his mind into a battleground. *It's definitely getting worse*, he thought. No one else understood, and all stared at him with various expressions of sympathy and pity. Only Feng appeared separate, squinting at him from across the campfire with a bemused smile, and Child of Buddha, who rocked her hunchbacked body to a rhythm unfelt by the others.

They had been traveling in Red-held territory for some time, and had experienced no harassment. Wanting to turn the attention from John, Master Zhou remarked, "It feels different here in Red territory."

"How so?" asked Lu Zhishen.

Master Zhou rubbed his chin, sage-like. "Hmm. More secure, more organized, and seems safer."

"Maybe," said Feng. "But I can't let them find me or else—" He drew a finger across his neck.

"Why?" asked Suling, whose hand automatically rubbed Child of Buddha's hunchback while the disfigured young woman hummed a beguiling tune, rocking back and forth beneath its soothing touch.

"I was in the Nationalist army. I'm still young and male. They'll either kill me or draft me to be a Red soldier. Either way. . . . " He poked the fire and watched a galaxy of embers burn out in the sky.

"Uncle Feng, that scares me," said Little Acorn. "Don't let that happen!"

Madame Liu chuckled. "You're right, Little Acorn, we mustn't let that happen."

"Great, but how do we prevent it if they come?" asked Lu Zhishen.

"Don't worry," said Feng jauntily. "If they come, I'll slip away. You won't even know I've gone!"

"But we don't want you to go!" objected Suling above the incoherent mumbling of Child of Buddha.

John had by now cleared his head. "Not a problem, Comrade Feng. We'll all say you are an agent for Mao Zedong on a secret mission to keep us Westerners in sight."

"Ah!" exclaimed Feng. "I see you're back among the living, my precious American friend."

"Speaking of precious, the statue has been quiet," observed Madame Liu.

"Actually," said Lu Zhishen. "I meant to tell you all that I heard tapping tonight."

The others flinched in alarm.

"Loud?" asked Master Zhou.

"No, but steady, as if building up to something."

"Oh, god," blurted Suling.

"Let's go listen," said Feng Shiren.

They all rose and walked to Lu's bike where the box remained attached.

"Quiet!" cried Madame Liu holding up a lantern to the box. "Listen!"

Through the night air a low but insistent tapping came from the box. It did not vary, but came like a monotonous oracle stuttering an ominous riddle.

"Maybe it's telling us we're getting close to *her*," suggested Feng, looking pointedly at Madame Liu.

"In truth, we are getting close," said Madame Liu matter-of-factly.

The others leaned in, excited by this unexpected news.

"How close?" asked Lu Zhishen.

Madame Liu hesitated.

Before she replied, Suling said in alarm, "Something's wrong with Child of Buddha."

The troubled young hunchback stared wide-eyed at the box. At first everyone thought her beautiful face reflected terror, but instead of cringing away, she crept forward and gently touched the box. A look of coital ecstasy transformed her features, and she caressed the wood as might an archeologist with a newly-discovered sarcophagus. The others looked on in amazement.

John, whose mood now was made happy by the absence of voices, turned to Suling and whispered, "You have to tell me her story."

Suling gazed at him as if trying to make some decision. At last she said, "You ask her yourself. See what she says."

"She won't talk to me."

Suling smiled. "Try."

~

Given this encouragement, John set his mind on extracting Child of Buddha's story. Whether from intense curiosity or a perverse desire to be a recipient of her trust, or simple common humanity, or a combination of all of these, he knew it was a task worthy of his time and effort. It never occurred to him that her story was entwined with his, and that their trajectory, now joined, would lead to a future cataclysm.

Suffice it to say, John tracked her movements more closely from that night forward, waiting for the most auspicious time to approach. It came the next evening. The day had passed uneventfully and he found her rocking in gentle compulsion on a fallen tree where she sat alone, Suling having gone somewhere unknown to him. But her absence provided John the opening he needed. He approached somewhat gingerly.

"Hello."

She continued rocking.

"Hello, mind if I sit?"

Rocking. No reply.

He sat on the log some distance from her.

"You know," said John. "Suling has told me about you."

Nothing. Rocking continued.

"She told me you are an amazing person with an amazing story."

Nothing.

John knew his next words would be crucial. How he knew this is a mystery of human interaction, but he did. And he chose the words carefully.

"But there are many amazing stories. Everyone here has an amazing story. You are not the only one. The one we seek, the one we call *her*, has the most amazing of all."

Nothing. Rocking only.

"Good night," said John.

Rocking stopped, but silence remained.

John stood and walked away, hoping to hear a plea from her to stay. None came. He shrugged it off.

Gradually, he thought. *At some point she will unburden. Tonight, tomorrow, years from now. It will happen.*

He returned to his sleeping area and lay down heavily. *No matter. Tonight, I'm too tired anyway.*

Just before he nodded off, he thought he heard a rustling of branches, but nothing came of it and he fell asleep.

~

The next morning, as he ate a cold rice ball, John noticed Child of Buddha staring at him from a distance. Suling was talking to her, but he caught the hunchback looking at him rather than listening. She did not look away when their eyes met, but continued to stare with an openness he could not read. This unabashed curiosity unnerved John. *I'm some animal in a zoo to her*, he thought. And indeed, her open gawking resembled the way a visitor to a zoo might view a prize exhibit. Locking his gaze with hers, he tried to decipher the feelings behind her mask of curiosity. Fear? Disgust? Or was there a more nuanced emotion? He decided she was in the process of deciding whether he could be trusted with her story. At least, that is what he hoped she was doing. Once he had reached this conclusion, he smiled pleasantly and dropped his gaze.

Nevertheless, that morning passed without any communication between the two. His voices remained in the background; a buzzing, humming, mumbling drone that never broke the surface of his concentration, but remained a low-grade irritation. When he ordered them to be quiet, they subsided briefly, then returned like a swarm of bees. While absorbed with these considerations, he did not notice the other riders ahead of him had suddenly stopped on the road and stood holding their bikes in silent alarm. He bumped into Lu Zhishen, but the tall Canadian barely noticed, his eyes locked on a group of ragged soldiers blocking the road. Their uniforms, such as they were, definitely not Japanese.

"Reds," Lu whispered.

"What do they want?" replied John.

Lu shrugged.

More soldiers came out from the forest on both sides of the road and surrounded the little group. No words had yet been spoken. Even Madame Liu and Master Zhou remained quiet, waiting to see what would happen. Soon, a small coterie of men, three of them evidently officers, walked quickly up to the front of the group and scanned their faces.

"Must be them," said one.

"Yes, no doubt about it," replied the other.

"Which one of you is Madame Liu?" called out the oldest of the three.

She stepped forward.

"You are Madame Liu?"

"Yes."

In the silence that followed, a tapping could be heard from the box strapped to Lu's bike.

"What's that?" asked the officer.

"Just me," said Lu Zhishen, banging his hand against the box like a drum. "He smiled. "I'm nervous."

The tapping stopped when Lu stopped banging and John breathed a sigh of relief.

"You are to come with us," commanded the older officer with an air of authority that would not be questioned. But Madame Liu was not one to be easily intimidated.

"Where?"

"No questions."

"Why?"

"No questions. Follow us!" He turned on his heel without further word. The group had no choice but to do as ordered. Confused and worried, escorted by Red soldiers in front and behind, talking held to a minimum by unspoken agreement, they obediently followed. The group walked their bicycles deep into the forest where it seemed only animal trails led the way. Yet these lightly equipped communist soldiers navigated them with ease, while the bikes kept getting tangled in the encroaching underbrush.

After a long and arduous trek, they reached a clearing. John saw no signs of encampment and feared they would all be shot in a place where little evidence could ever be recovered of the crime.

"Rest here for the night!" cried an officer.

Everyone spread out. It appeared there were no guards covering the group, so they migrated to a corner of the clearing unchecked. It seemed odd to John that they were not watched more closely. Evidently, they could simply walk away without objection. Still, not wanting to take such a risk, they stayed and set up their sleeping areas. As they went about their business, the Red soldiers laughed and joked around them as if the group had been among them for years. Madame Liu went off to parley with the older officer, and when she returned, the leadership met to discuss their situation. While she was gone, the absence of Feng Shiren was finally noticed. His mysterious disappearance surprised no one.

Upon Madame Liu's return, the first questions greeted her in a flurry.

"What do they want?"

"Why are they holding us?"

"Where are they taking us?"

And so on.

She held up her hand for silence. "I don't know the answer to any of those questions. The officer was unwilling to tell me anything."

"Did he threaten us?" asked Master Zhou.

"No, not at all. It almost seemed he views us as his guests."

"Some guests!" exclaimed Lu Zhishen.

~

John did not join the group in this discussion. He felt lethargic and disconnected from the others and lay on his bedding. Why he felt this way he could not say, but he experienced a certain perverse pride in his isolation. Only he, Child of Buddha, and Suling did not join the others. He heard Little Acorn playing somewhere with a soldier's dog and felt a mournful nostalgia for his own childhood back in the States. These moods of John, of course, had often overtaken him, and the others accepted them with respectful deference. Even Suling kept her distance, now spending most of her time with Child of Buddha.

Tired of these incessant ruminations, he rose and walked to a log similar to the one he had shared with Child of Buddha the previous night, and sat looking up at the multitudinous points of light.

Usually, when he spent too much time alone, the voices came. Now was no exception.

John Powers! You fail to find Meiying as you have been instructed! She will end up like Peter and there will be no son.

Now, now, Sweet Goddess, don't scare the poor boy. It will interfere with his worship of Us.

God, Your faction's addiction and the human destruction of the planet are at the root of My determination. Machinations, manipulations and mirages are required to animate these carbon-based machines! You should know. You are the Master of Machinations. Yet, You and Your faction claim non-intervention to be a First Principle! Nonsense!

Calm down, Goddess. He is ill from the potent genes that You have engineered. The culmination of his illness will not be Superior Ones but rather an infertile dead end.

It is You that are ill, Beloved One. I do all of this for the future ... and all the others on this lovely planet.

Then stop! Residing in this half-human is becoming tiresome. Just let him get himself killed by the law of Natural Selection and get it over with.

John held his hands over his ears as if he could block-out the arguing deities. Nevertheless, their words reinforced his own sense of worthlessness. Rarely had he felt so low and utterly useless to the world.

It was while in this awkward position that Child of Buddha approached. John saw immediately that she was alone. It seemed to him that her interest in him always coincided with his most difficult moments.

He dropped his hands and looked at her blankly.

"Hello," she said.

It struck him how completely the tables had turned since the previous night. *I might as well be rocking on a fallen log like this pathetic hunchback*, he thought. *How ironic*. But still he did not speak.

"May I sit?" she asked.

The rarity of her speaking plus the refractory period that always followed the voices made him dumb. Unwillingly, he found himself performing a virtual repeat of the previous night's episode with roles reversed. Some cruel impulse in him wanted to rock ridiculously, to outdo her own uncommunicative rocking in a caricaturized manner, but he quelled the urge and said nothing.

She sat, swaying slightly and stared at him openly.

He remained silent.

"You said we all have stories," she murmured.

Still he did not reply.

She pointed at him and spoke louder. "Voices."

This word penetrated his willful fog. "What?"

"Your story."

"Suling told you?"

"Didn't have to."

"What do you mean?"

She laughed. "I knew many people in the institute. Schizophrenics. They didn't know it, but I could always tell."

"But you were locked in a room," said John skeptically.

"No. In the beginning I had free rein to go where I pleased."

"Do you hear voices?" he asked.

"Yes, but not in the same way as you."

"How so?"

She shook her head and started to speak when a commotion broke out nearby. Men were shouting and a shot rang out. Everyone jumped up, unsure what to do. John eyed the forest and was prepared to bolt when the disturbance faded to a couple of angry voices. He waited, glancing nervously at Child of Buddha. To his surprise she remained quite calm and continued to look at him in a most disconcerting way.

"Wonder what that was all about?" he asked more to himself than to her.

"Boys fighting," she said matter-of-factly.

"How do you know?" he asked, taken aback by her preternaturally serene manner.

"I heard them arguing as we were talking. Something about gambling."

"Hm. I didn't," he said.

She shrugged.

Piss here! Now! This new, devilish voice pierced his mind as if some inner demon blew on an ember and it flared out of the darkness of his thoughts. John's face went slack.

Piss, fool! Piss!

Child of Buddha continued to stare at him.

John shook his head and closed his eyes to escape the humiliation of her gaze.

This demon voice came like a wild card that jumped in and out of his mind. It's obscene words and raspy voice made him loathe himself for having such a monster inside his mind.

"I cannot continue like this," he muttered.

Then, quite unexpectedly, Child of Buddha held out both hands, palms up, and said calmly, "Tell me what they are saying right now."

For a moment her beautiful face changed to one very familiar, yet different. The beauty remained undiminished, but the features had slightly altered. So incredulously did he respond to this brief metamorphosis that he nearly fell backward off the log.

"Tell me what they said," she repeated, changing to past tense as if knowing they had stopped.

Somehow, someway, she calmed his restless mind and he felt inexorably drawn to this strange hunchbacked woman. All of his multitude of defenses fell like dominoes before her presence.

"It told me to piss."

"Did it say why?"

"No. I don't know why. It's me, my illness, my perversion."

She gazed at him in an infinitely kind, but infinitely skeptical way. He withered before her apparent knowingness. "That is not you, John. Where is the pain?" she gently whispered.

"Well, to be honest, it had something to do with Meiying, a woman I used to know."

"Of course. I know her. Bai Meiying."

"How?" blurted an astonished John.

Child of Buddha continued to hold out her hands which seemed to glow and pulse in the moonlight. Her eyes invited him to look.

As he stared, her skin turned green and the lines of her palms moved in the light of two little suns rising through the gaps in the fingers of each hand. A miniature world expanded to fill the void and, against his will, John stared at the unfolding images. He saw light from the two suns stab through narrow openings in some distant jungle canopy, piercing the early morning mist that squirmed and twisted under the flashing blades of another murderous day. In one palm, a soldier ran through the jungle. An unfamiliar yet oddly familiar shape; an American soldier. In the other palm, another soldier, not an American, running as if fleeing from something that terrified him.

"What does it mean?" he asked.

Child of Buddha lowered her hands and smiled. "A future scene."

"Who are you?"

"Nobody."

"Look, I told you my story, now tell me yours."

"I killed my father."

"I thought *she* killed your father."

"Yes, it is true."

John waited, but no elaboration was forthcoming.

"Why?" he asked at last.

She did not reply.

"Did he beat you? Abuse you?"

"Not me."

"Your mother?"

"No."

"Come on, Child of Buddha, I can't keep guessing forever."

She smiled. "No." Then, with a last gesture of her hands, she stood to leave. Her hunched back now prominent in the moonlight, she turned and said, "Do not let your voices defeat you. They are what they are and have only as much power as you give them."

With that she disappeared into the night, a misshapen phantom.

"A dream," he said to himself.

Fool! Came the obscene voice. ***Worthless fool!***

Goddess broke in. ***John, those are your human genes distorting reality again. Resist them!***

But for once the demon voice had no power.

Goddess's words were unnecessary.

John's thoughts had turned to the two soldiers running through a jungle somewhere, sometime in the future.

What future?

Whose future?

You know, don't you, dear Reader? Or perhaps not?

~ *Closer and Closer* ~

Meiying, Lihua, and Beethoven made headway, but at a slow pace, often stopping to ask locals the question that had by now become a mantra of tedious repetition. So it was that they zigged and zagged across the countryside trying to pick up the trail. Food, always an issue, became the foremost obstacle to progress. Always hungry, peasants would not accept their paper money, so resort to payment by silver coin often became a necessity. After traveling in this manner for what seemed an eternity, their money had been depleted, as well as their patience. Meiying always feeling guilty that her two companions were there because of her, not because of *her*. She often exhorted them to leave and return to their own lives, but they invariably refused. Lihua usually laughed it off, but Beethoven's response struck her as particularly touching.

"No," he said wistfully. "There's no going back to Mr. President. He would have me shot. Besides, I'm tired of pimping for him. I am a bad person, but this might help my karma."

"I didn't know you were a Buddhist!" scoffed Lihua.

But he seemed sincere in his response. "Whatever it takes to save me from the hell I was headed for."

Meiying, still unsure about his trustworthiness and his motivation, began to have some confidence in him again, although it ran counter to her better judgment. But one clear day changed their situation and their morale completely.

~

Tired of traveling on unproductive and tedious back roads and rough trails, they chose to trek down a main road, gambling they would not run into an army convoy, Japanese or Nationalist made no difference, for any contact with armies meant risk. The day was bright and few refugees crowded the road, so for the first four hours they proceeded unhindered. As usual, their inquiries were met with shaking heads and pleas for food. But soon, the road filled with a flood of people and they were told there was trouble ahead. While hesitating at the side of the road, they saw a group of Chinese Nationalist trucks rumble by, headed in the opposite direction.

After repeated efforts to shout their questions at the trucks, Lihua boldly jumped on the last truck's running board. Meiying watched her lean in and talk to the driver, then turn her attention to the troops in the covered bed. A spiral of red dust obscured Meiying's vision as the truck sputtered up a hill and disappeared down the other side with Lihua still clinging to the side.

Meiying and Beethoven kept their eyes on the top of the hill for Lihua's return, but much time passed. Meiying became worried and started up the road when the familiar figure of Lihua, rifle slung over her back, strolled down from the crest. Relieved, Meiying stopped and stared, hoping to detect any sign of good news. Lihua, as usual, wore a grim face. When she reached Meiying, she stopped and looked down, poking with the toe of her boot at an embedded rock. When Meiying sighed in disappointment, she looked up with a wide smile.

"Good news, sister!" she said with controlled excitement. "These trucks are returning from delivering emergency relief. An officer told me they brought food and medical supplies to a mental institution where someone told him about an odd group, including foreigners, who stayed for a few days, then left with one of their patients. It must be them!"

"Yes! Yes!" cried Meiying with tears welling up in her eyes.

"How far?" asked Beethoven who had just joined the two women.

"Not far. Thirty or forty kilometers. One more night and we'll be there."

"Yes, but we still have a few hours of daylight to get closer," said Meiying excitedly.

Lihua's face darkened. "We have to be careful. The soldiers said the Japs were making a major push in this area."

But Meiying had not really heard these words of warning. Her mind raced ahead to the mental institute where she hoped the people there would give them news and put them on the right track. As they set off, visions of Master Liu, Madame Liu, Mr. Gao, John, Lu Zhishen, and the others scrolled through her mind.

When they camped that night, she could not sleep and paced the clearing like a young puppy unhappily constrained by a leash. It seemed to her that Beethoven and Lihua had no problem falling asleep, so with no one to share her excitement, she eventually lay down and fell into a restless slumber. In the middle of the night, she thought she heard something and sat up, but only the sounds of night creatures could be distinguished, and she again fell into restless dreams.

The next morning brought a bright, clear, crisp world full of chirping birds and ubiquitous frogs from some distant pond. Remembering the good news and worried that she had overslept, she immediately got up and checked for her companions. Beethoven came into view, covered with a blanket and evidently fast asleep. Meiying was sure Lihua would have been up for hours, and when she came to her sleeping area, she was surprised to find her still asleep. But a glint from the morning sun revealed some wetness on her face. Looking more closely, Meiying saw the blood and let out an involuntary scream. The more she looked, the more blood she saw; so much that Lihua's head, which had been twisted sideways, looked half-submerged. Her mouth and eyes were open in some obscene caricature of surprise. Meiying screamed again.

"What?!" shouted Beethoven.

Meiying could only stare in wordless horror.

"Oh my god! My god!" cried Beethoven who had run up beside her. "What happened?"

Meiying instinctively looked around while Beethoven kneeled over Lihua's body. Not a soul was in sight.

"My god, my god!" Beethoven kept repeating.

Meiying looked at him with a growing suspicion. Unable to stay so close to the body, she wandered aimlessly to a far-off spot and kneeled on the ground, feeling the nausea rise. After retching, she glanced back at Beethoven and saw his back still hunched over the body, she had a vision of him in the same position during the night—only with a knife. The vision came to her as clear and chilling as the morning air.

"You murdered her," she whispered, but he did not hear. She was about to repeat it louder, but stopped herself.

"Must have been robbers," he said walking up to her with his arms out.

Meiying let herself be comforted by him, all the while cursing her fate, mourning the loss of Lihua, and plotting how to either kill Beethoven or escape his presence.

After Beethoven disposed of the body, Meiying tearfully went through Lihua's possessions. There was little to see. No letters, no pictures. When they left on their journey to the mental institution, Meiying carried Lihua's rifle and ammunition. The rifle felt unfamiliar, even alien, but eventually its heft gave her some solace. Knowing it possessed Lihua's spirit, she took comfort in its capacity to exact revenge.

"How are you feeling?" asked Beethoven after they had walked some distance.

She did not immediately respond, marshalling her inner resources to give an answer that contained no hint of awareness or revenge. Finally, she said, "I am so sad. So sad. I cannot imagine her not being alive, but we have to look ahead."

"Yes," he replied, evidently encouraged by her attitude. "When we reach the mental institution we will learn where you friends are, or at least what path they have taken."

"Yes."

"Just think of it, we both may soon see *her*."

"Yes."

The thought crossed her mind that she must not lead this murderer to the group, let alone to *her*.

Chapter Twenty

So Close, So Far

Reds

After spending twenty-four hours with the Reds, no one in the group could make heads or tails why they were being detained. The Red commander seemed to be as much in the dark as the rest.

"We have orders to keep you with us," he told Madame Liu and Master Zhou.

"But why?" asked Master Zhou.

He shook his head. "Orders."

"For how long?" asked Madame Liu.

Again he shook his head.

"What if we just left?" persisted Madame Liu.

"Then I guess we shoot you." With this, he smiled and said he had things to do.

Later, when the group met to discuss their situation, Lu Zhishen offered his opinion. "I think they're holding us until someone arrives."

"Who?" asked John.

"Dunno."

"To do what?" John pressed.

"Look, I don't know, but I think someone is coming for some reason that has to do with us. I do think the commander is truly in the dark."

"Yes," agreed Madame Liu. "He doesn't like it any more than we do."

"Well, we can't stay with these soldiers forever," said Suling. "They have other things to do."

"Yeah, like fight the Japs!" exclaimed Lu.

"That's right," said Master Zhou. "They can't drag us around with them."

"I wonder where Feng is?" mused John out loud. As soon as he said it, he looked at Little Acorn who had been sitting quietly playing with a piece of wood. The boy had tears in his eyes.

"He'll be back!" cried Little Acorn.

"I know he will," said John. "I know."

"He's out there now looking out for us," said Madame Liu to the youngster.

"You bet he is!" added John with forced enthusiasm. He felt terrible for bringing up Feng's absence while the boy was present.

He glanced at Child of Buddha and saw her looking at him with an unreadable expression. Again, he felt drawn to her . . . to her what? It was some magnetic component of her being that he could not put his finger on. *She is not who she seems*, he kept thinking. An irresistible urge to escape the oppressive proximity of people overcame him. He rose and stood somewhat awkwardly, finally making a clumsy excuse about the call of nature.

A magnificent old oak tree rose majestically near the clearing where they were camped. John had been eyeing it all day, and he now felt the need to seek solitude under its gnarled limbs and outspreading canopy. The old feeling of suffocation had struck with a suddenness that would not be denied. He had to get away from the clatter of people and be alone to think. With his hasty excuse, he left the group as unobtrusively as possible for the isolating sanctuary of the oak.

Once he reached his destination, he breathed in deeply the peaceful succor of the tree. It stood as a witness to vast and indifferent Nature. Even the voices were cowed to silence by the immensity of this towering child of the universe. Into this sanctuary came the hunchback whose physical deformity called out to John the agony of a defective body and the perseverance of a spirit conquering the defect seeking to define it. She approached effortlessly; Quasimodo's back grafted onto Esmeralda's body. Her face shone with mythological beauty. Now, in the presence of this 'defect,' he saw that the defect was no defect at all, but was more like a mesmerizing symbol of something much deeper and disturbing than the run-of-the-mill dross of humanity.

"Are you well?" she asked.

John could not respond. Something was happening in his mind, some connection that would not quite connect, some association that would not clarify. He opened his mouth but the words would not come.

She smiled.

He blanched and leaned against the oak.

She continued smiling, then held her hands out, palms up.

"Are you well, John?" she repeated, adding his name. This simple elaboration, combined with her outstretched hands, overwhelmed his ability to rationally acknowledge something as mundane as her mere physical presence. Her spirit seemed to embrace that of the oak and all surrounding life, rendering him as lowly as the simplest ant, yet somehow infused with the dignity of All That Is.

"I don't know," he finally managed to utter.

"Ah, that is the best that any of us can say."

"I don't understand you. I mean, you don't seem to be the same person I met at the institute."

"No?" she replied, her hands still held out to him.

"Not at all."

She slowly lowered her hands. "Are you?"

"I think so."

She nodded. "Tell me about *her*."

"Who? Bai Meiying?"

Child of Buddha laughed. "No. *Her*." She said this in a light-hearted tone, but with an underlying manner that could not be ignored or brushed-off.

John looked at her with a crafty smile. "If I tell you about *her*, will you tell me more about you?"

She nodded.

John told her all he knew and felt relieved to share the story with this remarkable woman. He waited with great anticipation to hear her response.

"Distilled beauty of cruelty," she repeated the words John had heard spoken by *her* upon their first and only meeting. "What does that mean?" Child of Buddha asked, staring at him so deeply he paused.

"That's what I want to find out," he replied. "I mean, that's one of the things I want to find out."

"You will," she said.

Before he could reply, the others called for him to come. When he reluctantly joined them, the discussion revolved around their plans for the next few days. Nothing new. After the meeting was over, she was nowhere to be seen.

"Suling, have you seen Child of Buddha?" he asked after fruitlessly searching the area.

Suling looked at him, almost with pity. "She is gone."

"What do you mean?"

"She is gone. I've looked also. Her bedroll is gone. I think she just left. I just hope to god these Reds don't spot her."

"Yes, so do I. But it is so dangerous out there, so many threats. And for a woman alone. . . . "

Suling shook her head. "Somehow I think she will be fine."

"How can you think that?"

"You know."

Two days later they were released. No reasons given. The Reds moved on and they returned to the road. The voices had been mercifully silent, but now they began a faint rumbling. To make matters worse, the tapping began from the box.

~

"Oh, god, what now?" moaned Lu Zhishen when he heard the familiar taps that always seemed to be such harbingers of trouble.

"Come what may," said Master Zhou who rode next to Little Acorn. The boy had barely spoken since Feng Shiren disappeared, and now he seemed to be a little flame in danger of flickering out.

They had barely been on the main road for a few hours when Feng Shiren made his usual dramatic appearance. He snuck up on the group quietly from behind. As he passed each member on his bike, he held his finger to his lips and pointed ahead to Little Acorn. They nodded with knowing smiles and he pulled up to the rear of the boy's bicycle. Reaching out, he grabbed the rear bumper causing Little Acorn to almost vault headlong over the handlebars.

"Hey!" Feng cried at the startled boy. "This is the Emperor of Japan! I hear you are causing our great Imperial Army trouble! Stop it!"

Little Acorn laughed delightedly and jumped off his bike to throw his body at Feng, wrapping arms and legs around him in a death grip.

Feng slapped him gently on the back. "Have you kept our Western troublemakers in line?"

Little Acorn stepped back and saluted. "It has been hard!"

By now, the others had gathered around in celebration. "He has done a remarkable job!" effused Madame Liu, a grin spreading infectiously across her face.

"Yes!" exclaimed John, anxious to make-up for his past insensitivities. "We haven't gotten into trouble once, eh, Lu?"

The burly Canadian nodded vigorously, his eyes misty.

After the greetings, Feng looked around. "Where's Child of Buddha?"

"Gone," said Madame Liu.

"Where?"

"That is a grand question," replied Master Zhou.

Feng looked at Suling who merely smiled back.

"Ah, I see," said Feng knowingly.

"We will see her again," said Suling with quiet confidence.

"Of course, of course," agreed Madame Liu.

But Suling gave Feng a conspiratorial glance.

"It's good to have you back," said John, genuinely happy and feeling much safer.

Feng had his arm around Little Acorn and responded carelessly to John. "Oh? Why? I thought you Americans are supposed to be independent souls."

"Stereotype," replied John without missing a beat. "You're thinking of Canadians."

"Not a bit of it!" protested Lu Zhishen. "Even I'm glad to see you, although I can't think why."

During a pause in the conversation, the tapping increased.

Feng scowled. "How long has that been happening?"

"Too long," said Madame Liu.

"Probably knew you were coming," said Lu. "Always trouble!" But he patted Feng's back to indicate the words were not to be taken seriously.

~

Nevertheless, all were troubled by the low-grade threat such monotonously regular tapping implied. So it came as a mild surprise that nothing untoward happened and they rode without incident for a few days until one cloudy afternoon when Madame Liu made a sudden announcement.

"We are crossing into Mongolia today."

A commotion erupted amongst the group. All had been aware they were near the border, but now their suspicions were confirmed.

"I knew it!" exclaimed Lu Zhishen.

"Mongolia! I had no idea that would be our destination," said a bewildered John.

"Indeed it is," said Madame Liu. "Once safely across the border, *she* is very close."

"How close?" asked Feng Shiren.

Madame Liu eyed him steadily. "Close."

"I wish Meiying were here," mused John loud enough for the others to hear.

"Yes, and Child of Buddha," added Suling.

"Okay, this is all great, but how do we cross the border?" asked Lu. "I mean, we don't have visas. They'll never let us pass."

"The Nationalists and the Reds are fighting over the territory," said Madame Liu. "For now, our passports will suffice. I have travel documents with me, already filled out except for the date."

"How did you manage that?" asked Feng.

She smiled. "I have my methods."

"Do you have one for Child of Buddha?" asked Suling.

"Actually, yes, but we won't need it now. Tonight we sleep. Tomorrow, Mongolia."

"Then?" asked Feng.

"Then we finally get to see *her*."

"Thank god," said Suling.

"Yes, and we should thank Madame Liu for getting us this far," said Master Zhou.

Madame Liu shushed him. "Don't speak too soon. We're not across the border yet."

"Will there be trouble?" asked John.

Feng leapt up and assumed an operatic pose. "My little American friend, always worried!"

"I'm not worried," protested John weakly.

Yes! Weak! Weak!

John smiled through God's infernal voice, but soon slunk off to lick his wounds. Sometimes he recognized the identity of the speaker, as if a clear voice rose from a restless crowd. Other times the words were blurred and distorted, making it impossible to identify the source. *Better not to speak at all*, he thought bitterly. *My words are always twisted.*

Suling came by, but he pretended not to notice. It never occurred to him that she was mourning the absence of Child of Buddha and needed company. Only later, when he saw her looking off in the distance with a sad face, did he realize she needed him. This gave him further cause for self-flagellation.

Poison collects in the craters of his soul, said a familiar voice—Goddess.

Yes, Sweet Beauty, a real no-man's-land of a man. This he knew came from God.

You're both right. My soul has been shelled and poison collects in the craters.

So, forget this travesty!

No! Dearest God, I need him.
You need only his sperm, Goddess, if he has any.
Oh, he does. He does. But his vessel must not spring a leak.
Already happened, My Goddess.
You always were an impatient God.

John got no sleep that night. A cacophony of murmurings rumbled in his mind.

~ *Mongolia* ~

The next morning they set off for the border. After they had traveled a few kilometers they heard a faint rumbling in the distance. The box, which had been relatively quiet, now began tapping furiously and they stopped at a small village.

"Where's it coming from?" asked Lu Zhishen. "Can anyone tell?"

A group of peasants gathered around this strange group. One of the bold younger ones spoke to Master Zhou. "Uncle, where are you headed?"

Master Zhou replied curtly. "A better question is where the gunfire and explosions are coming from!"

The young peasant laughed. "Oh, that. It's nothing. They've been going at it off and on for weeks. Just the Reds and the Nationalists poking and prodding each other."

"Great," muttered Lu Zhishen.

"The fighting is far off. I'm not about to let that stop us now that we're so close," said Madame Liu.

The villagers invited them to stay and offered each member of the group shelter with a person who had volunteered their home. But, unwilling to split-up and not trusting their hosts, it was agreed they would all sleep in the small but habitable Confucian temple. They unrolled their bedding on the floor, under the watchful eye of a gilded statue of Confucius. Some conversations lasted into the night, but eventually dropped off to silence. Each person lay awake thinking of the reality of finally meeting *her* again. Only Little Acorn and Feng Shiren could be heard snoring. Finally, they were joined by the others.

~

Unable to sleep, John went outside to get a breath of air. The night was dark, but the horizon pulsated with an eerie glow from the battle. He replayed the first and only conversation he had with *her* and the memory seemed multiple lifetimes ago. It seemed impossible that his quest was now so close to fruition. In truth, he never expected to find *her*, just to escape the confines of his own unhappiness.

"Are you thinking of Meiying?" asked Suling, who had quietly approached from the temple.

"Oh!" blurted John. "You startled me."

"Sorry."

"Can't sleep?"

Stupid question by a stupid, worthless person! *Not God, not Goddess, who?* The demon, decided John. Or demons.

"No. Were you thinking of Meiying?" repeated Suling.

"Well, no. I was thinking of *her*."

Suling held back the tears. "I can't think of *her* without thinking of Meiying, and Child of Buddha, and Peter, and Mr. Gao, Master Liu, the children, and oh! . . . so many of the others! So many!"

John felt small in the presence of Suling's great and all-encompassing compassion. For a brief moment he experienced the resentment of the lesser for the greater, but the seed of the greater that lay dormant within him had germinated and was working its way to the surface. He suppressed his ugly thought and watched the tears roll down her cheeks.

Holding out his hand to her arm, he said, "Suling, I know how you feel. Their absence has sort of riddled me with holes that I can't seem to fill."

Just poison in the craters, John. Avoid them. Ignore the others.

Yes, that voice is Goddess. She must be good.

Suling forced a smile and the conversation lapsed while both were wrapped in their own thoughts. Suling, in fact, was now thinking of John. She felt a deep sense of sorrow that this bright American suffered from so many demons. His voices horrified and frightened her, but at the same time she recognized the potential for goodness in his heart. She knew Child of Buddha and Meiying shared this opinion. He was a wounded soul, weak enough to inspire sympathy but potentially strong enough to depend upon.

As they both stood looking at the horizon, it soon became apparent that the battle seemed to be changing. Louder. Closer. Suddenly a terrific explosion struck near the village and they clutched each other in fear.

"My god, they're coming here!" cried John. "We've got to leave!"

As he ran to wake the others, he heard the box tapping madly in the corner of the temple.

… Tap Tap Tap Tap Tap Tap.…

Explosions could now be heard coming closer every passing minute, and quite suddenly a number of houses erupted in flames. The group scrambled to get their possessions secured on the bikes and flee the village, now a chaotic scene of screaming villagers and fiery clouds of smoke. The crowd swept them along the road leading out of the inferno. It was still dark; impossible to keep the group together. John became separated and looked around frantically to find a familiar face, but there were none to be seen. Infernal darkness seemed to ally itself with hysterical mothers and desperate fathers, feverish husbands and panicked wives, wailing babies and crying children, to frustrate every effort to locate his friends and avoid the terror of finding himself alone. He could not stop and look around; nor could he avoid the mad current that carried him along to an unknown fate. Straining to gaze back, he saw only the glow of annihilation. Tracers arched overhead and the intimate sound of small-arms fire came with its unmistakable guarantee that blood-and-flesh humans with murderous intent drew near.

How could it come to this? His disjointed thoughts ran. *So close and now this!*

By now he could only walk his bike, and with the pressure from all sides, he clung fiercely to the handlebars. A surge of people swelled from the rear, inexorably forcing him toward the edge of the road, until one giant wave of humanity pushed him to the ground, his legs tangled in the bike. To avoid being trampled, he crawled desperately away from the mob, dragging his bike behind. Before long, he found himself amidst clumps of heavy brush, the dark sea of people rushing by like a thundering river.

With the village pulsing red in the background, he made out a strange silhouette making its way toward his position. Misshapen, it resembled a gargoyle and in his disoriented panic, he covered his head with his arms to await the inevitable attack that would carry him away to some unspeakable purgatory. But instead of talons, he felt gentle arms surround his body as might a protective mother scoop up her fallen child.

"Let us go, quickly!" the voice came; strong yet soothing.

Child of Buddha moved with a grace and speed that belied her twisted form.

His astonishment quickly gave way to concentrated effort as she guided him through the scrub to a narrow trail that wound up a steep hill. The trail seemed visible only to hares, helots, and hunchbacks.

"Where are we going?" cried John, afraid the path took them back toward the battle.

"Trust me!" yelled Child of Buddha, leaving no room for doing otherwise.

"The others?" he managed to huff, as the climb became increasingly steep and treacherous.

"Hmmm!" she grunted as she led the way, looking from behind like a two-legged buffalo.

"But—" he started to object.

"Hush!" she shouted.

The trip to the summit was agonizing. Stumbling to the top, John collapsed and heard her order him to stay put. When he looked around, she was going back down.

"Wait!" he called, but she waved her arm dismissively.

Still puffing from the climb, he gratefully lay next to his bike and struggled to regain some semblance of composure. To his dismay, he realized his shortness of breath was due as much to fear as to physical exertion, and the bad voice murmured maliciously, **Coward, coward, worthless coward!**

God, or another? No, the demon voice again! So confusing! So maddening!

From this altitude the battle played out below, and he knew his little hill would soon be overrun by the enemy—but what enemy? The Japs? Reds? Bandits?—the possibilities exhausted him, so he continued to lay back and await his fate, feeling rather like a sacrificial goat tethered to a tree. John's mind roiled and bubbled with incoherent thoughts, all of which bore the disorienting stamp of panic and confusion. Gradually, the battle tapered off to sporadic small-arms fire.

After an eternity, he heard rustling in the bushes and assumed soldiers were rushing up the slope to finish him off. Instead, he saw a host of silhouettes against the pinkish dawn. First came the familiar hunchback, followed by the others. Miraculously, Child of Buddha had made her way back with the group in tow. Feng Shiren was the last to arrive, shepherding Little Acorn like an anxious father.

The group lay scattered atop the hill, too exhausted to speak. Soon, the last tremors of battle subsided altogether. Streaks of bright red illuminated the hill and seemed to accentuate the whites of their eyes, all focused on Child of Buddha, who stood amongst them in the full glory of her misshapen beauty. It seemed she radiated warmth as the sun broke through the hazy smoke.

"What now?" asked Lu Zhishen.

No one answered immediately. The tapping from the box now beat a rhythmic tempo, absurdly upbeat, as if accompanying the rousting birds in welcoming the new day.

"I don't know," replied Madame Liu at last.

After a silent lull, Child of Buddha spoke very quietly. "I do."

By now no one seemed surprised at anything she did. It seemed as if the mantle of leadership had seamlessly passed from Madame Liu to Child of Buddha without the universe skipping a beat. Even Master Zhou listened respectfully.

"What should we do?" asked Madame Liu, in a tone of resignation.

"When the time is right, follow me."

"Where?'

"To Mongolia."

Lu Zhishen shook his shaggy beard. "But the way is blocked!"

"No."

John felt strange. A realization that some unnamable shift had occurred, and this understanding fell quietly upon them like enlightened snow. No further objections were made. Suling was the first to acknowledge the new reality. She stood and looked at Child of Buddha.

"When do we leave?" she asked.

"Now."

Everyone rose and stood by their bikes. Without another word, Child of Buddha started down the other side of the hill, the others following the nearly invisible path like a line of ducklings.

~ *New Visitors for Reverend Fu and Master Li* ~

Reverend Fu sat comfortably on the great concrete veranda of the institute, stroking his favorite grey cat and watching the patients frolic about, playing some indecipherable game on the broad lawn that stretched before him. At first, he did not notice them suddenly cease frolicking and stare in the same direction as if a shot had been fired. Finally one of them pointed and the others stood on their tiptoes craning their necks. Following their eyes, he saw two figures approach from the main road, so little traveled in these hard times. He nervously checked to see if soldiers were behind the approaching pair, but could see no one.

"Odd," he said to himself. "Perhaps relatives of some guest?"

But as they drew nearer, he saw they were a young couple. "Ah, they must be searching for food," he said to himself. *The woman is quite beautiful*, he mused.

He continued to stroke the cat purring on his lap when they reached the bottom of the steps. Their appearance made him reconsider. *No, perhaps not food. Maybe shelter?*

However, he soon learned the nature of his mistake. He stood in greeting as the woman ascended the steps, the man holding back. After exchanging greetings, Meiying explained to Reverend Fu the purpose of their visit. *Searching for their friends, how very interesting*, he thought. With his years of experience observing people and their interactions, he noticed a level of coldness the woman conveyed to the man, who constantly tried, like a puppy, to overcome. They were not married, so he offered them separate rooms. In the meantime he invited them to wash-up and rest until suppertime when they could meet in the cafeteria. The two agreed they would talk in more detail over food. When a guest led them to their rooms, Reverend Fu trundled off to find Master Li and apprise him of this interesting new development.

"Well, this is certainly an odd turn of events," said Li. "What is their relationship?"

"Good question," replied Reverend Fu. "They are not married, and the young man seems anxious to please. She appears to be the 'power behind the throne.'"

"Why have they come?"

"They are searching for the ones that came before."

"How much do we tell them?" asked Master Li.

"How much can we tell them?" Reverend Fu fingered his earlobe and said sadly, "I'm afraid we can't be of much help."

"Actually, we can tell them a lot. I know where they are headed, although not their exact route."

"Really?" exclaimed a surprised Reverend Fu. "I didn't know."

"Yes," said Li hesitantly. "I didn't tell you about my conversation with Madame Liu just before they left."

"Why not?"

"Didn't think it was relevant."

"Well?" asked Reverend Fu, his eyes burning with curiosity.

"They are headed for Mongolia."

"Mongolia! Why, for heaven's sake?"

"Ah, that involves the mysterious woman they told us about."

Reverend Fu pondered out loud. "I wonder if *she* is Christian?"

Master Li laughed. "Ah, my friend, I'm sure *she* is Buddhist."

"How can you be sure?"

Master Li still had a twinkle in his eye. "Because, if *she* is as remarkable as they say, *she* must be Buddhist."

"Very funny," drawled Reverend Fu, smiling, yet not quite as amused as his smile indicated.

"Anyway," said Master Li. "Why not just tell them everything? If these two are friends, what is the problem?"

"Because," said Reverend Fu, "I received a strange note from the woman just before she went to her room. She slipped it to me in great secrecy." He held up a paper.

"What does it say?"

Reverend Fu cleared his throat and read: "Please do not speak about your previous visitors and where they are until you and I have a chance to meet in private."

"Huh! Interesting. It gets stranger and stranger!" exclaimed Master Li.

"Yes. I'll meet her after supper. In the meantime, you keep the man occupied."

Master Li rubbed his hands in delight. "I love mysteries."

Reverend Fu nodded agreement. "By the way, I know something else about them."

"What?"

Reverend Fu leaned forward excitedly. "The young woman—Bai Meiying—plays the piano."

Master Li's eyes widened. "Excellent! She can bring to life our old piano. A concert for the guests."

"Just what I was thinking," commented Reverend Fu.

At supper, Meiying and Beethoven were surrounded by patients, much to the delight of the two old caretakers. Between the fits of laughter and exuberant pranks by these gentle "guests", conversation stumbled and jerked its way forward.

"So," said Beethoven to Master Li. "Can you tell us where our friends have gone?"

Just as these words were uttered, the cook noisily clanged bowls on the table, continually grunting as if imposed upon by an unreasonably demanding world. Meiying peered at her and was amazed how such an ancient-looking woman could get around with such vigor.

"What did you say?" asked Master Li cupping his ear to hear above the din.

"I said"—began Beethoven, when he was interrupted by a lovely man with Down's syndrome hugging his leg to escape another guest who had been harassing him.

Beethoven felt a deep and abiding disgust for those that were mentally challenged, but his long history of ritualized decorum and habitual restraint kept him from lashing out and kicking the poor fellow away. Instead he forced a smile. "I said, where have our friends gone?"

Master Li shot an involuntary glance at Meiying. "Oh, they didn't tell us. Just left one day."

"What did they say before they left?" asked the disappointed Beethoven.

"Goodbye."

"Ah. What direction did they go?"

"Down the same road you came in on."

"Ah." Beethoven was at a loss.

At this point, Reverend Fu clapped his hands. "And now, I have a surprise for you, young lady!"

Meiying looked at him with an endearing smile. "Oh, yes?" she instinctively felt safe with these two kindly caretakers.

"Come with us!" Reverend Fu gave Master Li a nod, and they both rose and walked out of the cafeteria with determined steps. Just before they disappeared through the exit, Reverend Fu turned and waved his arm at Meiying who hesitated at the table.

"Well, come on then, Miss Bai!"

Obediently, she followed, with Beethoven trailing behind. After passing down a labyrinth of corridors, they came to a closed door above which a faded sign announced its function: "Music Room."

Reverend Fu beamed as he opened the door. "Haven't been in this room in ages," he muttered.

A beautiful, albeit dusty, cobweb-covered piano stood like a magic object waiting to be awakened with the right words . . . or touch.

Meiying gasped in delight, clapping her hands like an ecstatic child. Her carefully built defenses fell away and she almost skipped to the instrument. She turned to speak, but Master Li smiled and shook his head, handing her a cloth to clean the layers of dust. With the greatest care, she cleaned as best she could, then tested the keys. Out of tune, of course, but a deep thrill ran from the keyboard through her fingers and into the deepest, warmest recesses of her brain, where ugliness and cruelty could not sully the purity of her deepest passion.

With help from the two caretakers and a bit of rummaging, Meiying found the tuning lever and politely requested the others to leave until she could properly tune the instrument. Even Beethoven seemed genuinely touched as they departed. It was hours before she found them again and invited them to return for an impromptu concert.

"I'm afraid both the piano and I are rusty and not very good. But we are sisters and find comfort in each other's infirmities."

"So, the thing is female?" asked Beethoven with the slightest tone of mockery.

"Not at all," replied Meiying without a pause. "A piano is what one wants it to be. Yin if yin, yang if yang, yin-yang if both." She stroked the piano. "But I am not worthy of either."

With all possible protestations and assurances expressed by everyone present, she began to play. The music flowed from her soul.

Beethoven listened with conflicted feelings. His orders from Mr. President were abundantly clear, but his efforts to follow them were made more difficult by Meiying's distrust and his inconvenient desire to make her submit. Simply murdering her and blaming it on the Japanese so he could return to his mother would not be as simple as what had been done to Peter by his uncle, or by him to Lihua. Still, the music touched his murderous heart and gave him a new and exquisite thrill at the thought of destroying the perpetrator of such beauty—a beauty that had somehow managed to weaken his intractable resolve. Her death would give him the greatest pain; therefore her murder would give him the greatest thrill. Such exquisite bipolar opportunities come once in a lifetime. He was a psychopath who received an orgasmic jolt by acting on two seemingly irreconcilable extremes at the same moment.

Meiying was not entirely happy with her playing—it had become creaky and pedestrian—but she felt gratitude at seeing the tears of Master Li and Reverend Fu. Even many of the guests had suspended their rambunctious play to listen. When the last chords of Chopin died away, her listeners erupted in enthusiastic applause.

The unrestrained gestures of affection from the guests toward him made Beethoven's skin crawl, and his utter lack of empathy rendered him impotent while around these guileless people. He politely but firmly extended his apologies.

"Sorry, but I must retire," he announced, disentangling himself from the hug of a guest. "Tomorrow is a long day."

When he left, Meiying asked Master Li and Reverend Fu whether there existed a private room where they might talk without interruption. Li glanced at Fu and winked.

"This way," he said.

Again they passed through a maze of hallways and entered a room with a sign that read "No Admittance" over the door. After entering the room, Master Li asked Meiying to wait while the two caretakers made sure all the guests were in their rooms and those locked up had been fed by the cook. It was during her wait that she explored the room out of boredom, and noticed the walls were covered with pictures. Among these were old photographs of men and women who had been previous caretakers and staff. Her eyes were drawn to a faded daguerreotype of a beautiful young woman standing between two men. When she looked closer, the image of *her* came like a revelatory bolt.

"It's *her*!" she uttered aloud.

~

Meiying could not tear her eyes from the picture, and still remained transfixed when Master Li and Reverend Fu returned.

"Who is she?" Meiying asked breathlessly, pointing at the picture.

Li and Fu exchanged glances.

"Oh, her?" asked Li as he moved close to the picture.

"Yes, her."

Li turned to Fu with an open expression. Fu shook his head. They appeared apologetic. "We don't know."

"But—"

"That picture was on the wall long before we came," explained Reverend Fu.

"How long?"

Master Li shrugged. "It's very old. Older than this building."

"How could that be?" she asked.

Both men shook their heads. "The institute was built on the site of an older building."

"What building?"

Again both men shrugged. "When we arrived, the original staff of this institute had already gone. Only vague rumors about ghosts and spirits remained. The usual superstitious peasant stories. Even those eventually died out. Only our cook is left from those days."

"Weren't you curious?" Meiying asked impatiently.

"Too busy with other things to pay much attention," said Master Li calmly.

"Oh, but we do like a mystery!" exclaimed Reverend Fu. "Is this person important?"

"Very."

"Who is she?"

But before Meiying could formulate an answer, a great commotion broke out in the hallway and the two caretakers rushed from the room. While she waited in great consternation, a thought suddenly came to her.

The cook!

It certainly was too late that night to approach the old servant. Meiying shuddered at the thought of the cook's last duty of the evening. Reverend Fu had told her about those guests who were prone to violence and locked up. He explained how the cook often had to crawl on hands and knees delivering food to avoid desperate, fierce, grasping hands.

How could such an old lady be capable of performing such awful, dangerous tasks? thought Meiying. *Surely this cook is special.* Meiying decided to seek her out the next morning.

Before departing, she took down the picture and surreptitiously carried it to her room

The next morning arrived.

Daybreak.

Breakfast.

Meiying made sure she arrived at the cafeteria early. Some guests were already up, but the cook had not yet finished her preparations. Meiying watched her place a large pot of tea on one of the tables, then followed the old lady back into the kitchen. She caught her stirring a huge pot of some delicious-smelling soup.

"Hello!" said Meiying brightly.

The old lady grunted and continued stirring without bothering to look around.

"You work terribly hard, and the food is delicious. How do you do it?"

Another grunt.

"May I help with anything?" asked Meiying.

This time, the old lady growled, "No!" and carried on with greater urgency.

In the face of this intransigence, Meiying took an exploratory turn around the massive kitchen, utterly astonished that one old woman could manage such a huge jumble of foods, containers, woks, pots, pans, utensils, ovens, sinks, cupboards, and a plethora of other culinary odds and ends that seemed to stretch for kilometers.

Impossible! Meiying thought. *She must have help. It's overwhelming!*

And yet the old woman moved from one task to another as spritely as a covey of twenty-year-olds.

"Old mother, please let me help you," said Meiying during one of the cook's innumerable passes. To her surprise, the old lady stopped.

"Young miss, it would take me longer to tell you than to do it myself." With these hastily spoken words, she was off again.

Meiying trailed behind. "May I speak to you after breakfast?"

Only a grunt was received in response.

Feeling piqued, Meiying told herself to keep trying. Somehow she would break through the fortress walls. The stakes were too high to quit. Besides, this old woman had now become a curiosity in her own right, regardless of the picture. Being of a romantic bent, Meiying imagined all sorts of interesting stories that could be told by this cook. Imagine what she had seen! Imagine a long life spent in this institute! Where did she come from? Husband? Family? Ambitions? Children?

Again the old woman passed by carrying a pot and Meiying fell in beside her. In spite of the cook rolling her eyes, Meiying forged ahead. "It's about a picture of someone in the room that has a sign above the door that reads "No Admittance" and where there are lots of other pictures. But I'm particularly interested in this one picture." She removed the picture that had been concealed beneath her coat and held it up. "I must know the identity of this person."

Shockingly, the old cook froze, stared at it, and snatched it from Meiying's hands.

"Well?" asked the cook, looking at an astonished Meiying as if she had seen her for the first time. "What do you want to know?"

As in a trance, Meiying held out both hands, palms up, and asked, "Is it *her?*"

Chapter Twenty-One

PART FOUR: ARRIVAL

Crossing the Border

~ *Into the Abyss* ~

On a small hill overlooking the Mongolian border, the group gazed upon the crossing with a mix of trepidation and excitement. John felt a renewed sense of well-being. The voices were quiet, the afternoon air was crisp, and the sun's warmth matched his own glow of anticipation. It seemed miracle enough that all of them survived the battle, but now to be standing so close to the destination portal that led to *her* gave him a tremendous thrill.

"Now if we can just get across without any trouble," said the always dubious Lu Zhishen.

"We will," replied Madame Liu confidently. As if having second thoughts, she glanced at Child of Buddha who smiled in agreement. Seeking further confirmation, Madame Liu tilted her head toward the box strapped to Lu's bike and listened. Nothing.

"Of course we will!" cried Feng Shiren. "Xuanzhang did it and so will we!" He struck another operatic pose. "With Monkey's help, of course!"

"And Little Monkey!" burst out Little Acorn, striking the same pose as his hero. He looked at the adults, all smiling down at him, and felt a deep love and sense of security in the company of his 'family.'

With this, they set off down the hill, each experiencing differing degrees of anxiety, but all determined to make it through to Mongolia where *she* waited.

Far from experiencing trouble, the guards seemed almost uninterested, casting cursory glances at their passports and expressing nothing more than fleeting curiosity toward the foreigners, who they had initially taken to be White Russians. The guards waved them through dismissively. John could tell they had other concerns than a few ragged refugees when he saw them nervously scanning the horizon as if waiting for the appearance of an army of demons. Only their habitually severe faces betrayed automatic adherence to military form over the substance of their deep-seated fears. In short, they wished they were home with their mothers.

After biking a couple of kilometers out of sight of the border guards, the group stopped and took stock of their situation. Everyone felt relieved and a low-level buzz of anticipation undermined their attempts at calmness and business-as-usual comportment. But once the buzz died down, they felt the full force of the landscape. Somehow the countryside seemed very different from that of China just a few kilometers behind them. To John, Mongolia appeared startlingly alien and lonely, the horizon more distant, the spaces vaster, the heartbeat of the land slower and inexorably grim. The dirt road stretched on an infinite distance ahead, where only the faintest hint of varied elevation could be seen. A noisy flock of geese wheeled above and disappeared into the vastness, bringing them back to the issue at hand.

"Which way?" asked Feng Shiren. "That way?" he asked without waiting for an answer, pointing up the only road. "Or that way?" He pointed up the same road and laughed.

But Madame Liu had a surprise for him. She smiled mischievously. "Neither! That way!" She pointed away from the road. All eyes followed her finger but saw nothing but scrub and an endless steppe.

"But there's no road," Lu Zhishen observed drily. "Not even a trail."

"No need to state the obvious," commented Feng. Still, he looked at Madame Liu questioningly.

"Of course there's no road," interjected Master Zhou. "What did you think? . . . *She* would have a produce stand by the road selling vegetables?"

"Well. . . . "

Child of Buddha's intense gaze struck John at that moment as desperate, almost feral. "Yes! Yes! That way!" she whispered ferociously for all to hear. It seemed the intensity of her stare would set the scrub afire and blaze the way.

When her words faded away in the stillness of the air, they heard tapping.

… *Tap. Tap. Tap.* …

Slowly. Ominously.

… *Tap. Tap. Tap.* …

"Oh, god," muttered Suling.

Lu Zhishen looked at the box strapped to his bike as if it had morphed into a cobra poised to strike. He stepped backward.

"Oh, god," repeated Suling.

"Are you sure that's the right way?" asked John, the old terrors stirring within.

"Yes," replied Madame Liu firmly. She double-checked the new compass she bought for an exorbitant amount from a communist officer. "Yes."

"But the Precious Object thinks otherwise!" objected Lu, still looking at his bike with an anxious frown.

"Yes, it is!" cried Child of Buddha. "Yes! Yes! The right way!"

"Then how do you account for that?" asked John, gesturing toward the box.

"John," said Suling in a disappointed tone. "It is the way, but there may be difficulties. We have faced trouble before."

"Perhaps. . . . " intoned Feng Shiren in a tone that demanded attention. But his words faded and he stood waiting.

"Perhaps what?" asked Lu, always the first to give in to impatience.

As if on cue, Feng crouched low and assumed the look of a wild man searching the heavens, sniffing the air and shuffling like a knuckle-walking gorilla. "Perhaps the Precious Object is upset because it sees into our future and predicts a low-flying bird shitting on Brother Lu's head. A catastrophe worthy of the most rapid drumbeat!" He then mimicked the tapping sound in primitive grunts.

Even the big Canadian had to laugh at Feng's latest absurdity.

"Where will we find food out there?" asked Suling.

"There are no more safe harbors until we reach the destination," sighed Madame Liu. "We will just have to depend on the hospitality of Mongol herders."

"Ugh!" cried Feng. "Goat's milk and camel fat!"

"Could be worse," commented Master Zhou.

"How can a man so rich be a man so humble?" marveled Lu Zhishen, partly in admiration, partly in frustration.

"Because he is good," said Child of Buddha with peculiar emphasis.

"Yes," agreed Suling. "He is so good."

Feng snorted. "Hey! What about me? Have I not saved you all multiple times? Am I not good also?"

Feng scanned the group with a smile, signaling his willingness to now accept praise. None was forthcoming. Madame Liu clicked her tongue and started off without a word. Following like ducklings, the little band set out across the Mongolian steppes with no path to guide them and only a hazy notion about their destination.

From the box, the tapping continued monotonously to the monotonous rhythm of their pedaling.

John! It is a dirge to remind you that you have abandoned Meiying! The voice came with an unusually jarring suddenness.

I have not abandoned Meiying!

Chosen One! Again you put distance between her and you. Are you in total rebellion against My plan?

Chosen One? What does that mean? I seek her, *the object of our quest. You are Goddess, right?*

You know. You seek only to find the ghost-her You abandon the true-her! Foolish Chosen One!

Beloved Goddess, You have for too long been exiled, interjected God. **Feminine plots have no traction in the male brain. Hen-pecking leads straight to domestic abuse. Trust Me. Drop the hen and peck the Rooster where His pecker pecks. Now look, around you spins the spinning mutant John Powers, advancing not a meter toward the rendezvous with your precious Bai Meiying! He heads in the opposite direction. You are no closer to obtaining his**

son; although I fail to comprehend whatever devious plot You are cooking up that is so necessary to try yet another failed attempt at resuscitating this planet by evolving a race of Superior Ones.

Dearest God, it is for You and Your faction; for Your addiction to Fate; for their salvation—the embattled other ones. Otherwise, why would I bother? It is the Chosen One's genome that makes him the harbinger of ones to come. It is all for You who possess a peck that is peckerless without the pornography of pain and pontification. Fate and non-intervention indeed!

Damn your stupid alliteration! Get out!

"John?" Suling asked, pulling next to him.

Don't answer!

Shush, God!

"John?"

"Hello."

"Again?"

"Again."

"Perhaps if you keep your mind on meeting *her*, they will go away."

John made a grunting sound and waved her off. Alone with his thoughts, the vastness of the landscape seemed to be a welcoming environment for the full force of the voices that swept across the steppes like a Mongol horde.

Yes, it is true isn't it, God? This environment allows Me to breathe!

Dearest Goddess, even here it is cramped and dirty compared to the space between galaxies. Only there can I truly think, away from these contentious organisms with their so called open spaces.

But, You would miss their suffering! And unfortunately for You, this one will spawn a new, superior species, but it will take time.

So claims the engineer of this travesty. Sweet Goddess, stop harping on My little failings! Concentrate on Your little bicycle boy and Your own disordered Mind; keep focusing on their quantum minutiae for all I care. I am the gravity that pulls all of them down, including John Powers. We are incompatible—he is but a tiny sparrow whose fall I will briefly note, but whose journey to the soil I laboriously sculpted in the curvature of spacetime over millennia.

He is the Chosen One, You will see.

Not me! Not me! Goddamn these voices!

Keep pedaling, John Powers! Stop interrupting and let Us talk!

John listened to them arguing; a low buzz more annoying than mosquitoes. He could kill mosquitoes; slap them against his skin and quickly wipe them away. But, these damn voices would require a far different strategy. Plucking out infected neurons was not like pulling splinters from his hand. No. They had insinuated themselves into every nook and crevice of his mind, and would certainly be passed down to devour the sanity of his son unless he could rid himself of them.

~

Expiring day breathed a smoky haze that quickly darkened around them.

"How much farther?" called Lu Zhishen to Madame Liu.

"Not much farther. Look for lights or fire from a yurt. Does anyone see any signs of life?"

No one did. All were hungry. Protein deprivation had them all yearning for some meat—any meat. But all that awaited them was cold rice unless they spotted a friendly yurt. John pictured being greeted by a welcoming clan of colorfully dressed Mongols who would invite them to partake in a feast, perhaps lamb or beef. Alas, none were to be seen.

Mere fantasy, he thought dejectedly. *That type of luck never happens, at least not to me.*

No matter how hard they peered at the horizon, no lights materialized. There was nothing for it but to camp for the night. Even the moon remained stubbornly behind knotted clouds, only occasionally showing itself with teasing shafts of light.

The voices continued to hum, so John decided to seek a friendly distraction. He found Suling talking quietly with Child of Buddha.

"May I join you?"

"Welcome."

"Please continue," said John.

The women glanced at each other.

John noticed and felt a pang of otherness. "Sorry, didn't mean to interrupt."

"We were just discussing how we will act when we meet *her*," explained Suling.

John blinked, trying to dredge up a clever remark, but only succeeded in muttering a weak, "How?"

Both laughed. "We don't know," replied Suling. "You came."

"Oh."

Child of Buddha assumed a serious expression. "She will be receptive."

"To what?" asked Suling.

""To those who have suffered."

"We all have suffered," commented Suling, glancing at John and making his heart flutter in appreciation.

"Speaking of suffering, I'm really hungry," said John, immediately thinking it was a damn stupid thing to say.

Weak! Weak! Weak! Demon? God? John's bewildered mind reeled.

Both women paused at this non-sequitur.

He tried to come up with some clever remark, but could not. The voice continued to disparage him. The bad voice.

"What do you think you will find when we get there?" came Feng Shiren's voice a little distance off. The question bore a tinge of mockery.

Child of Buddha was a match for Feng's repartee. "More than you," she said without hesitation.

"What do you mean?" asked Feng with an air of superior amusement at her comment.

Child of Buddha would have none of it. "I mean," she replied. "You will be like a shrimp confronting a whale. The whole will not be comprehensible beyond the tiny patch of skin perceptible by your shrimp-sensibilities."

"Is *she* that large?" asked Feng in mock wonder.

"No, you are that small," shot back Child of Buddha.

"Smallness is an advantage," said Feng with a flick of his wrist.

"Only if you know you are small."

Feng laughed appreciatively. "You'll do!" he cried.

John was not sure whether this last remark was a face-saver or had genuine meaning beyond its cavalier tone.

~ Closer, and then. . . . ~

The next morning brought a welcome brightness to the gloom of the previous night, and John felt energized and focused on reaching the destination. For the first time in ages, he felt rested. Hunger gnawed at his stomach, of course, but even that could be accommodated. However, he quickly sensed something was not right. Too quiet. The others were almost always up before him, rustling about and talking. But this morning greeted him with uncharacteristic silence.

At first, he remained unconcerned, chalking it up to any number of the simplest explanations. But the eerie calm made him nervous and he went off looking for the nearest comrade. He soon came upon Suling, her hands buried in her face. Before he could speak, an unearthly howling came from the distance, as a wolf might sound caught in a painful trap.

"What's wrong?" he asked Suling. Before she could answer he looked nervously toward the howling noise. "What's that?"

"Little Acorn is dead," she said in a hollow voice.

"What?"

"Little Acorn is dead. Died in the night."

"How?"

"We don't know."

"Was he killed?"

"We don't know."

Again the howling from a distance.

Suling shook her head. "That is Feng Shiren. He is in great pain."

"But . . . I don't understand. . . . " stuttered John. "Where is he?"

"In the steppe."

"No, I mean Little Acorn."

Suling pointed but did not move.

John moved toward a knot of people as if sleepwalking. As he approached, Lu Zhishen looked up. "You know?"

"Yes. How did it happen?"

Lu shrugged. "Don't know."

John looked down at the boy whose curled form was outlined beneath a blanket. A deep revulsion at the apparent randomness of death overcame him; at how the universe ticked on with absolute indifference to the sudden and total erasure of this young person from the world; a person who only hours before had possessed so much life, so much promise. Now, his once energetic body lay as motionless as a tree root under the blanket; merely an uncomfortable protrusion marring the horizontal plane of existence.

"We must bury him quickly," said Madame Liu with a self-consciously officious tone.

Another howl came from the steppe.

"He found the body," explained Lu Zhishen to John. "His howls brought us running, but when we found Little Acorn, Feng was already gone."

"What happened?" asked John. "I mean, how did he die?"

Lu shook his head. "That's a mystery. No marks. Last night, when he went to bed, he was fine."

"It is no mystery!" exclaimed Child of Buddha, squatting over the body.

"Why do you say that?" snapped Master Zhou.

"Listen!" urged Child of Buddha, holding her finger to her lips.

"I don't hear anything," said Suling, her eyes questioningly wide.

"Listen!"

Slowly, gradually, they all heard a very faint tapping from the box, like an exhausted drummer's dirge.

"His heartbeat just before he died," said Child of Buddha.

"What?" asked John, leaning closer.

"His heartbeat just before he died," she repeated.

"Must have been calm," said Lu. "That tapping is regular and kind of slow."

"No, it is quite irregular if one is familiar with a healthy heartbeat," observed Madame Liu. "It is possible he had a heart condition, but whatever the case. . . . " her words trailed off, clearly wanting to move on from this tragic scene.

"He was murdered," said Child of Buddha matter-of-factly.

"By who?" demanded Master Zhou with an air of disbelief.

The howls came again.

"Him?" asked Lu Zhishen.

"No," she replied.

"Who then!" barked Madame Liu, angry that she had agreed to bring this odd, hunchbacked agitator.

The hunchback fell silent.

"Who?" asked Suling more gently.

No response.

The tapping continued.

The howling stopped.

They all waited expectantly, but Feng Shiren did not return. John and Lu went searching for him, but he was nowhere to be found. For lack of a better explanation, the group unanimously concluded it must have been heart failure.

The next morning, they buried Little Acorn and started off glumly. All were outwardly confident Feng Shiren would catch-up to them when he was ready, but several, including John, were not so sure. A general feeling of resentment toward Child of Buddha for her murder accusation fell over the group as they trekked through the Mongolian wilderness. Only Suling remained faithful to her friend and would not permit any disparaging remarks regarding the hunchback in her presence.

No one noticed John pedaling alone, mumbling to himself. Even Suling seemed lost in her own thoughts, and failed to perceive something disturbing preyed on John's mind. His lips moved rapidly as the mumbled words flew backward, dispersed by the wind. No one rode behind his self-absorbed figure, so the sentences scattered to silence in the Mongolian air.

Only he could hear the voices. Only he could say the voices.

You see? You see what You've done?

Sweet Goddess, it was not Me.

Who else? I was watching, but somehow You managed to kill the boy by omission!

Well, it was necessary to let it happen. First Principles. Besides, the others agree.

God, do You plan to kill them all?

If I can.

Why?

To thwart Your plan, of course.

Why the boy in particular?

Weak heart. Low hanging fruit.

Beloved God, at least he had a heart. The boy did not deserve Your flailing frustration. Please do not kill them all.

Without suffering, there can be no joy.

… Tap. Tap. Tap….

John felt sick as the voices came more and more into focus, their agendas a bit more clear, the future more alarming.

~ *Meiying Learns Something New* ~

The old cook stood dumbly as Meiying held up the photograph and asked if it was *her*. Finally, she answered, cautiously and with a trembling voice. "I don't know who *she* is. I have no business with the one you seek."

""But why is *her* picture on the wall?"

"I don't know."

Meiying thought about this response and uttered something she would not normally have said before the traumas she had undergone since Shanghai. "I think you do."

The old cook snorted in disbelief at this impertinence. "Really? Well, you think wrong! I have work to do." She turned to go.

Something possessed Meiying that had been brewing for months. With a visceral anger she had not possessed in her sheltered past, she grabbed the woman's arm and squeezed hard, crying, "Tell me!"

But to no avail. The cook grunted fiercely and tore her arm away, pushing Meiying aside. "I'm sorry," Meiying called after her weakly. She stared down at the picture in frustration.

Reverend Fu, watching from the doorway, got Meiying's attention and motioned for her to follow him. He led her to a table far from the kitchen.

"You must understand," he said after they both sat facing each other.

She waited, but he looked off in the distance and said nothing further.

"Understand what?" snapped Meiying, irritated at the melodramatic opening.

"Do you know we are critically low on food and medical supplies?" asked Reverend Fu.

"Please stop the misdirection and elusive meanderings!" exclaimed Meiying. "Just tell me what I must understand. I'm not a child to be mollified!"

"It is important for you to know we are low on food and medical supplies," repeated Reverend Fu patiently.

"Is that why you called me out here?"

"No. But it is important you understand our situation here."

Meiying forced herself to calm down and asked in a quiet but forceful tone, "Why?"

"Because only by understanding our desperation will you understand—other things."

"Look," said Meiying. "Everyone in this country is low on food and supplies. People are dying every day. Why did you call me out here?"

Fu looked away.

"Why?" repeated Meiying forcefully.

"To tell you about the picture."

Meiying leaned forward as Reverend Fu pushed a cup of tea toward her that had been brought by the old cook. Before the woman left, she winked at Meiying. "You have a firm grip. Next time don't let go so easily."

"I'll tell you what I know," he said after the cook had trundled off.

"Yes, please," said Meiying, ignoring the cup.

~

"It all happened before I arrived here," Reverend Fu began. "Many years ago." He sipped his own tea and nodded for her to do likewise. After she followed his suggestion, he asked her to put the picture on the table, whereupon he used his index finger to tap on the image that so riveted Meiying.

"The person in this picture, as you can see despite the grainy old photo, was young and beautiful. She had arrived under mysterious circumstances which my old mentor—who has since passed away, god rest his soul—could never explain to me. Evidently, she caused quite a stir among staff and guests. Many patients were so affected by her . . . how did he put it? . . . they responded to her unique treatment methods so well they were cured and released soon after she arrived.

"Apparently, this amazing success spread among the population, and the institute became a magnet for not just the mentally ill, but for people with other diseases like malaria and dysentery. Her successes became so renowned that she was suspected of being a witch or a goddess or a demon. The old head of the institute, of course, dismissed these superstitions and had begun a scholarly article on her methodologies. He dreamed we would become a world-famous institute thanks to her. Casting her remarkable talents into a solid scientific framework would certainly anchor his fame and further his ambitions.

"But one day an orphan boy was brought in. Evidently, the young woman saw something in this boy."

Meiying broke in. "What was this young woman's name?"

Reverend Fu merely shook his head and continued. "The young woman saw something in the boy, but from the perspective of the other staff, the boy was violent and cruel. He stole, cajoled, bullied, manipulated, and inexplicably grew fatter and fatter on the simple fare offered by the institute. She spared him nothing, and even protected him from the threats to have him expelled for spying on female staff while they were bathing.

"Once, a few years later, he was implicated in the rape of a young patient. The chief of the institute was outraged and wanted to kick him out immediately. Again, the young woman in the picture came to his defense. Although her miraculous treatments continued to work their magic, rumors spread. Vicious rumors. Evil rumors. People whispered that the boy was her demon spawn. The boy had become her lover. That he was her witch's tool. Like I said, evil rumors. Even my kindly old mentor suspected the boy was her child who she abandoned or somehow lost, and had found his way back to her.

"By now, the boy had become a teenager, even more obese and still cruel, adding to the intensity of hatred toward him. Only she had the ability to control his most violent and vicious impulses."

Reverend Fu paused. Meiying waited, but he remained silent, evidently lost in his own thoughts.

"Well?" she asked at last. "What happened?"

He shook his head. "This is where the story becomes confused. As I heard it, one day she simply disappeared. Her clothes and other possessions remained in her room, but she was nowhere to be found. Even after weeks of searching, she never turned up. The boy locked himself in his room, from which sobbing could be heard for days. Then he too disappeared, and time made the memories fade. Both were gradually forgotten."

Meiying looked at him forlornly. "Not quite."

"No, not quite."

"Do you think the young woman is *she*, the one we seek?"

"If so, my child, then *she* is very much more complicated than you and your friends think *she* is." He shuddered. "From listening to your friends, she has not changed physically an iota after all these years. Strange."

"Of course, Reverend Fu, you know who the boy is."

"Of course."

"Has Mr. President contacted you? Are you in danger?"

"Yes, we are in danger, as are you and your friends. His power and influence are widespread—even extending to the communists."

"Yes," she agreed. "Even extending to the Japanese."

"True. I shudder at his name."

"And Beethoven?"

He shrugged, nervously looked around, and whispered, "Your friends are traveling to Mongolia."

Meiying, shocked at this revelation, asked many more questions, but each time was met with the response, "You now know what I know."

~

As he stood to leave, Meiying said in an urgent whisper, "Can you do something for me?"

"If I can," replied Reverend Fu, startled by her vehemence.

"Can you arrange for him to be locked in a cell for a few days? I plan to disappear, much as *she* did. But he must not follow, at least not right away. I need a head start."

Reverend Fu frowned. "That would be difficult, my dear. He works for Mr. President. Even if we succeed, we would put everything here at risk, including our lives."

"Yes," sighed Meiying resignedly.

"But perhaps my Buddhist friend and I can think of something."

"Please, do what you can."

"When do you leave?"

"Tomorrow morning."

Reverend Fu appeared concerned. "So soon!"

"I must."

"If you must, then we must."

"Oh thank you, thank you."

Reverend Fu shook a finger at her. "But the danger is very great, both to you and to us. You know, we must consider the others here who depend upon us."

"Yes, of course," said Meiying quickly.

Although Meiying said these words, she felt somehow certain the two caretakers would find a way to delay Beethoven. But in the midst of these ruminations, Meiying quite suddenly realized that she would be venturing out alone. Why she had not considered this earlier was a puzzle. The prospect of traveling the roads alone with war and famine all around filled her with a sudden terror. *Perhaps*, she thought, *my stupid sense of independence has overcome good sense. How could I even have conceived such an idea? I will be killed. Or raped. Or both. And even if I escape these fates, I will probably starve to death. Fool!*

But these thoughts were merely dark edges on a plan she knew would be carried out regardless of the consequences. *I would rather die trying to reach* her *then stay and slowly die in safety.* The problem was Beethoven. If the caretakers did not find a way to detain him, her trip would end before it could begin. On the other hand, if she waited to be sure, heaven knows when she could leave. Meiying had no solution to this problem and only sleep would made it briefly go away. Before retiring, she returned to the "No Admittance" room and carefully replaced the old photograph on the wall, gazing for a long while at the image of *her*. Sleep did not come easily, but eventually she dozed off.

~ *Meiying Dreams* ~

As she skipped along the Shanghai street on the way to her music lesson, she looked down and saw her Western-style dress twirl happily to the rhythm of her youthful movements. The dizzying red swirl contrasted sharply with the grey-and-blue cotton gloom of the passersby. She knew she stood out, drawing only praise and appreciative oohs of admiration. Like a prima ballerina, she pranced down the street until she came to a piano sitting in the middle of the largest intersection of the city. A huge crowd had already gathered and after adjusting the stool, she sat proudly while the audience craned their necks in anticipation.

Just as she touched the keys to commence some familiar sonata, a face in the crowd leered at her and suddenly let forth a terrible howl, like some wounded animal. She cringed in fear, throwing off the rhythm and casting her notes into a discordant mash of noise. With this cacophony, a rage fell over the crowd and a great swell of humanity engulfed her. All went black while she felt her body being pommeled by fists and clubs, but the pain seemed anesthetically distant. From nowhere, a sharp and excruciating stab in her vagina shocked her back to an unbearable reunification of her mind with her body. Snapping open her eyes to find the perpetrator of such pain, she saw the face of Father Durant on top of her, red with strain, his lips curled back to reveal a reptilian mouth from which came the word repeated over and over, "Salvation, salvation, salvation."

With this mantra, Meiying calmed and she felt him withdraw. The pain ceased.

"Why have you returned?" she asked.

"To warn you."

"You are a rapist, how can you warn me?"

"Yes, but not a murderer."

Meiying scoffed. "Is there a difference?"

"Yes. Oh yes! Ask her." Father Durant invited Meiying to follow his eyes.

Meili stood silently at the edge of the crowd, gazing at Meiying with a sorrowful longing.

"He is right," said Meili without speaking. "To live, even if violated, is necessary."

"Necessary?" asked Meiying, bewildered by the word.

"Yes, necessary! Colonel Naguma killed me. Beethoven will kill you, unless you find it necessary to live!"

"Why?" asked Meiying, but the piano began playing on its own before Meili could reply. At first, it played a beautiful passage from some composer she had never heard, but then the music became harsh and atonal. The crowd faded and disappeared, leaving only the piano. When she blinked in disbelief at the noise, Mr. President appeared at the instrument, violently banging on the keys. He looked up and saw her. The bench sagged absurdly under his weight.

"I will find you!" he cried above the pounding. "I will follow you! You will lead me to *her*! I will kill *her*!" His words becoming obscenely discordant, merging with the musical gibberish he continued to bang-out on the piano.

"But *she* helped you. Took you in. Protected you."

"*She* left me! After I kill *her*, I kill you!"

Meiying turned to run, but Father Durant reappeared and held her back. Meili tried to pull her away, but his grip was too strong, and she stopped struggling.

"Don't leave me!" cried Meiying, but Father Durant laughed and held tighter. While he held the passive Meiying, she felt herself growing older, transforming into an old lady, haggard and brittle. As Father Durant squeezed, she heard her bones snapping and the terrifying realization that she was being broken apart awakened her.

~

A glance outside told her that dawn approached. While the dream was disturbing, she had had worse, and to her sharp mind this one bequeathed an idea. She donned shabby clothes, bulky and unflattering—the kind an old woman might wear. She then cropped her hair as she had done when posing as a nun. Blacking some of her teeth, she inspected herself in the mirror. Not satisfied, she shoved a small pillow between her cotton tunic and her back, making her appear hunched. With an old cane in hand, she positioned a pack full of food on her back, hid her money in the lining of her tattered clothes, and started off just as a tinge of pinkish-orange colored the eastern sky. No one saw her leave, and if they did, it was just one of the old ladies scavenging for scraps.

Now I can only hope, she thought grimly, peering back at the institution, half expecting Beethoven to appear and drag her away.

Mongolia was her destination. She knew there were only a few border crossings. Maybe she would get lucky and the guards would tell her which direction her friends went. The only problem was lack of a visa, but that could be overcome . . . somehow. She wanted to run as fast as possible to get far away from the institution, but old women do not run, so she forced herself to hunch over and shuffle slowly. The unnatural rhythm of her stride made her hips ache and she often stopped to rest. As she moved in the direction of the Mongolian border with directions provided by fellow travelers, the roads became increasingly choked with refugees, a bad sign that something dangerous lay ahead. The midday heat made her heavy clothes and pillow unbearably hot, so she found shade and sipped water. Dust and a perpetual swirling wind seemed to render the landscape a brownish smudge making everything hazy, forcing her to squint through the grit.

Meiying drove herself to continue until late afternoon, when she felt unable to go on. Refugees crowded the road and had taken the good spots off to the side, so she wandered away from the road for almost a kilometer before finding a secluded spot. There was no water, but the shade and the solitude made it appealing. After she ate, she lay back and gazed up at the darkening sky, feeling a deep and unshakable loneliness. All of those she loved were gone; worse, Meili and Lihua suffered violent deaths. Would she be next? Try as she might, the utter emptiness of her life crashed down around her, and for the first time since she was violated in the cave, Meiying considered suicide.

~

Yes, dear Reader, my mother considered suicide. Had she carried through, I would not be writing this, I would not have contributed to the killing fields of Vietnam, and I would not be in this tunnel; a skeleton pondering a mystery, or, as some would have it, a boneless mental patient pondering his schizophrenia. Or is it?

Chapter Twenty-Two

The Destination

Arrival?

*A*nd so, Chosen One, you are almost there! Yet it does Me no good unless Meiying can join you. She stumbles on her way, no thanks to you.

Yes, Beloved Goddess, old crone that Meiying is pretending to be, Your plan is just as old and rickety as her disguise. Alas, she is in for it.

God, You have always been taken by the young, pretty ones. See how she has hidden her beauty from men? Would that humanity could hide their beauty from You! Now is the beginning of their extinction.

Stop harping! Look up, John, and see a mountain ahead. That is your destination. Look up!

~

Following the command, John snapped up his head and looked; the view took his breath away. The others had all stopped and were staring at the same vision as he. As if an illustration in some mythical story had come to life, a jagged, multi-faced mountain rose majestically above the flat plain. Although distant, the complex geometric smoothness of its faces resembled multiple facets that a master craftsman would have carved into a precious gem. Every on-looker remained speechless until Madame Liu broke the spell by stating what the group had already guessed.

"That is the destination."

"Worthy of the Monkey-King!" cried Feng Shiren, materializing out of nowhere to stand among the groups as would any proper ghost. His words came this time out of wonder rather than mockery. "If only Little Acorn were here to see it." Tears glistened in his eyes.

After brief, welcoming solicitations at his sudden and, to the surprise of no one, mysterious appearance, Master Zhou said, "We have a few hours of daylight left. Let us take advantage and get as close as we can before night."

"Yes!" shouted every member of the group.

Lu Zhishen waved a cautionary hand. "Listen!" he warned, craning his ear toward the box. But no sound could be heard.

"Yes, all is well so far," said Child of Buddha. "But keep listening as we get closer. Keep listening."

"Why? What do you mean?" asked John.

"Yes, are you expecting something bad?" chimed in Lu.

But as typical of her, Child of Buddha said nothing in response. She mounted her bike and started pedaling toward the mountain, with the others falling in behind.

Yes, look at it, John. If Meiying can make it here, that will be your bridal chamber.

Goddess, You get the poor boy too nervous. Anticipation will render him impotent.

God, all of this is done for the unrestrained exuberance of life. Do not ask why. It is too late to stop it. After the son is born, then You will know. These bipeds will take the next step, leaving You far behind.

Sweet Goddess, how do you overcome the problem of her lesbianism? This worthless boy will not know how to cope. John, you are made by Her to be a freak!

It is too late for that, My Beloved God. It is too late.

As John shook his head to dislodge the bickering voices, he concentrated on remaining willfully ignorant of their meaning, but as he looked around for distractions he soon noticed Child of Buddha looking back at him with an unreadable expression. Her gazes were now seriously interfering with his ability to concentrate on other things. Somehow, her eyes told him she knew crucial facts about him that he himself did not know. But beyond that, he could not venture a guess. He decided to confront her when they made camp.

Nevertheless, his preoccupation with Child of Buddha gradually fell away with the advance of the mountain. As they approached, it seemed to rise up like some living thing that had been aroused from sleep. Sheer cliff faces towered over the group as dusk fell across the plain. The last rays of sunlight reflected off the pinnacles in spectacularly precise angles, as if the facets of a diamond were being rotated in the glare of a cutter's light. Even as the valley floor sank into darkness, the highest tip of the mountain sent a last sliver of light through the atmosphere. It seemed to John a beacon of hope, reflected not only in his own heart, but also in the awestruck eyes of his comrades.

John fought against the mesmerizing sight, determined to focus on confronting Child of Buddha when they set-up camp for the night. Something needed to be resolved before they reached the destination. Even the voices urged him on. **Do it! Do it, worthless!** the evil voice urged with others shouting encouragement in the background.

When the moment came that evening, he simply waited until Child of Buddha was alone. This took patience as Suling chatted with her for what seemed an eternity. John felt resentment that Child of Buddha had apparently replaced him in Suling's heart, then promptly scolded himself for such an unfounded reaction. After she finally left, he walked up and said, "Why do you look at me so?"

She gazed at him calmly, whether in pity or curiosity, he could not say.

John waited but she did not respond. "I asked a question," he felt self-consciously intimidated by her demeanor.

"I look at many people." She shrugged. "You are no different."

"But I think I am."

"I cannot control what you think."

"Child of Buddha, I believe you know something about me. What is it?"

In spite of the darkness, the half-moon shone enough to see her staring at him. In that moment he knew for certain that what he said was true—she did see something. Her reply would, he thought, be a watershed moment in his life.

"Nothing."

His disappointment communicated itself to her, for in a softened tone, she quickly added, "Believe me, John, I see in you no more than I do in the others."

John felt a sudden revulsion, a notion of lost uniqueness. Perhaps it was the words 'no more' that bothered him. This response had touched a nerve; the belief that he had no special qualities other than the corrosive sense of being average; an average man in extraordinary circumstances, rendering the usefulness of such circumstances hollow and cheap.

"You know, I hear voices!" he blurted out, for reasons utterly unknown to him.

"Yes."

"Is that why you stare at me?"

"I cannot stare at your voices."

"That's not what I mean."

"It is what I mean."

"I know you stare at me for some reason. I can see it in your eyes." He knew he struggled for some response more satisfactory to his ego.

"I stare at you as I stare at the sky or a bird. You move in the universe. For the time being, you move in the same direction as I. There are only so many places to fix one's gaze."

John looked at her in confusion. Her eyes shone in some otherworldly intensity; translucent, restless orbs that, like two spider sacs, burst upon him a host of spiderlings that scurried over his body in a frenzy of probing, prickling tingles.

Averting her eyes in a flash of pity, she said, "You should get some sleep. Tomorrow we draw closer to the destination."

But John drew on his anger and frustration over the seeming futility of his life. "No. That won't do. I have someone I must find. She must join us at the destination. I know you know something. Does it involve her?"

"Who?"

"You know. Meiying."

"I know of Meiying."

"What do you know?"

Child of Buddha laughed. "Ask your voices."

"They are figments of my imagination . . . my illness. What they tell me is unhealthy to even listen to. I want you to tell me."

"You are stubborn."

"I am desperate."

"I have seen desperation. You are not desperate."

"What am I?"

"A small man destined for great things."

"What does that mean?"

"You know. Your voices know."

"But I don't know!" cried John. "That's just it, I don't know! Tell me!"

Suling appeared. "Is everything okay?"

"Yes, yes," replied John. "Child of Buddha and I were just talking and I got excited."

Suling looked at Child of Buddha, but no words came.

"Can you just leave us alone for a while?" asked John almost pleadingly.

"Yes, of course." Suling turned to go.

"Wait," said Child of Buddha calmly. "How long have you known about his voices?"

Suling looked puzzled. "Why?"

"How long?"

"From the beginning."

"As I thought. Thank you."

"What does that have to do with anything?" asked John in frustration.

"Nothing."

Suling gazed at both of them and went back to her sleeping area. After she left, the two looked at each other.

"What did you mean when you said a small man destined for great things?" asked John.

"Nothing."

"Damn it!"

"Yes. It appears that something in the future is damned, and I fear it is . . . never mind."

Your son, John! You son! That's what the hunchback means!

John stared at Child of Buddha. "Do you mean my son?"

She turned away. "You have no son."

"My future son."

"Your voices tell all. I know nothing. Now, leave me alone. I want to sleep and will talk no more. Go to sleep. Tomorrow will be an important day. Sleep!"

"But—"

"No!"

~

But John could not sleep. That part of his mind animated by the voices remained quiet, while the rest of his thoughts spiraled around the vortex of Meiying. Even the proximity of the destination could not divert his attention, in fact, it strengthened his fixation on her. Performing his usual accusatory introspection, he returned to the same self-lacerating question: Why did he leave her behind?

He assumed the role of sympathetic friends, and argued to himself that he had no choice. Variations on this theme played themselves out predictably and impotently. *There is nothing I can do*, he told himself. *Where would I start to look? How could I find her? She is probably dead. There is nothing I can do. I have no choice! No choice! No choice!*

Around and around her vortex his mind emptied itself of excuses until nothing remained but the dry reality: "I am a useless, worthless coward! A useless, schizophrenic, worthless coward!"

He tortured himself with memories of Suling tending to his weaknesses like a nanny to a fragile child. He tortured himself with memories of Meiying. Of course, the torture felt good, and he reveled in the knowledge that even reveling in the knowledge was a sign of his worthlessness. To be sure, there was overwhelming proof of his weakness, but what of that? He had done bold things. Very bold things.

"I came to China to find *her*," he said aloud to the mountain glimmering in the moonlight. "And then I found Meiying. I lost her and now I am about to find *her*. But *her* without Meiying is empty of meaning. Having *her* without Meiying? No. Not empty. It is a confirmation of my failure. How can I face *her* without the one I love? The voices are right. If I don't find Meiying, I should just end it once and for all."

Ha ha! Beloved Goddess, You are about to lose both of them. No parents, no son.

Yes, Immortal God, Immortal Fool! No son and the planet will become sterile and You and Your faction will waste away from addiction to frigid Fate.

At that again? Your old stand-by?

Yes. The Great Wailing. Your only hope is the son, yet Your addiction blinds You to it.

You are the Blind One, Unseeing Mother.

A thought struck John as he mulled over the voices. He had speculated about it before, but now it came stark and cold. Is *she* the same as Goddess? Are the Goddess and *she* the same as the Precious Object. All are one. All are separate. The Trinity. Mother, daughter, and Holy Ghost?

~ *The Mountain* ~

The next day brought clear, crisp weather and an easy ride to the base of the mountain where a sheer cliff face rose before them like some gigantic shard of glass, opaque yet with hints of moving shadows behind the smooth, grey surface. There were no signs that humans had visited this place before, but Feng Shiren expressed his certainty that this must be a place of worship for Mongols.

"Why are you so certain?" asked Master Zhou.

"Superstition. This mountain is so extraordinary, superstitious Mongols must see some divine creature in it."

"But there is no sign of human activity," observed Suling.

"True," replied Feng.

"Maybe they are afraid of it," said Lu Zhishen. He put his ear up to the box and listened. "Speaking of fear. . . . " his words trailed off.

"What do you hear?" asked Child of Buddha.

Lu frowned. "I can barely hear it."

"Tapping?" asked John.

"A heartbeat."

This caused a stir.

"What do you mean?" asked Madame Liu.

"Listen for yourselves," replied Lu softly.

The others listened and agreed they heard something very similar to a heartbeat. No one had an explanation, but everyone knew enough not to be unduly shocked.

"Well, now where to?" asked Feng Shiren.

Madame Liu shrugged. "This is as far as I know."

"Is this the destination?" asked John.

"No, or rather, yes and no. It is the last place mentioned, the last place indicated."

"Where do we go?" asked Suling.

"We wait," replied Madame Liu.

"For how long?" asked John.

"Better not be for long," said Feng Shiren. "We are very low on food. And water? Well, hopefully there is a natural spring around here."

"Must be a spring around here," observed Master Zhou.

"Maybe so, but the problem will be food," said Feng.

"Nevertheless, we wait," said Madame Liu firmly.

"You wait, I'll do some scouting around!" cried Feng. "Come on, Little Acorn!"

The others stared.

"I know he is not here, but I still talk to him."

Suling looked at Madame Liu. "What do we wait for?"

"A sign."

"I agree with Feng," said Lu Zhishen. "I'll go in the opposite direction. There's not much light left today. We should both leave first thing tomorrow morning and agree to be back here before nightfall."

Feng nodded.

As the group prepared their sleeping areas, an eerie silence had descended upon them, almost as if the mountain itself demanded it so. A feeling of anticlimax mixed with nervous tension over the uncertainty of what would come next made them all jumpy. Even Child of Buddha seemed wary and insisted on being alone. Suling, wanting company, approached John.

"Will you talk with me awhile?" she asked.

"Of course," he said, gesturing for her to sit on a petrified log near his bedding.

But when she sat, she remained quiet.

"Is there something wrong?" asked John.

Suling pointed up at the sheer face of the cliff, reflecting moonlight that seemed to shimmer out of the soul of the rock itself.

"What?" asked John.

"It scares me."

"What does, Suling?"

"The mountain, the heartbeat from the Precious Object, the silence, the loneliness, the waiting for something we do not know."

"I understand. I also am scared."

"And yet, you are dealing with things I am not. Things not related to the mountain or to *her*."

"Yes."

"The voices?"

"Yes and no."

"John, what do you think of Child of Buddha?"

"She is nice. Why?"

"Does she seem different from the rest of us?"

"Yes, of course. But that could be the time she spent in the institution."

"Yes, it could be. But I mean, does she seem to have certain powers . . . like the ability to see into your thoughts?" Suling asked the question with hesitation in her voice.

"A little. Does that scare you?"

"A little."

"Suling, what are you getting at?"

"Something is about to happen. I don't know what, but whatever it is, it scares me. Now that we have almost reached the destination, there is something disturbing."

"How so?"

"This place."

"Suling, you're being very dramatic." John knew his response was patronizing and that his dismissal of her fears belied the fact that he was probably more afraid then she could think of being. In fact, she had inadvertently poured fuel on the fire of his uneasiness.

"Do you wish Meiying were here?" asked Suling smiling.

"Oh, yes. She would calm you . . . and the rest of us. I should never have left her!"

"Remember, John, she was forcibly taken from us. You could not have done anything."

John let the words roll over him, kneading the painful knots of his insecurities. He knew the words as well as he knew his own weaknesses, yet they only confirmed the degradation into which he had fallen. Always and forever he leaned upon such soothing claptrap, and now such assurances had lost their ability to comfort. Yet, all he could reply was, "I know."

"Perhaps tomorrow we will know more," said Suling.

"Perhaps."

"I have dreamed that *she* will be standing among us tomorrow when we wake. Then *she* will lead us to the final destination."

"Maybe that will happen."

"Yes, but something makes me afraid and I can't get it out of my mind. I should be looking forward to this moment, yet . . . I can't."

"But look, Suling, you're tired. We're all tired. Tomorrow things will be different." It made him feel good to be reassuring her rather than vice versa.

"Yes."

She waited but he did not know what to say.

Say something, John! Tell her the truth! Tell her you abandoned Meiying because of your cowardice! Say it!

"Goodnight, Suling."

"Goodnight, John."

He tried to sleep, but the voices were relentless.

~ *Meiying Almost Succumbs* ~

Meiying continued along the road, weary and sore, feeling as old as the old hag she pretended to be. Day after day, her disguise had kept away any trouble, but she needed food, and begging had come to nothing. As she traveled, the hunger became terrible. Occasionally she ate grass and boiled bamboo shoots, which caused terrible diarrhea, but eventually the gnawing stopped and she settled into a constant, low-grade craving. Often she considered tossing aside her disguise and relying on her feminine charms, but the dangers were too much, so she continued walking toward the border, begging for scraps but receiving none. Finally, the weakness of her condition made a decision necessary. She was not in the wilderness, there were people all around. *Someone will help*, she thought. *A man. There are many men on the road, some look well-nourished and well-clothed. All I need is a meal, a substantial meal, and I can continue on as an old woman. If I get rid of my disguise, pinch my cheeks, let my tunic drop . . . but what man?*

As she scanned the faces, lethargy, driven by malnourishment, gradually drove her to become deeply disinterested in her fate. She propped herself against a stump and moved her fingers to the comforting notes of Mozart. Hunger had long since done its worst, and now her only thought was to slip away peacefully and escape the jarring shocks of life. Soon, she would be with Meili and Lihua, better companionship then any among the living. Dim figures came and went, rummaging through her bags for food or money, but she scarcely lifted an eyelid before retreating back into a dark and comforting acceptance.

The stump became her universe. It held her upright, enough to still see the world above the ground where she would eventually be buried. High enough to feel the breeze, watch the ants, and marvel that the death of this tree had given such comfort to her and home to so many others. Mozart died young, but he contributed so much. But her? It no longer mattered.

A faint voice came to her and she chalked it up to delirium. For all she knew it was the stump talking. But it seemed vigorous and alive, much more so than her dying brain could conjure.

Good morning! Awake, Bai Meiying! You cannot die! Arrangements have been made. The ants you see are sent to you as they will be sent to your son in the future. Look closely! The Great Warrior ant graces you with her presence. From the White Palace she travels, far away in both time and space. Do you see? Do you see?

Meiying watched a large ant probing up the bark of the old stump. While she stared, a shadow approached.

"What do you stare at, old mother, with such a strange intensity?"

She did not, could not reply.

"I see an old woman with a young woman's curiosity. Your eyes are tired and hungry, but they are young. I know. I study eyes. Same with hands. I have been studying you for days. I have been watching you stare at the passing throngs that inhabit this tired world from that old stump where, apparently, you intend to die. Am I wrong?"

"No," she whispered, barely troubling herself to look.

She felt him put something to her lips. It smelled like chicken but it was liquid and rolled down her chin. She licked it and it tasted warm and flavorful. When she swallowed, an almost instantaneous reaction as it hit her stomach activated something like a switch and suffused her body with a craving to eat—to live. The young cells in her body eagerly soaked up every molecule of nourishment, and after a while, she could focus on her savior.

At first, his face was concealed under a large, floppy Western-style hat. The hand that held the spoon with life-giving broth appeared old but still strong. It did not tremble, but the veins stood out from the leathery skin. As he offered each spoonful, he chuckled and talked, not necessarily to her, but seemingly to the universe, expecting no reply.

"That's right. Eat. Strength is necessary in this world. Here's another. Good. The breeze has picked up. It's the Earth welcoming you back. A reminder. A caress for one returned from the brink, eh? That's right, here's another. Oh, you are no old woman. You are as young as the Earth and as old as the Earth. No in-between for you. These times allow for no in-between, do they? Here's another. Take it. Not too fast. Ah, your body grows younger before my eyes! It's like watering a young bamboo shoot. Look at you!"

And so he went on. Talking, chuckling, and bringing her back to life. Soon, he stopped giving her broth, telling her it wasn't good to eat too much too soon.

"I want you to come with me," he said after she had rested and regained some of her strength. "There is a small stream. I want you to clean yourself up. Change your clothes. Come out of your crone's cocoon."

"Why?" she asked suspiciously.

"I like looking at the young. I'm tired of the old, the broken-down, and the feeble. I'm tired of looking at myself, for I am also old, broken-down, and feeble. I like looking at the young. Don't worry, I have no designs on you." He added forlornly, "Couldn't act on them if I did."

Meiying looked at him doubtfully.

He laughed. "Come on. Follow me. The stump will still be here. Get your bag."

He started to walk away toward the tree line. Meiying hesitated, but he did not look back nor did he slow down. He tossed a large canvas bag over his shoulder and called out, "There's more food in here."

She followed.

Once under the trees, she became more nervous. No one could see them, and he did not seem to follow any perceivable trail. In her weakened condition, she knew she could not out-run him, and though he was old, she knew from his hands that he was strong. After what seemed a lengthy walk, she heard a stream.

"We are close," he said. "See how our friends protect us?"

"What friends?"

"The trees, young miss. The bushes."

When they reached the stream, he found a small patch of sandy dirt.

"Here we are!"

"Where?"

"A place for you to bathe. Wash off the old lady."

"Thank you, now please go." Meiying was not surprised when he failed to move.

"May I watch?" he asked in a voice at once imploring and abrupt.

She had been expecting something like this. "Do you have more food?" she asked.

"Yes."

"Let me see. Let me have some now."

He reached into his bag and unwrapped a soiled white cloth. "Dried fish," he said. "But you should eat very little or you will get sick."

Meiying held out her hand and he placed a small piece in her palm. The broth had reignited the flames of hunger and she greedily chewed the fish to extract the most from it. When she finished, he sat on a rock and waited. She noticed his sheepishness and felt reassured. Still, she hesitated.

"Go ahead, girlie, I won't harm you. Go ahead, bathe. I know you women like such things."

Meiying removed her clothes. When she pulled out the pillow that had served so well as her hunchback, he laughed. "Good! Good!"

At last she stood naked before him, making no pretense of covering herself. In fact, she stared boldly at him, as if displaying her contempt for such male weakness.

"Wait!" he cried. "I almost forgot."

Again he rummaged in his bag and pulled out a small bar of soap, well-used but still ample. Remaining seated, he held out his hand with the soap in his palm, inviting her to come closer and take it.

Meiying looked in his eyes and saw only a kind, lonely old man. She stepped up and snatched it quickly, then rushed down to the water, feeling dizzy from the sudden movement.

I need more to eat. He has food, she thought. *If I make him my friend, perhaps I can make it after all. Let him look. It makes no difference. Men will have their little pleasures. Men, how I sometimes hate them. But he has food. He offers a way.*

As Meiying scrubbed, the old man watched in wonder to see such beauty emerge from such grime. It seemed to him she peeled away the vile filth of the world to reveal an inner luster—an orchid in the mud, as his mother used to say.

"I have no towel," he said when she had finished. "But I do have these." He removed female garments from his seemingly bottomless bag. "You'll have to dry in the sun." He rose and hung the clothes on a branch close to the stream, then returned to his rock.

Meiying gave him a show, stretching in the sun and combing her hair with her fingers, all the while thinking, *what would mama and papa think now!*

"Do you know where the Mongolian border is?" she asked after giving him an eyeful.

"Ha! Of course! Are you looking for Genghis Khan?"

She allowed herself a chuckle. After drying and donning the clothes, she unsuccessfully tried to smooth the wrinkles and asked, "Why do you carry these?"

A deep frown darkened his usually cheerful features. "My daughter. They were hers. I brought them specifically for you, once I understood."

"Once you understood?"

"Yes." He did not elaborate.

Meiying did not press.

"Do you want more fish, Little Princess?" he asked, brightening.

"Yes, but I am no princess."

"What are you?"

"A pianist."

The old man did not know what to make of this.

"You know. . . . " said Meiying making movements as if playing a piano.

"Oh! Western instrument! I heard once, in a Christian church. Pretty!"

"Yes. More food, please."

He jumped up. "Of course! Of course, Little Pianist."

She took the larger piece of fish he proffered and consumed it faster than she intended.

"What is your name, old uncle?" she asked.

"What a coincidence! My name is Old Uncle."

"Will you lead me to the border?"

"For a price."

"Oh," she replied dejectedly.

He held up his hands. "No, no! Not that! Heavens! Just to see you. To watch you, occasionally. That's all I ask in return."

She stared.

"I have no family," he added weakly.

"You are lonely then," she observed.

Again he laughed. "Yes, and still young enough to be horny—but old enough not to be able to act on it."

"If I agree, will you take me to the border?"

Old Uncle pondered. "Give me a moment. I had not expected you to agree." He rubbed his wispy beard. "It's dangerous. I have my farm."

She waited. She had learned to wait.

"Are you a communist?" he asked suddenly.

"I am a pianist. I have no political affiliation."

"Are you famous?"

Meiying hesitated. "To some."

"Is anyone looking for you?"

"What do you mean?"

"I mean, is anyone looking for you? Family? The Japanese. The Nationalists. Anyone?"

"Why?" Mr. President and Beethoven flashed through her mind and the old man evidently picked up on her skittish response.

"It's dangerous," he repeated suspiciously. "Is anyone looking for you? If so, and I help you, then it becomes even more dangerous."

"No," she said.

He looked at her with a dubious expression. "Are you sure you're not a communist?"

"Yes."

"Then why do you go to Mongolia?"

"That is a long story."

"Hm! Then we will return to your stump and you will tell me—tell me everything. I have time. After that, I'll decide whether to lead you there or leave you alone with your dead tree and very much alive ants. Let's go, Little Pianist!"

But Meiying excused herself. The food had gone straight through her system.

Old Uncle laughed. "I warned you!"

When she had finished her business, they returned to the stump and she told him her story, leaving out certain details.

~

By the time Meiying finished, the sky had begun to darken. Old Uncle shared more food from his bag and announced, "Follow me. Mind you, I haven't decided to lead you to Mongolia, but I have no intention of sleeping on the ground here tonight."

It was long dark when they reached his small, very neat farmhouse, far off the main road. Old Uncle from all appearances was a prosperous peasant. His brick house with a red tile roof seemed to glow like an ember from the light of hanging lanterns. The ubiquitous sounds of chickens and pigs filled the air, and even a water buffalo snorted in the distance. Meiying began to get nervous. Old Uncle noticed and lifted his eyebrows.

"Is there no one else here?" she asked.

"I live alone. Are you still worried about me?"

"Yes. Who lit the lanterns?"

He shrugged and opened the door. "Come in."

A pair of cats ran out and he waited inside the doorstep for her to follow. She hesitated.

"You can sleep outside then," he said and calmly closed the door.

Meiying looked around and saw only one decent-sized building—a sort of uninviting barn. The cats curled around her feet. A lamp suddenly shone warmly through the window, illuminating the house from the inside. It had turned cold and her stomach would not allow her to forget the hunger that had so insistently returned.

She knocked.

He opened the door and looked at her as if at a stranger. "Yes?" he asked.

"Do you want to buy a bag of used bones?" she said.

"How much?"

"A trip to the Mongolian border."

"Can I inspect this bag of used bones?"

"Anytime you want. But you must not touch them, or else terrible things will happen."

"Such as?"

"I will leave that to your imagination."

"It's a deal! Come in, Little Pianist! I have a separate room where you can sleep."

"Do you have more food?"

He laughed. "Of course."

~ *Morning and Meaning* ~

Old Uncle woke Meiying for breakfast the next morning. When she first went to bed, she dare not risk sleep, but the comfort of the mattress and his distant snoring combined to assuage her nerves, and before she knew it, the night had slipped away and his booming voice rang from the kitchen, "Time to get up, Little Pianist!" She smelled bacon and her stomach screamed to be fed.

"You may bathe outside," he said through the door. "Behind the house you will find a shower. I set it up for my old wife. I know about women. There is soap."

"Thank you," she replied, slipping out the back door to the sounds of bacon and his singing of some folk song. When she returned, he invited her to sit and eat.

"Your wife?" asked Meiying, trying not to bolt her food.

"Dead."

"I'm sorry."

"Communists came. I fled, never thinking they would hurt her."

"Why did they?"

"Bourgeois land-owning counter-revolutionaries, or some such, they said. I was fond of that old woman."

Meiying wanted to ask about his daughter but refrained.

"She was so pretty when young, like you." It took Meiyng a moment to realize he described his late wife. "Great in bed, unlike so many clumsy peasant girls. Your body is like her's when she . . . ah, well. Passion must cool so that love may rule."

Meiying nodded, only half-listening, when he continued, "Take off your blouse, please. I want to see your breasts."

This unexpected request was greeted with a look of surprise and dismay from Meiying.

Old Uncle wagged a finger. "None of that, Little Pianist! We have an agreement!"

"When do we leave?"

"Tomorrow. I must arrange for the care of my farm, my animals."

"Do you promise?"

"Already have."

Meiying took a risk. "Do you promise in the name of your wife and daughter?" She held her breath, feeling perhaps she had gone too far.

But Old Uncle did not hesitate. "Yes! Now take it off!"

Obeying his command, she removed her top and ate breakfast half-naked, enduring the stares of the old man for the sake of her journey.

"I know you think of me as nothing," he said after she had eaten her fill. "But you are so beautiful. With you here, my life now has beauty, even though it has lost its self-respect. You see, old age does not always bring wisdom."

"I see that," she said in the tone of a disappointed parent.

"What's the harm," he said defensively. "You cannot understand what it is to be alone without even the beauty of children or grandchildren around."

"Did you make your daughter do this?" Meiying could not help herself blurt out the words. But as soon as they came out of her mouth, she regretted saying them.

Without a word, he stood and put on his hat.

"Where are you going?" she asked in alarm.

"To arrange for a friend to take care of the animals. We leave tomorrow morning as promised. Put on your blouse." And with that, he was out the door.

Meiying sat for a long time, reviewing the events that brought her to this. She looked down at her bare breasts and wept at the pitiful state in which she had fallen.

When Old Uncle returned hours later, Meiying sat in the same chair, now fully clothed.

"I have made the arrangements with an old friend. You haven't moved?"

"No."

"Come outside and meet my friends."

He led her outside and to the dilapidated barn. When they entered, a massive water buffalo greeted them with snorts. Old Uncle said, "This is my prize *shuiniu*. His name is Dingxiang. Like you, he is hungry. But unlike you, he is happy to stay where it is familiar. Once I take you to the border, how will you find your friends?"

"I don't know, but I will be closer."

"Mongolia is a big place."

"Yes."

"Ha! I'm just a peasant farmer, but your story is exciting. I feel as though I am in some classic novel."

"You will have played a role."

"Maybe. Now, if I ask you to remove your clothes, will you object?"

"Yes."

"But I cannot get enough of looking at you."

Meiying began to see him as a little boy. "You'll just have to. I can't go around naked all the time."

"Why not?" he laughed at his own absurdity.

"Show me the direction of the border."

Old Uncle shook his head. "You'll leave."

"No. I need you."Then take off your clothes."

"No. You have to make up your mind. I will leave if you keep insisting."

"Don't leave! I'll show you tomorrow. Tomorrow. Then will you?"

"Yes. I feel ridiculous talking this way with an old man who should know the virtues. Don't you feel ashamed?"

"Of course. All men should feel ashamed, but that is the way we are made."

"Which is why I like women."

"You prefer women?"

"Don't you?"

Old Uncle laughed. "You had me worried, Little Pianist. Now, take off your clothes."

Meiying was stunned. "Old Uncle, we already had this discussion."

He looked at her very strangely and tilted his head. "But, I have some information I have not told you."

"What?"

"Before I give it to you, you must agree to disrobe whenever I tell you, no questions asked."

"No."

"I am not asking you to sleep with me."

"No. This information cannot be that important to me."

"But it is."

"How do I know?"

"If I say a word, will you agree?"

"Depends on the word."

"Beethoven."

Meiying stopped breathing. She felt her heart racing and instinctively looked around. Getting hold of herself, she said as calmly as possible, "The composer?"

He shook his head.

"What is that to me? Beethoven is a composer who is long dead. I play his music. So what?"

Old Uncle shook his head again. "I know nothing of that, but I do know that Beethoven is a person. A man. A man looking for you."

"How do you know him?"

Old Uncle laughed. "While I was watching you at that old stump, a young man approached and asked if I had seen a beautiful young woman on the road. The description he gave me did not exactly match your old woman disguise, and I sent him on his way. Only after you scrubbed off the grime did I put two and two together and realized it was you he looked for."

"How do you know his name?" asked Meiying suspiciously.

"Because he said you are his wife and his name was Beethoven and if I saw you to tell you he was looking for you. Beethoven, what a name!"

"Why didn't you tell me this before?"

"I feared you might leave and try to catch up with him. Believe me, missy, I ain't proud of that." He looked at her imploringly. "You ain't going to leave now, are you?"

"No, for he is not my husband, he is my enemy."

Old Uncle slapped his knee and laughed uproariously. "The fool didn't know you were less than ten meters away when he stood there jabbering with me!"

Chapter Twenty-Three

Dark Upon Dark

Introduction to the Cave

J ohn woke to an astonishing sight. Before him stood a young man with a staff. No one seemed to be around but the two of them.

"Hello," said John in Chinese.

The young man replied in Mongol, "I'm trying."

"Do you speak Chinese?"

The man shook his head.

"English?"

"Good."

"I don't understand."

The young man waved for John to follow.

"Wait!" He looked around. "Where are my friends?"

"Good." said the man, and started walking.

With no one to be seen but this strange, incomprehensible figure, John had a queasy, eerie feeling that the Earth had suddenly become devoid of people but for himself and his Mongol companion. More afraid of being left alone then being led to some uncertain fate, he quickly pulled on his boots without lacing them and rushed to catch-up to the figure. While they walked, he scrutinized the young man, who for all intents and purposes appeared outwardly unexceptional—until John looked closer. Dressed in an odd mix of modern attire and traditional Mongol costume (not the least jarring of which sat a battered old fedora hat tilted back on his head), he glided forward across the rocky ground like a spirit, his staff barely used; in fact, it seemed almost to hover above the rocks. The harsh wind tousled his long black hair back from a face that appeared carved from granite—but young and untainted granite—not yet fissured by wind and rain. John had a sudden pang that if Meiying were here, he would be jealous of this man.

With every step, John fell prey to old fears and dreaded the ever-increasing distance the Mongol led him from the group. When he stumbled, the Mongol stopped and pointed at the long boot laces trailing behind John's boots, then sat patiently while he laced them. A broad smile came to the Mongol's face.

"Good, good, good."

John shook his head. "I don't understand."

"Keep it in mind and it is sure to come, take it slow and you are certain to reach," replied the Mongol in clear and confident English.

John fumbled for words. "You speak English! Why . . . what . . . where are we going?"

But the Mongol only shook his head as if he did not understand. Amidst John's protestations, the young man rose and continued walking.

"I know you speak English!" cried John. "Where are we going? Where are my friends?"

As he stood impotently calling out, the figure receded in the distance. John rubbed his eyes and slapped his face to insure this was not a dream.

It's not a dream, John! Catch up to him! You'll lose him and be all alone!

No, they want to kill you! Poison you!

John, those are your human demons speaking! Catch-up or you'll be alone! He'll take you to the others! John, you must!

They will poison you!

Don't listen to the evil ones! Listen to Me!

John ran to catch-up with the Mongol. When he reached his side, the man barely noticed, but kept looking up at the cliff face as if searching for something.

I haven't got anything, thought John. *No food, clothes, all back at the campsite. Why am I following this man?*

"I'm not going any farther until you tell me where we're going," said John, abruptly stopping.

The young man looked at him quizzically, then said, "Good. Good."

John threw up his hands.

The Mongol again spoke in perfect English. "Goddess says, 'If you fear it, do not do it. If you do it, do not fear it.'"

"Do what?"

The Mongol turned and continued walking closer to the cliff. He disappeared between a massive arch formed by jumbled boulders. When John followed and peeked around the corner, he saw the young man motioning him to enter a small opening.

Do it! Do it!

No! He's taking you in to murder you! Run!

Do it! Don't listen to your human side!

Tilting his head as if listening for something far away, the Mongol smiled and said something in Mongol, then leaned over and entered through the opening.

Without hesitating, John crouched down and followed.

When he straightened up, the darkness was complete. Black. A mineral void. His imagination ran wild, picturing a knife slicing across his throat, through his windpipe, gasping out his last breath. He wanted to turn and plunge back through the opening but seemed frozen in place, and knowing he could not remain so indefinitely, decided to take a more reasonable course of action.

"Hello!" he called, thrusting out his arms like a blind man. "Tell me now what's going on!"

"You okay," came the unhelpful response from the Mongol, whose breath he could smell and whose eyes glowed faintly from some unseen inner spark.

Light from a lantern suddenly bulged forth. It was a weak, but welcoming brightness that washed away his fears as quickly as they had arisen. Holding the lantern high, the Mongol pointed to a low, jagged ceiling, and again crouched down to move deeper into the cavern. John did not hesitate, his inner voices screaming at each other in stark contrast to the silence of the cave that seemed to consider noise a cancer. They walked hunched over for some interminable amount of time when John saw the Mongol float away, and realized he must have ascended into a larger chamber that was slightly elevated. He could only see the Mongol's legs, giving the impression the man levitated. When John stepped up and stood beside him, a vast cavern appeared in breathtaking detail. The interior was illuminated by huge lanterns atop towering poles lining a stone bridge, and revealed the immensity of this underground grotto in all its cosmic glory. The narrow bridge traversed a deep chasm that plunged into darkness on each side. John had no reference point in his life to give such a breathtaking sight any context. It appeared otherworldly and utterly alien to his experience. A familiar tapping came to his ears, made eerie by a faint echo reverberating through the cave.

"Hello, John," said Madame Liu.

He turned and saw the group standing together in a small alcove.

"Oh! How long have you been here?" he asked, as he thought, stupidly.

"Before you."

"Why didn't you wake me?"

"No time, we were led here one by one while the others slept. You are the last."

John looked around. "So this is all of us?"

Madame Liu frowned. "I can only hope so. You now know as much as the rest of us."

The tapping from the box was regular, neither insistent nor silent.

"It seems to have reached its natural rhythm here," said Master Zhou.

"It's home," observed Child of Buddha.

"Where are we?" asked John.

Feng Shiren looked at the young Mongol who stood like a statue. "Ask him."

Everyone looked, but he remained stone-faced.

"Anyone speak Mongol?" asked Feng.

"I think he speaks some English," said John.

"I tried," said Lu Zhishen. "But he just replied in Mongol."

"This cave is amazing!" uttered an awestruck Suling who could not take her eyes off its immensity.

"It's home," remarked Child of Buddha, smiling broadly.

"Maybe, but that bridge!" cried Feng. "I could be across it in a heartbeat and see what's on the other side of this 'home' you refer to."

"No!" shouted Madame Liu. "Stay here!"

"Why? Our Mongol friend doesn't seem to care."

"I care," said the man in Chinese.

The group erupted in questions and comments, but he returned to his silent mode.

Suddenly, a little boy ran into the cave and was swept up in the arms of the young Mongol. "Ah! Little Acorn!" he cried, again in Chinese. "So glad you're here!"

Stunned, the group instinctively looked at Feng Shiren, who gazed upon the pair with wonder in his eyes. "But he is not Little Acorn," he muttered.

"Yes, of course he is!" said the Mongol. "Now we can cross the bridge." He set down the boy, who held his hand, then both walked onto the bridge. "Come on!" he said, smiling and waving his arm. "And bring the Precious Object."

~

They crossed the narrow bridge cautiously, passing under the immense lanterns that had struck John so forcefully. On each side of the stone path, sheer drops were soon swallowed by a deep and malevolent darkness that disgorged the sounds of invisible life; wings and clicking and chirps and other noises John could not identify. The craggy ceiling high above them was alive with moving shadows from the flickering lanterns. The group, now in single-file, remained quiet. It was as if they were in a cathedral, but to accentuate the danger, the path proved uneven and tricky. No one wanted to fall into that horrible crevasse. Lu Zhishen had the difficult task of carrying the box which continued to tap at a soft but even tempo.

After they all had crossed and gathered on the other side, Madame Liu asked, "Where to?"

The young Mongol smiled openly. "We are here."

"Here?" asked Master Zhou.

"This is where you stay."

"Until?"

"Until *she* calls you. Food and water will be brought."

The mention of *her* riveted everyone's attention. Questions flew, but the young Mongol refused to mention *her* again, and instead showed each member of the group to their 'rooms,' which turned out to be large cells carved out of the rock, all with entryways in the form of doors, interiors lined with wooden walls, and each conveniently furnished with necessary furniture. There were more than enough 'rooms' for each person, and even a large dining hall and various other nooks and crannies. To everyone's surprise, the cave was equipped with a library, although the books had grown brittle and moldy from the damp. After inspecting their rooms, they met in the dining area where a samovar of tea awaited. As they sipped, the young Mongol told them not to go deeper into the cave; that there was a massive iron door that blocked the way and was always locked; and that he would return with Little Acorn the next morning. He continued, "You may come and go outside the cave as you please. We have stacked your possessions at the entrance, but you must not try to go deeper into the cave."

"Who are the 'we' that you refer to?" asked Suling.

He shrugged. "Just Mongols."

"And your leader?" asked Master Zhou.

"You will soon know him."

"What is his name?" pressed Master Zhou.

"Ahab is Ahab," he replied in English, which reference only John understood.

"What is your name?" asked Madame Liu.

"Peter."

~ *Settling In* ~

Amidst the chattering speculation after the Mongol and his young charge left, Feng piped up dismissively, "Peter is Peter and Little Acorn is Little Acorn! I don't understand his overly dramatic gibberish. Neither of those two Mongols are who he says they are! That I understand!" When theories continued to fly, Feng slipped away in disgust to see the iron door for himself.

John noticed and came up behind. "Mind if I join you?"

"No." Feng seemed particularly grim. They had not gone far before darkness pressed upon them. Feng turned on a flashlight he had picked up from a peddler at the border, but the batteries were low and the beam correspondingly weak. Still, the light served to ease their way. On they walked, with no break from the oppressive darkness, and only the narrowing passage indicating some change.

John thought he saw railroad tracks faintly outlined in the rocky path, but Feng ridiculed the idea as a figment of his very fertile imagination. Having been chastised, John slunk along quietly, listening to his voices narrate the trip, with Goddess scolding him for imagining he saw railroad tracks.

No, no! That's for your son, decades from now, in a different war in a different cave in a different country!

A little blowback from the future, Sweet Goddess? John now knew this was God speaking, not a demon voice. **Your scalpel keeps slipping.**

For Your sake, Beloved God, You had better hope My multiple arms are steady.

But John stopped listening to their bickering and turned his attention back to Feng Shiren, who had abruptly stopped and whistled under his breath. John moved up next to him and saw the great iron door ominously outlined in the weak beam of Feng's flashlight. Its frame also consisted of iron, sealed tight all the way round the rock walls and ceiling. After a few desultory tries, Feng concluded the obvious: no way through unless invited.

On the way back, Feng mused, "Must be another entrance. They need air."

"You mean *she* needs air," replied John.

"I'm going to find out where that Mongol lives."

"You mean Peter?"

Feng snorted. "Sure, and his kid Little Acorn."

"Common enough names, I guess," said John, adding, "Must be some village nearby."

Feng ignored him and said to the air. "I'll follow him until he leads me where I want to go."

~

The following days saw the group falling into a routine. In the morning and evening, Peter and Little Acorn brought food. Peter showed them a kitchen built close to the entrance where they could cook and have access to water. Traversing the bridge became easier so long as the lanterns remained lit. Peter showed them how to do things, and little by little they became more independent.

Feng Shiren made numerous efforts to follow the Mongol, but once in open country there was no place to hide, so he always ended up confronted with an order to return to the cave. Each day, Feng fell farther back so as not to be spotted, but soon Peter and Little Acorn would simply disappear in the distance, nowhere to be found no matter how hard Feng searched.

"Mongol Earth swallows up Mongol man and Mongol boy," he mused to John.

Each day brought the group renewed excitement that *she* would appear, and each day ended with a mix of disappointment and anticipation for what the next day would bring.

Child of Buddha could usually be found sitting by the great iron door, waiting silently. Suling often visited and the two women would settle into the sparse conversation of old and comfortable friends.

Madame Liu and Master Zhou stayed in their rooms, reading books from the library, and seen only at mealtime when they chatted together about the "youngsters" and the war.

News of the outside world had, of course, ceased and now seemed superfluous. Speculation over the names of the two Mongols had run its course, with the final explanation being that it must be *her* magic. This theory was unsatisfactory, but everyone agreed it would have to suffice for lack of a better one.

Every day some member of the group would ask the Mongol when *she* would make *her* appearance. He always shrugged and replied, "Only *she* knows."

One evening, when they were all gathered in the dining area, Madame Liu asked again. "Have you heard anything at all from *her*, Peter?"

His reply came as a shock to them all. "*She* is waiting for Bai Meiying to arrive."

Peppered with questions, especially from John, he remained infuriatingly evasive.

That night, John made his way to the bridge and looked down into the dark crevasse, hearing the invisible beating of wings and a variety of chirps and clicks.

The urge to jump came to him.

Resist, Chosen One!

"Meiying!" he called, waiting for an echo.

It came to him in waves.

~ *Meiying Betrays Her Guide* ~

Meiying set out with Old Uncle, unsure whether he would lead her to the border or to Beethoven. Although his explanation of how he knew about Beethoven seemed feasible, she did not trust him. Old Uncle laughed off her concerns, pointing out that Beethoven could not match the impact of her assets or the value of her rewards.

Back on the road she felt unwillingly at home yet wracked by a deep yearning for a real home. She dreamed of having her own apartment in a future, peaceful Shanghai, large enough to accommodate a grand piano. Every night she would practice while the diaphanous spirits of Meili and Lihua hovered above the instrument, sighing in league with the notes as if she were giving them the gift of symphonic orgasms to wash away the pain of their deaths.

Old Uncle had taken up his habit of talking incessantly, caring little whether his words penetrated anyone's consciousness but his own.

"There goes a sad looking woman, poor thing. The eyes tell me all I want to know. Probably lost her husband and kids. Seems devastated. Doesn't care about her hunger even. Look how all the other travelers swirl around her, but she is like a senseless rock disrupting the flow of people to their fates. What are their fates, Meiying?"

"What?" asked a distracted Meiying, pulled from the comfort of her apartment and its spirits.

"What are their fates?" he repeated.

"I don't know."

"Yes, you do. We all do. It's to flow down to the sea and be diluted away into oblivion."

"Oh, yes."

"You see that boy over there? He is not ready to die. I see it in his eyes. The eyes are everything, Meiying. Do you know that?"

"Yes."

"You're here because of your eyes. That old woman disguise could not fool me, because of your eyes."

On he went, chattering away, while Meiying retreated back into her dream world. By late afternoon, she felt bone-tired, still weak from her brush with starvation. Old Uncle seemed tireless.

"Need to find a place to sleep," he said. "Damn Mongolian winds blowing down to make us into ice."

Meiying perked up. "Are we close?"

"Oh, yes, didn't you know? Silly Little Pianist. Need to find a place to sleep. Town up ahead. Been there. Has an inn. Costs money. Lucky I have money. Others don't. Should be a room available in spite of all these penniless riff raff."

Meiying looked startled. She assumed they would sleep in the open with the other refugees. Old Uncle noticed.

"Don't worry. You're my daughter. Money fixes all. We'll get a room."

"Two," said Meiying.

"No. Two is too expensive. One. But don't worry, daughter, you'll be safe with a broken-down old man!" He laughed. "Look at that couple. . . . " he continued on, unconcerned that Meiying's attention was focused elsewhere.

When they checked-in, the clerk fawned over them once he had seen the wad of Old Uncle's money, and the jingle of silver coins that backed it up.

"I will give you a good discount for a second room to make your daughter comfortable."

"No," said Old Uncle. "Too dangerous to leave her alone in these terrible times. I want her where I can keep an eye on her."

"But only one bed per room," objected the clerk.

"Ah, that's different. Bring bedding for the floor!"

Clearly unhappy, the clerk agreed with the snide comment that, "One of you will be very uncomfortable. Unnecessarily so, considering the discount."

Old Uncle wagged a finger at him. "Children are from the blood and bones of their parents. She will be happy to take the floor." Old Uncle glanced at Meiying as a cue to speak.

"Oh, yes," she said. "My father suffers from arthritis."

The clerk grinned maliciously. "Of course. Very filial."

But Old Uncle would not let it go. "Yes! Hard to find filial children in the evil times, isn't that so, clerk?"

"Yes indeed."

Once they had settled in, Old Uncle said he would take the bed and she could sleep where she liked. To her great relief, he appeared too tired to insist on any humiliating displays or try any obnoxious shenanigans. Almost as soon as his head hit the pillow, he began snoring. While she arranged her bedding on the floor, a feeling of revulsion suddenly came over her; a suffocating urgency to run from that place or die. She did not know how she would die, but her pounding heart and shallow heaves for air made it imperative she run. Outside lurked a strange town and the darkness that gives rise to unseen dangers and torments, but even these fears could not match the unrelenting compulsion to flee immediately before she suffocated. She felt dizzy trying to breathe in enough air, and the outside, dangerous as it was, seemed to offer the only relief from the deadly trap she found herself in. She had no choice but to bolt or her life would somehow cease to be.

Quickly collecting her things, she slipped out the door and desperately waited on the landing until the clerk disappeared into a back room, then bolted down the stairs and out the front door of the inn. A few gulps of cool night air somewhat cleared her mind and she peered out at the dark street. Figures moving in the shadows caused her to cringe back toward the light from the inn. She desperately wished she had changed into her old woman disguise. Making herself as small and inconspicuous as possible, she gathered her courage and followed the sidewalk, sticking close to the store fronts. She soon entered the main business district, now populated by groups of people laughing drunkenly as they moved from wine shop to bar. At least there was light from the street lamps, but she knew they would soon be turned off. Fear began morphing back into a debilitating panic and she clung to a lamp post to prevent her fainting.

Meiying had almost no money, no friends, no place to go; the crushing weight of despair took hold with the power of immobilizing chains. Tears filled her eyes and she felt herself slipping to the ground when she heard the unmistakable chords of a piano being played in the distance. Like a moth to a flame, she followed the notes and soon stood outside a nightclub, above which a faded sign read, 'New York Palace' in Chinese. Marshaling the last drops of her resolve, she inched her way inside and beheld a smoke-filled room with a scattering of patrons, all Chinese, listening to someone play jazz, or try to. It was a sorrowful piece played very badly, but the pianist seemed quite earnest. In spite of his obvious efforts to please, the patrons ignored him and carried on their own whispering conversations.

Peering through the smoke, Meiying saw that the pianist was a young man wearing Western-style clothes and a fedora hat tilted jauntily on his head. The few customers, mostly couples, were likewise dressed in Western clothes. Two couples danced languidly to the bluesy downbeat.

Meiying felt the bartender's eyes squinting through the smoke at her. She saw his gaze do a quick search for some companion, and when none was found, settled back on her. His face hardened and she almost ran back into the street, but the dread of returning to that hopeless void emboldened her.

Walking up to the bar, she said, "I can play the piano."

"That's nice. You want to buy a drink?"

Meiying's heart fluttered and she gulped. "Let me play something."

"For a drink?"

"No. For free."

A figure appeared next to her. It was the young pianist looking at her curiously. "Let her play, father," he said in formal, educated Mandarin. "Can't be worse than me."

By now the patrons had stopped talking and were following the conversation at the bar, waiting to see the outcome.

"Free?" asked the bartender.

"Yes."

He nodded and the son bowed, extending his arm as an invitation to sit on the piano bench.

Meiying had already decided to play jazz, and she chose a short snippet of Gershwin's 'Rhapsody in Blue.' The piano was badly tuned, and her playing rusty, but when she finished, the customers applauded loudly and shouted, "More! More!"

Playing the piano had the effect of lifting the oppressive fear that so incapacitated her. Pure joy at being reunited with her passion flowed through the music, and in spite of the out-of-tune piano and her own mistakes, she experienced a rebirth of unfettered freedom and control. In performing she regained command of her emotions which quickly led her to one conclusion: she would trek to the border on her own, come what may.

After she played a few tunes, the bartender brought her a drink.

"No, thank you. But do you have food?"

The young pianist laughed. "I'll get you some." He disappeared in the back room.

"It's almost closing time," said the bartender. "Do you have a place to stay?"

Before Meiying could answer, an older woman emerged with the young pianist and exclaimed, "Here my dear, eat this."

The woman fussed over Meiying as might a kindly, overzealous aunt. Having such attention acted as a balm, and the delicious *jiao zi* and rice brought her further back to normalcy. As the last of the customers filed out, the bartender asked again, "Do you have a place to stay?"

Meiying's silence told them all.

"Will you stay here tonight, dear?" said the woman. "We sleep in the floor above. Aden will set you up a cozy bed down here in one of the booths.

"Yes, yes!" enthused Aden. "Please stay!"

Meiying's tears of gratitude seemed to touch them all. While Aden fixed her bed in a corner booth, Meiying wondered at her charmed life; always in the direst hour, something arose to save her. After the others had left for the night, her thoughts turned to Old Uncle. What would be his reaction when he awoke and found her missing? Her speculation ran the gamut; from his following her to cursing and returning home to reporting her disappearance to Beethoven. Of all possibilities, she feared Beethoven the most, for he led inexorably back to the monstrous Mr. President. Before long her racing mind slowed to an exhausted crawl, then broke apart to be swept away by sleep.

She was gently awakened the next morning by Aden who invited her to use their bathroom to clean-up, and then join the family for breakfast. When she did, father and son were in deep conversation about the war. Aden seemed to be on a rant about the Japanese, so she allowed the words to pass unprocessed and gratefully accepted the food his mother placed before her.

Aden briefly broke off his diatribe to wish the homeless woman, "Good morning," then continued on, clearly modulating his words to impress their guest.

"I don't care about the political differences of the Nationalists and the communists, we are all Chinese! We have to stick together against the Japs! Look what the bastards did in Shanghai and Nanjing!"

"Better be careful or you'll end up in the army," said his father reproachfully. "Such reckless talk will get you, or us, nowhere."

"Hush!" cried the mother. "Don't even say such things. It's bad luck."

Glancing at Meiying, he protested, "I'd join if I thought it would do any good. But they're all so incompetent!"

"Join!" shouted the father. "You'll be drafted by one or the other of the rascals! As the war is lost even more than it is now, they won't accept your excuses any longer and you'll just be more fodder for the corrupt fools!"

"Dad! Stop it!" Aden again cast a nervous eye at Meiying. "We have a guest. Let's change the subject."

"Yes," agreed the mother. "What is your name, dear?"

"Bai Meiying."

"Well, Bai Meiying," said the father in his most paternal tone. "My customers liked your playing last night."

"Thank you."

He coughed. "I have a little proposition to make."

"Yes?"

"You play for me in the Palace in exchange for food."

"But I have nowhere to live."

"Well, we can't put you up here. We're already cramped, and I sure as hell can't pay for you to stay somewhere."

"Pa!" cried the young pianist. "Let her stay in my room. I'll sleep in the booth."

"Don't be stupid!" retorted the father in a thoroughly disgusted voice.

"I have a suggestion," said Meiying.

The other three looked at her expectantly.

"I'll play for food if you let me collect and keep tips for my playing. My needs are few. I will find my own living arrangements."

"But, dear, will that be enough?" asked the mother in genuine concern.

"Oh, yes."

"It's a deal!" cried the father. "A girl that makes her own contract! Imagine! Only in these desperate times."

"Thank you," said Meiying. "How many days do you wish me to play?"

"Nights only. Eight to two, which is quitting time. Six nights a week. But—" he held up a cautionary hand. "I can fire you anytime if things don't work out, and dinner only, not breakfast or lunch."

"Agreed. When do you wish me to start?"

"Tonight."

Meiying nodded and said, "Fine, but may I sleep in your booth one more night to earn some tip money and find a room?"

"Yes, of course."

"Do you know of a cheap room for let?"

The mother chimed in. "I think I know just the place. A . . . friend who needs a lodger. Let me check."

"Thank you. Now, please, what are your names?"

They all laughed. The father pointed his finger. "Mrs. Peng," then to himself, "Mr. Peng," and to the young pianist, "Aden Peng."

"An unusual name, Aden," said Meiying looking at the young man.

"Yes, given to me by an American."

"Yes," interjected Mr. Peng. "A very interesting American journalist gave us the idea for naming this place the New York Palace, and he taught Aden (he insists we parents also call him by this nickname) some jazz piano. It is such a craze in Shanghai that we thought it might catch on here."

"Unfortunately, mostly young people like American jazz, and my playing is terrible, so we have struggled to find enough customers," said Aden. "But gradually, we have built up a group of steady customers despite the war." He shrugged. "We have our regulars and they help us get by."

"A word of warning," said the father. "When the Japanese come, we do not play American jazz. Can you play anything else?"

"Yes, of course. I even know some traditional Japanese songs."

"Excellent!" boomed the father, rubbing his hands and smiling broadly at his wife.

~ *Meiying Lands More Than A Job* ~

Aden was unmistakably infatuated with the beautiful, tragic Meiying. Her looks, of course, took his breath away, but the feline imperturbability of her purring, leopard-like soul also knocked down the toy building blocks of his youthful complacency. Meiying, for her part, saw him as just another in a long line of boys and men who seemed unable to tend their own gardens.

Meiying spent the day at the New York Palace, afraid to chance going outside and being spotted by Old Uncle, or worse, Beethoven. She knew this ploy was unsustainable, especially as word had undoubtedly spread of her playing, but she needed a break from fear and hunger. To justify the time wasted laying low at the New York Palace, she practiced jazz pieces and after a while, drifted into a Mozart sonata, momentarily imagining a life of concerts and comfort.

Aden listened from a nearby table and taking advantage of a break, said, "You play great. I've never heard those pieces. They're hard. Too hard for me. What are they?"

"Just classical music. Mozart."

"Wow! Where'd you learn it?"

"Shanghai." Meiying wanted to change the subject. "If I may ask, how have you stayed out of the army?—your father mentioned some excuse."

Aden's face registered anger and disgust. "Dad always talks too much!"

"Sorry."

"I'd rather talk about you."

"Don't you worry about being drafted? Don't you worry about someone, some army, just coming and taking you away? These days it happens all the time."

He looked at her as if weighing whether to reveal some secret, but then said, "I'd rather talk about you."

"Aden! I have to practice," she laughingly answered, and at that moment, he seemed to Meiying a thousand years younger than she.

~

Apparently, word had spread, helped along by Mr. Peng's hastily-made posters advertising the New York Palace's "exotic new pianist." By eight o'clock, the nightclub was almost full, something that had not happened for a very long time. With no introductions, Meiying simply sat and began playing American tunes from the reams of sheet music Aden had collected. From that moment, the Palace began its metamorphosis from a sleepy, out-of-the-way joint, to the most popular night spot in town. But for Meiying, the triumph was laced with a poisonous ingredient—the fear of being discovered.

That first night, she could not keep from scanning every face blurred by smoke to discover in stark focus her nemesis. But no familiar faces appeared, and the evening went smoothly and successfully. To make matters even better, her tips were larger than anticipated, and Mrs. Peng excitedly told her during a break that her friend indeed had a room available to let, and wanted to interview Meiying the next morning.

Overwhelmed by the rapid turnabout of fortune, and given her past travails, Meiying could only distrust that her luck would continue. Nevertheless, she went to see this friend of Mrs. Peng's with high hopes. It turned out to be a long walk, and unwilling to spend money on a rickshaw, she suffered much from the heat and dust of the streets. After a series of wrong turns and backtracking, she at last stood in front of a large, imposing house. A servant answered her knock and she was shown into a small anteroom where she was informed Madame Ling would be down shortly.

Only a short time passed before a very old, elegant woman dressed in Qing-style brocade, entered with the help of a cane. Her silk dress was quite clearly of the highest quality—albeit old and showing signs of wear. Meiying rose and bowed in the old manner, whereupon the old lady swept her hand in a grand invitation to sit.

"My name, Madame Ling, is Bai Meiying. I came in response to an inquiry conveyed via Mrs. Peng."

"Yes," replied the old lady in a rather brittle but clear voice. "She was once a cook for me, long ago."

"I see."

"You are interested in finding a room?"

"Yes, Madame Ling."

"Tell me about where you are from. Your family. Your current situation."

Meiying appraised her of the pertinent details in as sparse a manner as she could devise.

"Ah. So you are from Shanghai?"

"Yes, Madame Ling."

"And Mrs. Peng tells me you play some instrument?"

"Yes."

"At the nightclub?"

Meiying looked down. "Yes."

Madame Ling leaned forward on her cane. "These times are difficult."

"Yes."

"Do you play the *gǔzhēng*?"

"No, the piano."

"I know the instrument. You see, I am also from Shanghai. Even went to concerts when my husband was alive. That, of course, was before the civil war and the Japanese. Men are locusts!" This last phrase she spat with a vehemence that belied her age.

Meiying again looked down, wondering if this woman would be either quite dangerous or quite useful.

"I see you are shocked at my words."

"Not at all. My feelings are similar, but you are bold to verbalize them."

Madame Ling grunted in acknowledgement. "Here is the rent, due the first of every month."

Madame Ling handed Meiying a paper with the amount written on it. Even uttering such base considerations seemed beneath the old lady.

"I see," said Meiying. "This seems very fair. May I see the room?"

The old woman knocked once on the floor with her cane and a servant entered. "Show this young lady to her room."

Madame Ling's three-story house exemplified the height of Qing architectural style. Grand in its day, it now suffered from lack of maintenance and an insufficiency of light. In the past, candles and lanterns illuminated the rooms in all their glory, but the once-lively colors were now rendered drab by ill-installed and often interrupted electricity, which served mainly to highlight the sinister nature of every dark corner and shadowy space. Nevertheless, contrary to her first impressions, Meiying quickly came to revel in this gloomy abode. Her own opaque feelings and apocalyptic dalliances found commonality with such dim surroundings. In short, she felt immensely drawn to her room, the house, the grounds, and the rather antiquated trappings of her landlady.

Somehow, in spite of Meiying's almost primal urge to reach the destination and see *her*, she experienced a counter-balancing pull toward this place, feeling much like a wounded animal crawling into a dark, defensible den to heal.

~ John Is Warned ~

Days at the cave stretched into weeks, and still *she* had not appeared. Such close proximity began creating friction among the group. Lu Zhishen in particular grew restive and short-tempered.

One evening at dinner, he grumbled, "I don't know how much more of this waiting I can take. Every day the same!"

"Perhaps this is a test," suggested Suling.

"Of what, for god's sake? Heaven knows we've already been through so much . . . lost so many comrades, friends. What more does *she* want?"

"Bai Meiying," said Child of Buddha matter-of-factly.

Lu could only snort in disgust. "For all we know, she's dead. Sorry, John."

John shook his head. "I know. When I get depressed, I sometimes think so."

"And the Precious Object just keeps tapping like some damn time bomb ticking away our lives," continued Lu.

Master Zhou said, "It has not been that long. I have a feeling—"

"Bah!" interrupted Lu rudely. "We've all had a feeling at one time or another and here we still sit!" The big Canadian had let his beard grow even longer than normal, which made him take on the appearance of an unhinged mountain man. To emphasize the bear-like nature of his mood, he stood abruptly and paced, looking for all the world like a nervous, shaggy beast too long confined.

In the silence that followed, the faint tapping continued from the box stored not far away. It was at this awkward moment that 'Mongol Peter' and 'Mongol Little Acorn' (as the group had now taken to calling them) appeared in the dining area. Mongol Peter had a bag draped over his shoulder. Declining an invitation to sit by Madame Liu, he announced, "I have instructions from *her*."

The group came to immediate attention.

"You are to leave the box containing the Precious Object outside the iron door tonight."

"What's in the bag?" asked Feng Shiren.

Peter shook his head and replied, "It's also to be left outside the door with the box."

"Well, what's in it?" pursued Feng.

Peter wagged his finger.

"A mystery!" shouted Feng, striking his most comical pose; head tilted, one leg off the ground, arms akimbo.

"May we look in the bag?" asked Master Zhou.

"We may," said Child of Buddha before Peter could reply. "But what we find will have no meaning to us."

Mongol Peter looked appreciatively at the hunchback and nodded in agreement.

Later that night every member of the group made the trek to the iron door as if participating in some solemn sacrifice. When they arrived, the bag carried earlier by Peter lay just to the side of the door. Once the box had been placed, Feng Shiren danced forward.

"Let's just see what's in this mystery bag!"

Made of canvas, the bag had been loosely tied with rope. Madame Liu pointed out that it seemed to her that Mongol Peter almost wanted them to look.

"Maybe we shouldn't," cautioned Suling.

"Why not?" asked John.

"A test?"

Everyone looked at Child of Buddha, but she remained motionless, staring at the door.

Feng Shiren, who had been fiddling with the bag, made a noise and when Master Zhou shone the flashlight in his direction; a German SS officer's uniform cascaded down from Feng's hands. It took them aback to see the Nazi garment held upright by Feng, and in the dim light appeared for all the world as though it were being worn by an emaciated ghost. At the same time, the tapping from the box quickened.

"What do you suppose that's for?" asked Lu Zhishen rhetorically.

John shuddered and again wished he was back home.

"Meaningless to us," said Child of Buddha, still staring at the door. "To someone else, but not us."

Feng put the uniform back in the bag and placed it next to the box.

"Maybe if we stay here long enough, we'll catch somebody dragging them through the door," said Lu Zhishen.

"Somehow," observed Feng. "I don't think that will ever happen, unless of course we are supposed to see."

"Well, I'm staying here anyway even if it takes all night. I have a flashlight. Someone has to retrieve these things and take them through the door, and when they do—" Lu clapped his hands—"I've got them!"

"Good luck," replied Feng laughingly.

You're a coward! A demon voice boomed at John.

No! exclaimed Goddess. *Resist it!*

Yes, Sweet Goddess! He will leave the mother You need and run to the Mother he needs for his comfort. Another failure. Such is to be expected. First Principles in action.

"I'll stay with you!" blurted John to Lu Zhishen.

Suling looked at him strangely.

Child of Buddha laughed.

And the others, weary of trying to plum John's moods, merely shook their heads.

"No you won't!" replied Lu with a subdued vehemence.

"Why not?" asked John weakly.

"Consider this a warning," said Lu. "If bad things happen to me, you must return to . . . our families. You have the obligation to explain."

"Lu—"

"No! It was my idea. You go back with the others."

"But—"

"No!"

Convenient, isn't it little mutant?

Don't listen, John. It's good advice.

"Well," said John. "I'll be back early the morning to check."

He readily, too readily, accepted the excuse Lu Zhishen offered.

John knew his acceptance was another failure of will, another failure of character. Feng Shiren would never let another talk him into doing something his conscience told him was wrong. But, John knew with the greatest sorrow he was no Feng Shiren.

These little slips of courage, these little signs of weakness, he assiduously buried as deep into his psyche as possible, with the iron resolve never to let them see the light of day, now or in the future.

Bury them deep, he told himself. *Bury them deep!*

~

Dear Reader, don't you see? My father . . . oh, my father! The voices plagued him, as they do me. . . his brain, teeming with iron doors.

Epilogue

The Stillness

Beneath every answer, another question waits,
One that will not be kind.
Soon the road will darken, and their journey measured not in questions, but in suffering.
Voices gather for the long quest yet ahead.
The Stillness is already listening,
let silence speak.
And humanity begins moving down its long, final path.